The Luna City Compendium #1

Containing: The Luna City Chronicles,
The Second Chronicle of Luna City,
And
Luna City 3.1
In One Complete Volume

By
Celia Hayes
& Jeanne Hayden

Geron GA & Associates

San Antonio, 2019

Dedications and Acknowledgments

Thank you to the readers who love the series, and demanded a further chronicle of events, lives, and loves in Luna City. To my family, friends and the memory of those who have gone before. *Semper Fidelis!*

Jeanne Hayden

The Luna City series is dedicated with affection to those residents of Texas small towns who have not only welcomed us over the past half-dozen years of doing book events and markets, but who have also served as an inspiration by telling stories which are woven into this continuing chronicle: Fredericksburg, Boerne, Bulverde, Beeville, Goliad, Gonzalez, Comfort, Richmond, Junction, San Saba and Harper, Giddings, Llano and Lockhart, Richmond, New Braunfels and Kerrville. Thank you all for your continuing inspiration. Special thanks are due again to Larry H. for expert advice on the cooking, classic French kitchen-management, and catering aspects of this and the previous Luna City chronicles, and gratitude to J. "Pouncer" Melcher, of Lancaster, Texas for attentive beta reading and extensive suggestions, and to the late Professor John Igo, of San Antonio, who read an early version of the first Luna City Chronicle and encouraged us to continue with the tale.

Celia Hayes,
San Antonio, 2019

Contents

Luna City & Environs

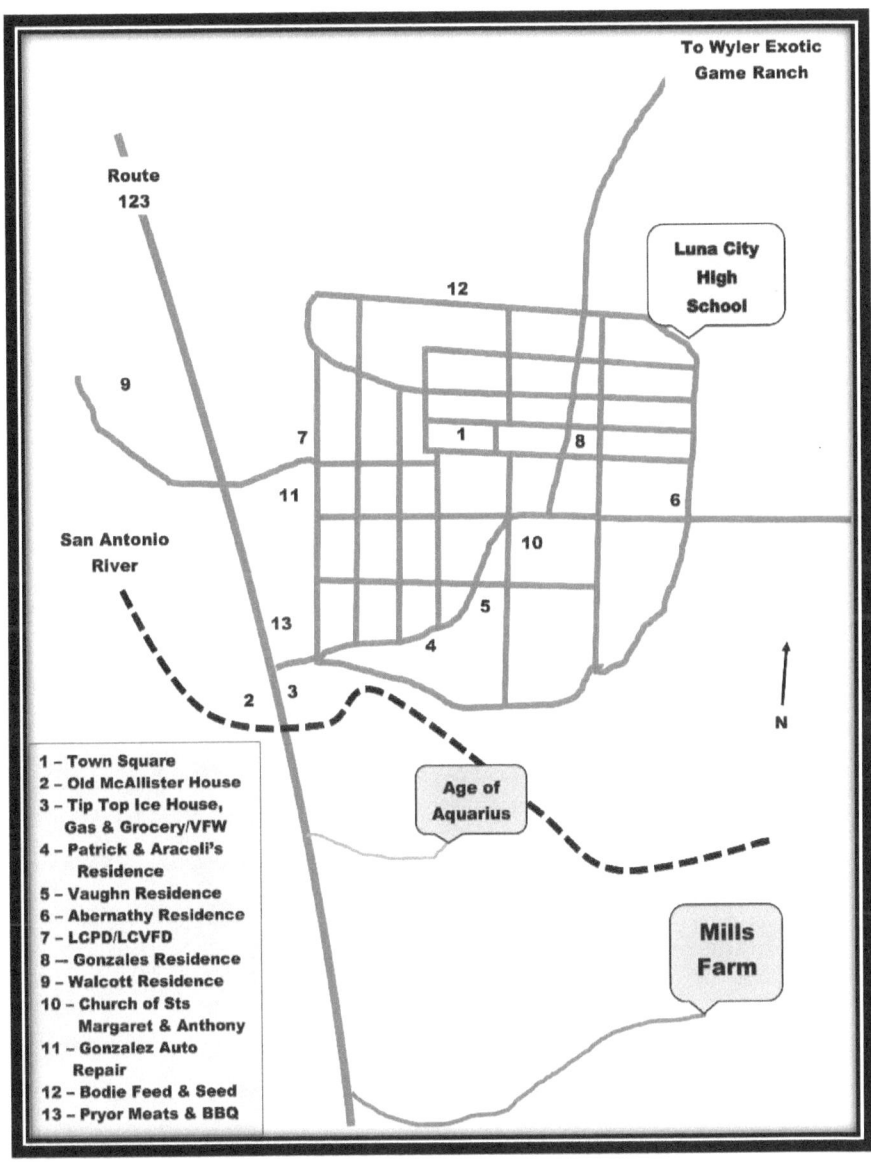

To Wyler Exotic Game Ranch

Route 123

Luna City High School

San Antonio River

N

1 – Town Square
2 – Old McAllister House
3 – Tip Top Ice House, Gas & Grocery/VFW
4 – Patrick & Araceli's Residence
5 – Vaughn Residence
6 – Abernathy Residence
7 – LCPD/LCVFD
8 – Gonzales Residence
9 – Walcott Residence
10 – Church of Sts Margaret & Anthony
11 – Gonzalez Auto Repair
12 – Bodie Feed & Seed
13 – Pryor Meats & BBQ

Age of Aquarius

Mills Farm

Luna City Town Square

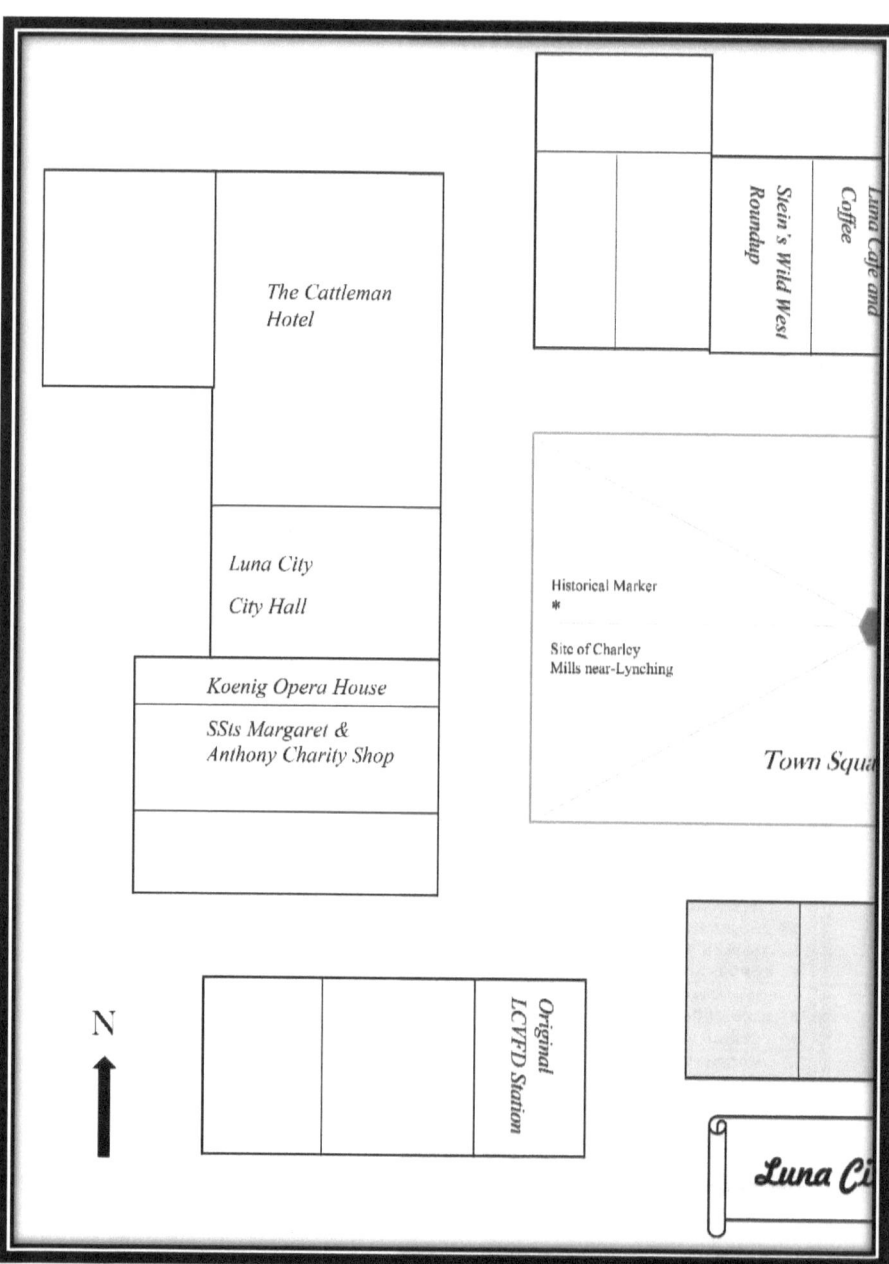

The Cattleman Hotel

Luna Cafe and Coffee

Stein's Wild West Roundup

Luna City
City Hall

Koenig Opera House

SSts Margaret &
Anthony Charity Shop

Historical Marker
✳

Site of Charley
Mills near-Lynching

Town Squa

N

Original
LCVFD Station

Luna Ci

First Bank of Luna City
(Now the Chamber of
Commerce offices)

1st Methodist Church of Luna City

Mercantile Bldg.

Luna Cafe and

• Historical Marker
– Last Gunfight

War *
Memorial

Luna City ISD Offices

Present-day Elementary School and Playground

are – Luna City

Abernathy Hardware Building

ity Historic Town Square – Est. 1876

Cast of Characters

(An asterisk marks those who are deceased)

Richard Astor-Hall

(Ricardo to his friends in Luna City, Rich Hall in his previous life)

A former celebrity chef, who through a chain of circumstances, finished up in Luna City, managing the Luna City Café and doing the occasional catering event.

Martin Abernathy

Widower, father of Jess, mayor of Luna City, hereditary owner of Abernathy Hardware.

Jessica "Jess" Abernathy

Daughter of Martin, qualified CPA, Air Force Reservist, champion barrel-racer, significant other to Joe Vaughn.

Benny Cordova

The devious and ninja-skilled general manager of Mills Farm.

Samantha "Sammi" Colquhoun

Sometime actress, media personality, and ex-girlfriend of Richard.

James Wyler "J.W." Ellis*

Grandson of Doc Stephen Wyler, once boyfriend to Jess Abernathy, best friend of Chris Mayall.

Dwight David "Music Man" Garrett

Coach of the Mighty Fighting Moths and band music master.

Alberto "Berto" Gonzales

Student and part-time limo driver, younger brother of Araceli Gonzalez, friend of Richard, and grandson of *Abuelita* Adeliza Gonzalez.

Sylvester Gonzales	Gaming geek, computer nerd, USMC veteran.
Roman Gonzales	Construction contractor.
Roman "Romeo" Gonzales	Cousin of Berto and Araceli, former oilfield worker, currently top male model, married to Susannah Wyatt, no longer an unwitting focus for strange and unearthly energies.
Adeliza "Abuelita" Gonzalez	The revered and feared matriarch of the Gonzales/Gonzalez clan, dedicated Food Channel watcher, and Richard's biggest fan.
Araceli Gonzales-Gonzalez	Older sister of Berto, married to Patrico, mother of Angelika and Mateo, manager, assistant cook, head waitress at the Luna Café & Coffee.
Patrico "Pat" Gonzalez	Husband to Araceli, drives a tanker truck for an oil company in the Eagle Ford Shale Oil Field.
Hernando "Nando" Gonzalez*	Korean War fighter ace, local hero, for whom the high school gymnasium is named.
Judith "Judy" Stillwell Grant	With her husband Sefton, the owner of the Age of Aquarius Campground and Goat Farm, the last two holdouts of a 1960s commune.
Sefton Grant	Husband of Judy, landlord of Richard.
Katherine "Kate" Heisel	Gonzales cousin, reporter for the *Karnesville Weekly Beacon*, significant other to Richard.

Christopher "Chris" Mayall	Manager, Tip-Top Icehouse, Gas & Grocery, bartender at the VFW, Navy veteran, amputee participant in marathons, medic - Luna City VFD, best friend of J.W. Ellis, and friend of Richard.
Leticia "Miss Letty" McAllister	Oldest person in Luna City, WWII Red Cross service, kindergarten teacher, friend to Chris Mayall.
Douglas McAllister, Phd *	Miss Letty's older brother, professor of history, and author of *The History of Luna City*.
Phillip Noel-Barrett	Actor, media personality, once romantic rival and frenemy of Richard.
Xavier Gunnison-Penn	Unsuccessful international treasure-hunter.
Andrew Pryor	Oilfield geologist, headquartered in Karnesville, owner of small BBQ restaurant
Patricia Wyler Pryor	Granddaughter of Dr. Stephen Wyler and Miss Alice, wife of Andrew Pryor, HS girlfriend of Joe Vaughn.
Georg Stein	Native of Germany, a retired corporate lawyer, passionate reenactor, owner of Stein's Wild West Round-up, married to Annise.
Annise Stein	Co-owner of Stein's Wild West Round-up.

Joseph "Joe" Vaughn	Army veteran, local football hero, chief of the Luna City Police Department, significant other to Jess Abernathy.
Clovis Walcott, (Colonel, USAR/Ret.)	Retired US Army Reservist, currently consulting engineer, keen reenactor.
Sook "Isabel" Walcott	Korean-born wife of Clovis, socially ambitious, and the tiger-mother from Hell.
Jeremy "Jerry" Walcott	Oldest child of Clovis and Sook, a student nurse and family care-giver.
Robbie Walcott	Younger son of Clovis and Sook, bright and wildly curious, potential kitchen trainee.
Belle Walcott	Daughter of Clovis and Sook, lead trumpet in the Mighty Fighting Moths Marching Band
Susannah Wyatt-Gonzales	Regional manager, at VPI, sexually stalker of Richard
Collin Wyler	Son of Doc Wyler and Miz Alice, father of Patricia, international financier, serial husband, and treasure-hunting enthusiast.
Stephen "Doc" Wyler	Owner of the Wyler Exotic Game Ranch, a qualified veterinarian, part-owner of the Café and second-oldest resident. Father of Collin, grandfather of Patricia Pryor and J.W. Ellis.
Marigold Amy Yasbeck	A student, and semi-girlfriend of Berto, formerly known as the child actress Amy Butler.

The Chronicles of Luna City – Volume 1

An Introduction to Luna City

The little town of Luna City is not a city at all, as most people understand these things. It is a small Texas town grown from a single stone house built by an immigrant Bohemian stonemason in 1857, at a place where an old road between San Antonio, Beeville, and points south forded a shallow stretch of river. The railway was supposed to come through where Luna City was planned to be – and the city fathers confidently expected it to become the county seat. Alas, when Dr. Stephen Wyler's Aunt Bessie eloped with a smooth-talking engineer on the Galveston, Harrisburg and San Antonio Railway, her father – who owned much of the land in the district – was furious. The railway, he stormed, was an invitation to vice and debauchery of every kind, a threat to the virtue of young women and girls – and so he saw that it never came to Luna City; although there had been a generous space allotted in early plans of Luna City for the usual magnificent Beaux Arts-style county courthouse in the square at the center of town. That expectation also came to naught; the county seat stayed in Karnesville, and since then, Luna City has made very little effort to attract the casual tourist.

Travelers on the farm-to-market road going north or south will pass by the Tip-Top Ice House, Grocery and Gas, perhaps note the four-square house of limestone blocks owned by the last descendant of Arthur Wells McAllister – the surveyor who first drew up the plat of Luna City in 1876, and drive on. They might also note the metal towers, ladders and chutes of Bodie Feed & Seed Supply, looming on the distant horizon – but definitely will miss the disintegrating sign advertising the Age of Aquarius Campground and Goat Farm. Anyone looking for that establishment already knows where it is … and that clothing there is optional. Jess Abernathy, who does the finances for Sefton and Judy Grant has mentioned to them now and again, that they ought to get a new sign or have the old one repainted and repaired, but Sefton and Judy aren't into the realities of advertising and commerce in this … or really, any age. This exasperates Jess, but then she is the fifth generation of a Luna family with commerce bred into their bones and blood; her father and grandfather run Abernathy Hardware, housed for all this century, every decade of the previous and fifteen years of the one before that in a looming Victorian commercial building on Town Square with a cornice which looks as if it is about to topple over onto the sidewalk below.

Sefton and Judy arrived sometime in the summer of 1968 in a colorful cavalcade of carefree spirits intending to establish a communal farm; forty-five years later, they are the only members of it who remain. Odd as it may seem at first or even second glance, they are valued members of the community. They set up in Town Square every other Saturday morning, under the biggest of the oak trees, and sell produce – which are sometimes a slow-seller, because in Luna City, most residents have a vegetable garden themselves – but also eggs, honey, home-made goat-milk cheeses, herbs, and hand-made soap. The Grant's vegetable patch has the advantage of deep and rich soil on the bank of the river, and generous applications of well-cured compost seasoned with goat-manure. A single disintegrating Airstream trailer is still parked there in the field which is supposed to be the campground, a relic of the past. Sometimes a relatively broke or undiscriminating traveler rents it for a couple of days or weeks; the Englishman who manages the Luna City Café and Coffee lives there now. Only a few residents of Luna City refer scornfully to the Grant place as Hippie Hollow. Mrs. Sook Walcott is one of these; if Jess Abernathy has commerce in her bones and blood, Sook Walcott has all that, tempered with the acid of pure acquisitive capitalism. The Grants are liked, and Sook Walcott is not … more about that, later.

The tea room and thrift shop housed in the front room of the old McAllister house is open only two days a week which discourages casual visitors, but not anyone who knows Miss Leticia McAllister; the last woman in this part of the world who always wears a hat and gloves when she leaves the house, not just for early Sunday services at the Luna City First Methodist Church. The formidable Leticia McAllister – known as Miss Letty, even during those decades when she taught first grade in the Luna City Elementary school – is notoriously impatient, especially of anything reputed to be humorous. On the occasion of the centenary of Luna City, Miss Letty and her older brother, Doctor Douglas McAllister (the doctorate was in history, which he taught at a private university in San Antonio) compiled a commemorative volume of local history, gleaned from the memories of the oldest residents; scandals, shenanigans both political and sexual, the last gunfight in Luna City (which happened in front of the Luna Café and Coffee) old feuds and new, controversies over every imaginable small-town issue – it's all there in *A Brief History of Luna City, Texas*, published privately in San Antonio, 1976, price $18.25

plus sales tax. The Luna Café & Coffee still has a small and dusty stack of them behind the cash register counter – although the manager/chef at the Luna Café & Coffee has no idea of what they are or what to do with them. Where he comes from, a hundred years is practically yesterday. Miss Letty's erratically-open tea room also has a couple of boxes in inventory. Dr. McAllister, whose puckish sense of humor was not appreciated by his sister, was dissuaded from titling it *A Hundred Years of Lunacy in South Texas* on the very fair grounds that other places possessed a history every bit as scandalous, and that it would somehow encourage local residents to be called Lunatics, rather than Lunaites … and that simply would not do at all.

Luna City, you will gather from this short introduction, does not precisely discourage visitors, but neither does it welcome them effusively. Luna-tes prefer to take a quiet measure of such visitors who do venture into the heart of downtown, and treat them with exquisite Texas courtesy. Those who choose to remain longer than a quiet stroll around the square or stop for a lunch at the Luna Café & Coffee – never doubt their welcome. If they fall under the spell and stay, within four or five years, they are as established and respected as any of the original Luna-ite families; McAllisters, Gonzalez-with-a-z and Gonzales-with-an-s, Abernathy-who runs-the-hardware-store, Wyler-of-the-Lazy W Ranch, the Bodies of the feed mill and all the rest. Lunaites have no urge or need to disdain relative newcomers. They know exactly who they are and do not need proving it to anyone.

The End of the Road

It was Berto Gonzales who brought the Englishman to Luna City –
the year that Berto was in his freshman year at Palo Alto on San Antonio's
south side and driving a luxury town car at night for his uncle Tony. Uncle
Tony Gonzales lived in Elmendorf, but ran his business based in San
Antonio, and Berto was living with Uncle Tony's family while he attended
college. Berto was one of the bookish Gonzaleses, but had no objection to
driving for Uncle Tony, who was both a third-cousin once removed, and
married to Berto's Aunt Lucy.

"You get to meet all kindsa people," Uncle Tony was fond of
expounding. "I drove Bryant Gumbel, once … and Spurs players? All the
time; I got Tony Parkers' autograph, even."

On one particular summer evening around six PM, Berto got a call
in the town car from Uncle Tony's dispatch office. "Got a pick-up at
Stinson – half an hour. It's a special – he'll be waiting for you out in front."

"Cool," said Berto. "Is it a celebrity? Where's the pick-up to go?" Stinson was the old airport on the South Side which served mostly corporate and private aircraft; a quieter, less frenetic place. And if the pick-up was someone famous, that would give him something to brag about on Monday morning. Dropping down to Mission Road was a snap compared to fighting heavy rush-hour traffic around San Antonio International on a Friday. Stinson was nearly out into the country on the edge of Espada Park.

"He'll tell you when you get there," the dispatcher replied.

Berto nearly gave up in dismay when he pulled into one of the parking spaces in front of the brand-spanking new little terminal. There was no one out on the sidewalk who looked like a passenger – and there was already another town car pulled in. After ten minutes there still wasn't any sign of a pick-up. Out beyond the terminal building and row of hangars and warehouses which lined that side of Mission Road was the ramp and a pair of runways. The airport was separated from Mission Road by nothing more imposing than some chain-link fences hung with any number of threatening signs. Presently, a silver and blue Gulfstream dropped low on approach and touched down with a roar. It flashed past the terminal, came around at the end, and taxied up to the terminal, being lost to sight but not hearing. Berto opened the door and got out of the car, wilting briefly in the blast of heat after the coolness of the air-conditioned car. The driver of the other car was already out, standing in front of his car with a sign in his hand – Wilson written in block letters in felt-tip. The other driver acknowledged him with a brief nod.

"Busy day," he commented and Berto sighed.

"Sooner here than SA International."

"That's for certain," the other driver grunted. Another small jet dropped down from the blue sky – a Learjet with a t-tail and wings which turned sharply upwards at the very tips.

"Looks like my fare," Berto observed. No, passenger pick-up at Stinson did not usually take long. The Lear rolled down the ramp with an ear-piercing shriek from its engines and vanished behind the terminal. Three minutes, four minutes … a single person appeared from the glass doors leading out to the apron of paving, interspersed with raised beds and patches of grass which formed the forecourt. Berto watched his pick-up approach – a young man carrying a small overnight bag in one hand and a half-empty bottle in the other.

"Oh-oh," the other driver remarked, with considerable sympathy, as the man seemed to pause, look in their direction and focus with an effort. "You got yourself a drunk, it looks like. Sooner you than me, *hijito*."

"I hope he don't barf on Uncle Tony's upholstery, 'cause he will kill me." Berto watched his fare approach; a young man, with dark straight hair cut short, as if he were going out for football this season. His clothes were wrinkled as if he had slept in them for a week. He staggered over to the bicycle rack set out by the flagpole and the handicapped parking. On his way, he dropped the bottle into the hedge. Then, clutching the bicycle rack for support, he began throwing up.

"Looks like he got that taken care of already," the other driver remarked. He held up the Wilson sign as a knot of people appeared in the terminal doorway. "Good luck, *hijito* … you wanna couple plastic bags? I got some in the trunk, just for this kind of thing."

"Yeah, sure." Berto's fare made one last heave, straightened himself from the bicycle rack, and approached the two town cars, walking as carefully as if he were on eggshells.

"I say, chaps," He spoke carefully, enunciating every word – oh, yes; English. He talked like some of those characters on those PBS programs that Aunt Lucy was so fond of. "I only needed the one car… I am, as you may observe, traveling very light."

"If you aren't Wilson, then he's all yours." The other driver jerked his thumb at Berto, adding in a low tone, "I'll get you those items I mentioned."

"Alas, I am not Wilson," the fare admitted, sounding rather sad about that. "But rather – Richard Astor-Hall, or what remains of him. Have you heard of me?"

"I gotta say that I haven't," Berto replied, disappointed. He had so been hoping for a celebrity on this pick-up. Unexpectedly this seemed to cheer Mr. Astor-Hall. Berto opened the passenger door and asked, "Where am I supposed to take you, Mr. Hall?"

Mr. Astor-Hall drew himself up to his full height and tossed his overnight bag into the front passenger seat. He fished into his pants pocket, drew out a roll of bills the size of which Berto had never seen before, not even at Uncle Jesus' garage, where many of the old customers preferred paying in cash and pressed it into Berto's hand.

"As far from here as that will take me," he said grandly and passed out cold.

Berto caught him one-handed as he sagged and directed Mr. Astor-Hall's unconscious body into the back seat of the town car. The other driver shook his head, in sympathy, as he helped Berto tuck in Mr. Astor-Hall's legs and close the door.

"Turn his head sideways, so he won't choke on it if he's sick again. What are you gonna do with him? That's one heck of a roll, *hijito* – enough to take him a good long way."

"Three – four hundred bucks," Berto hastily counted out the fifties and twenties, then folded them away, deep in thought. Meanwhile, the other driver's fare gathered around, busy with getting their expensive luggage stowed away. A Friday evening, an unlimited expense account – and Uncle Tony would understand.

"We're going home to Luna," Berto said out loud to his unconscious passenger, as he backed out of the parking place, and turned south, towards

Presa Street, and the road towards Luna City. Mr. Astor-Hall snored comfortably in the back seat – if he had no particular place in mind, then Luna City would do as well as any.

At about the time Berto was coming up to Floresville a cellphone rang, rang insistently from deep inside Mr. Astor-Hall's little bag. Berto let it go, let it ring several times, but whoever was calling didn't want to give up. Finally, he pulled over into the Whattaburger parking lot and fished the phone out of the bottom of the bag, underneath some clothes and two unopened bottles of Cristal; a Blackberry with a black and red plaid bandanna wrapped around it. Berto hastily untangled phone from bandanna. The ID of the caller said only "Morty."

"Hello?" Berto said, tentatively into it. The voice on the other end – presumably Morty exclaimed, in a burst of impatient profanity;

"Oh, for f—ks sake, Rich – you finally pick up the damned phone. You gotta be in LA by now. Look, I've been leaving messages on your voicemail for hours … no, don't talk, just listen, things are happening too damned fast. I'm trying to put the kibosh on the paparazzi, but you know how it is; a few dozen A-listers puking on the pavement in front of Carême on opening night no less … and you running stark-naked through the streets, with a colander on your head, screaming 'I'm a little teapot short and stout' as you bang two pots together! That's made the news on three continents, Rich; what the f—k were you thinking? Never mind, that's why I get paid the big bucks to get ahead of PR disasters. I got you booked into that fancy place in Malibu for as long as it will take for you to deal with your personal demons – but I gotta have you promise you'll stay in LA and keep your yap shut until I can get ahead of this thing. Damage control – it can be fixed, you can make a come-back, just let ol' Morty work his magic. Don't talk to anyone. Rich – are you listening to me?"

"Hello?" Berto said again.

Morty exploded. "Who the f—k is this?"

"No one," Berto hung up the phone. It buzzed again almost at once. Berto turned the phone off and carefully put it back into Mr. Astor-Hall's bag. It was almost sundown, and he had another hour and a half on the road. Uncle Tony always said that you couldn't and shouldn't drive distracted.

The Gonzalez/Gonzales Clan

The main farm-to-market county road, which skims past Luna City does not actually go into the heart of Luna, *per se*. The old McAllister house is there, of course, set back from the roadside in a lavish and well-tended garden set out in Victorian design – a lady tastefully withdrawing her immaculate skirt from the dirt of vulgar commerce and transportation. The house itself is set at a slight but perceptible angle from the roadway itself, which the cognoscenti know is proof that the house predates the road by any number of years. Miss Letty McAllister, whose family home this is – is now in her mid 90s, the oldest living inhabitant of Luna City, and the living repository of civic memory, public and private. It has been at least twenty years since Miss Letty has seen to maintaining the garden; one of the myriad Gonzalez-with-an-z family enterprises sees to that.

The sprawling and interrelated clans of Gonzales-with-an-s and the Gonzalez-with-a-z are acknowledged freely by all Lunaites to be the oldest family in the area. Their shifting residency within five or six miles of the place where the road between San Antonio and the coast crosses the river – where Luna City would come to be – predates the founding by at least a hundred and twenty years and possibly more. There are supposed to be records in the colonial archives in Madrid, Spain, of a royal grant to a Don Diego Manuel Hernando Ruiz y Gonzalez or Gonzales of a league and a labor of land in the area. In 1968, there was a careful archeological excavation made of the foundations of a small adobe brick building not far from the present-day main gate to the Wyler Lazy W Ranch. The results were included in *A Brief History of Luna City* since Dr. McAllister was privy to the reports of findings. It was judged to be a residence by the eminent archeologist from San Antonio who oversaw the dig – but a relatively comfortless and primitive one: two thick-walled rooms, sheltering humans in one and draft animals and goats in the other.

At the presentation of the results of that dig at the regular meeting of the Luna City Historical Society in August, 1970, the eminent archeologist gave it as his considered opinion that it had merely been a barn and bunkhouse for hired shepherds, and never a permanent residence. Jesus Gonzalez, Senior, then paterfamilias of that branch of the clan insisted heatedly that no, the site thus excavated had been that of the ancestral home – nay, mansion – which family folklore insisted had been adorned with many imported refinements, furnishings and ornaments. Since the elder Mr. Gonzalez had come straight from his place of business – the Gonzalez Auto Engine and Body Repair shop, after a frustrating day of doing battle with an ancient and recalcitrant tow truck – the eminent archeologist was curtly dismissive in his reply. He riposted that if so, his excavation had failed to find the slightest trace of evidence for such an establishment, to which Jesus Gonzalez gave as his considered opinion that the archeologist was incapable of locating his posterior with a compass and topological map and moreover that the archeologist's female ancestors had engaged routinely in unnatural congress with barnyard animals. A lively and stimulating discussion emerged, which was only concluded when Dr. Wyler, chairing the meeting in his office as president of the Historical Society, drew his ancient 1911 model Colt pistol from his briefcase and forcefully requested a return to civility and decorum. Meetings of the Luna City Historical Society occasionally become that heated.

The Gonzales and Gonzalez families – so tightly braided together by two hundred years of intermarriage that the family tree is a kind of Gordian knot, resistant to all mapping by genealogists – are a considerable force in the daily doings of Luna City and environs. Jesus Gonzalez, Junior, inherited the familial auto repair shop along with his father's position as head of the clan. His sons and nephews drive the wrecker which will come in response to a call for help from unlucky motorists along a twenty-mile stretch of county road, and tend to all aspects of maintaining and repairing automobiles, trucks, motorcycles, and farm machinery. Gonzalez and Gonzales brothers, sons, nephews, and cousins of every degree are profitably employed in a construction company which has built those few structures in Luna City which date from later than the middle of the last century, the HVAC company – always in demand during the 100-degree summers for which South Texas is so famed – cesspool pumping, and lawn and garden maintenance. The residences of the Gonzalezes and Gonzaleses are salted fairly evenly throughout Luna City and those fringes where town begins raveling out into open countryside. They tend to live in small, early 20th century bungalows with sagging porches, or plain stick-built bungalows of a later date which resemble Monopoly houses with sagging roofs, or in aging double and triple-wide trailers, surrounded by construction vehicles, trailers, tractors, and off-road vehicles. It is indeed curious and more than a little ironic that for people so deeply and professionally involved in construction, landscape maintenance and auto repair, their own residences usually could do with repairs and paint, the yards are most often a wilderness of tall grass and overgrown shrubs seeded with junk, and their own motor vehicles are aging miracles of rust held together with Bondo and bailing wire, splotched with primer, and the occasional missing window replaced by a piece of plastic sheeting and duct tape.

As a general rule, the Gonzaleses tend to be rather more bookish, cerebral, even. The slightly younger brother of Jaimie Gonzales – head of that branch of the clan – was moved as a young man to apply to join the State Department and was subsequently assigned all over South America for thirty years. He now lives in an upscale townhouse in San Antonio where he is writing a beautifully illustrated book about opera houses in South American cities. Jaimie Gonzales's nephew, Sylvester, who served in the US Marines for a much shorter period as a field wireman, now sees to the maintenance needs of those Lunaites who have computers and cellphones.

It should also be noted that Gonzalezes and Gonzaleses make up better than half of the surnames on the membership rolls of the Luna City VFW post both past and present, and about a third of the names carved onto the four facets of the war memorial in the corner of Town Square, opposite Abernathy Hardware. Fifteen Lunaites currently serve on active duty – Army, Navy, Marines, Air Force ... and a single volunteer for the Coast Guard. Young Horatio Gonzales was always a non-conformist. Miss Letty noticed his disinclination to color between the lines, when she taught him in the first grade at Luna Elementary, and confidently predicted his eventual career.

Members of the VFW meet informally on Saturday afternoons in the VFW hall, around in back of the Tip-Top Icehouse, Grocery and Gas. This is the faded desert-pink building which used to be a temporary classroom at the high school, until construction of the consolidated high school in 1989 made the old temporary structures surplus to needs. Roman

Gonzalez, construction foreman, did not want to see a perfectly sound building go to waste, not when the previous VFW post building was disintegrating under a simultaneous attack by carpenter ants, black mold and general rot. He rounded up the required equipment and volunteers, raised the building on wheeled jacks, and then carefully inched the old pink classroom down Oak Street, around the great oak that sits at the intersection of Oak and West Town Square, and out to its present position. The presence of the Mighty Fighting Moth Marching Band – who happened to be in practice on the day when Roman and his friends came to move the building – added considerably to the occasion by playing um pah-band selections and slow-marching in front, as it advanced from its old to the new location.

Yes, indeed – every day is an excuse for a parade, in Luna City.

Sunrise at the Age of Aquarius

On Saturday morning, Berto Gonzales slept in, knowing that he should have the town car back to Uncle Tony's place in Elmendorf by mid-day. He came yawning from the tiny back bedroom at his father's house, drawn by the smell of bacon frying, coffee brewing, and the sound of the cable Univision channel on rather loudly. His grandmother, Adeliza Gonzales, had never learned fluent English and was slightly deaf besides – but in spite of that and being relatively homebound at the age of 89, Adeliza Gonzales didn't miss much, even though the only English-language programs she ever watched were on the Food Network. Berto's father had bought a wide-screen television specifically to put in the kitchen so that Abuela Adeliza could watch her cooking shows in the comfort of the room that she loved the best.

"Morning, Abuela," Berto said, and then repeated himself, slightly louder. Abuela Adeliza's attention was riveted to the television screen, where an excited announcer was yammering on about … Berto wasn't sure. It looked shaky camera-phone footage of a naked man with something metallic on his head, running down the street in a foreign city – a brief clip, then to steadier footage of an important-looking storefront building, with numerous ambulances parked in front, their rotating flashing lights casting flares everywhere.

Abuela Adeliza shook her head in dismay. "Poor, poor fellow! Such a shame … he had such a fine future before him. 'Morning, Berto; did you sleep well, then?"

"Always," Berto dropped a brief kiss on the top of Abuela Adeliza's head. "Abuelita, may I have some *migos* and bacon? No one cooks *migos* like you do," he added with calculation. Just as expected, Abela Adeliza rose from her rocking chair. The bacon was already cooked; a bowl of fresh-gathered eggs sat on the counter by the stove.

"Of course, Berto," she replied, but Berto's attention was suddenly riveted by the television, all hunger forgotten. On the screen appeared a series of pictures – some of them intended for maximum dangerous glamor – of a youngish and rather handsome man in his thirties in a series of poses, alone or with others. In most of them, his head was covered by a black and red plaid handkerchief tied do-rag fashion; his lower face adorned by carefully cultivated designer stubble; he held a knife, a cooking fork or a mixing bowl and whisk, standing in front of a truly ferocious stainless steel restaurant stove. The handkerchief seemed oddly familiar to Berto … and come to think of it, so did the young man's features.

"Abuelita – who is he? That man – do you know him?"

"Why, of course I do, Berto – it's Rich Hall – they call him the Bad Boy Chef. He was coming up in the world, on television cooking shows so often… I thought he looked so much like your Abuelo Jesus when he was young – so dashing and handsome, so I always watched when he was on."

"Well, damn," Berto exclaimed. "So he is a celebrity, after all! That's the guy I picked up at Stinson last night. I practically don't recognize him when he isn't barfing or dead to the world."

"Oh, Berto!" Abuela Adeliza dropped the fork she had been scrambling eggs with. "Are you certain? But you must call Chief Vaughn at once and tell him! Everyone is searching for him, *pobrecito*! He has disappeared!"

"No, he hasn't, Abuelita – I dropped him off at Hippie Hollow!"

Abuela Adeliza assumed her sternest expression, commanding, "Berto – you will obey! You will call the police, at once."

"Why?" Berto was no longer eight years old, even if Abuela Adeliza still seemed to think so, sometimes. Abuela Adeliza told him. Before she was even finished, Berto had picked up the phone and dialed Joe Vaughn's office.

"I swear to God, Jess," Dr. Stephen Wyler examined the sludge at the bottom of his coffee mug, "if things don't get better around here, I might as well stay home and poison myself with my own coffee."

"No, you old poop, you have too much fun, carrying on complaining," Jess Abernathy replied, with a notable lack of sympathy.

"I'll thank you to keep a civil tongue in your head, young woman," Dr. Wyler replied, and Jess grinned at him. They were actually quite good friends, despite a distance of sixty years of age between them, Jess being a qualified CPA and Dr. Wyler one of her clients. As he was materially the wealthiest among them, Jess spent a good many hours untangling and keeping his complicated finances more or less in apple-pie order. There wasn't much Jess didn't know about Dr. Wyler. If no man was a hero to his valet, he most certainly isn't to his CPA. Jess regarded him very much as a kind of honorary uncle, aside from the professional considerations. And being both Lunaites from birth, she had known him all of her life.

"We might advertise for a replacement cook," she suggested. "The *Bee-Picayune* has rather reasonable rates. I'll call and see if they have room in next weeks' classifieds."

"That's how I got whats-his-name," Dr. Wyler scowled. "And he left without notice as soon as he got a better offer from those bastards at Mills Farm … damn, is that your phone?"

"No, it's yours," Jess replied. She and Dr. Wyler were sitting at one of the outside tables at the Luna Café and Coffee, enjoying the relative coolness of the morning, if not the current dismal state of the Café's menu selections.

"Damn fool invention." Dr. Wyler unsnapped the catches of the ageing leather medical bag that accompanied him everywhere. He fished out the insistently buzzing cellphone from its depths and regarded it with mystification.

"Finger on the circle and slide over," Jess hinted broadly.

"I knew that … Hello? Wyler here, what's your major malfunction? Oh, hullo, Sefton." Jess listened to the faint squawking emanating from Dr. Wyler's phone. At last, he broke the connection. "Sorry, my dear – duty calls. Azúcar has developed a cyst on his neck which simply defies all of Judy's home remedies."

Azúcar was the Grant's pet snow-white llama, who because he had been bottle-fed since shortly after birth, had grown up to be almost two hundred pounds of bossiness with regard to humans.

"I'll come with you," Jess hastily stuffed her notebook, and took out some change for a tip, for Araceli the senior waitress and the long-suffering high school girls who tended tables during the summer. At ninety-four, Dr. Wyler was as wiry and weathered as a lifetime of riding, working cattle, and tending to the medical needs of large recalcitrant animals could have made him, but still … ninety-four, against a two-hundred pound, obnoxious llama? Jess would have never forgiven herself if Dr. Wyler came to harm. "Heads driver, tails shotgun?"

"Tails."

Jess deftly flipped the largest coin, caught it in her palm and slapped it down on the table.

"Heads. I drive, Doc."

The Age of Aquarius Campground and Goat Farm was but a short distance away; it would have been little trouble for Jess to walk, but the day was already becoming warm, and mid-summers in South Texas are merciless to the elderly, no matter how hardened by a lifetime of work in it. Dr. Wyler's late model extended-cab pickup truck with the custom design – the brand of the Lazy W Exotic Game Ranch on the front doors – bumped down the unpaved ruts between the pasture where the Grants' goat herd spent their days, and the smaller meadow scarred with regular tracks which – if you squinted and the light was dim – did somewhat resemble a campground. The only evidence of this for most of the year was the aged Airstream trailer with long-disintegrated tires parked at the top of the slope, under a fringe of trees farthest from the riverbank, as the solstice had been last month. The last of the mid-summer nudists had been gone for weeks and the campground reverted to its usual dilapidated appearance. A heavy old-style picnic table with attached benches sat in a patch of shade near the Airstream, a table gone grey with weathering, and scarred with the many sets of initials and graffiti carved into it by bored hippies and teenagers.

As Dr. Wyler's truck came around the last bend, they both saw the single Luna City Police Department cruiser parked by the moldering Airstream, and Joe Vaughn – every crease of his crisp tan short-sleeved summer uniform as sharp as if it had just came from the cleaners not ten minutes ago – leaning against the fender, deep in conversation with Sefton and Judy. In marked contrast, the Grants were not crisp in their attire. In point of fact, neither of them were attired, although in deference to local sensibilities and the expectation of visitors, both had donned simple hand-loomed loincloths. It has long been a truism, and one deeply appreciated by Lunaites that in just about every case, those who proudly and defiantly forswear clothing really ought not to indulge themselves, as a matter of aesthetics. Judy's long hair covered the top half of her body rather efficiently, and Sefton wore battered cowboy boots.

"What's going on, Chief?" Dr. Wyler spoke first. Joe Vaughn tilted his white felt Stetson a little farther back on his head and nodded politely to Judy. Joe was tall, hawk-faced with a direct gaze – also like a hawk – and very, very fit. Part of a military tattoo with the motto "Death from Above" showed below the bottom of his shirt sleeve, which barely constrained the arm it clothed. His very muscles had muscles of their own.

"Welfare check on a guest," Joe replied. "Berto Gonzales called me up, first thing this morning, with a tale of how he brought out a fare last night from San Antonio – and he saw him on the TV this morning. Miz Adeliza told him some cock and bull about the fare being some TV celebrity chef that went 'round the bend. Just as soon as I put the phone down, Miz Grant calls and tells me that their guest from last night is nowhere to be found. His clothes, his bag and wallet are all here."

"And two empty bottles of Cristal," Judy Grant put in, her pleasant round face the picture of worry. "I think he must have drunk it all. You don't think he's done away with himself, do you?"

"Overpriced gnat-piss," Dr. Wyler put in, *à propos* of nothing in particular. "A man with real taste wouldn't swill anything but Krug for a last drink."

"Young Berto says his grandma told him this runaway chef is a bad boy named Rich Hall," Joe Vaughn answered. "But this joker's Green Card and visa say that he is Richard Astor-Hall, and that he came in through New York two days ago. The paperwork says that he is a chef, though."

"You don't say," Dr. Wyler's expression brightened, but just then, the screaming started.

Welcome to Luna City: Town Square

The heart of Luna City is known as the "Square." On maps it is called "Town Square." It is one of the most formidably charming central squares in South Texas, although it never has been adorned with the county courthouse which would have been its lot, had the railway come through as originally intended. Karnesville, thirty miles distant to the east became the county seat, snatching the prize from the hands of Arthur Wells McAllister and his patrons in the real estate business. Luna City may have been left with a hole in its civic heart, but as Dr. Stephen Wyler was often wont to observe; when life gives you lemons, get out the blender and plenty of tequila and make margaritas out of them. And so did the founding fathers of Luna City; they made civic margaritas from their blasted hopes for regional prominence.

Arthur Wells McAllister sighed and put away his architectural designs for a massive Beaux Arts-style courthouse, and revised his vision for Town Square as a public park, an outdoor ballroom and public space. A number of wide promenades delineated the edges of the space. At the time of the planning of Luna City, the space designated to be an open square was adorned with a stand of massive, thick-limbed native oak trees, which trees were sensibly retained, and a swath of lawn encouraged to establish itself around and beneath. Four more promenades began from the corners of the square and mid-point of each side, meeting in the center, for which Arthur Wells McAllister designed an elaborate Beaux Arts style bandstand, into which he poured all the elements which had previously distinguished his courthouse design. A greatly simplified bandstand was eventually constructed (including the public lavatories on the lower level) and inaugurated with a festival concert in 1893. The performing band was supposed to be conducted by the great John Philips Sousa, who declined an invitation to perform, pleading a previous engagement. Nonetheless, the bandstand still exists – a generous donation from the Wyler family in 1993 allowed it to be completely rebuilt and renovated on the centenary of its construction. The lavatories underneath the bandstand are now the office of the Luna City Parks and Recreation and garage for their riding lawnmower although the facility still smells faintly of ancient urine on the hottest of summer days.

The remainder of the Square is only particularly notable for the War Memorial in the northwest corner, and a historical marker at the foot of the second tree to the north of the intersection of Oak Street and Town Square. This was the tree from which an enraged lynch mob nearly hanged Charley Mills in 1926. Charley Mills had been caught, in flagrante, as it were – the exact nature of the crime for which he was apprehended on that particular occasion is somewhat uncertain, but his criminal record in the archives of the Luna City police force take up nearly half a file drawer in Joe Vaughn's office, and the list of crimes charged against his name in

1926 alone include domestic abuse, interferences with underage females, bootlegging, attempted arson, speeding – in a horse-drawn wagon – buggery, impersonation of a nun, maintenance of an illicit still, cattle rustling, unspecified thievery, public brawling, forgery of public documents, and indecent conduct in a public place, the exact nature of which is mercifully unspecified. Charley Mills – a deep-dyed blotch on the civic escutcheon and specific inspiration for any number of laws enacted by the state and county – was rescued from the hands of the 1926 lynch mob and survived to a ripe and disgraceful old age. He was resuscitated, in a manner of speaking some four decades later, by the marketing division of the corporation which owns and operates Mills Farm, just down the road to the south, as the official host and public face for the enterprise which offers an event venue for weddings, parties and corporate events, a specimen garden, wildflower fields and a small store selling organic nuts, dried fruits, jams, jellies, pickles and soup mixes. More of Mills Farm and Charley Mills, later.

Town Square is surrounded on three sides by classic brick and stone late Victorian and early 20th century shop fronts, two and three stories tall; Abernathy Hardware (established 1885 as spelled out in white bricks on the façade) the Cattleman Hotel, which has a wide covered gallery on the second floor, and takes up nearly half of the east side of Town Square, the Luna City Savings & Loan – which breaks the Victorian mold, as it presents a neo-classical red brick front, with four round white columns holding up a classic pediment. Across the western side of the square is another two-story neoclassical red brick building with white columns holding up the temple-like entryway; this is the old unified school building, which once housed all grades but now is the elementary and middle school, with the offices of the Luna City Independent School District occupying two of the downstairs offices. Science * Religion * Patriotism is engraved in two-foot letters across the entablature. The school building takes up nearly all of that side of Town Square, and as generously stately a building as it was, by the mid-fifties, a new building had to be put up at the edge of town to accommodate the high school. Luna City experienced a small population boom at that time, with constriction of several streets of post-war ranch-style houses on the north side of town. A narrow shopfront next to the town hall and Chamber of Commerce houses the Steins' used book and antique store, with the Luna City Café and Coffee just beyond. On fair days, there are always people sitting out at the tables and chairs set out on the wide sidewalk underneath the awnings which offer shade and shelter where the oak trees do not reach. Conventional wisdom has it that if you sit there for long enough, you will see everyone you know in Luna City. This has never happened for the Englishman who runs the Café now – but then, he came to Luna City hoping never to see most everyone he knows ever again.

A Free Man in Paris – or Luna City

"Oh, god!" Jess exclaimed.

"Oh, f__k!" growled Joe Vaughn, as he unsnapped the strap on his holster.

"Jumping Jesus Key-rist on a pogo-stick!" Dr. Wyler raised his reading glasses and squinted across the raddled meadow that was the campground at the frantically leaping, sun-browned and vaguely human figure leaping and twisting like an agonized gazelle on the riverbank.

"Oh, dear," said Judy, wringing her hands. "I think he found a fire-ant nest the hard way."

"Oh, sh*t!" responded her husband. "Judikins, you know we don't wanna use all those artificial insecticides on the property … but for the happiness and safety of our visitors …"

"Seftie, sweetie," Judy replied, with the most obdurate expression that her otherwise sweetly bland countenance could muster, "We agreed. No inorganics."

"But fire ants!" Sefton protested in a half-hearted way, as Dr. Wyler snorted contemptuously, "You morons, everything is organic; if you are going to pretend to be scientifically knowledgeable, at least get the terminology down right."

"Cool it, Doc." Jess whispered, warningly. The Grants were also her clients. And Luna City was a small place, in which conventional courtesies greased social interaction among those with wildly differing social and political philosophies to achieve a sometimes startling degree of amity when it came to outsiders.

"Well, sports fans, I think we found the missing guest," Joe Vaughn re-snapped the strap across the top of his side-arm holster, regarding the empty campground with a particularly sour mien. "And a damn-good broken-field runner – pity he can't play for the Moths next season."

"Looks like he will fit in here real well, Seftie," Judy commented, as the naked runner galloped across the intervening meadow at top speed. He was being chased by a very small Nubian goat, bleating enthusiastically. "He has already made friends with one of Rigoberta's babies! How sweet!"

The naked runner arrived, just short of the interested cluster of observers, his chest – clearly visible to them all – heaving like a bellows – and his eyes showing white all the way around.

"What the blooming hell!" he gasped. "Where am I? What is going on, and why is this … this thing following me. I couldn't find the dunny in this benighted place … and I woke up … oh, flaming hell!"

He swatted ineffectually at his thighs and nether parts. "Get them off me! Flaming hell, that stings!"

"He found the fire ants," Joe Vaughn announced to the world at large. "Jesus, sport – get a grip and put on your pants – there's ladies present. You're in Luna City, Texas."

"I don't think I am seeing anything I don't already know about," Jess replied, with an edge in her voice which unaccountably caused Joe Vaughn to turn faintly red, underneath his tan.

"Aloe vera," Judy Grant announced, with a great deal of satisfaction. "Seftie, you know where my aloe vera patch is … can you be a sweetie and break off a length – about as long as your hand. It's the least we can do, to make up for the fire ants. There's a bottle of witch hazel under the sink in the workroom – bring that, too." As her spouse trotted away obediently, she regarded their visitor with appreciative interest.

"Fire ants!" The naked runner had recovered control of his voice. "The ants of hell, escaped when the hatch was open! Is it too much to request that you can blast them from orbit as it were?"

"No can do, sport," Joe Vaughn replied, with a notable lack of sympathy. "Your hosts at the Age of Aquarius Campground and Goat Farm believe in organic solutions to organic problems."

"Everything is organic." Dr. Wyler sized up the situation with the analytical eye of long practice and opened his medical bag. "And compared to screw-worms and bot-flies, fire ants are a walk in the park. Painful, but a walk in the park. You don't have any open wounds on you, do you, son? Aside from the ant bites?" He soaked a wad of cotton gauze with rubbing alcohol and handed it to suffering patient. Meanwhile, the small goat continued to frolic around him, occasionally emitting a plaintive baaaa and darting at his knees.

"Let it go, Doctor Wy," Jess hissed, as Dr. Wyler continued, "Never mind the witch hazel, just wipe 'em off. And put on some pants as the Chief said. You're embarrassing the horses with delusions of adequacy."

"Your papers say that you are Richard Astor-Hall," Joe Vaughn thoughtfully examined the skyline, as the Grant's guest swabbed the gauze over his mid-section and buttocks, front and back. "If so – then who is this Rich Hall person? I'll wait on an answer, until whichever one you are puts on some clothes."

"Appreciate the delicate consideration, my dear chap," the Grant's guest replied, with a great deal more urbanity than any of the other two men present could have mustered under the same circumstances. In a few moments, Sefton came panting down the path from the Grant's eccentric and rickety home-built yurt with tree-house and cave additions, bearing a length of thick green cactus spear in one hand, and a gallon jug in the other. The naked guest vanished into the depths of the near-derelict Airstream. The small goat waited, forlorn, at the foot of the steps into it, restrained by Judy, who called into the trailer before the door banged shut,

"Just rub the cut end over the worst of the bites … it's organic and healthful …"

"Everything…" Dr. Wyler snarled, and Jess reminded him, sotto voice, "I said – let it go, Doc."

By mutual consent, everyone moved to the battered picnic table, where a small live oak afforded a patch of shade, relief from the blazing sun which was already making the reflected heat shimmer over the hoods and roofs of Joe Vaughn's cruiser and Dr. Wyler's pick-up. They waited, in more or less companionable silence, for the odd Englishman to emerge from the Airstream.

"I meant to ask," Jess said to Judy, "For a quart of that honey, if you have any. And Dad is out of that rosemary-flavored soap that he likes. I know it's not your market Saturday, but I thought I would just ask."

"Not a problem," Judy smiled, beatifically. "I'll bring it around this afternoon. Just credit the account, when you get to it, sweetie."

The door to the Airstream opened, and the Englishman emerged – to Sefton and Judy's slight yet obvious disappointment, clad somewhat decently in a pair of crumpled draw-string pants and a wife-beater undershirt. Neither of those garments seemed particularly fresh from the laundry – but the only being who seemed to care was the baby Nubian goat. It bleated in happy joy when the Englishman sat down and nuzzled against his thigh.

"Why is that bloody creature doing that?" he asked, after a moment.

"Che likes you," Judy replied, happily oblivious to the elbow that Jess shot into Dr. Wyler's ribs as soon as the old veterinarian opened his mouth. "You must have a pure soul. Animals are sensitive to these kinds of things.".

Dr. Wyler subsided, muttering, "Tell that to old Gonzalez' piebald mule in '53 – a broken rib and half a dozen stitches."

Joe Vaughn cleared his throat. "You were saying … who really is Rich Hall?"

"A phantasm," the Englishman answered, sadly. "An ephemeral creation of the star-making machinery…"

"Behind the popular song," Judy Grant brightened. "So, you'd rather be a free man in Paris?"

"There's a lot of people looking for that special paradise," Sefton nodded in perfect comprehension, a lugubrious expression on his face. "Darned few ever found it here, though."

"Seftie, sweetie, don't be a downer. It isn't our fault," Judy explained to the world at large, and Joe Vaughn cleared his throat again. The very sound had a dangerous hint in it. The Englishman took his cue to continue with the deftness of a professional.

"A character in a play put on for the amusement of the masses, a manqué and a fraud. Rich Hall is a puppet. Raised in a sink estate, the oldest son of pair of alcoholic benefits scroungers …"

"That's your problem, right there," Dr. Wyler glared sideways at Jess before she could apply the elbow again. "Shush!" she hissed, and the strange Englishman continued as if there hadn't been an interruption. "Who learned to cook out of cookery books from the local lending library, to feed his ten younger brothers and sisters, all of whom would have starved and been taken into care, otherwise."

"A touching tale," Joe Vaughn observed, in a caustic tone of voice.

"Yes, I thought so," the Englishman agreed, rather smugly, "As did the publicists for the show; they ate it up as if it were the finest *flaugnarde* imaginable and so did the public."

Judy exclaimed, "How tragic! This should not properly happen … where were the child protection authorities? Someone should have done something!"

The Englishman sighed, heavily. "No, dear lady; it is not what you assume; were you not paying attention when I said that Rich Hall is a mere character, a creation put on for the masses? To continue; nearly a decade ago, he placed second in one of those popular television cooking competitions. Subsequently, he launched a career of his own, starring as a celebrity chef and all-around arsehole. He's not a nice person, you see," he added with an air of confiding in them all. "He throws tantrums on camera, flamboyantly dates other celebrities, generally makes a fool of himself in public … drinks too much, parties too hard, is rude to his friends … I can't stand the git any more, myself. I <u>would</u> rather be a free man in Paris. Or anywhere, really."

"But you are …" Judy Grant began, quite baffled, and the Englishman shook his head, mournfully.

"No," he answered, with a tragic sigh. "I am merely Richard Astor-Hall, the only child of well-to-do professionals. They lived in Bickley when I was growing up and now in the South of France – in a villa with a vineyard that I bought for them. I boarded at Charterhouse, and when I finished there, my parents paid for a full course of study in Paris at Cordon Bleu."

"Nice!" Dr. Wyler applauded. He had already assessed the Englishman with the same eye that he brought to all of his professional encounters.

"So, it was all a pretense?" Judy's face brightened, and the Englishman nodded. "What should we call you then?"

"Astor-Hall, if you simply must be formal," he replied. "But plain Richard will do."

"So, that's my job done," Joe Vaughn rose from his seat with some difficulty. He leaned across the table to extend a hand to Richard Astor-Hall. "Gotta be rolling, folks. Nice to meet you, Richard; welcome to Luna City – it's a small place, but people love it, or they get used to it after a while. Let me know if there is anything I can do."

"There is one thing, officer," Richard Astor-Hall ventured. "If there should be any inquiries after Rich Hall, from anyone at all …"

"Rich who?" Joe Vaughn grinned. "Never heard of him. G'day, ladies, Doc, Sefton. Crime waits for no man…"

He sauntered back to his cruiser, fired it up, circled around to the road again, and was soon only visible as a cloud of settling dust in the wake. Dr. Wyler spoke first.

"Best see to Azúcar, then – I ain't getting any younger. I got a question for you, Richard. What do you want to do with yourself, now?"

"Cook for people," Richard replied, at once. "That's it, mostly. The celebrity chef thing took me away from that. I spent all my time traveling. Being seen. Judging other people's cooking. Existence was an utter and complete bore."

"Then I have a business proposition, once I've seen to business here," the old veterinarian also rose – like Joe Vaughn, untangling himself from the picnic table bench with some difficulty, and gathered up his medical bag. He looked at the younger man for a long moment. "Masks, young fellow – we all wear 'em, to one degree or another. But a mask that's not got the slightest resemblance to what you really are underneath is a mask that don't fit – best take it off, and try another before it smothers you under the weight."

"I will consider that, sir, and thank you," Richard looked down at the tabletop. "I will be more than happy to consider your business proposition – and your advice about masks."

"Good. Coming, Jess?" Dr. Wyler shot over his shoulder. "Mr. Astor-Hall, if you are still here in the morning, report to me at the Luna Café and Coffee at 10 AM sharp, clean, dressed, and sober. Miss Judy, darlin', take me to your llama."

"Where?"

"The café is on Town Square," the old veterinarian answered. "Luna City is small – Judy and Sefton can tell you where the café is, give you a ride there, even. See you at ten. Is that your cellphone?"

"I'm afraid so," Richard signed. He ignored the incessant beeping from inside the Airstream, sitting at the table, as Sefton and Judy also untangled themselves from it.

"Aren't you going to pick up?" Judy asked, with concern.

"Not until I have to," Richard replied, morosely.

Mills Farm

Oh, what is there to say about Mills Farm, the destination event-venue, country-themed retail emporium, petting zoo, specimen garden, and country amusement park just to the south of Luna City which has not been said a thousand times already in expensive full-page advertisements in glossy lifestyle and travel magazines, or in television spots that are enticing mini-movies all crammed into sixty seconds? Because Mills Farm is owned and run by a large corporation who also own and run many similar properties – all tailored to local idiom and conditions – star-scattered across the United States and Europe, the money and expertise is most definitely there.

Nothing shows of this, of course, with regard to Mills Farm. It's all a carefully crafted down-home Texas experience, down to the cherubic and beaming countenance of Mills Farm's official greeter, Old Charley Mills himself, resplendent in immaculate overalls and calico shirt, with a carefully ragged straw hat on the back of his head, presiding over the entrance and occasionally throwing down a pitchfork of hay into the calf enclosure, or riding around seated on a carefully restored small-front Farmall F-20 tractor. Mills Farm is all about the theater.

There is a theater, by the way – an open-air amphitheater, with a series of expertly graded, terraced and grass-grown slopes, where the audience can spread out picnic blankets or folding chairs. There is also a carefully quaintified old-fashioned style dance hall for smaller, more intimate gatherings and dances. The Mills farmstead – a turn of the last century ginger-bread cottage painted white and adorned all the way around with covered screen-porches – is a bed-and-breakfast. It is not the original Mills farmhouse; oh, dear no – that was an unsavory shack which burned to the ground in 1927, possibly by the last private owner of Mills Farm for the insurance money. This present building was moved with great care from the lot in Beeville where it had originally been situated. Other, smaller cottages on the property are also available for overnight stays.

Most of the other structures at Mills Farm have also been brought in, or reconstructed to serve the various purposes. They host weddings, corporate retreats, concerts and what-have-you; but the traveling public is always encouraged to drop in for a brief visit to the general store, to wander in a herb garden laid out in the form of an acre-sized Texas flag and then to restore themselves with a meal at the Mills Farm Country Restaurant; part of the dining area is in a wide screened porch above a scenic bend in the river, with a grove of noble oak trees and a seasonal wild-flower meadow beyond. Every aspect pleases – and no expense has been spared in making and keeping it so.

Mills Farm is one of the largest single employers in the area. Since it opened, some thirty years ago, two generations of Luna City teenagers have cut their teeth in the job market by working there in the summer – waiting tables, working the cash register in the general store, or helping set up for events. The Gonzales and Gonzalez family enterprises are also important cogs in the machinery of Mills Farm, for facility-maintenance and grounds-keeping, mainly, although Cousin Teodoro "Teddy"

Gonzalez also plays an extremely vital role in the grand theater of Mills Farm.

Teddy Gonzalez was raised in Chicago after his father – Jaime Gonzalez's younger brother Alfredo – went to work in Henry Ford's River Run aircraft plant during World War II and married an Anglo girl from Minnesota. Teddy didn't come back to Luna City for good until he retired and got tired of shoveling show in the winter. Teddy sports a snowy white Santa Claus beard, and when he forgets, he sounds more like a Minnesotan when he speaks, but mainly, all he has to say is, 'Howdy, partner – welcome to Mills Farm!' or 'Bye, folks – y'all come back here right soon, you hear?' "

Yes, Cousin Teodoro plays Old Charley Mills: he and his wife live in one of the staff cottages on the grounds, so that he is always on hand. It's an easy job for him, though – the general manager, Benny Cordova takes care of all the heavy lifting. Benny Cordova is mildly renowned for being the only local Hispanic employee not related in any way to the Gonzaleses or Gonzalezes. He is, in fact, a foreigner from Beeville, and has only a vague notion of the true history of the real Old Charley Mills; reprobate, bootlegger, drunkard, bigamist and all-around blot on the civic escutcheon.

Only a few of the oldest inhabitants of Luna City have any first-hand recollection of Old Charley Mills: Miss Letty McAllister, Dr. Wyler, and perhaps one or two others. Charley Mills was in his final disgraceful decade of life when they were children; he was the sort of character whom small children were sternly warned against by their mothers, so vivid memories of his malign and drunken presence persisted. An accounting of his criminal and antisocial deeds take up a full chapter of *A Brief History of Luna City, Texas,* and are memorialized by the historical marker in Town Square at the foot of the tree from which he was nearly lynched in 1926 by long-suffering and wholly exasperated citizens. Upon his death, during the depths of the Depression – from natural old age, much to the surprise of the county coroner and the Luna City police department, and the disappointment of any number of his present and former common-law wives – the property comprising the farm fell even more into disrepair. The surviving wives, assorted Mills family heirs, and associates, and the even more numerous creditors fought over it like the gingham dog and calico cat for the next thirty years, until there was nothing left but a collection of ragged scraps and forty acres of derelict farmland. The corporation which now runs the revived Mills Farm purchased it from the last heir left standing in the 1970s and dedicated another decade to rebuilding it to their vision. Now and again, the corporate managers give a thought to expanding the attractions in the direction of Luna City, but then someone reminds them of the Charley Mills files in the offices of the Luna City Police Department, and soberer judgement reins in such plans. For now, anyway.

Making It Do

Left alone, save for the overly-friendly goat and the throbbing of an acute hangover, Richard sat at the table, listening to the incessant buzzing of his cellphone, with a musical accompaniment of a cicada in the tree over his head. The Airstream, while not actually a charmless pit of nonfunctioning domestic despair, was where a generation of small insects had gone to die in the dust, neglected and bare of comforts. Better to sit outside, listening to the cicadas. Presently another plume of dust appeared; a car bumping slowly over the ruts and bumps; an oddly familiar town car, which pulled into the same patch of trampled grass and came to a halt. The driver was also strangely familiar; a gangly young man with dark hair, and a curiously innocent face. Richard squinted against the bright sunshine, trying to figure out why car and driver seemed so familiar.

"Good morning, Mr. Astor-Hall ... you don't remember me, do you? I'm Berto Gonzales. I brought you here last night – you said you wanted to go anywhere, and I thought … well, Luna City would do. It's where I'm from when I'm not going to school or driving for Uncle Tony in Elmendorf."

Berto Gonzales opened the passenger door and assisted a very tiny and elderly lady from the car. She carried a small covered pot in her hands, padded with a pair of oven mitts. Richard, in attempting to rise from the picnic table, was entangled briefly by the bench and table legs. "This is my grandmother – everyone around here calls her Abuelita Adeliza … she watches the Food Channel a lot. She's a fan of yours. I said you were pretty drunk last night, so she brought you some *caldo* … it's good for you, 'specially if you aren't feeling well." As Abuelita Adeliza beamed at Richard, Berto Gonzales added, "She don't speak English."

Abuelita Adeliza said something in Spanish to her grandson, who relayed the message. "She says she is going to put the *caldo* on the stove burner, so that it will keep warm. It's real good *caldo*, home-made chicken broth, with lots of *fideo* in it … you might like it, even if it's only home cooking an' not from your fancy restaurant."

"I appreciate your grandmother's consideration," Richard sketched a gallant half-bow, as Abuelita Adeliza marched across the trampled grass, and spryly mounted the sagging steps of the Airstream without any assistance.

"So, what do you think of Luna City?" Berto ventured, after a moment. It was an awkward moment: Berto didn't quite know what to do with himself, and Richard couldn't think of anything to say save, "I haven't seen all that much, actually!"

They sat in silence for some moments.

"Berto!"

That came as a steam-whistle shriek of outrage from inside the Airstream. Both men started, the baby goat fled emitting a frightened bleat or two. Even the cicada shrilling in the tree overhead was briefly silenced.

Abuelita Adeliza appeared in the doorway, snapping, "Berto, *su teléfono, ahora!*"

Berto obediently fished out his cellphone from his jeans pocket and handed it to her. Both men listened to a stream of Spanish, like rising floodwaters overflowing the riverbank, as Abuelita Adeliza dialed call after call, snapping out what sounded like peremptory orders. Finally, she returned Berto's cellphone and marched to the car, commanding, "*Llévame a casa, Berto!*" She also directed a comment at Richard, who of course didn't understand a single word.

"What did she say?"

"She said 'take me home, Berto.' But before that, she said 'this won't do at all,' and she said some pretty raw things about Miz Grant's housekeeping, which I won't repeat 'cause they are rude, and anyway, it's not like anyone who stays here for long, they bring their own things."

"But what did she say before all that?" Richard repeated, still amazingly baffled. His head ached so fiercely, he feared that it might split.

"Berto!" Abuelita Adeliza shrieked again from the back seat. Richard winced and Berto opened the driver's side door. "She said, not to worry. The Family is on the way and they will fix it," he replied, cryptically. The town car bumped away, trailing a plume of dust and leaving Richard even more baffled than before, and wondering if he should answer his cellphone, or just leave it ring and ring and go to voicemail. It was getting hot out here, as the sun was nearly overhead, but the inside of the Airstream was even hotter – an oven, even with the glass windows cranked open to their farthest extent. The cicada shrilled, louder and louder overhead.

Twenty minutes passed, and Richard's phone kept on ringing. He kept on ignoring it, in the faint hope that it would go away or at least stop ringing. He had just about decided to stand up, walk over to the Airstream, retrieve his phone and throw it into the deepest pool of the river at the bottom of the campground, when he saw that telltale plume of dust rising over the dirt road leading into the campground field; a bigger, denser and longer plume of dust than ever raised by a single town car or the pick-up truck with the custom paint-job. The noise of multiple engines quite drowned out the cicada, and the insistent buzzing of his cellphone, as a whole cavalcade of vehicles spilled into the campground, and parked in a ragged line just short of the picnic table; vans and pick-up trucks of every degree, make, and condition of repair, many surmounted by welded-metal racks holding ladders, lengths of pipe and lumber, or towing low-bed trailers full of ... Richard couldn't quite tell what they were full of, although one of them at least held a medium-sized cement-mixer and a couple of portable generators, and another held half a pallet of heavy concrete pavers, and sacks of sand, all neatly piled, while a third held a small earth-mover. People spilled out of the vehicles – men with serious-looking tool-boxes and equally serious-looking faces topped with construction hard-hats, calling brisk remarks in Spanish to each other. Three women in crisp pinafore aprons emerged from the most well-kept van, lugging a vacuum-cleaner and a cart of cleaning supplies between them, although the youngest carried a large laundry-basket piled high with ... Richard couldn't tell what it was piled with, but all was neatly folded.

The first man out of the nearest truck carried a heavy and official-looking clipboard. "Hey, Ricardo," he drawled. "*Que pasa,* dude – Abuelita sent us."

"If you say so," Richard answered, eying the clip-board nervously, certain that the man was some kind of busy-body council authority. "I'm not sure ..."

"Look, *hijito* – when Abuelita says to us 'jump', the only right answer is 'yes ma'am and how high?' Abuelita told us 'this place won't do' so now it's our job to make it do. It's a Saturday; the big game starts in two hours, so ..." the man winked broadly, "A Gonzalez gotta do what a Gonzalez gotta do."

"If you say so, I'm sure," Richard watched, slack-jawed in astonishment. With the rapidity of one of those speeded-up time-lapse films, the various trucks and trailers disgorged their contents. First one and then a second generator roared into life, then the cement-mixer. One of the women emerged from the Airstream with the end of an electrical cord which went to one generator. If there was any sound from the vacuum-cleaner, it was drowned out in the racket from the generator. Richard's head felt as if it would not only split, but fly apart into small fragments. Someone tapped on his shoulder and he whirled around as if he were a cat and his tail had just been stepped on. It was the youngest of the apron-clad women, his cellphone in her hand. She pointed at the river edge, and her lips moved, but of course neither of them could hear a single word in the uproar. Richard took the hint and his phone. As he stumbled away from the controlled chaos, the baby earth-mover was already busily scraping away the top six inches of soil in a rough oblong in front of the Airstream.

It was quieter at the river side although he was careful to avoid the fire-ant nest he had inadvertently discovered upon waking. The watercourse here formed a long and curving pool, with steep banks on either side. The water was deep green – it didn't look as if there were any current in it. Richard found a place to sit, on a length of long-fallen tree trunk above the bank, sighed, and began playing back the accumulated messages left.

"Rich ... this is Morty! Pick up the f—king phone, dammit!"

-delete-

"Rich, I swear ..."

"You always do," Richard muttered.

-delete-

"Rich, I know you aren't in LA ... where the f—k are –"

-delete-

"Rich, you got trouble ... pick up the phone and call..."

-delete-

48

"OK, Rich, there's a <u>hell</u> of a difference between LA and SA..."

"Tell me about it, Morty," Richard said to the phone.

-delete-

"Rich, that bastard Noel-Barrett is all over the place, telling everyone how he knew you were cruising towards a crack-up and he tried to help you ... pick up the phone, this is a diast—"

-delete-

Halfway through deleting the voice messages, Richard's phone dinged – the signal for a text message registering. He switched screens to read it.

"Rich. Sorry, it is all over between us. Stay friends? Sammi."

"Bitch," Richard commented to the phone and went back to deleting voicemail messages.

"Pick up the phone, Rich ... a little bird just tipped me – that t**t Sammi just sold the inside story of your crack-up to the *Sun* for 50-thousand simoleons, or whatever the f—k they use in Brit-land for money..."

-delete-

"Mr. Hall, this is Thorne, from the law offices of Thorne, Bellamy and Thorne, regarding our client..."

-delete-

"Mr. Hall, Jacinta Perry, calling from Erdoes & Blankenship, Attorneys at Law – would you be so kind as to return my ..."

"She's got a dead sexy voice," Richard remarked to the phone. "Pity, that – she's probably twenty stone and looks like the arse of a diseased hippopotamus."

-delete-

"Mr. Hall, Aspin, from Wellesley, Aspin & Rivers here. Our firm has been retained on behalf of ..."

-delete-

"Mr. Hall, this is Audrey Donovan, of the *Daily Mail*, calling for a com ..."

-delete-

"Rich, for the last goddamn time ..."

-delete-

"Rich, old chap, this is Phillip. I know we've had our moments in the past, but I wanted to reach out to you..."

"You f—king tosser!" Richard said to the phone.

-delete-

"Richard, this is Mum – we're worried about you, dearest. Please call."

-save-

Richard continued listening to the first few words and deleting messages although new messages were being posted at nearly the same rate. He had quite lost track of time, and barely noticed that the construction noise at the top of the campground had diminished, from the mechanical roar of generators and the earthmover to something more like the voices of men shouting cheerily and profanely to each other.

Lost in scrolling through text messages and voice-mail, he was just aware of a feminine giggle behind him. Startled, he turned from where he sat on the fallen tree trunk at two girls – nearly identical teenage girls, enough alike to be sisters, if not twins. Richard guessed they were thirteen or fourteen and dressed to look ten years older. They each carried an overflowing pair of reusable shopping bags with the inexplicable letters "HEB" emblazoned in various designs upon them.

"Hi, Mr. Astor-Hall," the first one giggled. "Uncle Roman said you were down here. Abuelita said we should see which of Sylvester's old clothes from before he enlisted in the Marines might fit you. Abuelita an' Berto, they said you didn't have any clothes at all with you."

"Abuelita said you were about the same size as he was then," the second girl explained, also with a giggle. "An' Sylvester dressed so sharp, all the girls were in love with him ..."

"Oh, shut up, Blanca, they were not!" the first girl blushed. "Here – let me hold this up against your back." She drew out a long-sleeved t-shirt, and Richard obliged. "Yes, definitely the same size as Sylvester back then. He had a 34-inch waist in jeans, but he is taller than you."

"You are such a slut, Beatriz," Blanca giggled, with a slight passive-aggressive edge in her tone which almost passed it off as a joke. To forestall any further embryonic femme fatale bitcheries, Richard cleared his throat.

"Ladies, thank you but the true test for fit is to actually put clothes on. Just leave them in the trailer. I'll try them all on later ... what <u>are</u> they doing up there?"

"Everything," Blanca giggled again, and the two girls withdrew. As they walked away, Blanca added, "*Él tiene un buen culo.*" And both girls giggled.

Richard returned to clearing out messages and texts. Sometime after the incoming flood diminished to a trickle, and his hangover to a mild pounding, he realized that the campground field was nearly as quiet as it had been in the morning. All but the van and the largest of the pick-up trucks had gone, as swiftly as they had arrived and with a lot less fanfare, leaving behind a radically changed landscape. In the mad flurry of activity, the amassed forces of the Gonzalez clan had re-balanced the Airstream on its pair of wheels and hitch-brace so that it sat level. Before the door lay a neatly paved stretch of concrete blocks set in sand, upon which sat a pair of folding lawn chairs and a small table. At the edge of this patio, someone had installed a pair of pink plastic flamingos, on wire legs thrust into the turf. Over patio and Airstream there was now a simple metal canopy, raised on four tall pipe legs anchored in concrete, and the picnic table had been removed some distance to another patch of shade.

The man with the clipboard – apparently this was Uncle Roman Gonzalez stood, arms akimbo, surveying it all with quiet satisfaction. He grinned at Richard.

"Not bad, Ricardo; not bad at all, even if I say so myself. I'll bring Abuelita out after the game sometime, so she can approve. What do you think?"

"I am lost for words," Richard answered honestly, his attention riveted by the pink plastic flamingoes. One of them bore a small sign from a length of string around its neck: *"Bienvenido a casa."*

"Hey, it's all part of the game," Roman Gonzalez expanded with pride, producing a small sheaf of pasteboard cards from his pants pocket with the aplomb of a stage magician with an endless string of handkerchiefs. "We do a good job – none better. The old Airstream's a pretty nice piece of work to start with. OK – Tomas, he fixed the AC, so it blows good and cold, once again. Here's his card … he does HVAC service for half the county. Rudy dropped off two full propane bottles for the stove and hot water … you can trade them in at the Walmart over in Karnesville when they run out, or you can just give Rudy a jingle." He handed Richard another business card. "Now, we hooked up the antenna, and Sylvester says that you got internet service out here. The TV set's old, Sylvester rebuilt it for fun… but if you want more channels, here's a card for my good buddy Sullivan at Grande… he's the local rep, tell him that you got the recommendation from me and he'll fix you up with a good deal. And Diego sorted out the plumbing so that the crapper flushes like a champ, but you might have to jiggle the handle a bit, and you have hot and cold running in the sinks and shower. Conchita and the girls cleaned up everything – she has this housekeeping service, and Marisol runs a second-hand shop in Karnesville so she set you up with pots and pans an' stuff from stock she was gonna hand off to Goodwill 'cause it wasn't selling. Conchita's card; if you want to call her and set up a regular appointment. She had the girls put in some basic groceries for you … they set up a tab at the Tip-Top, just pay it next time you drop in. This is Chris's card, with the receipt stapled to it. There's an extra key to the trailer on the dinette table – Rudy did a run to Abernathy's getting a key cut, but hey – no one locks their doors around here, anyway. Oh – and if you need any of those clothes taken in, here's Patricia's card. She does sewing and alterations. And this," he handed over a final pair of business cards, "This is mine and Sylvester's. Call us if you have any questions… but, hey – not for another couple of hours, OK? The big game started ten minutes ago and I wanna get going. Welcome home, Ricardo."

He shook hands briefly with Richard, leaving him with a dealer's fan of business cards in his hand. The pickup and the van bumped slowly away, leaving silence and settling dust in their wake. In the pocket of his trousers, the cellphone buzzed imperiously. Richard ignored it.

The metal canopy put the old trailer in shade as well as the brief patio. The Gonzalez crew had also installed a more stable and permanent step into the trailer itself. He opened the outer door, with the flimsier inner screened-door hitched to it. A gust of chilly air came to meet him as refreshing as a cool ocean breeze.

The inside of the Airstream was totally transformed – no longer a dusty, decrepit wreck, squatted in by god knows how many generations of insects and hippies. It was sparkling clean, and the little pot of Abuelita Adeliza's *caldo* simmered on one of the burners of the tiny stove. There was a single setting laid out on the dinette table – a plate and bowl of mismatched but clean china, and a place setting of equally mismatched silver on either side. The banquette seats had been re-covered in cheerfully mismatching flowered cushions, with a couple of extra small pillows added. The tiny lavatory at the back was also scoured clean and supplied with towels and a lavish assortment of hotel-sized toiletries. The bed had been made with clean sheets and a faded pieced quilt of somewhat unfortunate and clashing colors, but the pillows were fluffy and encased in crisp white cases. It all presented an appearance of comfortable random shabbiness; Richard had recently paid a bomb to an expensive designer to achieve much the same effect in Sammi's London flat.

The cellphone buzzed insistently again; Richard took it from his pocket and slid into one of the banquette seats. The wraparound window at this end of the Airstream offered an attractively rural view of a scrub-oak studded meadow with goats romping in it. He answered the phone with a sigh.

"Hullo, Mum... I know. I was on the road, and then I was dead asleep for hours. Jet lag, you know... I know, I know... sorry, Mum. I know you were both worried after seeing the news stories..." There was a long pause, while he watched the goats. "No, I'm all right now... look; I'm going to stay here for a while. No, I don't know for how long. I have to get some things straight... Where? Some place in Texas. I think. I might not be calling for a while, Mum. Don't talk to any reporters... yes, of course I trust you both..." Down along the unseen road, a telltale plume of dust arose above the line of scrub trees which formed a rough hedge. In a moment a pale pink SUV appeared and bumped carefully across the derelict campground. "I have to let you go, Mum... I think I have more visitors. Bye, Mum... I'll call when I can."

The pale pink SUV parked carefully before the Airstream, and Richard closed the cellphone. "Fantastic," he observed to no one in particular. "The clown-car has finally arrived."

As he opened the Airstream door, the drivers' side and passenger side doors opened simultaneously, and a pair of ladies emerged – ladies of certain years. The driver was short and matronly, about the age of Abuelita Adeliza, and fussily dressed in a vividly pink blouse and straight-legged blue jeans battened into pink cowboy books. She was carrying a small plastic bag. Her companion looked to be about twenty years younger, carrying a couple of books, and rather more plainly clad in tan slacks and a gauzy embroidered peasant blouse.

"Good afternoon, Mr. Hall," the older lady said, seeming to be rather relieved. "I'm Sarah Abernathy – my granddaughter said that you would be staying here. Oh, my – this is such an improvement – Jess Abernathy, if you remember. She was with Doctor Wyler."

Richard wracked his memory although much of the morning had been one which he would sooner prefer to forget entirely. Yes, there had been a woman here this morning… thirtyish, attractive, dressed like a cowgirl.

"I recollect Miss Abernathy," he ventured, and the older lady tittered.

"I am sure that you do," she replied, and held out the bag. "Well, Dr. Wyler said you got ant-bitten and sunburned pretty bad. I thought you might like to have the use of some of our Mary Kay product line for men. I put in some shaving cream, and a couple of cologne samples, too. There's one of my business cards…"

"If I need to call," Richard completed the thought for her with a sigh. Another card; at this rate, by the end of the day he might have a full deck.

"It's every bit as important for men to look after their skin as it is for women," Sarah Abernathy pronounced, in the tones of someone repeating holy writ.

"So they say," Richard agreed, as the other woman presented him with the books – one thick, and one considerably smaller.

"We have in the shop a copy of *Larousse Gastronomique*, and Sarah said that you are a cook, and might make better use of it, then collecting dust," she explained. She had a touch of a German accent, barely more than an attractive sprinkle. "I am Annise Stein – we have a shop in the Square, next to the Town Hall. And the other is a history of Luna City… from forty years ago, but little has changed."

"Thank you so very much," Richard exclaimed – more touched by the Larousse than he could bring himself to say. "I have… I had a copy, but I did not bring it with me. Would you ladies like to come in? I don't know if I can offer you any proper refreshment."

"No matter," Annise replied. "You are welcome."

"We can't stay long, dear," Sarah shook her head, regretfully. "It's a busy day for me, since I have a party today at the Walcott's. We just wanted to drop off these small things and welcome you to Luna City. Let's go, Annise – or I will be late, and Sook will be furious… again."

"Thank you again, ladies," Richard said, just as his phone began buzzing again. The pink SUV backed away in a half circle and bumped away across the field. Richard listened to the phone click over to voicemail and came to a decision.

He walked down to the riverbank and flung the phone into the deepest, murkiest part of the pool.

"*But hark, the cry is Astur, and lo the ranks divide,*" he remarked to himself as the phone sank with barely a bubble. "*And the great Lord of Luna, comes forth with his stately stride …*"

Besides, the *caldo* smelled entirely delicious.

Home of the Mighty Fighting Moths

The marquee sign outside Luna City High School makes note of the fact that the school is home to the Mighty Fighting Moth Football Team – District Champions – 1967 – 1971 – 1974. That there is only a small space left to insert another champion year or two is clear indication that the Mighty Fighting Moths football coach, school administrators and team boosters have completed their journey through denial, anger, bargaining, depression, and accepted the sure and certain knowledge that there will likely never be another district championship in their future with quiet fortitude. It's not that the Moths lack heart and determination; players and boosters alike begin each football season in the spirit of game optimism, and in the hope that maybe this year the Karnesville Knights or the Falls City Beavers – which are the two regional football powerhouses and die-hard rivals – will not be able to defeat them 80+ to 6 with the casual absentmindedness of a man swatting a fly while thinking of something important. Texans live for high school football; it is simply the expected thing to do, and Lunaites are heart and soul Texans, even those who came from somewhere else, like the Walcotts or the Steins, or Chris who bartends at the VFW and manages the Tip-Top Ice House, Gas & Grocery.

It is simply the Done Thing – although why the Moths have not had a purely winning season in four decades is a matter of passionate discussion at the Café & Coffee, the Icehouse and regular BBQ picnics at the VFW. The usual conclusion is that this is due to the relative shallowness of the bench as Luna City High School is a relatively small one. However, Dr. Stephen Wyler suspects dark machinations on the part of realtors in Falls City and Karnesville. He is convinced they have carried on a forty-year plot to offer absurdly good deals on residential real estate to families of sturdy youths with good athletic prospects in an organized effort to maintain a large pool of players. Most Moth boosters dismiss that theory, as well as criticism of the Moth's current coach, Dwight Douglas "Music Man" Garrett, for he has only been coaching for the past decade. His immediate predecessors were renowned coaches of football in the old-school style, and one of them had overseen the Fighting Moth's last winning streak. Otherwise, it is as much a mystery as the wholly unexplained random disasters which strike the Moth's homecoming games with disturbing frequency, ensuring that liability insurance for participants and spectators is always paid up.

The Mighty Moth Homecoming game is most usually held in conjunction with Founder's Day – a local celebration marked by a parade through Luna City led by the Mighty Moth Marching Band, a carnival set up in Town Square, and numerous other events, culminating in a football game on the Luna High School home field.

It is a matter of historical record, however, that every few years, the game is disrupted, delayed, or even cancelled entirely due to an unforeseen accident. Sometimes this is due to human agency, or a suspected misfiring prank, and sometimes to what can only be described as a freak of nature, such as in 1988 when Hurricane Gilbert roared through Texas, and a small tornado touched down on the Luna High playing field shortly before game time. Four years previously, excessive flooding from another tropical storm produced the interesting phenomena of a plague of frogs invading the field. During one Homecoming game (the year is a matter for intense disagreement) excessive leaking from a cracked water main dissolved a layer of limestone underlying the end zone, resulting in a substantial sinkhole opening up in the guest-team end zone – fortunately during half-time. The only near-casualty was the Falls City Beavers mascot, who happened to be standing in the end zone, but he was pulled clear by quick-thinking bystanders who caught hold of his costume tail. In the mid-1990s, the Beavers mascot was a casualty of yet another Moth Homecoming incident; attacked by a live beaver which inexplicably appeared just before the game. A human prankster was suspected; since then, Falls City has since been reluctant to participate in Moths Homecoming games.

Human agency was involved in the stampede of nilgai antelope from the Lazy W Ranch, which broke up the 2000 Homecoming game. A section of high-fenced game pasture abutted on a paved service road near the high school. A quartet of poachers, taking advantage of Founders' Day festivities appeared with a stock-hauling trailer, and having lured a dozen nilgai close to the fence, cut the fence and attempted to load them into the trailer. The nilgai were not cooperative and galloped away in a body... straight across Moth Field. The most recent Homecoming game disruption was also in the form of an escaped large animal: one of the Wyler's breeding bulls, who upon escaping from durance vile, inexplicably became enamored of one of the marching band's tubas. The tuba player, understandably traumatized by the experience, immediately gave up marching band and switched over to playing the piano.

Which brings me to the Mighty Fighting Moth Marching band; the redeeming bright spot in Luna City's sports program. Under the direction of Coach "Music Man" Garrett, they have swept band competitions from Laredo to Richmond, to Amarillo and Texarkana for the last ten years, with a combination of razzle-dazzle formations and mind-blowing musical selections. Their marching band rendition of Orff's *O Fortuna* is a show-stopper, although at least half the student body is convinced that the number is really called *Gopher Tuna*. Moth boosters comfort themselves over yet another double-digit to single-figure stomping on the football field by contemplating the case full of glorious band competition trophies on display in a glass case in the main foyer of the high school. And of those graduating Luna City students to go on to college? A good number of them go on band and music scholarships.

The PTA and Booster Club, though, keep a particularly thick cushion of funds, on hand, in expectation of the next Moth Homecoming disaster. As the last one was three years ago, the time is more than ripe for the next.

Café Audition

Mindful of Dr. Wyler's admonition – to appear at the Luna City Café at 10 AM, clean, sharp, sober and dressed, Richard Astor-Hall did not overindulge; that evening, he had a glass or two of the rather nice Texas chardonnay from the bottle in the tiny fridge which the Gonzalez housekeeping ladies had thoughtfully placed there, along with some milk, a package of bacon, a box of teabags and another of sugar cubes, half a dozen eggs and a loaf of bread. The wine and bread went splendidly with the *caldo*. He whiled away the remainder of the day trying on the castoff clothing – which generally fitted him well and had the additional and supremely attractive virtue of being clean – and reading *Larousse Gastronomique,* while wondering what it was that Dr. Wyler had in mind. It was an amazingly restful afternoon and evening, unmarred by the constant buzzing and beeping of his cellphone.

He woke with the sunrise – no, it could not possibly be anywhere near 10 AM – the sunrise was a mere pale primrose band, just above the wooded horizon. Richard dressed hastily in a pair of board shorts and a tee-shirt chosen totally at random. The tee-shirt had FBI written in large letters across the chest, and something below it in smaller letters. Looking out across the deserted campground, he watched a brief pale mist rising like smoke from the river, and noted that one of his erstwhile hosts was out in the goat field, towing a small cart on spindly bicycle wheels. From the manner in which goats, large and small, were gathering enthusiastically around the cart, Richard assumed that it must contain something which they wanted to eat... and wanted to eat, very much.

He went hastily across the campground and leaned over the haphazard combination of fence and spindly hedge which enclosed – not very efficiently – the goat pasture.

"Oi!" Richard shouted, and the man with the cart looked up, distracted from the herd of goats, jostling each other for his urgent attention. "I've got to be at someplace called the Luna Café at ten of the morning... can you tell me how to get there from here?"

"Better yet," his informant called back; Sefton Grant, in his customary at-home working attire of battered cowboy boots and nothing else. "I can take you there, as soon as I'm done with the kids. We have a regular delivery, mid-morning. When you are ready, just come to the yurt. You can't miss it."

"I hope not," Richard said, but only to himself; a yurt, here in the highlands of Texas.

Twenty minutes later – after affirming the time through the medium of the television set, and having a quick and unsatisfactory cup of tea, Richard switched off the television set. The picture it broadcast was black and white and grainy in the extreme, and the lead story seemed to be a breathless update regarding a fugitive celebrity. The celebrity wasn't him; Richard didn't know whether to be relieved or slighted by the lack of interest. He also didn't know whether to lock the Airstream caravan or not. Nothing in it was his personal property at all, strictly speaking, save the chef's jacket which he was taking with him. Roman Gonzalez had commented that no one locked their doors in Luna City. Richard did make certain that the door was closed all the way, to preserve the delicious coolness inside. Three steps away from the shelter of the metal awning, in the full glare of the morning sun – and it was already hotter than a brilliant English summer day in Bickley.

He walked down a small and winding path that seemed to lead back into a grove of monumental trees – tall trees, with massive trunks and small and dark green leaves. There was musical sound of chimes coming from that direction, and the regular flashing blades of a small windmill at the apex of a weathered metal-frame tower. Cloth banners fluttered from here and there, some of them faded, some of them bright. He passed by a vegetable garden, surrounded on all sides by a tall metal-mesh fence in a surprisingly good state of repair, and... even more surprising, a line of whitewashed square beehives. And in that way, Richard came upon the eccentric and colorful establishment which housed the Grants, their assortment of livestock, and the occasional visiting kin or former commune members. A number of small structures – a metal-sided garden shed, a chicken run and coop made of reclaimed doors and windows, an even more rambling greenhouse constructed of even more reclaimed windows, an Indian teepee, another ancient caravan, with wheels long decayed, a water tank on tall stilt legs, and a towering pile of cut firewood, scattered throughout a half-acre stand of oak trees.

All these structures orbited around the central sun of a towering fabric-covered yurt. Overhead, the windmill turned with a slight metallic clatter, and chickens wandered freely, scratching industriously in the dirt and leaf-mast. A tall white llama looked at him scornfully and then wandered away – to Richard's relief. A most extraordinary vehicle sat before the yurt's single entrance. The front half, all the way back to the first pair of doors looked like – and was, by proof of a large, circular Volkswagen logo adorning it center front – an ancient VW bus. But the back half had been replaced by an open truck bed, and the whole adorned by random free-hand graffiti in brilliant spray-painted designs. It was impossible to tell what color, aside from rust, that this contraption had been originally. Sefton Grant, now more conventionally clad in jeans and an old Grateful Dead concert tee shirt, was loading the back of the bus-truck with flats of eggs, and a box of garden produce. Judy Grant emerged from the caravan with a large jar and a small brown-paper bag in hand. She was dressed – or more accurately – undressed in the Grants customary manner

"Good morning!" she greeted Richard, and Sefton dusted off his hands on the seat of his jeans. "Up with the chickens, I see – but not as early as our chickens! Seftie-dear, these are for the Abernathys, if you can drop them off as well. And don't forget – supper tonight is Lentil Surprise. Mr. Hall, you'd be welcome to join us."

"Got it, Judikins," Sefton replied, with a notable lack of enthusiasm, as he turned to Richard. "Sure – Judikin's Lentil Surprise is… unforgettable." As the combination van-truck bumped down the unpaved dirt track, and Richard tried to keep himself more or less steady in the passenger seat with the aid of a tattered seat-belt, Sefton added, "Yeah, and I wish that she would go ahead and forget the recipe… but wish in one hand, and cr*p in the other; see which hand fills up first. That's what the damned stuff tastes like, too."

"My sympathies," Richard offered. "I'll consult *Larousse Gastronomique* and see if there is some tastier surprise one can achieve with lentils."

"Don't worry about it," Sefton answered. "As soon as I drop all this off, I'm driving over to Karnesville and grab a double-bacon-cheeseburger at the Dairy Queen." He winked at Richard and added, "Keep my secret, 'kay?"

"My lips are sealed," Richard assured him. The motley van-truck emerged from the dusty farm track, and onto a narrow paved road – which, within a few hundred feet, went from pastures and cultivated fields – of something, Richard wasn't the least certain – to scattered houses, surrounded by ragged lawns and gardens ornamented with items like planters made from inside-out truck tires.

"This is the short-cut into town," Sefton explained. "Straight on to the right, there's the high-school and one block past the lone oak, there's Town Square." Sefton carefully edged the van-truck around a gargantuan oak, sprouting inexplicably from the center of the road.

"Singular place to have an oak tree," Richard commented, and Sefton replied,

"Well, folks around here, they loved these big oak trees. Seriously, that's one of the reasons that Judikins and the commune decided to come here… because of how they respected the trees. When old McAllister platted out the town, the story is that Old Antonio Gonzalez swore that if they cut down any of the big old oaks, then town would only last for as long as the stumps rotted. They'd already lost the railroad, through Bessie Wyler running off with an engineer on the GH&SA. Ol' Antonio, he knew his curses, so they say, and folk hereabouts didn't want to take a chance of them sticking. Ah… here we are. A mountainous pile of capitalist-pig enterprise, but we do what we can."

Richard regarded the pleasant tree-grown square with mild pleasure. This was so much better than what he had half-expected. When Dr. Wyler mentioned that the Café was on something called Town Square, Richard had automatically assumed some barren and charmless concrete square rimmed with geometrical shop-fronts in brutal Bauhaus modern style, all plate glass windows, a few discouraged sapling trees with uncomfortable bench seats underneath them, and a fountain; a plain geometric shape with a formless metal turd in the center. The aspect before him was the complete antithesis of that dismal late 20th century urban vision; instead a sweep of lawn underneath the heavy branches of ancient oaks, crowned with a tall domed bandstand in the center, and late Victorian storefronts on three sides, all lavishly ornamented with balconies, window pediments and colorful brick and tile work. The building on the fourth side of the square took up the entire block and sat a little way back from the sidewalk. A playground – with swings and slides, and yellow squares marked out on the paving for games – made the letters across the porch reading "Luna City Unified School District" entirely redundant. Sefton turned to the left, and drove around two sides of the square, before finally parking. Gold block letters on a pair of tall old-fashioned shop windows spelled out Luna Café & Coffee. A number of tables surrounded by chairs were arrayed in the shade of a hefty wooden awning which covered nearly all the sidewalk.

"This is it," Sefton announced, rather unnecessarily. "And you said ten? I see Doc Wyler is already waiting for you."

Yes, there was the old veterinarian, sitting at a table just inside. Richard sighed inwardly. He had not felt quite like this since he was at school and summoned to the headmaster's study. He took up the folded chef's jacket and sauntered inside, assuming a confidence he did not really feel. Two women and another young man shared Dr. Wyler's table, but otherwise the place was empty. A small ice-chest sat at their feet. The younger woman was the sandy-haired young woman with her hair in cowgirl plaits – the girl who had been at the campground the day before. A handbag large enough to be a briefcase hung from the back of her chair. Richard did not want to recall the embarrassing moment of that previous meeting. The older lady, impeccably turned out in an old-fashioned rayon shirt-dress with matching hat, gloves, and handbag, looked as if she just come from a fashion-magazine shoot for a publication featuring vintage clothing for the old-age pensioner set.

"Ah… good of you to join us, Mr. Astor-Hall; take a pew – you've already met my financial advisor, Jess Abernathy, I think. This is my business associate, Leticia McAllister, and Christopher Mayall – a good man to know." Dr. Wyler rose, and gestured Richard to a chair, whereupon the young man stood, stuck out his hand and said, "Take mine – I gotta get back to the Icehouse. Just call me Chris, Mr. Hall."

"I think I owe you for groceries," Richard said, and Chris Mayall shrugged. He looked to be about Richard's age, gangly and smooth-faced, the light-brown color of excellent café au lait. "Pay when you can," he replied. "I know where you live. Miss Letty, you promise you call me when you're done, and I'll come get you," he added, and to Richard's utter astonishment, he leaned down and dropped a brief and chivalrous kiss on the back of Miss Letty's raised hand.

"You're a good boy, Chris," Miss Letty replied, and Richard wondered if his eyebrows were up in his hairline already. He took the seat indicated, and Dr. Wyler got straight down to the point.

"Your papers say that you're a chef, son – Paris-trained and all that. Well, we here in Luna City may live in a bitty little town in the sticks, but we got newspapers, TV, and the internet, too. We heard tell that got yourself into a pickle in your life. Well, we've got ourselves a situation, too. This here little enterprise is crying out for lack of a good chef since those bastards at Mills Farm…"

"Language," Miss Letty interjected in a warning tone of voice.

"Sorry, Miss Letty." Dr. Wyler didn't sound particularly contrite. "See here, Mr. Hall – this place is the heart of Luna City. Sit here long enough, you'd see everyone you know in town. It's the only place to get a decent cup of coffee without driving to Karnesville and the only place aside from the Icehouse, and Pryor's Good Meats BBQ where you can get a bite to eat. The Icehouse does hot grill sandwiches in the evenings, and Pryor's is only open on weekends. We can only get along for so long on Costco cinnamon rolls and Little Debbie cakes. Hell, if that's what people want, they can get it at home, or out at the Icehouse. You told me that you liked cooking for folks? I'd consider offering you a position straight off the bat, but Miss Letty is the skeptical sort and don't know you from a hole in the ground. So we thought we'd ask you to audition. Fix us a lunch."

"Sole Meunière," Miss Letty announced. "With a green salad, and everything scratch made."

Richard gaped at them, and Dr. Wyler indicated the ice chest at their feet. "There's two pounds of New England sole filets in there – I had 'em flown in overnight on ice. Butter, parsley, lemons. Everything you need is in there or back in the kitchen. Sefton just brung in the salad greens, so – if you want to acquaint yourself with the kitchen facility, give yourself an hour and a half. Dazzle us with your Paris-trained brilliance, and the job is yours. And," he added, with a faint touch of menace. "I've et meals at five-star places <u>and</u> in Paris in my time; don't even think you can fool <u>this</u> ol' Texas cowboy."

"You might also want to reconsider your shirt," Jess Abernathy murmured. It was the first time she had spoken.

"It says FBI," Richard answered, utterly baffled. "I thought the FBI was something you Yanks were in favor of…"

"Do not, if you value your possible future career here," Jess Abernathy replied, with an edge in her voice that one could have sliced carpaccio with, "Refer to us as Yanks, or even Yankees…"

"My Grandfather Arthur Wells was a Confederate man," Miss Letty put in. "And he would have called you out for insult, on that account alone – although likely he would have made allowances for a foreigner."

"Read the small print," Jess Abernathy sighed. "So many of my clients could have been spared by reading the small print."

Richard looked down at his own upper abdomen, baffled by not being especially skilled at deciphering upside-down lettering. "So, what does it say?" he asked, being fairly certain that he did not want to hear the reply.

"Female Body Inspector," Jess answered. No, not an answer that he wanted to hear. Good thing he had the chef's coat with him. In silence he put it on and picked up the ice chest while Miss Letty nodded in grim approval.

"Lunch will be at 11:40 precisely," he said, silently committing what he had left of his soul to his Maker, knowing that the two geriatrics at the café table likely had first call on his mortal backside.

Now, to investigate the mysteries of the café kitchen, behind the door at the back; he had to admit, not bad, not bad at all. There was only the one gas range, but it was a massive one, with ten burners and two ovens. The refrigerator – a three-door model – was equally massive. Walk-in freezer – very good; he tested the door. Alas, the freezer was nearly empty. So was the refrigerator, save for two flats of eggs and the box of vegetables which Sefton Grant had placed within. The racks of dry storage was a little better; oh, good. The array of pots and pans, not quite so good, but… eh, he could deal with it. A massive Hobart mixer – Richard felt his spirits rising. Pastries and breads; he always liked making them, and that was one of his strong suits. Cinnamon rolls… Do. Wyler had mentioned commercial cinnamon rolls. The restaurant dishwasher was humming away, so there was proof already that someone was minding the shop.

"I can do better," he said, aloud.

Knives… that was sad. Nothing had a good edge. Where to begin? Find the knife sharpener. And within another ten minutes, Richard was agreeably lost, swimming in his own element, doing that which he loved best. Not even the pretty, dark-haired young woman who came in with a tray of dirty cups and plates to feed into the dishwasher could entirely break his adamantine concentration.

"You the new cook?" she asked, interested. "Your coat says Carême – I'm Araceli Gonzales, and boy, am I glad to see you! I've been holding down the fort since the last guy quit, and I'm about run off my feet."

"Chef," Richard corrected her.

"Chef Carême… that's a cute name – you're new in Luna City, aren't you?"

"I am but recently arrived," Richard agreed, absently. "Araceli, my darling, your devotion to duty is doubtless appreciated. And now would you be so kind as to set three places for luncheon at the table by the window?"

"On it, Chef Carême," she answered, with a becoming show of enthusiasm.

"Thank you, Araceli. If there is such a thing as proper linen napkins in this establishment, please use them. Fine food deserves the best."

"If there isn't, I'll find them," Araceli promised. "Say, Chef Carême... you talk a bit like that TV chef that my grandma likes. Are you related to him?"

"Probably not," Richard answered, concentrating absolutely on properly browning the butter. Oh, yes – it was coming together nicely. And service for only three and the same entrée? Piece of cake; he set the browned butter aside and went to explore the food storage shelves and the refrigerator again. Olive oil, lemon juice, a dash of Dijon mustard and a quick grind of pepper; the salad greens wouldn't need much other than their own exquisitely fresh selves. "Gilding the lily," Richard said to himself. Alone in the kitchen, he liked talking to himself. Sammi once asked him why he did that; his reply of "Because it's the only chance I have of an intelligent conversation," was not received well. Just as well they had broken up. Sammi was spectacularly gorgeous, but wit had never been her strong suit.

Alone in the kitchen, absorbed in the moment: that was where he liked to be. Food was not just one of those needed things; it was an art, a calling, and at that moment, Richard realized how he had been so badly distracted into becoming something else... a clown, fretting and strutting upon a stage. No, never again – here, in this neglected café kitchen in a small town that no one had ever heard of – this was the pure, unfiltered experience of creation and skill, merged. Everything else prepared and in readiness – lemons sliced, parsley chopped; Richard opened the last package in Dr.

Wyler's ice-chest; the filets of sole were excellent; fresh, nearly odorless, and expertly trimmed. His spirits rose again, and he became wholly lost in the simple art of haute cuisine… the portion-sized fillets dipped into milk and then dredged in flour. 11:35 of the clock; Araceli arrived in the kitchen, panting slightly from exertion.

"There weren't any cloth napkins, Chef Carême, so I took some funds from the register, and went and bought some at Abernathy's."

"Good," Richard hardly heard her. "Wine, damn it… only lunch, but wine! A nice white: Crisp and not too sweet. God… I miss having a good sommelier! That bitch Sammi ran away with him, poor chap; he doesn't know what he is getting into."

"Dr. Wyler is on it, Chef," Araceli assured him. "He has a bottle that he brought with him."

"Open it," Richard commanded. "Let it breathe… glasses! White wine glasses… God!"

"I already put them out," she replied, slightly reproving. "You shouldn't take the Lord's name in vain, Chef Carême. It's not approved of, around here."

"My dear Araceli, you would hear worse in any high-class kitchen in the capitals of the world," Richard replied, feeling slightly waspish and out of the mood, even as he said it. For some reason, Araceli reminded him of someone … oh, yes; Berto and Abuelita Adeliza. They must be related. He turned the sole fillets and viewed the delicate brown and mottled crispiness of their top sides with relief. "Plate the salads. If we are going to work together, you must know how I want things done."

"And how do you want things," Araceli ventured. "Since we are not in the capitals of the world?" Richard fixed her with the ferocious glare which on many previous occasions had reduced kitchen and wait-staff to hysterical tears and screaming death threats.

"Perfectly!" Richard barked.

With aplomb, Araceli straightened her shoulders and glared back at him. "Whatever you say, Chef Carême; Perfectly it will be, then."

"I like you, Araceli," Richard replied, obscurely pleased that she hadn't crumbled. "You have something resembling a spine. Here – we have hungry guests. See to them." He plated the three portions of sole, sprinkled each with a careless dash of chopped parsley, a little dab of brown butter, and a judicious squeeze of lemon, and Araceli carried them away on a large tray. When she returned, the tray under her arm, they both watched from behind the kitchen doorway.

A sudden question popped up in Richard's mind, and he whispered, "Araceli, you speak Spanish, do you?"

"Well, of course," she replied with heavy sarcasm.

"What does '*Él tiene un buen culo*' mean?"

Araceli giggled. "Nice ass. Not the donkey sort… They like your fish, I think," she breathed. There was no need for either of them to hear the words, the attitude and what they could see of the faces of Jess, Miss Letty and Dr. Wyler said it all.

"Of course," Richard replied. "It was perfect… Ah; the Doctor wishes a word with me."

Wiping his hands on a towel, he approached the table. "I trust that your meal was satisfactory?"

"Don't be such a snot," Dr. Wyler grunted. "Of course it was – only the best damn meal I've set down at in years. You've got the job. Sit down; I'm getting a crick in my neck looking up at you."

Richard obeyed – not that he had been in any particular doubt. Jess Abernathy took out a manila folder from her briefcase and pushed it across the table at him. "Everything you need is in there," she said.

Dr. Wyler continued, "I can't authorize hiring more staff until the Café turns in more of a profit, so if you can manage with Araceli – more power to you. The place has always done breakfasts. Coffee and pastries at mid-morning, hot sandwiches and soups for luncheons; not much call for suppers, but if and when demand justifies it, I suggest Friday and Saturday evenings only. Most folk here have jobs and prefer eating supper at home during the week. Jess has given you a monthly budget to get started with on that basis – just bare bones. Includes your salary, too. I know it's not what you're accustomed to, but…"

"I've already made up my mind to take it," Richard answered.

"Good. Araceli!" Dr. Wyler bellowed, and she popped out of the kitchen.

"Yes, Doc?"

"Another glass for Richard here – I want to drink a toast to the management with the last of this."

And with that, Richard Astor-Hall became a Lunaite, a mere thirty-six hours after arriving.

A (Very) Brief History of Luna City

Luna City is an incorporated township, located in Karnes County, Texas, at approximately 28°57'29"N 97°53'50"W, a point where Texas Rte 123 crosses the San Antonio River. The population of Luna City and environs in the 2010 Census was 2,453. The nearest large town is Karnesville, the county seat, approximately ten miles south of Luna City. Those residents of Luna City not employed in their own small businesses commute to Karnesville for work, or to nearby enterprises such as the entertainment/ spa/commercial venue of Mills Farm, the Lazy W Exotic Game Ranch, or in various oil-production ventures associated with the Eagle Ford shale oil formation. Notable people from Luna City include the prima ballerina Johanna Gonzales Garcia, international financier Collin Wyler, noted historian Douglas McAllister, Korean War jet-fighter ace Hernando "Nando" Gonzalez, and the legendary bootlegger Charles "Old Charley" Mills.

The land on which Luna City was later established was part of a 1769 Spanish land grant of a league and a labor to one Don Diego Manuel Hernando Ruiz y Gonzalez (or Gonzales), who may have been already settled in the area at the time that his grant was recorded. It is a matter of undisputed archeological record that Don Diego, members of his family or in his employ were engaged in grazing cattle, goats and sheep in the area, as an adobe structure on the northern outskirts of Luna City was extensively excavated and studied in the late 1960s. The structure apparently served as a shelter for both animals and people. Evidence of regular camping and hunting by elements of the native Tonkawa people at a fairly early date was also found in later excavations in the area. The first recorded permanent dwelling in the area was built in 1857 adjacent to an easily forded stretch of the San Antonio River, by Herman Borgfeld, an immigrant stonemason from Bohemia, who ran a small general store, tavern, and inn catering to travelers between San Antonio and the coast.

In 1867, a large portion of the tract originally part of the Gonzales or Gonzalez grant were purchased by Herbert Kling Wyler, formerly a captain in the Confederate Army, assigned during the hostilities to various garrisons west of the Mississippi and in Texas. Captain Wyler had been involved in various capacities with operations to move Confederate cotton to Brownsville and thence over the border to the Mexican port of Baghdad, from where it was shipped to Europe. He emerged from his wartime service with sufficient wherewithal to purchase outright what is presently the Lazy W Ranch, still run by his grandson, Dr. Stephen Wyler. Captain Wyler caused to be built a palatial residence, modeled after the magnificent Greek Revival-style mansion of Windsor, at Port Gibson, Mississippi, a mansion distinguished by a series of ornate columns all around the perimeter of the structure which extended from the main floor through two stories to the roofline and supported a wide veranda on the main floor, and wrap-around galleries on the second. It is thought that the local economy revived to a not inconsiderable degree as construction of the house itself employed hundreds of local workers at a time and in a place where money was scarce. *(The ranch residence and gardens are open to the public once yearly, for the term of a week in mid-September, as part of the observances of Founders' Day, although application for private tour may be made through the website for the Wyler Exotic Game Ranch.)*

Around 1884, or 1885, having made another considerable fortune in trailing herds of cattle north to Kansas, Captain Wyler became intensely interested in the possibility of establishing a town on his property, since the proposed town-site lay along a possible route proposed for the as-then-unbuilt San Antonio & Aransas Pass Railway. Along with Don Antonio Gonzalez, presumed descendent of Don Diego Manuel Hernando Ruiz y Gonzalez (or Gonzales) and the second largest landowner in the district, Captain Wyler formed a corporation to build attract investors and businessmen willing to settle in a new town. Captain Wyler brought in as a partner in the project, an ambitious surveyor and engineer who dabbled in architecture, Arthur Wells 'A.W.' McAllister, to not only survey the site and create the city plat, but to design various public buildings, including a suitably impressive courthouse. It was confidently expected that Luna City, as Captain Wyler dubbed his project, would become the county seat. Arthur Wells McAllister in turn was so confident of success and committed to the project that he moved his family to the site, after purchasing, expanding and renovating the original Borgfeld stone house. *(The house still stands amid spacious and well-maintained gardens along Rte. 123 and is lived in by his descendants.)*

Alas for Captain Wyler's ambitious plans; they were undone by love – specifically that of his daughter, Myra Elizabeth "Bessie" Wyler. Married relatively late in life, his progeny numbered only three; two sons and Mary Elizabeth, the youngest. He doted upon them to a considerable degree, and especially on Myra Elizabeth – beautiful, indulged and impetuous. On returning from a year in a finishing school in New Orleans, which the Captain and his wife had hoped would curb Bessie's naturally youthful high spirits, the young woman fell hopelessly in love with one Edward Standifor, some ten years her senior and employed as a locomotive engineer on the GH & SA Railway. Bessie Wyler eloped with Edward Standifor; they were married by a Justice of the Peace in Fort Worth and settled down to a life of respectable tranquility – but Captain Wyler's fury knew no bounds. He not only disowned his daughter, but declared that his enmity against the railway – all its works, ways, establishments and personnel – was unremitting. The railway was, he declared in an impassioned statement to the *San Antonio Express News*, an open invitation to the establishment of vice and debauchery of every kind, a threat to the virtue of susceptible young women and girls everywhere... and he vehemently withdrew any support previously rendered to the establishment of a route for the San Antonio & Aransas Pass Railway which led through his property. From surviving correspondence, it appears that A. W. McAllister blithely assumed that this was an attempt by Captain Wyler to pressure the builders of the SA & AP into offering a higher price for the right-of-way through his property. A.W. had a basis for this belief, as Captain Wyler had a long-established reputation for driving a hard bargain, using every possible means at his disposal – including treachery and personal tragedy, as they served his immediate purpose.

Alas for the future of Luna City as a station on the SA & AP – Captain Wyler was completely in earnest. The managers of the proposed railway line shifted the proposed route to run through Karnesville – and all the investors in the Luna City project were left high and dry, including A.W. McAllister, who had sunk all of his own funds into the project and therefore had to make the best of it. Fittingly enough, he did prosper in a mild way – although not to the degree that he would have, if the whole project had come about as originally projected. Still – he was respected and honored, as the decades wore on; the man who originated the vision of Luna City and designed nearly every one of its surviving public buildings. Architectural historians and aficionados for this kind of thing laud Luna City as a peerless and harmonic jewel of minor late Victorian and Beaux Arts city planning.

As for Bessie Wyler Standifor, she and her husband lived to a ripe and happy old age, parents of a large and prosperous family. In the early years of the 20th century, she and whoever of her children wanted to accompany her were frequent guests of honor at Founders Day observances. It is noted, however, that her father throughout the remainder of his life eschewed railway travel, choosing to travel in a horse and buggy until the development of other means of transportation. Captain Wyler was the first recorded owner of an automobile in Karnes County in 1901 – a Columbia Electric Runabout – and the first to die in an automobile accident five years later, when – at the wheel of it and against the advice of his chauffeur – he collided with another motorized vehicle on what would become Rte. 123. There is a historical marker alongside the roadway where this occurred. Folk memory has it that the driver of the other vehicle was none other than Charley Mills, with a load of illicit whiskey.

Homecoming Curse Avoidance

Autumn had begun to touch the oaks and sycamores with gold; the nights and days were already cooler by several degrees. Both Luna City schools began their fall term; once again, the strains of Sousa, Alford and Orff floated on the early morning air early on Tuesday and Thursday mornings, for Coach Garrett was a martinet when it came to band practice. The new school bus – with all the latest and most high-end bells and whistles available – circulated through the streets and country roads like some mammoth orange fish, retractable stop signs on either side flapping open and shut like monstrous gills, and all lights blinking on and off. Petra Gonzalez, the regular Luna City School District bus driver had not quite gotten the hang of the new bus, being that it was a considerable leap forward, technologically speaking from the previous iteration. *(The previous bus had become unreliable in the extreme, to the point of barely making it out of the school bus barn, and so the Luna City PTA held a series of fund drives.)*

"It's quiet," Joe Vaughn complained one morning, as he sat with Jess Abernathy at a sidewalk table out in front of the Luna Café and Coffee. "Too quiet; like the lull before the storm."

"You always say that before Founder's Day," Jess reminded him, and Joe scowled.

"It's not Founder's Day," he replied. "That's only a matter of practicing good community policing... and keeping ready to drop on visiting dirtbags. It's the Homecoming game that keeps me up at night."

"Yeah, I've been meaning to talk to you about that," Jess quoted their conversation of the night before. "'Come to bed, sweetie,' 'Sorry babe, I can't sleep' – because you are walking the floor, worrying about what fresh hell awaits. Nothing happened last year, the year before, or the year before that."

"But something will happen," Joe scowled even more. "That it didn't happen last year, or the year before ups the odds that something will happen this year. Something always happens, every three or four years."

"I think you're being unnecessarily paranoid, Joe," Jess argued, although she was also well aware of the erratic series of disasters which had plagued Moths homecoming game since time immemorial.

"It's not paranoid to take a realistic view of the situation," Joe replied, and began ticking off events on his fingers. "The plague of frogs in '84, Hurricane Gilbert in '88, the sudden sink-hole in the end zone in '91 or '92, the *sshole prankster with the live beaver in '96... and no, that was not my circus and not my monkey."

"I don't think Falls City has ever forgiven us," Jess sighed.

"They damned near lost two mascots in a row," Joe observed, and continued his countdown. "The nilgai stampede in 2000... what did I say about keeping an eye on the dirtbag element? I still have my suspicions of

Sefton Grant that he let Doc Wyler's prize bull out in 2003 on account of his whacko animal rights sympathies…"

"Sefton is not a whacko," Jess stuck up for one of her best clients. "He just believes that animals ought not to be exploited…"

"I suppose that their chickens, goats and bees are happy, eager volunteers?" Joe retorted, and Jess wisely returned to the original subject. "The hailstorm in '07 was a natural disaster. There was no human agency involved in hailstones the size of baseballs; just pure bad luck."

"Human agency? I'll give you human agency – how I had to beg the city council afterwards for extra funds in the police department budget to pay Gonzalez's Body Shop for pounding out the dents in the city cruiser. It was an embarrassment, driving around; as if someone has taken a baseball bat to the cruiser. Might give the dirtbag element ideas. And no one ever figured out who or what was responsible for the food poisoning in '10."

"Tell me about it," Jess shuddered. "I've not been able to stomach a chili-dog since. Once you've gotten sick on something, you can never face it again…"

"And the accelerator jammed on the open convertible carrying the Homecoming queen and her court in '13… fortunately it was in first gear, and the driver and girls all had time to bail out."

"And then it hit the field house." Both Jess and Joe contemplated that vivid memory until Jess made another determined effort to change the subject. "Look, sweetie – you should try the sweet rolls. Richard is really making a go of the café. The baked goods are scrumptious."

"Thanks, but no thanks. I've heard enough jokes about cops and donuts to last a lifetime," Joe replied, but he compromised by taking a bite from Jess's. He took one last swig of his coffee, dropped a brief kiss on her forehead and said, "Gotta run, babe – crime waits…"

"For no man," Jess completed the sentence. "Don't forget about the planning meeting for Founders' Day. It's the last one before everything gets crazy."

"Etched on my heart, babe," Joe said, and made his escape.

"So what is this town's Founders' Day all about?" Richard came out from the café, wiping his hands on a towel, after the morning rush was finished. He and Jess had a regular appointment to review the budget and expenses for the café. While Araceli bustled about inside, collecting up dirty crockery and crumbs – of which there was not actually very much left on various plates and napkins. Even Abuelita Adeliza acknowledged with pleasure that he had an excellent hand with the pastry and breads. The café freezer was now packed full of trays of unbaked frozen cinnamon rolls, hot cross buns, Danish pastries, tartlet and pie shells of every size and composition, waiting to be finished off and baked on the day they were wanted. The Café was more crowded in the mornings than it had ever been.

"Pretty much the standard community bash," Jess explained. "The churches and fraternal organizations all have food and game booths set up in the square. There's carnival rides for the kidlets, and live music at the bandstand… the Moths Marching Band, Los Maldonados – they're a *conjunto* band from Karnesville, the Sons of Herman polka band…"

"Polka?" Richard shuddered. "Should I top myself now or wait until the day?"

"God, no, Richard; it would make a mess and Joe would kill you himself for causing extra work. It's also a hell of an opportunity for the café. Run out some extra tables, and Doc Wyler will allow the budget to cover a couple of extra temp waiters for those days, and you'll sell pastries and sandwich lunches, hand over fist. We have visitors for the day come all the way from Houston, Corpus and Dallas… it's a lot of work, but it's fun, when everyone joins in. It might be a good strategy to open for dinner on those two days. But think about serving anything but BBQ, since the Pryor's will have a booth, too."

"So… what is it all in aid of – these founders?"

"Didn't you read Dr. McAllister's *Brief History of Luna*? Never mind… much of it is pretty dry. Luna City was established in the 1880s when they were planning to build a railroad line from San Antonio to Corpus Christi and Brownsville. One of the best routes for it would have been through here, where a local consortium of landowners got together and decided they would establish a town and that it should become the county seat as well. Back in the day, having the railroad come through your town was golden. Dr. Wyler's grandfather was all for it. The Lazy W owned a lot of the land hereabouts, and what they didn't own, Antonio Gonzalez did… he was the descendent in the main line from the original grantee, Don Diego Manuel Hernando Ruiz y Gonzalez or Gonzales. Please don't ask me exactly how he is related to the Gonzalezes and the Gonzaleses. That question has reduced any number of genealogists to tears and psychotic breakdowns. They're not even certain if he was a Gonzalez with a z or a Gonzales with an s. The handwriting on the original paperwork was so bad, it could go either way. They found his tombstone, about twenty years ago in Mexico City, but the corner with the last letter was broken off. It's a controversy doomed never to be settled. "

"I know the feeling," Richard sighed, and Jess continued, in full lecture mode.

"As I said, Senor Antonio held the last bits of that original Spanish land grant. He and Dr. Wyler's great-grandfather assumed they would make a fortune. They brought in some investors and hired an engineer-architect to design the whole city. Cleverly, they paid him in advance, with a good few acres of land; Arthur Wells McAllister; Miss Letty's grandfather. He saw to surveying the whole tract, marked out the square and the streets, drew up plans for the major buildings, including a courthouse. They planned on this to be the county seat, of course. Miss

Letty donated her grandfather's scale model that they built to show investors to the Historical Society a couple of years ago."

"Thought big, did they?" Richard scratched his jaw, and Jess nodded.

"A bit too faux-gothic for my taste, but never mind. Just when half the town plots were sold, and buildings were going up on every street... disaster. Or that's what everyone said at the time."

"Flood? Fire? Famine? Jimmy Savile visiting the local orphanage?"

"That's not funny," Jess tried to look severe, but blew it by giggling. "No, even worse; Miss Bessie Wyler, our Dr. Wyler's aunt, eloped with a handsome engineer on the GH & SA railroad, as she was coming home from a turn in a finishing school in New Orleans. Doc has a picture of her in his place at the ranch."

"Pretty?"

"Looked like Evelyn Nesbitt's twin sister... anyway, she ran off with the train engineer, and from what her father had to say about it, you'd have thought this was Sodom and Gomorrah, Part Two. He went on about vice and debauchery of every kind, the railway was a threat to the virtue of womanhood, blah, blah, blah ... and the eventual upshot was that he backed out of the deal, and refused to sell land for the right-of-way. There'd be ice-skating in Hell before he would back down, and the railway people shrugged and said 'fine' and the railway went through Karnesville instead."

"What happened to Miss Bessie and the engineer?"

"Married him, and they settled down in California, raised a family, and her father never relented. Don't think she cared a bit which might be why he never relented. Anyway, it meant that Luna City would never be the county seat so things just developed in the normal way. Founder's Day is the anniversary of the unveiling of the town model – they had a nice little festival where the square would be... and it just seemed natural to have a celebration every year. People who have moved away from Luna

City come back for the weekend. Some of them even park their RVs in the Grant's campground."

"Any excuse for a party will do," Richard observed, and Jess replied,

"Well, there is that... anyway, the next day – Sunday – that is the Homecoming game for the Luna Moths. There's kind of an unfortunate tradition involved in that, too."

"What kind of unfortunate tradition?"

"Best not get into it," Jess said. "Don't want to draw bad luck... but getting back to the Café; think about starting out dinner service then. Maybe some nice *prix fixe* selections, for Friday and Saturday evenings, since there will be a lot of people staying at the Cattleman."

"Fine," Richard nodded. "I'll talk it over with Araceli. Just a personal question; you and Chief Vaughn – are you an item?"

"Just very good friends," Jess answered, in a particularly curt manner which indicated the question was a closed one. "Come and sit with us at the Homecoming game, if you are free on Sunday afternoon."

She gathered up the contents of the folder and departed with a crisp nod. Richard looked after her for a moment, and when Araceli came out to clear away the table, he asked her.

"Just how good friends are they? Miss Abernathy and Chief Vaughn." Araceli burst out laughing. She held up her hand, the first two fingers crossed together.

"You have to ask, Chef? She's spending half the nights at his place or him at hers."

"Jesus... sorry Araceli, forgot myself – why don't they just get married?"

Araceli's face went from amusement to a somber expression. "You'd have to ask them yourself, Chef. It's probably to do with them both having been in love with other people, once. Joe's girl married someone else, and Jess... her boy got killed."

"Ah. Small towns, everyone knows everyone else's business. What did I have for breakfast this morning?"

"Coffee, two cups, cream and no sugar," Araceli replied at once. "A bran muffin from the Costco in Karnesville and half a grapefruit."

"Jesus!" Richard could only stare at her in horror, until she burst out laughing again.

"You forget, Chef – Auntie Conchita cleans your place every Tuesday and takes out the trash."

"For a minute there," Richard was still feeling the prickle of cold sweat, "I was sure you must have planted a spy camera in the caravan."

"No, that would be Cousin Sylvester," Araceli gathered up the remaining detritus from the table. "He's the one with all that computer and camera stuff."

Interlude – From the Daily Mail UK

Dateline May 30, 2014

Glamorous super-model Samantha "Sammi" Colquhoun has a new steady escort, say friends of the former Page-3 girl, and it is serious this time, so they insist. She is dating oft-married international banking mogul Collin Wyler and recently accompanied him on a safari to Kenya with a party of similarly high-flying friends. Wyler, based in Hong Kong, has been frequently spotted dining with Sammi in London in the last few weeks, where he maintains a *pied-à-terre* in an exclusive Mayfair building. Wyler first gained notoriety in the 1990s for frequently squiring the then-recently divorced Duchess of York. Sammi's former relationship with celebrity chef Rich Hall came to an end following the latter's well-publicized breakdown six months ago at the inauguration of his exclusive restaurant, Carême. Hall, who has not been seen publically since, is reputed to be traveling abroad, and not available for comment…

By the Rocket's Red Glare

Founder's Day passed in a blur for Richard; a blur of music coming from the distant bandstand, of a constant cacophony of voices, and carnival rides, the odor of food – funnel cakes and BBQ, cotton candy and corn-dogs – and faces at constantly crowded tables in the Café. He reckoned that he had only gotten three or four hours of sleep on the two nights leading up to Founder's Day. After closing on Saturday – after an epic twenty-hour day in the Café kitchen, he had pedaled home in a daze sometime after midnight, and slept as if dead. Araceli and the three temporarily hired waitresses – all of them cousins of hers, would open Sunday morning, and serve up only the usual pastries and coffee, so he could sleep in, oblivious to the unaccustomed lights and music coming from the gaggle of RVs and caravans parked in the normally empty field by the Airstream. Although there was someone tapping on the Airstream door at 7 AM; a camper asking if he had any milk to spare. Richard couldn't remember if he had thrown the half-gallon of milk at them or not. Probably just as well. It was almost empty anyway.

Now, he lost himself in thought, having chosen to walk the quarter mile or so from the Age of Aquarius Campground to the Luna City High School athletic field. Today was the first genuinely cool and comfortable day; he would have opened the windows of the caravan to let fresh air in, but for the unaccustomed noise of the for-once-occupied campground. He could rest assured that Araceli would be running a tight ship on a Sunday. From the way that festivities in Town Square were still roaring on Saturday night, between hangovers and church services there likely wouldn't be many customers lining up during the morning. The Homecoming game was scheduled to begin at 3 PM, on Moth Field. Richard had no notion of what, exactly, to expect – although he was fairly certain that it would be thoroughly not what he had been led to expect.

At about halfway through the walk, and just past a bend in the road where he could see the top of the blocky brick and concrete main building of the school, he was suddenly overtaken by four schoolboys on bicycles – about fifteen or sixteen of age, Richard reckoned, although he was not all that good at estimating the ages of the less-than-legal. *(There had been a brief scandal in his past over this, involving his alter-ego and a girl who appeared all of a jaded 25, but was actually twelve years younger. Of this, the less said the better.)*

Alerted by the skimming sound of their bicycle wheels, Richard had already turned around to greet them with a cheerful 'hello' – as was the apparent custom in these parts, but instead they all looked startled at his presence. Apparently, they had not expected to encounter anyone else on this back-road short-cut to Moth Field. Only one boy – and very nervously – replied "Hi!" as they flashed past. As they passed, Richard noted each of them carried a bulging black Hefty trash bag over their shoulders, or bungee-corded onto the back of their bikes. Well, that was curious…

Richard thought for a moment, then recalled the overflowing drums of trash in various strategic locations on Town Square – the boys must be part of the trash-removal detail. In another moment, they were all out of sight.

This road paralleled the high-fence line of the Wyler property, and eventually terminated in the back reaches of Luna City High School – the athletic field, the service area where the dumpsters were parked, a high-fenced area with a lift and a couple of dismembered motor vehicles which served as the school auto shop. On this momentous occasion, a row of four bright-blue porta-loo chemical toilets had been brought in for the use of an expected overflow crowd, backed up in a row, right by a pair of school trash dumpsters some distance from the bleachers. Ah, that's what the boys were up to; rather than taking it to the dump, they were taking a short-cut by sneaking the filled bags into someone else's dumpster. As Richard came around the last bend, past the auto shop enclosure, he saw the four boys who had passed him on the road, riding around the perimeter of the football ground – and the trash bags were gone. He wondered if he should stop in at the porta-loo, but the faint chemical odor, even at a distance, dissuaded him.

It didn't seem to have discouraged Clovis Walcott, though; lingering out of sight of the bleachers and smoking a cigar with evident enjoyment. Likely the cigar masked the miasma emanating from the chemical toilet.

"Hey – Chef Richard!" he called, when Richard was in earshot. "Good to see you – nothing like taking an interest in Luna traditions! I meant to have a quiet word if you have a moment."

"Right, Colonel – a quick moment, then." Richard concealed a small sigh. He supposed that Colonel (Ret.) Walcott wanted to bring up the question of catering a special private dinner."

"You given any more thought to my proposal?" Clovis Walcott ventured.

"I didn't have time, what with the rush over Founder's Day," Richard admitted, trying not to breathe in too much cigar-smoke or porta-loo stink. "And I wanted to talk it over with Doctor Wyler before I committed to anything. He is my regular employer, you see – I'd definitely want to know that he had no objections to my catering your dinner."

"Understood, understood," the older man drew deeply on the cigar. "I doubt he'd have anything against it. He's a close friend of mine; he'll understand. Matter of fact, this is one of his cigars … a damned good Havana, too. A bit past the best, but still… if you got 'em, smoke 'em, as they used to say in the Army. It's just that my Little Bride has been bending my ear about getting an answer, *eti-wah-chop-chop-balli-balli*."

"As soon as I can talk to Doctor Wyler," Richard said again, as a steam-whistle screech cut through the distant hum of the crowd slowly assembling in the bleachers and on the field.

"Wah-cott! Where are you! Wah-cott!" Yes, that was Sook Walcott, five-foot-two inches of imperious Tiger-motherhood and towering social ambition, now marching across the field and the now-assembling band parting like the Dead Sea before her. Clovis Walcott started, guiltily, stubbed out the half-smoked cigar on the sole of his shoe, and tossed it into the nearest dumpster.

"She doesn't like me smoking," he explained, while his spouse was still out of their earshot.

"I didn't see a thing," Richard excused himself in some haste. He nodded to Sook, who brandished a digital camera in one hand and the tripod for it in the other.

"Wah-cott – I can no' get this camera to work! You know; you must come, Homecoming Queen arriving any minute!"

All the more reason to hasten to the bleachers, to where Dr. Wyler as head of the Moths Booster Club, Jess Abernathy and Chief Vaughn had seats on the first tier of benches, with Martin Abernathy, in his official capacity as acting mayor next to them. There were the Steins, Richard noted, and Miss Letty, impeccably dressed as ever and holding up a dainty parasol against the thin afternoon sunshine. Araceli and Patrick sat on the highest row in the bleachers, with Mateo and Angelica sitting on their parents' laps.

"Glad you could make it," Jess greeted him. She seemed a little distracted. Richard assumed it was because the whole pageantry of the arrival of the Homecoming game was about to begin. He based the assumption of pageantry on the curious sight of the Karnesville Knights mascot – who was indeed wearing half-armor, greaves, breastplate and helmet (with a plume). He and the Knights cheerleaders were working up enthusiasm in the guest bleachers... but curiously, it seemed to be an uphill job. Most of the audience seemed to be looking around with nervous attention even as they cheered. Richard couldn't help noticing that the Luna City Volunteer Fire Department's only ambulance was parked, relatively unobtrusively behind the field house. He hoped that it was the normal custom, and not that anyone anticipated a dire need for it.

A mighty roar erupted from the home-town bleachers as the decorated carriage bearing the Homecoming queen and her court hove into sight. No, it really was a carriage; an antique loaned from the Luna City Historical Society exhibits, normally on display in the Old Fire Station, just off the Square which housed the Luna City Museum – and thrillingly, not drawn not by a team of spirited horses, but the spirited starting squad of the Fighting Luna Moths at a dead run, resplendent in their colors. *(A sort of pale mint green with sea-blue and white trim, if you absolutely must know.)*

"Not taking any chances, after '13," Doctor Wyler growled at Richard's elbow. "Nothing mechanical to break down or animal to run amuck... I'm getting tired of paying for therapy."

The Moth Marching Band – likewise resplendent in pale green with sea-blue and white trim – struck up a lively marching band version of Handel's *Arrival of the Queen of Sheba* as the Queen and her court were seated. The home crowd roared in lusty approval; if truth were to be told, the Moth Marching Band was several degrees more highly thought of than the football team itself, although no one would actually come out and say so. Because – tradition; back in the day, most of the fit men of Luna City had either played on the Fighting Moth team, or wished devoutly that they had.

Richard noted that the Homecoming queen and her court of four attendants – all pretty and self-assured teenage girls dressed in formal evening-wear which showed just a little more of their shoulders and arms than he thought essential, given the massive sunburn that he had suffered on arrival, on a summer morning passed out cold on the riverbank. Everyone rose in deference to the Homecoming Queen *(which he thought faintly ridiculous, having had done several times in earnest to Her Highness, Elizabeth II)*, then sat down, then rose again for the invocation, sat again for opening remarks by Martin Abernathy, and then rose once more for the playing of the National Anthem.

"I think I am getting more of a workout, standing and sitting, then the footballers do," he murmured to Jess, at his right hand; she neatly elbowed him in the ribs and told him to shut up. Next to Jess, Joe Vaughn stood at rigid attention, bringing up his right hand in a salute – and then his cellphone rang, shrill and insistent.

"I gotta answer that," he hissed, as the Moth Marching band crashed into the opening bars of *The Star Spangled Banner*. "It's Milo… he says there's been a break-in at the evidence trailer." The evidence trailer was nothing but a locked metal shipping container moldering away in the yard behind the City offices, holding a rag-bag assortment of materiel and objects confiscated during various investigations.

"Is there anything missing?" Jess asked, while her father said, "What did they take?"

Joe pressed the cellphone closer to his ear, shook his head and listened intently. Far across the field, beyond the porta-loos, Richard wondered if that wasn't a tiny thread of smoke, rising from the dumpster… or perhaps just the potent chemical reek from the porta-loos manifesting itself in visible form. Out on the field, some of the young football players – absurdly weedy figures under their massive shoulder-pads and helmets – were singing along with the band.

"… Rocket's red glare… the bombs bursting in air…"

"They took what?" Richard heard Joe exclaim, and then everything was lost in a single, earth-shattering roar and a blinding flash of light in that space where the porta-loos were. Every military veteran on Moth Field at that moment hit the ground. The last notes of the national anthem were extinguished unheard in a secondary explosion and screaming from the audience in the stands and the players and band on the field.

"What the…" Richard could only gape, stunned to silence. Joe Vaughn had dropped himself on top of Jess, sheltering her with his own body – but had retained the presence of mind to keep hold of his cellphone.

A single porta-loo arched gracefully up, up, up into the serene blue sky, the centerpiece of a brilliant red fireball, broken by showers of white-hot sparks falling gracefully back to earth, as larger sparks arched higher, higher into the air, to burst into more chrysanthemums of gold, green and red, accompanied by a shrill demented wailing. The top, sides, door and interior parts of a second porta-loo shot away in a separate but loose formation across the end zone of Moth Field. The hinged lid of the dumpster spun lazily in the air like a thrown Frisbee, before gliding down, down, down and crashing into the auto shop enclosure.

As his hearing returned – and the din of smaller explosions lessened, Richard heard Doctor Wyler cursing with an almost literary inventiveness. Someone – Coach Garrett? – begged for calm over a bullhorn, and for everyone to evacuate the area immediately in a calm and orderly fashion. Martin Abernathy had his own cellphone out and punching in an urgent number.

"Alert the whole team," he said into it. "Most everyone is here at the field, but we need the pumper truck… it's going like a blowtorch, but isolated. No structures in immediate danger, but we'd better dampen everything around, stat… yeah, my gear is in my car, but it will only take me as long to get it as you need to get here. Meet you by the stands. Ten-four."

"I think I know what they took from the evidence trailer," Joe Vaughn said into his own cellphone, as he helped Jess to stand. "Get over here, quick. Notify the county sheriff, and the Karnesville Med-Center. I'm on scene, I don't see any immediate casualties… oh, wait. The Karnes City mascot just got beaned by a flying toilet seat. Good thing they got that helmet thing going, eh? Gotta go, babe."

He set off at a trot in the direction of the fallen mascot, intersecting the path of Chris from the Icehouse, also at a trot. Chris carried a substantial bag of First Aid equipment, in his capacity as the LCVFD medic. He was was followed by a pair of Moths band-members carrying a rolled-up stretcher between them, and Miss Letty at a more dignified pace. The crowd in the bleachers slowly emptied out, streaming on foot towards the school's main gate. Only a handful remained, watching the fireworks cook off, to the siren-tune of the distant but approaching fire engine, most of them men and a handful of women hastily pulling on turnout gear and helmets emblazoned with LCVFD.

"Well, you might not have a game this afternoon," Richard said, recovering his composure, his voice, and his hearing more or less simultaneously. "But I have to admit, you chaps do put on a first-rate fireworks exhibit."

"The Moths Homecoming curse strikes again," Martin Abernathy sighed. "You know – we probably won't get the deposit back on those portajohns."

"What do you mean, Pop?" Jess said, in tones of bleak humor. "There's deposits all over the field."

"No shit, darling," Martin answered, with a complete lack of humor. "It looks like the Booster Club will be covering the cost of another team mascot's therapist."

The LCVFD's shiny red pumper truck arrived, edging carefully out onto the field, trailing lengths of heavy canvas hose, as volunteer firefighters converged upon it with the alacrity of wasps locating a dribble of something sweet. Doctor Wyler ripped off one more vivid and scatological obscenity, and regarded a particularly spectacular waterfall of sparks raining down upon the demolished porta-loos and the dumpsters, which could not be clearly seen for the cloud of billowing, multi-colored smoke surrounding them.

"Between us," he snarled, "Martin, Joe, and I thought we had covered every single and possible angle. Weather-forecast clear for a week in advance, come down hard on food-safety with the vendors; double-checked the city water mains; patrolled the fences… but some idiot setting fire to a dumpster full of fireworks?"

A vivid mental image of the boys with the trash bags, and Clovis Walcott and his hastily snuffed cigar came to Richard's mind. He opened his mouth – and then thought better of it.

Luna City In the News – Part One

From the Karnesville Weekly Beacon, dateline 24 September 2014

MASSIVE EXPLOSION ON FOOTBALL FIELD!

The apparent curse on the Luna City Fighting Moths Homecoming game appears to have struck once more, last Sunday at approximately 3:47 PM, as the Moth's marching band finished playing the National Anthem. A quantity of illicit fireworks confiscated from an unlicensed vendor early in July were stolen from the Luna City Police Department evidence storage unit by four juveniles and abandoned in the dumpster behind a series of four porta potties rented for the occasion from Lion Sanitation of San Antonio for an expected overflow crowd for the annual Homecoming Game, held in conjunction with Founder's Day observances. *(See related story, pg. 3)*. The source for the resulting explosion is not known at this time although it is assumed to have been caused by a discarded cigarette. The names of the four charged with the theft are withheld, due to their status as minors.

The investigation is ongoing; according to Luna City police Chief Joseph P. Vaughn, who declined to provide any further comment to our reporter, although he assured us that the offenders are being appropriately dealt with. There was a single casualty requiring the able assistance of the Luna City Volunteer Fire Department EMS technician; the mascot of the Karnesville Knights team mascot, slightly injured by falling debris. His name is also withheld, due to status as a minor. *(See page 5)* The game itself was cancelled, due to contamination of the field itself, and in the interests of safety to participants and audience alike.

Damage is estimated to be $18,000, due to complete destruction of the porta potties and an additional $4,000 for damage to the dumpster, the property of the Luna City Independent School District, and to Moths Field itself. Hazardous waste cleanup was observed on the following day, supervised personally by Chief Vaughn, president of the Mighty Moths Booster Club, Dr. Stephen Wyler, and the parents of the juvenile offenders involved…

(A review of previous Moths Homecoming Game disasters follows: edited as extraneous)

Hunting Season Weekend

"So – are you invited for Doc Wyler's hunting weekend?" Araceli asked, on an early morning in November, as she carefully sliced root vegetables in precise planks, and then into uniform cubes, as Richard directed. It was late afternoon in the cafe's kitchen. At the worktable, Marco and Angelika sat on high stools, carefully folding the starched white linen napkins which had come in a bale from the commercial laundry in Karnesville, tucking a knife and fork into each fold. Their heels dangled a good eighteen inches from the ground.

"Really," Richard had observed caustically to his waitress-assistant-trainee-chef some weeks ago, when her two children began showing up at the Café after school, "Children are such an easily drafted workforce! It's almost worth the expense of raising the little blighters. In putting them to work early on, they will learn useful habits!"

"Blow it out yours, Chef!" Araceli had responded. "My kids, OK? Quality time – Pat isn't done with his route until 5, and this place doesn't get internet. Better they are doing something to help, not playing those nasty video games!"

Now Richard said in reply, "The good doctor invited me – yet I am not altogether enthusiastic regarding a response in the affirmative, though he is essentially our employer. A hunting weekend... I have visions of an obscene combination of *Deliverance*, crossed with the campfire scene from *Blazing Saddles*, and I am not enthusiastic regarding the prospect."

Araceli giggled, and shot a sideways glance at her offspring, earnest young faces bent over the task before them. "Yeah, Chef – all that and a pig-roast on Sunday. Better say 'yes.'" Her expression turned earnest, completely serious. "Doc Wyler invites all the important men of town, every year... it's a guy weekend, you know? You rate an invite, 'kay? Go with the flow, Chef. Say yes." Her expression turned speculative, even calculating. "Think what you could do, with a supply of venison sausage in the freezer."

"I don't have a hunting piece... rifle... gun... whatever you call it," Richard replied.

"No prob, Chef – Doc will loan you something," Araceli replied. She fixed Richard with a particularly earnest look. "You gotta go – it's a big thing in Luna. Pat, he's been hankering for an invite since forever. He says that he'll know he's arrived when he is on Doc's guest list. And think of what you can get for the menu... It's dove season, too." Her face turned speculative, and Richard answered,

"Thank you, Mrs. Nimrod the mighty hunter. There's no real way that I can get out of this, is there?"

"At deaths' door from Ebola should do the trick; that or having your liver explode," Araceli replied. "But nothing short of that. Six PM sharp, next Friday at Doc's place. Get a four-day license and have Chief Vaughn check you out on hunter safety. I'll see if Pat can drive you. Wear heavy shoes, and camo, if you can get it cheap. Don't look at me like that, Chef – it's supposed to be a fun guy weekend."

"Sleeping in the woods and brushing my teeth with a twig," Richard answered morosely, as Patrick Gonzalez came in from the front of Luna Café and Coffee, silent in his heavy petroleum- product-stained work boots. "It sounds like some kind of ghastly endurance exercise."

"Hey, Babe – you off yet?" Patrick asked, as Marco and Angelika slipped down from their stools, abandoning silverware with happy shrieks of *"Papi!"* as they launched themselves at him. Patrick, a big, amiable young man with a broad face and the same brown eyes as his cousin Berto swooped up Angelika over his head until she begged to be let down, all the while wriggling in puppy-like delight, while Marco latched onto one of his legs, heedless of the grime and grease on Pat's aged Dickie's work pants.

"Just finishing up, *querido*," Araceli hastily sliced the last few planks, and emptied the diced vegetables into a covered tub. She wiped her hands and untied her apron. "In the morning, Chef... hey, Patricio – next Friday, can we drop Chef off at Doc Wyler's on our way home?"

"It's out of the way, but sure." Pat's work-besmirched countenance lit with curiosity, unmixed with envy. "Man! You got an invite! Congratulations... oh, man – that is so righteous. You gotta tell us all about it, afterwards."

"To be honest, I'd rather give it a miss, and see someone who really wants it go in my place," Richard answered, "Someone like you." But Patrick was already shaking his head, saying, "No, dude – Doc's invites are not transferable. Anyway, I'm going with Uncle Jesus next weekend, hunting hog down in the river bottom below Mills Farm. Go on, Dude – enjoy! Some weekend, I'll have earned my own invite."

"I'm stuck then?" Richard murmured to Araceli as she shrugged on her heavy sweater and fetched her purse from under the cash-stand, concealed behind a dusty stack of copies of *A Brief History of Luna City*. Patrick staggered door wards, Angelika on his shoulders, and Marco wrapped around one of his father's legs, both children shrieking happily while Patrick made a loud pretense and protest of being overwhelmed.

"You are, Chef," Araceli replied, with what Richard considered to be offensively good cheer. "Be a good sport – you'll have fun."

"I had other plans," Richard watched after them, suddenly morose. Patrick's rust-splattered pick-up was parked out in front, in the space usually claimed by Dr. Wyler. Patrick was laughing, Araceli too – and the children's obvious affection and happiness was such that the very sight stabbed at the heart of a conformed bachelor. There was a family, one of those happy ones which were all alike. For a single envious moment, Richard wondered where he could get one as well.

But then – the stock for a simple pristine minestrone soup for tomorrow's luncheon called his attention.

When Patrick dropped him off, the following Friday evening, he was left agog as Pat's pick-up came over the first hill, and the splendor of the Wyler ranch headquarters house was revealed in all its majestic, architectural glory before them.

"That is the most splendidly vulgar structure I have seen since the last time I visited Trump Tower," he said, in awe.

"Yeah, it is kind of over the top," Patrick replied, as he down-shifted to negotiate the narrow graveled driveway. "But hey – the Doc's grand-dad loved it, and half the county was employed... still employed, keeping it running. Cousin Tomas cusses a blue streak that you wouldn't believe, every time he gets a call from Doc about the HVAC system."

The Wyler mansion crowned a small hill, surrounded on three sides by terraces, lovingly and lavishly planted with roses and ornamental shrubbery. It was a four-square block with a gently pitched roof of honey-pink Spanish tile, in a peculiar style which mingled elements of Greek Revival and Spanish colonial. A series of enormous fluted columns extended from the raised main floor through to the roof, supporting a wide veranda which extended all the way around the main floor and wrap-around galleries on the second. The sweep of gravel before the wide stairway which went to the front door looked like the parking lot of the Tip-Top on VFW night; mostly pick-up trucks of varying vintages and conditions, the Walcott's enormous black SUV with all the extra chrome trim, Chris Mayall's red Honda Civic and others that Richard didn't recognize. Patrick pulled to a stop at the foot of the stairs saying, "If you need a ride home on Sunday, just call 'Celi's phone. One of us will come and get you, if you can't scrounge a ride."

"Thanks," Richard replied glumly. He took up the gym-bag at his feet and hopped down from the truck; Patrick was away in a splatter of gravel before Richard could beg for a ride back to town. Oh, too late – he had been spotted. Half of the ornate double door swung open. The irascible old veterinarian and uncrowned king of Luna City had the doorknob in one hand and a highball glass in the other.

"Good, good," he exclaimed. "Come in, you're just in time to whet your whistle before we head out!"

"Where are we going, exactly?" Richard couldn't help but be impressed by the inside of the Wyler place. The entry hall opened into a grand atrium, topped by an arched glass skylight. The atrium, lightly scattered with upholstered chairs, settees and occasional tables, looked like nothing so much as the lobby of a very upscale and old-fashioned European hotel, a resemblance emphasized by a bar instead of a desk set up at one end. A vaguely familiar-appearing woman, in a maid's traditional black dress, white apron, and quiet shoes circulated with a tray, collecting empties and dispensing glasses of tasty adult beverages. The other guests for the hunting weekend were gathered around the bar end of the atrium; to his relief, Richard knew or recognized them all: Clovis Walcott, Chris from the Tip-Top, Hiram and Martin Abernathy, Roman Gonzalez the builder, Georg Stein the dealer in antiquarian books, Sylvester Gonzalez and his father Jaimie, Coach Garrett from the school.

"To the lodge," Doc Wyler replied, carelessly. "This isn't everyone; Chief Vaughn has crooks to chase and speeders to ticket, but he'll be there on Sunday for the pig roast, and Andy does his big business at the barbeque on weekends. Meant to ask – didn't you need a rifle?"

"I do," Richard answered. "I'm not... well, this isn't the kind of thing I normally participate in. I cook the food; I don't necessarily hunt it down for slaughter."

"You do now, son – it's deer season in Texas," Doc Wyler clapped him on the shoulder. "There's some rifles in the locker at the lodge. We're just waiting on Tony and Berto, and Benny to come back with the cart, and then we can get this party started!"

"I can hardly wait," Richard mumbled, almost certain that the only reason Doc Wyler had invited him in the first place was to cook.

"Son, sometimes you just have to step back and relax," the elderly veterinarian assured him, as the front door opened. "About damn time," he added. The latecomers were Berto and an older man whom Richard didn't recognize personally but knew at once that he was another Gonzalez. Both of them were clad in what Richard was beginning to recognize as hunting clothes colored in various randomly jagged leaf and stick shaped blotches of greens and browns. Besides a couple of soft-sided sage-green canvas bags, and two padded gun cases, they also carried laden manila-paper grocery bags – a great many of them, all emblazoned with the scrawling hand-written logo of 'Central Market.'

"Sorry we're late, Doc," drawled the older man. "Traffic was murder on the 35 this afternoon."

"Never mind," Doc Wyler snapped. "We leave the world behind and get back to our primitive roots, as soon as Benny gets back with the cart. He's five minutes out." he raised his voice. "Sound the chime, Chris. In five minutes we leave the mundane world behind. Gentlemen, turn off your cell-phones. We are out of pocket for the duration of this weekend. Only turn yours on in the case of a heart attack or arterial bleeding and only to call for the Karnesville medivac chopper. If anything serious happens in the outside world, Chief Vaughn will drive out to the lodge and let us know, personally. As of now…"

"Party time!" Chris Mayall drawled. "One more drink, Benny is driving, so feel free … but dawn comes early in hunting season, and accuracy is always appreciated."

Only Clovis Walcott, Doc Wyler and Tony Gonzales bellied up to the bar for one last drink. Richard turned to Berto and Sylvester as two of the other three males present within two decades of his own age. They were lingering on the edge of the cluster, as if uncertain of their welcome or status, sneaking awed looks around at the magnificent interior.

"I don't know why I rated an invitation to this," he murmured. "Either of you two been put in the way of a clue?"

"Sure," Sylvester replied. "I got the internet in Luna in the palm of my hand." Berto looked abashed.

"I ain't sure of that myself, Chef. I think Uncle Tony asked on my behalf. And he needs a break, for sure. That last Spurs championship kept us hopping like you wouldn't believe. I 'spec you got asked because of the Café. Everyone goes to the cafe, and most folk hereabouts know you used to be famous."

"Rich Hall used to be famous," Richard sighed. "But I get the point."

The front door opened at this point, and another man put his head around the door. Richard did not know him although he thought he appeared vaguely familiar; middle-aged, greying dark hair and olive of complexion. "We ready to rock-and-roll, sports-fans?" he called.

"A revolting metaphor, Benny," replied Doc Wyler, setting down his glass with a click on the bar countertop. "Conchita, darlin', finish up and turn off the lights when we're gone, I'll see you on Monday morning."

"Sure, Doc," the maid replied. "You all have fun – an' be careful out there at the lodge. Don't let the bedbugs bite."

Bedbugs? Richard suppressed a shudder, but it seemed that she was only joking. Now he recognized her – that near-invisible Conchita who kept the Airstream he called home tidy and neat in her visits once a week while he worked away at the Café, aunt in some untraceable way to Araceli. He followed the rest of the party out to the verandah and regarded with bewilderment the vehicle at the foot of the stairs; a twelve-passenger electric golf cart – the extended model. There was just barely room for all, with the last seat piled full of Tony and Berto's luggage and grocery bags. Richard stuffed his bag at his feet, in the seat that he shared with Chris Mayall.

"So – why do you also rate an invite to this exclusive event?" he murmured, and Chris grinned.

"Well… the Tip-Top. But mostly because of J.W…. that's Doc's grandson. He was my best friend, so I got myself adopted, in a manner of speaking."

"So – where's this best friend of yours, these days?" Richard asked, in a convivial and lighthearted manner, only to be sobered as if he had been dashed with a bucket of ice water when Chris answered flatly, "Since you ask – under a nice stone marker in the Fort Sam cemetery."

At that moment, the electric cart jerked as Benny climbed into the front set and released the brake. The cart rolled over the gravel with a slight crunching sound. Richard said,

"Sorry about that; I didn't know."

"Sh*t happens," Chris had his eyes fixed straight ahead. "Don't worry about it, none."

The electric cart lurched slightly as it went from gravel to a narrow and smoothly paved road at the side of the mansion which at first seemed to lead to outbuildings – one of which appeared to be a pool-house. There was a garage too – a long building with an immaculate forecourt, and a ways past it, a paddock and stables, spreading green paddocks marked out with immaculate white plank fences.

The sun in the west was a dark orange sphere, fringed with rags of purple cloud, and shadows stretched long across those meadows. The electric cart hummed almost noiselessly past them. The light conversation among the passengers was nearly the loudest sound.

At the bottom of the pasture, the narrow roadway plunged into woodlands of standing trees; oak and pecan, with smaller shrubs tangled in the undergrowth, or the occasional dell, with lank grasses grown knee-deep. In places, wild grapevines tangled the thickets together in one grey-green mass. Woodland alternated with natural-appearing hayfields grown deep in thigh-high grass. The western sky flushed to a dark orange-rose color, the color of the sun turning a deeper and more luminous orange as it edged towards the horizon. Now and again they passed by a feeder – a dull-green square box mounted on long legs, dispensing corn, scattered on the ground below.

"There they are," Doc Wyler observed with satisfaction from the seat next to Benny, as the cart came around a bend. A brace of deer with noble racks of horns held high, moved slowly from light into shade, haughtily unaware of the silent cart and the freight of hunters that it bore.

"Looks good," Clovis Walcott said, from the seat behind. "Prime beasts, Doc. My compliments."

"Nothing but the finest kind," Dr. Wyler replied, as the electric cart swooped into another patch of woods. At the end of a journey of twenty minutes or so, the cart hummed silently around yet another bend – and there was an angled metal roof, unnaturally smooth against the rough texture of the surrounding woods, but not as glimmer-glass smooth as the stretch of silvered water beyond. The roof and the lake flirted coyly with them, appearing and disappearing behind trees and undergrowth lining the road, only revealed at the last as a rambling rustic structure weathered to a subtle grey-brown. Peeled branches and log uprights supported and defined a wide-roofed verandah all the way around and connected to a simple roofed shelter meant to serve as garaging for the cart, although one end of it was closed in; a tool shed of some kind. Doc Wyler sprang up the steps, taking out a ring of keys from his trouser pocket, saying,

"Grab your bags and pick your bunks, gentlemen – we get an early start tomorrow morning."

Richard followed after the others, all of whom save Berto seemed familiar with Doc Wyler's lodge, which to his vague surprise, turned out to be a comfortably shabby, rustic-style place, full of chairs and tables made of peeled logs and upholstered in leather or fabric which at a squint looked like trade blankets. There was a fully equipped kitchen, where Berto and Tony's grocery bags were dropped, opening out into a great room where tall windows offered a limitless view of the reed-fringed lake and rolling brush country beyond. Richard paused to admire it – so much for sitting around a campfire in the open – while the older men passed by with barely a glance.

He only realized why, when he followed them upstairs and discovered that the only bunk left was one of two in the smallest bedroom – barely the size of the sleeping quarters in the Airstream – with a view out the window of the roof of the garage, and he and Berto had to share.

"Never mind," Berto commented cheerfully, "I hear from Uncle Tony that we won't spend all that much time sleeping. I'm pretty hungry, aren't you? We got take-out from the Central Market on Broadway for everyone... rosemary-lemon chicken, green beans almandine, and potato cakes. Pecan tart for dessert. And a pastry platter for tomorrow morning. Then we got meatloaf and other stuff for tomorrow night. They do food almost as good as yours."

"Classic," Richard replied. "And here I was thinking we would be eating beans out of a can, sitting around an open fire."

"Well, you can take your plate out to the fire-pit and eat there if you want to," Berto said with a complete lack of humor. "Uncle Tony says that Doc always fires it up at sundown, so the logs burn down for the pig overnight."

"The pig?" Richard felt his eyes going all the way to his hairline.

"Yeah… they roast a whole big overnight for Sunday."

"A whole bloody pig on a spit?"

Berto looked at him as if he were an imbecile.

"No," he explained patiently. "They wrap it in tinfoil and chicken-wire and bury it in the ground on top of the coals. It cooks overnight. It's real good, too. Didn't you ever do a pig-roast, Ricardo?"

"I cannot say that I ever contemplated doing it that way," Richard was still boggled. Here he thought he had heard about nearly everything there was to know about Luna City.

So much for roughing it in the wilderness; although they did eat supper from paper plates, either on the deck which overlooked the lake, or watching football on the large-screen television in the great room. Richard, not being particularly interested in American football, chose the deck, watching dusk fall, and waterfowl came down to the lake. The piled-up logs of the bonfire burned, crackling and sending up red-gold sparks, which reminded him vividly of the great and inadvertent firework display on Moth Field.

"Like the view?" Doc Wyler spoke at his elbow.

"Very much," Richard replied. "I had no idea there was a place like this anywhere near Luna City."

"I'm not surprised," Doc settled with a sigh into the rustic wooden chair next to Richard's. "You've been working like a dog in the Café ever since you got here. Miz Alice was always very fond of this place, Collin and the girls, too, when they were younger. They thought of it as our own little summer camp; I reckon that we still do. J.W. – our grandson – he couldn't get enough of the Lodge when he visited during the summers. Liked to come out and stay here, rather than up at the Big House. Not that I blame him," Doc added with a wry grin. "I've always wished that Grandfather Herbert hadn't gotten so big for his britches when it came to tastes in architecture. Ah, well… a man of his time, I guess. He built to show off what a big man he was. This place used to be a line camp. My father rebuilt it in the Twenties; he and my mother lived out here at first when they couldn't stand being under the same roof as Grandfather Herbert."

"Personally," Richard remarked, mellowed by supper – which was quite good, considering – "I was expecting something a great deal more strenuous. You know, stumbling around in the dark…"

Doc Wyler barked a short laugh. "That's what the wives and ladies think. No, this is meant to be a relaxing weekend for us. We come back with a deer each, a sack of doves, no questions asked as to how long it took. Have a beer, let your hair down, commune with the spirit of the Great Outdoors… now, if you want to take a long hike, I think Clovis intends to go dove-hunting tomorrow afternoon and that involves all the strenuous you want."

"An enticing invitation, but I believe I shall commune from this deck," Richard said, and Doc clapped him on the knee and replied, "Smart choice, young man… but remember, the deer-hunting part is obligatory. The season begins officially half an hour before sunrise, 6:13 on the dot."

Samantha "Sammi" Colquhoun

- *Wiki Entry* -

Samantha 'Sammi' Doris Colquhoun (born 8 July 1981), is an English glamour model, actress and social media personality, who first became known as a so-called 'Page 3 Girl' in the tabloid newspaper, *The Sun*, beginning in 1997. She appeared in various television shows, while continuing to model for various publications, including the *Daily Star*, the British edition of *Playboy*, *Vogue*, *Maxim*, and *Esquire*. She is currently unmarried, although her most notable long-time relationships have included Phillip Noel-Barrett, star of the BBC's hit television costume drama *Turpin the Highwayman*, and celebrity bad boy chef Rich Hall, who was featured with her in Series Three of *I'm a Celebrity Chef... Get Me Out of Here*. She is currently in a relationship with Hong Kong-based international financier Collin Wyler. [citation needed]

Born in 1981 in Wallington, Greater London, she was the oldest child of Linda (nee Parker-Rees) and Winston Leonard Colquhoun. She attended Wallington High School for Girls [citation needed] but left school at the age of 16 to pursue her modeling career. Upon success as a Page 3 Girl, she turned to acting. Throughout the decade following, she regularly appeared in bit parts such as 'blonde girl in Rovers Return' in the 2004 season of *Coronation Street*, 'parishioner in front pew' in the 2006 Christmas special of *The Vicar of Dibbley*, and as 'first saucy tavern wench' in the second season of *Turpin the Highwayman*. She was also featured in ITV's failed 2006 version of *Baywatch*: *Surf Rescue Cornwall*. She and Phillip Noel-Barrett also hosted a 'fly on the wall' reality series charting the progress of their relationship, which was critically panned and only lasted a single season. Attempts to sell a self-leaked sex tape of the couple together backfired, when it was hilariously reviewed as "the most vanilla porn tape ever' by viewers. She also appeared on a recent episode of *Dr. Who* as herself and is a frequent guest on British and American talk shows. She currently has her own popular lifestyle website *www.AtHome WithSammi.com.*

Strenuous Relaxation

Accustomed to early rising, it was no great challenge for Richard to be up and dressed at five. Berto, as the very youngest in the party had been nominated as the one to get up first and start coffee percolating had begun thrashing around as soon as the old-fashioned wind-up alarm clock began ringing. Richard nobly refrained from flinging the wretched thing across the room as it was obviously a vintage one and the property of his host anyway.

Sufficient it was for him to stumble after the other men in the pre-dawn darkness, bundled into jackets and coats, armored with thermoses of coffee and their hunting gear. Clovis Walcott in particular, seemed to be carrying a representative sample of Cabela's inventory over his shoulders and around his waist.

A few moths fluttered around the dim lights in the electric cart shelter, and from the lakeshore came the sound of a chorus of frogs peeping. Not even the birds were wholly wakened.

"All aboard?" Doc Wyler was a shadow among shadows. "Richard – you'll want to go with Berto and Tony, since it's your first hunt. Remember, the season opens at 6:13. First out, last to be picked up, and Andy will be along with the reefer truck as soon as the sun rises."

Overhead, the stars had begun to fade out, although Venus still hung bright and unwinking, almost as if in orbit around the three-quarter moon. The electric cart hummed along the paved road in near-silence. Richard could not tell if they were continuing along around the lake or backtracking along the way they had come the evening before. Whoever was driving had doused the headlamps – they must have had the eyes of a cat in the dark. Five or six minutes out from the lodge, the cart eased to a halt. By that time, his own eyes had adjusted somewhat, and he could distinguish between the paved road, the star-frosted surface of leaves, blades of grass, and the shadows under and between them.

"Your stop," Dr. Wyler whispered. "Cross over, take the path that goes towards the north. At the tree-line, there's a big ol' fallen log. Got a good line of sight over the clearing, all the way across to the feeder. Good luck."

"Thanks, man," That was Uncle Tony, and the shadow in his wake must be Berto. Richard stumbled after them, feeling clumsy, inept and out of place. He was a man of the city, accustomed to paved roads, sidewalks, street-lights, tall buildings and traffic. This silent, dark country, asleep in the faint starlight was as alien to him as the surface of another planet. After what seemed to be an interminable length of time, they came to Doc Wyler's fallen log. After Berto's example, Richard knelt clumsily behind it

"Here," Uncle Tony whispered, a breath in the shadows, a dark silhouette against the open meadow beyond. "Quiet, now. No wind. See them?"

After the dark woods, the meadow appeared daylight-bright in comparison. A layer of mist hovered just above the grass, belly-high to the creatures grazing in it; solid backs and branching horns, their white chins and the undersides of their tails a blaze in the dark. Richard could swear he could hear their teeth as they crunched grass and what must be corn scattered from the feeder that he could see only as a dark square against the sky. He was not at all certain of how many there were – half a dozen, moving as quietly as shadows themselves.

Uncle Tony uncased his rifle, Berto and Richard following suit. Tony pulled back his sleeve an inch or so to reveal his watch, whose hands pointed at five past six.

"Seven minutes," he breathed. "Mark and target your animals. Full-grown buck for choice. Take your time, make it it a clean kill, 'cause you'll only get one shot."

"I'm not sure I want to be doing this," Richard whispered, and on one side, Berto said,

"*Aiee*, Ricardo – think of venison steaks. Venison sausage with scrambled eggs…"

"*Hijito*, just pretend your deer is your worst enemy," Uncle Tony advised. He sounded mildly exasperated.

Richard considered Tony's advice. Yes, that particular person would do. He grounded the barrel of his loaned rifle on the fallen tree, settled the stock against his shoulder, and peered through the scope. Dr. Wyler had assured him that the rifle was a good piece, and the sights accurate at the distance that the grazing deer were at. Uncle Tony's rifle had a bigger scope mounted on it – a serious-looking one, at that.

"Two minutes," Uncle Tony whispered. Richard studied the deer, marked out the one straying a little from the others. Overhead the sky paled to the color of the inside of an abalone shell, a color without color, cloudless. Seconds ticked past, and Uncle Tony said, "On my count – three, two, one – fire away."

Their shots crashed out simultaneously. Four deer leaped away in alarm, their white tails flashing an alarm, and were gone from sight in a moment.

Berto vaulted over the fallen log, exclaiming, "Three for three! Good for you, Ricardo… you got yours! Bring out your tag, or it ain't legal."

Uncle Tony scrambled to his feet with more difficulty. "*Hijito*, be careful. Make certain of your kill before you start with the field-dressing." He looked sideways at Richard, adding, "Nothing like getting gored or slashed, when the bastard turns out to be only wounded."

"Field dressing?" Richard queried. He hadn't expected that – although, now that he did think on it, he should have. A hundred and fifty pounds of deer didn't just magically transform itself into chops, steak, sausage and stewing meat.

"Sure – gotta be done, else the meat will spoil." Uncle Tony slung his rifle and reached into his pockets. It was light enough to see that he took out a couple of pairs of rubber gloves and a heavy zip-lock bag. "Don't worry – I'll do yours."

The zip-lock bag turned out to be for the livers and hearts.

"Good eating," Berto explained. It felt as if it were noon already, but it was only mid-morning. Berto and Richard were taking it in turns to carry each gutted deer to the roadside, feet tied together and hanging from a long pole over their shoulders. Uncle Tony heartily approved of Richard's kill, guessing that it was about at the top end of the weight spectrum for white-tail bucks. "He'll be kinda tough, so tell Andy Pryor you want him dressed out as sausage and stewing meat. You want the head as a trophy, you tell him so."

"I don't think I'd have room in the Airstream for a trophy," Richard was horrified at the thought of his deer, staring down from the wall at him, with indignant brown glass eyes. Richard could imagine the deer talking in Berto's voice. *Really, Ricardo – it wasn't enough to be shot and eaten, now you wanna look at me, forever and ever?*

Uncle Tony shrugged. "Well, have him save the rack – Cousin Hernando can make you a chandelier, or barbeque tools with bone handles, or something."

Three field-dressed deer carcasses carried to the side of the paved roadway, and Richard was just beginning to wonder how much more would be required of him on this day, when a large van came around the corner – a van with solid sides emblazoned with the emblem of Pryor's Meats & BBQ, a van with a refrigerating unit perched on the top of it, and swooped to a stop, the sound of the engine loud in the silence of Doc Wyler's game reserve and in comparison to the equal silence of the electric limousine.

"Hey, fellas!" the driver exclaimed, as he pulled over, and stepped out of the cab with a clipboard in hand. Richard repressed a small shudder. *Here came the officious busybodies, puffed full of overbearing authority, just to put their own special blight on the morning.* "Three on three – good hunting!"

Richard placed him, after a second – Andrew Pryor, some kind of middle-aged techic-engineer in the shale oil field, who ran the BBQ place on weekends, and a relation through kin-marriage to Doc Wyler. Now Richard comprehended what the 'meats' part of the logo on the side of the van meant.

"'lo, Andy," said Berto, in his usual slightly bashful mode. "Don't want a trophy… but keep the horns. Dad and I, we're saving up to make a chair for Abuelita. Do mine in what ever Uncle Tony has, delivered to his place."

"The usual," Uncle Tony said briskly. "The horns for Abuelita's chair. God, like I need another stag rack!"

"Right," Andy Pryor said, scribbling madly on his clipboard of forms, and then he turned towards Richard, pen expectantly raised over a new form. "And you?"

"Sausage and stew meat," Richard replied, trusting to luck in all things Gonzalez. "As for the horns, no, not a trophy... Mr. Gonzalez said something about a chair from horns... yes, one to that... as for the other, there was something said to me about bespoke kitchen tools with deer horn handles? Save the other for that and refer me to that artisan. Christmas is coming, you see."

"A very good choice," Andy Pryor replied, even as he wrote, a talent which Richard envied. Try as he might, he had never been able to get 'the hang of that', as Araceli expressed it – speaking and writing at the same time. "I'll send a text message or call, when we've got everything all finished and packaged for you."

"How did the others do?" Uncle Tony asked as Andy Pryor re-capped his pen and closed up the door of the refrigerated van. By the brief look that Richard saw of the inside, it appeared that most of the hunters in the party had bagged a deer, for the van was packed almost full.

"Pretty well, considering... Clovis needed another shot to finish off his."

"He might be Army, but the man's an engineering consultant, and not a marksman," Uncle Tony shook his head.

"I'll drop off the pig, then get going," Andy looked back along the road. "Oh, hey – there's Benny with the cart. See ya at the lodge, fellows." The engine of his van masked whatever faint noise from the electric cart, which swooped around the last turn and rolled to a silent halt in front of three, with Doc Wyler leaning from the front seat, beaming and holding a victorious 'thumbs up.

"Now that the work is done, time for breakfast and a long hard day of relaxing!" he exclaimed, as Richard, Tony and Berto climbed aboard.

"I really didn't expect this weekend to turn out this way," Richard murmured to Berto. "The efficiency of this operation is so ... so overwhelmingly American."

"Land of the free, home of the brave," Berto replied, with a complete lack of irony. Richard looked around at the other hunters, seeing one rather noticeable absence and wondered why Chris was still back at the Lodge.

They piled out of the cart; it seemed to Richard that the other hunters were torn between exhilaration and yawns for having been roused hours before their normal time. He was hungry and for more than coffee; he craved enlightenment as to what Andy had meant when he mentioned the pig. The Pryor van was parked before the Lodge door; Andy and Chris were already lugging from the van a curiously shaped form wrapped in what looked like layers of tinfoil and chicken wire stitched together with heavier wire.

"Splendid!" Doc Wyler sounded disgustingly energized for a man of his age and in spite of the early hour. "To the pit, gentlemen ... there's work for shovels! Chris, are the gunny-sacks soaked and ready?"

"They sure are," Chris replied, somewhat out of breath. Curious, Richard followed the two with their burden around the side of the Lodge to where the logs in the fire-pit had burned down to a seething bed of coals, even as everyone but Doc and Berto scattered into the lodge, drawn by the odor of hot coffee and bacon. Richard could feel the heat almost as a palpable thing, radiating from the bottom of the pit which now that the wood had burned down looked to be about three feet deep. *A method of cooking new to him?* This he would have to see, up close.

There were a couple of long lengths of the kind of galvanized tin that served to side and roof barns and sheds in this part of the country. They were stacked on one side, next to a big galvanized tin tub full of water and gunny-sacks. The tin sheets looked as if they had been scorched by fire before.

"Hey, Richard, man," Chris gasped. "Can you take one of those sheets and throw it down longwise on the coals? Yeah, just like that; perfect."

The length of tin dropped into pit; Richard had calculated it so it fell almost evenly centered, with about three inches clearance on all sides, sending up a puff of sparks, and ash on the far side.

"Right – now, piggy – your almost-final resting place," Andy said, with macabre good cheer. He and Chris, standing at either end of the trench maneuvered the long, chicken-wire wrapped form, and lowered it carefully into the pit to rest on top of the tin. "And now – the bags."

"Good eating, pit-cooked pig," Doc Wyler remarked to Richard, taking one and then another of the sopping gunny-sacks out of the tub and dropping them into the pit on top of the wire and tinfoil-shrouded form. "That bastard was a wild-caught hog, spent all his life eating acorns on the ranch."

"I look forward to the experience," Richard said dryly, and Doc replied, "Don't you get snotty on me, son, showing off your ignorance. Wait until you taste of this Texas prime cuisine." He and Andy draped half a dozen sacks over the wire-wrapped form, and Chris dropped the other tin sheet over top.

"I filled piggy up top with whole garlic," Andy Pryor reported. "And apples, onions and a couple of jalapeno peppers... after a good rub with our house special barbeque-seasoning mix. I'll leave you all a quart of our special fiery-sauce."

"Seal it up good and tight, boys." Doc ordered. It seemed that Richard was expected to take one of the shovels... well; he had wondered why there was a pile of excavated earth, just by the fire pit, with three shovels set into it. Doc Wyler appeared to have this as carefully planned as a debutante presentation at Court, everything mapped out to the exact step, although Richard did wonder aloud why he hadn't been drafted into cooking.

"Because this is down time for all of us," Doc fixed him with another one of his patent, irascible glares. "Something different… like sitting quietly in a closed room. Take up that shovel and cover that pig good and tight, then go apply yourself to relaxing. Those are my orders, son."

It seemed a damned curious way to cook a whole pig – but Richard restrained himself from making any further remarks. Together with Chris and Andy, they scooped the earth back into the pit, with Doc Wyler watching, gimlet-eyed for any trace of escaping smoke, once the mound was tamped down.

Andy dusted off his hands, saying, "It should ready around noon tomorrow… see ya then."

"You ain't never tasted anything so good as pit-cooked Texas wild hog," Doc Wyler said again. "Tender enough to fall right off the bone… a side of Andy's *borracho* beans, and a bottle of beer. Given my druthers that's what I'd have as my last meal on this green earth."

"So… now what?" Richard asked, and Doc waved a hand.

"Whatever you want, son; Clovis and Tony are going dove-shooting after lunch. Me and Benny and Hiram and Jaime, we have a deck of cards callin' our names. The other fellas, they all have plans."

"I don't have any plans," Richard answered, feeling as if he was suddenly at the edge of a precipice as his host stumped up the stairs into the Lodge, and the sounds of Andy Pryor's truck diminished in the distance. *An empty afternoon with nothing to fill in the frantic hours?* He was an adrenaline addict, a man of ceaseless motion; he didn't think he had faced an empty and unplanned day since he was about ten years old.

Doc Wyler advised, "Then make some plans, son – even if it's just to sit on the deck and watch the clouds. You ought to dial it back, once in a while, just for the sake of your own health. Back in the day, Pascal said that all of our problems stem from an inability to sit quietly in a room alone."

"I'll try it," Richard answered. He appealed to Chris, now gathering up the shovels. "What are you going to do this afternoon, Chris – dove hunting?"

"Jesus, no," Christ replied with a barely concealed shudder. "I just this year stopped having flashbacks. Hunting isn't really my thing any more."

"If that's the case, why the hell do you come out here then, on Doc's little house-party?" Richard demanded, as puzzled as he was annoyed.

"Because of A.W.," Chris explained patiently but with an unmistakable edge in his voice. "Man, he loved this place so much – it was one of those things he never stopped talking about when we were out in the 'Stan. I come out here for him, 'cause he can't no more… and because Doc asked me; least I could do for them. A.W.'s people are the nearest thing I got in the world to family, so I owe them… what wouldn't you do for your people, Richard?"

"They live in Provence," Richard replied, still annoyed. "And know better than to press-gang me into some ghastly excursion that bores the hell out of me."

"Well, that's the difference between you and me," Chris answered, scowling. "I'll bet they're nice folks, an' you feel perfectly OK being shitty to them 'cause you know they'll overlook it all. Me? I came from trash – and I don't got that luxury of being a shit to Doc an' Miss Letty." He turned on his heel and walked away with the shovels over his shoulder, leaving Richard wishing that he had thought to appeal to Andy Pryor for a ride back to Luna. The afternoon stretched out before him as barren as a desert.

Having neither interest in nor skill at hunting, or interest in Doc's marathon poker game, that lack eventually drove Richard to the bookshelf at the left of the massive field-stone fireplace in the lodge's main room. It was filled with rather elderly books; worn cloth covers fraying around the edges or paperbacks with lurid covers and yellowing pages so fragile that they cracked easily. He concluded that likely the cloth-covered editions were a better bet and drew out one at random. Ah, a boy's adventure – *The Tower Treasure*, one of a series filling up almost an entire shelf. Well, better than most, for whiling away an afternoon. Let no one ever say that he suffered from an inability to sit quietly in a room alone. He retreated with it to the deck, hoping that no one else had claimed seductively comfortable knotted-rope hammock.

No one had; the only person on the deck was Chris, in gym shorts and shirtless, sitting cross-legged in a motionless yoga meditation position. Richard opened his mouth to ask where everyone else had gone, but thought better of it upon noting the web of knotted scars that seemed to climb up Chris' right leg, and the complex metal and plastic construction of the prosthetic limb which served as his left.

It must be one of those new high-tech things, Richard thought, as he settled quietly into the hammock. *I would never have thought it. I've never seen him even limp.*

Very gradually, something of the peace of the lodge, with the apron of lake before it seemed to seep into his restless soul. The story – after some befuddlement regarding language and setting in the 1920s – was strangely compelling, redolent of summer afternoons in Bickley reading the bound vintage copies of *The Boy's Own Paper* which had belonged to his own father. At some point, when he was most deeply engrossed, Chris finished his meditation unnoticed. When Richard raised his head from the book, it was to see that now he shared with deck with Georg Stein, armed with a folding easel and a paint-box, intent on doing a watercolor landscape. Down in the water, Martin Abernathy stood in waders, near to waist-deep in the lake, rhythmically casting out a dry fly, and drawing it expertly back across the gently rippling water.

An errant little breeze wandered by, lightly stirring the tree branches. Very faintly in the distance, Richard could hear the sound of gunfire – a regular popping, at such a distance that it sounded like pebbles falling. Movement along the lakeshore drew his attention, and he shaded his eyes to look. Ah – Coach Garrett hung about with a truly impressive camera with an immense lens and a binocular case. It looked like his interests this weekend lay in bird-watching. There certainly were enough birds around the margin of the water; a few white egrets, and an odd looking heron which could stand so still it merged with the litter of sticks and dead reads. He showed them all pictures saved onto the cameras' digital memory over supper.

By then, Richard was on his third Hardy Boys adventure. Yes, Doc Wyler was likely right about that sitting in a quiet room.

And the pit-roasted pig was the most sublime bit of roasted pork that he had ever tasted; delicately flavored, falling into tender shreds at the touch of a fork. All around him on the deck and in the patio area below, Doc Wyler's guests were tucking into plates piled high with pork, with beans and cornbread, tender flour tortillas moistened with a bit of Pryor's sweet fiery sauce and tart coleslaw weeping buttermilk dressing into everything else. *God, it was magnificent!*

I wonder, he thought... *if I could do this at the Café... there's that bit of ground out at the back. Does the budget allow for rental of a back-hoe to dig the hole deep enough?*

Day of the Dead

The dead are always with us – their memories, if not their actual presence. Some of the residents of Luna City do claim a casual speaking relationship with the dead, through some medium or other. Judy Grant claims to see auras and to sense otherworldly presences. The rest, especially those over a certain age – are acquainted with the dead. The oldest residents; Miss Letty McAllister, Dr. Wyler, Adeliza Gonzales, all of whom have passed into their eighth decade at the very least, are now in the curious position of having more friends among the dead than they do the living. Such is the custom in the borderlands, which includes Luna City; a time in the wheel of the year to formally acknowledge those gone on before.

In the Catholic Church, the first and second days of November – All Saint's and All Soul's Days – are set aside to honor and celebrate saints and martyrs, and then to remember all the others. Such orthodox Catholic rites and traditions of observing All Saints and All Souls merged, or were grafted onto more ancient customs. In Mexico, such observances merged with a traditional festival honoring an Aztec goddess of the underworld. It is believed that over the Days of the Dead, they are allowed to return for a visit to the living. It is considered a fond and courteous gesture to put out refreshments for those visitors, especially the deceased's favorite food and drink. In Mexico and in the southern borderlands, the dead are honored with representations of skulls, and offerings of marigolds and special food and drink. Families visit the graveyard, and adorn the grave of a loved one with flowers, or build special private altars adorned with pictures of the deceased, with flowers, candles and significant memorabilia. It's just one of those things.

The most visible Day of the Dead observance in Luna City appears stealthily around the War Memorial on Town Square – a grey granite obelisk on a four-square base, upon which are carved names of local men from both world wars, Korea, and Vietnam, and a single freshly incised name of a Marine, LCpl. J.W. Ellis, dead in the aftermath of an ambush near Fallujah in 2004. There is also the name of a single woman; an Army nurse who perished at Anzio in the Second World War. She was a girlhood friend of Miss Letty's – who brings and leaves for three days a bright red lipstick and a tiny vial of Coty *Emeraude*. Bottles of beer also appear, almost by magic – Pabst, Shiner, Lone Star and Pearl. On his way out to the Wyler ranch to participate in Doc Wyler's hunting trip (the first days of hunting season coincide with Day of the Dead – a coincidence which some have found bitterly ironic) Chris Mayall brings a half-dozen cellophane-wrapped Moon Pies for J.W. Ellis. Those were J.W.'s favorite, and he always shared them out with his buddies in the company when they got care packages from home.

In the little office in the Abernathy building, Jess brings out the silver-framed picture of her mother Beth, luminous in a bridal gown and veil.

She waits until after Martin and her grandfather have gone to the Wyler ranch, wondering if Martin still grieves for her mother... if he does or doesn't, Jess doesn't want him to think that she is reproaching him. Martin has been the best and most devoted Dad ever. Perhaps he has finally dealt with the death of his wife since it has been twenty years and a bit. Jess was ten when Beth died; if she has come to grips with her loss, she is not certain she wants to know for certain if Martin has. She sets up a modestly Anglo version of a Day of the Dead altar; some yellow and white silk irises in a glass jar and a small Franciscan Desert Rose-patterned plate with some home-made raisin oatmeal cookies on them. Yellow was Beth Abernathy's favorite color... and she always made raisin oatmeal cookies for Jess. The smell of oatmeal cookies baking – butter, brown sugar, cinnamon brings the memory of her mother most piercingly back to Jess: but not as she last saw her mom, skeletal and shrunken, stuck full of needles and plastic tubes in a hospital room in a big hospital in San Antonio. Jess' fondest memory is of her mother mopping the floor of the Abernathy's little house three blocks from Town square, her hair tied up in a scarf, and scolding Jess affectionately for tracking across the clean floor with dirt on her shoes, while the smell of baking cookies perfumed the air.

Miss Letty, sternly Methodist and with no inclination otherwise to follow any custom or practice which smacks of either high church or pagan practices, does nonetheless put out a dusty bottle of aged Courvoisier on the mantle of the old-fashioned parlor, where a tinted sepia portrait of her grandfather, Arthur Wells McAllister sits beside a smaller one of her brother, Douglas... the professor of history at the notable university in San Antonio. Douglas was three years older than Miss Letty, and she recalls him quite fondly – although with some disapproval over what she viewed as his inappropriate sense of humor.

Joe Vaughn and the half-dozen officers of the Luna City Police Department do set up regular memorial alter in the little foyer of the police department building, at the edge of town. It honors those officers of notable memory who served Luna City over the years, a few with some distinction, but most with quiet day-to-day devotion to their fellow citizens, their town, their community. Joe brings in a large box of doughnuts from the Krispy-Kreme in Karnesville. There is one picture not of a police officer among them; Hernando 'Nando' Gonzalez, who was a jet fighter ace in the Korean War. His taste for speed and dangerous living unappeased by the end of that war, Nando worked as a stunt pilot in Hollywood for several decades afterwards. As he was barely tall enough to qualify as a military pilot back in the day, and as lightly built as a jockey, he also performed (disguised with suitable padding, costume and wigs) as a stunt double for a number of different actresses and child actors. In retirement, crippled by arthritis, age, and the inevitable accidents attendant on that kind of life, he returned to Luna City, and lived in contented retirement in a comfortable residence just down Rte 123 from Miss Letty. He was in the habit of driving into town every day at 11:00 AM sharp for lunch at the Café… at the wheel of a massive boat-like late 60's Cadillac… which in the beginning was in pristine condition. Alas, as the trials of old-age shrank Nando even farther, he could barely see or be seen over the dashboard of the Caddy. In fact, the Caddy usually appeared to be driving itself, with a pair of tiny gnarled hands and the top of Nando's jaunty tweed flat cap just visible over the steering wheel. The Caddy suffered from a number of glancing collisions with the curb, telephone poles, fire hydrants, trash cans, the massive oak tree in the middle of Oak Street and West Town Square, the ornamental bollards in front of the Café itself, and numerous other motorists. Damage was never extensive, mostly as Nando usually wasn't traveling much faster than fifteen miles an hour. Still – Nando and his Caddy posed a hazard, especially to pedestrians. Nando could not be made to stop driving; someone who in his time had faced Chinese MIGs over the Yalu River was disinclined to follow the orders of a police officer who most likely was one of his nephews anyway. Lunaites had no real stomach for revoking his driver's license, either.

Chief Vaughn's predecessor devised an interim solution at last. When alerted by a phone call from Miss Letty upon observing Nando's Caddy rolling menacingly past her house, the duty officer, or the chief himself would set the ancient air raid siren to roar briefly into life – alerting everyone along Nando's favored route to get the hell out of his way. Nando, quite deaf by that time, was happily unaware of the daily siren alert.

This is why the air raid siren at the Luna City Police station sounds at 11:00 AM on the 1st of November every year. In case you were wondering.

A Very Luna Christmas

There are towns all across South Texas who go more all-out for Christmas than Luna City; illuminations, parades, evening street parties, complete with snow-making machinery and live music, craft markets set up in the central town square, pageants and posadas, with Joseph and Mary on a donkey walking through town looking for shelter... Luna City does a little of that. Usually the parade of Santa arriving is on the last Saturday before Christmas Day, although what with the development of inexpensive mini-light strings, nets and icicle lights, the city management has taken a lead in illuminating the trees in Town Square, beginning the first weekend in December. Volunteers from the Chamber of Commerce, fraternal organizations and the Scout troop assist in running and securing dozens of extension cords from the electrical main in the storeroom underneath the bandstand, and wrapping the tree trunks and branches with strings of white mini-lights. There are lights ornamenting the dome roof, columns and railings of the bandstand as well. Most of the businesses lining the Square also put up lights, along with decorated trees and wreaths.

Martin Abernathy emerges from his apartment over the hardware store last thing at 10 PM (when the evening news ends) with the bandstand storeroom keys and turns off the lights. Keeping the square lit up throughout every night in December would place a considerable burden on the city budget. Besides; the Abernathys, the Steins, and a handful of other Lunaites live upstairs from their businesses, and who wants all that light pouring into your bedroom windows at night? It's the courteous thing to do. So, the lights go off at 10 PM; peaceful moonlight and the lights from the four old-fashioned street lamps fall undisturbed on the sleeping town. Still, almost everyone enjoys the seasonal lighting which transforms Town Square into a fairytale land of sparkling trees. The oldest residents even grudgingly acknowledge that modern technology has wrought some improvement to the Christmastime appearance of the square... back in their day, it was just a string or two of colored lights around the ground-floor store windows and they were grateful for it!

On that Saturday before Christmas, organizations such as the ladies' auxiliaries of various churches set up booth between the trees. They are selling handicrafts, raffling a quilt or two, or homemade baked goods. A couple of food trucks from Karnesville and as far as San Antonio set up on the side opposite from the Café, and Andy Pryor's family brings their enormous portable BBQ in time for a lunch crowd. The Grants are always there, with their free-range eggs, honey and goat-milk soaps. In the last couple of years, they have taken to bringing some of their younger goats, as a sort of impromptu petting zoo. By noon, all vehicle traffic is stopped from going into the square. One of the fraternal organizations has a very elaborate miniature train made from 55-gallon drums, powered by the engine out of an old industrial mower. A couple of drums and some bits of creatively cut galvanized roofing made the locomotive. The cars are made from single drums, with a generous oval cut from one side, and then the other mounted on a set of wheels. The train goes trundling around the square, usually with a full load of excited toddlers and small children.

As darkness falls, the activity increases. The kids from the Luna High School chorus perform, standing in the steps of the bandstand; they perform a brief program of traditional carols for about half an hour, followed by elements of the Mighty Moth Marching band – not marching, and usually playing the same set of carols. No one minds very much. People walk around the square, admiring the lights and visiting with friends. A number of the businesses remain open into the early evening, offering hospitality; plates of Christmas cookies and stollen, slices of fruitcake, and hot drinks to all. The Abernathys have hot chocolate, and the Steins began offering mulled wine a few years ago which proved enormously popular. Hot spiced apple cider is also very popular. The café, as always, has hot coffee.

At about eight in the evening, Santa Claus arrives; sometimes on the back of the Luna City Volunteer Fire Department's old hook and ladder truck – which was replaced decades ago and relegated to the historical society's car barn. The VFD members have usually set up a throne for Santa under the domed roof of the bandstand, and for the next hour and a half, children line up (the smaller ones holding on to their parents' hands) to tell Santa what they want for Christmas. Santa – white-bearded and clad in a long red robe rather like the traditional Germanic Santa – curiously sounds like Doc Wyler. For most – especially the children – this is the height of the season, only matched by unwrapping presents on Christmas morning. And when the last child has confided their Christmas wishes, and taken away, yawning and confidently expecting those wishes to be granted within days, Lunaites gradually disperse to their homes. The Café closes, the Steins and the Abernathys close and lock their doors, although when the square is finally deserted, Martin goes across the Square with the bandstand storeroom key to turn off the lights.

And that is a very merry Luna Christmas.

Luna City in the News – Part Two

From the Karnesville Weekly Beacon, dateline 26 December 2014
LUNA CITY HS MARCHING BAND DEPARTS FOR CALIFORNIA

The Mighty Fighting Moth Marching Band departed this morning for Pasadena, California, where they are scheduled to march in the famed Rose Parade on New Years Day. This will be the second appearance of the Moth Marching Band in the Rose Parade since Dwight D. Garrett assumed the position of band director, and launched them on their decade-long championship sweep of Texas marching band competition. Accompanying the Moths Marching band are members of the Booster Club as chaperones, including Booster Club President Dr. Stephen Wyler, Col. (USAR-Ret.) Clovis and Mrs. Isabelle Walcott, Mr. and Mrs. Hiram Abernathy, and representing the corporate sponsor of Venue Properties, Intl., Chief of Marketing Susanna Wyatt.

The Dinner Party – The First Plan

"So, it's a go for catering the Walcott party?" Araceli remarked. Christmas had come and gone, the Mighty Moth Marching Band had come and gone to Southern California to participate in the Rose Parade, and school was back in session, so Araceli and Richard had the Café kitchen to themselves once the midday lunch rush was over. A bitter-cold Norther had descended, almost overnight, leading Richard to turn on the heat in the Airstream for only the second or third time since arrival, and to sleep under a full load of blankets and quilts. But the café kitchen was comfortably warm, even if there were slight drafts around the edges of the big plate glass windows out front.

"Doc approved, way back in November," Richard replied. He threw a couple of onions and a whole clove of garlic onto the tray of beef bones that he was roasting to make broth for soups, and slid the tray into the heated oven, from which Araceli had just removed tomorrow's sweet rolls. Cold weather was good soup weather. "But what with Christmas and all, Clovis said that he wasn't even going to begin thinking about it until they got back from California. He asked me to come up with a menu and a budget. Forty guests, including spouses and whatevers, sit-down dinner, with canapes beforehand, appropriate wines, coffee, ices and desserts for afters. An open bar, circulating and attentive waiters, and live music. At their house, which he assures me is sufficiently palatial to handle hospitality for twice as many. He... or rather, I infer that Clovis' dear Little Bride... wants everything of the finest quality and most elaborate service. I assume that if it is not, Clovis will catch all hell from Little Bride, and much of her considerable displeasure will splash over onto me."

"Going all top dog, is she?"

Richard shuddered. "That expression should not cross your lips anywhere within earshot of Mrs. Walcott. They do eat dog in Korea, you know. Even in this day and age."

"Oh they do not," Araceli exclaimed in disbelief.

Richard sighed. "I regret to say that they do. An esoteric taste, admittedly, and rather looked down upon as backwards by the more cosmopolitan. One of those wretched TV food and travel shows I was briefly involved with did a stop a place in Seoul that featured roast puppy."

"You didn't eat dog, did you?" Araceli looked horrified.

"I did not," Richard sighed. "Open-minded as I usually am when it comes to strange and unusual meats... I just could not overcome my cultural conditioning with regard to woof-woof soup. Silly, I know. I've eaten horsemeat, rabbit, and camel without hesitation, but I draw a line at man's best friend."

"So, what are you considering for the Walcott dinner, if dog isn't an option?" Araceli asked. She was mixing up a batch of maple icing to drizzle over a pan of fresh-baked cinnamon rolls, just out of the oven.

"Main course – beef wellington, with a green pepper sauce. I can do the sauce beforehand. I never want to do something extravagant with potatoes for a side dish; simple roasted fingerling potatoes with parsley. Another side dish – green vegetables for contrast. Asparagus, maybe sprouts. Beef wellington is so bloody rich that the side dishes absolutely must be simple, pristine, and complimentary. Soup – cream of cauliflower, with buttermilk instead of cream for a crisp finish… the salad course must likewise be simple greens. Anything but a creamy dressing. And then dessert…"

"Chess pie, or pecan," Araceli suggested and Richard shook his head.

"Too plain or too rich; I am considering a pastry of assorted bite-sized cakes and tartlets, and a plain fruit ice. The menu itself is so rich; I doubt that anyone will want anything more than a bite or two of a sweet. As for the canapes… crudités, most definitely. And I should do my signature appetizer: miniature Scotch eggs."

"Scotch eggs?" Araceli's eyebrows lifted. "What's so special about that… and what is a Scotch egg anyway?"

"Pub food, a nearly indigestible culinary abortion in the original incarnation – a hard-boiled egg wrapped in a layer of sausage, rolled in breadcrumbs, and then briefly deep-fried until the sausage is done."

"Yuck," Araceli made a face and Richard replied in indignation,

"Yes, but when I do my version, they are sublime; hard-boiled quail eggs, wrapped in seasoned ground veal sausage with an outer crust of finely crushed panko crumbs. I won a second prize with the recipe in one of those endless cooking competitions; two bites of sheer gastronomic heaven, and I swear to you, it would have had first prize if one of the judges – the greedy bastard – hadn't tried to swallow one in a single bite and nearly choked to death. They also have the additional virtue of being just as good prepared in advance and cooked on the spot."

"So… who's going to work this important dinner," Araceli nodded. "I guess you and I can handle the kitchen between us, since we can prep just about everything in advance. What about wait-staff, bartender and all?"

"Clovis mentioned using some staff from the Mills Farm organization," Richard answered. "Which would mean Benny Cordova and his regulars; I have no worry about them. You can pick at least four girls whom you trust to work the drinks and the table. We're set for a planning session next week at Chez Walcott. I'll do up a suggested menu and alternates and suggest the wines. He's putting a lot of thought into this dinner – I wonder why?"

"I guess that he wants to impress his guests," Araceli mused. "I suppose that it's something important. Mr. Walcott is a big wheeler-dealer in Luna."

"He would like to be an even bigger wheeler-dealer," Richard replied. "But between you, me and the gatepost, it's Mrs. Walcott who has the towering social ambition to be the uncrowned queen of Luna City. This dinner must have something to do with it."

"Like hell," Araceli blew an inelegant raspberry. "She'd have to import a lot of new people to Luna to get away with that. She sets too many people's teeth on edge, ordering people around as if they were her slaves or something. Mr. Walcott, he's OK. People like him. Abuelita Adeliza and Min Kim are tight, although how they even manage to talk when Abuelita only speaks Spanish and Min Kim only Korean is a mystery to all. Daniel was a freshman when I was a senior, and he's a sweetie. Belle and Robbie are lovely kids… but Sook? Give me a break. If ever there were someone murdered here in Luna, most folk would bet on her being the victim. Honestly, sometimes I wonder why Mr. Walcott ever married her to begin with!"

"Madly entertaining in bed is the usual rationale" Richard answered.

Araceli scowled. "You're disgusting, Chef."

"No, just bitter experience," he said, to which Araceli replied tartly, "Well, what do you guys expect, when they let the little head make all their important life decisions?"

There was no real answer for that, and Richard had acquired just enough worldly wisdom to know that he had best change the subject.

"So… what kind of soup would go over best in the café if it stays cold?"

"Chicken tortilla," Araceli mused. "That's always a great favorite around here, but since you've started roasting those beef bones… beef minestrone, I guess… oh, hey, Chef – Jess Abernathy forgot and left a new issue of *People Magazine* at the front table this morning. Do you mind if I take it home to read? I'll bring it back in the morning."

Richard snorted. "Be my guest – although why relatively intelligent women like you and Jess Abernathy want to kill brain cells reading garbage like that instead of something properly edifying like Larousse… you do want to be a chef yourself, someday, don't you?"

Araceli just laughed. "Chef, sometimes we just like to give our minds a rest. I thought the feature story looked interesting. There's this English actor trying to make a comeback after getting religion in Thailand… Phillip Noel-Barrett. Do you know him?"

"Only by his reputation as a right prat," Richard answered, after a momentary hesitation. "We got in a fistfight on the sidewalk in front of the Ministry of Sound a couple of years ago. At least I think it was him; nancy-looking hurray-Henry with perfect teeth and bad taste in haberdashery." Richard snickered, rather nastily. "I spoiled the teeth, and his haberdashery too, before the bouncers broke it up. Ah well, long time ago and in another country, and besides the wench has moved on to some other poor chap with a weakness for crazy in bed. Several of them, in sequence, if you can believe the tabloids. Minestrone it will be, then, for the soup of the day."

Up Close and Personal, with Phillip Noel-Barrett

– *People Magazine*, January, 2015

Joy Faircloth

"Just call me Pip," he says, when we meet for lunch at the lovely and casual Wolfgang Puck restaurant at the Hotel Bel Air. Our meeting has been arranged by Noel-Barrett personally, instead of his publicist. "I'm trying to pare down," he says, gazing at me with those intensely blue eyes which have mesmerized audiences throughout his long career, from child actor in British television, through sizzling performances in film and on stage. No one can easily ignore the charismatic presence of a star like Phillip Noel-Barrett – not even in a celebrity-heavy venue like the Bel Air. I sense intense interest from a scattering of diners at those tables, guests at a mid-afternoon and middle of the week. "I've become a Buddhist, you see," he explains, taking my hand and fixing me with that dazzling sky-blue gaze. "And part of that involves becoming more in touch with the world. Joy… that suits you. You have an old soul and a cheerful one; I can see that very clearly now. So… which one of my roles is your favorite? I know that you must be one of my fans."

"I am," I reply, delighted that he has agreed to meet with me on such short notice. "My very favorite is one of your early ones; Dick Turpin, in *Turpin the Highwayman*. I first watched it on Masterpiece Theater, in the early Nineties, when I was just was a child. I loved it – and my parents…"

"Indeed," he says, and the assurance wavers ever so slightly. "I was just a kid myself… that series was my first starring turn, after simply years as a child actor. So you have an affection for rebellious outlaws? I find that… fascinating."

"Tell me how you started in the business," I ask, knowing how much actors love discussing their favorite subject. With a cheerfully ironic air of detachment, which I sense has come of having endured personal trials, disappointments and tragedies large and small, Noel-Barrett – I simply cannot bring myself to the point of addressing him as 'Pip' – enlarges most amusingly on his early career. A bit part in *The Story Teller*, another in the long-running series *Grange Hill*; he paid his dues. And then, I ask – "What happened after that?"

"Dear Joy, I got to that awkward age, although mercifully, it didn't last long. Amazing what qualified dermatologists can do these days with regards to the age of spots – how long has it been since you saw a teenager with a truly hideous case of acne? And then there were those unpredictable teenage growth spurts – suddenly becoming six inches taller and sprouting whiskers and a basso-profundo voice between one season and the next? Agents positively begin tearing their hair out at that stage, I assure you. I pottered about with work on stage… glorious, that period of my life was," He assures me. Such energy, such joy in life and its various experiences is infectious.

"So, you launched the third phase of your career in your twenties," I say. "Critics say that you did your best work in the late 1990s – there was the Merchant-Ivory production of *The Longest Journey*…"

"Oh, that," he says modestly. "A doddle… a walk in the park. Moody evocatizing in soft focus, with my shirt undone to the navel; I still get fan mail for that, can you believe?"

"You were everywhere in the late 1990s to early 2000s," I say. "And then… suddenly, you were off to Thailand. Your publicist at the time released a statement saying that you were re-thinking your life and seeking spiritual renewal."

"Ah, yes… Morrie. Worth every penny I paid him. The thing is," and here he fixed me with that intense blue gaze. "I had begun to think of it all as the most dreadful sham; a spiritual dead-end, in a manner of speaking. I had to go away. I wanted to do some work on my soul, you see."

"Some sources have speculated that your motivation was guilt over your breakup with Tiffany Rand, since that led to her breakdown and near-fatal overdose," I suggested, knowing that this would be a sensitive subject, but Noel-Barrett nods.

"She was such a fragile soul," he agrees. "A gentle butterfly; I – of all people – should have sensed that. So talented, and with such a promising future – but our profession is a brutal place for fragile souls, even one who had the affection and support of so many friends! So many of them blamed me, you see. I have tried to forgive them – would you believe that my agent tells me there are directors who refuse to consider me for roles on that account? Poor Tiffany; she has never entirely recovered. I tried to reach out to her… but she has never answered my messages and emails."

"So, what are your plans now?" I ask, intensely curious. It is hard to imagine Noel-Barrett behind the camera and not in front of it, but that appears to be the next phase of his life plan.

"Producing!" he exclaims. "Actors are but poor puppets, you see! I want to be the one telling the stories and pulling the strings. I have the right experience, the right connections… and the right investors – and it's here in Hollywood, where they are extraordinarily fond of those of us with a solid background in British television and the stage. I am about to finalize my first project."

"Can you tell me anything at about it?" I ask, at which Noel-Barrett smiles that heart-meltingly mischievous smile, and replies, "Well, it's a very up to the minute project – a kind of alternate history, science-fiction adventure… think *Abraham Lincoln Vampire Hunter*, but with a Texas setting. I can't tell you any more than that, dear Joy. Promise you won't spill everything to your readers?"

"Of course I will," I reply.

The Dinner Party – Evolving with Sook

"I feel like Sisyphus," Richard moaned, the morning after the first planning meeting at the Walcott's, after the morning rush was over in the Café.

"They make a medicated cream for that," Araceli replied, with a shocking lack of sympathy. "You can pick up a tube at the CVS in Karnesville. So… what part of your proposed menu didn't pass muster with the most demanding tiger mother in Luna City?"

"The shorter list is what did," Richard was taking out his frustrations by punishing an innocent and harmless bowl of pastry dough, rolling, and folding, slamming it down on the worktable top. "The beef wellington. Naturally – oh, and the tiny pastries. Both because they are time-intensive, complicated to create and expensive. Everything else – pah! She wants a seafood course – lobster, I believe. Or maybe oysters Rockefeller. Cream of something or other for the soup course... can you feel the arteries of their guests clogging all the way from the Walcott manse? I can. She might as well just set up a vomitorium, next to the bar, in the imperial Roman tradition. Hollandaise sauce on the asparagus and do not ask me about what she wanted for the appetizers. Individual quiches, for the love of God! I could not make the stupid b—" Araceli cleared her throat meaningfully, and Richard bit off the rest of the word.

"It's the vulgarity of it all that gets up my nose. That, and the fury. She goes from calm and rational to screaming rage faster than anyone I have ever known. She knows nothing of taste, or artistry, of the tradition of fine cuisine – only if it's complicated and expensive, it must be good, and she must have it. And Clovis..."

"What did he do?" Araceli finished stacking the last load of dishes into the dishwasher.

"Sat there like a tailor's dummy, nodding his head and agreeing with whatever she said."

"Well, he has to endure her when she's in a bad temper," Araceli said. "Look, Chef; I'll bet you anything you like, she'll change her mind at least three times before the day, anyway. And you _have_ to have the menu finalized before putting in the grocery order. I'd just tell her that what she wants – lobster and oysters – just aren't in the market. And ignore the screaming furies. She only does it for effect."

"She wants a signed contract," Richard thumped the pastry dough with vicious force upon the worktop, obviously wishing it were Sook Walcott, or a part thereof. "Specifying exactly what will be served..."

"So, put in a clause saying that if the necessary ingredients for those menu items are not available to you at a fair market price, then you may use your own best judgement. Georg Stein used to practice law... I'll bet if you ask him, he'll tell you how to phrase it. You are the expert chef, Chef," Araceli fixed him with a slightly exasperated look. "She is paying you for your expertise in providing a grand culinary experience for her guests. All that other stuff that she says that she wants? Sook is just talking about what she <u>thinks</u> she wants because it's expensive and it's what she <u>thinks</u> that high-class people have at their dinners. You know what she <u>should</u> want, and I bet that Clovis does, too. Don't let her bulldoze you with a tantrum. Call her bluff – don't worry so, Chef!"

"We have to have it settled by next Saturday," Richard regarded the helpless mound of pastry dough cowering on the work-top under a dusting of four, beaten thoroughly into submission. "So that Chris and I can finish shopping; he's tending bar."

"Oh, good," Araceli beamed approval. "If he can make all of her drinks doubles during the cocktail hour, she'll be too sloshed to start fussing when the first course is served. Beatrice and Bianca will be waitressing that evening – and you know that I've trained them up to do things right. Berto is a bit raw, but he's a good boy, and he used to bus tables at Mills Farm during the summers."

"Benny Cordova and some of his boys are going to manage the valet parking," Richard plopped the dough into a bowl for the second rising, and dusted off his hands. "And he's also setting up for the musical entertainment. Benny has many talents, apparently – and one of them is as a roadie. Apparently, there's going to be dancing, after supper, though I'll be surprised if anyone can manage to find the dance floor."

"Who's going to play?" Araceli asked, curiously, and frowned when Richard said,

"I think they're called *Los Maldonados* – they were here for Founder's Day, weren't they?"

"They were," Araceli replied. "I guess Walcott doesn't know about the feud, or he would never have booked them."

Richard cursed, with a richness and invention that Araceli had hitherto not encountered save when Dr. Wyler was particularly inspired and slammed a new bolus of pastry dough down onto the worktable with a crash that shook the kitchen.

"It's not like the Hatfields and the McCoys," Araceli explained, when she could get a word in edgewise. It's not like there's been gunfire in the streets when the Maldonados and the Gonzalezes and Gonzaleses meet although there was that one time in 1919. In front of this very building though; Old Don Antonio Gonzales got into a shoving match on the sidewalk with a Maldonado and challenged him to a duel. Before they could be stopped by the police, they emptied their pistols at each other. You see… around here, men went on going about heeled for a good long time. It was just the way things were."

"So what happened?" Richard was fascinated and horrified all at once. Every story that he had ever heard about Texans and guns was about to be proved accurate.

"Well, they both missed. Each other, anyway; crippled a mule, broke a streetlight mantle, and holed the radiator of Don Antonio's Model A Ford. Didn't you ever note the historical plaque? That was the very last gunfight in Luna City unless you count the time that the Newton gang tried to hold up the Bank of Luna."

"This just keeps getting better," Richard said. "It sounds more like a tale of the border reivers. How did it all start?"

"With a dead chicken," Araceli was clearly enjoying this. "Miss Letty McAllister's brother went and researched it all when he was a young man for his doctoral thesis, although by that time all he had to go on was the stories that the abuelas told. As near as anyone could make out, there was a fight at a fandango in old Goliad about 1820. We Gonzalezes had a fine rancho here on the San Antonio River. The Maldonados… they were quarrelsome trash, tenants of the De Leons, up in Victoria. They came to the fandango… oh, it must have been grand, a week of festival, you see; gathered for trading, for dancing and exchanging news, racing horses, games of skill, gossip and gambling. The story is that a prize fighting rooster belonging to a Gonzalez was killed by a Maldonado. And of course, there was a brawl among the young men over that."

"Simple but stupid, like young men everywhere," Richard agreed. Yes, he could see that happening, quite easily. "And then it all grew from that one dead chicken?"

"We-l-l-l, it was a little more complicated than that, according to Dr. McAllister. It turned out that the Maldonados were always on a different side from us. They were *Centralistas*, we were *Federalistas* – allied to the cause of independence for Texas and loyal to the Constitution of 1824. The Maldonados were partisans of General Lopez de Santa Anna – that pig of a dictator. We were proud Tejanos, they were…" Araceli made a face. "Hungry jackals, following after the lion, hoping for a mouthful or two, although we were both treated alike in being contemptuously by the Anglos, in the end. There were other controversies… like when they were planning the San Antonio-Aransas Pass Railroad. We wanted it to go through Luna City, the Maldonados sided with Karnesville. I don't suppose there is any more to the feud now than schoolboys taunting each other after a game between the Moths and the Knights. Anyway, we are still a family of substance and property, and they are traveling musicians. Although… rather good ones," Araceli hastened to add. "They have a following; very popular in this part of the country. But not quite respectable; when I was allowed to date boys my mother and Abuelita did not permit me to go out with a Maldonado boy. Abuelita said they are shiftless and improvident, and beat their wives when they bothered to marry them at all. Don't worry, Chef – it won't get out of hand, not at a big party like the Walcotts. We will be busy in the dining room and in the kitchen; they will be busy making music."

"Well, keep an eye on your girls and Berto," Richard commanded, still sweating at the thought of a long-established family feud breaking out anew among the staff at his first high-end catering event.

As Araceli had suggested, he did walk over to the Steins' bookstore that afternoon, to seek the advice of Georg. He had wondered how on earth a pair of middle-aged German nationals had finished up in Luna City, but never had the opportunity to ask. The Steins owned one of the most attractive buildings on Town Square, against considerable competition; a narrow storefront adorned with colorful flowering plants, and baskets of ferns hanging from the edge of the verandah which sheltered the length of sidewalk in front of it. The old-style ornate street lamp which stood before the shop also had a pair of baskets planted with bright flowers and trailing vines hanging from it. "Stein's Wild West Roundup" was stenciled in ornate gold Victorian letters on the glass shop window. Richard paused for a moment to admire the display in the window; a scattering of books, some of them open to colorful illustrations of cowboys and soldiers, artfully arranged among a welter of relics of the old west; knives in fringed and beaded sheaths, a Navaho patterned blanket and a Western saddle on a stand.

When he pushed opened the door, a small bell on a spring at the top jingled: the store was empty at this mid-week. Empty of people, but not of books, paintings and Western relics. As in the other old shop buildings, the first floor had a high ceiling. The space between the tops of tall book-cases was filled in with framed posters and paintings, some featuring landscapes of Texas and the southwest, rather than cowboys, horses, cattle, and Indians. More western memorabilia of every imaginable kind and materiel filled glass-fronted display cases, and the tops of the standing bookshelves. A dozen heavy and old-fashioned long-barreled revolvers were displayed in a glass case with their necessary tools. Apparently these were the black powder and lead ball sort, which probably reduced their attractiveness to potential thieves. A large German-language movie poster of John Wayne in a movie called *Die Comancheros* dominated the wall over the door to Georg Stein's office in the back. A fluffy grey cat briefly twined himself around his ankles, before retreating to a basket underneath the nearest display case, regarding Richard with unblinking green eyes.

"Ah, Mr. Astor-Hall," Georg emerged from the office, pushing his reading glasses to his forehead and addressed another cat – a black one with white paws and chin, hunching meaningfully with tail lifted and his hindquarters aimed at the side of the tall counter which served as the cash stand. "Behave yourself, Beethoven! How pleasant to see you! I meant to say how delicious your pastries are – Annise and I find dining in the café to be so enjoyable since you have taken over management!"

"My pleasure," Richard replied. He was always rather taken back when diners complimented him; of course his pastries – indeed, everything he prepared – were delicious. They couldn't be anything else, barring deliberate sabotage. He outlined Araceli's suggestion for a clause to the contract.

Georg frowned, slightly. "I am not qualified to advise formally on legal matters in this country," he said. "So take my opinion as that of a layman only. Such a clause worded in that manner should offer you... cover against legal fire, so to speak. Being acquainted with the other party to this proposed contract, I agree with Mrs. Gonzalez in her estimation of the situation."

"Oh, good," Richard was relieved; not so much that Georg couldn't speak officially, but that his reading of Sook Walcott harmonized with Araceli's. He had already learned to put stock in her judgements. "You know... I should spend some time in your shop. I didn't realize that you specialized in the old west."

"It is my passion, rather than law," Georg seemed to expand with pride and enthusiasm. "Law was my profession – you are a lucky man, in that your profession is your passion."

"I've wondered how you and Mrs. Stein finished up here," Richard ventured.

"Ah, that was a mistake, you know. Beethoven – behave yourself!" Georg snatched up a plastic spray bottle and aimed a squirt at the black and white cat, now sinking his claws into the tattered Oriental rug which covered part of the floor. The cat shot away and vanished among the shelves.

"He is a very bad cat," Georg sighed. "But Annise... she will spoil them. How we came here? By accident! When I retired, and our children were grown, Annise and I decided we should travel. She has distant cousins in Texas, you see; in Fredericksburg. I was so much a fan of Karl May... Zane Grey... John Wayne, always, since I was a boy. It was my hobby, all things to do with the Wild West. My collection of relics and things; it was the marvel among all of our neighbors. Well, we decided to travel, so I could see all of these places that we had only dreamed of! So – my dear Annise's cousins. And then – the Alamo! It is very small, you know," Georg sighed. "And in the movies – a fortress, a veritable fortress! So then we wanted to see the Grand Canyon. But we got lost. So very lost... by the time we found ourselves we were here. We drove into Town Square, looking for the Grand Canyon, which was not here, of course. It is three days drive in the other direction! But here is the shop, and it is for sale, with all the contents. Just from curiosity, we ask at Abernathy's... they have the keys, you see." Georg explained.

"What was the shop, then?"

"Oh, it was full of junk, dark and very dusty. Annise nearly cried. But we saw the upstairs – there is this little apartment, you see... and a garden in the back, and it reminded her of where she lived when she was a girl. A little apartment, over a shop, looking out onto a green square; Annise, she said; how very well the old furniture from her parent's house would look in it! And behind a pile of junk in the downstairs, I see that poster! John Wayne – in German! It is a sign – and I look a little more, and see that all this... these shelves and cases, they are good. Good wood, fine carving. There are many books – and I look among them, and some are valuable. And I think of how I would have space for my collections and my books. I have one of the best collections of Texiana, outside of a university. I could collect and sell even more books about the glorious West! I say then,

Anni, my dearest; what would you think if I bought this place, and we moved here?"

"I can just imagine what your wife would have said," Richard ventured. Yes, he could imagine what Sammi might have said, if he suggested that she leave London and take up housekeeping in tiny flat above the business. The screaming defiant hysteria would have made the front page of the *Sun* and the *Daily Mail*, at the very least.

Georg beamed happily. "Oh, she liked it. We went out to see the garden and there was a cat in it, which came up to her and purred. We never saw the Grand Canyon... not on that trip, anyway. And Annise has three cats, and I have my business with books and sufficient room for all my collection. I sell fine books and western memorabilia through my website and we are happier than we have ever been."

"Ah. I did wonder," Richard thanked him for his expert opinion and began to take his departure. Halfway to the door, he turned around. "Georg... you wouldn't by any chance have any of the Hardy Boys series – the original set from the 1920s, written by Franklin Dixon?"

"I do not believe so," Georg looked thoughtful. "But if you would like, I will search. We buy books by the box at estate auctions... or Anni can look if they are available from dealers. She would like that – and she is very good at locating items, you would not believe."

"Thanks, Georg... tell me if you find any of them. I'll pay whatever you're asking."

Yes, happy accidents had a way of happening in Luna.

A Small Town Treasure: Stein's Wild West Roundup

From the San Antonio Weekly Current - Archives

A bare hour and a half drive south of San Antonio lies a hidden treasure of Texiana – Stein's Wild West Round-up; concealed behind a quaintly ornate storefront in the historic main square of Luna City. Yes, there is a Stein; Georg Stein, from Mannheim, Germany, a retired corporate lawyer. A decade and a half ago, Georg and his wife Annise came as tourists to San Antonio. Fascinated since boyhood with tales of the Wild West, Georg had long been a collector; of books, of Indian relics, of artifacts, art and reproductions focusing on the mythic West. A long-time participant in various German re-enactment groups, Georg's dreams of partaking in that mythos came true, when he and his wife set out on a road trip. By mistake, the found themselves in the charming and relatively unspoiled hamlet of Luna City, where the nearest McDonalds is at least a ten-mile drive away.

There was a building for sale on Luna City's scenic and sleepy Town Square; as Georg tells it, an idle impulse let him to ask to look at the property which once had been a dry-goods store, with a small apartment on the upper floor.

"It was not immaculate – no, not by any means!" Georg says today, sitting in the small office at the back of the store, now tastefully arranged and organized to the degree that the proprietors know if a single item has been replaced a half-inch out of place. "It was filled, indiscriminately with anything and everything old. Most was trash, piled up here and there. We could not say so, of course, when we purchased the building. It is one of those things; where you come to live as a newcomer – do not say to your news neighbors that which may unthinkingly insult them. But ah—the store! For me, for my wife, it was perfect!"

The storefront property, previously a dry-goods emporium and then a second-hand store was indeed perfect. The building itself needed very little in the way of renovation; updating of the plumbing and HVAC systems has been sensitively performed on the 19th-century fabric. The dark oak woodwork of the shelves and display cases gleam like satin; the perfect setting for Stein's vast collection of books, memorabilia, and Western-inspired art. His collection of Texiana is unparalleled, nearly rivaling the library archives of the Amon Carter Museum of American Art in Fort Worth.

This meticulously curated gallery is the base from which Georg and Annise run an on-line business in antiquarian books. Annise, a native of Munich, took up bookbinding as a hobby when she was employed by the publisher Urban & Schwarzenberg. Now she has a small workroom in back of Georg's office where she meticulously repairs and restores the damaged bindings of vintage and antique volumes, precisely replicating what cannot be repaired. They share the premises with three cats: Beethoven, Bach and Mozart, who have the run of the show room, and warmly greet all visitors.

Stein's Wild West Roundup is on the corner of West Town Square and River Road, open on weekdays from 10 AM to 5 PM and on Saturdays from 10 AM to 3 PM. Look for the hanging baskets of ferns and flowers, opposite the bandstand in Luna City's Town Square.

The Trouble with Los Maldonados

Richard had to appeal to the Pryors, for the use of their refrigerated van, and for Berto Gonzales to drive it, on the afternoon of the planned grand dinner at the Walcotts.

"You never learned to drive, Ricardo?" Berto asked. He expertly crashed the gears of the van into low gear as they pulled away from the Café.

"No," Richard answered. He and Araceli squeezed onto the long bench seat of the van, elbow to elbow.

"Why is that?" Berto negotiated the turn from out of Town Square onto the road which lead, through several easy turns, to the edge of town and the low eminence upon which had been deposited – as if by some almighty defecation on the part of the architectural gods – the Walcott establishment. This was a structure not unpleasing to the viewer; just one dreadfully out of place considered by every esthetic standard imaginable.

It was a grey and vaguely French-style chateau, in a country where more organic buildings were constructed of native cream limestone, and one topped with blue slate tiles in a place where honey-reddish tiles or weathered cedar shingles would have blended more perfectly. Some square and unadorned glass and concrete Bauhaus cube would have appeared far less alien. A paved driveway circled the hill, leading by gradual stages around and up, from a pair of extremely ornate gateposts at the bottom. There was a neatly mown meadow just inside the gates, on which parking spaces were already being marked out by a sweating young man with a shaker-can of powdered chalk.

"I've always lived where there was public transportation," Richard answered. "And then I always had the services of a driver."

"La-de-dah!" Araceli snorted. "You'd better learn to drive yourself, Chef; nothing of the one here and you haven't any of the other available!"

"I have my bicycle," Richard protested, as the van gained the top of the hill, with the full arrogant splendor of the baby French chateau lay revealed before them; a terrace edged with massive urns, in which grew topiary shrubs tortured into geometric shapes.

"Yeah, like now?" Araceli replied, even as Berto earnestly promised, "I'll drive you wherever you have to go, Ricardo. My word on it."

Everything that they would need – the finished trays of desserts and appetizers, the prepared vegetables and ingredients measured out and sealed in plastic tubs – all were loaded into the back, with the necessary pots, pans and culinary tools from the café's kitchen. While the kitchen in the Walcott's was nearly twice the size of that in the Café, Richard had judged that everything but the workspace and the range itself were inadequate for his purposes. Without a word, Berto drove the van around to the back of the chateau, to a graveled courtyard set in an angle of one of the wings and a series of garages. Almost at once, Sook Walcott popped out of the back door, an imperious dynamo barely five feet tall, and apoplectic with rage.

"Reeechard!" She screamed, "You late! Arready people call – they on way!"

Richard resisted the temptation to look at his watch.

"Mrs. Walcott, I am never late," he said patiently. "Nor am I early… I arrive exactly when I need to arrive. Is there anyone here who can help us carry all this in so that we can begin cooking?"

Sook Walcott turned around and screamed into the house. "Wah-cott! He come!" she added to the three of them and vanished into the back door. Araceli muttered, "Chris better get here and start setting her up with doubles, or I'm going to wallop her with the biggest cheese tray I can find."

Distantly, they could hear Sook arguing fiercely in Korean inside the house with another woman – who from the sound of it, was giving as good as she got. No one appeared to help, until Berto had already opened the back of the van, and carried in the first of those boxes in which everything had been sorted and packed. A teenaged boy and girl appeared; both of them dark-haired and sloe-eyed. The girl was very pretty, but her fingernails were bitten down to the quick.

"Hi, Belle," Araceli greeted her, warmly. "Hi, Robbie; Sorry, didn't mean to set your mom off on a tear. We just need a hand with all this stuff."

The girl shrugged and brushed back a long lock of her ink-dark hair. "'S Okay… Mom's not much tighter-wound than normal. This dinner is huge for her and Dad though."

"She's fighting with Grandma now," offered the boy. "It's your chance to escape while she is distracted."

"Tempting suggestion," Richard sighed. "But I have to say 'no.'"

At that very moment, a dapper figure in jeans and a western-style shirt with a sharp crease and mother-of-pearl snaps appeared around the back of the van. It was purely amazing, Richard reflected, how very quietly

Benny Cordova could move, even in cowboy boots on gravel. The man must be some kind of Hispanic ninja.

"Help you all with that?" he offered.

With Benny and the two Walcotts, they had everything moved from the van in about two trips. Benny and the teenagers vanished, at the sound of Sook's high-heeled pumps tapping indignantly on the terrazzo floor, coming back into the kitchen from the farther portions of the house, as a door slammed in a distant wing, away from the kitchen.

"Reechard!" She appeared in the kitchen. "You rate! Thees a mess! You muss feeex!"

"No, it is not, Mrs. Walcott," Richard explained patiently. "Compose yourself. It is not a mess, we are exactly on time. It is exactly one hour and fifteen minutes until your guests arrive, two hours until dinner is announced, two hours and ten minutes to begin dinner service. I have just sufficient time to become familiar with your kitchen and to finish prepping the appetizers..." Beyond Sook Walcott, he could see that Araceli was looking speculatively at the largest of the cheese boards in her hands – from it to the furious chatelaine. "I must request that you allow us to do our jobs," He raised his voice. "I cannot work with this kind of interference. Either get out of this kitchen and leave us to do it, or we will leave... and your guests will have nothing but boxes of groceries to look at."

"We have contract!" Sook hissed, her normally ivory-tinted complexion pink with fury. "You no reave – cannot break contract!"

"I can," Richard replied, tranquilly. After any number of furious ex-girlfriends, insane celebs and certifiable BBC producers, Sook Walcott was a small, hissing kitten in comparison. "I can give verbal notice and walk out. It's in the fine print. Araceli, start putting the Café equipment in the van..."

"Hokay, I leave." Sook announced, without turning an eyelash and suddenly, surprisingly agreeable. "You work now, Reechard."

"Thank you, Mrs. Walcott," Richard gallantly kissed her hand – he thought he ought to lard on some old-world charm to sooth her loss in this battle of wills. "I can promise – your dinner tonight will be amazing. Don't worry about anything, save being your usual charming self for your guests."

He thought Araceli did an admirable job of converting a snort of laughter into a cough. The door closed behind Sook, leaving Richard in command of the field.

"Right then," He rolled up the sleeves of his chef's jacket. "Let us now begin committing acts of culinary genius!"

Absorbed in the assembly of the beef wellington, Richard did not at first detect any unusual disturbance of the atmosphere in Château Walcott. Between them, he and Araceli had prepared most everything that could be prepared in advance without diminution of flavor. Fingerling potatoes scrubbed and dashed with seasonings and a splash of olive oil, the raw vegetables for crudités cut and bagged, dips and sauces assembled... practically everything but the beef could be plated or slung into a cook-pot or the oven and then plated. He was aware, in a peripheral kind of way, of other people passing through the kitchen coming and going through various doors to other parts of the house, and once of angry voices outside – possibly one of them might be Sook, but they were all male voices and in Spanish. As long as Sook stayed out of his hair, there was no cause to break his adamantine concentration on the tasks at hand. The four waitresses and a single bus-boy/pot walloper would soon be arriving; all vetted and approved by Araceli, tempered by working at the Café or in the Mills Farm restaurant.

He was briefly distracted by Berto in his waiter's formal white dinner jacket, and dark cummerbund and trousers, looking rather embarrassed... and was that Abuelita Adeliza with him? And Araceli – she scowled, as she straightened from a large burbling pot of hot oil, a wire kitchen scoop full of miniature Scotch eggs in one hand.

"*Qué está haciendo la abuela aquí?*" Araceli demanded, and Berto looked thoroughly miserable.

"She demanded that I bring her here," he replied in English. "Because of Blanca an' Beatriz... she didn't take it well when she heard that *Los Maldonados* were going to play tonight. You know what *los viejos* always said. So Abuelita said – if she couldn't stop the girls from working tonight, I had darned well better take her to see her friend Min Kim, and between the two, they would chaperone Blanca an' Beatriz properly."

"Oh, for the love of all that's holy!" Richard snarled, little mollified by Abuelita Adeliza beaming at him with doting affection. *Did the old biddy just blow him a kiss?* "What is this – are we back in the days of *Pride and Prejudice*, with a duenna in black lurking around every corner to guard a young lady's virtue..."

Berto blinked. "Yeah, sure, if it's Blanca an' Beatriz's virtue; especially if it's los Maldonados."

Richard drew a deep breath, struggling to maintain focus on the work of preparing the beef tenderloin in its delicate seasoned layer of mushrooms. Through his teeth, he said, "Take your Gran to her friend. Tell her I am always glad to see her, but at this moment I cannot socialize. Tell both the old biddies that they can chaperone the girls every minute that they are not in the dining room, as long as they don't interfere with their work, or get in <u>my</u> way. Their much treasured chastity will be quite safe in this room as well. This place is full of knives and I have no hesitation about using them; on the strolling musicians, or anyone else. Savvy me?"

"Sure, Ricardo," Berto agreed, serenely oblivious to Richard's anger, bubbling as threateningly as the cooking oil in which the miniature eggs were cooking. As Berto and Abuelita departed, nearly colliding with Chris at the door, Richard looked across at Araceli and said, "You should start plating them as soon as they are cool. Half an hour to Mrs. Walcott's start time..."

"Hey, Richard," Chris said, urgently. "Do you have a first aid kit anywhere? I left mine in my car at the bottom of the hill."

"There's one in the van," Berto said, over his shoulder. "Underneath the driver's seat. Did someone get hurt?"

"Yeah," Chris answered. "Don't worry, I've got it under control." He left without saying anything more. Richard made a conscious effort to loosen the punishing grip that he had on the largest kitchen spatula.

"Araceli, my sweet, do you suppose that I can have the next twenty minutes uninterrupted and undistracted? Will that too much to ask, do you think?"

"Take it easy, Chef," Araceli replied, in the same tones that she used to reassure her children. "Chris says he has it under control."

He had approximately fifteen minutes of intense concentration before the four girls appeared; Blanca and Beatriz as usual, giggling with their heads close together.

"Hi, Chef," Blanca said. "Hey, Berto said that Abuelita was here, and that we should change into our waitressing things in Mrs. Kim's place. That OK?"

"Perfectly splendid," Richard replied, absently glancing at the clock. "You're due to be on duty in ten minutes, so don't take all bloody evening about it."

"Sure, Chef," Beatriz giggled and tossed her hair back from her face. Araceli regarded her niece and second cousin with a severe expression.

"Put up your hair in a proper net... no one likes finding long hair in their food. And be sure to wash your hands. No one likes to see dirty fingernails."

"Yes, 'Celi," they chorused. Richard was extraordinarily relieved to see that they obeyed instantly, reappearing exactly eight minutes later, utterly transformed.

"Good heavens," he exclaimed. "Don't tell me – someone boosted maids' costumes from *Downton Abbey*? You all look absolutely perfect!"

And they were; clad in identical black dresses, with the classical white aprons over them, and the little white lace and black velveteen ribbon-trimmed headbands.

Araceli grinned. "I thought you'd approve. Patricia is a wiz with dress-making with only a picture of the outfit to go on."

Beatriz giggled again. "Well, Miz Walcott told 'Celi that she wanted us proper old-school maids."

"I think I'm going to dress in this for Halloween," Blanca confided. Richard repressed an impulse to tell her that if she shortened the skirt about two feet, lost the bodice, and wore fishnet stockings, she would be a wild success. Araceli was standing altogether too close to the knife-block.

Instead, he snapped, "Never mind your future costuming needs. Two minutes. Prepare to circulate among the guests. Mrs. Walcott wants perfection – and perfection she will have."

"Yeah," Blanca said, "But I'll bet she didn't count on the Los Maldonados getting into a fistfight and two of them falling over the side of the terrace…"

"They what?" Richard was horrified. Los Maldonados playing live music on the terrace outside the cavernous salon where the guests were to assemble and socialize was a key element to Sook's detailed plan for the evening. Having that fall through would be an excuse for the pint-size domestic tyrant to indulge in another high-decibel fit of temper.

Blanca giggled and twirled one of the dangling black ribbons on her headband around her finger. "Yeah, Vincente an' Anselmo got into a fight, 'cause Anselmo is dating Vincente's old girlfriend, an' when Sebastian tried to break it up Vincente socked him in the jaw… an' then when he hit Anselmo, they both went over the railing."

"God save us," Richard muttered to himself, just as Chris put his head around the back door. "Hey, Rich," Chris asked, with an urgent tone in his voice. "Can you get me a small container with about a quarter-cup of milk in it?"

"What?"

"Milk," Chris repeated. "For some loose teeth. A dentist can save them, maybe. Sebastian plays the trumpet, he's gotta have his teeth."

"I'll get it," Araceli had finished garnishing a vast silver salver with sprigs of parsley and curly lettuce and filling it with miniature scotch eggs, every one stuck through with a toothpick. "Beatriz, take this into the salon and begin circulating... milk?" She rummaged briefly in the vast monolith of a refrigerator and found a half-gallon of milk. Another brief search produced a small Tupperware container. "Ok, then – is anyone else hurt?"

Chris sighed. "Anselmo's arm is broken in two places that I can see, and I'm pretty certain Vincente has a concussion. One of Benny's boys is going to drive them to the emergency room in Karnesville."

Araceli added the three small bowls of dip to the tray with crudités and nodded to Blanca. "Circulate – but come back to recharge when it's below half-empty. Nothing looks sadder than a half-empty tray. That's half of the band, accordion, sexto and trumpet. How are Los Maldonados going to perform?"

"Belle plays the trumpet," Blanca added over her shoulder as she followed Beatriz out of the kitchen. "She's good – she's First in the marching band."

"No idea," Chris replied. "Not my circus, not my monkeys." He was out of the door with the Tupperware jar. Richard and Araceli looked at each other.

"Not mine, either," Richard said, and Araceli shook her head. "I don't think we're going to escape the Wrath of Sook, Chef."

"Balls," Richard could feel the cold fingers of despair reaching out for him. Things were about to go catastrophically wrong, all over again and there was nothing he could do about it. "I say that we carry on with dinner for now. The Wrath shouldn't land on us full-force until later. God, I hope Chris is loading up her drinks…"

"We got us a problem, Ricardo," Again, Benny Cordova, appearing noiselessly from nowhere. "But I think I may have a solution."

"Christ, Benny – sorry, Araceli – you've got to stop startling me like that! I know <u>we</u> have a problem, but when did it become MY problem that the hired band is conducting themselves in the manner that others have doubtless come to expect of them?"

"Well, now that you put it that way," Benny thoughtfully sucked his teeth. "I don't suppose that it is… but there is a viable work-around."

"You have my undivided attention," Richard consulted the kitchen clock again. An hour before serving up supper to the Walcott's important guests, and he was out of all ideas, as well as energy for doing much else other than supervising the kitchen.

"We field some substitutes," Benny said, in complete earnest.

"I'll do a lot to make this evening a success," Richard replied, "But putting on a suit of lights and pretending to play the accordion is not something I'm prepared to do."

"No," Benny agreed. "That would be me – I play the button accordion. We have our own little house *conjunto* band at Mills Farm for special events. Berto, he can hold his own, on the twelve-string. All we need is a trumpet player, like…"

"Belle," Araceli's face lit up.

"You are not serious," Richard looked from face to face.

"Hey, where's Chris? We need ice at the bar," Berto – as if on cue – came in through the door to the rest of the house, with a large square container in his hands. Araceli took it from him.

"On it!" She began filling the container from the ice-maker in the Walcott's cavernous refrigerator-freezer. "Berto, there might be a change of plans. Benny wants you to fill in for Vincente tonight."

"That's cool," Berto shrugged. "Benny and I – we've played together. I know it's the Maldonados, but hey… that feud is old school. I'm new school."

"Right." Araceli began filling a small plate with a few crudites and some of the miniature eggs. "Chef, I'm taking this to Abuelita and Min Kim. When either of you sees Chris, tell him he's managing the bar alone. If Belle is with Mrs. Kim, I'll let her know."

"Would she play with us, too?" Berto looked interested. "That would be so cool!"

"We'll see what she says." When the door opened, Richard could hear the buzz of conversation in the salon on one direction, and the sound of a foreign-language television drama from the other.

"I like it, Ricardo, I like it." Benny grinned. "We'll grab some quick rehearsal round in back and then! Showtime!"

"It's stupid," Richard answered. "It's stupid, and it will never work."

"Hey, if it works, then it ain't stupid. C'mon, Berto – for those about to rock, we salute you!"

Benny and Berto vanished through the outside door. Richard began to feel that he was in one of those lunatic cartoons where everyone chased each other in and out of doors along an endless corridor. Just as he had that thought, Chris appeared, unexpectedly debonair in a white dinner jacket, over a black cummerbund and trousers.

"We need ice for the b—"

"Here," Richard jerked his chin towards the bin of ice cubes sitting next to the refrigerator-freezer. "Your assistant has been drafted to the band, so you're on your own. How're your damaged Maldonados doing?"

"Halfway to Karnesville by now," Chris didn't turn a hair; no, he was likely quite accustomed to mayhem of all sorts.

"Good… are you keeping Mrs. Walcott sufficiently well-supplied with her favorite tipple?"

"Yeah," Chris actually cracked a grin as he headed back to the bar. "But she's got hollow legs and the hardest head in Luna City."

"We live in hope," Richard riposted, just as the girls returned with half-empty trays – and as usual for them, giggling together.

"Those little fried things are fantastic!" Blanca exulted. "Everyone just adores them… we're not going to run out, are we?"

"If anyone asks," Richard said, "tell them no."

He darted another quick glance at the clock; yes, counting down the minutes. Araceli, trailed by Belle Walcott marched into the kitchen, Belle protesting, "But I've never played in a band like that…"

"First time for everything," Araceli began refilling the empty serving salvers. "Go get your trumpet."

"Hi, B," Beatriz enthused. "You gonna play with Los Maldonados? That's awesome! Go, Moths!"

"Yeah, go Moths!" Blanca echoed, and with a quick glance at each other, they assumed a cheerleading stance, side by side, chanting and clapping in unison, "Who rocks the house? Yeah - B rocks the house! And when B rocks the house, we go all the way down! Go, B!"

"Thanks, guys – you're so…" Belle started to say, but Richard snapped,

"Can we forget cheerleading practice and get back to work? This is a kitchen!"

"Yes, Chef," Blanca and Beatriz chorused. All three girls bundled through the same door. The kitchen felt emptier for their going, but the quiet and lack of adolescent giggling was refreshing.

"Better start some more of the eggs," Richard commanded. "They're as popular as I thought."

"Good thing we made a hundred and fifty," Araceli replied. "Oh, hey – Abuelita thought they were fabulous."

"What are the old dears up to?" He asked, for the television was turned up quite loud. Araceli laughed, fondly. "They are watching some overwrought Korean historical telenovela with Spanish subtitles and having a good old time... especially since Min Kim snagged a bottle of good Scotch. I'll make up two plates for them, later on."

"Oh, good – at least someone is having a riotously enjoyable evening around here," Richard opened the oven door to surveille the progress of the beef. Around in back, he could now hear music... music in fits and starts; accordion and guitar, pierced now and again by a pure trumpet threading all together. With the vegetables roasting in the oven, and the soups just beginning to simmer gently, he took a moment to open the back door and observe unseen the ad hoc rehearsal.

The six musicians stood in a semi-circle – apparently the middle-aged Maldonado with a saxophone was directing. Belle Walcott stood next to him, pink and flustered.

"... You're too stiff, *hija* – there is not a rhythm of marching, crash-crash-crash. This is improvisation – like jazz. Feel the melody, feel the notes and let them take you. Now, again – and feel it, feel it like Mangione... don't worry, *hija* – we will carry you on our notes when you crash..."

"How are they doing?" Araceli looked up anxiously from stirring the roasting fingerlings.

"Not bad," Richard answered. "For all that I know about this peculiar ethnic style of music..."

"*Conjunto*," Araceli giggled, sounding most unsettling like her niece and second cousin. "Created when the traveling musicians of *Mejico* collided full on with Poles and Germans, with their um pah-pah, their accordions and their polkas."

"An unseemly congress," Richard shuddered at the mention of polkas.

In the interim as the cocktail hour wound down, and before the formal dinner commenced – that brief few moments when Richard could take a breath, he slipped outside for some fresh air. It seemed that the rehearsal had gone well. Now the musicians had moved around to the terrace which commanded an astounding view of distant Luna City to the north, with roofs and hints of buildings half-concealed by trees, and the columned grandeur of the Wyler home-place in the distance.

Out to the west, the vista was of the winding green ribbon of the river, marked by the green of the cypress trees lining the banks, a dash of silver where the sunlight reflected on the water, and duller silver where the winding road caught the light, coyly as it wound around bends and over the hills. The sun slid down towards the western horizon, veiled in dark violet clouds trimmed in fiery orange, while the music floated in the still spring air. He had not heard Sook Walcott in screaming temper, so he assumed that everything was going well, or that Chris had been able to make her drinks generous ones.

Inside the kitchen, Blanca and Beatriz and the other two girls had returned with almost empty trays. Araceli swiftly stored away those few leftovers in Tupperware containers. Likely they would all dine on them later, when the guests were on the final course of nuts, raisins and candied fruit. The girls were – as he instructed – plating individual green salads; forty-three fine china plates, in rows on the immense island in the middle of the Walcott kitchen, in preparation for when the diners were ready for it.

Richard couldn't think of any household in Luna who had dinner service for fifty and two dishwashers unless it might be the Wylers. When the guests were all seated, they would carry in the soup course; a choice of either cauliflower or clear consume which Richard had finally agreed to, for service *a la Russe*.

"Oh, so that's what they call it!" Blanca had mused, much impressed. "It's a lot more trouble than a buffet, isn't it?"

"That's why all the silverware is laid out and the plates stacked up at each place they way they are," Beatriz explained. "It saves a bit of trouble."

"It would save even more trouble if they kept one plate and ate with a spork," Richard said, "But *haute cuisine* has some bloody standards!"

"Does Mrs. Walcott seem happy so far?" Araceli asked, from the stove where she was filling the first of the four soup tureens; two of cauliflower cream, two of consume.

"I guess," Blanca replied. "She's mostly talking with that Mizz Wyatt. You know, that bleached-blond witch from Corporate, who always wears pink cowboy boots when she comes out to the Farm?"

"Does she?" Araceli was diverted, and Blanca made a face.

"Yeah... always pink shoes. She told Uncle Teddy once that it was her 'personal fashion signature.' She's really tight with B's mom – like her BFF, or something."

"Right, then – once everyone is seated, bring out the soups," Araceli directed. "Remember – serve from the right, clear from the left."

"We know," chorused the girls, and Araceli snapped, "Do not roll your eyes at me; Abuelita is just around the corner. Now... off you go."

"Six courses," Richard muttered. "Two down, four to go."

He couldn't help himself; when the soup plates were cleared, and one of Benny's Mills Farm boys began loading up the first dishwasher, overwhelming curiosity led him to peek around the corner of the door to the dining room; another cavernous salon, decorated in a manner suggesting that no expense had been spared. It looked rather like one of the private dining rooms at a high-end Los Vegas casino; lots of mirrors, gilt frames and amber-colored velveteen upholstery, flowers, candles and every expensive table ornament there was for a socially ambitious hostess to aspire towards. Sook had directed that the tables be lined up in a formal 'U' – the whole banquet set-up. Yes, it was all going well; Chris and Berto circulating with wine bottles, the girls with their trays of salad plates. One more course to the big reveal – the beef wellingtons, in all their rich splendor.

"Downhill after that," Richard felt much more assured of success, upon returning to the kitchen. Left to himself, he would have liked twice the staff – but that would have strained the working space in what was after all, only a home kitchen, if a very large one. He set himself to slicing the wellingtons, arranging them precisely on the serving platters. Araceli positioned the garnishes as he worked, centering a sauce-boat in the center of each platter, and silver serving-tongs across the end. He found it gratifying that they worked in silence; Araceli was coming along very well as a sous-chef.

"Perfect," he said, nodding to the girls, as the last of the salad plates stacked up by the dishwasher. The girls were exclaiming over the magnificence of the platters: Richard reveled in their excitement over working such a classy event. It quite made up for their relative inexperience.

"Perfect you shall have," Araceli grinned, as the last of the primly black-and-white clad waitresses vanished through the doorway.

"A small thing, but all I have ever asked for." Richard felt the tension beginning to melt from the back of his neck, between his shoulders. "I'm back in the game, Araceli – back in the game and in top form."

"You were worried? I wasn't – not after you told Sook to stay out of the kitchen. So… as soon as the girls dish up the main course, I'll tell them to pull up a chair and eat while the guests are eating. Then all we need do is set up the dessert course and the final nibbles… Is that why people say 'from soup to nuts?' – I'd always wondered. Then, all we have to do is clean up… Pat is going to pick me up here, when he's done with his shift. I won't leave until everything is packed to go back to the Café. You won't mind, will you? He's gonna take me out to the all-night Whattaburger in Karnesville… just the two of us. I will be so glad to sit down."

"From the sublime to the ridiculous," Richard sighed. "Chris'll give me a ride home – since he has to close out the bar. And I'm staying until I get the final check from Clovis… hamburgers; really?"

"A meal that I didn't fix, with my sweetie, after a long day at work and the kids spending the night at my Mom's? Chef, I'll take my revelry and romance where and when I get it."

"Patrick's a lucky man," Richard admitted, more than a bit wistfully. Araceli was not his cup of romantic tea in any way. Even considering her for a moment in that regard would wreck a perfectly satisfactory work relationship. But he wished most sincerely that he could toddle on home to the Airstream tonight, pour out two glasses of good white wine, and relax over a mess of scrambled eggs or something comfortable with an undemanding, even-tempered bit of female company. This triumph wouldn't be complete until he could review it in tranquility with someone who had a sympathetic ear.

Araceli looked across the kitchen at him; yes, that hawk-sharp judgement which was the other thing preventing him from ever contemplating her as anything more than a level-headed gal-pal.

"You ought to have a best girl, Chef... ever thought of dating anyone here? There are plenty of single women your age about Luna City – Karnesville, even. Nice ladies, not sluts... stay away from the bars, you know. Give a cooking class to one of the churches. That would give you a chance to meet..."

"Alas, my dear Araceli – I am a right bastard when it comes to the fair sex," Had to be confessed, Richard told himself, recalling Sammi and all those previous to her. They all seemed to blur into one single type; harpy-hysterical, shrieking, and self-centered, but madly entertaining privately, given the right mood. "My judgement of women in general is so horribly flawed, I am disinclined to put any trust in it whatsoever; it is just the way it is. After a certain age – the person that you are at that point is likely to be the person you are for the remainder of your life."

"If you say so, Chef," Araceli replied, shrewd and skeptical. "Give it some time, I think. Unexpected things have a way of happening in Luna City."

At the shank end of the evening, close on half-past ten, after the final courses had all been served and cleared away, Richard was left alone in the vast kitchen, wrapping up the last few details in the echoes of a culinary triumph, and waiting for Chris. A handful of lingering guests were finishing out the evening with coffee and brandy in the reception salon; Richard honestly wondered where they had room to put it all and if any of them were still able to walk a straight line. The two dishwashers were humming away through their cycles, Araceli and Pat had gone, Berto had driven away in the van, delivering the waitresses to their homes and their no-doubt anxiously waiting parents. Abuelita Adeliza and Min Kim were still up – the television soundtrack of a Korean dramatic epic resounding in the quietness of what Richard had been told was the 'granny wing.'

The lonely sound of a trumpet essaying some Alpert and Mangione soloes echoed from the other end of the house. Likely this had been a good ego-boosting experience for Belle Walcott, with her bitten fingernails and vaguely hunted look. The survivors of Los Maldonados were gone likewise. Benny Cordova had appeared – noiselessly as was his habit – nearly causing Richard to drop one of the soup tureens to the floor.

"We're off, Ricardo," he announced blandly ignoring Richard's startled expression. "You OK? There's nothing left for us to do, since the last guests are spending the night. Good event, eh? Next one, a hundred per-cent better, as Teddy says. You got a ride?"

"Yeah – Chris. I'm just waiting on him."

"Don't think much longer," Benny commented. "Hey, that little girl of the Walcotts' – she did OK, didn't she – filling in with the band. Berto, he did swell, too. It was a blast, playing with them, I hafta say. Maybe there's an end to this family feud crap? Yeah... no. Around here, they cherish them, like prize hunting dogs. Family pride, I guess. Me, I'm from Beeville, and my folks never fought with nobody, not over a decade or two. Yeah, my mom had it out with Tia Consuela over the right way of making menudo, about fifteen years ago. They haven't spoken since, but it's not like they're going to have it out in the street. Anyway… a good night, Ricardo."

"Thanks, Benny – it was a fantastic evening."

"Yeah, it was," Benny agreed. He was gone from the kitchen as silently as a ghost. Richard thought about hitting up Chris for a stiff nightcap and decided against it. Better a cup of coffee. He located the Walcott's coffee-maker – a high-end Keurig, of course – with the stash of single-serving cups next to it. The Keurig bubbled happily away to itself, and presently Chris appeared, with a hefty box in his arms.

"I've got two more boxes to go back in the wine cellar, then I'm done," he announced.

"Christ, you mean this place has a wine cellar?" That had not been included on the initial familiarization tour.

Chris laughed. "No expense spared. Believe it or not, Clovis has his own helicopter pad, as well. Never know when you're going to have high-powered clients drop in for a quick consult."

"Guess not… want some coffee?"

"Sure." Chris padded away – now Richard knew where that door led. He went to search the behemoth of a refrigerator for some cream if not some half-and-half. When he closed the refrigerator door, there was another person in the kitchen with him. Not Chris; a fortyish woman in an evening gown that was too plain in material and too elegant in cut to be anything but designer and expensive. Tired to the bone, Richard also registered serious and understated jewelry, chiseled features distinguished rather than beautiful, and piled-up masses of hair just a little too perfectly honey-blond to be entirely natural. And… hot-pink Jimmy Choos. She was looking at him in a manner which irresistibly brought to mind a hungry gourmand surveying a box of designer chocolates… or a snake looking over a baby bird. Blanca's words earlier in the evening popped into his mind -- *that bleached-blond witch from Corporate… always pink shoes… her 'personal fashion signature.'*

"Miss Wyatt, is it – from Corporate?" Richard ventured, quite thoroughly unsettled. The woman laughed a throaty and knowing laugh.

"My reputation precedes me," She drawled, while walking... no, slithering across the kitchen to where he stood transfixed with a bottle of half and half in hand. "Suzanna Wyatt... chief of Marketing for Venue Properties, International. And I know you; you're Rich Hall. Your reputation has also preceded you. Those little sausage and egg appetizers are a dead giveaway."

"I got the recipe from a TV cooking show," he protested. "And Scotch eggs are... well, they've been around for years. You have me mixed up with that Rich Hall chap... common mistake, you know. I'm Richard Astor-Hall and as far as I know, I've never been on a TV show in my life."

"Oh, on a TV show?" Suzanna Wyatt ran the tip of her tongue around her lips. "I never said how I knew you... give it up, Rich. Admit all." Her voice lowered to a seductive purr. "I know who you really are and I have an offer you can't refuse."

"Watch me," Richard dodged around the edge of the massive kitchen island... damn, she was between him and the Keurig.

"An exclusive contract with Venue Properties," Susanna Wyatt purred. "A free hand in designing the menus for all our locations, overseeing the catering of all our high-end international events... it doesn't stop there, of course..."

"Yes it does," Richard circled around farther around the island, wondering if he should just make a break for the door; any door would do. "I'm Richard Astor-Hall, I run the Luna Café and Coffee in town... and I don't want anything to do with high-end international events. I'm fine with doing dinners like this. Really. Cross my heart, Miss Wyatt..."

"Playing hard to get, are you?" Susanna Wyatt feinted towards one end of the island and doubled back with the swiftness of a striking cobra. *Damn – now he was cornered.* "Holding out for a better deal? Ohhh, I like it when a man plays hardball. I like it when a man plays hard... anything."

Forget about the coffee, Richard decided in a moment of wild despair. *Forget about the ride from Chris. Make a mad run for it… after all, how fast could she chase him in high-heeled Jimmy Choos.*

"Why-att!" He never thought he would be glad to hear Sook Walcott's steam-whistle shriek. "Why you make goo-goo-eye with help! We have night-cap! Talk plan for extension – no time for monkey-shine business!"

Sook had two glasses in one hand, a bottle in the other; tiny, imperious and infuriated.

"Oh, but this is important business," Susanna Wyatt's voice returned to what Richard judged must be her normal clipped and professional queen-of-the-boardroom tones. "Didn't you know – this is Rich Hall, the Bad-boy Chef! What he could do for VPI…"

Sook swept them both with a dismissive look. "No, Why-att – he only cook for crummy café. He do catering – a favor for Wah-cott."

"I…" Susanna Wyatt began, but if Richard still was any judge of predatory womanhood, a certain doubt had been instilled.

Sook shook the bottle in her hand – a very fine Scotch, if Richard was any judge at a distance. "You come, Why-att – serious business." As they left, Sook looked over her shoulder, saying, "Wah-cott, he drop off check tomorrow, OK?"

"OK," Richard answered – no, forgoing payment until tomorrow was worth the chance to make a clean getaway tonight. Especially since it looked as if Sook had winked at him in a meaningful way.

"Oh, man," Chris spoke from the door, another box in his hands. "Looks like you got yourself a real bunny-boiler there, Rich."

"Bunny-boiler?" Richard, still deeply shaken, decided that he wanted that coffee after all.

"As in serious cray-cray obsession; a stalker in the of the *Fatal Attraction* variety… I thought you were pretty experienced with crazy in women."

"Yes, which is why I'd have been legging it down the hill alone in another thirty seconds, if Sook Walcott hadn't pulled her off me, metaphorically. You know – that's almost the most humiliating part," Richard poured out two mugs of coffee, and warmed his hands around his own. Chris propped his lean length against the island and added cream and sugar to his own cup.

"What is? That she would have ripped off your clothes and performed the unspeakable, right here on this kitchen island?"

"No," Richard sighed. "That I am indebted to Sook Walcott. As for Miss Wyatt…"

"Not gonna ride the crazy train?"

"No." Richard added a pungent description of the circumstances under which he would, which involved borrowing certain essential gear for the purpose from Chris, who laughed enormously.

"Well, if she does start to haunt your place, Rich – you can come hide out with me, out behind Miz Letty's. Guarantee Miz Letty will run off that bleached-blond harpy without breaking a sweat."

"Shouldn't come to that, old chap, but I am grateful. Adopted sons of Luna should stick together."

"Yes, we certainly should." Chris agreed.

Charley Mills, Unexpurgated

Charles Everett Mills, born 1876 (the year of the Great Centennial) is perhaps the most widely famed native son of Luna City, responsible for at least three historical markers in the vicinity of his birthplace, and the small farm/ranch which provided a living for his parents, in the decades following the Civil War. He was the youngest child of James Bowie Mills, and his wife, Jane Everett: James Bowie Mills was the son of an old Texas family, reputed to be one of Stephen Austin's original 300. Jane Everett was of a similarly old and respectable lineage, settling in South Texas shortly after the Civil War. At the time of Charles' birth, James and Jane were the parents of three daughters, attractive and intelligent girls known familiarly as the Three Graces: Mary Faith, Elizabeth Hope, and Annabelle Charity.

James B. Mills' property lay somewhat to the south of Luna City, and under his management prospered sufficiently to enable James and Jane to educate their son and three daughters at private academies in San Antonio during the 1880s. Charles, as the only son was much-treasured by his parents and sisters; it would not be too much to say that he was spoiled rotten. The youthful Charley Mills was tall, athletic, handsome and charming, and appeared bound for every success in the world, the pride of his parents and community. Alas, this was not to be; Charley had a taste for fast women, easy living, and not to put too fine a point on it, a dissolute and criminal life-style. This did not become immediately obvious; to the end of their respective lives, his parents defended him as a good son and an upright citizen, claiming that Charley was the innocent victim of jealousy and slander.

At the age of 22, Charley was supposedly attending a business college in Topeka, Kansas. As it turned out, he was actually a member of the Doolin-Dalton 'Wild Bunch' Gang, and then of a relatively obscure group of professional robbers known as the 'Bent Cactus Gang' for a mocking scrawl left at the site of various robberies, the most famous of which was that of a Santa Fe train west of Cimarron, which netted several thousand dollars worth of silver and gold, both coin and ingots. A quantity of this loot was never recovered, leading to apocryphal stories of Old Charley's Treasure being secreted somewhere around Mills Farm early in the 20th century. Charley, whose sense of self-preservation became sufficiently acute to override his affection for making an easy living through train, bank and store robberies, prudently severed his association with the Wild Bunch and the Bent Cactus Gang by mid-decade, and so escaped the various violent ends dealt out by law enforcement to his former associates. Doubtless he reasoned that a living from immoral earnings might be a little safer.

His movements in the decade afterwards remain obscure; some accounts have it that he was serving as a mercenary in the service of

Pancho Villa, but that kind of strenuous adventure seems out of character for Charley, whose bent towards indolence became even more pronounced. He returned to take over management of Mills Farm following upon his father's death in 1903. His three sisters were all married by then; his mother went to live in Houston with Mary Faith and her family.

Sometime during the years following, he built a still, or hired someone to build a still, and began distributing various home-distilled spirits. By the time that Prohibition became the law of the land, Charley was a full-time bootlegger. He made not the slightest pretense of farming; and the well-ordered and profitable enterprise that his parents had established fell into rack and ruin. The pastures and fields became overgrown with cedar, cactus and impassible canebrakes along the length of river which formed a boundary of the property. The largest stock-pond became home to a pair of native alligators; the source of the legend that Charley Mills disposed of the bodies of his rival bootleggers by dumping them in the pond and letting the alligators feed.

It is presumed that Old Charley and his confederates in the local bootlegging business made sufficient from it to maintain a prosperous living throughout Prohibition. It was during this period, though, that close neighbors and his sisters – perhaps with some regret – gave up any public pretense of Charles Everett Mills being a solid and respectable citizen. His inclinations towards sloth, debauchery and general low-level criminality made him notorious as far as Karnesville, a constant burr under the saddle of local law enforcement, and those of his neighbors who suffered from that petty thievery, vandalism, and drunken misconduct which could be laid at his door. As frequently as charges were brought against him, very few actually came to court, and those were often dismissed. Charley, by whatever means, was always able to pay for the services of an excellent and combative lawyer. Community frustrations came to the point of him nearly being lynched from a tree in Luna City's Town Square in 1926.

Rescued by several of the more sober citizens, Charley thereafter became somewhat of a recluse.

The beginning of the Great Depression and the repeal of the Volstead act spelled an end to whatever shreds of prosperity Charles Everett Mills had been able to hang on to. The last of a series of female companions or common-law wives, Carolina de san Pedro, reported finding him one morning early in March, 1935, slumped over the fence which enclosed the alligator pond. He had been dead for hours. Much to the surprise of the official Karnes County coroner, death was from natural causes.

The disposition of the Mills family acres then descended into a kind of Texas version of Jarndyce vs Jarndyce. Charles Everett Mills had seventeen acknowledged children, resulting from 45 years of cohabitation, affairs and brief encounters with a dozen women who can be named with certainty, and another two dozen whose names are a matter of conjecture. In the cases of the acknowledged children, Charles Everett Mills did make some kind of provision for them, in that he handed most off on his sisters and the others set out on their own as soon as they were able. Of his various paramours, three stand out; the first being the only one who actually achieved the status of legal marriage with him, sometime in 1892.

That would be Josephine Courtemanche allegedly from Paris: a brothel-keeper in Tulsa more readily known by her real name, Bertha Potts from Poughkeepsie. She was nearing forty when she and Charley married before a justice of the peace. She choked to death on a fishbone on their wedding night, and Charley was chased out of Tulsa by the brothel's real owners; a pair of gamblers who took exception to the then-twenty-one-year old Charley trying to throw his weight around.

It is considered likely that his next significant female companion was the woman suspected of being the real brains behind the Bent Cactus Gang, Odette Peterson, dubiously a widow who kept a livery stable in Fort Worth. She was described as a 'fine figure of a woman' by those who admired her and 'Gargantua in a blond wig' by those who didn't. It is a recorded fact that when the Bent Cactus Gang held up a bank in Spearville, Kansas, Odette Peterson was eight months pregnant, brandishing a sawed-off shotgun and a pistol... and smoking a Cuban cigar. She and Charley Mills eventually separated; Charley to return to Texas with their two children while she became the mistress of a US Senator and learned more subtle forms of looting money from the common people.

Carolina de San Pedro, Charley's final common-law wife, was three decades his junior at the time of his death. It eventually came out that she had been overseeing his illicit distilling operations for a number of years, and that she was quite the expert at filtering, blending, and aging. Her various concoctions were popular in the most discriminating and expensive speakeasies in the United States during Prohibition. Her Mills Farm scotch whiskey led to her being hired by Hiram Walker and Sons, of Windsor, Ontario. She settled there with her new husband, Ambrosiano Gonzales, of the Luna City Gonzalez/Gonzales clan. An eighty-year old bottle of Carolina's Mills Farm Scotch recently sold after a furious bidding war at Sotheby's in New York for $28,000, reportedly to international financier Collin Wyler.

The Battling B's

"Utter piffle," Dr. Wyler stated, categorically, to a dining room half-full of morning patrons. "The only damned thing the History Channel knows anything about is Hitler, and I swear, they get half of that wrong anyway. It's not a hundred percent certain that Charley Mills ever was a member of the Wild Bunch ... or the Bent Cactus Gang. And if he was, he never came home to Luna with any of the takings. Collin was fascinated by Old Charley when he was a teenager – if there was anything left unknown about the old scoundrel's miserable existence, my son would have found it ... and then bored Miz Alice and I to death with it over the dinner table. "

It seemed that some kind of treasure-hunting documentary on cable TV the night before had touched on matters local – that is, Luna City local. Richard had opened the Café doors at 7 AM to hear that just about all of those waiting for coffee, cinnamon rolls and scrambled eggs were also hungry to talk about it. It was a mild spring morning, and the diners had spilled out onto the sidewalk tables.

"So, what is this treasure supposed to be?" Richard was honestly curious. He knew of Old Charley Mills; bootlegger, lifetime career blot on the civic escutcheon, and the disgraceful son of an otherwise respectable family. After all, there were three historical markers around Luna City noting his presence, or participation in certain events, but the possibility of buried treasure had never been noted on any of them. He, along with other Lunaites found the old rip's scabrous reputation of a hundred years ago to be an amusing contrast to the corporate image of him in this present century as the genial official host and public face of Mills' Farm.

"$19,000 in silver and gold ingots, from his share of the Spearville Express robbery," Georg Stein answered his pleasant face alight with the passion of enthusiasm. "And he was most definitely a member of the Bent Cactus Gang; that is most assured, Herr Doctor Wyler. There is a daguerreotype, in my own collection, certified by experts to be of the Bent Cactus Gang … him and Odette Peterson and the others, all very plain and clearly identifiable…"

"That may very well be," Doc Wyler replied. "But if Old Charley ever had $19,000 – or $19.00 in his possession, it went out of his hands as soon as it came into them. Lazy, improvident wastrel … and there were a thousand places between here and Spearville where he likely blew it all on good whiskey and bad company. Furthermore," and Doc Wyler pointed his fork emphatically at Georg Stein. "He was too lazy to spend the effort to dig a hole and hide it. My father knew him pretty well; Papa said you could trust him about as far as you could throw the bandstand in the Square and that a more indolent rascal never walked the earth. About the only thing he ever demonstrated any energy about was in stealing anything not nailed down, distilling rot-gut whiskey and breeding bastard children. No, there's no treasure buried about Mills Farm, much as it grieves me to agree with those corporate slugs. Not that it ever stops treasure-hunters from trying. Guess we'd better prepare for another onslaught of them, now that the goddam History Channel has revived the rumors once again."

"It's an ill-wind that blows no good for anyone," Georg Stein bit into his fresh-baked cinnamon roll, with renewed enthusiasm.

"Wait and say that when you wake up in the middle of the night and find some addle-pate digging in the middle of your lawn, because his metal detector has alerted on a set of old horseshoes," Doc Wyler answered, and the talk drifted off into some mild speculation of exactly how much the renewed influx of treasure-hunters would bring to Luna City – in additional income and in annoyance.

Richard wondered if the rumored treasure-hunters would disrupt his peaceful existence at the Age of Aquarius. He had become accustomed to the peace and quiet there, a peace only occasionally interrupted by the friendly goats, the roosters crowing at ungodly hours, and the shriek of a peafowl who insisted on roosting in the tree by the Airstream. So far, the only remotely disturbing trespasser had been Susanna Wyatt, several days after the Walcott dinner. He had woken early, to the noise of someone tapping experimentally on the side of the trailer. Fortunately, he thought to look out between a narrow gap in the curtains before answering the door, and he was barefoot, so made no noise inside. She went away after five minutes, and hadn't been back since. Thinking of how Chris had described her as a 'bunny boiler', Richard wondered if he hadn't had a fortunate escape.

About mid-morning, as he busied himself with a new recipe for a salad dressing based on a reduction of blood-orange juice, Araceli came in from the front, saying, "If you have a moment, Chef … Uncle Roman and Uncle Jaime would like a word. It's about Beatriz and Blanca."

"I never laid a hand on either of them," Richard protested, assuming that this must have something to do with the girls' stint at waitressing for the Walcott dinner. "And Abelita Adeliza made such a big too-do about chaperoning them…"

"She and Min Kim were half-sloshed on Mr. Walcott's Scotch," Araceli replied tartly. "And no, it's not that, although I would remind you about the guilty fleeing where none pursue. It's about planning their *quinceanera*."

"Their what?" Another quaint local custom had caught him by surprise.

"Their *quinceanera* … their fifteenth birthday celebration." Araceli explained patiently.

"Strike me blind," Richard observed, "but I would sworn that both of them are a hell of a lot older than fifteen. I don't do birthday parties for the kiddies, in any case."

"It's not the kind of party that you are thinking of," Araceli assumed her most patient voice. "It's very formal, very ceremonial … it's their debut. It is the custom here, you see. A girl, as soon as she is fifteen she may wear makeup … well, with the approval of her mother and all. Beatriz and Blanca probably keep their makeup in their school lockers. But now they can do it at home. They can go to dances and parties, wear high-heeled shoes. They will be young ladies, you see. Not children."

"A bit young to have them married off, though," Richard observed, and Araceli giggled.

"No – that will not happen until they are eighteen, at the very least. But, Chef – the point I am trying to make is that this will be a very big party. Uncle Roman and Uncle Jaime … Beatriz and Bianca are their eldest daughters, and they were born two weeks apart. There's been a lot of fuss among the families about them … well, anyway, my other point is that Uncle Roman and Uncle Jaime have agreed to ask you to cater a joint party. You did good with the Walcotts, and Abuelita Adeliza thinks the world of you … and Uncle Roman's place, and Uncle Jaime's place might not be as grand as the Walcott's, but they are willing to splurge almost as much for their darling little girls. Likely more, even, since neither of them was ever been fool enough to spend a fortune to impress passing strangers."

"So – they've enough dosh between them?" Richard asked – well, he ought to have known. Roman had a lock on any construction work going for thirty miles around, and Jaime the auto-maintenance concession. As an Englishman, he should have known all about proud and independent local nabobs not giving a damn for the opinions of foreigners.

"Well, they won't sign off on lobster and fresh oysters," Araceli appeared very serious. "And probably not anything as high-end as beef wellington and service *a la Russe*; buffet will be fine. But this … it's personal, and a bit complicated. Come and talk to Roman and Jaime."

Richard sighed, and put the pan of blood-orange reduction off the burner. He was curious, though – about how exactly this kind of bash differed from anything else he had ever done.

"Hey, Ricardo, thanks for taking the time," Roman said, as Richard sat down. "How's it working out for you with the Airstream? Conchita says you've settled in Ok. Let me know if you ever want to move to something a bit more permanent … Cousin Bacilio in Karnesville can hook you up through his realty."

"I'm quite content living in the caravan," Richard answered. "It suits my needs, and I relish the peace and privacy … well, not when the campground is full, but it seems that is a rare occurrence."

"Yeah, the midsummer solstice and Founder's Day are really the only times that Judy and Sefton have a crowd," Jaimie agreed. Richard was afraid they would spend another twenty minutes or so, getting through the social pleasantries, so he plunged right in.

"Araceli says that you are considering asking me to cater another event, one for your daughter's birthday celebration."

"Yep," Roman agreed, appearing somewhat relieved. "See, it's been a bit of a problem for us both. See, the girls are so close in age, and all of their friends, and all of our friends are pretty much the same crowd. So – we thought at first, hey, let's throw a party at the same time, so that everyone can come. We set up a date and booked it with Mills Farm – their dance hall is the only space big enough … but last week, they notified us that they had to cancel our reservation. Some big corporate wing-ding…"

"It must be a big wing-ding, if they had to cancel paying customers," Jaimie put in, with barely concealed resentment. "And we are locked into the date because of the Church being available."

"What about the parish hall?" Richard said. "Or the VFW, or the school gymnasium?" to which both fathers shook their heads.

"Maribel and Carmencita both nixed the VFW," Roman explained. "And the girls had conniptions at the thought of the gym … it's school. They're there every day. A quinceanera out to be … special. And the parish hall would have been OK … but they were working on the new HVAC system last month, they found asbestos insulation in the ceiling, and that won't be sorted out until fall…"

"Of next year," Jaimie sighed.

"But we came up with another plan … and cleared it with Martin. A big-ass tent put up in Town Square and a dance floor laid out in front of the bandstand. Three weeks from this Saturday."

"Where there's a will, there's a way," Roman nodded. "That sorts out the venue … but not the catering. Beatriz couldn't stop telling us about the Walcott dinner, and the bang-up job that you and Araceli did, so…"

"We thought – why not ask if you would cater this job," Jaime completed the sentence. "Come up with a budget, work with Maribel and Carmencita and the girls on what they want. Cake. Don't forget the cake. See, it's kind of like a wedding … only before a wedding."

"Clear as mud," Richard sighed. "But yes – I'll do it. Easy enough – a doddle out the front door of the café."

"Excellent, Ricardo!" Both men beamed at him, and rose as if to leave, and Roman added, "You still have my card – call my office number and set up a good time to meet with the girls, and Carmencita and Maribel to thrash out the details."

"Three weeks should be enough," Richard allowed. "If everyone is willing to make firm decisions, compromise if necessary … and work together."

"Yeah? Your words in God's ear," Jaimie said, in a voice so dry that Ricard didn't realize for days that it was a warning. And by then, it was too late.

Quinceanera

Where are the markers, the ceremony, the milestone marking that absolute dividing line between childhood and full membership among the adults of the tribe? They are few and far between, and increasingly appear to more a matter of custom than the definitive markers that they were in the past. In the western world they seem to be more an acknowledgement of having moved from dependency towards independence: getting a drivers' license, getting that first part-time job, enlisting in the military or going off to college. In religious life – everything from Amish, through Catholic, various flavors of Protestantism, LDS and Jewish – there are those milestones of being confirmed, baptized, First Communioned, sent on a mission and mitzvahed. One is considered an adult in the eyes of the religious community, if not strictly speaking, in the eyes of the family, or the larger society for a good few more years.

A quinceanera – the celebration of a girl's 15th birthday in the Hispanic communities in North America, and in much of South America – combines elements of the first with the second. If anything, it has rather more resemblance to the archaic custom of 'coming out' among the upper classes of the last century and the one before that, although at a slightly younger age: a young woman was formally presented to her parents' circle of friends as now being of age to be courted by suitable men, without any fear of charges of indecency to a minor being brought. A suitable dress, a formal dance, a certain amount of pomp and circumstance to mark the occasion, perhaps a few personal liberties and privileges granted to the young lady following the observation; in many Hispanic communities, a quinceanera can generate as much fuss as an elaborate wedding.

Like a wedding, though – the party is preceded by a Mass of Thanksgiving, where the girl is escorted by her parents, godparents, nearest family and her court of honor; the seven or fourteen boys and girls. Some rituals call for the girl to be presented with a necklace bearing a charm of the Virgin of Guadalupe, blessed by the higher clergy, and a tiara – signifying that in the eyes of those who love her she is and will always be a princess. Sometimes the tiara comes later … or sometimes she is already wearing it on arrival.

Customs vary, from country to country – even from family to family; two of the most charming, I think are the presentation of a doll, often dressed in a miniature of the honoree's gown. This is the 'Last Doll' – an acknowledgement that she is no longer a child playing with toys. The other is the presentation of a pair of high-heeled shoes, for a similar reason; she is a young lady now. In old-line Hispanic families, at the quinceanera party is also an important signifier for the girl; that is her first dance in public at a formal event, other than at chaperoned school dances and family parties. She and her court of attendants, seven boys and seven girls, or sometimes fourteen of each, perform a very elaborate dance, often choreographed and rehearsed for weeks or months in advance – again, very much like a formal wedding. Sometimes the first dance is with a boy escort, or sometimes her father.

Like a wedding, there are toasts, and more formal dancing, an elegant decorated cake … and when all these are done, then there is general merriment, feasting, dancing and all.

Decisions, Decisions

As it was mutually arranged, with Araceli volunteering to serve as a go-between, Richard, the girls, and their mothers met the following afternoon after school, at the café. Since luncheon service was done, Richard had thoughtfully arranged his usual afternoon duties to accommodate several hours to consult regarding the buffet menu, and the cake.

"I trust that they already have a pretty good notion of what they want," he said to Araceli at about fifteen minutes before three, "So, I think we can have this wrapped up pretty much by five … you know, it worries me when you start laughing in that manner."

Araceli shook her head. "Chef, I think that you had better set aside another couple of days for this. "You're thinking Anglo-time, but this will be on Gonzalez time. And … well, Carmencita and Maribel already had a screaming fight with Patricia over the color of the dresses for the *damas* and the shirts for the chamberlains ... that is, the court of honor for the girls."

"Not my problem," Richard answered.

"Yes, but the cake will be," Araceli prophesied darkly. "The flavor, the color of the icing, the decorations on it ... the color of the table linens..."

"White," Richard said, flatly. "White table linens. White frosting. White sugar paste decorations on the cake, white flowers ... why do you keep laughing like that?"

"Oh, Chef ... you sweet innocent Anglo! This. Is. Luna. City! Nahh, I won't pitch you into the Grant's water tank ... we do colors here. Lots of colors. And flavors. Lots of wild flavors." Araceli sighed, very deeply, and suddenly sober. "You might want me to sit in on this meet. As far as I can tell, Beatriz and Blanca haven't decided on much of anything. They haven't even agreed on the menu – that's simple enough, though. *Cabrito*, for certain ... and tamales. Rice pudding. Abuelita fixes amazing rice pudding, I can ask her for her secret recipe."

"I'm certain I can handle them," Richard replied.

"Sure, Chef." Araceli agreed, although she sounded most skeptical.

***

Twenty-Four Hours Later

***

"I did warn you," Araceli was doing her best to hide her amusement the following day, as Richard made an omelet for Dr. Wyler.

"Three hours later, all they had decided was that there should be three cakes – chocolate, red-velvet and vanilla ... one tall in the middle, and the other two on stands on either side. We did not come to any conclusion as to the colors of the frosting or the decorations." Richard looked haunted. "Or much of anything else ... this is going to be the catering job from hell. I knew it the minute the ladies began to fight in Spanish ... say, who is that third woman? Madame Johanna Gonzales-something or other?"

"Aunt Johanna from Mexico City," Araceli explained. "She's choreographing the court-dance and rehearsing the *damas* and chamberlains. Way back in the day, she was a principal dancer with a couple of different companies in Europe."

"I might have guessed she was a dancer," Richard sighed. "There is something terribly Black Swanish about her. So the cake is sorted; we can do it here. I was always a good hand at the gum-paste flowers, and as long as we keep it simple and elegant, I can't foresee any real problems get it done ... once they stop fighting over it all."

"It's a big thing, a *quince*," Araceli mused. "Nearly as big as their weddings will be..."

"Remind me," Richard said, between his teeth, "That when that comes up, I will be vacationing. Traveling in Outer Mongolia. Otherwise unavailable."

"So ... another meeting today?" Araceli turned to plating the finished omelet, quickly adorning it with a sprig of parsley and a small cup of fresh salsa which Dr. Wyler preferred. (This is one of the secret menu choices at the Luna City Café and Coffee.)

"No," Richard groaned. "Cheerleading practice this afternoon. I'm free to conduct my regular business until tomorrow afternoon ... and if you do not mind and your own duties allow – might you sit in with me during the meeting?"

"Not certain what I can do to help," Araceli replied. "Pat will tell you, I'm not the most polished diplomat around."

"At least, when they start yelling at each other in Spanish, you can tell me what they are on about. Araceli, my dear sous-chef, we need to get this sorted. Another couple of days like this it will begin affecting the true business of the Café most horribly."

"I'm certain that another day or so, and everything will be worked out," Araceli replied comfortably.

***

Another Twenty-Four Hours Later

***

"Hey, Ricardo, what's happening, dude?" Berto came in through the kitchen entrance of the café, unaccountably dressed in his town-car livery, to find Richard glumly contemplating the gallon-jug of cooking sherry. The sound of female voices raised in ferocious barrages of Spanish came from the front.

"The ladies are conferring," Richard answered. "With passion and enthusiasm; I decided to withdraw to the kitchen and hide the knives."

"Oh, wow," Berto peeked around the door. "They're going at it hot and heavy, aren't they? I haven't seen 'Celi so agitated since Carmencita decided she wanted to wear a blue dress to be matron of honor in 'Celi's wedding party. I think 'Celi wanted aquamarine…"

"Agitated?" Richard looked wildly around the Café's kitchen. "Any more agitation, I'm going to call Chief Vaughn and ask if Luna City has a riot-suppression squad."

"It's just our passionate Latin nature," Berto shrugged. "Don't worry about it, Ricardo."

"You know," Richard mused. "For one supposed to have a madly passionate Latin temperament, your own is extraordinarily phlegmatic, Berto. Were you perhaps dropped on your head as an infant, or inadvertently exchanged by the fairies?"

"I don't think so," Berto appeared to consider the question with full and careful consideration. Armored in a completely literal mind, sarcasm

194

bounced off him like marbles thrown at a dreadnaught battleship. "Mama was real careful, and Abuelita says that I look like Uncle Nando ... not Uncle Nando the ace pilot, but her second cousin Nando who used to drive booze for Charley Mills."

"Never mind," Richard sighed. "Hyperbole – to you, it's just something that happened to other people, isn't it?"

"I guess." Berto's round face brightened. "Hey, Ricardo – I was supposed to drive Aunt Johanna to Karnesville at 5 for her master class at the Y ... she sounds like she's pretty busy and we've got forty minutes anyway ... you look like you need a drink. We're just got time enough to slip down to the VFW – it's guest night tonight, so we can get in. Although," he peered earnestly at Richard and added, "You be certain an' go easy, Ricardo."

"Oh, yes," Richard agreed. "The last time I got totally pissed, I wound up here."

"Exactly," Berto nodded. "Who knows where you might finish up, if you did it again?"

They left very quietly out of the back door. With a grin and a flourish, Berto opened the rear door for Richard, and once he was ensconced in the back seat of Uncle Tony's commodious town car, driven the two blocks to the edge of town, the Tip-Top Gas and Grocery – on the verge of the road between San Antonio and Beeville, with the pale-pink Monopoly-house shape of the VFW behind it. There was a scattering of cars, haphazardly parked on the asphalt apron in front of the Tip-Top, a few more around in back on the gravel in front of the VFW. Richard recognized Roman's battered and work-rusted pick-up, and Jaimie's only slightly less battered light tow-truck next to it.

"We can't stay too long, or Aunt Johanna will create," Berto announced, as he pulled around the Tip-Top. He looked down earnestly at

Richard as he came around and opened the door with a flourish. "Hey, feel that you are back on the red carpet, Ricardo?"

"No, not especially," Richard sighed. That was one aspect of the past celebrity existence that he genuinely missed; being expeditiously delivered and on time to wherever he had to be, instead of depending on the charity of friends with vehicles, and on his own muscles propelling the bicycle. There was something to be said about learning to drive … perhaps he should take lessons or something.

The VFW post – housed in a re-purposed former temporary classroom building laboriously moved from the Luna City High School Campus when the big new modern extension was finished – still bore the marks of having once been a classroom. A rank of windows looked out on the banks of the river, and a patio of concrete blocks which bore a resemblance to the patio in front of the vintage Airstream which Richard now called home. A BBQ grill, of the kind made from metal 50-gallon drums cut in half and installed on metal legs held pride of place in back, along with a couple of weathered picnic table/bench combination units.

Where the blackboard once had been was now the back-bar; shelves made of stained and varnished plywood held ranks of bottles, glasses, and beer steins. The bar itself was also made out of stained and varnished plywood; serviceable and battered. A single pool table and a miscellaneous collection of chairs and small tables filled the rest of the place. A large dartboard hung in an out-of-foot-traffic corner. Other walls were decorated with patriotic posters, an American flag in a large frame, and a couple of military unit patches done in paint on pieces of plywood cut to shape. It had been clear to Richard on his very first visit on guest night shortly after arriving in Luna City that this was what passed for a male refuge – although there were a handful of female members, of whom Jess Abernathy was the most notable.

"Air Force Reserve," she had explained curtly, upon being asked. "Activated for a tour in the Middle East, a couple of times."

Miss Letty was also a full member, having been a member of the Red Cross and also overseas in World War Two – which did not startle Richard nearly as much, since Miss Letty was of the generation in which participation in a war effort had been nearly universal. But Miss Letty and Jess were not here on this particular late afternoon; only Jaimie and Roman, commiserating over a couple of beers, and Chris idly throwing darts in the general direction of the dart-board. They both looked up, at the sound of footsteps, and waved Berto and Richard over to join them.

Chris flung a last aimless dart and came over, wiping his hands on the towel tucked into his belt. "What's your pleasure, gents?" he asked.

"Lemon-lime soda for me," Berto confessed, bashfully. "I'm driving."

"Good for you," Jaimie approved. "Beer for you, Ricardo – put it on my tab, Chris. I owe ya, and I reckon you need it."

"Oh?" Richard sat down, wondering why this largess, until Roman said knowingly,

"The girls still at it? Yeah, thought so. I feel your pain, bub – sorry to land you with a share of it, but a Gonzalez gotta do what a Gonzalez gotta do … and we've been feeling the pain since when?"

"Since Beatriz an' Blanca were ten years old," Jaime regarded his own beer with gloom. "But it kicked into high gear a couple months ago. We thought we had it all sorted with Mills Farm, and the girls were thrilled to bits. But it all fell through when they cancelled …"

"Any idea why they would?" Richard mused, more as a way of making conversation. "I mean, I relish the challenge of catering an event the like of which I had never heard of before, even if no one can make up their mind over a single blasted thing … well, I owe you all. But why they might cancel and return your deposit and not give a reason; they did return your deposit, didn't they?"

"Hey, Ricardo, it's not like we just fell off the turnip truck," Roman drawled. "Nope, they returned it in full. I still wonder what was going on

– something to do with Corporate, they said. Jeez, I'm glad that I don't have a head office to answer to ..."

"Only Carmencita," Jaime remarked. Roman slapped the tabletop and laughed.

"You got that right, amigo ... still; I wonder what would make them ditch a paying customer."

"A dead-certain chance of landing a bigger one," Richard ventured, and they speculated in an idle manner over this, while a few more members wandered in, including Clovis Walcott and Dr. Wyler, who settled at a nearby table with a copy of the *Journal of the American Veterinary Medical Association*, and became so engrossed in it almost at once that he never noticed the beer at his elbow.

"I heard Benny say that it was something to do with a major renovation on the guest suites..." Jaimie ventured at last, and Roman shook his head.

"Nope – if it's anything more than swapping out the curtains and pictures, they'd be calling me, or someone that I do business with."

"May I join you gentlemen?" Clovis Walcott stood with his own drink in hand. "I ... don't like to push in on a private conversation, but I couldn't help overhearing yours. I've also had a cancellation for a date at Mills Farm, too. Like you, I've been wondering why as well ... it's not like them; I've had an understanding with the management for years, and they've always been most accommodating."

"Pull up a pew, Clovis," Roman nodded at the nearest chair and grinned. "The Little Bride took her eye off you long enough that you can come hang with this disreputable crowd of honest working men?"

Clovis grinned as well; obviously he was used to being ribbed over his indulgence of his uber-demanding spouse. "She's in Dallas – Fort Worth for the week, with a friend. You are right – Mills Farm corporate has demanded a redecoration of the concierge suites – that's what Sook and Susanna are shopping for, in Dallas."

"Susanna ...what's her name, with the bright pink shoes? You'd think that your wife being tight with her would have kept your event on the books," Jaime gestured at Chris at the bar. "'Nother round, Chris – on me, this time."

Richard kept quiet; visions of being chased around the Walcott's kitchen by Susanna Wyatt were still vivid.

"You'd have thought," Clovis agreed. "Half a dozen of my associates from Houston regularly come out for a weekend in the spring for some serious discussion regarding future projects. I can put them up at my place, so I didn't sweat the small stuff. But I don't believe in coincidences..."

"Neither do I," Jaime agreed. "When was your date, Clovis?"

"Next month," Clovis replied. "I asked for another couple of weekends – but all they would tell me was that accommodations were booked solid until July."

"It must be something huge," Roman shook his head.

From the other table, Dr. Wyler adjusted his hearing aid and rasped, "Those bastards at Mills Farm always think big – you ought to know that by now, every one of you. And trust me, they are thinking big!"

"Man, oh, man, Doc – you have spies everywhere," Roman said. "You may as well spill what you know: what are they planning and how do you know?"

Dr. Wyler moved himself, his *Journal*, and neglected drink to their table, as Chris hurried over and shifted another chair. It was getting quite crowded around that single table now.

"I know, because God love him, Mike at the post office is slightly dyslexic, and half the time something addressed to S. Wyatt, Luna City gets mixed up with something addressed to S. Wyler instead. This week, it was an especially thick express envelope with a return address of Glendale, California, from some enterprise called Six Feet Deep Films. It's a movie production company – I had Sylvester look it up for me."

"I don't think I've ever heard of them before," Richard ventured, racking his memory. "But most of my projects had to do with TV producers. So what do you think they're planning with Mills Farm?"

"Some kind of massive corporate conference is my bet," Dr. Wyler replied. "But in any case, it's probably sneaky, underhanded, bad for Luna City ... they're just carrying on with Old Charley's method of civic disruption."

Just then, Berto's cellphone buzzed. "Sorry," he apologized, after listening to it squawk and squeak for half a minute. "I gotta get back with the car. Aunt Johanna's ready."

"I guess I had better come with you," Richard sighed. "I don't suppose they came to any firm decisions today?"

"She didn't say," Berto answered. "Maybe tomorrow. You know, Ricardo ... this is getting kinda serious."

"Any more serious," Richard said, as Berto opened the town car door for him, "And I won't have time to do any other business."

"Is it that bad?" Berto's pleasant and slightly vacant countenance bore the expression of a small child just informed of the mythical nature of Santa Claus. "What are you going to do, Ricardo?"

"I have no earthly idea." Richard leaned his head back against the padded head-rest. Berto started the engine, and the town car rolled out onto Rte. 123 at a stately pace. "As near as I can tell, Beatriz and Blanca cannot agree – on anything. Their mothers take sides – not always with their own daughters, just to change things up. Araceli or Johanna floats a compromise which no one likes, and in the space of a heartbeat, they are all screaming at each other. This is very wearing, Berto. I cannot get anything done."

"Maybe I should talk to Abuelita?" Berto ventured, and Richard replied, "If you think it would do any good, have at it."

"I think I will," Berto sounded supremely confident. "Abuelita can get anything done. They should make her president of the United States, Ricardo."

Yet Another Twenty-Four Hours Later

***

"The girls have a game tomorrow," Araceli said, when she and Richard opened the Café the following day. "So … it's all going to be settled today."

"Promise?" Richard asked, without any hope at all that it would.

"Look, Chef … I'm as tired of this as you are." Araceli brushed a loose strand of hair out of her eyes and came as close to snapping as she ever had. "It's in two weeks. The menu has to be settled today, if it means we all stay here until midnight. We must order the groceries, and the drinks, start notifying waiters and pot-wallopers. I'll make everyone understand that this silliness has to come to an end."

"For myself, I wish I had never agreed," Richard was just discouraged sufficiently to say it out loud.

"Me too, Chef … but it was too good a chance to let go – you'd be the first choice for every Gonzalez in the county, and more catering business then you could shake a stick at."

"I know … best-laid plans, and all." Richard sighed; mourning the coming slaughter of his afternoon, an afternoon which he could have spent doing useful things for the Café … like perfecting the blood-orange reduction. When the Café bell jingled at 3:10 and a murmur of female voices made it obvious that the fatal hour was upon him, he washed his hands, took up his notebook, and put on a brave face. Araceli was already out in the dining room, having arranged seven chairs around the largest table. But as he came out from the kitchen, she was dragging one more chair towards the table.

The girls and their mothers were already seated, with the tragically elegant Aunt Johanna ... and at the head of the table, the indomitable Abuelita Adeliza. Abuelita Adeliza had a particularly grim expression on her face; at that moment somewhat resembling the late Margaret Thatcher about to dress down a subordinate with extreme prejudice. The expression broke into a fond smile when she spotted Richard.

"She says that everything has been decided," Araceli took up her own seat, at Richard's right hand."

"Stone the crows ... it has?" Richard was gob-smacked. Araceli nodded; the other women looked into the medium-distance, slanting an occasional nervous glance at Abuelita Adeliza, as they also nodded. Abuelita Adeliza brought out a large and battered cardboard portfolio, and opened it.

"Yes ... she will now tell us what has been decided." Araceli cleared her throat. She had her own notepad and pen. Abuelita Adeliza began to speak, pausing now and again so that Araceli could translate, and both she and Richard could take notes.

"Blanca's court will wear lavender color, and Beatriz's will wear yellow. The girls will have garlands of lilies and roses in a matching color in their hair, the boys will have matching shirts and boutonnieres. That has been decided."

A large filing card with two swatches of fabric stapled to it appeared from the portfolio and passed from hand to hand to Richard.

"This is to guide you in the color of the decorations for the cakes; yellow and lavender ribbons, sugar roses and lilies. The cakes will be plain vanilla; Abuelita will trust your own excellent taste as to the overall design."

"As for the tablecloths, and decorations in the church and in the pavilion where the dance and meal will take place, Marisol will shop in Karnesville for all that will be required. She will be provided with the color swatches as well. The tablecloths will be white, with ribbons and flowers of lavender and yellow."

"I ..." Beatriz started to speak but was quashed instantly by a furious hiss of outrage from Abuelita Adeliza.

"For the menu," Araceli began, as a sheaf of papers journeyed from the portfolio all the length of the table to a resting place beside Richard's notepad. "There have been 150 invitations set out to families, with responses of 83, so expect to feed at least 400 people. Barbequed brisket, chickens, and roasted goat, with suitable condiments and sauces. Likely only one or two *cabrito*, since usually only the old people like it. This is the number for the best supplier, if Pryor's cannot obtain *cabrito*. Plenty of tortillas, corn and flour, and bread. Plain bread, Abuelita says. Beans, and macaroni salad, and three more side dishes of your choosing to compliment the meats. A pan of rice pudding – this is Abuelita's own recipe, which may be multiplied as many times as needed. Cupcakes in *tres leches* flavor, frosted to match the cakes."

Abuelita Adeliza continued, hampered only now and again by a half-hearted and readily-squashed interjection from Blanca, Beatriz and their mothers. Richard had to hand it to the old woman – and with considerable respect – she knew her stuff. Some of the lists were of ingredients unfamiliar to him, and not stocked in the Cafe's kitchen. She suggested the best places to procure them, along with names and phone numbers. But Abuelita also rendered him the respect of leaving final decisions to him, which was deeply appreciated.

"Tamales ... we will make them, the girls and their mothers and I, with their godmothers. It is a tradition among the Gonzales and Gonzalez families. But here, in the café kitchen, where there is room to work. Here is a list of what should be ordered; we will come on the Saturday before to prepare the tamales, if that is agreeable to you." Finally, Abuelita Adeliza finished, snapping the elastic around her now-empty portfolio and Araceli said, "That is it, Chef. Any questions?"

"Not a single bloody one." Richard gathered up the stack of papers, profoundly glad to have had every last decision made final, and beyond all appeal to a higher court. And it was only coming up on four o'clock. "Ladies ... it has been a pleasure, this afternoon. You will have the most amazing buffet supper at your party ... doubtless I will have the cakes ready for a final viewing on the day before the event."

"It will be the most splendid quinceanera ever seen in Luna City," Araceli promised, and the women and girls all hugged, every bit of overwrought temper quite forgiven and forgotten. Even Cousin Johanna unbent sufficiently for Richard to reconsider embracing her, but kissed her hand instead. To his surprise, Abuelita Adeliza went on tip-toe and kissed him very firmly, one cheek and then the other, before patting his cheek as if he were only eight years old.

"She likes you, very much," Araceli explained as the ladies departed. "I think it's because you remind her of Abuelo Jesus. He was a cook, too ... in the Army."

"Interesting comparison," Richard said, as the Café doorbell tinkled one last time. "And remind me to be grateful for her intervention ... I should do something very special for her, in gratitude. If she hadn't put her foot down and got it sorted, we might have spent another week as we spent the last three days."

"Include Berto in whatever you do," Araceli replied. "He was the one who said it was time for Abuelita to get involved."

"I was thinking ... an autographed copy of one of my books and a bottle of forty-year old Scotch," Richard frowned, as Araceli sighed. "Work on it, Chef. Work on it."

***

Two Weeks Later
***

It all went flawlessly – every element as perfect as Richard had ever wanted. The cake especially; the center cake towering three tiers high, the flaking single-tier cakes on lower stands, all twined together by garlands of pale violet and yellow flowers bound with bows and streamers of matching sugar-paste ribbons.

On the morning of the quinceanera, as Richard, Araceli and their helpers were setting up in the decorated pavilion, a reporter-photographer from the *Karnesville Weekly Beacon* insisted on taking a number of pictures, exclaiming with cheerful irreverence, "Oh, boy, Chef – you are going to set the bar high around here! Once everyone sees this, they are going to beat down the door of the Café, begging you to do a cake for them." She was a comfortably plump young lady, dark-haired and somewhat resembling Araceli, with a round face, sparkling with merriment and intelligence. She wore an ageing tan trench coat several sizes too large, over a very proper and businesslike skirt suit. The pockets of the trench coat bulged with several notebooks and extra camera lenses, as if she were copying the look of legendary news correspondents of old.

"I do not think how this could possibly be of interest to the news media," Richard protested. The reporter – who had been introduced to him but whose name had gone out of his memory almost as it was told – replied,

"Oh, anything and everything is newsworthy in a small town. Just think of it as gossip in print and in our blog. Say, you aren't from around here, are you? May I take a picture of you next …?"

"No," Richard answered, his heart hammering in apprehension. "I… I'm really a rather private person, Miss…"

"Kate. Kate Heisel …" She squinted at Richard with sudden acute attention. "You look awfully familiar; do I know you from someplace?"

"I don't believe we've had the pleasure," Richard stammered. "Although … you also remind me of someone … are you from Luna City?"

"From Karnesville," Kate Heisel replied, with a grin. "But my mom is a Gonzales ... and everyone says I look like her side of the family."

"Ah ... that would explain it," Richard nodded, and made his escape to the relative safety of the Café's kitchen. For a good few hours, he was too busy to worry about the sharp-eyed Miss Heisel, overseeing the kitchen, and the relays of waiters taking food across the street to replenish the buffet table, although he did note the arrival of Blanca and Beatriz, in fluffy white dresses, crowned with diamanté tiaras – in an open barouche, drawn by a pair of white horses. He did see Miss Heisel, taking a picture; yes, that would have been a lovely picture for a slow news week in Karnesville.

The feasting and dancing seemed like they were going to go on well into the evening. Richard was not adverse to a little of both. After all, it had been another long day, a successful day. Considering it all, Richard found himself to be happier, more content, well-settled in a place in this world where he could do the work that he wanted to do, knowing that he had friends, real friends. He was a valuable part of a community; perhaps just a small and relatively obscure one, which he didn't mind at all. The old life and everyone in it but his parents – all that could fall away, forgotten, unwanted, and unlamented.

But he ought to finish closing out the till, first. Then lock the doors, and go listen to the music, watch Blanca and Beatriz and their friends in their flower-trimmed dresses, dancing in the twilight under the trees in the square, while the cornices and windows of the Beaux-Arts brick storefronts of Luna City looked down on them.

He had his head down over the opened till, counting out the bills and coins taken in that morning, for coffee and cinnamon rolls, when the bell over the door chimed, once as it opened, again as it closed.

"We're closed for the day," Richard said, without looking up. "I'm just now locking up."

The person who had just come in spoke in dreadfully familiar voice and accent, and a thrill of horror ran down his spine in the next second.

"'ullo, Rich; aren't you glad to see me?"

The Second Chronicle of Luna City

Chamber of Commerce Spring Newsletter

Spring 2016 Newsletter

Luna City Chamber of Commerce

5 North Town Square, Suite 4

Reminder: The Luna City Chamber of Commerce has a Facebook Page

Help support those who help you – the Luna City Fire Department hold their yearly benefit pancake breakfast in the Methodist Church Parish Hall, on Saturday, 6 February- three days before Shrove Tuesday. They will start serving up breakfast at 8 AM, continuing for as long as supplies last. The goal this year is to purchase sufficient high-quality turnout gear for an additional five volunteers. Come early – and bring your appetite.

Parish Church of St Margaret & St Anthony Spaghetti Feed – April 2

The venue for the yearly Spaghetti Feast has been changed *(due to asbestos remediation work in the SSt M&A parish hall)* to the Luna City VFW Post, on Rt 123. All are welcome. Anna-Maria Constaza Gonzales will oversee kitchen prep day, on Tuesday afternoon before the Spaghetti Feed. This will be in the kitchen of the Luna Café and Coffee; volunteers will be preparing mass quantities of her prize-winning meatballs.

Anna-Maria's Famous Authentic Italian Polpette

Combine 3 pounds ground meat (beef, pork and veal to taste) 1 loaf stale Italian bread, soaked in water then squeezed and crumbled, ½ cup grated Parmesan cheese, ¼ cup chopped parsley, four eggs, 4 cloves garlic minced or mashed, 2 Tbsp salt and 1 tsp ground black pepper. Roll into small balls and fry in oil or shortening. Makes approximately 45 meatballs.

Luna City. Texas – Home of the Mighty Fighting Moths

Upcoming Events

February 23

Moths Booster Club bus trip to San Antonio Stock Show &Rodeo semi-finals. Our own Jessica Abernathy and her horse Sweet-Pea have reached the semi-finals in barrel-racing! Come along and cheer for our hometown champion!

March 3

Spring Rally of Karnes Company Living History Association on Town Square

March 19

Children's Easter Egg Hunt at Mills Farm

Spring Square Dance Festival - Rescheduled

The Luna City Trotters Square Dance Club has rescheduled their regular Spring Dance-Off from the Mills Farm Dance Hall to the Karnesville Senior Citizen's Center on Saturday, April 9.

Celia Hayes & Jeanne Hayden

Luna City ISD News

Tryouts for Fall Season Moths Football

Eligible sophomore and junior students who wish to try out for the Fall season are invited to do so, beginning Monday, March 21, beginning at 10 AM on Moth Field. Members of the 2015 Moth Varsity team are reminded that they must turn in helmets, pads and other issued team uniforms before the end of February.

Permission Slips for Senior Trip

Signed parental permission slips for the Senior trip to Enchanted Rock and Natural Bridge Caverns must be turned in no later than March 1. Payment for the overnight hotel stay at the Sunday House Inn, Fredericksburg, must also be made at that time.

Canned Food Drive

There will be a large container in the foyer of the Luna City High School to collect canned goods to benefit the Karnesville Community Food Bank, through the end of March. Canned goods, shelf-stable and dry foods such as pasta, cornmeal, spices and bottled sauces are requested. Please be careful when adding your contribution to this container. Consider the breakability and stain-producing capacity of those items already donated.

LCISD PTA Book Sale

The yearly PTA book sale will be held in the Luna City High School Gymnasium on Saturday, April 2, from 9 AM until 4 PM. Hardbound books $1, paperbacks 50¢. No exceptions. You buy it, our volunteers will carry it to your car. No checks, no holds.

Community Marketplace

Valentine's Day Special

Judy Grant has a special romantic Valentine's Day offer; honey-scented soaps available in exotic "lingam" and "yoni" shapes. These will be available only at their booth on Saturday, February 13, or by special order through the Age of Aquarius Campground and Goat Farm website. Because of the adult nature of these items, they will not be on display, so purchasers must ask for them. These will be sold only to those over the age of 21.

From Chief Vaughn, Luna City PD

The stop sign at the intersection of School Road and East Oak has been stolen again, likely as part of the customary Luna City High School senior class prank day. Chief Vaughn is not amused, and requests that the sign be turned in to the mayor's office, the Chamber of Commerce office, or the the Luna City Police station. Drivers are warned that yes, that is a controlled intersection, and care would be appreciated by all until the sign can be replaced.

Breakfast Special at Luna Café and Coffee

For the month of February, Richard at the Luna Café and Coffee will be offering a full English Breakfast on Saturdays only, from 8 AM to 10 AM: eggs, bacon, sausage, fried bread, hash-brown potatoes, and baked beans, with grilled tomatoes and mushrooms. If this proves popular, it will be added to the regular breakfast menu.

That's Show-biz

In the early morning, before the sun was more than a brief bright apricot rumor along the eastern horizon, Richard Astor-Hall pedaled grimly along the back road from the aged Airstream caravan at the Age of Aquarius Campground and Goat Farm towards the site of his daily labors. At least now the Airstream was beautifully and comfortably-maintained, since he appeared to have been informally adopted by the sprawling and omnipresent Gonzales-Gonzalez clan, on top of paying rent to Sefton and Judy Grant from his income from the Café. This was managed through Jess Abernathy, whose firm hands channeled the financial streams of a myriad of Luna City enterprises, including that of the Café and of the Age of Aquarius Campground and Goat Farm.

"Rent. I manage all of Sefton and Judy's financials as well as those of the Café," Jess informed him, some months ago when he asked for an explanation for a certain deduction marked every month in his stipend from the Café paid into a bank account at a bank in Karnesville.

"Why?" Richard had asked. "Can't they manage for themselves?"

Jess frowned. "They are communists," she explained, in a patient kind of voice which absolutely rubbed him the wrong way.

"I thought you Yanks disapproved of communists in the most strenuous fashion," Richard replied, to which Jess snapped, "In the old sense, Richard; the lower case-c sense. Judy and Sefton are the last of an idealistic colony of true believers in a system which is only practical when it involves volunteers who work hard to benefit the collective and when it comes to finance, they don't have the sense that God gave a goose. But they do good work and a lot of it," she fixed Richard with a commanding glare. "So – I see to handling the takings from the goats and the campground and their Saturday market. I make certain that their taxes, utilities, health insurance and license fees are all paid … so the Grants can go on with tending their goats and worrying about whether it is ethical to weave with machine-made yarns. Never mind Judy twittering on about all that New Agey crap; she and Sefton show up when anyone needs help, and Judy hasn't yet met a suffering animal that she doesn't want to rescue. Who do you think fosters all those cats and dogs dumped out here in the country by idiot former owners? From each according to their abilities," Jess added with a particularly cutting turn of sarcasm, "And to each, according to their needs. Or as we call it around here, supply and demand. I demand regular supplies of their honey, eggs, and goat-milk rosemary soap in return for economic services rendered and Judy supplies them: a win-win, all the way around."

"I regret even asking," Richard said and Jess snorted. On further consideration, though, he had to admit to himself that he rather favored Jess's system of intelligent budgeting and rigid cost-to-benefit analysis. *('Can we afford this for the Café?' 'No, not until ….' Or sometimes, 'Yes, but only up to this amount.')*

In his past life, he had been spectacularly careless with money. *I had millions of pounds in income once and blew most on loose women and abuse-worthy substances. The rest I wasted.* That recollection led to a dire contemplation of the other recently-arrived element of that old life.

Now he pedaled the bicycle along the verge of one of the unpaved back roads which eventually led into the heart of Main Square, Luna City, still pondering on the unfairness of it all. The bike was a mountain model, which had come to him through the largess of the Gonzales/Gonzalez clan, through one or another the the seniors bashfully admitting that it was a great bike, but the son – or possibly the grandson – had outgrown it or moved on to other and less environmentally-sustainable means of getting around. *Hey, Ricardo, it's a good way to get to work! You want it? Twenty-five dollars; I'll tell Jess and it's paid for.*

As he came up on Route 123, he saw the lights of an automobile at a distance – ah, one of those grossly over-chromed SUVs. Knowing that drivers were apt to speed, in spite of the efforts of Chief Vaughn's patrol cars and the much more substantial hazard posed by deer insouciantly wandering into the traffic lanes, Richard braked the bicycle, went onto the narrow gravel-and-weed shoulder of the road and waited for the SUV to pass. Which it did – about fifty yards farther along Route 123, where a number of unaccustomed lumps lay, slightly off the tarmac.

It looked, from where Richard stood, as if a deer had gone *mano-a-deero* against a mechanized vehicle, with predictable results. *Hundred-pound deer, five-thousand-pound motor vehicle – which was going to win that contest?* To his mild curiosity, the SUV slowed abruptly and went off into the shoulder. The blinking hazard lights flicked on, and someone emerged from the vehicle … a masculine outline, a male someone followed by a faintly overheard burst of indignant Korean in a familiar and feminine steam-whistle shriek. Ah; Clovis and Sook Walcott. Richard wondered why on earth Clovis should be interested in roadkill – but not for very long. To the tune of a final machine-gun burst of Korean, the shadowy figure of Clovis got back into the driver's side, the blinking red hazard lights resumed their steady beam and with a roar the SUV pulled back onto the road and vanished around the next bend. Now that the road was empty, Richard remounted the bike and carried on – he had another fifteen minutes before he was due at the Café.

When he got to the place where the Walcotts had pulled off the road he saw that yes – indeed a deer; relatively undamaged from the impact but quite plainly dead; neck at a grotesquely unnatural angle. Nearby lay another roadkill; this one a hulking black bird of the kind he was given to know was called a 'turkey-buzzard,' also sprawled on the edge of the pavement with one wing upraised like a small black sail. The turkey-buzzard stank like a charnel-house. Why this unlovely spectacle of vehicular/wildlife mayhem had drawn Clovis Walcott's intense interest was a mystery indeed. In the seven months or so that Richard had lived in Luna City and bicycled back and forth between the Café and the Age, he had seen it often enough himself … and even more often, the live deer creatures, wandering dainty and long-legged in the open spaces between thickets, or the turkey-vultures soaring on motionless dark wings in the faultless azure midday sky. But – he said to himself, in a grumpy acknowledgement he had made a thousand times in the last six months and would doubtless make a hundred thousand times more – this was Luna City, Texas.

He continued pedaling through the pre-dawn dimness, relishing the welcome chill of it all after the ungodly summer heat, a chill which had left a slight crunch of frost on certain grassy spaces. The sky was the color of mother-of-pearl, an elusive shimmering shade flushed with pink and apricot-orange, evanescent. He passed the bright orange Luna City Independent School District bus, pausing briefly at an intersection on the outskirts of town to collect a gaggle of small children, swathed in their winter coats and burdened with small rucksacks. These children were also burdened with the attention of watchful mothers and the occasional father who went scattering to their own daily devices once the school bus bore their offspring away.

He waved to Patrick Gonzalez, rumpled in his oil-stained coveralls, and sleepy-eyed from a night of driving a tanker truck; it seemed to be his morning to see Angelika and Mateo off to school, while Araceli turned on the lights and the coffee-machines at the Café.

Still ruminating alternately over why Clovis Walcott was so interested in fresh roadkill and his own predicament with regard to the recent inconvenient visitor to Luna City, Richard turned down the narrow street which ran along the back of that block of buildings. Most of them housed garaging or at least a place to park a car, and in the case of the Café, the rubbish bin, a small weed-grown space and a small loading dock. The Steins, in the next building over, had a garage and a small shed at the very back, with a walled little garden between it and the rear windows of the main shop. As Richard wheeled into the back of the Café, he saw Georg's bare-bones sedan backing out of their garage. He wondered vaguely what brought out Georg so early; on most mornings, he and Annise were over in the Café at that large table in front of the front window – what Georg jokingly called the *'stammtisch'* – where the regular patrons gathered.

He let himself in through the back door into the kitchen, which smelt divinely of fresh coffee and baking cinnamon rolls. Araceli was empting out the dishwasher, stacking plates and mugs with nervous efficiently and a great deal more force than strictly necessary. She glared at Richard, as he shrugged off his winter coat; this was a vintage military field jacket from Marisol Gonzalez' second-hand shop in Karnesville. Chris Mayall at the Gas & Grocery had already been humorous about it, but the jacket was well-made and warm.

"That friend of yours is here," She said, sounding if she were speaking around a clenched jaw. "The English one."

"Not a friend," Richard sighed. "More like an associate … and I regret like hell that it was ever that close."

"Oh, Rich," drawled the visitor in tones of tragic disappointment. Alas, Richard's visitor was leaning picturesquely in the door way to the main room of the Café. "I am cut to the quick. I thought we were best chums, always."

"Nope." Richard was inordinately proud of the way that he thought he had adopted something of the classic western bent towards the taciturn. Besides it was past time to fire up the griddle and start the bacon, then those slivered ham slices that everyone called Canadian bacon, and finally a nice vat of scrambled eggs.

"You're a brute, Rich; a cold, cold unfeeling brute."

"All a part of my happy, inconsequent charm," Richard answered, sternly unmoved.

"I come all the way to this out-of-the way hole," his visitor protested; tragically wounded as to expression, languid as to posture in the doorway, "I endeavor to make myself pleasant to your friends, rekindle our old relationship, relish the charms of this quaint little village, and this is my reward?"

"We were never friends," Richard replied, his attention bent upon the griddle, and preparations for the morning rush of breakfast customers. "It was a mutually-advantageous association; friendship had bloody-all to do with it. Are you going to stand in the door all morning, with Araceli and the girls constantly stepping around you? You'll be trampled underfoot in the morning rush for cinnamon rolls – consider yourself warned."

"If you truly feel that way, Rich," there came the deep and wounded sigh. "I've tried to reach out to you so many times! You never replied."

"Life is full of these little tragedies," Richard brought out a bowl of eggs from the refrigerator and began cracking them with deft and systematic skill into another. After some moments, he looked up from this task. "'Ere – you still there?"

"I am," replied the visitor. Araceli took up a tray upon hearing the front door open and close with a musical chime, and interjected, "Well better find another wall to hold up. Your special order is ready. Best eat it before it gets cold, then."

"You take such good care of me, dear girl," the visitor answered, without a blush. Richard thought it a testimony to good manners and excellent customer relations training that Araceli refrained from bouncing the tray off the visitor's skull as she carried the breakfast special order into the dining room. After a moment, she returned, not visibly fuming, although Richard could read the signs accurately.

"Pip Noel-Barrett was never a bosom chum of mine," he confessed with a long sigh. "Truly – I have better taste than taking that poser to my … well, to my confidence, anyway. He is, as practically everyone eventually realizes, an insufferable, inconsiderate, and amoral git; I deduce that we are in accord in that matter. Ordered off-menu, I take it? Told you to add it to his running tab?"

"Of course," Araceli snapped. "As always; I do not mind taking the trouble, Chef, I really don't. What I do mind, is that he picks over it with an expression on his face like Mateo when he doesn't like what's for supper, leaving most of it on the plate and never saying a darned thing about what's wrong with it. If he calls me 'dear girl' or 'Araceli-my-darling' one more time, I WILL hit him with the heaviest iron skillet in the Café."

"No, you won't," Richard answered. "It will make a mess on the floor, and assaulting one of Clovis Walcott's business associates will reflect badly on everyone. Speaking of business, has he done anything about paying?"

"Nope," Araceli's expression was thunderous. "It's always – sorry love, left the card in my room, sorry, bit short of the dosh at the moment, tomorrow, Araceli-my-darling. Jess will be furious."

"If it comes to that," Richard sighed. "I will set Miss Abernathy on him. That would give me the greatest pleasure. He owes for more than a fortnight of breakfasts and sandwich luncheons since he took up a room at the Cattleman."

"A month is more like it. You'd think if he was in the movie business," Araceli continued grumbling. "He'd be a lot better about paying his bills." For some reason that Richard couldn't fathom – save that Araceli was one of the most hard-headed women of his acquaintance and that she was badly offended by a customer pick-pick-picking at the Café's food offerings like a dyspeptic hen – she was immune to the fabled Noel-Barrett charm. The front door chimed again and then again almost at once. Yes, the first of the morning regulars. Araceli bustled out with carafes of fresh coffee and hot milk.

When she returned, Richard explained, "Araceli, my dear rural innocent, Pip Noel-Barrett is just not in the movie business, as it were. He's a celebrity! A bit past his best-if-used-by date, admittedly; but in his world, he has people – call them assistants who take care of all that. Commonly, he is comped for silly little things like meals. Drinks. Tickets to popular events. Waved through the velvet-covered rope. Because … celebrity. We little people should be grateful for the attention, you see."

Araceli gave her pungently expressed opinion on that and where she would <u>really</u> like to place the tray with Phillip Noel-Barrett's special off-menu breakfast on it.

Richard chuckled. "Does Patrick ever hear you use words like that? I admit only to relishing that mental image; but I suppose the medical team would administer anesthetic — before extracting your serving tray from his …"

The bell chimed again, Araceli vanished with her carafes and Richard finished the sentence to an empty kitchen. "…and that would take all the fun out of the exercise! Likely it wouldn't fit, but given all those rumors about how he cultivated his early career, perhaps it would after all."

The grill demanded his immediate attention. After some minutes, the meats crisping on it – sausage, bacon, Canadian bacon, the usual patties of hash-browned potatoes – were at a point where he could tear his attention from them and look out into the dining room. It was a bustle of activity – tables crowded with happy people, feeding on breakfast pastries, coffee … even tea *(strong tea and piping-hot, a hearty brew of the sort that his Gran had always insisted that one could 'trot a mouse over')* and good, expertly-brewed coffee. For Richard, there was an enormous personal satisfaction in regarding the Café at the peak breakfast-time; hungry people, happily tucking into excellent food, perfectly cooked. The only blight in the pleasing aspect was Noel-Barrett, alternately pushing around the food on his plate or ignoring it entirely. Lending insult to injury, he was doing so at the regular's table, with Clovis Walcott, sitting down at the empty place next to him, and Andy Pryor sitting across, absently eating sausage and looking into the far distance as if he were considering how the flavor could be improved. *(That sausage was sourced locally from Pryor's Meats & BBQ - a tiny specialty business that Andy, who in his weekday life was employed as a petroleum engineer, ran with the aid of his dazzlingly competent wife, Patricia and their three handsome and well-spoken sons. Andy Pryor's mind might have been devoted to extracting oil from the Eagle Ford Shale formation – but his heart was in the business of game processing and the provision of quality barbequed meats and bespoke sausages.)*

What were they up to? Of course, the detestable Pip was up to something. Of course, it was to no good. And there was Georg Stein, appearing well-pleased, as he hung up his European-style wool winter overcoat on the coat-and-hat rack by the *stammtisch* – an item so rarely used that Richard sometimes thought it must be more of a set design element in the Café dining room than an actual usable piece of furniture. But now with the chill of an early spring in Texas, the ornate old rack was getting a full workout. From across the Georg caught Richard's eye, and beaming expansively, waved to him.

"'Allo, Richard – the usual, please! Anni will be long in a moment! Mozart – poor Mozzie – he has had an accident on the carpet and Anni says she must clean it up before it leaves a stain. Ah, excellent!"

Araceli, frantically busy with serving coffee and taking orders, cast him a desperate glance from across the room. No – his duty. Richard piled a platter with cinnamon buns and brought them to the *stammtisch.*

"Perfect!" Georg was exclaiming as Richard approached the *stammtisch* with his platter and Andy Pryor said, "As long as you wash them with a mild hand-soap and set them to air-dry. That should take out the smell … and a little mineral oil on a cotton-ball to replenish the natural moisture. Oh, hi, Richard! Thanks!"

"It shall be an enormously popular item," Georg burbled, as enthusiastic as a dog with two tails. "I have a source in Canada for red osier dogwood for the shafts; not strictly authentic for Comanche or Apache exact reproduction but refreshing to work with. And thank you for the animal gut and sinews."

"My pleasure," Andy Pryor replied, with his mouth full. "One of the fellows in the Company does absolutely stunning beadwork on hide. Let me know if you want any fancy accessories to go with. He's a high-powered bank executive in San Antonio and doesn't need the money, but he loves for a wider audience to gain an appreciation for the craft."

"Ah," Georg replied, "That they will have flint heads – that will do for most of them, although perhaps I should construct some with bone points …"

"Business over pleasure," Phillip Noel-Barrett drawled.

Clovis Walcott cleared his throat. "Right, gents. So – Phillip, your bottom line question is 'How much cooperation would you have from the Karnes Company Rangers Living History Association for your production?' That would depend…"

On that note, Phillip Noel-Barrett shot Richard a perfectly vicious look and Richard said, smoothly, "I'll have Araceli bring you more coffee and take your orders for dishes from the grill. The eggs were delivered fresh this morning. Will there be any more? Just let Araceli or one of the girls know."

He made his escape to the refuge of the kitchen; a sinking feeling in his heart. Yes, Noel-Barrett was up to something and had somehow gathered up a good portion of the respectable citizens of Luna City in whatever ghastly toils he had planned. There was nothing good to come of this, whatever it was. How could he warn the good citizenry of Luna City? He was only lately arrived himself. The implied friendship which Phillip Noel-Barrett was trading on as if it were his last hope of heaven would likely not assist his credibility any. But still – and on this consideration, Richard's confidence was restored, albeit in a somewhat limited fashion: Doc Wyler thought well enough of him to include him in the ritual yearly first-day-hunt. The deeply entangled and even more deeply influential Gonzales-Gonzalez clan were also firmly in his corner through the enduring and adoring fan- worship of the clan matriarch, Granny Adeliza, and the magnificent spread provided for the *quinceanera* of two of her great-granddaughters. The eccentric Grants seemed fond of him and the affection of the small goat, Che, was as everlasting as embarrassing, but how would that stand up against the power and glamor of show business?

But by the time that the Café telephone rang, shortly before midday – just when the Café was once again, near to capacity, he had thought of something, something that he could do, with regards to the ever-obnoxious Phillip Noel-Barrett, which would restore his own and perhaps Araceli's good humor.

"Rich, I'm having a midday confab with the Steins and Clovis Walcott," drawled the hated voice. "Since we are now rather peckish – I'd like to order a sandwich luncheon for … oh, make it five people. And delivered next door? Thank you so much."

"Fifteen minutes," Richard said into the phone and Noel-Barrett replied, "The shop is closed today. You'd best bring it around through the back."

"I'll bring your bill, too, shall I?" Richard was pretty certain that Phillip Noel-Barrett had already hung up.

It was the practiced work of a few moments to assemble a platter of sandwiches and fresh fruit – a few minutes more to write up the bill for it, and assemble the pages of previous bills. Araceli had circled the complete total in red ink on top of the first page.

"Back in a tick and with payment," Richard promised with grim determination and let himself out through the back of the Café. The gate to the Stein's garden was unlocked, the portal to a much more attractive prospect of a tiny city garden; a pocket-handkerchief of lawn, an arbor dripping with pale lavender wisteria. Georg also had a shed at the back of his home and place of business – but one offering a much more pleasant aspect, although Richard did wonder about the folding drying rack sitting in a patch of sunshine. It looked as if there were little black strips of cloth hanging on it … no, they were feathers. Black feathers.

Georg Stein waved from across the garden, where there were some patio chairs, a small garden bench and a glass-topped table set underneath the arbor. The detestable Noel-Barrett sat there, along with Clovis Walcott, Benny Cordova, the manager at Mills Farm, and a fifth man whom Richard did not recognize, though he was fairly certain he was not from Luna City. After eight months, he had a pretty certain knowledge of who lived there and who was just a stranger, passing through.

"You are admiring the feathers, no?" Georg beamed, jovially. "I am using them to replicate arrows … for the fletching. There is a great interest in authentic Indian weaponry, you know. I did not realize when I first came here – that Colonel Walcott was also an enthusiast!"

"Retired, Georg – retired," Clovis Walcott allowed with a smile. "Set 'em here, Richard. I do portray a colonel now and again, as part of an event

… but more often a plain soldier, and sometimes even the exalted rank of a sergeant. Say, these look great, better than any grub we cook for show when we're in the field. If my Little Bride didn't have the most splendid kitchen in Luna City, I'd be eating at the Café, morning, noon and night. Our friends still talk about your beef Wellington dinner party."

"Thank you," Richard nodded. Of course with Clovis Walcott being an officer and a gentleman, he had paid up and handsomely for the catered supper, upon being presented with Richard's final invoice for that event. Now Phillip Noel-Barrett was looking impatient.

"Was there anything more, Rich?" He demanded, all but tapping his fingers impatiently on the tabletop.

"There is," Richard answered, putting down the stack of bills; a considerable pile, covering at least two meals daily for the past three and a half weeks. "The matter of payment being past due. I'll wait," he added, with faint malice, "For you to fetch your card. Or cash."

"Really, Rich," Phillip protested, the very picture of injured innocence. "Can't this wait – since it's between friends?"

"No," Richard answered. "It's nothing personal, Pip – just business."

There was a sudden, fraught silence around the table; Georg, Benny and Clovis Walcott's sudden attention rested entirely on Phillip Noel-Barrett. A considerable weight in their regard and all three being in possession of something that the obnoxious Noel-Barrett wanted, and wanted most desperately to have hinted at the significance of this exchange. Richard, not an especially subtle man, sensed the undercurrent– and the very certain knowledge that he was on the verge of queering whatever pitch Phillip Noel-Barrett was making, although he didn't quite grasp how or way.

Clovis Walcott was the first to speak and provide a clue by opining gravely, "A good businessman always sees that the bills are paid; the ones he owes and the ones he owes to others, otherwise his reputation suffers. We can break for a few moments while you see to business, Phillip."

"Grateful to you all," Noel-Barrett sounded as if he was grinding his teeth. "Back in a tick. A moment of your time, Rich."

"Agreeable, as long as your bill is paid at the end of it," Richard replied, now serenely certain of victory. He accompanied Noel-Barrett out to the narrow street running behind the two establishments, well out of earshot of anyone in the Stein garden, before the latter rounded on Richard, snarling, "What d'you think you are playing at, Rich!"

"Not playing at anything, Pip – just trying to run a little business in a small town. Not some sort of ghastly reality show, I'll have you know. Just real people, real life, and a real cash-flow situation. The people I have to report to are merciless. Not that I think they would take out their frustrations over an unpaid bill out on on your knees, or your peerless profile, but you never know. They might. The bill, Pip. Pay it in full or your reputation in this town is sunk. I have friends here, too. Among them, the chief of the police department. You might have seen him; that traffic bollard in khaki…"

"I am trying to get a movie being made here," Phillip snarled, as he dug out a wallet with a full hand of cards in it. "You would think that these fly-over country bumpkins would be f**king grateful for the consideration."

"That all depends," Richard accepted the card, with a feeling of triumph. "On your facility in hiding your bloody condescension and on how well you tip for the privilege. Shall I bring your receipt out to you? This way it spares you embarrassment in front of Clovis Walcott if your card is declined."

"Suit yourself," Phillip Noel-Barrett's expression was thunderous. "And don't wait for me to walk in the door of your dingy little caff ever again."

"An effort – but I imagine that I shall be able to bear the loss with fortitude," Richard deliberately radiated good cheer and whispered, "Tosser!" once his back was turned on Phillip Noel-Barrett.

Of course, Phillip didn't add a tip when he signed the receipt but then Richard hadn't really been expecting anything of the sort. Within a day or two, Phillip Noel-Barrett moved into digs at Mills Farm, and shortly thereafter was gone entirely from Luna City, to Richard's profound relief.

For weeks, he entertained a fond hope that Noel-Barrett's movie project would die aborning, but a story in the *Karnesville Weekly Beacon* dashed them, quite comprehensively.

Lights, Camera, Action for Luna City Movie Location

From the <u>Karnesville Weekly Beacon</u> – February 29, 2016 By Katherine Heisel – Staff Writer

The Glendale, California based movie production company Six-Foot-Deep Films has announced that they will begin filming on location in and around Luna City, for two months, beginning in late June. The film, a historical epic about Sam Houston and the retreat of his army east to San Jacinto in the spring of 1836 has the working title of *The Road to San Jacinto* and will be directed by Michael "M.A." Lydecker, three-time Academy Award-winner for Best Director. The cast includes former Disney child star Amy Butler, star of the long-running TV series *Family Tree,* Cal Fenwick as Sam Houston, and Diego Leon Sepulveda, who has starred in a number of Spanish-language telenovelas, as General Antonio Lopez de Santa Anna. The tentative premiere and general release set for summer, 2017. The Mills Farm resort will serve as temporary headquarters for stars, production staff and film crew; the parent company of Mills Farm, Venue Properties International are also investors in the production. The Karnes Company Rangers Living History Association has been recruited to serve as extras for major battle scenes. Six-Foot- Deep Films representatives will also be hiring extensively in San Antonio, Karnesville, Luna City, and Beeville for actors to play minor speaking parts and as additional extras. Studio filming with the lead actors has already begun, says producer Phillip Noel-Barrett. Negotiations are underway for extensive location shooting on the grounds of the scenic Wyler Exotic Game Ranch, which offers a suitably wide variety of landscapes within a fairly small area for exterior scenes.

Talk of the Town

The story in the *Karnesville Beacon*, amplified in Kate Heisel's "Talk of the Town Blog" about the movie production revived every one of Richard's fears with regard to Phillip Noel-Barrett. No, the wretched movie project was back again, like a ghastly reanimated corpse in an old Hammer Horror production. And as excitement built among Lunaites in the Café every morning, Richards' concern deepened, correspondingly. His only sympathetic confident was Araceli, and her feelings were based more on a visceral dislike of Phillip Noel-Barrett rather than Richard's suspicion that whatever the detestable wanker was pursuing, it would be only to his own benefit and the detriment of everyone else.

"Well, it's a movie," Araceli said, practically, one afternoon as they were preparing a massive batch of cinnamon rolls. She was mixing together a small vat of brown sugar, grated lemon peel, nutmeg, cinnamon and chopped walnuts for the filling, while Richard shaped an enormous log of dough the length of the worktable, and then began patting it gently to flatten. "Besides the thrill of it all – there's money to be made. Uncle Roman has already contracted a full two crews to set up pavilions and construct sets. Uncle Tony has signed an exclusive on transportation – every town car, van and minibus is locked up for six weeks, transporting the actors and crew ... and never mind people hiring as extras. They even hired Jess as a horse-riding double for Amy Butler! The Luna Players are thrilled to the maximum – they've all sent in headshots and lists of their credits ..."

"There's a difference between regional amateur theater and a major movie production," Richard observed in a sour tone, and Araceli laughed indulgently.

"Well, of course – they know! But they are thrilled anyway – it just looks like so much fun!"

"It's not," Richard argued. "It's one of the most mind-numbingly, skull-crushingly tedious activities you can imagine – one tiny detail can wreck three hours of setting up the shot. Do you know that there is about an hour or two of work for every minute you see on screen, and that's only counting the actual shooting? You sit around, waiting for the grips to finish setting up, for the lighting chap to fiddle with the lights so they fall just so ... and some luckless wight to gather up a bit of trash that has blown into the area, and then the makeup artist is grooming the stars' chest hair just so, and the costumer is fiddling with the starlet's ruffles so her nipples peek demurely just sufficiently ... oh, I've been there, don't ask for the ghastly details or the name of the ..."

"Samantha Colquhoun," Araceli replied, "Better known as Sammi, of *At Home With Sammi*. One of your exes, although she seems to have been a lot of mens' exes."

"You've been spying on me again," Richard scowled and Araceli laughed indulgently. "Well, Abuelita is your biggest fan. She says that

Sammi was <u>very</u> bad for you, and you should find a nice girl who doesn't behave like a cheap *puta* and never mind the rest of it. Is there enough dough that we can make a pan of orange rolls; sugar, orange juice and pecans on the inside, orange sugar glaze on the top? That would be a new taste thrill."

"Just one pan," Richard cautioned. "Until we see how it takes. As for the other, leave my love life out of this discussion. This movie is not going to be a good thing. I know it in my bones, and I cannot for the life of me figure out why men like Clovis Walcott and even Doc Wyler are going all out for it."

"Because it's history, and a grand story – heroes, villains, narrow escapes, murder, treachery, derring-do, survival by the skin of the teeth, and a sudden turn of good fortune," Araceli explained. "All they've ever made big-name-movies before is about the Alamo. Last stand, everybody dies – that's the only thing that everybody knows."

"There was more?"

Araceli muttered in absolutely volcanic Spanish, "Yes there was more. A lot more."

"Enlighten me, then," Richard said, rather afraid that he would be sorry later.

"All right then," Araceli began spreading her filling along the two-thirds of flattened sweet roll dough. "While they were fortifying the Alamo, Sam Houston who had been once governor of Tennessee and then went on a prolonged drunk bender among the Cherokee upon being divorced from a wife who had not been in love with him all that much – so the story goes – came to Texas when he sobered up, and got himself named by delegates to the Constitutional convention in Washington-on-the-Brazos to be the leader of the Texian Army ..."

By the time she was finished, four whole pans of cinnamon rolls and one of orange-pecan were rising in the warming cupboard, perfuming the air with the scent of spice and citrus. "And independence was granted, by Santa Anna, right then and there," Araceli came to a fine triumphant finish.

Richard said in awe, "Stone the bloody crows – eighteen minutes? He won the whole bloody battle in eighteen minutes?" He could feel some sympathy for Sam Houston – the drunken bender aspect, mostly.

Araceli nodded. "And with only about a dozen casualties on his side. Now, you see? Besides being good for business in Luna City, it would be a fantastic movie for Texas. They'd be showing it to kids in classrooms for a history credit for years after it went to theaters."

"So it would," Richard agreed. "But I just cannot make myself believe that Pip Noel-Barrett is the right man to make it. There is something rotten in the state of Denmark, Araceli – mark my words … who is supposed to play the part of Sam Houston, I wonder?"

"Cal Fenwick," Araceli replied, with a faint frown creasing her brow. "Never heard of him," Richard said. "I was never really into American TV, except maybe for detective shows."

"Well, he's getting a bit up there," Araceli said. "He was on a couple of Western shows, when they still did TV westerns. He was pretty young then. He hasn't done much lately. Got a heck of a substance abuse problem, at least that's what all the magazines say."

"Noel-Barrett probably got him pretty cheaply," Richard said, still unable to shed the feeling that the whole project was a disaster in the making.

Karnes Company Rangers Living History Association

The Karnes Company Rangers Living History Association is a non-profit corporation of volunteer reenactors whose mission is to interest and educate the general public in local history in South Texas, with special emphasis on life in South Texas before and during the Texas War for Independence, and in the days of the Republic of Texas. The organization was formally incorporated in 1989, after several years of volunteer reenactment events centered around commemorations of the Gonzales "Come and Take It" Fight, the departure of the Gonzales mounted volunteers to relieve the Alamo, and the Plum Creek fight with the Penateka Comanche. It was the suggestion of an early enthusiast, Clovis Walcott (Colonel, USA, Ret.) of Luna City, to formally organize and schedule regular encampments throughout the year.

Since many members of Karnes Company are residents of rural areas, a fair number of them own and train horses, and so are able to reenact mounted events. Members are able to role-play members of a ranging company of mounted volunteers, Sam Houston's cavalry detachment at San Jacinto, a ranging company in the Plum Creek fight, and Penateka Comanche warriors. They regularly coordinate with other living history associations in Texas, in commemorating events such as the siege of the Alamo and the Battle of Coleto Creek. At least as important as anniversary events are regular educational events, where members demonstrate 19th century practices and technologies, either live and in person, or for filmed documentaries.

The Karnes Company is often called upon to demonstrate their expertise for such educational productions, counting it as part of their mission. Currently, the Karnes Company is set to participate in filming a significant motion picture, *The Road to San Jacinto*, produced by Six-Foot-Deep Films, and directed by three-time Oscar Award-winner, M. A. Lydecker. Members of the Company are also serving as historical consultants for this production, which is being described enthusiastically by producers and the director as the most authentic recreation yet filmed of Sam Houston's 1836 campaign against Mexican General Antonio Lopez de Santa Anna. The movie project and the Karnes Company's participation were the subjects of an extensive feature in a recent issue of *Texas Monthly*.

The Unexpected Egg

"So, they do this, every year?" Richard asked. He sat with Araceli and Patrick on the terrace of the old wooden dance hall at Mills Farm, a terrace which overlooked a sweep of rich green lawn which lapped the edge of the lush flower plantings surrounding the Mills Farm farmhouse, a pole-fence-enclosed stand of cornstalks already waist-high, and beyond that, the golfing range, which went on and on, spread like a lush green velvet comforter, starred with the occasional pools of water hazards and pure white sand-traps. The nearer view was all a Grandma Moses version of a quaint 19th century farmstead brought to life and tailored in Texas style, a stage-set in real life; a tall cistern on stilts, a daisy-wheel of a metal wind-vane spinning away overhead. The wind-vane formed the basis of Mills Farm's corporate logo ... and the flower borders were a stand-out in every southern gardening magazine they had ever been featured in. A crack squad of garden maintenance technicians took care of that.

"Every year," Patrick affirmed. "And there is a pumpkin patch just before Halloween, too. The kids look forward to it."

"I should think they would," Richard looked out across the inviting prospect; green and bountiful, under a flawlessly blue sky ornamented with a few self-conscious white clouds. Late spring, and the weather was glorious. The gardens of Mills Farm were at their best, bright with many-colored salvias, with white and blue wild iris ... there was even a pale lavender wisteria draped over the loggia behind the farmhouse which had graciously consented to bloom in full glory just in time for Easter. There was a small corral beside the barn, where a couple of small donkeys and a young colt hung their heads over the top rail, watching the activity with mild equine curiosity. The barn itself – classically painted red, with white trim, and with locks of golden hay bulging theatrically from the upper door which represented the loft – actually housed an administrative facility on the upper level.

Around on the other side was the chicken enclosure and petting zoo. The chickens – all exotic breeds, of course – were housed, for the purposes of the petting zoo, in a chicken house which mimicked the appearance of the main farmhouse, even down to color and a small weather-vane at the highest roof-peak. Now the petting zoo stood abandoned, for the traditional Easter egg hunt was about to begin on the main lawn, and in the flower borders which surrounded it. Fifty or sixty small children stood behind the gate to the garden and lawn, practically vibrating with excitement. Teodoro Gonzales, in his representation of Old Charley Mills, the official host and greeter of Mills Farm, stood with his hand on the gate latch, beaming with practiced affection on the gathering of eager children.

Their parents lounged around on the terrace of the dance hall which overlooked the egg-hunting grounds, the most experienced with indulgent eyes fixed on their offspring. Others were lined up at the bar, just inside the dance hall premises. The terrace was set with many small tables, each surrounded with comfortable rustic chairs or tall stools made of weathered grey wood. Cannily, the management of Mills Farm had lavishly distributed half-priced coupons, as part of their Easter Egg Hunt package.

For a small entrance fee, each child received a small chip-woven basket from China with a wad of green waxed-paper "grass" in the bottom of it, a pair of white and pink bunny ears on a headband, also manufactured in China, and any number of drink and meal coupons, redeemable at the dance hall bar, or at the Mills Farm Country Restaurant, the standing tin-metal roof of which was just barely visible over the grove of trees at the other end of the golf course. Each basket also contained a ticket for a drawing to be held following the hunt; a grand prize of a $500 gift card, which could be used for any merchandise or service provided by Mills Farm or any other Venue Properties location, and a number of $100 cards for merchandise or meals at Mills Farm.

These tickets usually didn't interest the children nearly as much as those special eggs; hidden among the many ordinary, pastel-colored Easter eggs were three gold-colored ones, which would entitle the lucky child finding one of them to claim a huge hollow milk-chocolate egg filled with more chocolates. The corporate owners of Mills Farm rarely missed an opportunity to cultivate visitors and to cultivate them as young as possible.

A dark-haired young woman in an oversized old-fashioned beige trench coat stood a little beyond the crowd of children, aiming a serious and meaningful camera with a Brobdingnagian lens attached. It was a pretty scene – the children with their baskets, the genial bearded Teodoro in his blue denim overalls and artfully tattered straw hat, and the sweep of lawn and garden beyond. She looked familiar. Richard now remembered that he had seen her, taking pictures of the grand Gonzales-Gonzalez *quinceanera*: Kate Heisel, Araceli's cousin who worked for the Karnesville weekly newspaper.

Now she looked up from the camera, and waved to Patrick and Araceli, as Teodoro opened the gate. "And they're off!" she called, in the manner of a race-track announcer as the children scattered, focused with but one intent on the hunt and the prize.

"Come sit with us, Katie," Araceli called, and Kate replied, "Let me get a few more pics, OK?"

She wandered off with her camera, the outsized overcoat flapping like a sail. Richard was hardly enthused about sharing a table with a professionally paid-up member of the print media tribe, and one armed with a serious camera to boot, but on the other hand, Kate Heisel was a Gonzales. Media or not, Abuelita Adeliza ruled the clan with an iron fist. It was too late to run, anyway. He had come with Patrick and Araceli in their pick-up, with the children. With luck, Kate Heisel wasn't a Food Channel fan. It was the best that he could hope for – sit still, and excite no notice or comment.

Patrick had dived fearlessly into the scrum around the bar. He returned carrying four generous mugs, two by two by their handles in each faintly oil-stained fist by the time Kate climbed the stairs and sank into the empty chair, placing her heavy camera upon the tabletop, where Richard eyed it as warily as if it were a coiled and poisonous adder.

"I love this," she exclaimed, beaming cheerily on all and sundry. "The Easter Egg hunt! Remember when Abuelita and Abuelito Jesus used to bring us every year, 'Celi? The kidlets look so cute in their little bunny ears!"

"I remember the year you found a Golden Egg," Araceli replied, with the same tone of reminiscent affection. "You and the other kids who found them all got your pictures in the *San Antonio Express News*, holding those ginormous chocolate eggs!"

"Yeah, but I got sick on so much chocolate," Kate shuddered. "I haven't been able to stomach the stuff since. Hi, Rich ... it is Richard, isn't it? From the Café. You did that fantastic cake for Blanca and Beatriz' *quinceanera*! It even tasted good, too. 'Celi says that you are training her – you're a real Paris-trained chef! That's fantastic! What brought you here to Luna City?"

"Cordon Bleu-trained, actually" Richard corrected, hoping that the curiosity was neighborly and not professional. "As for what brought me here? Generally, a spirit of wanderlust aided by massive quantities of alcohol. Specifically – Berto in a hire-car."

"He's a good kid, Berto," Kate replied, and he couldn't help noticing that the corners of her eyes crinkled most engagingly when she smiled. And also that those eyes were blue-green, almost the color of beryl – a startling contrast to ink-black hair, drawn up into a lop-sided bun stuck through with two ornamental hair-sticks and a number 2 pencil with a worn-down eraser. "And you're still here, too! The kid did OK by you, Rich."

"It's a special place," Richard said, meaning it in the non-ironic way, "I can see why people come by accident, and are tempted to stay forever." He was thinking of those cosmopolitans, Georg and Annise Stein, his landlords, the hopeful New Age drop-outs Sefton and Judy Grant, and Chris at the Tip-Top, with his scars and prosthetic leg – all of whom had arrived by accident and remained ever since.

Kate beamed upon him. "Oh, yes. I love it myself. I'd not go anywhere else, if I had a choice." She sank the first inch and a half of beer in her tumbler in a thoroughly professional manner, and admitted, "OK, maybe I'd go as far as San Antonio, Austin, even, if I got a tempting offer. But absolutely no farther. I'm not a big city person at all."

"Just a small-town girl," Richard said, somewhat waspishly, "Living in a lonely world."

Kate blinked at him. "I am so not living in a lonely world! I had an internship for a year after J-school at a media company in Chicago. I was offered a permanent position, but I hated the big city and the winters were brutal. It filled a square and I leaped at the chance to come back home. Besides," she added. "What with the internet, you can be anyway a n d have an international audience... look at W.C. Brann and the *Iconoclast*!"

"Tell Richard about the blog you started for the *Weekly Beacon* website," Araceli interjected when Richard only looked blank, but Kate leaped to that new topic with passionate enthusiasm.

"I wouldn't say that print publishing is entirely dead," she explained, as Richard feared it was obvious that his eyes were glazing over, under the full spate of such enthusiasm. "Paper and printing presses are expensive but with more and more services and commerce going on-line, there isn't the structure to pay for it any more. Honestly, the big money- maker for the *Weekly Beacon* isn't advertising or want-ads so much anymore – it's the legal notices being published. And obituaries. But people still want to know what's going on. It's like the buggy-whip business, after automobiles replaced the horse and carriage," she fixed Richard with that intense, blue-green, beryl-colored gaze.

"They thought they were in the buggy-whip business, you see – and they held on to that thought and went broke because no one bought buggy-whips any more. No, what they were actually in was the personal transportation accessory business. They made a huge mistake, not thinking of it in that light. Think of all the automobile accessory items they might have turned to making, if they had not been so hung up on buggy-whips! I'm not in the newspaper business," she made a gesture with her fingers, installing air-quotes on either side of the words. "What I am in is the information dissemination business. I'm not hung up on the actual transmission vehicle."

She continued in that vein for some minutes, while Patrick grinned in deep private amusement and Araceli's eyes wandered beyond the rail of the dance hall terrace, following the children as they ran from bush to flowerbed, stooping and reaching into the plantings. Now and again, a child shrieked in triumph, holding a pastel-colored egg on high. At this distance, and with so many children wearing bunny-ear headbands, Richard could not distinguish Angelika or Mateo among any of them, since he had taken no notice of what they were wearing otherwise.

"I can't see Mateo!" Araceli exclaimed in sudden alarm. "Where has he gone!"

"Easy, 'Celi," Patrick didn't sound upset in the least. "He's probably gone into the shrubbery. Don't worry. This whole garden is fenced, and under camera surveillance. They got rid of Old Charley's alligator pond years ago."

(Which they had. The skeletal remains of an alligator – found during a hurried initial excavation by the contractors hired by Venue Properties, International to land-sculpt that portion of the property intended to be part of the golf course – were mounted and on prominent display in a glass case in the Mills Farm Country Store, on the wall above the comic Texas souvenirs.)

"He's only seven years old," Araceli – if she were a Victorian mother, she would have been wringing her hands, or searching for her smelling salts. Ah, thought Richard: *The mother tiger, ferociously protecting her brood. In another moment, she is going to roar out into the garden and turn the place upside down.*

"He's a boy," Patrick answered, sounding indulgent. "And how much trouble can he get into, here at Mills Farm? They pad the trees and geld the male goats and sheep, just in case of a lawsuit."

"Mateo ..." Araceli began, and Kate, cool-headedly looking through her camera – obviously one of those with a long-distance zoom lens, lowered it from her face and said, "He's over there by that big esperanza – he looks very happy, as if he has found a Golden Egg."

Indeed, even in the distant view of Mateo's infant face – the very image of his father's, a resemblance which Richard had always thought rather comic – was lit with triumph.

"Do you think that he has?" Araceli asked, anxiously. "We'd best take it away, and only let him have little bits at a time. Or maybe we might let him share it out with his friends. That's what Miss Letty said to me, when I was in her class – if I ever found a Golden Egg in the Mills Farm egg hunt – I should bring the prize to school and let everyone share."

"I wish that Mom had taken that advice," Kate's pleasant round countenance reflected the memory of horrific indigestion.

"Napalm that bridge when we get to it," Patrick suggested. "Anyone want a top-up? One's my limit since I'm driving, but we still have three tickets."

"Save them for another time," Araceli said, quite firmly.

"I write more colorfully when I'm slightly buzzed," Kate Heisel confided, with another one of those intense blue-green beryl gazes. "But my typing goes to heck, and so does my picture-taking. I still have to take pictures of the kidlets and the drawing winners, so I'd best not."

Below the terrace, the frenzied search-and-retrieve activity had died down. Most of the children lost interest in the hunt, once that intensive searching resulted in few discoveries of eggs, hidden coyly among the plantings, although Richard thought that he could see a bright yellow egg balanced among the branches of a yellow-flowering shrub directly below the terrace, not four feet away.

"Look – the kiddiwinks have missed one," Richard called the attention of his companions to it and Kate Heisel grinned. The color of the egg exactly matched the color of the blossoms, which was why it had been missed, although it was in plain sight of the earnest young searchers.

"Someone has been subtle. I used to do that at Abuelita's, once I graduated from looking for eggs to hiding them. Put one the same color as the flowers in an azalea bush – they would be forever finding it. Ohh ..." and she took up her camera. "Call one of the kids – and I can get a picture of the expression on their face when they find it!"

"That's not fair," Araceli objected. "You shouldn't tell them outright!"

"Just give them a hint," Patrick said, obviously relishing the small drama. Richard had the feeling that Patrick – absent a devious bone in his entire stocky body – did not approve of subterfuge in pursuit of that one perfect photo shot.

"Right, then. All's fair in love, war, and Easter Egg hunts," Richard answered, casting his gaze across the lawn below, feeling somewhat charitable towards the small and earnest searchers. He called to the nearest tot, a boy of about seven or eight, standing there with his basket. The basket contained a single forlorn egg.

"Hey! Psst ... young fellow. Look up – no, over there. There's something nice for you ... up above. Look, you ..."

"Mommy!" Shrieked the innocent young tot. "Stranger-danger! Mommy!"

That particular young hunter went off across the lawn, running towards the now open gate into the garden, while a slightly older girl, with a narrow-eyed, predatory expression on her face – and a basket nearly full of pastel-colored eggs – looked into the direction of Richard's gaze. She leaped up and collected the yellow egg, likewise running off across the Mills Farm garden lawn.

"Damn ... it's blurred. She was gone in a heartbeat," Kate Heisel lamented, as she set the camera down on the table.

"They'll think you're a pervert, Rich!" Patrick laughed so hard he looked likely to fall off of his chair, while Richard consoled Kate. "You have got an early picture of some grasping celebrity wife ... that little tyke was fast enough off the mark. Only time until she reaches for the golden goolies, and then where will some unfortunate berk be? Probably in divorce court, or assisting the police with their inquiries."

At that moment, Mateo appeared at the table, his Mills Farm-provided Easter Egg basket in one hand, a modest quantity of eggs contained therein, and something in his other closed fist, a triumphant smile on his face.

"You didn't find a Golden Egg?" Araceli said, with a quick look at the contents of her son's basket. "Well, never mind – we'll go over to the Country Store and have some ice-cream..."

"But I did," Mateo replied. He opened his closed hand and something gold-colored fell out of it with a solid thunking sound onto the wooden table top. Richard thought at first it was one of those gold-foil covered chocolate coins, for it was the right size and color, but candy and foil did not fall with that kind of sound. It lay on the tabletop between Araceli and Kate; bright yellow gold gleaming radiantly between damp earth crusted on it.

"You are not eating that," Araceli commanded, firmly – obviously, she thought it was a chocolate coin. "You don't know where that has been and the germs …"

Kate picked up the coin, quickly polishing away the dirt with the damp cocktail napkin which had been absorbing the condensation dribbling down from the sides of her beer.

"Holy moly, Batman," she breathed. "It's gold. From 1892. A twenty-dollar gold piece! If it's real…" She grabbed up her cellphone and snapped a quick picture, one each side of Mateo's magnificent gold coin. One side featured a woman's head, crowned with a tiara and a semi-circle of stars, the other a shield with an eagle's head and wings outspread.

"Where did you find this!" Araceli demanded.

"It's mine," Mateo replied, suddenly downcast. "I found it."

"You must give it back," Araceli insisted. "It's valuable – it wasn't just lying around."

"Yes it was," Mateo insisted, as stubborn as only a seven-year-old could me. "It was, and I found it. It's mine."

"Where did you find it, *hijo*?" Patrick asked, the calmest of the three. Richard was still inwardly panicking over the little tyke who had run off screaming.

"In the hunt," Mateo's lower lip stuck out mutinously. "It's mine, and I found it."

"But where …" Araceli began and at that, the people at the next table were craning their heads to look at the gold coin.

"Will you look at that … they always did say that Old Charley hid a fortune … no kidding … where did the kid find it? Willya look at that!" The whisper spread, from table to table, distracting other parents from contemplating their own children's Easter Egg haul and by extension, the management team of Mills Farm, standing with microphone in hand at a white-covered table by the closed gate to the egg-hunting grounds. Old Charley Mills – Teodoro "Teddy" Gonzalez, Benny Cordova and the regional marketing manager – the sight of whom made Richard cringe away and contemplate diving underneath the table, or pleading a sudden bladder emergency and hiding in the nearest loo. This was the bunny boiler herself; Susannah Wyatt, in a pale pink business suit, tastefully accessorized by her ultrahigh-heeled Jimmy Choo pumps.

They all three looked impatient, vaguely hostile, even. Something had happened to derail their carefully-calculated and staged event. With a sinking feeling in his heart, Richard essayed a guess at exactly what that was. She hadn't spotted him … yet, anyways, although it was only a matter of time.

A matter of time.

A LUCKY FIND!A CLUE TO THE MILLS TREASURE?

From the <u>Karnesville Weekly Beacon</u> – March 21st 2016 By Katherine Heisel – Staff Writer

The seven-year old son of Luna City residents Araceli and Patrick Gonzalez made a lucky find at the Mills Farm's Easter Egg Hunt this past Saturday. While searching for eggs in the manicured landscaped grounds of the Mills Farm homestead, Mateo Gonzalez discovered a near-mint-condition, 124-year old $20 gold coin. Young Mateo will not say exactly where in the Mills Farm gardens he found the coin, valued conservatively at $2,000, and reportedly one of the most coveted of the so-called 1892 gold "Double Eagles." When pressed by his parents and Mills Farm management, he would only repeat, "It's mine," and "I found it."

Mateo's parents, and representatives of Mills Farm's corporate management all declined further comment when questioned by this reporter, although according to Venue Properties VP for Marketing, Susannah Wyatt, Mills Farm and Venue Properties will not contest actual ownership of the rare coin.

"Finders, keepers," MS Wyatt replied, when first interviewed by this reporter, who happened to be present and covering the Easter Egg Hunt for this newspaper. "He found it, he should keep it. Do we look like people who would take candy from a baby, or a shiny golden coin from a little boy? Honestly, the bad publicity wouldn't be worth it."

This unusual find is the latest and most convincing evidence for the existence of the Mills Treasure, a trove of coin and gold ingots supposedly hidden somewhere on the property at the turn-of-the-last century by the last private owner of Mills Farm, the legendary bootlegger, Charles Everett "Old Charley" Mills. Treasure hunters have long believed that Mills – as a member of the Dalton and Bent Cactus robbery gangs – returned with his share of the loot from a series of bank and train robberies in the 1890s and concealed it somewhere on the family farm, near Luna

City. Local expert Dr. Stephen Wyler, a past president of the Luna City Historical Association has long insisted that there had never been any such treasure, citing as proof the fact that Charles Everett Mills was all but a pauper by the end of his life. Various representatives of Venue Properties, International, the current owners of Mills Farm have also vigorously denied the existence of the Mills Treasure, insisting that if it did exist, it would have almost certainly been discovered during the period that Mills Farm was undergoing extensive reconstruction of the buildings and grounds. Only two presently-existing Mills Farm buildings date from the lifetime of Charles Everett Mills, and both were moved to their present locations from elsewhere in Bee and Kendall Counties. The grounds themselves have been extensively landscaped and terraced, especially around the area of the original homestead site.

But Saturday's find will revive interest in the treasure hunt at Mills Farm. The very date of the coin and its excellent condition is, in the mind of long-time searchers such as Xavier Gunnison Penn, of Toronto, Canada, proof that the Mills Treasure does exist and remains hidden somewhere on the site of the original Mills homestead. In 2005, a similar 1892 $20 gold "Double Eagle" sold at a private auction for an undisclosed sum to a collector with a particular interest in the Mills Treasure. The coin sold together with several personal letters exchanged by Charles Everett Mills' sisters, Mrs. Mary F. Davis and Mrs. Elizabeth Olson. The letters purportedly dated 1911-1912 and are said to provide a provenance for the coin itself, and proof of the existence of the Mills Treasure. Do the letters, now in the hands of a private collector, hint at a possible location? For now, the only clue remains in the existence of the coin found last Saturday by a seven-year-old boy.

Upstairs in Mills Farm Security Central...

Drawn window blinds over the window of the Mills Farm security office put the end of the room housing the central monitoring station into a grey twilight, illuminated only by banks of monitors and the flickering multi-colored lights of the control panel. Three people sat before the monitoring station; the regular security specialist in his comfortable chair, his supervisor and Susannah Wyatt in slightly less comfortable chairs drawn into a huddle. Susannah Wyatt wore jeans and a rather ornate Southwestern-style tunic, accented by her trademark pink cowboy boots. The two security specialists, bland and anonymous men of no particular age or appearance, wore plain, unidentifiable overalls.

"There," Susannah Wyatt said, pointing to a particular screen, where pale, blobby masses jittered like microbes in a Petrie dish. "That's him.

There he goes, away from the other children. See if you can pick him up on another camera, matching that time-code."

"This is the camera that covers the petting zoo," Larry, the security specialist replied, punching buttons with the brio of a concert pianist in mid-Rachmaninoff. "Ahhh … wait for it, wait for it; there he is." He slowed the fast-forward, and the three of them watched a single small and tentative blob wander through the petting zoo area. Past the corral with the colts and the donkey, past the sheep, and the rabbit hutches…

"It looks like he's headed for the chicken enclosure," remarked his supervisor, Morris.

"On it, boss," replied Larry, with another nimble-fingered pass over the control bank. "Ah, here we go. Never pick your nose around here, ladies and gents – it will be recorded on at least two cameras."

They watched in silence, as the barely-recognizable figure of Mateo, his basket in hand, opened the gate to the chicken's pen. Tinier blobs – the chickens, of course – bounced around at his feet. He walked around the back of the henhouse. Without a word, Larry brought up the second camera covering that area.

"I guess if you were a kid looking for eggs, the chicken house is where you would start," Morris observed, after several moments of watching the blurred form of Mateo drift around the chicken enclosure. Now and again, he stooped and poked at something in the dirt. The last time he did so, he straightened up and practically ran out of the enclosure – although he did pause long enough to close the chicken enclosure gate after him.

"We got him coming straight back to the lawn," Larry replied. "He went straight to the terrace, to where Mrs. and Mr. Gonzalez were sitting with that girl reporter. He didn't stop to pick up anything else. He found that coin in the chicken enclosure – no doubt about it."

At that moment, the outside door to the security center opened, admitting a burst of light and Benny Cordova with his arms full of long scrolls of rolled-up paper and several file folders.

"I had to go way back in the archive storage, for these, Miss Wyatt," he said, with a sneeze. "But I think they'll give us a notion of the old layout, and then what Venue Properties had installed over top of it all. I got some of the court files, and a copy of the county tax records, too. You don't really believe in Old Charley's treasure, do you?"

"I don't," Susannah Wyatt replied, grimly, "but there are enough people who do. That damned gold Double Eagle is just the excuse they'll need to make trouble here. I want to make certain there isn't anything more, just laying around for any fool to find."

"If there is anything at all," Morris ventured, as he was old enough to remember the reconstruction of Mills Farm, "It's gotta be in the ground, someplace. There wasn't a plank of a building large enough to make a good bonfire out of, when Venue Properties bought the place."

"Damned little left below ground level, either," Benny Cordova agreed, spreading the first of the rolls flat on the nearest desktop. "I remember when they first brought in the 'dozers and began scraping away the brush and topsoil. This used to be a little bitty hill, where teenagers dared each other to bring their girlfriends – but they leveled all that out. Anything in the ground must have been buried deep, way back when. What are you looking for, Miss Wyatt?"

"This," Susannah unrolled a second sheet. "So, this is what they were looking at, when they started, and this is the topographic map showing the old place. The original farmhouse was here," Her immaculately French-manicured fingertip out lined a rough square on the developer's plan for the New Improved and Sanitary Mills Farm.

Benny Cordova mused, "I hafta say the new place is really nice. The old one was a dime-a-dozen ranch house ..."

"A dump," Susannah's gaze flickered back and forth, comparing the maps, the plans, the expanded copy of a turn-of-the-last century panoramic view of the original Mills Farm home place, as Larry mumbled a protest. "It wasn't that bad. Miz Wyatt!"

Charley Mills' parents had been very proud of their prosperity, and the comfortable yet modest home place. The original photograph which documented it all in loving detail – house, barn, outbuildings, corrals and all – had long adorned Mary Faith Mills Davis' parlor, in an ornate gilded frame.

Susannah Wyatt continued as if she had not heard. "Although we would have made the best of it, in the interests of the direct historical connection. All of this was gone by the time Venue Properties started work?"

"Every stick and stone," Morris nodded. "The old house burned, everything else fell down of neglect and wood-rot by about 1960. VPI had to rebuild from the ground up."

"Just as well," Susannah Wyatt agreed. The immaculately lacquered fingernail went to a small, shed-like structure, to one side of and rather distant from the original farmhouse. "We could have made it work, of course. But starting from a clean slate worked out best in the long run. So, what is this little outbuilding?"

"Most likely, the shitter," Larry answered, and Morris coughed, warningly. "The outside latrine," he corrected his underling.

"Interesting," Susannah's gaze went to the ground plan of the new Mills Farm. "So. As I estimate, that charmingly rural feature would have been about ... here."

The French-manicured fingertip outlined a certain area – by coincidence, just outside of the very building they were sitting in. Benny, Morris and Larry studied the maps, the old photograph, compared them all, and concurred. Yes, the boss-lady might have her moments, but all three did agree – she had a gift.

Now she commanded, crisply. "Benny – put out a press release; the petting zoo, and the chicken house are closed tomorrow and until further notice."

"It's Easter week," Benny protested, unhappily. "We'll lose business with the families – the kids are out of school …"

"No help for it, Benny," Susannah Wyatt answered, in her chairwoman-of-the-board voice. "The next kid who digs a near-mint condition Double Eagle out of the chicken yard? The value of that coin lost to VPI will be deducted from your salary and pension." She turned, decisively to Morris and Larry. "We'll need to set up a quickie dig – over the site of the original outhouse. But we need to keep tight security over this – understood? Especially if we find anything of significance."

"Think we will, Boss-lady?" Benny drawled; his tenure and proven ability in managing the day-to-day matters at Mills Farm allowed him a certain degree of impertinence when it came to VPI's resident gender-equality warrior.

"No," Susannah answered, with confidence. "But even so – when we don't find anything, that's another location for the treasure-hunters to cross off their to-do list, isn't it?"

Xavier "X" Gunnison Penn

- Wiki Entry -

Xavier Gunnison Penn (born 4 June 1949), is a Canadian citizen and self-proclaimed expert treasure-hunter, currently resident in Toronto [citation needed] although he is known to travel frequently throughout Canada, the United States, Mexico, Great Britain and Europe. He is chiefly known for his frequent appearances on *Coast to Coast*, his appearances in various courts on charges ranging from trespass, fraud and public brawling, his notorious lack of success in actually finding any such missing treasure troves, and his high-profile lawsuits against author Dan Brown for plagiarism, actor Nicholas Cage and producers of the *National Treasure* movie franchise for plagiarism, financier Collin Wyler for defamation of character, the PBS corporation, and *Entertainment Weekly* for the same, as well as the managers of INTERPOL's database of stolen works of art. He is banned for lifetime from the premises of all Sotheby's and Christie's auction locations, from the Smithsonian Institution, and from the British Museum. He is the author of a number of self-published books, including an autobiography, *Memoirs of a Treasure-Hunting Man,* outlining his various and largely unsuccessful searches for – among other items of note – the Oak Island Money Pit, the Amber Room, the Charley Mills hoard, the so-called Yamashita's gold, the missing Civil War-era Confederate treasury, the crown jewels of Ireland, the treasury of the Templars, a valuable gold shipment on the *RMS Republic*, King John's trove lost near Wisbech, England, and the treasure of Lima.

Penn was born in Manchester, England, the youngest son of Mavis (Gunnison) and William Gordon Penn, who emigrated to Canada in 1956 with their family. He attended various local elementary and secondary schools of no particular note in and around Toronto and Mississauga, and graduated from University of Windsor after eight years of various study programmes with degrees in History, Geology, and International Law. [citation needed]

Penn's first and abortive search for buried treasure occurred in the late 1960s, when as a teenager, he participated in the effort by Triton Alliance to excavate the Oak Island Money Pit, on a small island off the coast of Nova Scotia. The Money Pit is theorized to contain everything from pirate loot, through treasuries of several different nations and organizations secreted there for any one of a dozen reasons and over any number of decades. To date, in spite of numerous attempts to excavate it, nothing of much significance has ever been found, leading some to suggest that it was nothing more than a naturally-occurring sink-hole, into which soil and organic material such as burned logs from forest fires had washed over centuries.

In searching for the Charley Mills treasure hoard, supposedly hidden somewhere on the family farm once owned by Charles Everett Mills, near Karnesville, Texas. Gunnison Penn was befriended by Collin Wyler, then a college student, whose family owned extensive property near the Mills Farm site. As a teenager, Wyler had long been fascinated by the possibility that Mills, reputed to have been a member of at least two late- 19th century organized robbery gangs, had concealed his share of the loot somewhere nearby. No such hoard has ever been found on the property, which is now a hospitality/event venue owned by VPI, Inc., although the search continued intermittently through 2015.

Penn's most famous search for treasure, and the one which resulted in a bitter feud and dueling lawsuits between him and fellow treasure-hunting enthusiast Collin Wyler involved the fabulous Amber Room. Penn propounded the unlikely theory that many if not all of the panels of sumptuously carved amber which had adorned a royal palace near St. Petersburg until removed by the invading Nazis at the end of WWII had been transported in a U-boat to the United States. The U-boat, he insisted – against every evidence and likelihood of such an occurrence – had been sunk in or near the Houston Ship Channel in the spring of 1945 and had lain at the bottom of the Channel ever since. He claimed to have proof of this, in the form of a sliver of carved amber, which he claimed to have found in a preliminary search of the site of the wrecked U-boat and proposed to use as collateral in seeking a loan from Collin Wyler to fund further explorations. Upon analysis by a third party, that supposed piece of amber proved to be part of a carved Bakelite radio cabinet from the 1920s. In 1992, Collin Wyler sued, claiming fraud.

Gunnison Penn was declared *persona non gratia* by the government of Costa Rica, for his activities in searching for the treasure of Lima, which was thought to have been concealed somewhere on Cocos Island in the early 19th century. Gunnison Penn was also deported from the Philippine Islands in 1975, while searching for a hoard of gold supposedly hidden by the Japanese authorities during the WWII Occupation of the islands. During that expedition, he was reportedly kidnapped by Huk guerrillas [citation needed] who demanded a substantial ransom for his return. The ransom was paid, against the wishes of the Marcos government, who subsequently also declared him *persona non gratia*.

Described by many as peppery-tempered, autocratic, and litigious, Penn is also extremely sensitive of criticism. A PBS documentary of his search across Wilkes County, Georgia, for the long-vanished Confederate States treasury – missing since the last days of the Civil War resulted in a series of lawsuits. Penn took violent exception to the voice-over commentary of the final broadcast version, which pointed out that the failure of his many treasure-hunting excursions usually involved serious disputes with his partners or investors, or with the host-nation government involved. He brought suit against the writer/producer of the documentary, as well as the narrator, and the PBS network itself. When *Entertainment Weekly* covered the controversy in a feature story, they were included in the suit as well.

Although the courts eventually found against Gunnison Penn, establishment broadcast channels and print publications have tended to avoid coverage of his activities since that time. His treasure-hunting expeditions are documented on his own website, and through frequent YouTube video releases.

Xavier Gunnison Penn is not married, and there are no records of any informal partnerships or children resulting from such.

Higher Ed

Many are the educational fads which have swept school districts across our fair land in the last half-century; New Math, Whole-word reading and other theories beloved of the advanced establishments purporting to teach our teachers. Fortunately, when it comes to the Luna City Independent School District, few of those ill-considered pedagogic fads have come to roost, or at least their roost was not of sufficient duration to damage without possibility of repair the intellectual development of those children trusted to the local educational establishment.

Of course, for those parents sufficiently unhappy with the LCISD, there was always the outlet of a grimly old-fashioned Catholic grade school, St. Scholastica's in Karnesville, where the children wore the traditional school uniforms – including white shirts and school-patterned-plaid neckties for the boys – and the handful of teaching nuns wielded stout rulers with the expertise of Babe Ruth in his prime.

But on the whole, the parents of Luna City and environs are content with the elementary and high schools in Luna City; after all, most of them attended and graduated from them in their day, often having been taught by the same teachers. Indeed, Miss Letty McAllister's tenure as kindergarten and first-grade teacher began in 1947 and ended – under half-hearted protest from all concerned – in 1990. It was entirely possible to have had a young student's grandmother or grandfather face the formidable Miss Letty on the first day of school in the high-ceilinged classroom arrayed with the small-sized desks which had been bought in 1920 … desks which were still equipped with little round holes in the top right corner to accommodate bottles of ink … a classroom in which the faint odor of chalk lingered like an exotic perfume. Miss Letty missed her classroom in her years of official retirement.

(The desks were eventually sold in the antique market for an eye-poppingly gratifying sum early in the 2000s and replaced with high-quality small-sized wooden tables and chairs.)

But retirement did not end Miss Letty's teaching career; dear me, no.

Among the educational practices which were dropped from the high school curriculum around the time that the new high school building was constructed were mandatory home economics classes; that is, cooking and sewing. Most parents – and indeed most students – had the vague sense that educational time given over to that was wasted time. Girls and boys who wanted to learn to cook and sew had already acquired those skills from their parents or by other means of instruction by the time they hit high school. And those *(admittedly few)* students who were passionately interested in haute cuisine and needlework had already gone far, far beyond learning to make meatloaf and construct a drawstring denim gym-bag. Pointless to waste five hours a week for a semester on those projects … but the home economics kitchen classroom with the adjoining room which could be set up as a dining area still remain in active use.

Geronimo "Jerry" Gonzales *(a second cousin of Jaimie)* while in his tenure as Luna City Superintendent of Schools *(which lasted about half as long as Miss Letty's as a teacher)* suggested sometime around the mid-1990s that some kind of life-skills class ought to be instituted in the curriculum for junior or perhaps sophomore-year students. Jerry, as one of the bookish and intellectual Gonzaleses, was singularly unencumbered by conventional pedagogic idiocies: the class was instituted in the following academic year and has been continued ever since.

Jerry's Gonzales' mind-blowing stroke of genius was to have a wide-ranging curriculum of practical skills taught by volunteer experts in the Luna City community, who might do a single classroom hour – or as long as two weeks' worth. Jess Abernathy, for instance; teaches financial management. How to set up a household budget, manage a checking account, fill out a simple tax return. Jaimie Gonzales does a down and dirty auto maintenance course; checking oil and fluids, and how to safely change a flat tire. Roman Gonzalez, the construction foreman, teaches simple household repairs and residential trouble-shooting. This comes in handy especially when graduates strike out on their own following graduation, and find their own apartment in Karnesville, or Beeville, or the big city, San Antonio. Even Doc Wyler contributes; a single hour-long class on how to interview for a job.

But Miss Letty's emergency First Aid class is a stand-out, and in more ways than one. Oh, yes, Miss Letty covers the usual First Aid classics; broken limbs, snake, spider and animal bites, splints and tourniquets, bandages and all that. Then there is the emergency child-birth portion of Miss Letty's class, for which she brings in some particularly graphic visual aids. *(Film in the early years, of late on a DVD.)* Graphic … as in no portion of the delivery process is veiled from the delicate sensibilities of the susceptible. That at least one student will either faint or throw up is a constant to be relied upon; Miss Letty merely incorporates the treatment of those conditions into the lesson plan. Most students depart from Miss Letty's classes firmly and silently swearing a vow of chastity. Romeo Gonzalez – a cousin of Araceli and Berto's – whose dramatic and persuasive skills were famed from an early age was one of the few exceptions.

But is a matter of quiet community pride that incidents of teenage pregnancy in Luna City are refreshingly well below the national average – as are also STD infection rates.

Miss Letty Disposes

"I wish that Mateo had never found that coin," Araceli was venting, on the first afternoon after the Easter holiday, when all the children resumed school. It had been a nine-day and more wonder. The Café was empty; Richard and Araceli were occupying themselves in preparations for the following day.

"Your friend Kate shouldn't have made such a story of it," Richard agreed, and Araceli shook her head.

"No, she couldn't not write the story – not after all the fuss at the Easter egg hunt. She wasn't the only reporter there, either. Any one of them could have written it up. The Mills Treasure is a legend that will never die, any more than the ghost riders of Agua Dulce ..."

"That is one that I hadn't heard of," Richard was diverted, but Araceli was not.

"It's one that Abuelita used to tell ... that the ghost riders would take you away, if you were bad. Teenage boys used to dare each other to come out to where they were supposed to ride along the river on the nights with a full moon. Judy Grant says she sees them all the time – spectral white horses with men on their backs, galloping along the riverbank by their place. I'm surprised you haven't heard about them by now. Anyway, we're at our wits' end. Strangers have been calling the house at all hours, wanting to know where Mateo found it..."

"He still won't say?" Richard was intrigued, for Mateo still remained adamantly close-mouthed about the $20 gold piece.

"It's his, and he found it. I think he is keeping it in a Gold Mine Nugget bubble-gum bag."

"You ought to take it away from him," Richard said, "For his safety and your peace of mind."

"Yes, but Pat and I just spent a couple of years impressing on him that just because he was bigger, and wanted it, he had no right to take something away from anyone else. I can't be a hypocrite in the eyes of my own kid."

"Well – tell him to put it in a safe deposit box or something."

"I'm trying to talk him into that, but he is so darned stubborn – not even Abuelita can get through to him."

The Café door chimed – it was a little after three o'clock, when Mateo and Angelika were accustomed to walk the short way across the square from the Luna City Elementary School to the Café and wait for Araceli to finish her work for the day. The two children were in the habit of making themselves useful – folding napkins and setting tables. They were quite good at that, after Richard took the time to school them in proper place settings. Usually, Patrick came in his pick-up to drive them all home; he spent the days sleeping, and his nights driving a tanker truck between pump and refineries across the Eagle Ford Shale country.

"Mama," that was Angelika's voice, aged ten and the neatest child Richard had ever laid eyes upon. Angelika wore her hair in twin pigtails, looped up and tied with ribbons in an old-fashioned style that Richard had only ever seen in old movies. "There was a strange man at the school, saying that he wanted to talk to Matty, so Miss Letty said she would walk with us."

"Oh my God," Araceli turned as pale as the tablecloths she was folding. "Who was it – did you recognize him? Miss Letty …"

"There was no danger," Miss Letty smiled, a rather wintery smile. Angelika was carrying the cane that Miss Letty hardly ever needed, with something of the manner of a squire bearing a sworn knight's own sword. Miss Letty had Mateo and Angelika by each hand; the most determined pedophile in the world would have had as much luck getting past her as a bank robber would have had in getting into Fort Knox. "He was just some metal-detecting enthusiast from Houston, come to try his luck. I sent him off with a flea in his ear…"

"This is really getting to be a pain," Araceli turned on her son. "Matty, you have to let us have your gold piece…"

"It's mine and I found it," Mateo replied, immovably stubborn. His lower lip stuck out like the pediment over Abernathy's Hardware. Before Araceli's own temper could explode, Miss Letty gently cleared her throat. "Mateo, I have something to discuss with you, about your find.

Araceli, dear – may I take Mateo across to the park? I have a small business proposal to make to this young man."

"Of course," Araceli stammered, and the Café door chimed again. She and Richard watched the two – the child and the very elderly woman walk across the street to the nearest bench under the towering oaks which were Town Square's most magnificent feature. Mateo and Miss Letty sat down. After a moment, Miss Letty took something from her handbag.

"What do you think she is asking him?" Richard ventured and Araceli replied, "No idea. But Miss Letty is magnificent with children. She always has been."

The talk lasted a few minutes. Mateo brought out something from his pocket and handed it to Miss Letty. Miss Letty in turn fastened something around his wrist, and the pair of them gravely shook hands. Then, the oddly-assorted pair returned to the Café.

"We came to an agreement," Miss Letty announced, as the front door closed behind them with a jingle. "Regarding Mateo's gold piece – he has agreed to loan it to me. As a security on that loan, I offered him the watch that my brother Douglas had when he served in the Army Air Force in the Second World War."

Mateo proudly lifted his wrist – now encircled by a plain dull-green fabric band, and a stout silver-cased watch with a black face and white numbers on it. "Miss Letty says it is a good watch to learn to tell time on," he announced. "Much handier. It can be read in the dark, too. And it has a sweep second hand. For putting people on the same time."

"Well…" Araceli looked as if the breath was knocked out of her. "That is very nice of Miss Letty. You remembered to say thank you? Now, you and Angelika go and do your homework. And take care of Doctor Douglas McAllister's watch – I'm sure that it is a very precious thing…"

"Not so much, really," Miss Letty looked most conspiratorial, as Angelika and Mateo settled with their books at the *stammtisch* table in front of the large window, Mateo proudly showing off the old watch to his sister. "They manufactured them by the thousands. Douglas had a white gold Swiss pocket watch that our father carried which is far more valuable. This has only the sentiment and a little history attached." She leaned towards Araceli and passed a small drawstring bag to her. "There, dear; put it away in a safe place, until Mateo comes of age and decides what he wants to do with it."

:Thank you, Miss Letty," Araceli breathed. "We've been ... this whole thing has turned our household upside down. I'll have it in the bank tomorrow, as soon as the morning rush is over."

"Good," Miss Letty nodded. Her voice lowered even farther. "You know; I have often wondered if Old Charley kept his hoard in the pit under the outhouse. Something that Douglas said to me, once, when he was writing the history of Luna City; he read an old letter from one of the Mills girls that said something of the sort, but it was years ago. The outhouse is about where the petting zoo is now. I do believe that is the reason the petting zoo was closed during Easter week. The Mills Farm people were making absolutely certain there was nothing else to be found there. I thought the coincidence was most curious."

"If they found anything at all, it'll certainly divert the treasure hunters," Richard agreed. "Can't say I envy anyone who has to dig through a hundred-year old *khazi*. If there's any more gold in it, they're more than welcome to it."

In the Telecommunications Center at Mills Farm

Susannah Wyatt, Morris – the head of Mills Farm's local security team – and Benny Cordova sat at one end of the large conference table, which had been set up to teleconference for a far larger number than just the three of them.

But as Morris had pointed out, "You know this is going to get out to the public, eventually. Corporate just needs a chance to formulate their response and get everyone on board with it."

"We required the archeological team to sign non-disclosure agreements," Susannah Wyatt pointed out. "Backed up by serious legal action."

Morris sighed, "Miss Wyatt, that is all well and good, and I am certain that everyone will consider themselves bound not to speak to a member of the media. But a casual word here and there; talk to a spouse, a friend over drinks, a girl they want to impress at a bar – I guarantee you, word will get out. The best we can do is slow down the flow of information to a trickle."

"You are through to Corporate, Miss Wyatt," Susannah's executive assistant called from the outside office."

"Thank you, Cecily – and close the door, please. Good morning, Harry," she addressed the conference phone in the center of the table. "I'm with Benny Cordova, the local manager, and Chief of Security Morris Dickenson, to brief you on the results of the excavation on the site of the petting zoo."

"Good morning, Susannah," replied the president of VPI. Benny and Morris exchanged a brief, eyebrow-raised glance. "I'm with Tim, from corporate security office, and Jerry Vale, of public relations. Let's just cut to the chase; what was found? Anything to concern us, good or bad?"

Susannah took a deep breath. "Good and bad both, Harry. No treasure-trove entire …"

There came a hearty chuckle from the conference phone. "A small fortune in gold bars and coin – a problem I would be glad to suffer, all for the good of VPI! Is that the good, or the bad news, Susannah?"

"It all depends," Susannah Wyatt replied in carefully guarded tones. "The excavation was performed in utmost secrecy, and findings documented thoroughly by a trusted member of our team; either Morris himself, or one of his people. Those materiel objects discovered are currently in our custody, although as part of our agreement with the experts conducting the dig, they retained photographic evidence."

"Well, good," Harry sounded quite jovial. "So – what was found? I trust that it will all be good materiel for an educational exhibit on the premises … make a note of that, Jerry, will you? Go on, Susannah. We are on tenterhooks, here."

"Well, much of what was discovered was very … prosaic, actually. What you might expect to find in a late 19th or early 20th century privy-pit, or so I was told by the local experts in this kind of enterprise. Some bits of leather strapping, a brass buckle which fit them – the experts speculated from a satchel of some kind. Empty glass bottles, mostly, and of no particular value. Medicine – laudanum-based concoctions, a couple of jars of beautifying concoctions, some liquor bottles, all of nominal value to a collector, although interesting from a purely local historical perspective

… you do know that Charles Everett Mills was notorious locally for his bootlegging activities? "

"I am cognizant of that," Harry suddenly sounded impatient. "Cut to the chase, Susannah. What did they find of specific interest with regard to the so-called Mills Treasure Hoard?"

"Some small silver coins, much degraded by the … er … original contents of the privy-pit. And another 1892 Double Eagle twenty-dollar gold coin. Buried among the same."

"Ah," replied the thoughtful and disembodied voice of Harry. "That rather complicates matters with regard to the Mills Treasure, doesn't it?"

"I knew you would see the matter clearly at once," Susannah Wyatt sounded much more cheerful. "The remains in the privy-pit do tend to indicate the presence of a substantial quantity of … well, loot … at an earlier date. But that it was removed, and perhaps concealed elsewhere. The coins, the photographs and the documentation will all be sent by secured priority currier to your office. The bottom line, Harry – and those present concur in this," Susannah Wyatt took a very deep breath. "As do our local experts. The findings of this excavation indicate a strong possibility that the Mills Treasure Hoard does exist, and may still be found, somewhere on the property. The privy was a temporary hiding place. Since it has never been found or accounted for, it is only logical to assume that the remainder of it may still be hidden, somewhere on the grounds,"

"Ah," the disembodied voice of Harry, the CEO of Venue Properties International sounded thoughtful over the tinny connection of the conference phone set-up. Benny and Morris drew an invisible and relieved breath. Yes; the Big Guy was an intelligent man, able to instantly grasp the nut. "So the treasure hunt will be inevitable, once word leaks out? Good of you to keep us posted up to the minute, Susannah. I think you are best suited and positioned to handle those situations which may present themselves, locally – with the help of your very able staff, of course. We'll send you a breakdown of our suggestions. Our assistance at a higher level – well, that comes without saying, eh, Sue – Susannah?"

"Of course; thank you for your confidence is us, Harry," Susannah Wyatt nodded briskly. "I think the best course to take is to go ahead and announce it in a small way, ourselves. Not with a full-blown press release of course. Jerry, will you insert a small announcement in the monthly VPI employee newsletter? Two lines, nothing more conspicuous, without mentioning the Mills Treasure itself – just that a second gold coin was found while doing routine maintenance in the Mills Farm petting zoo area."

"Can do, Susannah," Jerry answered. Tim, of VPI's corporate security broke in. "I'm just not following your reasoning on this, Susannah. Can you enlighten me?"

"The matter of the coin being found will eventually become known, as Morris so ably pointed out," Susannah replied, with a barely-concealed trace of impatience. "In announcing it in this manner, we are releasing the information without letting it be widely known. After all, who on the outside really reads corporate employee newsletters? By the time anyone thinks to ask questions, we can legitimately claim it as old news, and of relatively minor importance."

"The late Friday afternoon news-dump scenario," Jerry, a hard-bitten public-affairs expert sounded actually cordial in his explanation. "Bad news to be put out there? Late Friday afternoon, before a holiday weekend, if at all possible. If there is any news interest in it at all, it will die by Monday morning – guaranteed."

"Exactly, Jerry," Susannah Wyatt nodded. "I'll send you an email with my suggested text so that you can polish it."

"I think that pretty wraps up the situation," Harry, being a CEO with a dislike of long purposeless meetings, fell upon the first opportunity to draw a line under this matter. "Thank you for staying on top of it, Susannah. I'll leave the rest to you and Jerry between you. Let me know if anything does come of it. Do you believe there is any point to a quiet search of the grounds for the remaining treasure – if it exists at all?"

"I do not," Susannah replied, decisively. "The work done in establishing Mills Farm in the 1970s was so extensive, I believe that if it was there to find, anywhere on the grounds, it would have been found then."

"Good, then," Harry said. "We'll operate on that assumption, then. Thank you all."

The Age of Aquarius Lives Yet!

From *Texas Monthly*

The Age of Aquarius Campground and Goat Farm celebrates their 48th anniversary this year at mid-summer – a well-established institution after a rocky beginning during the Summer of Love. And rocky would be the correct term to describe the original property; five forlorn and overgrown acres in a gentle bend of the San Antonio River, a bare quarter-mile from the pleasant little town of Luna City. The property was in the distant past, a part of a generous tract granted by Spain to Don Diego Manuel Hernando Ruiz y Gonzalez or Gonzales. Over the last quarter of the 19th century, much of the tract was sold off to various new owners, including the family of Morgan P. Sheffield, a moderately well- to-do gentleman from Philadelphia. Morgan Sheffield was diagnosed with tuberculosis around 1895 and advised to move to a more temperate climate for his health.

While the climate of South Texas proved to be restorative to Mr. Sheffield's health, the five acres of land was too rocky to farm in a traditional manner and too small to support more than a handful of cows. When the town of Luna City itself was planned, there was some thought given to establishing a hotel and spa on what was undoubtedly a pleasant situation on the banks of the San Antonio River on the outskirts of the proposed town, as attempts to dig a deep well on the site struck a thermal spring of naturally hot water. Unfortunately, that was the last of that run of good luck for nearly seventy years. The San Antonio & Aransas Pass Railroad bypassed Luna City and Mr. Sheffield's property. The hotel and spa were never built and the hot water well capped. During the 1930s, Mr. Sheffield's heirs established a small motor court on the property, in the hopes of attracting vacationers; they built a row of small cottages, a combination bathhouse/lavatory built of concrete blocks, and paved areas for travel trailers, in the hopes of enticing travelers on Route 123 between

San Antonio and the coast to come and stay for a night or two. However, travelers and campers remained stubbornly un-enticed; the cottages disintegrated through a combination of cheap construction, disuse, and lack of maintenance. The acreage became severely overgrown.

In 1967 the property passed into the ownership of Morgan P. Sheffield's great-grand-niece, Judith "Judy" Stillwell, a native of Austin, mostly because no one else in the remaining family really wanted it. Judith Stillwell was then a sophomore at the University of Texas at Austin, and the despair of her upright and generally conventional middle- class family. 1968 was the so-called Summer of Love, and all things counter-culture swamped practically every college campus in the land – affecting students like Judy Stillwell and a circle of friends, which included her live-in boyfriend, Sefton Grant. They embraced practically every 'ism' going, with near-religious fervor; vegetarianism, pacifism, nudism, paganism, and small-c communism. At the beginning of summer vacation, Judy, Sefton and a group of about forty other devotees – most of them fellow students at UT – conceived a grand plan to establish a New Age commune, where they would all live in harmony with nature. Where to plant their ideal Age of Aquarius? Why of course, the parcel which Judy had inherited, sight unseen, would be perfect. Her family agreed, over considerable misgivings – although they did extract as a condition of their approval and initial monetary support – that she and Sefton marry. Much to the astonishment of the Stillwells, Judy and Sefton acceded to that demand, and were married before a Justice of the Peace within days.

They set out from Austin on the first day of the summer break; a long convoy of rattle-trap student vehicles, loaded down with everything thought necessary to set up their commune. Although students and therefore addled with more than the usual quantity of late Sixties nonsense, there was a substantial streak of practicality, and among some at least, a willingness to engage in hard work. Sefton Grant, the son of a livestock farmer from Noodle, in Jones County typified that minority element.

Sefton realized almost at once upon arriving at the site of the new commune – a substantial grove of oak and pecan trees, deeply tangled with wild mustang grape vines – that subsistence farming would purely be out of the question; it would be a project of years to rid the best soil of rocks and improve it with manure and compost. He suggested grazing goats, and raising chickens. This suggestion was discussed and ratified over the period of a week by the commune members, while they worked at setting up living quarters. To several trailers were added the first yurt, which eventually became the Grant family home, a series of tents, and a number of free-form shack/shed/hovels built from scrap lumber, cardboard, construction leftovers, and sheets of plywood. Early on, the members discovered a substantial source of raw materials for their projects at the Karnesville City Dump, some eight miles south of the commune site. The hot well was uncapped, and an old windmill repaired to pump hot water into the only remaining structure from the campground – the lavatory and bathhouse.

But before the end of the year – even before the end of summer – the commune itself began dissolving. Fully a dozen members felt obliged to return to UT and complete their studies there in the fall, although they continued to consider the Age of Aquarius their more or less permanent home and to return there at intervals, especially at the time of the mid-summer solstice. Two male commune members had draft numbers come up, and being no longer students, had to report for military service. Three more, being not yet of legal age, were tracked down and retrieved by their outraged families. The others, all but Judy and Sefton, drifted away before the decade was out, having concluded with some degree of chagrin, that living off the land and in harmony with nature involved too much backbreaking physical labor in the South Texas summer heat. It proved to be much more uncomfortable then it had sounded in long and substance-addled discussions in the Student Union. Only Sefton and Judy remained constant, eventually raising two sons and a daughter and achieving some degree of eccentric comfort in their chosen lifestyle.

They acquired beehives, goats, chickens – Judy being much more inclined than Sefton to consider them as pets – and the manure from the latter slowly improved the patch where they established a thriving truck garden. Judy, who dabbled in various arcane household skills, including weaving, herbal medicines, fortune-telling, and macramé-knotting, worked out recipes for hand-made soaps, and goat-milk cheeses, and established a tiny but thriving business selling them at local markets, along with honey and fresh vegetables in season. In time, they were able to pay to have an electric line run out to the campground, on the grounds that people paying to camp there expected it, although their own home establishment depended on solar panels, a windmill and kerosene lanterns. And every mid-summer, the long-dispersed commune members return; middle-aged and prosperous, to fill up the campground and reminisce about that long-ago summer with Judy and Sefton, recalling youthful dreams and illusions, to light a bonfire in the grove and dance sky-clad to the Stones, the Doors and Janis.

The Grants' three children – all now well-grown, also prosperous and utterly conventional – do not come to visit during that week. There are things which once seen, cannot be unseen.

Celia Hayes & Jeanne Hayden

Chamber of Commerce Summer Newsletter

Summer 2016 Newsletter

Luna City Chamber of Commerce

5 North Town Square, Suite 4

Reminder: The Luna City Chamber of Commerce has a Facebook Page

Due to commitments to the movie project, the Mills Farm Country Restaurant will not be open for their customary Mother's Day Luncheon special – but Richard at the Luna Café & Coffee will offer a special Champagne Sunday Brunch, May 8th From 11:00 – 2:00. Reservations are requested, in order to prevent a lengthy wait on the day of this event.

Richard's Famous Café Butter Cookies

These lovely cookies are available every day in the Café. Richard's secret is that there is simply one basic recipe, with several easy variations. Sift together 2 ½ c. flour, 1 tsp soda, 1 tsp cream of tartar, ¼ tsp salt, and set aside. Cream together 1 cup butter, 1 ½ c. powdered sugar, 1 egg and 1 Tbsp. vanilla, and combine with dry ingredients. The basic cookie may be chilled, rolled out, and baked at 400 d. on parchment paper, 5-8 minutes.

Snowballs – Stir 1 ½ cup chopped nuts to basic dough, chill and shape into small balls, Bake as above, and roll warm cookies in powdered sugar.

Cinnamon-Nut – Shape chilled dough into small balls, roll in ¼ c. sugar mixed with 1 tsp cinnamon and bake.

Chocolate Sandwiches: add 2 squares melted unsweetened baking chocolate. Chill, roll out, cut into rounds, and bake as above. Sandwich two cookies with icing of choice.

Jelly Cookies – shape dough into walnut-sized balls. With the end of a wooden spoon, indent a hole into each, and fill with ½ tsp jelly or jam of choice. Bake as above.

Luna City, Texas – Home of the Mighty Fighting Moths

Upcoming Events

May 20

Graduation ceremonies for the Luna City High School S Class of '16 will be held, beginning at 5:30 in the Nando Gonzalez Memorial Auditorium.

May 30

Memorial Day BBQ at the VFW Post behind the Tip-Top beginning at 4:00 PM

July 4

The day begins with a parade through Town Square at 10:30 AM, and concludes with fireworks at 9:15. Bring the family for a day of patriotic observances.

Luna City Players

Patricia Pryor invites all members to a meeting at the Pryor residence Saturday, June 11 at 4:00 to discuss the fall theatrical season.

The Second Chronicle of Luna City

Luna City ISD News

Fall Season Moths Football Practice

Moths Football Boot camp will be held for those selected for the Fall '16 Mighty Fighting Moths Varsity Football team will be held every Saturday morning beginning Saturday, May 28. Team members are allowed to miss only two boot camp sessions over summer.

Permission Slips for Band Camp

Signed parental permission slips for the Summer Band camp trip to beautiful Camp Stewart in the Hill Country must be turned in to Coach Garrett's office no later than mid-May.

Senior Project Community Garden

The Senior class of 2017 is asking for donations of seeds, starts, fertilizers, and other garden-related materiel for their community project garden. Materials to be donated may be brought to the Luna HS Auto Shop garage, or call Martin Abernathy at Abernathy Hardware to make arrangements for pick-up of bulky items.

Permit Slips for Fall Life Skills Classes

Parental permission slips for students scheduled to participate in Fall '16 Life Skills classes must have them signed and turned into the school registrar before the start of classes in August. No exceptions

Community Marketplace

Summer is Mosquito and Fire Ant Season!

Martin at Abernathy Hardware reminds everyone that summer is mosquito and ant season, and now is the time to order foggers, insecticides, repellents, bug-zappers, and fire ant killer.

From Chief Vaughn, Luna City PD

The summer solstice falls on June 21, and for the week of June 19th-26th, the original members of the Age of Aquarius commune will be holding their annual reunion. Chief Vaughn reminds Lunaites that the Campground and Goat Farm is private property, the Grants are valuable members of our community, and that spying on their guests through binoculars during that week is rude, inconsiderate and contrary to Luna City civic ordinances.

Mills Farm Country Store

While our Country Restaurant will be closed during the month of May, the management of Mills Farm encourages you to shop for that special gift for Mom in the Country Store. The country store offers a selection of gourmet chocolates and sweets, specialty perfumes, soaps, and a limited selection of original and hand-crafted jewelry items.

Stop by, and pick up something special for that someone special ... and you might also have a chance to ask movie stars Amy Butler, Phillip Noel-Barrett, Diego Sepulveda or Cal Fenwick for an autograph!

It's a Go for The Road to San Jacinto!

From Talk of The Town – <u>The Karnesville Weekly</u> Bulletin Blog By Katherine Heisel

Location shooting begins next week in and around Luna City for the epic Texas historic adventure movie, *The Road to San Jacinto!* Although most interior scenes have already been staged and shot, in studios in San Antonio and in Burbank, California, those scheduled to be filmed here in Karnes County are expected to set the visual tone of the production. It's an exciting time for residents of Luna City, since nearby Mills Farm is serving as home headquarters for the production crew and stars.

Actor and now producer Phillip Noel-Barrett has become a familiar sight around town, as he was visiting earlier this year to scout locations and recruit the assistance of historical experts such as Clovis Walcott of the Karnes Company Rangers Living History Association, and Georg Stein of Stein's Wild West Round-Up. Jess Abernathy, who placed fourth this year in the barrel-racing event of the San Antonio Stock Show and Rodeo has been hired as the horse-riding double for Amy Butler, the former child star of the TV series *Family Tree*. A little bird wants to know – was there a female scout, spy, or messenger associated with Sam Houston's retreat across Texas in the spring of 1836? Since I have been repeatedly assured that every effort towards historical accuracy is being made, I can only assume that this is an addition for the sake of pure story-telling.

Memorial Day in Luna City

Luna City is well-equipped with military veterans, as are many small towns in fly-over country – especially the old South. The draft is only somewhat responsible for this. After all, it was ended formally more than four decades past. But the habit and tradition of volunteering for military service continues down to this very day, with the result that veterans of various services and eras are thick on the ground in Luna City – while a good few continue as reservists. There are not very many pensioned retirees, though; Clovis Walcott is one of those few, having made a solid Army career in the Corps of Engineers, and then in the same capacity as a Reservist. He is the exception; Lunaites mostly have served a single hitch or two, or for the duration of a wartime mobilization. They come home, pick up those threads of the life they put aside, or weave together the tapestry of a new one. What they did when they were in the military most

usually lies lightly on them, sometimes only as skin-deep as a tattoo …
and sometimes as deep as a scar.

The oldest veterans among present-day Lunaites are from the Big One
– World War Two, although that number has diminished to a handful in
recent years. Doc Wyler, who served in the Army Air Corps is the most
notable representative of that cohort. Miss Letty's late brother Douglas
McAllister, the eminent historian, was also in the Army Air Corps, and
Miss Letty herself served in the European theater as a Red Cross volunteer.
The greater portion of the Luna City VFW post, though, are Vietnam and
Vietnam-era veterans, with a younger cohort – to include   Joe Vaughn,
Sylvester Gonzales, and Chris Mayall – serving in various capacities in
more recent operations in Africa, Afghanistan, and the Middle East.

There is not much need in Luna City for elaborate observances of
Memorial Day; flowers and wreaths appear on the steps of the pale obelisk
in Town Square which is the war memorial. The Abernathys' display
window has a pair of American flags with the staffs crossed, over a large
vase of red, white, and blue artificial flowers, and a fan of those magnets
shaped like loops of yellow ribbon with various patriotic and veteran-
supporting mottoes on them. The notice boards outside of the various
churches make respectful note of the day, but in the main, the most notable
civic event marking Memorial Day is the late afternoon BBQ at the VFW
post. This is more of an open pot-luck; the VFW members pass the hat for
the purchase of brisket, pork roasts, sausages and chicken quarters … and
everyone else brings salads, bread, chips, and relishes. The bar has been
well-stocked with beer and soft drinks for weeks. The weather is usually
mild – neither hot or cold, although spring rain has threatened in some
years – so the party spills out from the clubhouse, out onto the paved patio
under the trees which line the riverbank. The air is rich with the good
smells of roasting meats slathered with the spicy sauce provided by
Pryor's Good Meats BBQ. The veterans and their families and guests
nibble on a bit of this and that, as they reminisce and gossip. Sometimes

someone works up an impromptu flag football game, played on the mown grass out in back of the Tip-Top. Joe Vaughn, who had been the star quarterback for the Mighty Fighting Luna Months in his senior year, sits out the game with considerable regret. Three hitches of particularly strenuous Army service have blown out his knees; jumping out of perfectly usable aircraft or fast-roping down from helicopters in full battle-rattle will have that effect on mortal joints and bones.

The only thing which might strike a casual visitor as curious is that table set up in the corner with a plate and silverware for one, a beer mug empty and turned upside down, even as unopened bottles of beer accumulate during the afternoon and evening. There is a small square of black fabric draping this table, which is centered underneath the POW/MIA banner which hangs on the wall – the table set for those who are not able to return to Luna City for the Memorial Day BBQ at the VFW. Their friends buy them a beer, though. By unspoken understanding, the money paid for those beers goes into a gallon glass jar which once contained pickle relish and at the end of the evening the cans and bottles lined up on the black-draped table are put back into the storeroom. The day after the BBQ, the money in the pickle relish jar is forwarded to a military charity which sends comforts to those troops deployed overseas.

And that is Memorial Day in Luna City.

The Legend of the Agua Dulce Ghost Riders

From the <u>Karnesville Weekly Beacon</u> – May 2, 2016
By Katherine Heisel – Staff Writer

The legend of the Agua Dulce ghost riders varies in details, depending on who is telling it and the year of the telling. It is one of those ephemeral stories – a folk legend – as wispy and insubstantial as the ghosts themselves; a dozen horses and their riders, who are seen on the night of the full moon, riding at a silent gallop along the bank of the San Antonio River, along wooded stretches between Floresville and Goliad. Always the horses, their riders leaning forward in their saddles, as if in dreadful haste. How the appellation of Agua Dulce – or sweet water – became attached to them is as much a mystery as their origin, since those places in Texas called by that name are somewhat removed from the area where it is claimed they have been most frequently seen.

This writer first heard of the ghost riders of Agua Dulce when visiting relations in Luna City during summer holidays – tales told in whispers by teenaged boys hoping to impress with their bravery, and by aged elders reaching into the storehouse of their own legends; *La Llorona*, the wailing mother of drowned children, the ghost children who pushed cars out of the intersection which they had been killed in years before, the fearsome *chupacabra* – the animal vampire who preyed on goats – and a hundred others, all intended to raise shivers around a campfire. The ghost riders are just as impossible to pin down; the version most frequently circulated is that they are the souls of a company of Tejano – or perhaps Texian – volunteers during Texas' War for Independence; part of the garrison at La Bahia, the Goliad citadel. They were pursued, run down, and fought to the last man by Mexican cavalry – and buried in an unmarked mass grave, somewhere along the banks of the San Antonio River.

But there are other versions. One variant is that the Agua Dulce ghost riders were actually a detachment of Mexican cavalry from the command of Santa Anna's subordinate commander, Jose Urrea, pursued and executed by Texians, during the war or after it upon the victory of Sam Houston at San Jacinto. The historical experts are all mute upon this point – but this is where historical fact goes wandering off in the mists of legend, even as the mist rises from the surface of the water on a moon-lit midnight.

There is one last alternate version of the Agua Dulce legend – one supposed to be told in the Comanche reservation in Oklahoma – a small war-party of Comanche fighters who were pursued and defeated by a mounted ranging company. The riders, the last stand, the mass grave, unblessed and those in it unshriven – that is the constant. Many people, even today have claimed they saw the ghost riders, riding soundlessly through the shallows, or among the trees that fringe the river. They say that seeing them is a portent of certain misfortune and disaster, although those who claim to have seen them lately say there is nothing more to them than the wandering of lost souls. No one can really say with any certainty – but the legend endures, throughout Karnes County.

Things That Go Bump in the Night

It gratified Richard no end, to discover that there were a number of weeks – months, even – during which it was possible to be comfortable in the little Airstream without running the air conditioning or heating. It seemed at first, that Texas had only two temperature settings; Broil/Roast and Blazingly Hot. To someone accustomed to the fairly mild summers of Northern Europe, alternated with the occasional frigid winter blast, it had all come very much as a shock, especially when such extremes could sometimes be experienced within a single day. However, once he discovered that autumn, winter, and spring were very much like an English summer, he was prepared to be more philosophical about it. The only bad thing about leaving the windows of the Airstream open at night, for the fresh air was the occasional scream of a pea-fowl who preferred to roost in a nearby tree, *(until he took steps to discourage the blasted creature)*, the distant crowing of the Grant's half a dozen roosters, and now and again something that sounded like a dog suffering from fits of nervous laughter.

"Coyote," Sefton Grant explained to him, the morning that Richard first mentioned this. Sefton, who was lean and stringy and looked like a slightly younger, fitter and less run-to-seed Willie Nelson, was putting out morning feed for the goats, clad in his usual working attire of battered cowboy boots, a pair of baggy cut-off jeans and a wide-brimmed 'boonie' hat which had once been military green but was now weathered to no particular color at all, and nothing much else besides. "Yeah, there're are coyotes all over in the brush. You won't see them in the daytime, though."

"Do they present any danger?" Richard asked, nervously – since he had coyotes and wolves rather muddled in his own mind.

"Only if you are a housecat, or a chicken," Sefton replied, grinning. "That's why we lock up them both at night and give the dogs free run. Judikens says that the coyotes gotta live, too … but not on our damned chickens."

The dogs – a couple of houndish-looking mutts and one which looked rather like a standard poodle – were usually to be found lazing in any convenient patch of sunshine in the Grant's yurt-centered compound, where they had all found a happy refuge. Richard didn't think any of the three were energetic enough to be effective guard dogs, but you never knew. The Grants hadn't selected the dogs for particular guarding-skills in any case; it was more a case of the dogs – all strays or cruelly dumped in the countryside by irresponsible owners – selecting the Grants as their chosen humans.

"The goats now," Sefton added, with some satisfaction. "They look after each other. Don't worry about anything you hear at night, Richard – the dogs are on guard."

This conversation was the first thing to come to Richard's mind – actually the second thing, after, "What the hell was that?" when something woke him in the middle of the night. Something; he sat up in the dark, trying to recollect what it was, or might be. Yes, a sudden kind of 'whumping' noise, as of something heavy hitting the ground. Without turning on any of the interior lights, he slid out of bed and padded through to the front of the caravan, where the larger windows offered views of the goat pastures, and the lumpy meadow leading down to the river, with the forlorn campground bathhouse and lavatory, standing foursquare with moonlight silvering the white-washed walls and tin roof. The moon drifted, a milk-pale orb, above the tree line at the water's edge, where mist tangled like shredded gauze among the distant shrubs and stands of rushes. Was there something moving, there among the brush? Something white; Richard was not certain of what, exactly. Could it be Azúcar, the Grant's infamously bad-tempered pet llama?

He shrugged – likely it was. Well, no matter to him; and Azúcar was big enough and sufficiently aggressive to look after himself very well. Richard would have thought no more about it – and then he recalled what Araceli had said about ghost riders, along the bank of the river at full moon. Nope – didn't look anything like ghost riders on spectral horses at all.

But something woke him the following night; not the 'whump!' noise that he had heard before. This was more like a regular squeaking sound, like a supermarket trolley with a bad wheel. It went on for about fifteen minutes, finally diminishing into silence, and Richard went back to sleep, muzzily thinking to himself that it was someone passing in the street below … only to recall upon waking very early – that there was no street and no 'below' from an Airstream caravan parked in a deserted campground. This was curious at the very least. He could not be certain that it wasn't a dream anyway.

He mentioned it to Araceli, about mid-morning, when the breakfast rush was over.

"I've been wakened in the early morning, a couple of times," he ventured. "The place is usually so quiet that I sleep like a log … but there is something queer going on."

"Not that," Araceli said, in much alarm. "Judy and Sefton are nudists

... and totally against any kind of exploitation in any form!"

"No, not that," Richard sighed. "Not the way that it sounded. It's just ... odd. The place is quiet as a tomb, when the old commune or Founder's Day isn't in session. But I can't help thinking that something strange is going on. Two nights in a row, and something waking me up in the wee hours."

"Not the ghost riders, is it?" Araceli ventured. "That's a tale told by teenagers to frighten each other or by the *abuelitas* to frighten disobedient children."

"The ghost riders?" Richard raised a skeptical eyebrow. "Pull the other one, Araceli my sweet country innocent. Britain is haunted several times over every inch by the ghosts of two thousand years. I doubt that there is a square inch of the place completely un-haunted. Spectral riders, of a mere hundred- and fifty-years' provenance? Please."

"Well, you're living there, you figure out a way to put up with them," Araceli replied smartly and then their conversation wandered on, perforce, to more immediate topics.

But on the next night, Richard was wakened again. This night was a one where a storm front had blown through, dropping quantities of rain, and now the warmer temperatures were bringing moisture up from the ground and the water. The entire campground was shrouded in mist. It was not quite solid enough to be called a 'fog' – but it did wrap the low- lying area adjacent to the river-bottom in a silvery-white veil. And there came that same squeaky-wheel sound again. Only this time, he recognized it for what it undoubtedly was – the hand-cart that Sefton hauled heavy things like goat-fodder and straw bedding from the yurt compound to the series of ramshackle sheds which sheltered the goats in bad weather.

"I wonder what the old berk is up to?" he wondered. Well, nothing much could startle him with regard to Judy and Sefton, but why they were doing it in the middle of the night was a puzzlement. On that note, he rolled over and went back to sleep. He did make mention of it, the following afternoon, after bicycling home from the Café. He stopped at the yurt to ask for half a dozen eggs for himself.

Judy beamed at him, saying, "Sure – let me see what the girls have produced! Can't get any fresher than straight from the hen's butt, can we?"

"No, I think not," Richard replied, slightly unnerved by Judy's way of putting it and also by a sudden mental vision of a hen on a gynecologist's examining table, with feet in the stirrups. She bustled off towards the henhouse, as Sefton came around from the main shed, rolling the wheeled cart before him.

"'Lo, Rich," he said. "How's it goin', man?"

"Pretty well," Richard answered. "Getting ready for the mid-summer solstice?"

"Yep. We're hoping for a good turn-out this year. The weather's gonna be nice." Sefton scratched his slightly bristly cheek with a faint scratching sound, and Richard suddenly recollected the sound of the cart, from the previous night.

"You might want to lock up that cart," he said. "I could swear that someone has been using it at night. I keep hearing someone or something out in the campground in the wee hours."

"Do ya?" Sefton shrugged, as if this was of little concern. "No one locks up anything around here. Mebbe ya heard the ghost riders, 'r something like that."

"Maybe," Richard agreed. There were large bottles of something in the cart, large, opaque plastic bottles, mostly covered by other bags of wood-shavings used for bedding the hens and goats. But not quite … and he did wonder why Sefton headed off to the goat pasture as soon as Judy emerged from the henhouse with a wire basket of eggs.

And that night, he was wakened again – this time, not by a squeaking wheel, but by a strange kind of 'chuff-chuff-chuffing' sound. Without turning on any lights, Richard padded silently to the banquette end of the caravan and looked out into a world of fog and mist, an eldritch world in which a single small light flared and bobbed. Up and down across the length of the deserted campground, bobbing as a man might walk with a small light affixed to his forehead, the regular 'chuff-chuff' noise now close, now distant and nearly inaudible.

"Good night, nurse!" Richard said to himself, having finally realized what he was seeing. He watched for a bit longer; until the figure in white, the small light bobbing in the fog passed close enough to the caravan for him to be absolutely certain. And then he went back to bed and slept the sleep of a man with a completely unworried mind.

In the morning, before the sun was more than a brief bright line on the eastern horizon, he went to the nearest goat shed with a battery torch in his hand. The small goats nuzzled at him in mild curiosity, and Che the now full-grown Nubian goat butted his thigh as if demanding the caress that was only his due.

Buried deep in the goat's bedding in the second ramshackle shed were some very curious items. And when Richard returned home that afternoon – how very strange to think of the Airstream as home! – with small shreds of bread dough still clinging to his hands, a dusting of flour on his shirt and in his hair from the weekly preparation of an enormous batch of cinnamon rolls, he put up his bicycle and wandered over towards the yurt. He was exhausted from the day of work, which had begun before dawn, and from pedaling the bike, for the summer heat was merciless, but he had just enough energy to look for Sefton.

He found him shoveling the latest accumulation of chicken dung into the serried rows of reeking piles that were the Grant's compost heaps. *(Used and reused wooden pallets, strung together in fours to make individual compost containers.)*

"Hard at work, I see," Richard observed, and Sefton hesitated and grinned – an expression which vanished completely from his bronzed countenance as soon as Richard added, "Near to twenty hours a day, that I can see, after last night."

"Er …" Sefton went several shades paler under his tan. "What did you … it was foggy last night. That's when people see the ghost riders! Judikens says that …"

"Likely she could see the whole mounted parade of Horse Guards, given the right encouragement," Richard drawled. "But what I saw was someone in a white cover-all, walking around fogging the whole place with insect-killer and the whole lot of bug-killer and fogger is presently hidden under the goat's bedding materiel in the second shed where you left it in the wee hours."

Sefton recovered something of his composure, squinting at Richard. "There hasn't been anyone living in the trailer long-term since the commune broke up, so there ain't no way that anyone took note before. Well, you know how Judikens makes such a big thing about natural remedies, and chemicals. She's been big on it for years, tell the truth. But the truth of it is that folk that are not used to the outdoors much; they can get sort of over-exposed, real easily. You know; mosquitoes. Fire ants…"

"Yes, I recollect that, very clearly," Richard answered with a reminiscent shudder. On his very first morning in Luna City, he had awakened from drunken slumber, lying naked on top of a large fire-ant hill on the riverbank, with predictable results. It had taken nearly two weeks for the small pustules left wherever they stung him to heal entirely.

"So, the usual environmentally-sensitive stuff that Judy wants us to use doesn't make a dent," Sefton looked at Richard – not quite imploring, but inviting comprehension. "And we can't have our guests, our old friends bitten six ways from Sunday. I do what needs to be done – been doing it for years, without her knowing. Hell, she was raised in the suburbs, had no idea of what farming and raising stuff really meant when we first came here. I did; I grew up on a ranch, outside of a little burg called Noodle … ever hear of it?"

"Can't say I have," Richard managed to swallow his astonishment. "Really – there's a place in Texas called Noodle?"

"You betcha," Sefton nodded. Richard thought about it some more, wondering for almost the first time how Sefton and Judy became a pair. A more oddly-assorted couple was hard to imagine.

Sefton answered the unasked question. "We were at UT, together. A thing, ya know? Turn on, tune in, drop out. Summer of Love, and all that. My folks were almighty pissed – hers' too. I was supposed to be studying agronomy. But Judikens had a way with her. Crook her little finger, guys come running. Goddess-power, ya know?" Sefton leaned against his shovel and sighed, reminiscently. "It seemed like the world was on fire, falling apart. We had to get back to the garden, get in touch with nature, withdraw from the materiel world an' all. So, Judikens had this little piece of worthless, overgrown land she inherited, and we had the notion to set up a commune on it." Sefton chuckled, wryly. "Yep – buncha college kids with a load of airy-fairy notions. Took most of the summer to kick that nonsense out of them. But us two – we stuck to it. No, it ain't much to look at, and I'm the first to admit it. But we don't owe nothin' to the man, and we don't call anyone boss. We're off the grid, got plenty to eat, a roof over our head. We get by – you know what they say 'bout how country boys can survive? Heck, I wish that Judikens was a better cook, but I'll bet there are folks like Mister Clovis Walcott who might live under a better roof'n ours but aren't any happier. You don't wanna give me away, do ya?"

"My lips are sealed," Richard replied, with perfect contentment. "I promise, I will say nothing to cause domestic dissention between yourself and your good lady. I have no great love for either mosquitoes or fire ants."

"Thanks, Richard," Sefton beamed at him. "It ain't much, but it's home … an' you're a part of the family."

"Looks like we're going to get another member of it, by extension," Richard observed. From where they stood, by the henhouse and the compost enclosures, they could see a battered RV crawling carefully down the rutted dirt road which led from Route 123 towards the campground enclosure. "Is this anyone you know?" he added, for Sefton had mumbled something uncomplimentary under his breath, upon noting the large logo applied, as a banner across the side of the RV. *"Treasure Hunters, International"* it read, in ornate letters, with a website in slightly smaller letters underneath and a portrait representation of a beaming, bearded gentleman alongside the logo.

"Yep," Sefton replied, and spat into the weeds which fringed the compost piles. "Xavier Gunnison Penn, the world-champion treasure-hunter as he calls himself. He's been coming here for years, looking for Charley Mills' treasure hoard. I'll bet that Araceli Gonzales' little boy finding a gold coin in the Easter Egg hunt has fired him up all over again."

"He's been here before?" Richard was frankly astonished; the only regular visitors to the Age of Aquarius were either members of the old commune on their regular mid-summer pilgrimage, or out-of-town residents returning for Founders' Day – in either case, visitors knowing well what fresh hell awaited. He had yet to see a casual traveler pull off the main road and find their way to the overgrown meadow; if they did, turning around and driving away as soon as they saw the place, as fast as they could risk their tires and shock absorbers on the rutted unpaved track. Now Sefton nodded glumly. "Yep. And aside from being about six kinds of nut, he's a cheap bastard. Guess I'd better call Joe Vaughn and let him know."

"He's not some kind of criminal, is he?"

"No, not that you'd notice so much," Sefton hesitated. In the campground, the RV trundled slowly across to the far edge where the single row of electric hook-ups was situated, several spaces down from the Airstream. The RV halted, then backed slowly into the space. "It's just that he's one of these enthusiasts. No discretion. Some crazy notion pops into his head, he's going with it three seconds later."

The driver-side door of the RV opened, and a man emerged; short, stocky and bearded. He saw the two of them and waved, not with any urgency. As the driver – presumably the impulsive Mr. Penn – went around settling the RV hook-ups, Sefton continued, "You ever hear how he got banned for life from the Smithsonian? I'll tell ya; I know it's a fact because he told me the story himself. He got it in his head that there was a map to a treasure, etched on the inside of one of those big dinosaur bones. And nothing would do but that he had to look at it, right that very moment. So, he jumped over the rope and shinnied up into the exhibit. You know – into it! One of those big bastards in the main exhibit hall. You gotta know that everything and everybody all around went all kinda ape. He got into a fist-fight with a nice lady docent, right on the spot, and that was when they banned him forever."

Sefton shook his head, sadly. "You know, any real sensible person woulda asked permission, written a letter asking real nice, pretty please. So, if he gets some sorta notion to pop over to the Wyler's or to Mills Farm with his metal detector and a coupla shovels, try to talk some sense into him. And if you can't manage that, then don't let him talk you inta going with him."

"I will keep your wise advice in mind," Richard replied. "Consider me warned. And thank you once more for the midnight mosquito-slaughter. Judy might not approve, but I do, most enthusiastically."

"No problem," Sefton grinned, revealing a most unexpectedly healthy set of good teeth. "Say, I know you're a two-fisted drinking man. I got a good batch of mustang grape wine made a couple years ago – k'n I bring you a coupla bottles, as a token of my esteem?"

"Certainly," Richard answered – really, considering some of the swill he had pounded down in his time, how bad could mustang grape wine really be – *and what was a mustang grape anyway?* He devoutly hoped that it wasn't some kind of rural slang, like road apples for horse droppings.

"Great!" Sefton replied. "Soon as I get finished with this, I'll bring it over." He looked over at the RV with the Treasure Hunters banner across the side, and sighed, his features returning to their usual expression of lugubrious gloom. "Guess you'll be seeing how long it takes for Gunnison Penn to come over and make friends, Rich. Inside-outside, about two minutes is my bet. Sorry 'bout that. But as Judikens says, it's our sacred obligation to make strangers welcome at the Age of Aquarius."

"A concept to be heartily embraced by all in the business of providing hospitality to the public," Richard answered, unable to think of anything else to say. He bade farewell to Sefton and strolled down the gentle slope to what he had begun to think of as home. Over the past fifteen years of his life, he thought – the old Airstream was the one place in which he had remained in residence for the longest unbroken period of time – a straight eighteen months. On that account alone, good reason to think of it as home. All the better reason to defend it – and by extension, the Grants, eccentric as they were, and as inconvenient as Che the goat and the unbearably noisy pea-fowl – that beast which had taken to roosting nightly in the tree adjacent to the Airstream and rousing Richard at ungodly hours with its' incessant screaming. Still … if he had his old income at his command, he could purchase the Airstream from the Grants, and move it to … no. To change anything about his situation was to make it something less than what he had become comfortable in.

He opened the door and closed it behind him, relishing as always the cool air inside which came to meet him, the tiny, tidy and comfortable interior; a quiet place to eat, sleep, and read *Larousse Gastronome,* to sit in the banquette seat, or in one of the patio chairs outside and watch the sun go down, after a long and rewarding day of work in the Café. Yes, he was a self-centered bastard. Never mind about the subjugation of enemies and listening to the lamentations of their women – life's greatest pleasure to him was watching the sun set on a day of honorable and rewarding work *… oh stone the bloody crows, was that someone tapping on the door?*

He opened the rounded-corner trailer door – yes, of course; there stood the driver of the Treasure Hunter RV. He was a gentleman of late middle age, balding above, and extraordinarily hirsute below the nose –

which organ was large and curved like a parrot's beak. He was clad in khaki shorts and an eye-wincingly multi-colored Hawaiian-style shirt patterned in palm-trees and electric pink canoes, alligators and hula-skirt clad dancing girls.

"Hi, neighbor," this person said. "Do you have a pint of milk to spare?"

Fruit of the Vine

The wild native grape, *vitis mustangensis,* is a species of grape native to the South and specifically Texas, where it grows in extravagant and weed-like abundance, especially at the edges of woodlands and along fences and hedgerows. The vine romps exuberantly up into the high branches of native scrub trees and tolerates heat and drought conditions with insouciance. The leaves of it are green on the top, greyish underneath and fuzzy to the touch, growing on runners that can be as long as 300 feet. The grapes grow in small bunches, normally dark purple to black, and are so tart and acidic as to be almost inedible when straight from the vine – in fact, it is always recommended to wear gloves when harvesting and handling them. Depending on whether the wine is made with skinned or unskinned grapes, and on the method of fermenting, mustang grape wine can be either white or red, or range from dry to semi-sweet to sweet. The grapes are usually ripened by mid-summer around Luna City and the Age of Aquarius Campground and Goat Farm. When Sefton and Judy Grant and their idealistic student friends first came to Luna City to establish the commune, the wild grape tangles were about the only thing that grew bounteously on the commune acreage … that and stands of cactus.

But Sefton and one of his companions, who came from an old Czech-German family in Texas, readily saw the promise in the mustang grape tangles … which, when they arrived, were heavy with a particularly large bumper crop of ripe black grapes. Sefton's friend immediately scrounged a number of plastic buckets, some old ceramic crocks and a wooden barrel, and set to making wine in the traditional method that his family had practiced for decades, filling the crocks and buckets with fresh-picked and rain-washed grapes, and crushing them with a length of clean and untreated lumber. The resulting naturally-fermented grape-must was strained and transferred to a number of glass carboys – also scrounged, and mixed half and half with a sugar water solution made by boiling 2 ½ gallons of water with ten pounds of sugar. That mixture was allowed to ferment for several weeks, until it stopped bubbling, and the containers were sealed. The tradition was to allow the wine to sit in the carboy for six months – until winter, when it can be siphoned off and bottled, a tradition which Sefton Grant follows to this day. The Grants maintain a rather nice wine cellar, inconspicuously housed in an eccentric structure made from rammed earth and adobe bricks, plastered inside and out, and with roofed with scrap plywood waterproofed with tar. Those members of the original commune who returned to their studies at the end of summer, spoke often and nostalgically of the wine-making at the Age of Aquarius as about the only aspect of the commune which succeeded beyond their wildest dreams.

Of Mustang Grape Wine and Memory

Richard blinked uncertainly at the newly-arrived treasure-hunter and his fruitless quest for milk. This must be none other than Xavier Gunnison Penn, as he did bear something of a resemblance to the more than life-sized countenance emblazoned on the RV, to the right of the Treasure Hunter logo. The man himself had accrued as many years, pounds and miles as the RV, but the likeness was undeniable.

"Sorry, old boy – no. I've just enough for tea tomorrow morning. But there's a little grocery store by the petrol station on the main road ..." "Nasty little pit of a place," the caller snorted, and Richard answered rather testily, "Well, that's the nearest, save the Walmart in Karnesville, unless you like the taste of goat-milk, in which case I am certain that Judy and Sefton can oblige ... although it's a bit late in the day for fresh ..."

"Never mind," Gunnison Penn snapped, irritably. "The least you can do is invite me in."

"Not certain why I should, exactly," Richard murmured." We've hardly been introduced. Richard Astor-Hall, sir. I presume that you are Mr. Penn, the treasure-hunter of note?"

"My fame proceeds me, as usual," Gunnison Penn. Richard was not quite certain how he managed it, but there he was, standing inside the door, having somehow shoved his way in. He moved fast, for a man of about sixty or so, with the reddened cheeks and white beard of an extremely bad-tempered St. Nicholas. "Astor-Hall, you say? British, by your speech, I take it. My, how this old place has been improved. Mrs. Grant must have discovered the benefits of cleanliness and order."

"No, my housekeeping service has," Richard replied. He could not recollect the last time that he took such an instant, visceral dislike of someone on so instant an acquaintance, unless it was Phillip Noel-Barrett, who possessed enough superficial charm to soften the blow of a first impression. "Conchita Gonzalez – her little company is called Luna City Ready-Maid. I can refer you to her with my highest recommendation; I think I have her card somewhere around here."

"This trailer was a dump, last time I was here," Mr. Penn looked around, scowling either in disappointment or disapproval. Richard couldn't make out which.

"Well, I have been living here … since a year ago in May," Richard wondered how on earth he was going to get this tosser removed from his personal space, after a long day in the Café; a day which began before dawn and involved a two-way bicycle ride. "And I have to say that my hosts could have not been more kind, or considerate … although most definitely eccentric."

"I'll say …" Mr. Penn leered in a most unpleasant manner, and Richard snapped,

"Please don't. Look, I have just finished a very long day of work, I would like to sit down and have a bit of my supper – and as I told you before, I don't have any milk to spare. Good evening, Mr. Penn."

"Well, good evening to you, Hall," Gunnison Penn scowled even more thunderously, just as there came another knock on the trailer door.

"No bloody rest for the wicked," Richard sighed. Before he could answer the knock, Gunnison Penn had jerked the door open, nearly sweeping Sefton Grant off the second step.

"Hey – you nearly made me drop the wine!" Sefton objected. He had one bottle in his hand, and another at his feet; hefty gallon jugs, one dark and mysterious, the other the natural green glass with a pale clear fluid inside. "I didn't know if you favored a semi-sweet red, or a dry white, so I brought ya a jug of both. Hiya, Penn; good to see ya again. I was just coming over to see if ya wanted anything, make sure ya were hooked up OK ."

"Milk," Richard said. "He came over to ask if I had any milk."

"No problem," Sefton handed the jugs to Richard, and removed a cellphone from the top of his cowboy boot. "Keep 'em in a cool place, Richard. Good ta have you stay with us again, Penn – lemme call Chris at the Tip-Top, see if he can drop off a half-gallon for ya on his way home. I'll just add it to your tab – that OK, Penn?" Without waiting for an answer, Sefton thumbed through his contacts list and selected a number, as Gunnison Penn glowered at them both impartially. "Hey, man – got a new guest here, needs a half-gallon of moo-juice … yeah, the big RV, three spaces up from Richard's. Right – see ya in a few." Sefton put away the phone with a decided air of triumph. "Ya'll have your milk in five minutes. Let me walk with ya back to your wheels. Judikens asked me to make certain you were hooked up all right, and see you knew where to flush your tanks. Cool – see ya round Aquarius, Richard."

With a wink to Richard over his shoulder, Sefton and Penn strolled away, and Richard thankfully closed the door. He was tired, more than tired – exhausted beyond even considering getting up and ransacking the tiny refrigerator for butter and cheese – which he thought he had in addition to eggs from the Grant's hens but was too tired to make certain of this. He was just surveying the two jugs of wine, wondering which of the two would be the less distasteful, if both would fit into the tiny refrigerator ... and how – if the wines proved equally nasty – would he get rid of them without bad feelings ensuing. No, he did not want to insult or alienate the Grants. This was a new and slightly uncomfortable feeling for Richard – an obligation to be considerate of others. He would just have to drink the damned stuff.

These ruminations were interrupted by yet another knock at the Airstream's door. Richard swore impatiently under his breath – *couldn't he get a moment of peace and quiet?* He was all ready to swear out loud, thinking it was the return of the obnoxious Penn, but instead it was Berto Gonzalez, standing bashfully at the bottom of the steps with an insulated food carrier at his feet.

"Hi, Ricardo," he said, "Abuelita sent you some homemade tortillas and a big pot of venison red-chili stew that she made. It's a New Mexico style, like what Abuelo Jesus used to like. After a long day in the Café, she says she thinks you don't really want to cook ... but you have to eat."

"She might be right," Richard admitted, touched and slightly embarrassed by the consideration. "I was just thinking that I was hungry, but too tired to cook up an omelet and too picky to warm up a frozen whatever."

"I'll put it on the stove for you," Berto offered. "Abuelita will want to know that you tried it ... oh, hey – you got some of Sefton's mustang wine! That's good stuff! It'll go great with the stew!"

I suppose it will," Richard agreed, although wondering what Berto's basis for judging wine was based upon; cheap stuff on the shelves at the Tip-Top, most likely. "I was about to pour myself some – would you like a glass?"

"Yeah, but just one," Berto was divesting Abuelita Adeliza's covered pot from the carrier and placing it gently on the hob. "Since I'm driving. Just keep the flame real low, so it stays warm. The tortillas are wrapped in tinfoil, so they'll stay nice and warm, too, Hey, is that someone at the door?"

"Afraid so," Richard groaned. This was becoming a farce. He opened the door, but it was Chris from the Tip-Top, lean and saturnine, a young man the color of good coffee with plenty of cream, jingling his car keys in his hand, with the little red coupe parked beyond him.

"Yo, Richard – you looked wiped, man. I brought over some milk for the Grant's new guest, and I thought I'd see if you wanted to go into Karnesville for a pizza or some burger action."

"Too tired," Richard replied, gratefully. "Berto's Gran just sent over some venison chili – you're invited to share, if you'd prefer that."

"Smells awesome, and yeah … oh dude! Is that some of Sefton's mustang wine? He usually only gives it out at Christmas!"

"It's too crowded to sit inside," Berto offered shyly. He had taken three wildly-assorted glasses out of the tiny dish cupboard. "The venison is from the deer I got at Doc's last fall. Abuelita finally got down to the bottom of the freezer. It cooked up real good."

"Glad to hear it," Chris said. "Venison, huh? I still hold a grudge. I got the left fender crunched this spring when one of those rats with hooves hit my car and it cost me $450 to get fixed."

They took the jug of red with them, and sat out on the patio, where a slight afternoon breeze alleviated some of the day's heat. Long golden fingers of light stretched across the empty campground, green alternating with the dun-colored parking places, shadows stretching out from underneath the scattered trees. Berto unfolded another patio chair, while Chris did the honors, ceremonially unscrewing the metal cap, and ostentatiously sniffing it.

"Very nice, I would judge – a prize 2014 vintage, an excellent harvest that year. Definite flavor of oak, with earthy undertones, nicely balanced with a faintly citrus perfume …"

"I thought it was just grapes," Berto looked worriedly into his glass.

"It is," Richard said – really, sometimes he wondered about Berto's sense of humor, or rather, lack of same. "Gentlemen, a toast!" He raised his glass, and Chris raised his as well. "Through the teeth and over the tongue, look out stomach, here it comes!" They drank, and Richard added, in complete astonishment. "Stone the bloody crows … that is good. Damn good. Magnificent, even."

"Sefton does a mean red," Chris allowed. Berto nodded – and it was; a rich, deep flavor, the transmuted soul of the grape, so filling and warming it was almost a nourishing as solid food.

Richard mentally took back every doubt that he had ever entertained about Sefton's homemade mustang wine. "The man's a genius," he said. "I could serve this to the Queen herself, without a touch of embarrassment. A little wine for thy stomach's sake …" It was a marvel, how the exhaustion of the day, of the hard pedal on the bike all melted away, in the gentle warmth of Sefton's mustang grape wine. "Rest to the weary, a balm to the soul, comfort to the distressed, food for the starving… damn, he could make a fortune with this stuff! I wonder why he doesn't?"

"Because it would take all the fun out of it," Chris drawled. "It would just be a job. This way, it's just a harmless hobby."

"Free man in Paris," Richard settled back in the patio chair. Beyond the goat's pasture, a thread of dust rose up – a vehicle coming up the road. Such was his state of satisfaction with the world after only a few sips of the wine that he could regard it only with mild interest – that possibly the second guest in a single day was approaching the Age of Aquarius. Outside of mid-summer and Founder's Day, that would be a record.

"Enter the po-po, stage left," Chris observed. "What's with the RV, Ricardo?"

"Some Canadian wanker of a treasure-hunter," Richard said. "Name of Xavier Gunnison Penn. Didn't you see the side of his caravan when you dropped off the milk? A thoroughly pushy and unpleasant gentleman, I must confess. I have already had the displeasure of his company this afternoon. He came to ask if I had any milk …"

Chris swore, rather briefly but with passion. "Oh, dude – that's him, back again? Doc will be completely pissed."

"The very one," Richard replied. "He's been here before? In Luna City?"

They watched, as Joe Vaughn parked the Luna City PD's cruiser by the ornamented RV and walk around to the far side. He remained there, and out of sight for some minutes, and it was too far away for them to hear what was being said.

Chris said, "I've only heard about this, second hand. Yeah, he's been here a couple of times over the years, but before my time. Hunting for the Mills Treasure. He was tight, early on – this would be around the time before any of us were born – with Doc Wyler's son. Collin. Collin's a money man, so they say. Also a bit of a real asshole, if you can read between the lines. He was in college then, and a real treasure-hunting fool himself."

"Hang on …" Richard had the sinking feeling that he recognized the name, and from another source than Doc Wyler. "Money man – financier, you mean? That Collin Wyler? He is our Doc Wyler's son and heir?"

"The very same – son, but probably not heir," Chris explained. "Don't work that way, in this part of the world. Likely, Patricia Pryor is Doc's main heir – you know her? Mrs. Pryor of Pryor Meats & BBQ? Yeah, the very same. Her mom was Collin Wyler's first wife. It seems that Collin became obsessed with screwing his way through the alphabet about the time that he decided to go for owning the world, so he divorced his wife, and dumped Patricia on Doc and Miz Alice to raise … again, back in times past. An' all I know is what I hear, so don't take it as gospel."

"I had no notion," Richard marveled. He knew Patricia Pryor by sight, of course. She was a habitué of the Café; on market days and special events, and also present with the Meats & BBQ food trailer, a fresh-looking matron in her mid-thirties, whose presence Richard had noted mostly because of her superficial resemblance to the late Princess Diana. A woman perfectly turned out on all occasions, even if it was making up BBQ sandwiches for the multitude, a woman with a heart-breakingly warm and lovely smile which never flagged. Yes, that was another reason that the likeness to Princess Diana drew Richard's attention. Except that Patricia Pryor generally looked happier – blindingly happy. "So ... how did you come to know all of this?"

"Got myself unofficially adopted by Doc and Miz Alice," Chris explained, with a suddenly bleak expression. He looked into his almost-empty glass. "Hit me with another, Berto. They talked ... they talked to me, when I was feeling blue. When I was in physical therapy and after I got medically discharged from the Navy. I believe they didn't know how much they were talking, how much they were saying, in between the lines. As much trouble as they had with their family ... with J.W. being killed and Collin being such an a**hole, it was still a thousand times better than what I came out from. You have no idea."

"Who is Miss Alice?" Richard held out his own glass, for a refill from Berto – obviously nominated as cup-bearer – poured another dose of the wonderful elixir from the gallon jug. Out beyond the RV, Joe Vaughn appeared. He looked back at the RV and quite obviously shook his head, before getting back into the cruiser.

"Miz Alice was Doc Wyler's wife. Died about four years ago. A lady. Of the best kind. She was also Miz Letty's best friend," Chris looked into the far distance. "It was their grandson who was my best buddy. J.W. Ellis."

"Doc's grandson," Richard recalled a certain brief mention. "A Marine ... killed out in Iraq, wasn't he?"

"Yep." Chris' jaw tightened. "IED. Happened like that – wham. One minute trundling along in convoy, talking shit with the guys – another minute, off on the side of the road, upside down, wondering what the hell.

It went off under the driver-side. I was in the front seat next to J.W. – he was driving … got real messed up myself. When I woke up for real, I was at BAMC – that's the big military hospital in San Antonio. Miz Letty, Miz Alice, they were there. They knew about me from J.W.'s letters – so they were there. Went on being there. Never let me go down, never let me feel sorry for myself."

"What about your family, then?" Richard asked, his natural incuriosity regarding other people's lives overcome with another sip of Sefton's wondrous elixir. "Didn't they … couldn't you have gone back to … wherever you were from?

"He don't have one, Ricardo," Berto explained, in a somber voice. "A family – I know, it seemed real hard for me to believe, at first."

"See, I'm from Detroit," Chris was slightly less tight-jawed. Over by Gunnison Penn's RV, the Luna City police cruiser started up, but instead of Joe driving away, he circled around, and parked by the Airstream. Chris continued, "My birth mom was an addict, she's dead, the guy everyone said was my dad was doing forty to life in the Federal pen. I was raised by my grandmother for a piece, and then into the system. You know – foster care. The last foster family, they were decent folk. I was with them four years. Foster dad, he'd been in the Navy, once; he told me I could make something of myself in the military, get the hell out of Detroit, anyway. So, they signed the paperwork for me, soon as I was old enough."

"Chris was a medic," Berto confided. "That's almost a doctor … Hi, Joe." He added as Joe Vaughn extracted himself from the cruiser. "Now, Joe was a policeman in the Army."

"And then I really got crazy and went to Ranger school," Joe drawled, looming over them all. "Evening, gentle-grunts all. Looks like a party, guys – why wasn't I invited?"

"We thought you Army troops were all on duty," Chris replied.

Joe looked around and then at his watch. "As of twenty minutes ago, I'm not. Chris, man, they tell me you are going to go all out for marathons.

You need to start working out and more than just running – strength training, too. I saw your car and thought I'd come over and tell you while it's fresh in my mind. We got some Nautilus machines in the back room at the cop shop – sort of a mini-gym. I can set it up so that you can come over in off-hours and work out."

"That would be great, Joe," Chris answered, warmly. "Save me the drive to the Y in Karnesville."

"No problem, Squid. Hey, is that some of Sefton's home-brew?"

"Yeah," Bert replied, opening up another chair, into which Joe sank with a faintly stifled groan. "Sefton brought him two whole jugs."

"Conniving Limey bastard," Joe said. "I only rate one at a time … you must have something on him. Thanks, Berto. The crime really must be epic."

"Sure, Joe." Unbidden, Berto fetched another glass from the trailer, and the four of them sat silent, letting the peace and mellow calm of excellent homemade mustang grape elixir smooth the rough edges off of existence and a long day of work. The sun, an orb of burning gold, dropped farther towards the horizon, and Joe ventured, "So what it is it, Rich – what do you have on Sefton?"

"Nothing really," Richard was feeling even more mellow than before. "Not a crime at all. It's just I caught him fogging the campground with insecticide over the last few nights and I promised not to tell Judy. It's not a bribe," he added, with small indignation. "Merely a token of his esteem, in appreciation for my silence and discretion. That's all."

Chris was laughing and began coughing as some of his wine went down the wrong way, when Berto said, completely in earnest, "She really wears the pants, doesn't Miz Grant? That's what Papi says. I've always wondered how she can make him do what she says."

"So noted, by the man whose' aged Gran has the rest of the clan jumping through hoops, at her express command," Richard observed. "It must be some exotic form witchcraft."

"Yeah, sure it is," Joe drawled. The wine had seemingly already fast-tracked his own mellowing, or perhaps Sefton's grapes had a very special witchcraft of their own. "There isn't a mystery about it at all, just plain old feminine wiles."

"Feminine wiles?" Berto asked, completely baffled. "Miz Grant? She's as old as my mother – older, even." Chris was still laughing and coughing.

Joe sighed in exasperation. "Look, sport, she wasn't always the age she is now. Years and gravity, you know. Happens to us all, believe it or not. Hit me again, Berto – easy; this stuff is for sipping and relishing, not chugalugging like it was Kool-Aid. See," he continued, when Berto had refreshed all their glasses with a discreet top-up. "Along about the summer that I was eight, nine, maybe – me and some buddies of mine came out here, on the other side of the river, opposite from here. They used to call that bit of river 'Hippy Hollow' for understandable reasons. This would have been round about 1980, 81' maybe. We were kids, you know, and curious. We hid in the bushes, opposite and watched Judy Grant and her girlfriends swimming."

"I can see girls swimming in the gym pool at Palo Alto any time," Berto was unimpressed and Joe regarded him with exasperation. "What was so great about that?"

"They were skinny-dipping, Berto. Swimming without any bathing suits on at all. Naked as jaybirds." Joe sighed, in reminiscent awe. "And she was magnificent … gorgeous … sexy like you wouldn't believe. I swear, my eyes were bugging out of my head like Tweety-Birds'. Mind you, I was only nine at the time, and had about as much clue about girls as your average nine-year-old. Less, maybe. But I swore then, that when I grew up, I wanted me one of those, just like her. I also had to sleep on my back for about a month for dreaming of her …" Joe added in a much more prosaic voice. "And I will swear to you right here, in all the porn tapes and dirty magazine centerfolds that are, or that I have ever seen, there was nothing so downright sexy as that memory of seeing Miz Grant skinny-dipping in Hippy Hollow. So, I can appreciate how she can have had Sefton dancing to her tune, all these years."

They all four were silent, either in reminiscence, or in consideration of a mental image of Judy Grant – or a twenty-five-year younger version of her – skinny-dipping in the river. Finally, Berto shook his head. "I just can't see it," he admitted at last.

Chris shrugged, "I can ... sort of." They contemplated the sunset, now spreading gold and apricot across the western horizon. Berto silently topped up the glasses again. "I've seen a picture of Miz Letty, when she was young," Chris said, finally. "When she was in the Red Cross, in World War Two. I gotta say – she was a babe in her day. Sharp as a tack, but this little bit of a teasing look, in her smile. Must be something about a woman in uniform to me; so prim and businesslike, don't-you-dare- whisper-a-naughty world to me, or I'll snip off your balls with one hand but you just know that once you'd skin them out of that issue kit, you'd have a tiger on your hands. An insatiable tiger-goddess; I wonder if Miss Letty was ever that, with the right man?"

Joe shuddered, "Look, Squid – this is my kindergarten teacher you are talking about. I'd just as soon that we not go there."

"You brought up the subject first," Chris pointed out, with perfect truth and they all watched the sunset for another few moments, each with their own thoughts on the subject, until Chris sighed again. "Women – can't live with, can't live without. Now Rich – that Miz Wyatt, over at Mills Farm – she'd be your tiger, given half a chance. And Jess Abernathy is one damn fine woman in the same way."

"Thank you, Captain Obvious," Richard answered, with a shudder. "I'd give a miss to the experience, odd as it might seem to the ladies who have previously shared my bed or my life or even a portion thereof. Show me the bound issues of any lad's magazine for the last ten years and I'd be able to point out every centerfold model and Page Three girl who flung themselves at me – for free. It's been a principle of mine ever since not to sleep with anyone crazier than I am."

"No brag? For real centerfolds? Did they come without the staple through their navel, or did you have to pull it yourself?" Chris asked with understandable skepticism.

Joe scowled. "Drop it about Jess, Squid. One warning, and one only."

"Tough guy-Army Ranger," Chris jeered. "You gonna make me? I hang with Marines, pal."

"A cream-puff Squid medic," Joe replied, not moving a muscle. "Hell, it's not worth it. I might break a fingernail, pounding your ass to the floor!"

"Cousin Kate likes you," Berto suggested to Richard in earnest, completely oblivious to the emotional landmines he was treading heavily upon. "Maybe you should date her."

"Alas," Richard said, "Miss Heisel is altogether too fine a woman altogether to be stuck with a bastard like me. "

"She is a nice woman," Berto agreed, and added in an undertone, as Chris and Joe continued with the service-oriented insults, "Yeah, I think it's time for supper now. Chris and Joe get real cranky when they get hungry."

"Do they get like this often?" Richard asked, as they dished up four generous bowls of rich, pepper-red venison stew, and Berto shrugged.

"All of the time … it's a service thing, so Sylvester says. But have a stranger come in and start talking trash, they'd all gang up on him."

When Richard and Berto, each carrying two bowls, came out of the Airstream, the trash-talking had moved on from inter-service personal abuse into general lamentations.

"I swear," Joe was saying. "Jungle … desert … desert and f**king barren mountains! Why the hell can't we ever invade someplace with a nice climate and women who aren't all covered in black curtains?"

"Like Europe – why can't we invade someplace nice like Europe?" Chris lamented, "Just for the variety, man!"

Richard set down a bowl of stew on the patio table and snapped, "You Yank bastards trashed it last time. Then to add insult to injury – you seduced a bunch of our women with Hershey bars and nylon stockings and bragged for seventy years afterwards about how we'd all have been speaking German otherwise!"

"If you can do it, it ain't bragging, princess." Joe riposted, and his tone changed entirely as Richard set down the tinfoil-wrapped stack of tortillas. "Hey, thanks, Richard – is this your own recipe?"

"No, Berto's Gran sent it over," Richard answered. "She was worried that I wasn't eating enough."

"God love her," Joe spoke through a mouthful of folded tortilla and chili scooped up in it. "Women – ya gotta love 'em, young and old. Where would we be without them?"

"Getting drunk in the dark," Chris said. "Hey, pass me some of those tortillas, man – or are you gonna hog them all to yourself."

And Richard sat back with his own bowl, listening to Joe and Chris banter with each other, as Berto passed out a handful of spoons. He watched the last bit of the sun spread a thread-line of gold along the horizon, and thought of how enjoyable it was, eating and drinking with friends, men who liked him – for a much better, yet still inexplicable reason other than transient celebrity.

* * *

In the midst of the breakfast rush that following morning, Richard thought he heard a dreadfully familiar voice, slightly raised over the pleasant buzz of conversation in the dining room. He peeked around the door from the kitchen. Yes, there was Xavier Gunnison Penn, wearing a slightly different but no less ghastly Hawaiian shirt, and standing over Doc Wyler, in a posture which suggested the former was being confrontational with the latter.

But Doc Wyler's own attitude suggested that he was more than equal in a set-too with a man half his age and twice his weight. Richard could hear him very clearly.

"If it's a matter of concern to you, Penn," the elderly veterinarian snapped, "Take it up with Chief Vaughn directly – but I suggest you verify for yourself his work schedule before you do. For the record, we don't give a damn how you do it in Canada, and they'll be hosting the Icecapades in Hades before <u>we'll </u>give a damn about a two-fisted Texas lawman having a drink with friends, any time of the day or night – or in uniform. Good morning to you, sir!"

Your Mission, Should You Accept It

"I might have to take you up on your kind invitation of hospitality very soon," Richard said morosely to Chris, late one afternoon at the VFW. It was visitors' evening, and the place was still relatively uncrowded. Mid-summer was at hand, and the Age of Aquarius Campground had filled almost to overflowing with the reunited members of the old commune. "Between the ongoing nightly drum-circle, and visitors constantly tapping at my door asking for this or that, and that obnoxious Canadian treasure-hunter Gunnison Penn yammering on and on about his latest test-pit and trying to recruit me into pulling a commando raid dig on Mills Farm on account of us both being British by birth and Commonwealth citizens, I hardly get a wink of sleep – God, that wanker is the worst kind of snob. How you Yanks can think that Canadians are the politest people in the world … it's a snare and delusion of the most malignant kind."

"You're more than welcome," Chris replied, shrugging. "I had trouble getting used to the country, because it was so damn quiet. I missed the sounds of sirens, gunshots, and fenders crunching."

"It's dark, usually," Richard continued. "I got used to that – seeing the stars, all clear of a night … Venus in the morning, clear and bright by the moon. The only moon I've seen lately is sagging old hippy bum."

"My sympathies," Chris murmured, nodding towards Sylvester Gonzalez who had just come in out of the harsh afternoon sunshine.

Sylvester was one of the bookish Gonzaleses, a lean and quiet young man in his late twenties, who cultivated a sort of retro-nerd look in wearing a pair of heavy-rimmed Buddy Holly-style glasses, button-down short-sleeve shirts and skinny ties. Sylvester nodded back and went to the pool table. He was followed by Benny Cordova, as usual drifting in as silent as a ghost. "Hey, Benny, man! How's show-biz?"

"Crazy," Benny answered. He joined them at the bar, shaking his head somberly. "Just a beer, Chris. They're supposed to start shooting next week, if they keep to schedule. The director himself flew in just this morning, on a private helicopter, no less. I don't recall the last time I took such a deep dislike of someone, just by shaking hands. And the star? You know – Cal Fenwick? Meeting him was enough to make me want to sponge myself off all over, with about a quart of hand sanitizer. And I used to be a fan of his, too, but the guy has gone way downhill. I can't wait until this movie stuff is all over and done with. I've got a bad, bad feeling about all of it now."

"Same here," Richard agreed with a lugubrious sigh. "This whole movie project has a definite pong … no, it stinks to high heaven, and I'd be saying so even if Pip Noel-Barrett wasn't involved."

"Funny you should say that," Benny regarded his beer bottle with a thoughtful expression. "That's the exact same thing as I've been thinking now." Almost inconsequentially, he added, "Anyone like to take a look at the shooting script? That script might explain a hell of a lot."

"Why? Did you get a look? Could you get ahold of one?" Richard's interest was piqued – not the least over why Benny had suddenly soured on Phillip Noel-Barrett's movie project.

"No can do," Benny drawled. "Tightly controlled items ... numbered, signed for individually and secured under lock and key. I'm not on the need-to-know distribution list. But Miz Wyatt has a copy. Board of directors and an investor; VPI has its privileges, after all." Benny directed a significant look at the wall, over Chris' head. "I had a look at a few pages of it. Not hard, cultivating the ability to read stuff when it's upside down. Required corporate survival skill. You ought to figure out a way to get a better look at Miz Wyatt's copy – the whole thing. And then do what you think best."

"Man, I thought you were all about company loyalty," Chris spoke, after a long silence.

Richard said, "What exactly is it that got up your nose, Benny? What did you see in that script?"

"I can't be specific, Ricardo," Benny replied, with carefully-selected words, and his countenance – usually reflecting professional good cheer – was somber. He considered for another moment, before addressing Chris' question. "Company loyalty – it's a give and take. I've been the GM for Mills Farm for eight, nine years, now. Best job I've ever had. Guess you can say that I love the place. My folks out there – they're like family. If something happened ... a huge, flaming corporate disaster with the result that VPI decides to close Mills Farm, you know how many people would be out of a job? I do. I sign their paychecks, every two weeks. You think many of them are going to be employed again soon, if they lose their jobs? In this economy – you gotta be kidding me."

"You're saying this movie will be such a massive stinker that having anything to do with it might sink Mills Farm?" Chris shook his head. "There are people in Luna City who wouldn't mind that at all."

"Clearly, I can see that," Benny agreed with a nod, still uncharacteristically grim of expression. "But if Mills Farm goes down, Luna City will feel the pain. This movie project is a stinker – not a single doubt of that in my local-level corporate management mind. We have a commonality of interests in preventing Mills Farm and VPI from committing a self-inflicted public relations disaster."

"Exactly how big a sh*t-storm will this blasted movie create?" Richard asked as a matter of self-preservation. He had survived several in his time and did not wish to participate, however peripherally, in another. But anything which could get Phillip Noel-Barrett out of Luna City would be all to the good.

"So enormous, that it is not measurable with current technology," Benny was examining the wall over their heads again. He spoke with a voice of absolute certainty. "Miz Wyatt is staying in the little pink guest cottage, round the other side of the Mills Farm Dance Hall – that's where her office is. You gotta know that Mills Farm security has cameras pretty much covering all the public areas, and the grounds between buildings. Figure out a way to fox security, and you're home free. I can't be seen to cover for you too obviously, but I'll do what I can."

"We'd welcome suggestions as to timing," Chris drew out another beer for himself and after due consideration, one more for Sylvester, who came drifting over from the pool table, as soon as Chris caught his eye and beckoned. Benny seemed to be conducting a detailed survey of the wall above their heads. Sylvester silently took a seat several stools away, as length along the bar went.

"This Saturday night, there's going to be an all-hands launch party at the Dance Hall," Benny explained. "A kind of meet and greet, for the out-of-town crew, the cast, and all the local folks involved. Lotsa people drifting in and out. Miz Wyatt, couple of investors, a VPI VIP or two, maybe. Lotsa alcohol and food, a live band. Best time? Maybe at the shank end of the evening. As for the rest, I'll leave it all up to you."

"We'll keep you posted," Chris lifted his own beer in a toast and salute.

Benny grinned, customary good cheer restored. "No, I'd rather you not. Plausible deniability; If you flub the mission, I was never part of this conversation."

"Got it," Chris replied. "This tape will self-destruct in three minutes."

"Good luck," Benny swallowed the last of his beer, and set the bottle on the bar with a small but definite clink of glass against tin countertop. "See you Saturday ... or not, depending on good luck. Ricardo," he fixed Richard with a particularly speculative gaze, "You know, Miz Wyatt has the hots for ya, in a not-wholesome way. If you choose to exploit that weakness, be a gentleman, 'kay? She might be a real PITA, in some ways – but she's an OK boss. Or at least, not near as rotten as some, in my experience. That's all I'm gonna say. An' now I'm gonna go, so that I won't have to testify later about what I heard, should this all go south and law enforcement have to become involved."

"Appreciate the consideration, dear chap," Richard sketched a brief bow. "I will be the complete gentleman; I assure you most sincerely on that account." Benny departed silently, still grinning, although how a man in cowboy boots could ghost though a room with a creaky wooden floor was a mystery beyond anyone's ken.

With a brief gesture, Chris summoned Sylvester even closer, to join the knot of conspiracy at that end of the bar. "OK, Comm-expert; you've been listening to all of this. What's your plan for foxing the Mills Farm security system?"

"You're gonna love it," Sylvester replied, a mad grin spreading across his face. Richard sighed. The manner in which this was shaping up, it appeared that his manly virtue was going to be sacrificed to the voracious appetite of the woman whom Chris had described as a 'bunny boiler.' His ticket for the crazy train seemed to be already punched...

Directive to Local Hires and Extras

Please report on time to the makeup and costume trailer on the date and time you have been assigned. The current list of names and scheduled days/times are attached. Please be aware that due to unforeseen circumstances, this schedule will in all likelihood be revised and amended. It will be your responsibility to keep up with these changes.

You are required to park your automobile outside the main gate of the Wyler Exotic Game Ranch. There will be a regular shuttle van operating between the gate and the production site.

All extras as well as local hires are required to turn in their cellphones, and IPad tablets which have a photo or video- recording capacity at the production security kiosk, which will be located at the gate of the Wyler Exotic Game Ranch. There will be no exceptions, save for drivers of the shuttle buses.

Those hired locally as extras or for small speaking parts are strictly forbidden to approach, speak to, or make eye contact with Ms. Butler, Mr. Fenwick, Mr. Sepulveda, any of the named cast members, Mr. Lydecker or Mr. Noel-Barrett, or any of the production staff. No exceptions.

Mills Farm, Inc. – Owned by VP, Intl.

With Catlike Tread...

"It's a wild party, isn't it?" Chris asked, late on Saturday evening, a week later.

"That it is, old chum," Richard answered. This was a rare moment he had to himself, late in the evening of an event that he had not wanted to have anything to do with in the first place – even with an open bar and a full buffet of food that he had not prepared himself.

The get-to-know-each-other party was in full swing in the Mills Farm Dance Hall – a barn-like structure which had been disassembled, stick by stick, from its original location in the Hill Country, where it had served the needs of an isolated community of German-Texans for nearly a hundred years before being purchased entire by the eagle-eyed acquisitions agent for VPI. Now, reconstructed on the edge of a low plateau, overlooking the gardens, grounds, and golf course of Mills Farm, it was a low, sturdy building, weathered to a pleasant grey color by decades of Texas sunshine, lighted during daylight hours by long horizontal windows along the sides. In the dance hall's original form, the windows had been covered only by window screens, and long shutters, which when raised had formed a kind of continuous awning. Now, in the interests of year-round comfort of guests, the original openings were glazed, the whole structure cunningly insulated and air-conditioned. There was a low stage and the necessary facilities at one end, a generous bar at the other, and a deck outside, on which in temperate weather, those gathering for events at Mills Farm were encouraged to spill. For intemperate weather, there were misters, and tall metal heaters.

But on this particular evening, there was no need of them – the gathering was firmly contained in the loving embrace of the dance hall, with the out-of-town talent meeting and mingling – in varying degrees of comity – with those local experts who would be adding so much of their expertise to what had been represented as a serious and well-budgeted exploration of a stirring event in Texas history. Yes, Clovis Walcott was very much in favor of that; he was the movie's biggest local booster. There he was, in the middle of a genial circle of his reenactor friends and some of the money men, investors from Houston. And one man who Richard would have sworn looked more like a scrawny, odoriferous derelict, fresh from a blackout-drinking session in a squat under the nearest overpass. Clovis Walcott kept looking at that man with a vaguely disbelieving expression on his own face.

"Who on earth is that?" Richard asked quietly of Chris. "That grotty-looking specimen talking to Clovis Walcott."

Chris replied in the same tone, "Don't you recognize him? That's Cal Fenwick. He's the star, supposedly. He's playing Sam Houston."

"You have got to be kidding me," Richard couldn't help recalling Araceli's flash-forward history lesson, in the Café kitchen over five pans of sweet rolls. "Sam Houston was what at the time – forty, strapping and vigorous – all right, he drank like a fish, so I suppose that is accurate enough. Costume, stage makeup and careful lighting can only go so far, they can't work miracles. No wonder Clovis looks like he's having second thoughts."

"Wouldn't surprise me none," Chris said. "I've got to be a bit of a history buff myself. I asked one of the Hollywood guys – he said he was a script doctor, or something – which books they had read up on, in a way of doing research. You know – historians. There are some darned fine books out there, and I wanted to know which ones they had based the script on."

"So what did he say?"

"He kind of looked sideways and told me that they had done original research – which didn't surprise me none, as practically every soldier at San Jacinto wrote a memoir about it all, later. So I asked – well, whose original account? And he hemmed and hawed and basically gave a lot of BS." Chris shook his head. "Yeah, I'm beginning to agree with Benny – there is something real sketchy about this whole movie thing."

Yes … Indeed. Richard's gaze wandered across the crowd, skipping with a repressed shudder over Phillip Noel-Barrett, over Susannah Wyatt with an accompanying cringe … and lighting on the director of this benighted movie with a feeling that slugs had just been crawling over his bare skin. M. A. Lydecker was the toast of the Motion Picture Academy and a hyper-demanding auteur director – mostly of elegant suspense thrillers – right up until a badly-mistimed stunt crash involving a car and truck chase killed a stunt-driver, an assistant cameraman, a pair of unbilled bit-players, and the star of the movie in a single horrific fireball. Since then, while M. A. Lydecker still had a career as a director, it was a given that mainstream audiences bolted for the exits at the multiplex before the professional film critics finished penning their glowing encomiums. *(Even if the movie – sorry, the film – in question even opened in a multiplex in the first place.)*

He was a tall, cadaverous man, long-jawed and with a high forehead, over which fell a fringe of unnaturally black hair. In fact, less the bolts in his neck and a certain unattractive smirk on his lips, M. A. Lydecker bore a decided resemblance to the movie version of Frankenstein's Monster. The talk in the Café among the Lunaites who followed this kind of thing was that M.A. Lydecker was aching to regain that lost movie-going audience by directing this movie project of Noel-Barrett's.

Richard had his doubts, although up until now he assumed those doubts were based on his own well-established animus regarding Phillip Noel-Barrett. Now there were additional reason to prejudice him in the matter: Beatriz and Blanca were replenishing the buffet and assisting guests tonight, and Phillip Noel-Barrett was lavishing his usual smarmy charm upon them. Well, Granny Adeliza Gonzalez had better not catch any wind of this; she knew people with earth-movers and cement trucks, and Richard would bet anything that the body would never be found, even by a law enforcement agent as dedicated and suspicious as Joe Vaughn.

Richard hoped that he himself would never come under the dedicated and professional regard of Joe Vaugh, six-foot something tall, and every inch as hard-muscled as cold-forged iron. Just the sight of Joe, white felt Stetson tilted forward above mirrored sunglasses, and a ghastly death-dealing military tattoo showing below the short sleeve of his tan uniform shirt was enough to turn most people to jelly – even if the off-duty Joe was a friend and fellow aficionado of Sefton Grant's marvelous mustang grape elixir. The terrifying prospect of the official Joe certainly worked on speeders along Rte. 123 – another excellent reason for Richard to stick to his bicycle and scrounging rides from responsible drivers.

Now the hands of the vintage clock *(or maybe an only vintage-appearing-clock)* on the section of wall over the bar – were creeping towards 11:30. Zero Hour, as the plotters had all agreed on, would be at the shank end of the evening. Richard didn't think that any of them had the stamina to last until dawn, which had been his experience of serious party-going. The success of their whole enterprise now waited upon him and on the double-loaded drinks that Chris had managed to send Susannah

Wyatt's way, while misting Richard's own drinks with a light sprinkle of gin. No, he was as sober as a judge, or near to it, whereas Susannah Wyatt was becoming more agreeably sloshed and commensurably more amorous with every quarter-hour marked off by the clock. It all depended on seizing the moment. The moment was coming upon them … now.

Sylvester Gonzalez was standing by in his current guise as a guest, lurking within close range of Richard. They had all agreed on that; he could not make this party as a waiter or pot-walloper, although it would have been easy enough to accomplish, with Benny Cordova's tacit influence. Sylvester simply had to have the freedom of movement allowed to a guest at the party. Richard didn't grasp exactly how this had been wrangled. Likely it involved something to do with the Gonzales/Gonzalez clan and Sylvester's widely-acclaimed talent at anything to do with computer and electronics skills. With Chris tied to the Dance Hall bar as a relief bartender, someone would have to be free to escort Richard to the pink guest cottage and do … do whatever had to be done.

Richard hoped profoundly that the necessary didn't involve anything indecent, although given the manner in which Susannah Wyatt had been pounding down the drinks anything was possible. He just hoped that it wasn't actionable, or that her condition didn't inspire any other guest at the party into a fit of chivalry. Without a sound – not especially surprising, considering the noise-level in the dance hall, Benny Cordova appeared at his elbow. Richard was becoming accustomed to this. They exchanged a nod, and Benny fixed his gaze on the back-bar shelves, as if he were mentally running an inventory.

"Getting late in the day," he said. "I don't think the party is going to run much longer, at least for some."

"Not for me," Richard answered, ostensibly yawning for extra effect. "I was up at the crack of dawn, opening the Café in time for the breakfast crowd."

"Know the feeling," Benny still had his eye on the back-bar. "That bit of a computer virus in our system kept the security guys really jumping for a couple of hours. They earned their pay, no sh*t. But they tell me the system will be back on-line, soon – if it isn't already."

Benny kept an admirable poker-face, considering that he had been the one who installed the virus, delivered on a thumb-drive provided by Sylvester, guaranteed to be untraceable and to essentially dissolve itself in twenty-four hours. In the meantime, it had thrown Mills Farm's security and information tech expert into paroxysms of panic. This was part of the plan – a distraction, as it were – chaff, thrown out to confound, confuse and distract Mills Farm security. After a moment Benny transferred his consideration from the back-bar to the gathering. "Miz Wyatt is looking a little the worse for wear, don't you think, Ricardo?"

"She seems extremely animated," Richard agreed. Susannah Wyatt was at the center of a small knot of men in dark suits, sparkling in a dark green evening gown sewn with pearls, sparkling crystals and sequins, which glittered with every restless movement. Somehow, he had grasped the essential wisdom that in her social appearances, Susannah Wyatt was one of those women who wanted to be the only woman in the room. "She does not ready to leave the party, yet, alas."

Benny winked, lowering his voice in a manner that only hinted at conspiracy. "One more double vodka and tonic ought to do it. When she starts laughing that way, she's about ten minutes from going nose-down into the drink, in a manner of speaking. Her glass is empty, Ricardo; show-time!"

Richard sighed; Chris – making a pretense of wiping the bar while making another pretense of not eavesdropping on the two of them – wordlessly set up another vodka and tonic, heavy on the vodka and practically nonexistent on the tonic. Richard exchanged a meaningful glance with Sylvester, who likewise had been making the same pretense.

With the fresh drink in his hand, Richard plunged into the crowd around the sparkling green evening gown, summoning every bit of theatrical chops that he possessed – knowing that however slight they might be considered next to Phillip Noel-Barrett, an English accent ruled them all as far as most Americans were concerned.

"My darling Susannah, I couldn't help seeing that your glass was empty … allow me!"

She beamed at him, in delighted surprise, drawling in that throaty and half-sozzled mezzo-soprano coo, "Rich, what a surprise! I didn't think you cared."

"The belle of the ball; how could I overlook your needs?'

"You have before, Rich," she pouted. Richard summoned up the powerful reserves of a practiced seducer, namely the sure and certain knowledge that the targeted candidate for it wishes, above all and anything, to believe in the seducer.

"I regret those unthinking actions, darling Susannah – you caught me by surprise, that is all. After a long and exhausting evening working the Walcott dinner party, I could barely think straight. There, here's your lovely drinky-poo. Just as you like it."

"Marvelous, simply marvelous!" she sank about a third of the glass. "What shall we do for a nightcap? Ohhh, I'm certain I can think of something!" Susannah Wyatt hiccupped, an involuntary reaction which seemed to take her by surprise. Since she had made her preference for subsequent male company completely clear, most of the gentlemanly circle around her took their cue and drifted away.

"I am certain of that," Richard mentally thought of anything else. Ah, yes; think of the rules for cricket. That ought to take his mind off whatever intimate plans Susannah Wyatt had for them both. Benny Cordova – *God, but the man was a lifesaver!* — now ghosted into the suddenly vacant space at their side.

"Miz Wyatt, are you OK? I think the party is winding down. Do you want Mr. Astor-Hall to walk you to your place?"

"More than anything!" Susannah Wyatt burbled. Richard thought she was going even more completely cross-eyed squiffy than before. *Oh, let Benny Cordova be correct!* With a motion which caught even him by surprise, Susannah Wyatt flung her arms about his neck. "I'm home, take me drunk, Rich!"

"Yeah, she's a goner," Benny confided in an undertone, as Susannah Wyatt sagged briefly and then seemed to recover herself. "If you will do the honors, Ricardo. Miz Wyatt, Mr. Astor-Hall is gonna take you to where you can get a good night's sleep. Remember, there's that meeting tomorrow morning. You're not fit enough to party any more, Miz Wyatt, and that's a fact."

"Oh, but I am!" Susannah Wyatt proclaimed. "I could go on for hours!"

"Yes, Miz Wyatt, surely you can," Benny summoned Sylvester with a barely-perceptible nod. "But you really ought to go and rest up for tomorrow. Mills Farm and VPI, we're all depending on you."

"Yes, you do – all you dear little people who keep Mills Farm all running ... running like a well-boiled machine!" Susannah Wyatt still submitted to Richard putting his arm around her waist and draping hers about his shoulders. "I will be generous to you, you know that I will ... Rich, have I told you how much I adored ... simply adored your show ... I had a reservation for the second night at Carême, don't you know? I was so diss ... siss ... diss ..."

"Well, so was I," Richard sighed. No, not a good memory, of how it all came crashing down, the opening night of his exclusive West End restaurant – with a mass food poisoning of his many celebrity guests. In fact, he retained no actual, personal, and first-hand remembrance of the epic disaster that was Carême's opening night and his own subsequent four day-long break with reality. But the video cellphone and news footage of the disaster was everywhere on the internet when he needed reminding.

"It never happened," Susannah Wyatt pouted. "The second night …"

Richard directed her staggering steps towards the side door of the dance hall, Sylvester a silent shadow at his elbow. Just as they reached the door, Sylvester reached inside his vintage sports-jacket, and kept his hand there for quite a while. At the edge of the terrace, where the limestone pavers glimmered in the moonlight, sketching a pretty winding path through the garden and out into a grove of pecan and oak trees, Sylvester caught Richard's eye and nodded.

"Phase two," he formed the words. "It's a go."

So, Sylvester's home-brew wireless video signal disrupter was working as planned. Richard was still a bit foggy on exactly how; Sylvester had patiently explained it to him, in words so technical that he might just as well have been speaking Chinese. Another layer of protection for them, just in case Mills Farm's IT team had managed to re-patch their security net.

The pink guest cottage where Susannah Wyatt lived for now was in a handkerchief-sized patch of garden all its own; a pretty little Victorian place with plenty of white-painted wooden lace, and a tiny covered front porch, just big enough for a pair of rocking chairs and a plant stand with a luxuriant Australian fern in it.

"'s locked," Susannah said, fretfully. She was already sagging against Richard.

"You have a key?" Richard kept a very tight rein on his exasperation. "Of course, you big silly – in m' bag."

A tiny evening-bag dangled from her wrist, beaded in the pattern of brilliant green and blue peacock feathers with matching bead fringe. Richard could have sworn it was just an outsized charm on a narrow beaded bracelet. He handled it to Sylvester, who fished out the key –

fortunately, it was all there was in the bag. Indeed, that was all there was room for.

"Who's that, Rich?" Susannah blinked suspiciously at Sylvester. "Ohh, a threesome! You're so naughty. It's what I love about you, you bad boy!"

"No," Richard repressed a shudder, even as Sylvester snickered. "He … Benny thought he should come and help me."

"'Zat's so nice of him," Susannah hiccupped again, wrapped both of her arms around Richard, and sagged, utterly senseless at last.

"About time," Richard said, as Sylvester closed the front door. "Can you get her feet? This is the office, I guess."

"The bedroom is through there," Sylvester, in true *Mission Impossible* form, had studied the ground plan of the cottages, available on the Mills Farm website, together with comprehensive tours of the amenities and decorations thereof in the interests of attracting moneyed vacationers. "I'd guess that the script is in her desk. If it's locked, I can pick it easily enough."

"You are a font of useful skills," Richard gasped, as he and Sylvester between them carried the limp and unconscious Susannah through the front room of the cottage – which had indeed been set up as a comfortable sitting area, with a small table and two chairs in one corner, and a computer console, office chair and filing cabinet in the other. Susannah's laptop computer sat in the desk, with a fairly substantial copier-printer-fax machine on top of the filing cabinet. All of the furniture and decorative accessories in the cottage ware substantial stuff, likely most of it vintage, or at least of a pretense to be vintage, attractively arranged to suggest the domestic aesthetic of the century before the last.

The master bedroom was furnished in the same quality, the bed made with crisp white sheets, and a duvet in a pale green cover folded back. Sylvester let go of Susannah's feet and pulled the covers down – as he did so, scooping up both of the wrapped gourmet chocolates laid on the pillows with his free hand.

"One, two three, and heave!" he whispered. Between them, they tossed her unceremoniously onto the sheet. The mattress and springs bounced under the sudden additional weight, and Susannah briefly roused long enough to cry, "Wheee!"

Richard slid off her rhinestone-spangled sandals and pulled the covers over her – now and at last, she was out like the proverbial light.

Sylvester ate one of the chocolates and offered the other to Richard. "Take the wrappers with us," he whispered. "DNA, you know."

"You are altogether too familiar with the thinking of criminals and detection," Richard whispered.

Sylvester whispered back, "Four years in the Corps, a hitch as a contractor, and a lotta watching the Investigation-Discovery Channel," He was now putting on a pair of vivid blue gloves, of the kind worn by people having to handle body fluids and other unsanitary materiel. "Hey, what are you doing?"

"Looking for a pen and some paper," Richard answered. "I just had an idea … don't you have a pair of those for me?"

"You're OK to be here, Ricardo – everyone knows about you and the Wyatt bunny boiler. Let me take pictures before we toss the place, so that we can put it all back together exactly as it was before."

It was not necessary for Sylvester to pick the lock, after all; the antique key was already in the center drawer. All Sylvester needed to do was open the drawer and there it was – a thick, three-ring binder, with a four-color illustration on the cover in the style of the finest classic pulp magazine covers.

"The working title is *The Road to San Jacinto* … but this says *Texians and Zombies*, all the way through," Sylvester whispered. He already sounded puzzled. This was nothing like what had been publicized for months regarding the movie project.

"Could be promising," Richard caught up a notepad and a pen, as Sylvester removed the thick wad of pages from within the binder. Richard perched on the nearest chair, as Sylvester loaded the printer with a full ream of paper and set the script on the top feed to copy, page by page.

"Is that going to take very long?"

"About 300 pages," Sylvester replied, as the copier commenced to humming and clunking, shooting through page, after page, after page, the original set into the upper receiver, the copy into the lower. "It'll take a bit. Glad you don't have to wait for me to photograph every page by hand? Then we have to police up this place, put everything back as it was. I'll call Chris as soon as we're done – he should be ready to close out the bar. And then we see what exactly this movie is really all about."

The cottage was a comfortable place – Richard could see why the B&B accommodations at Mills Farm commanded a high price. In his old life, he would have not given a second glance, accepting it only as his due. But the tiny Airstream – that was home now, friendly goats, demanding elderly nudists, and all. He wrote the note to be left on the bedside table in his best public-schooled hand.

My dearest Susannah – you are discomposed and not in anything like your usual clever and incisive mind on this occasion. I confess that I am a gentleman – and to take advantage of you in your current condition is not an act of which I am capable of with a clear conscience.

Adieu, good night, farewell, Your friend and admirer, Pip N-B

PS – we should never speak of this night again.

Just to ornament that, Richard added a scrawled heart with an arrow drawn through it at the bottom of the page. There – that ought to do it. Anything which sent confusion among the ranks of Mills Farm and Phillip Noel-Barrett's movie enterprise was all to the good.

When he came out from the bedroom – after leaving the note on the bedside table and turning off all but the small bedside light – Sylvester was replacing the original script into the binder.

"All right, Ricardo – these are the pictures of the office corner. We need to make certain that everything is back into place, exactly as we found it, then I'll call Chris."

Sylvester had even tucked the printed pages back into the wrapper from the ream of new copier paper. Richard appreciated a detail-oriented person. "Benny said that Miz Wyatt didn't much notice things like if the copier were low on paper. Always did notice if the bathroom vanity hadn't been polished to a new-issue shine … eh, command echelon has their priorities, ya know? We book now – at high speed. The door will lock itself after us."

And yes – it did so as they departed, trying to appear as if casually strolling in the direction of the gravel-paved parking lot behind the Dance Hall, lit with period street lights casting a series of irregular blobs of light. Under the nearest of them, Chris stood, with folded arms, leaning against the little red Honda coupe that was his ride.

"Got it," Sylvester said. "Everything left clean and ultra-sanitized. Tell Benny thanks – for God, country and Luna City, we salute you."
"A**-hole," Chris replied. "Get in – let's see what this is all about."

It was only a brief drive, out to Country Route 123 from the beautifully-graded spur which lead from that road to Mills Farm and from there, a short mile or two to the Tip-Top, the VFW, and the McAllister home, standing sentinel over the bridge that crossed the river. There was no light in the house, save for that at the back door, and another over the bottom of the stairway up the side of the old coach-house. Richard followed the other two up the narrow exterior staircase.

The tiny apartment over Miss Letty's carriage house was still several times larger than the Airstream, but every bit as tidy, comfortably set with solid old pieces of wooden furniture that looked as if they had been seconded from the main house. Richard often wondered if Conchita's cleaning service offered a discount to bachelors like himself.

Chris tossed his car keys into a brass dish on a stand by the door, saying, "Coffee OK with you guys? I have a feeling we'll be up for a while, reading this."

"Sure," Sylvester answered, stifling a yawn. He must be familiar with Chris' place. He knew where the light switches were and pulled a chair from the farther room to add to the pair at a narrow table which seemed to serve as a dining table and desk.

With a coffeepot beginning to gurgle in the tiny kitchen, and sending out a most tempting aroma, the three of them settled at the table. Chris opened the package of pages, and upon finishing the first page, handed it to Richard, who passed it on to Sylvester. The ensuing silence was broken only by the coffee pot seething, the rustle of pages, and an occasional interested comment.

"*Texians and Zombies* ... well, that could be interesting," Chris mused, after perusing the first. "Depends massively on the special effects, I guess, but it does seem to me that the zombie thing should be played out about now."

"Monkey see, monkey do," Sylvester shook his head. "Screw the movies, man; the really intense stuff is on-line multi-character gaming."

Another five minutes of paper-shuffling, with Richard sometimes interpreting the more arcane production short-hand for the other two.

"Hoooo, boy," Chris said, passing a page to Richard. "If my eyes aren't foolin' me, this scene is some hot interracial girl-on-girl action between Sam Houston's illegitimate lesbian daughter and Emily Morgan!"

"Soft focus, tasteful feminine nudity," Richard scanned the page. "What's not to like about that?"

More paper-shuffling; Chris got up to bring the coffee, a small beaker of milk and a handful of paper restaurant packets of sugar.

"So ... the anti-zombie serum is ... wait for this, guys ... concealed in a stone tomb in the crypt of the Alamo."

Sylvester cursed, very briefly and in Spanish, before returning to English. "Oh, man – you gotta be sh*tting me. Even Peewee Herman figured that out!"

"There isn't one at the Alamo?" Richard looked up from his page. "I thought all old churches had a crypt."

"Not the f**king Alamo, man!" Sylvester's voice was high-pitched with anguish. Richard considered several possible answers, rejected them all and kept silent.

"Easy, Marine," Chris said, soothingly. "We'll get through this. Power on and then we decide what to do."

Sylvester had several ideas on what he thought ought to be done immediately to M.A. Lydecker, to Phillip Noel-Barrett and whoever had written what he termed a 'rancid piece of cr*p'. He expounded on them at some length and in detail; most of which were painful, humiliating, permanently disfiguring, and contrary to the Geneva Convention.

"Keep your cool, Marine," Chris said, finally, when Sylvester took a deep breath and Richard put in, "It was one of Napoleon's maxims – never to let anger get above your chin."

"Napoleon didn't get sh*t on like this! Sam Houston an incompetent bumbling drunkard? Someone is gonna pay for this movie slander and pay big!" Sylvester replied, but seemed to take their admonitions for calm detachment to heart until they had got another hundred or so pages farther.

"Oh, man, Clovis is gonna about sh*t a brick the size of the bandstand when he sees this," Chris drew a long breath.

"May as well know the worst," Richard said, with a wary eye on Sylvester; game nerd and IT geek that he was, he probably contained unplumbed depths of fury, just waiting to be unleashed.

"The US Federal Army comes to the rescue of Sam Houston, who has been pictured throughout this as a drunken and incompetent buffoon … at San Jacinto."

"What the hell!"

That was about the most coherent statement they got out of Sylvester for some minutes. While he ranted in Spanish, Chris collected up the pages, making them into a neat stack. He and Richard exchanged a glance and an unspoken agreement to let Sylvester get it out of his system.

"I don't think there's anything to be gained in going on with this, tonight," Chris said in a low voice. "What Benny said is absolutely true – this will be disaster for Luna City, even if it turns out to be one of those cult classics they show at midnight and everyone acts along and that ain't no guarantee. If you think Sylvester is hopping-mad now, wait until Clovis and the Karnes County Rangers, and Doc Wyler get a load of this. When they find out how they got suckered into lending their support to a hack bit of exploitation, thinking it was a straight-up leaf from the history book, they're going to go nuclear."

"Damn straight, they will," Sylvester switched back into English. He was still ashen-pale with fury. "I know … you two didn't come from around here, but what this does to us, what this does to our history, man! Our people, our heroes, our places – exploited for some cheap-ass f*cking zombie movie! It can't stand! I wanna see this Lydecker POS vaporized. I wanna be able to clean up the rest of him with a paper towel and some Windex! I wanna …"

"Easy, Marine, I know," Chris was in his best soothing EMS-to-accident-victim manner. "You gotta cool the jets now. Firstly, Clovis and Doc Wyler will figure out something, as soon as they're in the picture, secondly …"

"I don't quite see how this will cause such a controversy," Richard ventured. "It's only a movie." Sylvester regarded him with renewed fury and horror, about to launch into another multi-fractured English, Spanish and military-language diatribe.

Chris interjected, "Look, Richard, it's like this. Suppose some big-name American movie director was to do a movie about ... about the Battle of Agincourt, and had a company of Spanish knights suddenly arrive and save the day for Henry V. Or have the Turkish fleet suddenly arrive, saving Queen Elizabeth I and Britain from the Spanish Armada. Or a battalion of American cavalry ride to the rescue of Wellington at Waterloo. Wouldn't you be pissed as hell?"

"I concede your point," Richard allowed. "And understand, totally. Count me in to whatever effort you are going to make, in throwing a spanner into the works of this production. But at this point, I am not at all certain what can be done to counter it. The contracts have all been signed; to judge from this document, at least three-quarters of it have already been shot. There's still the post-production, of course. Likely to be very extensive as well as expensive and by the way, I would purely love to see the White Cliffs of San Jacinto – but what can we really do?"

"We'll have men on that," Chris said, with a steely and meaningful look, as he gathered up the last pages. "Top. Men."

Sylvester shook his head. "I didn't think you knew all that stuff, Chris. Me – I am humbled."

"I read a lot," Chris replied. "So all this goes to Clovis and Doc, at first light. And then whatever happens, happens. And when the sh*t finishes falling, we don't know nothing. Agreed?"

"We do not know anything," Richard answered without hesitation, and Sylvester nodded, vigorously. "Yep. I have no idea what you're talking about and I never even laid eyes on this piece o' cr*p. Agreed."

A Dish Best Eaten Cold

Three days later, two men sat on the terrace of the Wyler home place, watching the sun slide down in the western sky, and the shadows lengthen across the formal garden below, and the green pastures beyond, where cows drifted idly hither and yon. A comfortably shabby set of rustic bentwood furniture contrasted rather oddly with the pillared splendors of the mansion built by Captain Herbert Wyler, in the first flush of his prosperity in the 1880s cattle markets. But they sat at the exact best place to watch the sun go down on the Wyler Exotic Game Ranch, and on the distant trees and church spires of Luna City, and so it was one of Doc Wyler's favorite places, even in the heat of a Texas mid-summer. The temporary headquarters for filming extensive location shots was also within view, a prospect in the farthest meadow, and now regarded by both men with extreme distaste.

"Good of you to drop everything, and hustle all the way from Houston," Doc Wyler said at last. The pages of the script lay on the table between them.

"You said it was an emergency in the note," Clovis Walcott replied, as grim as a stone face on Mount Rushmore. "By God, so it is. I'd like to smash that miss-representing little weasel into a bloody pulp with my bare hands. We got taken, Doc. And taken bad."

"That we did, Colonel – that we did. They told us what we wanted to hear, like any good convincing conman does." Doc Wyler sounded much the calmer of the two, although the half-consumed mint julep at his side may have had something to do with his air of relative equanimity. "The thing is now … what are we gonna do about it?"

"My lawyer's going to hear from me – first thing in the morning, if not by voicemail tonight," Clovis sounded as if he were grinding his teeth. "And my banker, as well. I invested in this travesty and I was near as dammit about to make it a bigger investment, on account of what those bastards said. I wouldn't have touched this travesty with a ten-foot-pole, no matter how sweet they talked. As it stands in this script, this movie will be a disaster, all the way around. I wonder if my lawyer can make a case for fraud?"

"Ah, but there was nothing in writing about the plot itself, was there?" Doc Wyler sipped meditatively at his julep. "All a verbal understanding between honorable men doing business together on a handshake understanding … sharp practice, Colonel. It'll be the death of this world. A man's word used to be a bond. I've always said 'trust but verify,' but when it turns out that you can't trust 'em after all…"

"Thought that was Ronnie Reagan who said that," Clovis Walcott sounded as if his own barely touched julep had just begun to mellow the edges of his fury.

"Yeah, he did, but he stole that line from me," Doc Wyler replied. "As I was saying; if it turns out to be that you can't verify, and don't trust … and that you have been, in fact, lied to in the most infamous fashion – what do you do then?"

"Destroy them," Clovis Walcott looked out upon where the temporary film headquarters had been set up; tents and generators, with tall lights on stilts, and elaborate RVs. Filming was set to begin in earnest on the outdoor scenes the following morning. "Destroy them, root and branch. Sue them into such oblivion that their grandchildren are still paying into the end of this century. I roped the Karnes Company into participating in this, on my word alone! I'll never be able to lift up my head in Texas reenactor organizations again, if this movie shows in any venue but a midnight cable freak-fest and even then, I know there'll be words spoken! It's my good name – my reputation on the line, every bit as much as the Karnes Company Rangers."

"Destroy them … what, with a lawyer, brandishing a brief and a court order?" Doc Wyler chuckled. "They'll use it as publicity, and then where will you and your history enthusiast friends be? Oh, yes, I agree with the overall aim, but not the immediate means. Look, son; they'll be done with the last filming before your lawyer can even draft the first cease-and-desist order. Time … time is against us in a legal sense, but not the opportunity for sabotage." Doc Wyler sank another third of his mint julep and regarded the distant movie camp with the same calculating, squint-eyed expression with which his grandfather *(had he but known)* regarded such obstacles in his path as Union Army foragers, Comanche raiders, cross-border Mexican cattle rustlers, and various Kansas rivers in flood-stage. "Suppose … just suppose, you tell your Karnes Company reenactor pals about the dirty trick that's been played on you … has been played on them all. Emphasis upon 'them all.'"

"I'm not sure that I follow," Clovis Walcott ventured, and Doc Wyler's gaze returned as if from a long-distance journey to the movie camp.

"No? The scene they are to film in a week, if this schedule is to be believed, is the climactic scene. The one that they gathered all of your reenactor folks to film, in wide-screen and thrilling detail, from every perceptible angle, including a very expensive helicopter and a tall bucket-truck or two. If I have been reading this script aright … it's the make or break for the whole production in a whole lotta ways. Now, between the two of us, we have a considerable force at our disposal, which, if we deploy them effectively, might damage this production beyond recall, and leave us with relatively clean hands. What say you to that, Colonel?"

"What can we do?" Clovis replied. "And who have we got? Who knows about the contents of this document?"

"A varied collection of volunteers," Doc Wyler replied, briskly. "You have your reenactors, of course. As for who has seen this script, besides you and I? Chris from the Tip-Top and Jaimie's boy, Sylvester – he was a Marine, too – like J.W. Richard from the Café. And Benny Cordova, who was the one who put them wise to it. Those last two, I'd rather leave on the sidelines, keep their hands clean; Benny especially. But we can count on Chris and Sylvester – boots on the ground as it were. Chris'll be one of the movie crew as the on-scene medic. Sylvester has got himself hired on to help with communications. I believe that your folks, though, have the very best opportunity to wreck the shoot of that big battle scene."

"I'll take those I can trust into my confidence," Clovis nodded. "We'll come up with something, my word on it."

"And if you could find a creative use for a couple of pints of methylene blue," Doc Wyler scratched his chin most thoughtfully. "I b'lieve I can lay hands on some in a day or two."

"Why, and what does it do?" Clovis Walcott looked doubtful at first, but a broad grin crept across his countenance, as Doc Wyler explained. "My hat is off to you, sir! I know just how this might be used to good effect. Confusion to our enemies, Doc." He lifted his julep glass and drank from it, looking happier than he had since reading the script.

"To confusion, humiliation, and pain." Doc Wyler lifted his own glass, and added, "It's an established fact, Colonel – old age, guile, and treachery will always beat out youth, speed and a handy lawyer."

Berto's Star

Berto Gonzales, on his summer break from college, congratulated himself again on how Uncle Tony had gotten the transportation concession for the movie production, and given Berto a special assignment. Driving a celebrity at last! Truth to tell, he had driven Richard many times, and Richard might have once been a celebrity of the first order, but now he was just the prickly Anglo-English guy who ran the Café, so in Berto's mind – that didn't quite count.

"Be polite, helpful ... and above all, keep your mouth shut!" Uncle Tony had briefed Berto many times, and yet once again with stern emphasis this last time. "Ya wanna act as if you have been there before, OK? No talking to the client unnecessarily, no asking for their autograph – don't be so classless as to do that. They're working people, in the main hard-working people. All they wanna do is get to their next job in peace and quiet. Ya wanna be one with the furniture, 'kay? Unless and until they invite ya not to be … then be discreet. That's the key to this business – and never, ever talk to a member of the media."

"Not even Kate?" Berto asked, in some confusion. Kate – Cousin Kate? Yeah, she did work for the *Weekly Beacon*, and had that blog and all, but Kate, who had been his babysitter when he was just a small child?

"Nah, Kate's a good kid, she knows that is what. But anyone else, Berto – poison. Say hello, and goodbye, and move on."

"Miss Butler – I am her designated driver? Is there a reason for that?" Berto asked, and Uncle Tony smiled. "Yeah, I know that you would wonder about that, but Lucy says that she is a good kid, smart, too. You look at where all those other kid-actors in the system have gone an' made a mess of their lives? Your aunt reads the entertainment magazines and never read anything bad about Miss Butler. She is one of those sensible ones, an' her people are looking out for her – the odds of it all, hey? So, you gotta pick up at the #3 guest cottage at Mills Farm, tomorrow morning at six sharp. Miss Butler has to be in makeup not later than half- past. She'll call you, when she needs you during the rest of the day, so stick close."

"Right," Berto agreed hastily, and spend the remainder of the day making certain that the town car was immaculate. Uncle Tony had his full fleet out for the length of this production, all six cars dedicated to transporting the various stars, the director and producer. Driving between Mills Farm, where all the out-of-towners were staying, and the various locations – most of them somewhere on the vast acres of the Wyler ranch – was to Berto, a huge improvement on driving in San Antonio. And he could live at home, too.

At five minutes to six – "If you're on time, you're late!" was Uncle Tony's mantra, or one of them, anyway – Berto pulled up in the graveled area in front of the guest cottage; this was the smallest of the dozen small Victorian or Craftsman-style houses star-scattered throughout the beautifully landscaped grounds and gardens. Most were vintage structures moved from their previous locations; attractive places, but usually too small to be considered renovation materiel by previous owners.

Berto knocked on the door; to the young woman who opened it, he said, bashfully, "I'm here to drive Miss Butler to the set for today's shooting – I'm a bit early. If you could tell her, I'll wait in the car until she's ready."

"Oh, I'm ready now," the young woman said, with a brilliant smile. "I'm Amy Butler – let me get my books."

Berto blinked, utterly confounded. She was a rather ordinary, yet brainy-looking girl; straight dark hair pulled back in a careless pony-tail, and serious glasses, kind of plain, right up until the moment she smiled.

"You are?" he ventured. "Are you sure?"

"Well, that's what Mom and Dad always told me," Amy Butler answered, dryly. She scooped up a full armload of books; the top one, which Berto could see was Charles Darwin's *Origin of Species*. The next down looked like a chemistry textbook. "What's your name?"

"Berto. Alberto Gonzales – Berto for short."

"Nice to meet you, Berto," Amy stuck out her right hand and shook Berto's with a firm and almost masculine grip. "Mine's really Marigold. Mom was having a counter-culture moment when she named me. Marigold Amy Yasbeck – Butler is Mom's maiden name. Let's get this show on the road, eh?"

"Of course," Berto fumbled with the passenger door. "You gotta lot of books there…"

"Yeah," Amy slid in, cradling the books in her arm. "I'm starting at Cal Tech in the fall, and I really need to bone up on chemistry."

"Cal Tech?" Berto was so utterly boggled at this bit of information that he totally forgot Uncle Tony's advice to be one with the furniture and not make unnecessary conversation. "Wow, that's unexpected. I thought you'd be more into … I dunno, theater arts, or something."

"Yeah, well, sometimes you just have to step back and do something different."

"That's different, all right," Berto agreed. "I'm a student, myself. Structural engineering is what I'm aiming for, but I'm doing all the lower-div classes at Palo Alto in San Antonio. Nothing like Cal Tech. Wow ... I guess you're pretty smart, huh? Top in all your classes, I guess."

"Home-schooled," Amy Butler replied. "Mom and Dad are really fanatical about education – and staying out of trouble. So you're a college man, yourself? That's fantastic; is that why you're driving cars? For tuition money?"

"Yeah," Berto confessed. "My folks are fanatical, too."

Amy giggled – she had a particularly musical giggle. "My brother Mark and I – that's why Mom and Dad let us get a SAG card and took us to tryouts. So that we would have a nice college education fund. This job alone is going to fund my freshman year. It's an unutterably schlocky movie, but like the man said, 'I didn't see the movie, but I saw the house that it paid for, and that was magnificent!'"

"Yeah, sometimes work is like that," Berto agreed. *Schlocky movie?* He wondered – but everyone who talked about it seemed to think it was going to be something serious and high-class. But he put those doubts aside, utterly charmed to realize that while Amy Butler might be a celebrity and a movie star and all, she was also smart and down-to-earth; a perfectly ordinary girl, delightfully curious about Luna City and everything else. By the time he delivered her to the range of RVs and trailers which housed the temporary facilities of Six-Foot-Deep Films, and they had exchanged cellphone numbers, it seemed like they were already good friends.

The 1922 Luna Savings & Loan Bank Robbery

There are three official historical markers in Town Square, much cherished by local citizens. The most noted is the one marking the site where Old Charley Mills was nearly lynched by infuriated citizens, which action was forestalled by the timely intervention of somewhat less-infuriated and more clear-thinking individuals, who included Doc Wyler's father, Albert Wyler and his younger brother Thomas Wyler, the Reverend Calvin Rowbottom, then senior minister of the Luna City First Methodist Church, and a handful of others whose irreproachable respectability was of such a degree that they were able with reason and persuasion, to turn their fellow citizens aside from such an irrevocable action. The second official historical marker is set into the wall of the building now housing Luna Café and Coffee and marks the site of the last officially noted personal gunfight on the streets of Luna City in 1919; this being a duel between Don Antonio Gonzales and Eusebio Garcia Maldonado. The only casualties were the radiator of Don Antonio's Model-A sedan, a city street-light and a mule hitched to a wagon parked farther down the square felled by a wild shot from Eusebio's revolver.

The third historical marker is set into the red brick and neo-classical style exterior wall of the what was once the Luna City Savings & Loan, but now houses city offices and the Chamber of Commerce. The Savings & Loan was a casualty of the Depression, closing its doors in 1933; since then, most Lunaites must do their bank business in Karnesville, but in the evanescently prosperous decade of the 1920s, it was a temple of the local economy. It even looked rather like a temple, a smaller mirror of the Luna City consolidated public school across Town Square. In January, 1922, that magnificent neo-classical façade concealed a weakness: the bank's massive safe was an older model, and vulnerable to a form of safe-cracking which was the forte of the quartet of bank- and railroad-robbing Newton brothers, of Uvalde, Texas. The mastermind of the gang, brother

Willis Newton had procured a list of banks with old safes from a corrupt insurance official, and methodically worked their way through it. None of their bank heists were particularly notable for the size of the haul but they regularly cleaned out everything of value from a targeted bank, including small change and the contents of safe deposit boxes, striking early *(usually in the middle of the night)* and often, and making a clean getaway as well. In other words, the Newton boys and their safe-cracking expert, Brentwood "Brent" Glasscock, practiced bank robbery assembly-line fashion. Regular and successful looting of small-town banks amounted to more in the aggregate over a long period than an occasional spectacular and more dangerous raid against a bigger target.

But Luna City proved to be more than a match for the Newton boys, through a couple of fortunate circumstances. The first was that the local telephone exchange had just that very week been relocated to new premises. The second was that Albert Wyler and a number of fellow ranch owners and cattlemen from across Karnes County were having a post-New-Years get-together at the Cattleman Hotel, a get-together involving much marathon yarn-telling and a certain amount of well-disguised alcohol consumption.

Although Karnes County was by tradition and practice not completely 'dry', at this time the United States labored under the burden of the Volstead Act, which likely only inconvenienced casual social drinkers … including Albert Wyler and his friends, some of whom – like Albert himself – had also been volunteer Rough Riders with Teddy Roosevelt's cavalry company twenty-five years before. Luna City was, after all, the home town of Charles Everett Mills, bootlegger extraordinaire. Sometime around two in the morning, Albert Wyler excused himself from the gathering in the Cattleman Hotel's second-floor small salon and smoking room, pleading a call of nature and retiring to the room which he had taken for the night, for convenience, rather than returning in the early morning hours to the Wyler main house, which was a mere two miles from the

Cattleman. Little did he expect the good fortune that would come from this circumstance. Even as Albert Wyler made his excuses to his fellows, receiving a certain amount of ribald teasing in response, Willis Newton was silently shimmying up the side of the building which had formerly housed the telephone exchange, and cutting what he assumed was the main line, thus rendering the whole of Luna City unable to communicate to the outside world … or even from telephone to telephone within city limits.

Unbeknown to Willis Newton, he had gone to the wrong building to sever the telephone wire, and during his brief absence from the gathering of cattlemen, Albert Wyler stepped out on the second-floor gallery for a breath of fresh air. Before rejoining his fellows, he looked down into the shadowed square, faintly illuminated by the streetlights of the time, and noticed a large Studebaker automobile, with headlamps dimmed, idling in the street before the Savings and Loan. Albert noted this initially with mild curiosity and then with growing concern. Automobiles were not uncommon in Luna City at that date; however, ownership of one was sufficiently rare so as to render each easily recognizable to a knowledgeable resident of the area. And Albert did not recognize the Studebaker at all. In those few moments, the conviction was formed in his mind – as he so related later – that there was nothing good going on, what with a strange automobile, its engine running in the street in front of the Luna City Savings and Loan. Indeed, this was the customary stratagem of the Newton gang; small town, dead of night in the middle of winter, fast and powerful automobile for a quick getaway.

So firm was Albert's instant conviction of this, that he hurried back to the gathering, exclaiming, "Fellows, grab your irons – I think there's a gang about to rob the bank!"

At that very instant and as if to add emphasis to Albert's words, Brent Glasscock blew the door of the massive safe, using a combination of nitroglycerine forced into the slight gap between the safe door and the safe itself, and setting it off with dynamite caps. The explosion was massive; not only did it open the safe, it also blew out the front door of the bank, every glass window along the front façade and rattled windows all along the square. It also wakened every resident – and there were more of them in that day than this – who lived over a shop on Town Square, including Charles Abernathy, of Abernathy Hardware. *(The father of Hiram Abernathy, grandfather of Martin and great-grandfather of Jess.)*

Charles also looked down from the second-floor window of the building which housed his enterprise and his family. Being closer to the Savings and Loan, he had an even better view, or would have, if he were not so near-sighted as to require thick eyeglasses. But he could see the Studebaker and the blurred forms of the robbers, even as three of the gang dashed back into the bank to grab what they could from the blown safe. Charles Abernathy caught up his father's lever-action Winchester shotgun which had ever been the Abernathy's first choice when it came to protect their home, business, and high-value stock, and blasted away.

Two of the Newton gang stood fast, with their own weapons and blasted back, not with any particular effect other than wakening everyone who had not been wakened by the explosion in the Savings & Loan. Albert Wyler and his friends were also doubling through Town Square from the front of the Cattleman Hotel, howling and whooping like banshees, and firing their own sidearms. That there were no human casualties in this encounter is doubtless due to several factors. The Newton boys, unlike a number of other robbery gangs of that and an earlier era, had a demonstrated reluctance to add murder charges to that of robbery, in the event that they were ever captured and brought to trial. They were scrupulous in that respect, preferring to menace, scoop and skedaddle; hence their preference for minimizing risk by robbing banks when no one was likely to be around. That they were not casualties themselves was due to a combination of Charles Abernathy's near-sightedness and the amount of alcohol consumed by Albert Wyler's companions.

Realizing that the element of surprise was lost, and the local citizenry were aroused, and perfectly willing to make a fight of it, the Newton gang prudently cut their losses and ran for safety, having only had time to empty out a small portion of the safe's contents. They fled with the Studebaker's engine roaring – waking up at last that small portion of Luna City which had managed to so far to sleep through the explosion and the subsequent exchange of gunfire. Law enforcement was alerted in a timely fashion, but fortune smiled belatedly on the Newton gang and they were able to shake off pursuit. It is a matter of record that they were somewhat shaken by their hairsbreadth escape in Luna City; their next recorded robbery of any substance took place in Toronto, Canada, the following year; as far away from Luna City as you could get, without departing the North American continent entirely.

There are still some obvious small chips and divots in the lower outside walls of the old building which housed the Savings and Loans, which are still pointed out to visitors – supposed to have been caused by one of Charles Abernathy's missed shots, on a chilly January early morning in 1922.

4th of July – Love and Rockets

The 4th of July in Luna City is celebrated in much the same manner as other holidays are; a parade around Town Square – just as there is at Christmas; the Might Fighting Moths band marches in the parade, of course, and later performing a concert of patriotic songs on the bandstand; a community picnic under the trees. In the evening there is a dance – music provided by various groups like *Los Maldonados* – and the evening finished out with everyone watching fireworks launched from the middle of Moth Field under the watchful eyes of volunteers from the Luna City Volunteer Fire Department. Children run around with sparklers, Martin Abernathy makes a short address, and solemnly reads the Declaration of Independence. Again, as at Christmas, many of the businesses lining Town Square remain open into the early evening.

This year, because of the movie being filmed out at the Wyler ranch, the Karnes Company Rangers Living History Association also made up a goodly part of the parade; marching as infantry soldiers of the Texas War for Independence, with six of their number as mounted scouts, and another six or seven pulling a small sturdy wagon with a replica six- pound iron cannon of the time mounted on it. They set up a small camp in a corner of Town Square and diverted those gathering for the celebrations by displaying many of their weapons and gear. One volunteer – Andy Pryor, who customarily wears a fringed leather hunting shirt and a cap made from the skin of a whole raccoon – enchanted many small boys by casting lead bullets in a patented bullet mold of the time, which has a little scissor-blade attachment which snips off the little sprue and pops out a perfectly round, bright silver-colored and still-warm bullet the size of a small marble. The boys all find this fascinating. Georg Stein also enthralls the small boys by dressing as a Comanche warrior, although one would have to go a very long way to find a man who physically less resembles a native Comanche Indian warrior than Georg Stein. His outfit – hide moccasins and leggings, a bright red blanket wrapped toga-fashion around him – is most marvelously authentic and entirely made by hand with authentic tools. He demonstrates chipping arrow points from flint and attaching them with sinew to straight shafts of willow to make arrows for hunting.

Six-Foot-Deep Films had originally scheduled filming to continue on Monday, the 4th of July. But there were so many local citizens who quite firmly and rightfully declined to participate that the producer and director conceded – although with a considerable lack of grace – that since they had been able to move ahead of schedule, they could yield on the matter of a day's holiday.

Berto called Amy with the good news, as soon as everyone was notified. "Hey, do you want to come with me to the 4th of July bash on Monday?" he asked. He could sense that brilliant smile, even over the phone.

"Sure, Berto!" she answered. "It sounds like fun – a parade, and kids with sparklers. I can hardly wait!"

"There'll be a dance, too," he promised. "I'm not all that good a dancer – but I'd love it if you danced with me at least once. And you can meet Abuelita, and my sister and her kids, and all. They're like normal people."

"You've been a great driver and good company," Amy said. "And I much prefer normal people, myself. Mega-A**hole creeps me out, and if Phillip Noel-Barrett tries to feel my behind one more time … ugh. He's my Dad's age, for Pete's sake!"

"He hasn't tried anything!" Berto was appalled. "I mean – you feel safe, working around those pervy creeps? Do you want me to to…?"

"Taken care of, Berto," Amy sounded quite unworried. "I've got my agent on speed-dial. She's all the dragon I need. One word from me, and there's a very expensive lawyer bringing up a sexual-harassment complaint, a nice splashy story about it in *Variety*, and me on TV, crying about the horror of it all on Oprah's shoulder."

"You know, Amy," Berto ventured. "If he is such a creep, why did your folks let you go off and do this movie?"

Amy sighed; he could hear <u>that</u> very clearly on the other end. "Well, they weren't keen, really. Mega-A**hole has got a bad reputation. But I <u>am</u> eighteen. You can join the Army at that age. A month in Texas with Mega-A**hole, Mr. Grabby, and the Witch in Pink Boots is a walk in the park by comparison and pays much, much more. For another, they'll be wrapping up shooting in time for the fall semester. And finally, I've got it in writing; no nudity. And absolutely no stunts. It's in my contract. Dad insisted. It'll be just another week for me, then."

"Well, darn!" Now it was Berto's turn to sigh. "I'm really gonna miss seeing you around."

"So will I, Berto." He thought she sounded quite sincere, but then she was an actress. "Let's not think about it. Let's just have a fantastic time on Monday."

"We will … we will." Berto promised solemnly.

Jess Abernathy sat, watching the dancers swirling across the dance floor as dusk fell in Town Square, thinking, *Honestly, the older the couple, the better they are at it. Of course, Pops and Johanna aren't any slouches, either, even if they aren't really old ... I wonder why she and Pops don't just get married – I wouldn't mind at all. At least Pops would have someone.* She watched them, with affection, while searching back in her own memory. Johanna – you can tell she was a ballet-dancer, even just waltzing with Pops. *Yep, Pops and Mom used to dance, until Mom got so sick. And when I was really little, I used to stand with my feet on Pops' feet, and he would dance me around the room like that. I danced with J.W. – at school, and then that one year at the Marine Ball. I haven't danced much since then – not the heart for it. And Joe is usually working. Look, there's Berto with a girl – must be a friend of his from college, she isn't from around here.*

Berto hadn't collected Amy in Uncle Tony's town car, because that would be wrong. This wasn't part of work, this was a private thing, and it would be unethical. Berto had a very strong sense of ethics, which had been inculcated in him by the combined efforts of his parents, his older sister, and most of all, Abuelita. He borrowed his father's aging pick-up truck – the one spotted with rust, a sprinkling of dents, and the bench seat in the cab tastefully patched with duct tape whose color was a distant match to the original upholstery color.

Berto, without a single devious bone in his body, considered it a waste of time and also mildly fraudulent to try and impress Amy by putting on a pretense. There was just no point, so why bother? He liked Amy too much to try and fool her. In any case, she was clever enough to see through most female-impressing stratagems. Of which Berto had little command, anyway.

Indeed, Amy laughed when she saw the truck and Berto handed her up into the seat. "That's such perfect casting for you, Berto! All you need for it is a gun rack and a couple of hounds in the back!"

She was also perfectly devoid of pretense, in jeans and a shabby tank-top with an oversized gauze shirt over it; no purse, as her keys and billfold were stuffed into her jeans pocket, and her hair was drawn back into her customary pony-tail. Berto said, "Papi's other truck has the gun rack – this is just the old beater for driving around town in."

"Don't change a thing about it," Amy giggled, her eyes as bright as if she was a small child being taken to Disney World. "It's perfect. I am so looking forward to this! There was this lovely quaint old book about the history of Luna City on the shelves in the cottage. A bunch of old books – I bet they put them there for décor, but I read that one, front to back. My goodness, I would never have guessed about some of the things that went on here! The very last gunfight in Luna City and the almost-lynching! I could about die with trying not to laugh, every time I see Mr. Gonzales, all dressed up like Charley Mills, and I try and picture the scene! Did he really dress up like a nun, and that was why they tried to hang him?"

"Well, Abuelita said," Berto wracked his memory for what it was that he had overheard Abuelita Adeliza and one of the distant great-aunts talking about in the kitchen when he was about six years old. "That was because he was sweet on a teenage girl whose parents sent her to boarding school at St. Scholastica's in Karnesville to get her away from him, and he dressed up like a nun to try an' get next to her, but there was a lot of other stuff that he had done."

He amused Amy, with what he could remember of what the abuelitas had said about Old Charley Mills during the rest of the drive to town. He found a parking place on a side street, helped Amy down from the truck – yes, that was one of those charming and effective courtesies which he stored away among his meagre collection of strategies for impressing those of the opposite sex, and they wandered away, hand in hand, into the beating heart of downtown Luna City.

"I'll bet all my old pals are wondering why I have a date with a movie star," Berto ventured, at about mid-point in their evening.

Amy laughed. "I'm not being a movie star," she explained, with an air of indulgence. "I'm Marigold Amy Yasbeck, my very own self. I'm not 'on' – there's a difference."

"What are you, when you're 'on'?" Berto inquired, honestly puzzled. "It's when … oh, heck, Berto, it's easiest to show you. Hold these and watch."

They were passing the front of the Café. Because of the holiday, the Café had a special supper menu, and were doing a booming business in coffee, cold drinks, cookies iced in red, white and blue, and the ever-popular cinnamon rolls. There was a good crowd at the tables, inside and out. Amy pulled off the gauzy shirt and handed it to Berto, along with her glasses, and the elastic band from her pony-tail. She took a deep breath, ran her fingers through her hair, which instantly became a thick, glamorous mane and before Berto's very eyes, Amy transformed. Her posture and bearing changed. She appeared to glow from within, as she stalked into the Café like a panther on the prowl – lissome, dangerous and drawing every eye to her, as if she was suddenly the most luminously gorgeous and confident woman in the world. Berto could swear that conversation in the Café paused momentarily, as Amy asked for two coffees and two of those lovely frosted cookies. She came out of the Café in the same manner, her hands full. She handed Berto the cups and the cookies, took back her shirt and in the same unsettling manner of her transformation, put on her glasses, and bound up her hair.

"See?" she said, biting into a cookie with ravenous appetite. "That's 'on.'"

"Wow!" Berto exclaimed. "That was totally awesome. You wanna do it again?"

"Nope," Amy replied, completely her every-day Amy-self again. "Wears out the batteries. You know that guy in the Café? That's Rich Hall, the Bad Boy Chef. I'd know him anywhere. I did a show with him, once; he's a real dick-head."

"Yeah," Berto replied, as he took a bite out of his own cookie. "I know, but he's got over it, mostly."

* * *

Jess Abernathy sat on the same bench, taking a kind of melancholy comfort in the whole familiar, traditional event unfolding around her; mesquite-scented smoke rising like perfume from the cooker hitched to the back of the Pryor's Meats & BBQ food truck, the lights along the facades of Town Square, dusk falling as gentle as a transparent silk scarf falling overhead, the music of *Los Maldonados,* and the aspect of people dancing. *Los Maldonados* had added another trumpet-player, Jess noted with mild interest; Belle Walcott, all dressed in black trousers trimmed with silver buttons, a white shirt and a red sash around her waist. Belle looked quite unexpectedly happy, flushed pink with excitement and exertion. *Well, who would be going around like a little ray of merry sunshine, with Sook Walcott for a mom?* Jess thought. *The poor kid must be embarrassed to death on a regular basis, in a small place like Luna City.*

I wonder what it'd be like, living in a big place like Dallas? Anonymous, I expect. Walk down a street – no one knows you, you know no one, Jess mused. This place was a part of her, bone of her bone, flesh of her flesh; she relished the very familiarity of those people, so affectionate and dear, doing as she loved to see them do – living ordinary, quiet lives. Oh, that was Berto Gonzales, dancing bashfully with that dark-haired girl, who looked kind of like the movie star Amy Butler – but honestly, couldn't possibly be … this was Berto, after all.

Johanna Gonzales-Garcia was dancing with someone else – it looked from a distance like she had partnered with Georg Stein, unexpectedly suave and debonair for someone who had spent most of the day dressed up in a leather loincloth and leggings and red blanket, being a Comanche and demonstrating how to make arrows from flint, osier-shafts and vulture-feathers.

When Martin Abernathy sank down onto the bench next to Jess, she ventured, "Hi, Pops – grand evening, isn't it?"

"It is that, Jessy-belle," he replied, and Jess leaned against him, recalling again how she had put her feet on top of his – when she was a little girl, and Pops seemed to be the tallest and most darlingly-commanding man in the whole of the world. That was when they all lived in the little house, two blocks away from Town Square, and Mom fixed the dinner meal from recipes she found in some fancy home and garden magazines. Jess and Pops waltzed in the living room to the music of the radio, while Mom laughed.

A long time ago and in a country far, far away, for the past is a distant country, and floating ever farther out of reach, as a helium balloon drifts from the hand of a careless child, letting the string go. The past floats out of reach, farther and farther away. Jess sighed; now she was as tall as Pops, so it was a bit awkward, leaning against his shoulder, never mind dancing with him with her feet on top of his.

"You know, Pops," she ventured. "It would be OK with me if you married Johanna. Really. No skin off mine, at all. It would be a good thing for you both."

"Jessy-belle, darlin'," Martin sounded as if he were groaning. "It's not that simple – as if anyone could replace your Mom! We like each other fine, Jo and I, but we both know that marriage isn't in the cards. She's a citizen of the world; she's never be happy here in Luna City for long without wanting to pop over to France for an opera premiere, or to Japan to teach a master class. She's always lived large; me, I like it small. I'd never be happy anywhere else. I saw enough of the world when I was in the Navy. Besides, Jessy-belle," Martin now sounded tentative, as if he were not certain how – or even if – he should broach the subject. "You're a fine one to bring up the subject. What of you and Joe? You know, your grandmother was telling me just the other day how much she wants to see you two settle down, start a family even. Gran and Grumpy aren't getting any younger, you know. Neither are you and Joe. They'd like to see a couple of great-grandchildren sometime soon."

"I just don't think it's going to happen, Pops," Jess answered. "Or not any time soon."

"Why not?" Martin asked, very gently. "Joe's a good man – you two have been going out for … what, three, four years now? Ever since he had to quit the Army through wrecking his knee and came home. J.W.'s been gone for more than ten years, Jessy-belle … I'm certain that he wouldn't have wanted you to …"

"No, Pops," Jess replied, a hard edge of grief in her voice, although she appreciated the heck out of her father's sense of tactful euphemism instead of baldly pointing out that she and Joe regularly spent nights together at her place or his. "Don't tell me what J.W. would have wanted, or not wanted! This is between Joe and I."

"Jessy-belle, the two of you really ought to be ready to settle down. I'd been married to your Mom near ten years by the time she was the age you are now."

"It's different now, Pops," Jess said. "Joe might be ready to settle, but I'm just not certain that I am."

Martin sat quiet, waiting for her to say something more, but when she didn't, he ventured, "You just haven't said anything about that Dallas offer to Joe, have you?"

"We still got that father-daughter ESP thing going, haven't we, Pops?" Jess replied. "No, I'm just not certain at this point. It's a great opportunity, professionally, but I'd be in Dallas or Houston most of the time. I could still take care of clients like Doc, and the Grants by email, but I don't know how Joe would handle me being out of pocket for weeks as a time."

"Other people handle long-distance relationships," Martin pointed out.

"It's just complicated, Pops. It would mean either that … or Joe quits his job here. I can't ask him that. Everything in his life is here in Luna City. Now and again I wonder if maybe I'm leading him on, when he could have spent the time on someone else, and I feel guilty. I do love him, Pops, but I just can't seem to make up my own mind; follow my own star, and turn Joe aside from his … or give my own star up, for him."

"No easy answers, Jessy-bell," her father said, very gently. "I can't tell you what to do on this one, anyway."

On the bandstand, *Los Maldonados* finished their next-to-last dance number, to a happy round of applause from the dancers, under the swaying, moth-freckled strings of lights. "But I think you have to tell him and the rest of us soon about the Dallas job. That's all I'm gonna say … I gotta go and announce the last dance – the fireworks are a go in fifteen minutes."

"I just don't know, Pops," Jess answered. "I really haven't made up my mind. You gonna dance the last dance with Johanna?"

"Of course," Martin said, briskly. "And you gonna come back to Gran and Grumpy's for dessert after the fireworks? Bring Joe, of course – unless he is caught up processing some fool into jail for committing acts contrary to public order."

"I will, Pops," Jess watched her father, threading his way through the crowd, and up the steps to the grand old bandstand. At that moment, her eye fell upon the Luna City PD's cruiser, pulling in to a parking place opposite, marked off for official vehicles in full confidence of the driver's authority and freedom to do so. Joe Vaughn emerged, as immaculate in tan summer uniform as only he could achieve, after a long, hot mid-summer day spent keeping a merciless eye on crime, misdemeanors and excessive speed on Route 123. Jess frequently wondered how on earth he could do that – herself always being crumpled and sweaty after about forty minutes' exposure to the full fell blast of Texas mid-summer heat.

She watched as Joe crossed the square. He paused long enough to tip his white Stetson to the Pryors, and exchange a few remarks with Andy and Patricia, and the boys; dishing out the last couple of plates of BBQ and settling up the Pryors' Meats & BBQ food truck for the evening. And after that eagle-gaze scanning the crowd in the square, his eyes fell on her and the expression of his face lightened.

"Hey, Babe – last dance with me?" he drawled, when he was close enough to speak.

"Of course," she replied, and they went hand in hand to the paved area before the bandstand, already well crowded with couples; Berto and his dark-haired girlfriend, Patrick and Araceli, the Steins, Gran and Grumpy, Patricia and Andy Pryor, Doc Wyler partnering Patricia Gonzalez, Beatrice and Blanca – the battling Bs with a pair of bashful swains who most likely were Gonzalez cousins. Pops and Johanna … and so many other Lunaites; there was barely room to move very far in dancing – it would have been hazardous in the extreme to venture a tango. *Los Maldonados* launched into a slow-dance version of "Waltz Across Texas With You," which was the traditional last dance on these occasions. Jess stood close, her nose buried in Joe's uniform shirtfront, with the hard metal star-shape of his Luna City PD badge pressing against her cheek as they moved together in time to the music. Jess could sense

Joe singing along to the chorus.

"Waltz across Texas with you in my arms, Waltz across Texas with you … Like a storybook ending I'm lost in your charms, I could waltz across Texas with you …"

"Nope," she said to herself. *"I won't tell him about the Dallas offer, not just yet."*

The Perils of Jess

The long last day of the horse-pursuit filming day ended when the sun sank too low in the western sky to match easily the footage shot on previous days. M. A. Lydecker allowed as how he was content and drew a slashing pen-stroke down the length of the last page in his shooting script, and thanked Jess Abernathy for her work.

"This is the last day that we need you to double for Miss Butler," he said, after a word with his hovering production secretary. "All the rest of her scenes do not involve any actual riding."

"Can't say that I'll have a broken heart over that," Jess allowed. She was exhausted, sweaty and covered with dust; only in slightly better shape than the horse, after a miserable day in the full heat of a Texas summer, galloping over the rolling landscape of the Wyler ranch's largest pasture. And the horse wasn't even her own beloved Sweet-Pea. "I'll see you around, of course." She slithered down from the saddle, annoyed yet again over the long skirt that tangled around her legs. The horse trainer came to take away the stunt horse. Jess exchanged a nod to him, and a rub on the nose for the horse, saying, "Who's the good boy then? Whoo, whoo – I'm free! Mama Abernathy's little girl is free at last!"

"Lucky you," said the trainer. He and his horse were part of the out-of-town contingent. "I have another week or more of this douche. Ya know that they say his initials stand for, don't cha?"

"Mega-A**hole," Jess answered. It was about one of the first things that the out-of-town movie crew had passed on to her; the makeup technician, the hairdresser and the costumer who had all done her up on that first morning, to make her look like Amy Butler from a good distance. Every single one of them had told her. "Eh – he's not so bad in small doses, I guess."

"You're on a fast horse, running away from him," the trainer added, before leading his charge away. Jess laughed; yes, she was more than glad to be done with this. Honestly, not even a hard day of barrel-racing competition on Sweet-Pea was this much of a drain. She barely had the energy to divest herself of the long dark calico period dress and the petticoats underneath it before the wave of total exhaustion overtook her.

"You want I should give you a shampoo, get started washing out that temporary dye?" the hairdresser asked, as Jess wiped globs of cold cream from her face.

"No, I'll just shower at home," Jess replied. They had sponged temporary hair color onto her naturally sandy hair so that it better matched Amy Butler's dark brown locks. "How long will it take this stuff to fade, entirely?"

"Three or four shampoos, usually. Live dangerously as a brunette for another week or so, I'd say."

"Thanks." Jess regarded her face in the lighted mirror, trying to work up enough energy to resume her own clothing. Eventually, she managed that herculean task, recovered her cellphone from the lowly assistant who had charge of them for that day of shooting – Jess wondered if it wasn't assigned to whoever had drawn Mega-A**hole's wrath most particularly that morning. There was one of Tony Gonzalez's shuttles just making the run down to the Wyler ranch front gate. From there, she walked the short distance to her own little bare-bones Jeep Wrangler. Nope, she was glad to be done with her little bit towards making Luna City a movie legend.

On an impulse, she got out her cellphone and called her grandmother. "Gran? I'm done here for the day. It's nearly five, so I'm gonna go over to Joe's – we'll go out for hamburgers or something. Tell Pops not to wait up for me."

"Of course, dear," Sarah Abernathy replied. "Give Joe my best – and tell him that we'll expect him for Sunday dinner."

"I will, Gran."

Jess closed up the phone window on her cellphone; she considered stopping by the Wyler place to say hi to Doc and pass on what she had heard from the movie company bookkeeper, during the long break while they set up the camera for that aerial shot … but on reconsideration, no. She was just too tired. And Doc had something up his sleeve; he always did, when he got cagy.

Joe's place was a little 1920's cottage that his grandparents had lived in with Joe was growing up. It was on the near side of town to the Wyler place, surrounded by a neat green patch of lawn that Joe kept mown and raked with meticulous attention. Jess parked in back, to one side of the detached one-car garage and let herself in through the back door. Joe wasn't home yet – he wouldn't leave the office a minute before five. She dropped her handbag/briefcase on the nearest kitchen chair, shed her clothes in the bathroom and stepped into the shower-stall with the water on full-blast. When Joe moved into the old place, he had the bathroom modernized – a tiled shower with one of those enormous, tropical-rainstorm-falling-on-you showerheads. Oh, that was better. Much better. Of course, she kept bottles of her own shampoo and conditioner here

– toothpaste and her own toothbrush, as well. There were two white terrycloth robes hanging up in the bathroom, too.

When she heard the screen door fall closed with a clatter, and the sounds of his footsteps on the kitchen floor, she yelled, "Joe – I'm in the bathroom, trying to get his gunk out of my hair. You done for the day?"

"Yep," he replied, a distant voice as he moved through the rooms. "And you?"

"They've finished all the scenes where I doubled for Amy Butler, so I'm good. I think I've finally found the one thing more boring than a deployment exercise."

"Oh?" Now the bathroom door opened. Over the sound of the shower, she could hear the small and fabric-rustling sounds of him taking off his own clothes, hanging them up as neatly as she had not. "Babe, you know the laundry hamper is right over there."

"Too tired," she answered; Joe, the eternal neat-nick. All that Army training, of course.

"And my knees are giving me hell and I'm too damned tired to wait for you to finish – move over. Save water, shower with a friend."

Obediently, she moved aside from the stream of fast-gushing water. "Can you reach my conditioner? Thanks, sweetie. I thought we might go over to Karnesville for a hamburger later, if you wanted – but I'm just too tired."

"So'm I. Combo pizza warming in the oven, Babe. Fair enough?" "Bliss," Jess replied. She took the bottle of conditioner from him, squeezed out a spritz of it into her palm and began to rub it into her wet hair. In just a moment, Joe took that over, and she leaned her back against him. Solid; Joe was like that – elemental, as solid as a granite boulder, with the shower water raining down on them both. He was earth and water, whereas J. W. had been air and fire …

"Stay in – watch a movie, if we can both stay awake long enough. Hey, I like you as a brunette. Exotic, even if the drapes don't match the rug. How long will this stuff last?"

"About a week, maybe two, so make the most of it."

"You gotta love show business," Joe put his arms around her, and they stood close, waiting for the conditioner to rinse out of Jess's temporarily dark hair. "Today, I ticketed an excessively-speeding minivan full of zombie Mexican soldiers. And it won't be Halloween for months yet."

"Part of the chase sequence," she giggled. "They were late. It's all supposed to be some kind of dream, I guess. Or at least, that's what Mega-A**hole was saying, this morning."

"Zombie soldiers on zombie horses?" Joe sounded quizzical. "I'm not even sure how that would work. Dead flesh perambulatin' across the Texas prairie … how do the buzzards an' all manage with zombies? I mean, they're scavengers, even if the carrion is still twitching. Babe, I just don't think they thought this whole zombie dream-sequence thing was thought out very well."

"I wonder if they have thought any of it out very well," Jess stepped out of the shower, reaching for her robe and the nearest towel. "It just doesn't seem like an entirely serious kind of movie, Joe. Not the kind that Clovis Walcott and his people think it is. From what some of the extras and actors let drop, I wonder. Everyone knows there isn't a crypt under the Alamo, don't they?"

"If they don't, Clovis will put them straight," Joe turned off the water, and emerged from the shower. "And he's an investor as well."

"I hope so," Jess answered, wrapping a towel around her head. "Pizza, you said?"

"Your favorite," Joe replied. "Canadian bacon, sausage and mushroom, with olives and extra cheese on my side." He kissed her very briefly, no more than an affectionate brush of his lips on hers. "Try to stay awake long enough to appreciate my own culinary skills, 'k' Babe? I might not be Richard Astor-Hall, but I do my best with what I have."

"So you do," Jess answered, utterly content. "Still … it's odd."

They fell asleep together on the sofa in mid-evening, with the movie playing out unseen in front of them, and the pizza half-eaten on paper plates in their laps.

And so passed another evening in Luna City.

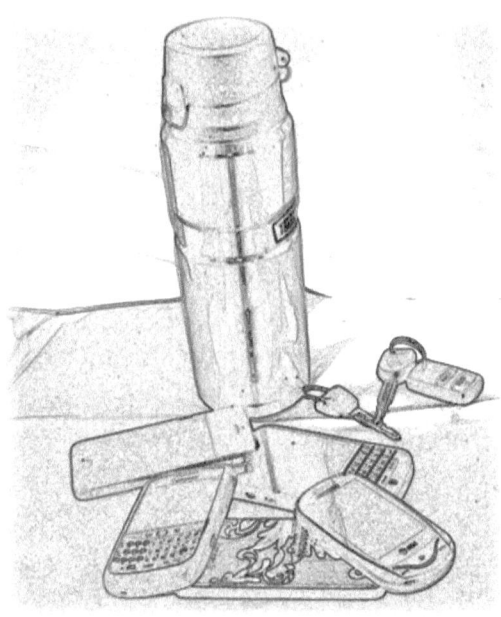

Errands and Diversions

Berto had the blues, when Amy departed for California and the fall term at Cal Tech, although she was assiduous about instant-messaging and calling. It was not the same as seeing her there, every day, and Berto was of the melancholy conviction that absence would not make the heart grow fonder; that their friendship was a brief and shining moment. Likely if she was as distracted by the coming academic year, then so was he – but at the moment, the last two weeks of filming *The Road to San Jacinto* filled most of his attention.

"OK, since Miss Butler is gone, I got you scheduled to drive one of the shuttle minivans," Uncle Tony handed him the set of keys, in the wee hours of early morning. It was still deeply dark, not even the slightest smidgeon of a hint of dawn on the eastern horizon, and the moon floated, a milk-white disc in the sky, attended by a bevy of stars. "Hey, I know   it don't have the cachet of being the personal driver, but it pays the same for the same hours. They're gonna do the big shoot today, so you're gonna be racking up the hours and miles. And don't let them take your cellphone – we gotta stay in touch. Keep on your toes, Berto. Hey, don't get down in the dumps over your Miss Amy girl, 'kay? Plenty of fish in the sea, ya know."

"Yeah, but only one of 'em I know can change in a minute to being the most beautiful girl in the world, and then back into your best friend in the next."

"Berto, *hijo* – when you love 'em that much and they love you back, they can do it in a heartbeat." Uncle Tony slapped Berto's shoulder affectionately. "Get cracking, hey? You gotta pick-up for extras at the Cattleman in fifteen minutes. Likely you'll be running back and forth for the next hour. There's another group staying at the Walcott's and one more at the Wyler place. The AD tells me they all have to be in costume and in position at 6:20 AM sharp."

"Where to I take them to?" Berto asked, rather relieved to have something to think about than Amy. California was two hours behind. Amy wouldn't be waking up for another five hours.

"Here," Uncle Tony passed a single-page map – obviously downloaded from Google-Earth – of the Wyler ranch. "They've got an assembly area set up for the reenactors, right where that big red X is drawn. What I'm told is they will go through costuming themselves, gather on point, and at a signal from the AD, assemble in battle-line and charge over this ridge." Uncle Tony shook his head, sadly. "*Hijo*, I gotta say that the potential for an epic cluster is enormous. They wanna catch the reenactors coming over the hill, with the sun just coming up in the sky behind them. They gonna set off explosives, fire off fireworks, and film all this through a dozen cameras, six ways from Sunday. They even got a helicopter crew standing by. Lydecker, man – he has a thing about explosions."

"Do or die," Berto nodded, and Uncle Tony grimaced.

"Hey, don't say that where Mega – where M. A. Lydecker can hear you. His lawyers only settled the last of the wrongful death lawsuits a coupla years ago. Fleet as the wind ... but keep an eye out for deer on the road. When you've collected the last load, stand by at the reenactor's location for further orders."

"Of course," Berto agreed, one eye on the clock.

The reenactor's rally-point was well-set up; only naturally, since Clovis Walcott and his reenactor organization had a substantial hand in it. Clovis was a retired Army Reserve engineer, and his compadres were all well-acquainted with setting up a temporary campsite in worlds both ancient and modern. There was one large pavilion, a bunch of horse trailers and some restless and annoyed horses moving around in a temporary corral. One single assistant director, who looked barely older than Berto himself – and armed with a walkie-talkie the size of a concrete brick – was being ignored, more or less, by the reenactors – both those delivered by Berto and the other assigned driver – one of Berto's Gonzalez cousins, who usually drove the wrecker truck for the garage.

On his second trip in, the assistant director came out to the van, as his passengers debarked. "Hey, you there. Can you stop by the commissary tent and bring me some coffee in this?" He held up a substantial thermos and allowed by way of excuse. "They're all out, here – or these pricks just won't let me fill up. Like – they say it's a membership thing, and I'm just not a paid-up member. That or they're getting pissy about Lydecker having everyone turn in their cell phones. Stupid redneck pricks ... I am so ready for this day – this whole shoot to be over."

Berto took the thermos and replied very politely that he would be glad to, on his next round, all the while thinking how cross and rude the assistant director sounded. Really, it seemed like Amy was the only real nice person among the whole lot of the Hollywood people. On the way out, he pulled in at the main location camp – a veritable wilderness of RVs and trailers, lighted by tall light standards on wheels, all orbiting around a large canvas pavilion, with generators already roaring away. That big pavilion was serving as an informal cafeteria, meeting area and theater for the review of what had been filmed every day. There was even a huge truck set up as a mobile production studio, a hulking beast the size of an 18-wheeler, with a padlocked door to secure all the most valuable camera gear and the footage already shot.

Berto parked the minivan next to it and ran towards the big pavilion; he had only a few minutes. There was no line at the table where trays of breakfast pastries and muffins, individual serving-boxes of cereal and a jug of milk were already laid out; his cousin Sylvester was just now replacing the lid on the top of the big coffee urn.

"Thought it wasn't perking just right," Sylvester said in an elaborately casual manner. Berto noticed that Sylvester had just taken up his own thermos from the table. "It's still not strong enough for me – they just now put it on."

"I'll catch it on my way back through," Berto said. "The assistant director out at the reenactor camp want some and wants it yesterday. Hey, this is going to be exciting today, isn't it?"

"You bet," Sylvester answered, and Berto wondered just why Sylvester had that peculiar quick grin on his face. "If you want good coffee for yourself, give a miss to this gack. I'll get mine from the Café, as soon as they open up and I'd advise you to do the same."

"I'm not a coffee in the morning person," Berto admitted, bashfully. "Grapefruit juice, or herb-tea. That's my vice and I'm sticking to it."

"Good," Sylvester replied, and Berto did wonder why he sounded so emphatic, as he drove into town. His second pick-up of the morning was at the Walcott house; a sprawling architectural monstrosity on the other side of town. He got there without nailing a grazing deer and ferried a dozen or fifteen reenactors back to the ranch site – Clovis and a number of his particular friends. Berto did wonder that if so many of them were gotten up in their 1836 garb already, then why did they all have such large bags with them. He did ask, and the one who seemed to have the most authority among them aside from Clovis, replied easily, "Spares. In case of them wanting to take a re-take."

Berto did wonder why the van-load of men chuckled in such a cynical and knowing manner. But all of that was not his business, he reminded himself – as Uncle Tony had so often advised – he was just there to drive, and not to concern himself with regard to the bigger picture.

"Sorry," he gasped, as he pulled in next to the big pavilion. "I gotta get some coffee for the AD out at your place. Won't be a moment."

"Take your time," drawled the big guy with a beard that made him look as if he belonged to some scruffy old-time hippy band. His name was Bill Weitzman; he taught history at Palo Alto, which is how Berto eventually recognized him. Most of the reenactor company boasted either beards, flamboyant mustaches or excessively ornamental sideburns. They were so serious about reenacting that most of them let them grow in real-time. Berto left the van running, though – with the air conditioner at full-blast, since the morning was proving to be uncomfortably muggy. He ran the thermos full of coffee, replacing the cap and top as he returned to the van. Just outside the pavilions' entrance, he spotted Clovis Walcott and Bill Weitzman talking with M.A. Lydecker. Or rather, they had him cornered and were talking at him, in low and furious voices.

"… one last chance," Berto heard Clovis Walcott say, clipped and curt. If he hadn't needed to go past them to get back to the van, Berto would have gone the other way, as he hated that kind of angry confrontation.

"This is not the time to be renegotiating!" M.A. Lydecker's voice sounded shrill. "If you stupid hicks didn't grasp the sense of what I am trying to do here, that is hardly my fault! No – you will come over the hill, exactly as instructed at the time you are given, in perfect period costume … as you are instructed, and in the manner to which you had previously agreed. I've no time for this … what do you want, you nincompoop!" he snarled at Berto.

"Coffee," Berto replied, rather hurt. "I was asked to get coffee for your assistant director."

"Then get it for him and get the hell out of my sight! And where the hell is Noel-Barrett! Anyone seen Noel-Barrett?" M.A. Lydecker shouldered past Berto, who at last concluded that M.A. Lydecker was not a really nice person, and chief among a whole lot of not really nice people.

"He's not a really nice person," Berto observed to Clovis Walcott, who replied, "What was your first clue? Well, then, the plan is on, I guess. Wish I could have talked sense into him," he added to the other reenactor as they followed Berto back to the minivan.

"There are certain men, Colonel," replied Bill Weitzman, "Who seem to have a sense-repelling field about them. That jack-wagon is definitely one."

Berto let the minivan out of 'park' and slowly drove away from the main encampment, hoping that he had not wasted too much time. In the back, Clovis Walcott said, in a firm voice meant to be heard all through the minivan, "All right fellows, it's a go. Pass the word."

What word? Berto wondered silently. As far as he knew, the whole order of what everyone called the money shot, had already been planned and marked out, rehearsed to the very step over the last few days.

At the reenactor camp, he handed over the thermos of coffee with relief, unloaded the dozen passengers and their gear – again wondering what it was they had all brought with them, in duffle-bags and grim pale green carry-alls, if all their gear was already here …

"To the Wyler place," the assistant director said, checking off a list on a clipboard, while relieving his inner man with a hearty slurp of coffee from the thermos in his other hand. "That's your last pick-up, it looks like. Hey, what's-your-name, remind everyone to turn off their cellphones –

and I mean it. The Big M.A. has standing orders, from 8:00 on. No distractions."

"If you see Doc Wyler," Clovis Walcott added, in an undertone to Berto, "Tell him that everything is going as planned. He'll know what I mean."

"Sure," Berto answered, totally baffled. But then, he reminded himself of what Uncle Tony said about what his job was; just drive people back and forth. Even when Clovis Walcott added, sotto voice, "It's always been a good military principle and one that I followed all of my service – know the names of those you command. Good advice for you, in your future career, Mr. Gonzales."

"Sure … Colonel," Berto replied, utterly baffled. But he did remember Clovis' additional cryptic message when he pulled up to the magnificent façade of the Wyler place. The guys he was to transport had so many extra bags that they had to be bungee-corded to the rack on top of the minivan. One of the reenactors produced a whole set of them, as Berto waited at the foot of the grand entrance to the Wyler Home Place. And Berto thought to himself – *Wow, these guys are really prepared!*

Doc Wyler was standing at the foot of the stairs – as the additional baggage was being secured to the top of the van, he came forward, saying, "Looks like everything is in train, Berto … "

"Yes," Berto replied. "Colonel Walcott said to tell you that everything is going as planned."

"Ah." Doc Wyler had an expression on his face that Berto could not quite fathom. "Good to know, then, Berto. Don't drink the coffee – take my advice; don't drink the coffee."

"I don't," Berto replied, entirely baffled, and Doc Wyler barked a short and completely menacing-sounding laugh. "Good for you, then – good for you. Let's get this show on the road, boy!"

Berto wondered to himself – *what was all that about, then?* It seemed that there was something going on, way above his head and even far above

Uncle Tony's pay-grade. He drove the van-load of reenactors the short distance to their camp. He was under the gun – or least the sunrise, which had already begun to pale the eastern horizon. Following Uncle Tony's instructions, he parked the minivan at the reenactor's camp to await further orders, rather regretting that he would miss the commanding view of the big scene … but he would see the reenactors forming up, with all their horses and their authentic gear, and that would be a sight for certain – Sam Houston's replica army on the march. Unless he missed it through being sent somewhere.

Electra Pee in Blue

About half-past seven, the phone in the Café kitchen rang, rang insistently. Richard, busy with warming up the vast griddle, upon which would be cooked bacon, sausage, pancakes and omelets to order, swore under his breath and picked up the receiver.

"Thank God!" It was Phillip Noel-Barrett, gasping. "At last, someone answered the phone! You've got to come let me out – I'm…"

"Arsehole!" Richard snapped and slammed the receiver down with considerably more force than required.

"Who was that?" Araceli demanded, arrested just short of the door with a breakfast order in one hand and the coffee carafe in the other.

"Your least-favorite customer in the whole world," Richard answered, as the phone rang again. "Who but Pip-Araceli-my-darling- Noel-Barrett? Yes?... Look, you inconsiderate prat, we're in the middle of the breakfast rush, and have no time for idiotic pranks!" He slammed it down again with even more force. Before Araceli returned, and the bacon Richard threw out on the griddle had even begun so go translucent around the edges, the phone rang again. "Go to hell!" Richard snarled into the receiver. Two minutes later – and there it began ringing again, insistent, shrill. Richard could feel his concentration beginning to fray. This kind of distraction put him off, jangled his nerves and made that little nerve under his left eyelid to begin twitching uncontrollably.

"I'll get it," Araceli set down the coffee carafe. "If you slam it down one more time, you'll break the phone and Jess will have a hard time justifying the expense of a replacement. Hello … yes, it's me … no, of course I won't hang up on you." A distant squawking sound emanated from the telephone. Araceli's tone of voice turned into that deliberately soothing one she adopted with fractious customers. "Can't open the door… locked in, you say? All right – now, calm down, Mr. Noel-Barrett. It's dark inside … oh, the camera and editing van. You say that no one is answering? I see. This was the only telephone number you could remember … the only one you could remember that anyone answers! Got it. Now, listen to me – calm down … Mr. Noel-Barrett, I do not appreciate that tone of voice! I'll see … I'll send someone out to the location. Yes, I promise. It's not all that far away. Look, you know that we're always busy in the mornings, so I have to hang up now. But if you call back … call every five minutes, I promise – I will pick up the phone. Don't worry, Mr. Noel-Barrett. Take a deep breath. Help is on the way."

She set down the receiver with exaggerated care, then picked it up and dialed again. She listened to it for a few minutes, and said, "OK – thanks. Not an emergency, we'll see what we can do here." She looked straight at Richard. "Chef, I think you might have to go out to where they are filming the movie. Your friend …"

"Pip Noel-Barrett is most definitely not my friend," Richard retorted. "And I don't care. Locked in a van or drowning at the bottom of a well. We have the morning rush on."

"Not so much that I can't handle myself," Araceli explained. "Everyone in town that is involved with that movie – they're working this morning, not having breakfast here. And no one is answering their phones. Mr. Noel-Barrett says that the director had everyone around the set-up turn off theirs, if they didn't hand them in. For security, he says – and because of distraction. I think you have to go. He doesn't sound in too good a shape, either. The electricity to the trailer got switched off, he's alone in the dark and says he's claustrophobic."

"What about the police?" Richard demanded. "Isn't this kind of thing the province of Chief Vaughn and his stalwart constables?"

"Normally, yes," Araceli said. "But Joe is out covering an accident situation, Milo is working security at Mills Farm, and all calls are being routed to the Karnes County sheriff's office in Karnesville. It's not a real emergency-emergency, so they couldn't possibly get here before noon. He sounded really shaken, Chef."

"He's an actor, of course he was playing on your sympathy," Richard answered, quite unmoved.

Araceli shook her head, "He's not that good an actor, Chef. Pat and I checked out some of his movies when this whole thing began. The man can't emote his way out of a wet paper bag. He's on the edge, for realsies, I am certain of it. Look – go and see what you can do. I'll manage here."

"Right," Richard accepted the inevitable with a sigh. As he wheeled out the trusty bike out onto the road, it occurred to him that it wasn't a dead loss as an opportunity, since it would allow him to torment Phillip Noel-Barrett – locked into the editing van of his own production. Oh, it would be delicious, and he could hardly wait.

As he pedaled up the winding road which led to the front gates of the Wyler ranch, the light paled to a delicate shade of oyster-shell, tinged with apricot.

* * *

Berto's first indication that something unusual – that something even more unusual than the movie shoot was going on – was when the young and rude assistant director emerged from the latrine trailer, grey-lipped with a face as pale as a ghost. He stumbled on the threshold.

Berto, waiting for his own turn, was naturally moved to ask, with concern. "Hey ... hey, guy – you all right?"

"No," the assistant director stammered. "No; I think I got something bad. I think I'm gonna die. My piss has turned blue."

"Wow!" Berto's eyes widened in astonishment. "That's horrible. I haven't ever heard of anything like that!"

"I have," Clovis Walcott materialized, as commanding in his reenactor gear as Sam Houston for the long shots as he was in his ordinary garb and doubtless had been as a Reserve Army officer. "In Korea; usually among smart young soldiers who had been sampling the bad stuff available in Itaewan. I'd advise you to seek medical attention immediately, son. The sooner the better..." And he outlined some of the possible side effects, including the possibility of a specifically male body- part rotting and falling off entirely. Berto was nauseous before Clovis was even halfway through, and the assistant director had gone from white to pale green and back to white again, even as he moaned, "But the shoot ... it's a million-dollar shoot, set to go in twenty-five minutes!" He brandished the brick-like walkie-talkie and Clovis Walcott continued in that firm, commanding voice, and Berto mentally blessed him. Clovis Walcott, like Uncle Tony, knew stuff, including what was best to do in any emergency.

"You get yourself seen to, son," Clovis replied. "Give me that walkie-talkie and I'll take the cue from that ... Lydecker. I know how to operate this unit, and by damn, I know how this thing is to play out. We'll get the great scene done, trust me. Leave it to me – just get yourself taken care of. You go with Berto, here; there's a qualified medic at the main site who can confirm my judgement, if you are in any doubt."

It all seemed to hang on a momentary decision; the assistant director hesitated, then handed over the brick-like walkie-talkie to Clovis Walcott. "Thank you," he said, about the first polite words from him that Berto had heard that morning. "I won't ask you to lie and cover for me, but don't blurt this out to Mr. Lydecker, if there is any way around it."

"Got your back," Clovis Walcott promised. The last that Berto saw of Colonel Walcott in the side-view mirror as the minivan bumped away, he had an expression of intense satisfaction on his face. Berto would have wondered why, if all heck hadn't been breaking loose at the main location tent. Fifteen distraught film production people awaited him there, men and women both, all looking pale, ill, and distressed. Cousin Sylvester and a couple of other people – obviously unaffected – hovered around, looking as if they wished there was something they could do. A single woman cried hysterically, waving her arms about. Chris and another woman attempted fruitlessly to restrain her, as Berto parked the minivan and cut the engine.

"There's nothing I can do for them, here," Chris said, over his shoulder to Berto, his face drawn with the strain of coping with this. "It's some kind of mass panic. Get 'em loaded into the van, take them to the emergency room at the Karnesville Med-center, as fast as you can go … ma'am, ma'am, please calm down…" To no effect; the woman wailed even louder. Suddenly, a man doubled over, vomiting.

"Aw, geez," Chris said, in resignation. "Couldn't you have used a bucket? OK, round 'em up, Berto … give us a hand. I'll call ahead, so they'll be expecting you." With cajoling and sometimes outright carrying the worst-affected, they got everyone loaded into the van, although it made a pretty tight fit.

"Oughtn't you to come, too?" Berto asked, uneasily, and Chris shook his head. "Can't – no room and I've got to stay on-scene here, anyway." He lowered his voice, adding, "There really ain't that much wrong with them, Berto. Just got over-agitated, 'cause most of them are peeing blue." "Them, too?" Berto stared at him, in horrified disbelief. "Here?"

"Yeah, here too," That was Cousin Sylvester, handing Berto the keys to the minivan. "Drive like the wind, cousin o'mine."

"Yeah," Berto said dubiously. But he held back on the accelerator until he got through the outskirts of Luna City, with his van-load of distressed, moaning humanity, to where he nearly ran someone on a bicycle off the road. No – never too fast in the streets of Luna City! He couldn't even pull over and apologize to the bicyclist. *Was it Richard?*

"Oh, man," Berto whispered to himself; yes, it was, and that was certainly an angry gesture flung in the direction of the rapidly-moving van. "I never run over anyone, before … 'specially not a friend!"

Just as he got past the turn-off for Mills Farm, the flashing red and blue police lights appeared in the rear-view mirror. His heart sank; better pull off to the side. His heart did an extra-double-deep sink when Joe Vaughn sauntered to the driver-side door. Berto rolled down the window, noting that Joe flinched when the smell of vomit and panic rolled out like a visible miasma.

"They're awful sick, Joe," he explained, over the agonized moaning and weeping. "From the movie set. Chris told me to take 'em all to the emergency room in Karnesville."

"You better just do that," Joe replied, looking faintly nauseated himself. "Can this crate of Tony's do eighty-five without a strong tail-wind?"

"Yeah, I guess," Berto said, somewhat dubiously.

"Then lock on to my rear bumper, Berto, and keep up. You got an escort all the way."

It was, thought Berto afterwards – totally exhilarating, if his passengers in the van hadn't been all so very unpleasantly and hysterically ill. He topped eighty-five easily, screaming into Karnesville with sirens before and another trailing, since Joe called in a patrol car from the Karnesville sheriff's department. It did nothing for the condition of his passengers, though, especially when he hooked a curb on a tight turn. But it was entirely gratifying, wheels squealing as he rocked the van to a stop under the awning over the emergency entrance at the Karnesville Medical Center. They were immediately converged on by nurses, orderlies and even doctors – with gurneys and wheel-chairs.

"Likely the most exciting thing to have happened here in months," Joe Vaughn remarked, as the last of the suffering movie people vanished into the depths behind the swinging glass doors. "You OK, Berto?"

"Joe, it was horrible," Berto confessed. "Really horrible. There was this one woman, screaming that she didn't want to die … an' then they were being sick all over each other. Uncle Tony's gonna be furious about the state of the van, too."

"Well, look – I'll lead you over to the Pit Stop. I think they got a car-wash bay and a vacuum-cleaner."

"Thanks, Joe." Berto pulled out his cellphone and looked at the time. "Awww … darn it, we're missing the big scene. They're supposed to be shooting it right this very minute."

"I kinda doubt it'll wind up being any more exciting than this," Joe tilted the Stetson a little further back on his head. *(He was wrong, but he and Berto had no way of knowing that until much later.)* Now Berto was distracted, looking at the ring of keys handing from the minivan's ignition.

"Hey, where did that extra key came from?" he wondered aloud. "I thought there was just the two, for the doors and the ignition."

"No idea," Joe replied. "You must have picked up someone else's keys by mistake. It happens all the time."

The Charge of the Karnes County Rangers

Narrowly missing being struck by the speeding van, Richard made a fruitlessly obscene gesture at the swiftly-vanishing tail-lights, and pedaled grimly on, down the paved road to the Wyler ranch, marked by a pair of ornamental gates, adorned by sheet-metal silhouettes of longhorns, horses and cowboys in a frieze overhead. He rumbled over the cattle grid. Now on the faint morning breeze, he could hear the distant roar of the electrical generators – not far to go now. The last of the stars winked out, all but the very brightest, Venus lingering coyly just out of reach of the crescent moon's embrace. Out beyond the huddle of lights, a helicopter rose from the ground, a dragonfly shape hovering in the pearl-colored sky.

He had not been out to the movie encampment before – mostly through having no wish to encounter Phillip Noel-Barrett, but it now looked as if an encounter with the despicable Pip was inevitable. No one stopped him – in fact, everyone seemed to be too busy to take any notion of him. A company of forty extras, in rags of period Mexican uniforms and full zombie makeup were being marshalled at the foot of the hill, with a gold-braid hung officer in a gaudy blue and red uniform just hauling himself into the saddle of a white horse. Richard stared, agog, thinking *'Stone the bloody crows, this is even worse than I thought it would be!'*

Fortunately, the first person he encountered who seemed to take any interest in him at all, when he approached the main pavilion were a pair whom he recognized, with considerable relief: Chris Mayall, lean and saturnine, and Sylvester Gonzales, looking uncommonly smug.

"Hey, man – come to see the fun?" Chris drawled. "They're about to start rolling on the big scene! Well, you saw the script."

"I was under the impression that there is some kind of scheme afoot to sabotage the whole thing," Richard answered, still panting and breathless from the furious pace. "Which I can hardly wait to hear all about. But I actually came all the way out here for Noel-Barrett. He keeps calling the Café, saying that he is locked in the editing van and no one is answering their cellphone."

"Yeah, we know," Sylvester replied, without turning a hair. Richard looked upon the conspirators with dawning comprehension, not unmixed with horror as well as envy.

"You did it," he whispered. "You two … you magnificent conniving bastards. Now get the key and let him out."

"We can't," Chris was entirely unmoved. "We do not, as a matter of fact, have the key in our physical possession."

"Well then, where is the key and who does have it?" Richard demanded. Sylvester, affecting the retro-nerd look even to the extent of wearing a vintage wristwatch, consulted that watch and replied with nerdish precision. "At this time and given the legal speed limit between here and Karnesville, Berto is likely at least halfway to that destination with the key in his possession. Chris sent him with the emergency cases," he added, parenthetically. "Likely, he won't be back for hours."

"Well, get a bolt-cutter!" Richard demanded, thinking only of the strips that Araceli would subtly rip off his hide – she being abominably soft-hearted with regard to the suffering of others. Frankly, when it came to Phillip Noel-Barrett suffering, Richard was one inclined to sit back and enjoy, even add a couple of more judicious brands to the flaming spectacle. On the other hand, he had heard Araceli promise to take Noel- Barrett's calls every five minutes or so – *and how could any work be done in the Café under such conditions!*

"Sorry, Ricardo; they are about to begin filming the grand scene," Chris replied, with a perfectly stunning lack of regret. "Likely you won't find anyone here with a bolt-cutter or the time to go for one until it's all done. Mega-A** Lydecker is real short of personnel this morning. I can't think how that could possibly have happened…" At that point, both he and Sylvester exchanged a meaningful look and laughed synchronistically.

Richard looked from one to the other, still torn between horror and envy. "All right, what else did the two of you do?" he asked, fairly certain that he would not welcome hearing the answer.

"What we had to do," Chris replied. "To sink this movie. Don't worry, Ricardo; your hands are clean. So are ours, if we have done it right and if Colonel Walcott and his reenactor command do their stuff – which he has promised they will do, come rain or shine. If you want to, come and tell what you see to that friend of yours through the keyhole. I guarantee – it will be the most awesome f**king thing you will ever see!"

"It's three minutes to rock and roll," Sylvester said, with another glance at his watch. "As I understand it, our fearless Mega-A** director wants to exceed the record for a single long unbroken tracking shot of a battle scene set by Kenneth Branagh in *Henry V*. They've been setting up the track and choreographing the extras in their moves for a week."

"Me, I don't want to miss a single minute. You want to tell Noel-Barret he'd better sit tight for a bit? We can watch it all from the back of the editing van and you can describe it to him through the door." Chris shouldered the bag that held his First Aid gear and supplies, and Richard followed after; they knew the layout well, after having worked at the site, day and night for three weeks.

A chaos of noise, of movement, three or four young assistant directors with heavy walkie-talkies running around like two-legged sheep-dogs with their ghastly, gore-dripping charges. The helicopter hovering overhead made speech impossible, unless one was right next to the person you were conversing with. Chris and Sylvester led the way, to a hulking 18-wheel truck trailer at the edge of the location encampment. He climbed up the four steps to the door – a solid door padlocked on the outside with a fairly substantial lock. He put his head next to the door, and shouted,

"Pip! Damn it, Pip – Noel-Barrett, it's Rich – can you hear me!" He thought that he heard someone inside replying, but the racket from the helicopter was so loud that he couldn't make out the words. Nonetheless, he yelled, "I'm here – but they can't find the key and they're about to start shooting! God is my witness, Noel-Barrett, they'll get you out as soon as they can. Just sit tight … you don't have to keep calling Araceli, you know! She has bloody work to do!"

At his side, Chris nudged his elbow, and when he saw that Richard's attention was turned towards them, he made a megaphone with his hands, and shouted, "There they go! See the sun, just above the hill? Watch there!"

The white-hot silver rim of the morning sun touched the crest of the gentle rise just east of location headquarters. It seared the eyes, to look at, as more and more of that blazing orb rose into that breathlessly blue sky. A pale thin mist hovered briefly over the grass, dissipating as the shadows lengthened. Richard flinched at the sound of the blast, as three explosions kicked up gouts of earth and smoke, about a quarter of the way down the hill. The sun floated higher and higher and suddenly silhouetted against it, the figure of a man on horseback. The horse pirouetted and reared, the man lifting a sabre in his right hand, sunlight flashing along its brazen length, and it seemed that the horse neighed a challenge ....

Richard had to appreciate the sheer heroic appeal of the image – say what you would about him, and many were eager to say the absolute worst about M.A. Lydecker – he did have skill at creating a heroic spectacle in the old-fashioned wide-screen and cinematic manner. The horse pirouetted once again, and now the ridgeline was lined with advancing shadows, silhouetted as the rider had been, against the bright hot sky – men brandishing flashing knives, with long rifles and glittering bayonets, bearded, burly men, in a long skirmish-line, advancing over the long ridge of that green hill, shouting as they came. Half a dozen riders followed after the first, a purposeful arrow after their leader. But ...

"Jumping Jesus on a pogo stick – they did it!" Sylvester exclaimed, and about doubled over with laughter. He pulled a cellphone out of his back pants pocket and held it up. "What –?" he shouted to Richard. "I gave Lydecker's people a cheap-ass burner phone! You think I would miss being able to document this!"

The ripple of dismay from the movie crew was almost palpable, although Richard could not hear any of what they were saying to each other, though the ubiquitous assistant directors with their brick-like communications devices barely hesitated. M.A. Lydecker, as stalwart upon his trolley as the captain of the Titanic as the boat deck began to slope under, moved unflinchingly along the path dictated by the tracks laid out with painful labor along the grass on the lower hillside. The smoke swirled in a cinematic – but doubtless historically inauthentic pattern – as the reenactors topped the ridge and began to charge downhill towards the zombie Mexican Army ... who, to give them credit, did not seem nearly as startled as everyone else.

"Stone the bloody crows!" Richard could hardly credit the evidence of his own eyes at first.

The first who caught his disbelieving gaze was a tall … person. A tall person, with an amazingly hairy and masculine décolletage revealed by the low-cut garb and made even taller by a commandingly towering white 18th century powdered wig, topped with a model of a ship under full sail, bobbing in an unsettling and realistic manner. The person underneath that white wig and boat was clad in full Versailles court dress, with sweeping brocade panniers to left and right. There might have been a train involved – but Richard could not take notice, in his utterly boggled astonishment at the sight of the company.

"The Widow Twankey goes touring!" was about the first thing he could think of to say, for every one of the reenactors had got themselves up in something approximating female period dress; crinoline skirts, bonnets bobbing and shawls flapping and trailing as they ran, incongruously brandishing their antique weaponry and shouting blood-thirsty war cries. A mounted scout, though, was fetchingly turned out in a 1920's beaded and brief flapper's dress, rucked up almost to the point of indecency. Half a dozen other reenactors looked to have taken Jane Austin for an inspiration, in high-waisted Empire-style gowns. But the weapons and accessories were most un-ladylike accouterments and Chris was laughing fit to cause injury to himself, even as several more thunderous explosions flung up another carefully-calculated round of dust, smoke and fire.

"Noel-Barrett! Can you hear me!" Richard shouted at the door. "This will be the most memorable bloody movie you'll ever have done!"

The moment of impact was a palpable thing, when the howling skirmish-line of cross-dressers slammed into the massed body of zombie soldiers.

"It looks pretty convincing!" Richard observed, still shouting over the sound of the helicopter. "I say; is Marie Antoinette getting the better over zombie General Santa Anna?"

"It would appear that way," Sylvester squinted at the fray, now devolving into an-every-cross-dresser-and-zombie for themselves brawl, complicated by the presence of the movie crew, who in trying to break it all up, were getting the worst from both sides. The man in the Versailles court costume was indeed getting the better of zombie Santa Anna, who seemed to be screaming a lot in hysterical Spanish, and attempting to rain blows upon his taller, and broader opponent – who, since the man in court costume was holding Santa Anna by his shirtfront at arm's length, could not seem to land anything like a serious blow. "They do these mock bouts fairly often. Not like what we did in the Corps, so much. But every so often, one of the guys gets a bloody nose."

"I don't know about you chaps," Richard answered, "But I wouldn't mind seeing this in a theater; alas, I suppose that nothing will come of it ... oh, dear – I think Mr. Lydecker is about to have words with our good Colonel over how his movie has been wrecked. I don't think the former is prepared to be especially sanguine in the face of adversity."

Indeed, the famed director appeared to have broken out of his state of shock; he came roaring off the camera trolley, and launched into the middle of the fray, straight towards Clovis Walcott. The latter stood out in the melee, for being the only one of the reenactors not in skirts or in special-effects gory zombie decrepitude. At this point, even though the helicopter still hovered overhead, like a giant mechanical dragonfly, Richard guessed that M.A. Lydecker's grand cinematic vision had devolved into the stuff of which internet video pratfalls are made. No wonder he had made a point of temporarily sequestering the cellphones of everyone involved, but Richard had no doubt that Sylvester had already posted the whole thing on-line – likely still was posting it, live. This was the first time in months that Richard seriously regretted throwing his own cellphone into the deepest pool of the river below the Age of Aquarius.

In the middle of it all, four of the reenactors mounted a Mexican Army ammunition limber and launched into a spirited barbershop quartet performance; Richard could barely make out the chorus;

"So, heave her up and away we go, Heave away, Santy Anno Heave her up and away we go, All on the plains of Mexico..."

"Should we do anything?" Sylvester ventured, as the helicopter lifted up and they could more easily hear what was going on and speak to each other without shouting.

"Aside from making popcorn? Hell, no, the Colonel can hold his own against this a-hole Hollywood jerk! Take a man out of the Army, but never take the Army out of the man!" Chris replied, but now with relief from the noise of the helicopter and explosions, they could clearly hear what was being said – or rather shouted – on the field of battle!

"You bastard!" screamed M.A. Lydecker, utterly unconscious of the cameras, official and otherwise, still rolling and the fact that now he could be heard clearly by all. "You unmitigated redneck bastard! You deliberately sabotaged this shoot! You promised that your people would be in appropriate period dress! You did! It was agreed and before witnesses, reliable witnesses! I'll sue you for breach of contract in every court..."

"It was a verbal agreement!" Clovis Walcott snarled, handily dodging the ineffectual fist which the infuriated auteur director swung in his general direction. "Let us demonstrate to you then, how effectively a verbal agreement stands up in court! That blade cuts two ways, Sirrah!"

Clovis seemed to have been momentarily overtaken by the courtly spirit of the early 19th century. "As for period dress, I promised authentic – but said nothing regarding sex-appropriate! You are no gentleman and you have sworn falsely to us, Sirrah – upon my own honor, the conventions of Texas gentility to not apply to you. Indeed, they do not!"

"You bastard!" M.A. Lydecker shouted, adding several more terms of colorful and more contemporary vernacular abuse, before taking another swing at Clovis Walcott with his fist.

At that point, and not before – Clovis Walcott swung with his own fist, weighted with the hilt of his cavalry sabre. M.A. Lydecker dropped like a stone. It was doubtless a testimony to the respect and affection with which he was held by the movie production crew that no one came to his aid, before Chris Mayall leaped down from the steps to the production van and shouldered his way through the mob.

"You got that, Sylvester?" he added, over his shoulder – and Sylvester nodded. "I gotta see to Mega-A**hole; looks like the Colonel hit him a good and fair one."

Richard had the impression that a plan – a convoluted and chancy plan of which he only knew the bare outline of – for which he thanked his Maker had been well-accomplished. He cast his eyes up to the ridge, over which the reenactors had ridden with such splendid effect. There was a single horseman, there – an erect and solitary figure, looking down upon the debacle with an attitude of fierce attention; Doc Wyler. Richard was pretty certain that if he could see Doc Wyler's face, it would be wearing an expression of grim triumph.

In the end, they loaded M.A. Lydecker into the LCVFD ambulance on a stretcher. When Chris held up three fingers before the dazed and downed director, asking urgently, "How many fingers do you see, sir – can you tell me?"

M.A. Lydecker only looked into an indeterminate distance with unfocused eyes and replied, "It went 'boom.' That's all. It just went 'boom.' Everyone likes to see it go 'boom.' It went boom."

"How many fingers, sir?" Chris repeated. An unseen wit in crowd behind them commented, "Just one – but it's the middle one!"

The general brawling had died away at that point, as the reenactors gathered their skirts and their dignity around them and withdrawn on foot and horseback to their encampment, jaunty and in possession of the day, such as it was. Chris vanished into the back of the ambulance with the stunned M. A. Lydecker, now supine on a gurney – and Richard was smugly satisfied to see that the director was well-strapped down on it. For himself, he managed to gain the brief attention of a walkie-talkie armed assistant and requested that someone locate a bolt-cutter and free Phillip Noel-Barrett from durance vile in the editing-suite van. Much to his astonishment, such an implement was readily produced, and the disheveled actor-cum-producer emerged, as angry as a wet pea-fowl.

(Richard had made that experiment at the Age of Aquarius, with a super- soaker borrowed from Araceli's son Mateo, on that shrieking avian pest which had insisted in roosting in the tree by the Airstream, and therefore was well-qualified in drawing the comparison.)

Noel-Barrett did manage to make a two-fingered gesture at Richard, leaning on his bicycle – from the back of one of Tony Gonzalez' fabulous black town cars as he was driven away in, bumping down the unpaved track, following after the ambulance.

"Pip, you ungrateful sod," Richard said, returning the gesture. "See if I ever do you a good turn again."

At his side, Sylvester sniggered. "Luna City rules – but you gotta love Brit class. Two fingers, instead of just one!"

"If a thing is worth doing," Richard answered. "It's worth doing well."

"Semper Fi, man," Sylvester agreed. "Hey, let's go over to the reenactor camp, and help them celebrate."

There was a palpable sense of satisfaction, righteously earned, about the reenactor encampment. Most of the reenactors had changed from their drag into either their regular 1830s garb, or into their mundane clothing – tending towards jeans or Dickie work pants with tee shirts. The burly Bill Weitzman, still in the Marie Antoinette court dress was sitting on a rickety camp chair, wig askew, smoking a large celebratory cigar and sporting a magnificent black eye, to which he was holding a contemporary ice-pack with his other hand. Clovis Walcott in particular, radiated triumphant good cheer, resting his hands on the hilt of his cavalry sabre in the midst of the crowd. There were celebratory and completely contemporary bottles and cans of beer in evidence, being handed out from a cooler full of ice at his side.

"We sure showed them, didn't we, Colonel!" exclaimed one of the cavalry riders – the man who Richard recognized as having been incongruously decked out in the beaded flapper dress.

"Well, and damned, Pete – and if you had showed any more, you'd likely have been arrested for indecent exposure. Didn't you get the memo about period-appropriate?"

"Hey," Pete protested. "By the time I got to Gibson's in Alamo Heights, they were out of everything period that would fit me. It was either this or sexy Cleopatra, so count yourself lucky."

"Narrow escape, that," Clovis Walcott agreed. He looked at the Bill Weitzman, resplendent in court dress, shaking head, saying, "Bill … you know, you didn't have to go all out, with the wig and all … the skirt and train would have been sufficient."

"Yes, but I've had the whole outfit for the longest time and this was the first good opportunity to wear it," Bill replied, around his cigar. Shaking his head again, Clovis caught sight of Sylvester and Richard and called out, "Hey, fellows! How did it look at your end?"

"Absolutely magnificent," Richard replied, warmly. "I cannot recall the last time I viewed a scene so absolutely farcical. If that doesn't absolutely destroy this bloody movie, I don't know what will, save perhaps a series of strategic assassinations."

"And I just uploaded the whole thing to YouTube," Sylvester added, smugly. "Including the part with your fight with Mega-A**hole."

"Excellent, gentlemen, excellent," Clovis beamed. "Call it the revenge of the Karnes Company! Those bastards – it could have been magnificent, if they had only gone ahead and made a straightforward and truthful epic. It would have made *Dances with Wolves* look like home movies at summer camp. Who's in charge over there now?"

"I have no idea," Richard admitted. "M.A. Lydecker is away in an ambulance to Karnesville, Phillip Noel-Barrett with him, I think. Half the assistant directors had some kind of sudden medical emergency, and the rest seem to be running around like chickens with their heads cut-off. Oh, and that actor playing Santa Anna was throwing a screaming tantrum and no one was paying attention to him, which I believe was making him even angrier."

"No proper leadership," Clovis Walcott nodded sagely. "Good, good. It's unworthy of me, I know – but I really did enjoy socking that bastard Lydecker. I didn't hurt him too badly, did I?"

"Richly deserved," Richard assured him. "And he swung at you twice, while being verbally abusive ... viciously abusive," he added, feeling virtuously smug. Although he didn't bear any particular animus against Lydecker, he did when it came to Phillip Noel-Barrett. "I think Chris was just being careful. The only downside, as far as I am concerned, is that now every time I watch you fellows do an old-fashioned drill, I'll be reminded of Monty Python's military fairy sketch. And I don't think I'll be the only one."

At his side, Sylvester choked on a laugh and Clovis Walcott laughed uncomfortably, admitting, "We did open ourselves up for that, I guess. But our personal embarrassment is but a temporary and passing thing, willingly sacrificed to the greater good of sinking that damned movie. Have a beer and celebrate. It's five o'clock somewhere in the world." Clovis urged them. Although only late morning, it was late   mid-summer in South Texas, and the day was turning hot now that the sun was sun well-up. Richard was feeling as if it were already late afternoon, with so much having gone on.

They had only just popped off the bottle tops, and drunk a toast, to cheers, to Clovis and to Sylvester, when Joe Vaughn's police cruiser nosed carefully across the meadow and into the edge of the encampment; the celebration had got decidedly merry at that point.

"Morning, ladies and gentle-grunts. Y'all having fun, now?" Joe drawled, to a chorus of cheerful assents.

"That we are, Chief," Clovis Walcott replied. "Have a beer – oh, sorry. You're on duty. Never mind."

"I am that, sir," Joe replied with a grin. "I understand there's been some considerable ruction around here and that you struck Mr. Hollywood Director Lydecker on the jaw."

"I did indeed," Clovis acknowledged, setting aside his own beer and grandly holding out his wrists, as if ready for the handcuffs, while Sylvester and Richard chorused, "He was provoked – it was wholly justified, and we were there… it's on Sylvester's phone …"

"Yeah, I know that," Joe silenced them with a stern look, as well as those reenactors within earshot who were also beginning to grumble in a most menacing manner. "Well, Colonel … I just came from Karnesville Medical Center – and on my way back from there I got a phone call. I have been told by Mr. Lydecker's representative that his jaw is fractured in two places, and he insists that you be officially reprimanded for this brutal and unnecessary violation of his human rights. You are hereby officially reprimanded: You have been bad, Colonel Walcott; very, very bad. Don't let it happen ever again, or I'll be forced to make a note on your permanent record."

"I most certainly won't, Chief," Clovis Walcott bowed his head in mock penitence. "Next time, I shall be certain to hit him hard enough to break his jaw in three places."

"Good," Joe grinned, even more widely. "Drink up, gentle-grunts. It's against city ordinances to let good beer get warm. Nice wig, by the way, Bill. Keep up the good work."

* * *

At 5:30 PM That Day at Mills Farm

* * *

Benny Cordova walked from his office in the main administrative facility at Mills Farm towards the small compound of staff cottages, tucked inconspicuously in a grove of well-grown oaks, concealed from the main grounds and facilities by a thick hedge of hackberry and cedar scrub-brush. Halfway there the cellphone in his pocked chimed – the particular note that he had a new email on his personal account – not his official Mills Farm work account. In the nearest pocket of shade, he pulled out the cellphone, and opened that message – brief and cryptic.

Victory is ours. Get a beer, close the door, put up your feet and watch this.

TweetyNemesis@gmail.com

The word "this" contained a link. Benny put the phone away and walked on. Five minutes brought him to his tidy bachelor cottage. He went in through the back door, got a beer from the fridge and opened up his home computer. Yes, there was the message. There was no need to close the door, since Benny lived alone. He popped the beer, clicked on the link … and as the video rolled, he sat back and laughed. When it was finished, he watched it again, lifting the bottle in salute.

"Mills Farm, boys, and to Karnes Company – may they ever endure!"

Comeback Launch Fail: The End of *Road to San Jacinto*

From *Entertainment Weekly*
Joy Faircloth – Exclusive to EW

The apparent failure of the independent movie production company Six-Foot-Deep Films has put the comeback dreams of controversial three-time Academy Award winning director Michael "M.A." Lydecker in jeopardy, it can now be revealed. Six-Foot-Deep Films was the brainchild of British television idol Phillip Noel-Barrett, whom I interviewed for this publication over a year ago. At that time, "Pip" *(as his friends call him)* was upbeat about the project, his first essay in filmmaking by his own independent production company. But after a dissention-plagued location shoot in Texas, and a post-production schedule derailed by financial reversals caused by the withdrawal of major backers and investors, the future of Six-Foot-Deep Films and the epic historical-zombie adventure *Texians and Zombies* (working title *The Road to San Jacinto*) remains in jeopardy.

A short video recorded on a cellphone and uploaded to YouTube by someone identified only as TweetyNemesis purported to be of a chaotic battle scene, concluding with M.A. Lydecker in a physical altercation with an unnamed extra. This video went viral, before representatives of Six-Foot-Deep Films were able to have it taken down. Attempts to reach the management of Six-Foot-Deep Films has been met with little success. Numerous telephone messages left on company voicemail have not been answered, nor have email messages sent through their website. The building housing their Glendale offices is, according my sources, empty and up for lease.

The main figures behind Six-Foot-Deep are similarly elusive: Michael Lydecker is rumored to be in seclusion in his mansion in an exclusive Bel Air neighborhood, while other sources suggest that he is undergoing extensive rehabilitation at a private clinic in Malibu, for injuries suffered in an accident during shooting. Cal Fenwick, who shared top billing as General Sam Houston, is also reportedly returned to rehab. Pip Noel- Barrett is in Thailand, according to his agent, incommunicado at a Buddhist monastery, undergoing a strict regimen of fasting, ritual and prayer.

Of those others directly involved in filming *Texians and Zombies*, few can be located, and fewer induced to speak on record. Mexican *telenovela* star Diego Leon Sepulveda – cast as dictator and General Santa Anna, in the expectation that this role would be his break-out into the major US film-scene – was contacted by an EW correspondent in Monterrey, Mexico, and asked for his perspective on the film project. Of his response in English, little is repeatable in a family-oriented magazine. It would appear that his experience was not a positive one. Former Disney child star Amy Butler also declined comment through her representative. MS Butler is currently on hiatus from acting, in favor of pursuing a degree in physics through the California Institute of Technology. Her representative confirmed that MS Butler enjoyed the experience of shooting on location in and around the tiny town of Luna City, Texas, and that she had been paid in advance for her top-billed role. She actually appeared in relatively few scenes, and that those scenes had already been shot before the trouble-plagued production was forced to close down. As far as Ms Butler is concerned, her representative emphasized, she had no particular further interest or concern in the completion or release of *Texians and Zombies* – although, per contract, she would be willing to make a certain number of appearances to publicize the move, upon completion and release.

Contact with individuals and parties who were associated locally in Luna City with the production were easier to locate, but no more forthcoming. Those members of the Karnes Company Living History Association contacted by this reporter all declined to comment. The president of the association, Clovis Walcott, referred us to his personal legal representative, when this reporter asked him to confirm that he had been the other party shown fighting with Michael Lydecker in the controversial and now-embargoed YouTube video. The resort and event venue of Mills Farm (owned by Venue Properties, International) was reported in local media to have hosted the production team and leading actors, as well as being investors in the film itself, but when contacted, the Mills Farm spokesperson referred us to their corporate public relations team, which also refused comment. Much of the outdoor location shooting, including the climactic battle scene, took place nearby on the scenic Wyler Exotic Game Ranch – but attempts to contact the current owner of the ranch were also rebuffed.

As it stands, it would seem that Michael Lydecker's most attempt to reboot his fading career as a director of popular and critically well-received films have been stymied by circumstance and his own difficult nature. For now, we can only conclude that *Texians and Zombies* is – to coin a phrase – a dead movie walking.

Celia Hayes & Jeanne Hayden

Chamber of Commerce Fall Newsletter

Fall 2016 Newsletter

Luna City Chamber of Commerce

5 North Town Square, Suite 4

Reminder: The Luna City Chamber of Commerce has a Facebook Page

With the completion of the movie project, Mills Farm will resume their regular calendar of fall events. The Pumpkin Patch will open on October 15th, on the main lawn below the Mills Farm Dance Hall. Bring the kids to find that perfect pumpkin for Halloween, and go for a good old fashioned hayride through the grounds.

Dinner Theater by the Luna City Players

The Luna City Players are staging a special, one-time-only dinner theater and audience participation event on Sunday, October 30th, to benefit the parish church of St. Margaret & St. Anthony rebuilding fund.

The performance is entitled *Let No True Hearts Admit Impediments*, and the conceit, according to Players stage manager and president, Patricia Pryor, is a wedding ceremony and reception plagued by suspense; as the groom has been arrested, the bride is about to melt down entirely, and the families involved hate each other, passionately. Almost but not quite like every wedding you have ever been to – or in – but a lot more fun.

Tickets will be in the form of wedding invitations, and may be purchased at most retail stores in Luna City. The bride and groom will be registered at Abernathy Hardware, at Gonzales Air and Heating, and Gonzalez & Sons Construction. (Items noted on their registry are also those necessary for the renovation of the Sts. Margaret & Anthony Parish Hall and are included so as to give an idea of the costs involved in this work.)

Luna City, Texas – Home of the Mighty Fighting Moths

Upcoming Events

August 22

School year begins for all Luna City Independent School District Students

September 2

Labor Day Weekend Muster Encampment of the Karnes Company Ranger Living History Association on Town Square – Continues through Sept 5

September 23

Founder's Day for Luna City – Celebrated on Town Square this weekend!

Luna City Players

Tickets will be on sale beginning October 1 for the Luna City Players dinner theater presentation *Let No True Hearts Admit Impediments*, to be performed October 30th.

Luna City ISD News

School Begins for Elementary and High Schools

The 2016-17 School semester begins on Monday, August 22 for Luna City students attending Luna City Elementary and High School. New students in the district should register at the respective school registrar's office during the week of August 15-17, if they had not been registered prior to the summer break. As a reminder, the elementary school serves kindergarten through 6th grade, and high school grades 7 through 12.

School Bus Route & Pick-up Times

Bus routes and pick-up schedule will be finalized by Monday, August 15, for all students eligible for school bus transportation between home and school. Elementary school students living more than half a mile from school and high school students living more than three quarters of a mile are our priority for transportation, as are students with physical disabilities. Other students may be considered on a by-request basis.

Mighty Fighting Moth Football!

Come out and support the Mighty Fighting Moth Varsity team and Marching band! Moth season begins August 26th and continues every other Friday until January, with a break over the Christmas holiday. Schedule of games and location will be posted on the Luna HS bulletin board.

Reminder: Permit Slips for Life Skills Classes

Parental permission slips for students scheduled to participate in Life Skills classes must be signed and turned into the school registrar before the start of classes. Without signed permission from a parent or legal guardian, students will not be permitted to attend Life Skills class.

Community Marketplace

Ready for Winter

Martin at Abernathy Hardware reminds everyone that winter is coming, and that it does get cold now and again in Karnes County. Now is the best time to call for maintenance on your heating system, to order fuel for that system and stock up on faucet covers and insulation for exterior plumbing.

From Chief Vaughn, Luna City PD

With the beginning of the new school year, drivers are urged to take care and slow down, especially at intersections where they may be students waiting for a bus, walking or bicycling to school, especially in the early morning hours when it is still dark outside. Currently, Luna City's population stands at 2,453, plus Jorge and Guadalupe Gonzales' triplets, Roman Gonzales' cousin Pedro and his family who moved to town over summer, and whoever may be presently living at the Age of Aquarius. Chief Vaughn would prefer not to see those numbers drop through someone being an inconsiderate dumba** behind the wheel.

Age of Aquarius Fall Specials

Judy and Sefton will begin taking orders for their specialty goat milk and honey holiday soaps in September, at their usual Saturday market booth. Judy makes only limited quantities of her rosemary, peppermint and cedar-scented holiday soaps, so order now to be assured of delivery in time for the upcoming holiday gift-giving season.

VJ+71

Early on an August Sunday morning, Miss Leticia McAllister combed out her long grey hair, rolling and neatly pinning it into an old-fashioned hair-net on the back of her neck. That done, she surveyed her appearance in the dressing table mirror. The hat, gloves and scarf that she would wear against the chill – for the sanctuary of the First Methodist Church of Luna City was enthusiastically air-conditioned against the blistering heat of a Texas late summer – all lay in order on the dressing table, next to Miss Letty's Sunday handbag, which held a fresh handkerchief, her house keys, and the envelope with her weekly offering. Hat, bag, scarf and all carefully matched, and coordinated beautifully with the colors of Miss Letty's flowered and full-skirted summer dress.

I never had beauty or elegance, Miss Letty told her reflection, with clinical satisfaction – *but I could manage chic by paying attention, and I had the brains enough to be charming. Alice was the one for elegance!*

Oh, my – did she turn heads! Hard to believe it has been seventy-one years to the day. Every man in Schilo's Delicatessen on Commerce on VJ-Day – they all turned to look at her, as she came in the door. You could have heard a pin drop; I think most of them thought that a movie star had come to San Antonio, but she was really only the chief secretary to an insurance company manager, for all that she was only twenty-four. And he kept trying half-heartedly to seduce her, the wretched little Lothario. She wrote complaining about that to me, all the time that I was in England, and then in France. Alice had a hatpin, though – and she could use it, too.

Miss Letty pinned her hat, with a long, straight old-fashioned pin, which went straight through the bun on the back of her neck, firmly anchoring the straw confection into place. She touched her lips with a pale pink lipstick, and gathered up gloves, scarf and bag, but her thoughts returned to that early afternoon, seventy-one years before, and Miss Alice Everett, stepping through the street door, squinting into the dimness inside; the dark paneled walls, floor tiled in tiny, hexagonal tiles, all of it old-fashioned even then. Alice was looking for Letty, sitting in a corner booth all by herself, waiting for her brother and his friend.

"Letty, sweetie – you look wonderful!" Alice exclaimed, hurrying between the tables, and flashing a brilliant smile at the nearest waiter. "Oh, it's simply divine, seeing you again! Tell me, did you buy that hat in Paris! You must have; there isn't anything half so chic at Joske's!"

"No – Bonwit-Tellers' in New York, on my way through," Letty rose from the banquet seat, and the two of them exchanged an embrace. "There wasn't anything in Paris worth buying. Just desperate refugees, too many Allied troops, and guilty collaborators hoping that everyone else had suddenly developed amnesia."

"But it's all over, now!" Alice said, with a sigh of happy rapture. "The war – and all that awfulness; no one in the office can get any work done, for the excitement, so Mr. Tradescent just told us to take a holiday. I have the rest of the day off! So let's have a lunch with your brother and his pal, and then let's all do something exciting, even if it is just walking along Commerce Street, looking at all the happy faces." She stripped off her gloves, beaming expectantly at Letty. "I expect that you will be coming home for good, now. You looked so brave in your Red Cross uniform, though. Will you miss all the excitement?"

"No," Letty answered, for there hadn't been much excitement, really. Just ward after ward of hospital beds draped in clean white sheets, full of men with broken bodies, broken spirits, and broken hearts. And after that it was Displaced Persons, poor skeletal shadows of the humans they had been, clad in striped rags, stumbling barefoot along muddy, rutted roads. "So much agony; I will not miss it in the least."

"You did your part," Alice said, bracingly. "You are ever so much braver than I am: I can't stand the sight of blood, or someone being sick, so I wouldn't have been any good at all. I am so envious!" She looked at Letty with such openhearted affection that Letty was reminded yet again of why they were fast friends – from the moment they had met at the Texas State College for Women on the first day of fall term of 1939, right up until the day that Alice died in 2005 – still elegant, perfectly groomed, and complaining about the color of the hospital gowns.

The thing about true heart-friends, Miss Letty thought, carefully negotiating the stairs from the back porch of the McAllister residence – *is that they look at you, see and believe the best that you are, without reservation.*

Seventy-one years. She was a little early. Chris Mayall's little red coupe was still parked in front of the old carriage house. Miss Letty shook her head; the dear boy was obviously still primping. Young men did have their vanity. Miss Letty approved of this on the whole; there were so very few dandies left in this modern world.

"So, tell me about your brother's best pal," Alice said, as they sat in Schilo's on that momentous day, with the sound of impromptu victory parades going up and down the street outside. Letty ordered soft drinks, which had been brought by the attentively-hovering waiter; ice-cold root beer, so cold that the frost was thick on the outside of the heavy glass mug. "Army Air Corps, you said – is he handsome and dashing?"

"That goes without saying," Letty replied, briefly amused. "They are all handsome and dashing … it's the uniform, you know. But you have met Douglas. He was already serving in 1942. Stephen didn't sign up until last year when he finished with his degree, and then he was training in transports. We grew up more or less together. Honestly, Alice – he was like another brother."

Miss Letty kept it forever in her heart that Stephen Wyler had once jokingly proposed marriage to her, the summer of the year they were both seventeen, with a crowd of other teenagers swimming in the deep pool in the bend of the San Antonio River, below where the Grant's commune and goat farm would eventually be established.

"Hey, Letty – we can do it!" He said, smiling as he walked carefully out along a dead and sun-bleached log, which had come down in a flood year, and deeply embedded in the riverbank. They had been taking turns, diving off the end of the log into the deepest part of the pool. "You and I – we like each other fine – and won't that set all the old hens to gossiping!"

"Ridiculous!" Letty splashed water at him. "I've known you forever – it would be like marrying Doug!"

"All right, but I won't ask again," Stephen replied.

Letty snorted, "Promises, promises!"

He cannon-balled into the water with an almighty splash, and everyone laughed, and there was an end to it, for they both went away to different colleges the following year, and then the war began. And now the war was over, with an abruptness that left everyone dizzy with happiness and relief. Stephen was twenty-four, Doug twenty-six. Because of this all-of-a-sudden, newfangled, and amazingly powerful bomb dropping on two cities that practically no one had heard of ever before,

Doug and Stephen and hundreds of thousands of other young men were assured of living to be another year older. For that, Miss Letty would be grateful for all the rest of her own life.

"Is that them?" Alice Everett had said, on that day in Schilo's Delicatessen, as the street door opened, and two men stepped in from the dazzle of sunshine outside; two handsome young men, gallant in Army 'pinks', with silver aviator wings on their chests. "Oh, my – I do believe that I am in love already!"

Letty had made a brief 'tisk' of mild disapproval at that, but upon seeing the dazzled expression on Stephen Wyler's face, and the delicate blush on Alice's – she recognized a certain truth at once; there was such a thing as love at first sight, and this love was no brief affection, for it lasted a full and devoted sixty years.

Now Miss Letty waited on the back porch of the McAllister house, leaning on the cane that she barely needed, as Chris Mayall trotted briskly the outside stairs from his apartment, in the old carriage house, car keys in hand.

("You must go with me," Alice could barely contain the sobs, that day in 2004, calling Letty on the telephone from San Antonio. "They've moved him to a ward at Brooke – You know how I feel about hospitals – but I simply must be there when he wakes up. Petty Officer Mayall was J.W.'s best friend, he was beside him when ... it happened. That poor boy has no family at all – certainly none out here who can visit ...")

"All ready?" Chris said, opening the passenger-side door with a flourish. He helped Miss Letty on the last step, and into the little red coupe. "I'll have to bring you home straightaway afterwards, though – I'm running a half-marathon in Beeville this afternoon. It's not one of those big races, but I'd like to have it under my belt when I start competing in the fall."

"You are serious about this, aren't you?" Miss Letty mused, as the little red coupe pulled out onto the road. "Have you thought about getting one of those special blade-running prosthetics? "

"It is a thought, Miss Letty," Chris mused. Miss Letty thought that yes, he would have been thinking about it. Running marathon races must be awfully hard on his regular prosthesis.

"Let me look into it," she said. "And I'll see what I can do. After all – I have been with the Red Cross a very long time. I know people."

Wherefore Art Thou Romeo?

"Oh, hey, Ricardo," said Sefton one afternoon in late August, when Richard stopped by the yurt for a pint of honey and some fresh eggs. "You're going to have some neighbors for a while, so I thought I'd give you a heads-up. We just got an email about an open-ended reservation; Romeo Gonzales is on his way back from North Dakota."

"I take it that he is one of the Luna City Gonzaleses?" Richard was only just amused. "And ... North Dakota? What was he doing there?"

"Shale oil fields – ripping the heart out of Mother Earth," Sefton replied, with a slightly sour expression. "But Romeo's OK. It's just that things happen, when he is around. Don't mean to say you should plant sandbags around the trailer, 'r anything. But if you got accident insurance, you might wanna make sure it's paid up."

"Singular concept," Richard murmured, and Sefton explained, "Judikens says he is a catalyst for unseen interdimensional forces, so you don't really want to stand too close to him. But a nice guy. Still amazed they let him work around high-powered machinery, though."

"He's mine and Berto's sort of half-brother," Araceli explained, when Richard made mention of it when he got to the Café and thought to ask. "A cousin by blood. Papi and Mama took him in when he was about ten. Uncle Roberto disappeared after his wife ran off with a guy she met clubbing in Matamoros." Araceli frowned, wiping her hands on a towel. "I'll bet he is out of work again."

"That happens often?"

"Yeah – he usually leaves a string of broken hearts behind him and sometimes some smoking rubble."

"Nothing wrong with that," Richard observed, a little smugly; Araceli's frown deepened.

"When those hearts belong to the wives of other men, it sometimes gets a little awkward."

"They should have expected that, when they named him Romeo," Richard answered.

"He was baptized Roman," Araceli explained with some indignation. "He got the nickname when he knocked up his high school girlfriend. Her name was …"

"Juliet? I might have guessed."

Araceli sighed again. "He hasn't been back home in about three years. I guess he's been fired again and can't find work. Abuelita says that he was born under a cursed star. That's the other usual thing about Romeo. I was not joking about the smoking rubble, either."

"You weren't? I thought it was just a turn of phrase."

"No," Araceli gave the luncheon soup of the day *(a hearty and vegetarian harvest vegetable chili)* a careful stir. "It's just that sometimes … many times … stuff just goes wrong around him. Thing just seem to happen. Oh, he doesn't deliberately sabotage things; Romeo just isn't that nasty and spiteful. He's a hard worker and a good one, too. He can go for weeks, months on a job site, without anything happening. And then without warning, something breaks down. Catastrophically.

Romeo usually isn't even in the same room, at the site, or on shift when it happens. And it usually isn't anything anyone can explain, even when there are survivors."

"As in for instance?" Richard asked.

Araceli replied, "Too many to count, but there is one that you might have heard about – he was working on the Deepwater Horizon rig on the Macondo Prospect ... was that five years ago? Guess it was. Anyway, he and his buddies, they had just gone off-duty when it all blew. Whatever happened in that well blow-out, Romeo was cleared of responsibility in all the inquiries afterwards – but guys working a dangerous job – Pat says they will for sure begin to talk when they notice a pattern."

"A Jonah, in other words," Richard ventured.

Araceli nodded in agreement. "Nobody managing rigs in the Gulf after that wanted to hire Romeo, although they were all very nice about it. Nice doesn't butter the bread, and oilfield work is all that Romeo knows how to do, so he went up to North Dakota to get work there." Araceli turned the stove burner down to a gentle simmer and replace the pot lid. "There haven't been any spectacular disasters in the Bakken Shale oil fields lately that you have read about? Maybe on the back pages?"

"Nothing comes to mind," Richard answered, after a hasty search of the mental headlines. It was kind of comforting to know that there was a man more prone to professional reversals than he was – although the knowledge that he was coming to live in the same campground was enough to give one pause. "So now that he is coming home, maybe he can park next to that wretched Canadian tosser."

"The treasure-hunting man?" Araceli's face fell even farther. "Mother of God, is he back again? Patrick says that he heard him the other night on *Coast to Coast*, still carrying on about the Mills Treasure."

"Alas, my dear sweet rural innocent – yes, he is. I can only hope that he was not thrown off Mills Farm with sufficient vigor last time. He is still rabbiting on about the Mills Treasure, claiming that the management admitted simply months ago that there was another $20-dollar gold coin, found in repairs to the petting zoo was how he explained it. He is convinced of the existence of that blasted treasure and is certain that Mills Farm management knows exactly where it is. Then he frowned darkly and said that he means to prove it for once and for all. Frankly, it was a relief when he stopped yammering at me. The man's obsessed and he will neither shut up or change the subject."

"Well, never mind – are you going to come over to our place on Saturday? Pat has three days off, because he volunteered to be stand-by on call driver, and he's firing up the smoker to do a whole brisket. Supper will be on us, and someone else to do the cooking."

"Brisket, eh? Throw in some sausages of Pryor's for me, and you'll not be able to keep me away," Richard answered. He had become quite fond of Texas style smoked brisket; a rather ordinary and normally tough cut of meat, but purely magical when slowly smoked over a mesquite-wood fire and sliced thinly across the grain.

"Saturday, then," Araceli nodded; for some reason, quite satisfied.

Araceli and Pat lived in a nicely-kept double-wide trailer on the outskirts of Luna City, where the older, late Victorian part of town raveled off in easy stages through mid-20th century bungalows to trailers and sheds, and thence into rural fields and thickets, and pastures patched with groves of oak trees. Richard passed their home every day as it lay along the shortest and safest route between the Café and the Age of Aquarius. On Saturday afternoon, he arrived at Araceli and Pat's to find a small gathering already assembled on the screened porch which ran along the back of the double-wide, while Pat tended the massive covered barbeque grill and attached smoker around in back. Angelika and Mateo romped with a handful of other children their age.

"Hey Ricardo – welcome! Get yourself a beer and tell me how you would punch up Pryor's finest mild. They only had a batch of mild left last weekend, and I thought – oh, what the hell."

"Not certain, actually," Richard replied, leaning his bicycle against the side of the porch. Pryor's mild sauce – served up in a large crockpot on weekends when Andy and Patricia opened their part-time restaurant always seemed fiery enough for him. *(The sauce also came in 'medium' and 'hot', which to Richard's refined palate, seemed more like tomato-based napalm.)*

"It suits me fine, just as it is."

"You have no sense of adventure," Pat averred. "What about a splash of siracha?"

"Tabasco," suggested Joe Vaughn from inside the porch. "Well known fact – everything goes better with Tabasco … except maybe MRE fruitcake. Hi, Rich – have a beer."

"Thanks," Richard climbed up the three steps and let the screen porch door close behind him. He practically did not recognize Joe, when not in uniform. Amazingly – he still looked as large as one of those concrete traffic bollards outside of significant government buildings in jeans and a *guayabera* shirt. The porch seemed to be the male hang-out of choice; Besides Joe, there was Berto, his Uncle Tony Gonzalez from Elmendorf and Roman Gonzalez, the construction contractor. How all the branches of the Gonzalez and Gonzales clan connected together was something that Richard had never been able to figure out. Araceli assured him that no one else had, either. "Where is Araceli?"

"The ladies are inside," Joe replied. "Finishing touches to the coleslaw an' *borracho* beans, and the apple cobbler for dessert … and girl talk. Especially the girl talk."

"Probably just telling rude stories," Richard observed. "Too rude for our shell-like – that or damaging to our delicate male sensibilities." He accepted the beer and found a free chair. It looked like the long table at the end of the porch was being set up for service; a pile of paper plates and napkins, a couple of bags of crisps, some loaves of supermarket sandwich bread and a pile of silverware.

"You got that, for sure," Joe agreed. "Hey, I hear that Romeo is coming home. Crazy dude – wonder how long he will stay this time?"

"You know him?" Richard marveled again at the speed at which information passed through Luna City.

"Well, yeah – we played together on the varsity Moths in '91," Joe said, as the interior door opened. Jess Abernathy, Araceli and Kate Heisel emerged, attended by the smells of good food cooking. Each of them bore a platter, a crockpot or a baking dish, and were followed by two older women; Carmencita Gonzalez – Roman's wife, whom he recalled most vividly from the epic battle of the *quinceanera* of the year before – and a woman he didn't know, who must therefore be Aunt Lucy, the espoused of Berto's Uncle Tony. *(Really, Richard reflected and not for the first time ... he should draw up a chart, just so that he could keep all the Gonzaleses and Gonzalezes straight.)* The ladies set their burdens down on the table, and found seats of their own; Jess claiming a space on the porch swing next to Joe, and Angelika and Mateo claiming seats to either side of Kate.

"He's going to be my neighbor at the Aquarius," Richard confessed with some trepidation, and Joe grinned.

"My sympathies, pal ..."

At that, Kate Heisel said, those eyes of hers which were the perfect blue-green of beryl jewels all alight with passionate fire, "Don't you dare say that! Patricia says that she wants him for the Luna City Players charity dinner theater production!"

"As soon as Romeo gets into town," Joe added in an aside to Richard, "Tell him about that – and if he knows what is good for him, he'll just keep moving on. What Patricia wants, she will have, come hell or high water."

"It's a good cause," Araceli added, in her starchiest tone of voice. "And she isn't even a member of the parish." Richard cringed inwardly. *What Araceli also wanted, she would have. What was it, about these Luna City women?*

And it was no good looking to the men – even the older men for support. Roman Gonzalez was also nodding somberly. "It's to rebuild the parish hall of St. Anthony and Margaret," he said. "You know, where they found asbestos in the ceiling last year? Well, it turns out that there's black mold in every place there isn't asbestos … and to remediate it all and build clean and new, it's gonna cost about three times as much as the diocese is prepared to pay and the parish can afford. Luna City isn't one of those places that is growing by leaps and bounds, you know. And we can't go back to Doc Wyler, every time an institution in Luna City runs into an economic roadblock. It's not fair – he has a business to run as well. So …"

"Patricia is the creative director of the Luna Players," Jess explained, as an aside to Richard. "She was a theater major in college. Never plays a part, though – she prefers stage design and directing."

"In addition to everything else," Araceli put in, with an exaggerated sigh. "I've never been able to figure out how she does it all. Perfect figure, perfect face, perfect family, perfect home, always beautifully dressed … honestly, I would hate her guts on general principles, but in addition to all that, she's a nice person and always has been."

"Perfect SAT score in high school," Joe added, with a nostalgic grin. "Not bad as a cheerleader, either."

"Not entirely perfect," Jess elbowed him in the ribs "She ditched you for Andy Pryor."

"History, babe – history," Joe said, while Kate Heisel exclaimed,

"We're doing a charity dinner theater fund-raiser! May as well give donors some fun and a good meal, in exchange for their contribution!" She turned that deep beryl regard on Richard. "Patricia wondered if you would be able to do catering ... a buffet menu very much like for Beatriz and Blanca's *quinceanera* last year. We'd work out the details and the costs, of course – if you'd be willing to consider doing it."

The existence of the Luna City Players had only come to Richard's attention during the detestable Phillip Noel-Barrett's attempt to film the ghastly zombie film, when all of the members had eagerly signed up to be extras, under the illusion – carefully cultivated by the movie production team – that it was to be a straight historical epic.

"What play are they going to perform?" he asked, mildly curious as to how this would tie into a catered buffet. "I'd try and work out a menu appropriate, of course – something with relevance to the play's title, perhaps."

"It's an improvisation," Araceli explained. "It doesn't actually have a title yet; but the plot is basically a wedding verging on a disaster, with the groom escaping from the county lock-up in Karnesville, and the bride and her family, and the groom's family waiting around the reception hall to see if the wedding is going to go off or not. Berto has a student friend who has done simply heaps of acting, who is going to be the bride. The customers are invited guests ... and the Players are all family members or in the wedding party. There's a lot of improvised bits and scenes, and the bride has tantrums and fights with everyone, the mothers hate each other and want to break the engagement ..."

"I've been to weddings that were like that," Richard observed. "It wasn't what I would call the least bit entertaining."

"It will be when the Players put their backs into it," Jess assured him. "And Patricia has written some amazing bits of dialogue, and some of the plot twists ... well, I don't want to ruin the surprises. We should be drawing audience from Karnesville and as far as San Antonio."

"I'm doing publicity, of course," Kate said. "And if you did the catering, that would be another draw. Say that you will consider it, Rich – it would add so much!"

"I'll think about it," Richard promised. From the smoker outside, Patrick called,

"Hey, you guys hungry or not? The sausages are done – you wanna get it when it's hot?" He raised the lid and began shifting the various meats with a long-handled fork and a set of tongs from the grill and the tall smoker into a large high-sided pan. He brought the savory odor of charred meats and mesquite smoke with him into the porch, where the hungry multitude fell gratefully upon it. For quite some time conversation was brief and centered mostly on appreciation of the simple bounty placed before them.

It was all very different from a solitary supper in the Airstream of an evening. Richard told himself that he wouldn't favor dining out with friends every evening, by any means – he needed a certain amount of solitude, as if he were a monk and the Airstream his symmetrical aluminum cell. But it was pleasant; the conversation, the undemanding company of Araceli and Patrick, Berto and the others – that sense of being part of the beating heart of Luna City. This pleasant spell was broken by Patrick's cellphone ringing, shortly before sundown, as Araceli and Kate were dishing up small plates of apple cobbler.

Patrick looked at the number calling, before swearing softly in Spanish.

"I thought since they hadn't called this afternoon…" Araceli's face was downcast.

"Sorry, 'Celi," Patrick listened to the faint squawking emanating from his cellphone. "Sorry, guys – hey, at least we got a chance to enjoy the brisket. I gotta run."

"Duty calls," Joe agreed. "Know the feeling – be careful out there tonight, Pat."

"Always," Patrick nodded. With his departure, the social evening began to break up and scatter, as moths batted against the porch lights in the dusk; Roman and Carmencita, Tony and Lucy for the drive back to

Elmendorf. A neighbors' dog barked at some stranger passing by in the road.

"We about done, babe?" Joe called into the kitchen, where Jess was helping Araceli sort out the serving dishes and the crockpot. Kate had gone to read a bedtime story to Angelika and Mateo – it appeared that she was one of their very favorite people in the world.

"In a minute," Jess emerged with a large trash bag, gathering up paper plates and cans for the trash. "Araceli says – do we want to take some of the brisket home for later? She has more of it left over then they can eat in a week."

Richard belatedly thought that he also ought to be making himself useful; he and Berto began helping Jess gather up stray silverware and bring it into the kitchen.

"Sure," Joe agreed. Another dog barked, this one closer.

A doorbell rang, and from inside the kitchen, Araceli called, "Can someone answer the door? I've got my hands all over grease and sauce."

"I'll get it," Richard offered, as he was the only person who didn't have something in his hands at the moment. Araceli, doing mortal battle with large chunks of aromatic brisket and several lengths of aluminum foil, lifted her chin in the direction of an interior door, saying as the doorbell rang again.

"Through the front room – thanks, Chef. I can't think who would be coming around to the front door and bothering with the bell on a Saturday night."

"Someone flogging life insurance?" Richard ventured, which earned a frazzled laugh from Araceli.

There were no lights on in the front room of the double-wide; a comfortably shabby room, furnished in no particular style. Obviously, a family with small children lived in it, though; Angelika and Mateo's school knapsacks hung from hooks by the door. Someone moved on the front porch on the other side of the door – someone rather heavy, Richard thought – or perhaps it was just because it was a trailer and the floor under his feet shimmied slightly as he moved.

He opened the door to an explosion of blinding light, of faces spectral in the portable flash, camera lenses, and veritable storm of voices, shouting, demanding –

"Where is it! Can you confirm or deny…! Comment – how long have you known! Who are you protecting?!"

The memories rolled over him, an ungovernable flood, a tidal wave of darkness, horror, helplessness. Richard screamed, an unearthly scream of terror, and knew nothing more.

Luna City 3.1

Public Matter, Private Affair

The first thing that Richard was conscious of – other than the brilliant after-image of photographic flashes and movie lights imprinted on the back of his eyeballs in throbbing shades of neon – was that his head hurt terrifically. And he wasn't laying where he had originally fallen; on the living room floor of Patrick and Araceli's double-wide trailer/caravan, draped artistically across the small hooked rug sitting before the door, a rug which had an elaborately worked motto on it – in Spanish. *Limpie sus pies*, the motto commanded. Wipe Your Feet. Now Richard looked at the rug from across the room, and also a bright light shining into his left eye – as a masterly hand held his eyelid open.

"F**k off, get that bloody thing out of my face!" he demanded, and pulled away.

"Okay, he's awake and back to his usual self," drawled Chris Mayall. The light winked out, and Richard blinked against the after-image dazzle, and demanded again, baffled beyond all words. "What the hell is going on, and what are you doing here?" All that he could recall was opening the door of Araceli and Patrick's down-market but simple, comfortable home, and the blast of lights and voices that met him, a wave of horror washing over him like some ghastly tsunami. Then darkness, nightmare, flashing lights and someone screaming. He was pretty certain that it had been him.

Well, that'll put me well to the rear of the pack in the Luna City manhood stakes!

There were faces beyond Chris' lean and cappuccino-colored one; the paler one of Araceli, and the yet even paler countenance of Jess Abernathy. All three were looking down upon him with matching expressions of deep concern, mixed now with some relief. Chris winked out the small silver medical torch, and tucked it into the pocket of his shirt-front – the navy-blue uniform shirt which bore the name *Mayall* embroidered above one pocket, and the logo of the *Luna City Volunteer Fire Department - Medic* on the other. Chris had a stethoscope in his hand now, and the earpieces already fixed; he scowled at Richard, saying, as he pressed the business end of it against Richard's chest, slightly to the left of his sternum.

"Shut the f**k up, Rich – your BP was in the stratosphere. You were merely having the mother-f**ker of all flashbacks and a serious panic attack. Just as a matter of record and professional respect, I'd prefer that you not stroke out on me. Looks bad for us and can really wreck your own day. You want the guys transport you to Karnesville Med Center? Get seen by a doctor?"

"No," Richard gasped, as soon as Chris took away the stethoscope. "I'm fine, now. I want to go home."

Chris snorted. "No, you ain't, asshole. Not to Blighty-land <u>or</u> the Age of Aquarius Campground and Goat-f**kery; not tonight, anyway. And not alone. You gotta be monitored. If you won't let us haul your ass to the hospital in Karnesville, you better spend the night here."

"He can stay the night," Araceli said. Richard noted with mild astonishment that she actually sounded concerned. "In the children's room. Katie is spending the night, too – she can look after him. She got every badge there was for First Aid when she was a Girl Scout."

"I suppose that will be all right," Chris admitted, grudgingly. He sat back on his heels, returning the stethoscope to his bag of emergency supplies and eyed Richard. "I gotta know, pal – who the hell were those guys Joe was chasing down the road to town? I passed them on the way when I got the call to come here. I thought I recognized that lard butt Canadian treasure hunter. He was making damn-good time for an old guy."

"Mr. Gunnison Penn," Jess Abernathy's own voice had that icy steel edge to it; the tone which could shave Parma ham into tissue-paper thin slices. "And some of his reporter friends. They came here with the intention of door-stopping Pat or 'Celi about the gold coin that Mateo found at the Easter Egg hunt, hounding them into telling them all where he found it by making a big fuss with the cameras and lights. It's a pretty crummy tactic; in the morning, Pops will call the judge in Karnesville and ask him to file an injunction ordering them not to come anywhere within fifty feet of this place, or the school. Although I think that some of them will have to sneak back to retrieve their cameras and light-stands."

"They weren't after me?" A blessed wave of ... something washed over Richard. He didn't know if it was sheer, lighthearted relief, or crushing disappointment. "Well, stone the crows. It was just a case of mistaken identity!"

Araceli sniffed, remarking, "I will be a nice person – I may gather up all their gear from the yard and pile it next to the mailbox, and if Tio Jaimie's old basset hound pisses all over it before they come back, it's so not my fault."

"You can take your time," Chris zipped up his medical kit and stood up. "Joe looked like he was gaining on them, coming around the turn-off to the high school, but with his knees, he ain't got any stamina when it comes to distance … speak of the devil," Chris added as the front door opened and shut, admitting the chief of Luna City's police department, panting only slightly. "You catch 'em, Joe?"

"No," Joe Vaughn limped into the room – most uncharacteristically sweating and disheveled. "But I put the fear of God into them before they got away. Last I saw, they were beating feet on 123, heading south. Bastards should be halfway to Karnesville. I'll send Milo with the patrol car, after a while, if I'm feeling generous. Is Ricardo gonna be OK?"

"Pretty certain," Chris looked thoughtful for a moment, "I wish he'd agree to going into Karnesville to see a for-real doctor …"

"You'll do, Squid, you'll do. Damn – I never thought civilians got PTSD. Gimme back the Kel-Tek, Jess – I guess no one tried to come through the door?"

"Yep, they sure can," Chris replied, "It all depends on the degree of initial trauma."

Jess silently handed Joe a small, evil-looking pistol. Before Richard's horrified gaze, Joe casually hiked up his pants leg and replaced the pistol in an ankle-holster.

"You don't need to talk about me as if I'm not here." Richard demanded. "Are you always armed while attending to your social obligations?"

"Sure, Ricardo – I'm never really off-duty; Colt in a shoulder harness, Kel-Tec in my sock, Ka-Bar in my other sock, switchblade in one pocket and a Gerber in the other. And those are just my social-occasion arms. The professional gear is locked in the station gun-safe safe."

"Singular," Richard searched for words and could only find that one. Joe Vaughn grinned, although he grimaced as he held out a hand to Jess.

"Break out the heating pads and the extra-strong Motrin when we get home, Babe – my knees are feeling it already. You better spend the night here, Ricardo – you don't look so hot."

"I guess so," Richard agreed.

Chris hefted his bag. "Don't forget, Joe – drink plenty of water with that Motrin. Look, Ricardo – since you won't see a doctor, here's what I'm gonna tell you to do: first, have a nice long hot relaxing soak in the bathtub tonight. I'm gonna bring you some nice special sedatives; take one when you get into bed, the other if you wake up with the jitters before morning. Don't take both at once – they're prescription, and OD'ing on them would be a professional strike against me for giving them to ya. Don't drink any more alcohol tonight. Maybe some nice herbal chamomile tea with honey to kill the taste, sleep in tomorrow as long as you need to. Talk to a friend, but don't dwell on it." Chris nodded towards Araceli. "I'll be back in a few."

"Right – I'll leave the back door unlocked for you," Araceli nodded, and saw Chris, Joe and Jess out. During the flurry of leave taking and goodbyes, Richard closed his eyes, for his head still ached abominably and he felt as if he had been either beaten-up or run through a tumble-dryer together with a duvet stuffed full of boulders. He may have dozed for some minutes, for between the headache and the beaten-up feeling, he was as exhausted as he had ever been, even the night when he first arrived in Luna City.

"Hey, Chef!" That was Araceli's whisper; he opened his eyes. She stood by the sofa, enveloped in a fleece housecoat that covered her like a monk's robe from neck to toes. She looked as tired as he felt. It was now fully dark outside the windows of the double-wide, so some considerable time may have passed, at that. "The bathtub is all yours. I've put a pair of Pat's clean PJs in there for you, and a fresh towel. Don't worry about opening the Café in the morning – I'll take care of it, and Pat'll take the kids to school. I'm afraid you're sharing the kid's room with Katie – so behave yourself, OK?"

"Araceli, my sweet, in my current physical and mental condition, I do not present a threat to anyone, sexually or otherwise," Richard stood with a groan, and Araceli eyed him with fresh concern.

"You OK, Chef?"

"No," Richard sighed. The horrible memories of last year in London, at the abortive opening of Restaurant Carême jangled along his nerves like animated skeletons, those brightly adorned ones that the local people favored for that quaint celebration of the deceased. Araceli's look of concern deepened, and to forestall her insisting upon a visit to the Karnesville Medical Center Emergency Room, he added, "But I'm certain I'll be better after a good night sleep."

"Right, Chef," Araceli still looked skeptical. "Chris brought those sedatives. Katie is holding them for you; and he says they will help, somewhat. OK, the bathroom is through there, and the kid's room is the door next to it. Don't worry about them; they're spending the night with me. They were pretty shaken up, and with Pat away tonight, Matty and Angelika will sleep better with me. When you're finished, I'll bring some chamomile tea to you both. Abuelita swears by chamomile tea, for a good night's sleep."

"Thank you, Araceli," Richard said – to his own ears, that came out as if someone at his back was hissing at him to remember his own manners. "You've been an absolute brick." He thought for another second – then took her hand with a splendid air of gallantry and kissed it, whereupon Araceli snatched it back, saying,

"You don't have to go all sentimental on me, Chef. Take your bath and go to bed; it's already after nine."

"Yes, ma'am," Richard answered, somewhat relieved that at least Araceli was in something like her usual authoritative mood. "Good night."

"Good night, Chef." With that, Araceli vanished into the brief hallway which led to the bedrooms and bathroom, although she left the light on for him. The one doorway open led into the bathroom, still warm and faintly scented with the odors of bath soap and a faint lingering odor of female toiletries. Somewhat surprisingly, the bathroom was fitted with not only a shower stall, but a generous oval-shaped bathtub, already filled halfway, and with a clean and neatly folded towel stacked on the closed seat of the necessary with a clean t-shirt and a pair of draw-string waist pajama trousers. Richard regard it all with amazed gratitude.

Was it possible, that if he had this to come back too, after the catastrophe that was the opening night of Restaurant Carême … perhaps the whole thing wouldn't have been so … so catastrophic. Or perhaps, it was something which had building for a long time, like one of those legendary Caribbean storms, which started as a small spot of depression out in the middle of the sea, and then swept ashore in a howling tempest of destruction. No – too much thinking. It made his head ache. Richard stripped off, and slid into the water, soothingly hot. He had not been in a bathtub for more than a year. The Airstream featured only a miniscule yet efficient shower stall. Bliss to braise himself, soaking in that bounteous tub but eventually the water cooled. By that time, he felt as limp and wobbly as if his muscles were made of rubber bands, and drawing on Pat's loaned tee-shirt and pajama drawers was an absolute effort.

There was a faint bluish light still showing under the door next to the bathroom; obviously, Mateo and Angelika's bedroom, now serving as quarters for unexpected overnight guests. For form's sake, Richard tapped on it twice and opened it without waiting for a response; it wasn't as if he had never shared a bedroom with a female acquaintance before, and frequently on a shorter acquaintance than that with Miss Kate Heisel.

A pair of twin beds almost filled the tiny bedroom. Even lined up against opposite walls, there was barely enough room between them for a tiny night-stand and a fuzzy hooked rug, obviously by same hand as the one by the front door. One was made up with Disney princess sheets and a pastel comforter; Kate Heisel sat cross-legged in the middle of it, with her laptop computer screen casting sufficient glow. She was wearing pink flannel pajamas patterned with white bunny rabbits and yellow daisies, and for once, her dark hair fell about her shoulders, instead of her customary sloppy bun. She looked about twelve years old.

"Oh, hey, Rich," she said casually, without looking up from the screen. "About time. I was thinking you were gonna fall asleep in the tub. Your first pill is there – 'Celi brought you the chamomile. Hope you don't mind Superman sheets."

"When in Rome," Richard edged carefully between the beds, and sat on the edge of what obviously was Mateo's bed. A pair of ceramic mugs sat on the night-stand, one almost empty, the other full. There was a pill in a little paper mini-muffin paper cup next to it; Richard downed it with half the contents of the full mug, and lay down, acutely aware that he was not at home in the Airstream, on his own familiar bed – and also aware in a purely intellectual way of Kate, absorbed in whatever she was doing on her laptop.

Until she closed it, and set it carefully aside, plunging the room into a dimness slightly alleviated by a night-light at the foot of their beds. The bedclothes rustled. Obviously, she was settling to sleep in a likewise unfamiliar bed. Richard devoutly wished for Chris' allegedly potent sedative to kick in. He was afraid that she would start to talk. Women always started to talk at the most inconvenient time.

And of course, she did.

"You feeling better now, Rich?" she asked, after a long moment.

"A bit, I think," he said – well, honestly, this was awkward, at least as much for her as for him. "I ... really didn't want to see a doctor. This is probably best, all the way around."

"You scared the living biscuits out of us all," Kate observed, with clinical detachment. "Probably scared Gunnison Penn's news-hound friends even more, though. Especially after Joe came bombing out of the kitchen with an automatic in each hand. I'll bet you anything they'll have a good long think about it, the next time they consider door-stopping some family in Luna City."

"True," The mental image that brought forth was worth a dry chuckle or two. "I've come to expect that kind of conduct from the press, though. Unfortunate though it is to be on the receiving end of it. Didn't you ever do that, Kate? It is your profession, after all."

"No," Kate answered, out of the dark. "I rely more on subtly and charm. And sometimes a bit of judicious stalking. Flies, honey, better bait than vinegar. So you flashed back to a previous bad experience tonight. Is that why you've been hiding out here in Luna City for the past year?"

"So much for subtlety," Richard sighed. "Like a brick through a plate glass window, your particular brand of subtlety. Yes ... for one ghastly moment, I thought my cover had been blown, I was being hunted to ground again by a mob, and it all came crashing back onto me."

"But they weren't hunting you, Rich," Kate replied. "It was purely an accident. Look – don't hold honesty against me, 'kay? You're old news. No one is seriously looking for you. Hey, maybe in about twenty years, when someone needs to fill up the bottom half of a *'where are they now?'* feature. But at present? Nada, zip-a-roony. On to the next celebrity crack-up, or some pop-tart busting out the seams of her dress on Academy Awards night – whichever draws more eyeballs."

"So no one gives a damn about the Bad Boy Chef?" Rich mused. Honestly, he wasn't nearly as crushed by this intelligence as he thought he would have been. Still – so many years of pursuing and suckling at the breast of the Great Goddess Publicity and now he was dropped like a used tampon; it still sent a pang through him – or might have, save for the aftermath of the hot soak, Chris's illicit sedative and his own bone-weariness.

"Nope." Kate sounded remarkably confident. "I checked, you know. No interest at all. Most everyone thinks you are locked away in some insanely expensive and private rehab facility somewhere on the West

Coast. Now, Abuelita always cared about Rich Hall – but that was only because she adores the Food Channel and you reminded her of Abuelo Jesus, God rest him. And you had some really nice recipes on your TV show. Now, as for Ricardo … Richard Astor-Hall; we do care about him. Prickly, bossy, self-centered, but he does the most amazing cinnamon rolls, and cakes and stuff … that's the person who matters in Luna City." He heard the bedcovers stirring as she moved in the other bed. "Look now – give me your hand, so that you know I am being totally honest."

"All right then," Richard stretched out his right hand, reaching across the narrow gap between the beds, felt her hand taking his in the darkness, thinking muzzily that the bath and sedative had really gotten to him, this time. "Now – given my hand for that assurance, tell me what you honestly think, Miss He… Kate. Although I have to confess that I have never understood women."

"I am being honest," Kate repeated, with patient emphasis. "And as a woman, I have to confess that sometimes, we don't actually understand ourselves, either. But you matter in Luna City. No one here gives a waffle-fried damn that you used to be the Bad Boy Chef. Anyone coming here looking for the Bad Boy Chef … we purely don't have any idea of what on earth they are talking about. And you can take that to the bank."

"Thank you," Richard replied. And yes; that was a reassurance indeed. Who would be looking for a has-been celebrity at a run-down campground in South Texas. He could open the door – any door – in Luna City in the perfect confidence that there would only be a friend on the other side.

Chamber of Commerce Winter Newsletter

Winter 2016 Newsletter

Luna City Chamber of Commerce

5 North Town Square, Suite 4

And check out our Facebook Page

The Mills Farm Country Store opens their Christmas Bazaar annex, on Saturday, December 3rd, at 10 AM. Hand-made gifts, gourmet candy and food, and original art will be offered for sale throughout the season. The Christmas Bazaar will be opened in Guest Cottage #2, which will be decorated throughout all the rooms with festive and seasonal ornaments, including a Christmas tree in the parlor. Santa and Mrs. Claus will be available for granting Christmas wishes and pictures with children, every Saturday until Christmas Eve, from 11-3.

Christmas on Town Square

The traditional lighting of Town Square is scheduled for December 3rd, at 8 PM. Mayor Abernathy will ceremoniously turn on the switch which will illuminate the Bandstand and the Trees in Town Square. Owners of storefronts lining the square will compete in decorating their own buildings and their shop-window displays. Lunaites may vote on the best display by casting a vote at Chamber offices through December 24th, when the winner and runners-up will be announced at the Annual Christmas Parade. Because this will be Christmas Eve, the schedule of events; the parade, Santa's Arrival and concerts by the Moths Band and High School chorus will be moved up an hour, to permit all of our participants and volunteers time to celebrate the season with their families.

This year, Jesus Gonzales has generously made his bucket truck available, to assist us in safely decorating the fine cypress tree in front of the 1st Luna City Methodist Church.

Upcoming Events

October 29

Luna City Players – Let No True Hearts – 5PM Town Square

November 10

Decoration of local veteran graves with American flags – volunteers assemble at the VFW at 2 PM

December 21

Winter Solstice Observance at Age of Aquarius

Holiday Food Drive

Contributions for the community food pantry Holiday Dinner baskets may be dropped off at the SSts. Margaret and Anthony Parish Thrift Store, on East Town Square any time that they are open, Monday Through Friday. Holiday Dinner baskets will be distributed to local families in need on Monday, November 21st, and on Monday, December 19th.

Luna City ISD News

Mighty Months Marching Band Practice

Regular band practice will be every Monday afternoon from 3-5, and every Thursday morning from 6-8. Band members should have received music for new selections prior to the start of the new school year, and to be familiar with their parts before the start of practice.

Life Skills Course - Update

Since Richard from the Café has kindly agreed to teach a segment on survival cooking, the parents of sophomores scheduled to take the Life Skills Course must amend the student permission slips to include any significant food allergies. Food will be prepared and consumed by the students as part of the class. Any potential adverse reactions will merit transportation by the fastest means possible to the Karnesville Med-Center for treatment.

Canned Food Drive

As in every holiday season, there will be a decorated container in High School foyer to collect food for the Karnesville Community Food Bank, through the end of December. Canned goods, shelf-stable and dry foods such as pasta, cornmeal, spices and bottled sauces are requested. Please be careful when adding your contribution to this container. Consider the breakability and stain-producing capacity of those items already donated.

LCISD PTA Hamburger and Hot Dog Stand

PTA volunteers will open and maintain a hamburger and hot-dog stand by the Moth Field stand, offering grilled hamburgers and dogs – with and without chili – chips and soft-drinks during all home games. Our thanks to Andy Pryor for spearheading this effort to provide refreshments at a reasonable cost to Moths fans.

Community Marketplace

Seasonal Celebration at Age of Aquarius

Judy and Sefton Grant will celebrate the winter solstice with their guests, beginning at sundown on December 21st, featuring a vegetarian pot-luck feast, the ceremonial lighting of the Yule log, and the launching of sky lanterns – subject to favorable environmental conditions. Since this year has been relatively damp, it is expected that the launch of sky lanterns will be allowed by the LCVFD.

From Chief Vaughn, Luna City PD

The graded pasture just off RT 123 adjacent to the VFW post and the Tip Top Gas, Ice and Grocery will be used as the main parking lot on Saturday, October 29th, for the guests attending the Luna Players performance of *Let no True Hearts Admit Impediment*. All vehicular traffic on Town Square will be blocked save for emergency vehicles after 3 PM

Daily Breakfast Specials at Luna Café and Coffee

Richard at the Café is offering in-house, fresh-from-the-oven daily pastries:

Monday – Doughnuts
Tuesday – Butter croissants
Wednesday – Assorted muffins
Thursday – English-style crumpets
Friday – Scones
Saturday – Assorted Danish pastries

Luna City, Texas – Home of the Mighty Fighting Moths   Page 2 of 2

Romeo

When Richard woke the next morning – having slept the sleep of the righteous in Superman sheets – he was alone in the Gonzales children's bedroom, where mid-morning summer sunlight leaked around the edges of the roller blind that covered the single window. The bed opposite, neatly made with Disney princess sheets, was empty and Kate Heisel was gone; Richard was unsure if he was regretful over that, or not. In telling him bluntly that he was very much a celebrity back number and that no one in his old life seemed inclined to seek him out for any purpose; that was a comfort in one way, but a definite kick in the crotch to his ego in another.

His clothing from the night before was freshly-laundered, folded and stacked at the foot of the bed where Kate had slept, his shoes next to them. Really, Araceli thought of everything. Richard dressed – his native good manners belatedly kicking into overdrive – and took his borrowed pajamas with him.

The smell of bacon frying greeted him out in the small kitchen, where a sleepy-eyed Patrick was scrambling eggs at the stove.

"Hi, Rich," Patrick yawned. "'Celi said you were sleeping like a rock – and not to bother you until you woke up. She's gone to work, the kids are at school – me, I'll hit the sack myself in another twenty minutes."

"What time is it?" Richard asked. "Thanks for the loan of the PJs. I was … not in good shape last night, but I am much better, now – thanks to yours' and Araceli's hospitality."

"Half past nine," Patrick answered. "Glad to hear it … 'Celi said it was quite a ruckus last night. I'm sorry to have missed the excitement. But on the other hand – I might not have been near as polite as Joe was. Just put those in the laundry basket in the bathroom, and siddown for a bit of breakfast. You want some hot sauce on your eggs?"

"No, I'm pretty much a traditionalist when it comes to my morning eggs," Richard replied, repressing a small shudder,

"You're missing a thrill," Patrick shrugged. "Everything goes better with a bit of siracha sauce."

"I'll take your word for it," Richard replied. They ate breakfast in companionable silence, Patrick stifling the occasional yawn. Richard, still feeling a little at odds through not having another day at work, decided that he would ride the bicycle home to the Airstream and spend a leisurely afternoon reading Larousse. The weather being temperate – cool autumn being welcomed after the searing blast of summer – he might even sit outside.

His bicycle was where he had left it the afternoon before, leaning against the stairs leading to the screened back porch. As he left by the front, where a low chain-link fence enclosed the front garden, he did note a single lonely news microphone covered with an enormous furry windscreen muff lying abandoned by the gate. It looked at first glance like a very large, very road-killed raccoon. A Basset hound with a lugubrious expression and drooping ears waddled over from across the road, cocked a leg and peed luxuriously on it, and looked at Richard as if seeking approval.

"Good boy!" Richard said. Gunnison Penn and his friends must have retrieved the rest of their jettisoned video gear under cover of darkness. He wheeled out his bicycle and set off, feeling as if he were on a bit of a holiday.

Coming up to the dirt road turn-off for the Age of Aquarius, he heard a truck behind him – slowing to make the turn. He took the prudent step of pulling entirely off the road and letting the truck pass him; a slightly battered but otherwise well-kept extended cab pick-up truck of the sort that half the working men around Luna City drove. There was a weathered twenty-foot Fifth-wheel travel trailer hitched to the back of the truck – one of the plain bare-bones models without any of the bump-outs that increased the living space when parked. Trailer and truck alike were layered in dust, and alike bore North Dakota license plates. Richard let the dust settle, before he followed after; it looked like Romeo Gonzales had not followed the advice of his friends to just keep going.

Well, thought Richard – a social gain for him, in having company at the Age of Aquarius, besides the over-friendly goats and the annoying Canadian treasure hunter, Gunnison Penn. By the time he got to the campground field proper, the driver of the truck had deftly backed the Fifth-wheel into a parking place at the other end of the field from the Airstream. Well – since the place was all but empty for much of the year, they might as well give each other space. As far as Richard was concerned, Gunnison Penn could give them all the space of the entire county.

"I wonder how much longer he'll be staying anyway," Richard wondered aloud. He really hoped that Romeo would be a more congenial neighbor, in spite of Sefton Grant's worrisome aside about Romeo's propensity for attracting strange energies, and Araceli's tale of how he was a particularly disaster-prone Jonah in the oil fields. So, good that his Fifth-wheel and pick-up were parked the length of the campground away. Richard propped his bicycle against one of the posts that held a metal awning over the Airstream and opened the door; he had adjusted so much to the ambiance of Luna City that he never locked door any more, either. He felt again the contentment of coming home, a feeling unknown to him since his school-days. When Romeo the walking disaster-area was done with settling his trailer in, he might walk over and introduce himself.

Some fifteen minutes later, a small yellow Jeep Wrangler appeared in the rutted and unpaved lane leading to the campground. Richard closed *Larousse Gastronomique*; Jess Abernathy; thirtyish CPA and championship barrel-racer, daughter of Martin the acting mayor, an Abernathy of the hardware store Abernathys, who as things went in Luna City were nearly one of the established old families. The Jeep bumped across the lumpy field and parked next to the Airstream, and Jess emerged from the driver's seat, her briefcase in one hand, and a strange sort of potted plant in the other.

"Hi, Rich," she said, with an expression of relief. "Doc said that I should check on you today, although Araceli says you seemed to be OK this morning. And this is for you also – from Miss Letty, for your little patio. She says that nothing like a green plant dresses up a patio or a front porch."

"I'm fine," Rich answered. "You needn't have gone to the trouble … and what in hell is that thing?"

"No trouble," Jess grinned, mischievously. She set the plant on the small patio table. "It's a spider plant – just water it a couple of times a week and take it inside when a freeze is expected. With luck and you don't kill it, there'll be little baby spider plants growing on the ends of long stems. I was coming out here anyway. When Doc heard about last night, he was pretty pissed-off. He considers you one of his personal projects, which is terribly patriarchal of him, but hey – he's a product of his age and upbringing. He had his personal lawyer get ahold of the district judge at the crack of dawn and write up an injunction. Mr. Gunnison Penn is hereby instructed on pain of arrest to not approach within thirty feet of your person, your place of residence, the Café, or any private or public place where you happen to be – such as the high school. You volunteered to teach a survival cooking segment to the life-skills class, and there's no way you can get out of it."

Jess drew out a large manila envelope from her briefcase. "And the same with regard to Araceli and Patrick and their kids. I was charged with delivering these copies of the injunction to Mr. Penn, since Doc was too angry to wait on the availability of a bailiff. Not an errand, but simply one of life's little pleasures. And this, for you also – in case of emergencies." She handed him a small, low-market cellphone. "This is officially a company phone, so don't go all crazy with the personal calls. We've already preprogrammed mine and Joe's number, the number for Doc, for Doc's personal lawyer, the Luna City PD and a couple of others. And this is the instruction manual for it." She handed over a small, thick volume.

"Ah – it seems this Monday morning has much to recommend it," Richard was feeling better and better. "And your friend Romeo has arrived safely – is that him?"

"It certainly is," Jess shaded her eyes. The distant driver of the truck with North Dakota plates was now busying himself with setting the braces to balance the trailer and unhitch it from the truck bed. She looked amused and exasperated. "But we really aren't friends, as it were. He was ... oh, three years ahead of me in high school and our social circles didn't intersect. He was a total jock. Around here, there is a sort of social pecking order, based on your sport. Did you play sports at your school, Rich?"

"Nothing brutal like rugger – I was on the rowing team, and on the school sailboat."

"La-de-dah," Jess snickered. "Then you wouldn't have rated at all, when it came to date-bait. Neither did I, back then."

"I presume that you were a total swot … what you Yanks call a bookworm?"

"Glasses and braces both," Jess nodded. "Romeo was always perfectly charming … but just a sort of charming male butterfly, flitting from flower to blooming flower. He usually didn't bother much with the barely-open buds."

"I was going to wait a while before I introduced myself," Richard ventured. At that moment, Sefton Grant appeared from the direction of the Grant's untidy yurt-based home site farther up the hill. He was carrying something over his shoulder – several very long slender poles, some of them tipped with … Richard blinked. Some kind of green glass insulating knobs, of the old-fashioned sort that used to be used to insulate electrical wires, a heavy sledge-hammer in the other. "What on earth …"

"We may as well go say howdy," Jess said, firmly. "And see what fresh lunacy Sefton and Judy are going to inflict on their guests. Mostly it's the fairly harmless kind, although the LCVFD safety officer did have to warn them sternly about that sweat-lodge they built at mid-summer…"

As they passed Gunnison Penn's RV with the fading Treasure Hunter International logo painted across the side, Sefton Grant had paced off the corners of the space surrounding Romeo Gonzales' Fifth-wheel. He was setting a pole in each corner, plunging the end deep into the ground – which had been mercifully soften by a series of recent rains – and then pounding it further in with blows from the sledge-hammer. Each blow clanged like a bell; once well-seated in the earth, the second, glass-tipped pole was set into it.

Jess muttered something under breath about New Age crapola, and demanded, "Sefton, what on earth is this?" as soon as they came close enough to speak without shouting. Sefton Grant, who looked like a younger, fitter and less-run-to-seed version of Willie Nelson, hefted the sledge-hammer, and picked up the last set of poles.

"Judy's idea," he explained, somewhat abashed. "Something to bleed off the excess psychic energies before they build up. I'd explained it already to Romeo ... hey, Romeo, you remember Jess Abernathy, don't you? And this is Richard – he runs the Café now, lives out in the old Airstream. He's from England."

Romeo, thus addressed, wiped grime off his hands with a somewhat less dirty bandanna, tilted his straw cowboy hat further back on his head, and stuck out his right hand. "Howdy, folks," he drawled. Richard was momentarily nonplussed. He had never, in his life, either before arriving in Texas or after, observed anyone tilting their hat and saying 'howdy, folks.' "Jess! Good to see you, girl! You don't say – England, huh? Man, I feel like I've driven from there, these last few days, instead of all the way from Missoula, Montana. Good to meet you!" he pumped Richard's hand with the strength which can only come from a man who has spent the last fifteen years wrangling heavy tools and machinery. "I guess we're neighbors, then!" Romeo added, with a cheerful and wholly openhearted grin.

"I guess that we are," Richard said, after searching his mind for something to say. "I've heard about you," he added. Which he had; but what he had not heard was that Romeo Gonzales was so very blindingly the winner in the lottery of good looks in a clan whose general appearance clustered around a norm of 'average' to 'pleasant' with an occasional outlier of younger Gonzalez/Gonzaleses in the direction of 'cute.' Physically, he was tall, lean-hipped big-shouldered wedge of a man, with chiseled facial features, and pale blue eyes which contrasted to devastating effect with black hair and a tan not acquired in a salon through artificial means.

"Yeah, I've heard of you, too – you're that chef guy, 'Celi's boss," Romeo exclaimed. "Say – when I get settled, we ought to go out honky-tonking together! It'll be a blast..."

"That's what we're all afraid of," Richard thought he heard Sefton say, in a discrete murmur, and to cover it, he replied, "Well … I have the Café, and they expect me to be there very early most mornings, so my evening social life is … for the moment, pretty constrained."

"No problem," Romeo favored him with another one of those blinding grins. "I'm gonna work driving the wrecker for Uncle Jesus at the garage, so I've gotta be careful myself about staying out of trouble, I reckon."

The Cattleman Hotel – Luna City

(From Texas Highways, 2005)

Among the dozen notable late 19th Century Beaux-Arts style buildings lining Luna City's historic Town Square is the Cattleman Hotel. Four stories tall, with a mansard-style roof which adds still another story, the exterior is a flamboyant combination of mellow rose-pink Texas granite, with architectural trimmings of imported white Carrera marble; window and door surrounds balustrades and pediments creating a notable contrast. The frieze, cornice and projecting modillions were also of Carrera marble, with primary highlights picked out in gold. A large half-circular bay formed the main ground-floor double-door entrance, sheltered with an ornate cast-iron and glass canopy, and extended through the upper floors to the cornice as a series of stacked bay windows with narrow balustrades.

The Cattleman Hotel originally was named the Grand Palazzo Vittoria Hotel; designed and constructed with no expense spared in 1885 by one of Luna City's original minor investors, an Italian gentleman and entrepreneur of means, Signor Afredo Vittorio di Barreca. At this time, Luna City's investors had expected the San Antonio and Aransas Pass Railway would pass through Luna City; Arthur Wells McAllister, the engineer and surveyor who had laid out the town and designed much of the still-extant public buildings, had designed a particularly ornate railway *station (which would have been constructed about where the Luna City Police Department and Volunteer Fire Department garages are located now).* Arthur Wells McAllister also expected Luna City to become the county seat, and accordingly planned a fabulously ornate courthouse to occupy Town Square instead of the pleasant square of oak trees, lawns and flowerbeds which adorn the space today. Signor di Barreca, therefore, designed and outfitted his enterprise in the full confidence that his palatial hotel would become the cynosure of local social life and a refuge for weary travelers; thirty-five guest rooms, including three suites, a gentleman's smoking room on the second floor, a lavish bar with back bar, etched mirror, glass shelves and fittings made from imported Circassian walnut, a dining room capable of seating a hundred diners at a time, and a ballroom with a stage at one end, suitable for concerts and theatrical performances.

Signor di Barreca, already middle-aged and prosperous through his previous hotel properties in Italy and in the eastern US, was married to a young woman barely half his age, Filomena Gismondi, who had ambitions as an opera singer. Although quite beautiful, vivacious and charming, and with a pleasing singing voice, young Signora Gismondi had neither the drive or luck to continue performing professionally on the opera stage, and it is assumed, gratefully accepted an offer of marriage. Signor di Barreca was, however, indulgent of his young wife, and it is said, had the ballroom and stage included in the design of his establishment so that she could continue giving recitals and concerts.

Alas; as has been related elsewhere, the grand ambitions of all those who invested in the vision of Luna City as a traveler's mecca, and county seat – were undone by love. Signor di Barreca, like Arthur Wells McAllister, was not unduly cast down by this misfortune, but zestfully turned his energies into carrying on his own vision of his hotel as a destination and show-place for winter visitors to Texas, refugees from the snow-clad north. In this he was successful for some two decades. Shortly after the turn of the last century, he invested in a motor-coach, which made daily journeys between the nearest railroad station in Karnesville and his hotel, emblazed with the name of the Grand Palazzo Vittoria Hotel, bearing visitors to and fro, while advertising his hotel. The di Barrecas were cosmopolitan in their tastes and travels, returning frequently to visit Europe and England during those years, the height of the so-called Belle Époque.

Signor and Signora di Barreca were the parents of one child, a son named after his father, born in 1896. The senior Signor di Barreca passed away while visiting his homeland in 1908 and his widow promptly remarried. The younger Signor Alfredo returned to Texas, and for several years managed the Grand Palazzo in much the same manner as his father had, although with much less ferocious energy. Upon the outbreak of the First World War, he sold the hotel to the then-owner of the Bodie Feed mill, Alexander Bodie, who was then waxing prosperous, and returned posthaste to Italy, where he enlisted in the Italian Army and perished in fighting on the Italio-Austrian front several years later.

Alexander Bodie tasked his younger sons, Curtis, with the management of the Grand Palazzo Vittoria. Almost his first act upon taking over was to change the name to "The Cattleman Hotel", although faint traces of the original name may still be seen, where they were emblazoned in gold letters on the façade over the third-story bay window. Under that name, the hotel continued to prosper through the first three decades of the twentieth century, although not quite on the same flamboyant scale as previously. A number of rooms were refitted to accommodate in-suite private bathrooms during this period, although such renovations were halted by the ravages of the Depression, which hit South Texas as hard as anywhere else. Wartime shortages and gas rationing had an effect as well, although there was a slight recovery observed in the late 1940s. Still, post-war prosperity and renewed travel opportunities could not repair twenty years of dwindling demand. Many of the smaller rooms on upper floors were emptied of furnishings and closed off permanently.

The second and third-floor rooms continued in sporadic use, as well as the hotel bar and the ballroom – often used for special receptions, meetings and community events, such as a visit by then vice-President Johnson in 1961. But what demand there was for rooms and special events fell precipitously with the development of Mills Farm ten years later. Mills Farm and VPI had the lock on providing entertainment and hospitality venues; with the added benefit of offering an old-fashioned classic Texas experience updated with every modern convenience. In a modern sense, the Cattleman Hotel was extraneous to needs, and in the centennial year of 1976, Curtis Bodie sold the place to a consortium of the Luna City municipality and the Luna City Historical Association for what amounted to a token payment. It was thought possible for a time to use part of the place as a museum, and indeed, the old main lobby is used to this day as a display space for various local historic relics. According to long-time Luna City Historical Association member, Leticia McAllister, there is no truth to the rumor that Mills Farm's parent company, Venue Properties, International, attempted to purchase the historic building outright and move it to the present Mills Farm Property, although that rumor was widely circulated at the time, and helped engender a considerable degree of local distrust towards Mills Farm. That distrust that continues to this day. The plan was, as Miss McAllister avers in a recent interview with our reporter, presented as using the old grand hotel as an adjunct hotel facility for Mills Farm/VPI, but the terms offered were so insulting, they were rejected after brief and acrimonious consultation.

The municipality and the Historical Association are able to maintain the ballroom and dining room as an event venue, although the electrical system is not normally equal to the demands which modern-day celebrations put on it. The Historical Association maintains an office a second-floor room and the city government does so with another two rooms. Many of the remaining rooms are used as overflow storage by the city, the Luna City Independent School District and the Historical Association. The three renovated suites are maintained, ready for rent to interested parties, although of late, this mostly means ghost-hunters.

Yes – the Cattleman Hotel is widely reputed to be haunted; there are the customary moving lights behind the windows of long-uninhabited rooms. Docents who volunteer at the lobby-area museum often insist that they hear the sounds of male voices, and bottles and glassware rattling in the old bar … a room which is customarily locked.

Guests in the three still-used suites have often claimed they detect the odor of pipe tobacco and cigars in the hallway adjacent to the old smoking salon on the second floor – also a room long emptied and locked. There are said to be three main ghosts in the old hotel. None can actually be tied to real people with certainty through historical records – although not from the want of trying on the part of folklorists and ghost-hunters.

The first is said to be that of a female guest; well-bred and traveling alone *(possibly to meet her lover?)* who killed herself with poison in a guest room on the second floor sometime in the late 1880s. Her spirit is said to be the one who roams the second floor, seeming to search for someone. The top floor, which housed hotel staff in the days when the place had live-in staff, is haunted by the spirit of another woman; a maid or housekeeper who was murdered by a spurned boyfriend; she is reported to manifest by the sounds of an invisible broom, sweeping dust … which is seen moving in brief spurts along the floor. The third ghost is that of a reckless young cowboy, who was robbed of his takings at a not-so-friendly poker game in the livery stable which once stood behind the Cattleman Hotel. It is this ghost who is reportedly responsible for the voices and the noises in the old bar.

The Cattleman Hotel is located at the western side of Luna City's historic Town Square. Tours of the building may be arranged by contacting the Historical Society, or the office of the Mayor. When not in his office in City Hall, the mayor may be found at his place of business, Abernathy Hardware.

Dance with the Bunny-Boiler in the Pale Moonlight

Some weeks after Romeo Gonzales arrived and set up his own campsite in the near-deserted Age of Aquarius, Richard pedaled up the road – deftly avoiding the ruts, bumps and puddles that nature and the passage of the occasional heavy vehicle had scoured into the clay-like soil with the skill of experience. It had rained lightly the night before, so puddles there were in plenty, and the fresh new grass had begun just raising tender new blades coyly between the old dead hay of the previous season.

On the whole, he had found Romeo Gonzales to be a congenial neighbor, given that it was hard to be anything else at half an acre space between their trailers and workplaces some blocks distant from each other. At least, Romeo showed no inclination to conspire together with malignantly-inclined micro-media operatives to ambush him at the door with lights, cameras and harassing commentary, unlike the egregious Penn. Who, in concordance with the injunction delivered through Jess, showed every inclination of making himself scarce whenever Richard was around. Richard was profoundly glad of that, not least because he treasured his afternoons of solitary contemplation of the pleasant but uninspiring landscape and his studies in Larousse.

Besides all that, Romeo was good at fixing things. He took it upon himself to shinny up and lubricate the old-fashioned windmill that drove the water-pump which supplied hot water to the old concrete block washhouse in the campground. Romeo adjusted the handbrakes and the chain of Richard's bicycle, and when completely bored and bereft of things to do, popped up the hood of his pick-up truck and tinkered with the mysteries within. Still, Richard had looked out of the Airstream's windows, very late at night, rubbing his eyes because he thought he could see some kind of ephemeral apparition – kind of like the Northern Lights, but rather more red-tinged than electric green, writhing and twisting in the air over Romeo's Fifth-wheel. But as soon as he blinked, that vision was gone.

Now, that very pick-up coasted slowly across the campground, and Romeo leaned out of the drivers' side window. "Hey, Rich – I'm heading out to Karnesville to swap out my propane bottles; you were saying that one of yours is empty and the other almost – you wanna come along?"

"Certainly – and thanks for the offer," Richard answered with honest gratitude. "Run over to the Airstream – I'll put them in." He had been experimenting with various interesting recipes on the tiny propane-powered cooker in the Airstream, which had completely drained one tank. To judge how the burner flame had been flickering of late, he was close to emptying the other. The tanks were heavy and the Walmart in Karnesville was a good ten or fifteen miles distant. In the space of a minute or two, his tanks were in the back of Romeo's sturdy workman's pick-up, and they were out on Route 123 – the back road between San Antonio and Aransas Pass, which gained in scenic qualities and relative lack of traffic in its soothing meandering across scenic portions of South Texas what it lacked in the boring celerity of the major highway.

But there was frequent traffic upon it; some miles along the way to Karnesville, the two of them witnessed evidence of that, in the form of a very late-model, velvet-black Mercedes sedan, off on the grassy verge on the other side of the road. The front left tire of the Mercedes was fatally, hopelessly flattened, and the driver stood uncertainly by it, very obviously boggled by this misfortune, although she held a cellphone in her hand.

"Oh, man," Said Roman, in admiration. "What a gorgeous piece of … and the Merc isn't hard on the eyes, either."

"I don't care!" Richard, recognizing the unfortunate driver, was horrified. He barely restrained his first impulse to dive under the passenger-side dashboard of Romeo's truck; which as one of these huge garish American vehicles, would have been big enough to hide at least two people, three of them if they were light of build. "Drive on – that's the horrible Susannah! She's a stalker, the bunny-boiler of Mills Farm! An executive of theirs! She has haunted me – chased after me! She came out to the trailer … for God's sake, man – don't stop! If you do, you'll regret it, I tell you!"

"She came out to the Aquarius?" Romeo answered. "Damn, Rich, she's way too classy for a lot lizard. I'll run that risk, sure. And that Merc is one awesome bit of machinery." He sighed, as the pick-up swept past the stranded Mercedes. "Sorry, man – you have issues with her. Your problem, not mine. I don't leave ladies with car trouble by the roadside – just my personal standard." He grinned sideways at Richard, who felt his heart sink right down to the level of his trainers. *(Bought at Marisol Gonzalez's thrift shop in Karnesville. He did wonder briefly if he could impose on Romeo to make a quick pit-stop there after trading in the gas bottles.)*

"She's a remora in human-guise," Richard gabbled, frantic and horrified, as Romeo made an easy U-turn and drove back towards the stranded Mercedes and Susannah Wyatt – as always, slim and dressed to the nines in elegant and high-fashion vacation wear. "Just drive on! Call your uncle with the garage and the wrecker – anything! Once she latches onto your flesh, she doesn't let go! A relentless succubus …"

"Sounds like my kind of woman!" Unmoved, Romeo did another U-turn and eased the pick-up off the road, backing up and parking just ahead of Susannah and her stranded Mercedes.

Richard slid down in the passenger seat, lower and lower, hissing between his teeth as Romeo turned off his engine, "I won't be a part of this – I can't be a part of this! For the love of God, don't let her see me! Don't tell her I am here! The woman is a menace: you have no idea of what you are letting yourself in for!"

"No problem, Bro," Romeo answered, with total assurance. He unsnapped his seat belt and opened the driver-side door. "I reckon maybe that I do, and I just won't leave a woman stranded by the roadside with car trouble. That's just not the Gonzales way."

"You'll live to regret it!" Richard made one final frantic and fruitless plea to no avail. He slid farther down in the passenger seat, certain that he would not be seen, since Romeo's truck sat so much higher than the Mercedes and had tinted windows in the back. But he could observe what transpired in the mirrors and hear Romeo's and Susannah's voices since the windows were open.

Romeo, swaggering just the tiniest bit like an old movie cowboy, doffed his hat and drawled, "Say there, little lady, you look like you've got a flat tire, there."

Richard sank even farther down in the seat. "Oh, God – the bloody stereotype. Kill me now." He couldn't hear Susannah's reply, but Romeo continued, "Don't you fret, ma'am, I can change it for ya. Just show me where your spare is. I got all the tools I need in the back of my truck. I'm Romeo Gonzales, by the way – of the Luna City Gonzaleses. You must be Miss Wyatt, from out at Mills Farm. I've heard so much about you."

Richard cringed. The man was absolutely shameless. Burying himself well below the level of the truck windows, Richard waited in an agony of apprehension and impatience. He heard the scrape and clang of metal as Romeo let down the tailgate and opened his toolbox. He risked a peek in the mirror. Good heavens, the man had a substantial auto-jack, of the sort more usually seen in a garage and other serious tools, distaining the usual flimsy accessories packed and forgotten in the trunks of cars for tire-changing purposes. Susannah Wyatt stood by, watching Romeo work with wholly focused attention. Richard had to admit he did a wickedly competent and swift tire change, perhaps a little more leisurely than a pit crew at Le Mans, but then, this wasn't a race. In the space of ten minutes, Romeo had the spare tire on and rolled the damaged one to stow away.

He stood looking down on Susannah, all six-foot something of devastatingly competent male pulchritude, accepting her thanks with touching earnestness, "Now, you be certain you get that patched right away, ma'am – Miz Wyatt. You don't want to be driving around with a bad spare tire … but if it happens again, you just call me, you hear? I'll come running."

Richard gagged: *had the man no pride, no self-respect at all?* But he stayed hidden below window-level, until the velvet-black Mercedes had zoomed away in the direction of Luna City, and he and Romeo had continued on their way towards Karnesville.

"She seems like a real nice woman," Romeo commented, tactfully forbearing to cast any aspersions on Richard's courage or lack thereof, and his taste in female companionship, which consideration Richard appreciated no end. "Takes good care of herself … and that car is a real daisy. Top of the line, with a special custom interior all done in light pink leather. That's serious quality, Rich."

"You are welcome to it," Richard replied, with a shudder at the very thought. "She probably still has the knives out for me, since your cousin Sylvester and I did a *Mission Impossible* for that movie script this summer – long story, that – if she even remembers how we got her drunk, so we could break into her desk."

"Thanks, man – I appreciate it," Romeo said, with same air of earnest literal-mindedness which so distinguished his cousin Berto.

And it was not a week later, on a mild night, when he slept with the windows of the Airstream open to the fresh air, that he woke to hear a thread of music, as if from a distant radio, floating in the night air. He looked out; yes, there was a light on in Romeo's trailer, and another light on the outside, casting a dim circle of illumination on the little paved patio area. In that distant pool of illumination, Romeo and a woman were slow-dancing, close in each other's arms. Oh, it couldn't possibly be …

But the following morning, in the dark before sunrise, as he set off on his bicycle, he pedaled past Romeo's Fifth-wheel … and there by the steps up to the door were a pair of women's fancy cowboy boots. He knew they were women's boots because they were pink leather, and fancifully adorned with flowers and embroidery in appropriate colors. In all of Luna City he knew of only one woman who sported such expensive decorated boots.

"A better man than I am, Gunga Din," Richard murmured to himself in dawning recognition, mixed with awe and sprinkled with a soupcon of relief.

It was curious, though, that he never again observed the red-tinged Northern Lights apparition, hanging in the air over Romeo's trailer. Many weeks later, when Romeo had gone from the Aquarius in spectacular fashion, he mentioned it casually to Judy, who nodded in complete understanding.

"It's sex-magick," she said with authority, clearly appending the mystical 'k' to the ordinary word. "The most powerful force in the world, seen and unseen – capable of diffusing the most powerful of the unseen energies." Judy looked at him wistfully, as she handed him a small wire basket filled with eight or nine smooth brown eggs, fresh from the hen's nests. "Romeo is one of those unfortunates who are a focus for those unseen energies … unless they are diverted usefully, they build up until they are violently expressed. There is so much harmful energy in the world which could be neutralized by vigorous practice of sex-magick ...properly organized and conducted, wars ... poverty, world hunger – these could all be abolished forever."

"Indeed," Richard took the basket of eggs, reflecting as he walked down from the Grant's eccentric and yurt-centered compound, that perhaps the energetic and semi-annual efforts in that direction on the part of the commune had certainly freed the small community of Luna City from the scourges of excessive violence, poverty and hunger.

Secondary Education

It was part of Richard's gradual acceptance into the community of Luna City – as a pillar of the same in his office as manager/cook of the Luna Café and Coffee – that he take a turn in the old home economics classroom of Luna City's secondary school teaching a necessary adult survival skill to twenty or so sixteen and seventeen year old students. The high school was named for Hernando "Nando" Gonzales, the legendary jet fighter ace of the Korean War and native son of Luna City; the adult survival skills course had been the mind-blowing stroke of genius on the part of Nando's second cousin once-removed, Geronimo "Jerry" Gonzales while serving as Luna City Superintendent of Schools. A series of adult experts offered an educational smorgasbord; household budgeting and basic income-tax return preparation, simple auto and household trouble-shooting, repairs and maintenance, First Aid … and Richard had been tapped for a week of cooking classes. The class met in a room which had been set up to facilitate cooking lessons, back in the decades when that meant cooking and sewing instruction for girls; five fully-equipped kitchenettes and a central instruction area with an overhead mirror over the prep-area and cooktop. Richard felt oddly at home on the very first day, although it was jarring to be addressed as 'sir' or Mr. Astor-Hall. And he felt terribly old, when he made a reference to Graham Kerr, the Galloping Gourmet, on the very first day, and had to explain it to a roomful of baffled teenagers.

"I could do a two-week segment, next semester," he remarked to Jess Abernathy, at mid-week, when they had their regular management consult. "They're a very promising lot. I had a brilliant inspiration, regarding roast chicken; you know, start with preparing a basic whole roast chicken with basic herbs and lemon on the first day, then move through several different recipes incorporating the leftover cooked chicken … simple dishes, exploring various cuisines … and then finish up with using the bones to make a stew, with dumplings. Tasty, economical, simple; what do you think?"

"The kids will eat it up," Jess said, and Richard replied, "Well, of course – that's the whole point. D'you think I could offer an internship over the summer to one or two of the most promising?"

"You'd have to pay them at least as much as they would earn, bussing tables at Mills Farm," Jess warned him. "We'll look at the finances at the end of this year, see if it can be done. I'm glad you like doing a part of the class, Rich – I was afraid you'd regret it as a waste of time."

"Teaching someone to cook for themselves is never a waste of time," Richard answered with adamantine conviction. "Every creature on earth eats – but cooking your food and cooking it well is the foundation building-block of civilization."

"Well, when you put it that way," Jess laughed. "Hey, if you happen to see Romeo this afternoon – remind him about the costume rehearsal tomorrow at the gym. Kate is going to come and take pictures of the main characters for the newspaper and website, so it's absolutely important that everyone be there."

"So he did get convinced to be the groom?" Richard had almost forgotten about the Luna City Players' benefit event to rebuild the church parish hall, free of the twin scourges of black mold and asbestos; an event which involved staging a terribly dramatic mock-wedding with all the required and traditional trimmings.

"Of course," Jess giggled. "Patricia is terribly persuasive, and Romeo has always been putty in the hands of strong-minded women who don't want to sleep with him."

"He's also putty in the hands of those who do," Rich said. Yes, the velvet-black Mercedes had made occasional appearances, discretely parking on the far side of Romeo's Fifth-wheel. The gossip that he couldn't help overhearing in the Café of a morning, had it that Susannah and Romeo spent many an evening and into the wee hours, honky-tonking in various bars and dance halls in Beeville, Karnesville and even as far afield as Victoria. To his relief, Susannah appeared to make every effort to avoid being seen, especially by Richard.

Romeo had jovially thanked Richard for the semi-introduction; he leered in quite a disgusting manner when he added, "If the trailer is a-rocking, then don't come knocking!"

"Point taken," Jess looked amused. Yes, she must also have heard the Café gossip, although since she and Joe Vaughn were an established couple, this intelligence may have come to her via pillow talk. "Yes, if you want to teach a two-week session next semester, I'm sure Jerry will approve."

"They're nice kids," Richard admitted, feeling somewhat foolish that he had never had much to do with the sub-adult specimens of his species since he ceased being one of them. "I'd like to see them off to a good start in life."

"So do we all." Jess gathered up her spread-sheets and receipts. "So do we all – since they're the ones who will be managing our assisted-living residences."

The adult-skills class was the final regular class of the day, which ended at 3 PM. Richard rather liked it, since it let him put full-time at the Café, and added an extra fillip to complete his working day. The final bell dismissed the class – and he was unexpectedly touched to see that most of the kids departed rather reluctantly, rather than jetting out the premises at full speed, a handful of them lingering to ask very specific food-preparation questions which suggested they were going to go right home and attempt them there that every evening.

Which he thought was all to the good – given his fake biography which involved fixing meals for a mythical starving and neglected family of younger brothers and sisters, and his real-life experience, in cooking for his parents – all pleased and appreciative they were, although some of his early experiments with fusion cuisine were not all that successful. Although his parents were, if anything, sporting about it, since they ate the results with a becoming show of pleasure. He went out the back of the school to where he had left his bicycle leaning against a handy rack, thinking again of how much he owed his parents.

He was mildly surprised, therefore, to observe two Luna City Police department *vehicles (about half the force, until there is sufficient funding to purchase a fifth SUV)* parked around in back of the school, in a sweep of gravel by the auto hobby shop enclosure, the gymnasium and the field house which served as an overflow parking-lot when the Moths played home games. And he noted, with a rising feeling of disquiet, that the Walcott's blinged-out monster SUV with all the extra add-on features was also parked next to a battered panel van with the logo of the popular local *conjunto* band, *Los Maldonados,* stenciled on the sides.

As he took up his bike from the rack where he had left it – for no one locked their bicycles any more than they locked their doors in Luna City – he heard Sook Walcott's steam-whistle shriek of outrage, emanating from the direction of the double doors to the gymnasium, followed very shortly by the pint-size domestic terror herself, dragging her teenage daughter Belle by the arm in one hand and flailing blows in the direction of a dark-haired teenaged boy with the other, while two civilians; Coach "Music Man" Garrett and an older Hispanic man whom Richard didn't recognize, but who was in the customary performance garb of *Los Maldonados*, as was the boy and Belle Walcott. Joe Vaughn with three of his officers was attempting to reason with the infuriated Sook.

"You no canoodle with crummy musician!" Sook shrieked at top decibels and her distraught daughter wailed in response, "Mom! Javi wasn't doing anything!"

"Mrs. Walcott!" That was Coach Garrett, mild-mannered middle-aged musician and football coach for the Luna City Mighty Fighting Moths, who hadn't won a game against any of their division opponents in three decades, although the Moths Marching Band, under his exacting tutelage were state and national champions in the marching band sweepstakes several times over. "Mrs. Walcott, please! Calm down and listen to me; there was no impropriety here, we were finishing up Belle's audition tape for …"

"My daughter not be crummy musician!" Sook screamed, unappeased. "She go to proper college, perfect SAT! No canoodle with stupid musician boy!"

"Mom! You're embarrassing me!" Belle pleaded, sobbing. "Javi – Coach – I'm sorry, I didn't know Mom would carry on like this!"

While Coach Garrett begged for reason and decorum and the older Maldonado attempted to pull the teenaged boy out of her reach, the four officers hovered uncertainly, although Rich could see that one officer, whose name badge read "Gonzalez" was already exchanging heated remarks in Spanish with the older Maldonado. Finally, Joe Vaughn shrugged, obviously giving up on reasoned diplomacy and settling for sheer lung-power.

"Enough!" he roared, in a parade-ground bellow which likely could have been heard in downtown Luna City and possibly as far as

Karnesville. "Miz Walcott, lay a hand on Javier Maldonado again, I'll have you in handcuffs on charges of assault and battery. Now – everyone, just calm the hell down. Milo, Jim-Bob, you two see Ignacio an' Javi to their vehicle un-assaulted. Coach, what in the blue blazes is this all about?" he added in slightly lower, but no less aggravated tones, as Sook Walcott shoved her weeping daughter into the Humvee. "Oh, hi, Rich. You got anything to add to this?"

"Not really," Rich ventured. "But I've been told that crime waits for no man."

"Not now, wise-ass," Joe said, as Sook Walcott spun the SUV out of the area in a spray of gravel.

Coach Garrett sighed very deeply. "Chief, I just don't know what gets into that woman, sometimes – but it was all my doing."

"She seemed pretty upset, regardless." Joe said, with remarkable patience, considering. "She must have had something to get fired up about, minor as it usually is. What were you doing here, with Javi and Ignacio and Belle, all dressed up?"

"It was an audition tape," Coach Garrett explained. "For Belle to send with her application to Julliard."

"Julliard – the college for musicians, the one in New York City? <u>That</u> Julliard?"

"My alma mater," Coach Garrett answered, with an air of modest pride. "We were putting together her pre-screening DVD. She's got the Ravel, Rossini and Mozart pieces down pat, but for the solo of her choice, she wanted to go with jazz; Mangione and Javi and Ignacio were just here for moral support, keep her feeling in the zone. She's ... wound pretty tight about all this, as you can imagine. Mrs. Walcott, she has it in her mind that Belle is going to one of those serious colleges, study medicine or law, or something heavy-duty like that."

Remarkably, that seemed to make sense to Joe, who nodded, very slowly. "Their oldest boy – Jerry, is it? He bailed out of all that, broke his parent's hearts like enough, when he went off to study nursing. At a public college, in San Antonio, no less. Don't see why they got all bent out of shape, though. It's a skilled calling, but …" he shrugged. "Kids, they have their own minds. I know that I did, when I was that age."

"So Sook and Clovis now have all their ambitions invested in Belle," Richard mused. He had been just long enough in Luna City to have had business dealings with both Walcotts, seen Belle playing the trumpet with the Moths Marching Band, and with *Los Maldonados* at various local fetes. She was a pretty, but nervous-looking girl with bitten fingernails. Who wouldn't be in her position, given her mother's towering and ear-splitting social and parental ambitions.

"That's it," Coach Garrett nodded, an expression of deep concern on his middle-aged and otherwise bland countenance. "That's it, and that's the trouble; because she is really, really good. All my band kids are good, or at least fair enough by the time I'm done working with them. But she could be world-class; is almost world-class as just as she is. She needs a place like Julliard, to have the space to stretch her wings and really learn. She needs music like normal people need air and water. I … just don't know how to deal with her mother."

"Join the club, pal," Joe tilted his white Stetson a little farther back on his head. They watched the Maldonado's van pull away, and Coach Garrett sighed again.

"At least we got the videotaping done," he said, with a determined air of good cheer. "I can tweak the final bits when Mrs. Walcott came busting in. It's only a prelim screening, anyway. If they accept her, they'll schedule a live audition, in New York."

"Do you think she has a chance of acceptance, Coach?" Joe asked, and Coach Garrett nodded. "Oh, yeah – depend on it. She is that good."

It was a momentary local drama; Richard pedaled away home, arriving with a sense of relief that no fresh installation of it awaited him there. Even Romeo Gonzales, the potential provider of that was gone –

doubtless tom-catting on his own, around the various clubs and bars dedicated to providing entertainment and alcohol to the attractive single man and those women looking to bag one.

But the matter came roaring back, Friday morning at the Café, just as the morning rush slowed to a crawl and he had the time to answer a phone call from a harassed Clovis Walcott.

"Richard, I'm so glad you picked up!" Normally urbane, authoritative, Clovis now sounded harassed and uncertain. "I have a very great favor to ask and I know that it is on short notice; but could you do a little spot of catering at my house on Sunday evening? Nothing like that fabulous dinner last year, but just a small, intimate family meal. For the usual consideration, of course."

"Of course," Richard agreed. "If I may ask; is this some kind of special occasion?"

"Of a sort," Clovis replied. "It's for my daughter, Bee ... you know – Belle. It's ... a special treat for her, because she already has three acceptances for college ... and her mother and I wanted to do something special to celebrate the occasion. Nothing really fancy, like the Wellington. Just special. And tempting. Bee is so ... well, she has ... she has to make up her mind between which college to honor, and it is such an important decision. She has ... well, she hasn't been eating well, and we wanted ... something special. Just for the family – that would be six, counting my mother-in-law."

"I'd be more than happy to do a private family meal," Richard agreed cheerfully. This meant a spot of extra cash, as well as the opportunity to work in the Walcott's gloriously appointed kitchen on what sounded like a fairly simple undertaking. "You wouldn't be needing extra staff – to serve, I take it."

"No, nothing like that," Clovis immediately sounded a touch more assured. "If you prepare the meal, we'll just do what we normally do at home for meals."

"Very good," Richard agreed, with relief. The grand beef Wellington dinner had involved four waitresses, a pot-walloper, two bartenders, Araceli as sous-chef … and strolling musicians. "So – do you have any preferences as to the menu?"

"No, I'll leave that all up to you," Clovis said. "Just that it be so good that no one can resist taking a single bite. Expense is no object. Just present me with your invoice afterwards."

"I'll come up with something this very afternoon, and do the shopping for it tomorrow in Karnesville," Richard promised.

"Probably won't be necessary to go that far," Clovis said. "We keep a pretty full pantry and freezer. Stop over sometime today or tomorrow and see what you can work with. I'm in Hong Kong today, leaving for home in the morning, but I'll let Sook or Min Kim know to expect you." Clovis rang off, after expressing his warmest gratitude, and Richard poured himself a belated mug of coffee and considered the menu for Sunday. It would depend on what the Walcott's had on hand; which, considering his recollection of the size of their kitchen, and the walk-in pantry with bountiful chest-freezer, would most likely render a trip to Karnesville unnecessary.

The Music and the Man

By Katherine Heisel, Staff Writer, Karnesville Weekly Beacon

The start of this school year marks a significant anniversary for Luna City High School's Mighty Moth Marching Band; it is the fifteenth year at the helm for Band Master, and Coach Dwight David "Music Man" Garrett, who arrived in the last week of September, 2001. Dwight Garrett appeared just in the nick of time to rescue the 2001 football season for the Moths. The previous coach Davis L. "Leadfoot" Oatman, who had served in that capacity for twenty-four years had been sidelined by a massive heart attack on the morning of the Moths first game, which impelled his retirement almost immediately. Dwight Garrett, who had played junior varsity football for Henrietta King High School in his hometown of Kingsville and had just taken up a position as Band Master at Luna City High, volunteered to step in as coach until a replacement could be found. Much to everyone's surprise, including his own as he confessed in later interviews, the Mighty Fighting Moths did very well that season, and he was persuaded to continue wearing two hats. While the Mighty Fighting Moths have never again reached the heights achieved by squads in their glory years as division champions during the late 1960s and early 70s, the Marching Band has gone from strength to strength under Coach Garrett's tutelage. They have been selected twice to march in the historic New Year's Rose Parade, in Pasadena, California, and routinely sweep the boards at band competitions the length and breadth of Texas and the Southwest. Over the last ten years, nearly every band member who wished to continue on to college was able to do so on a music scholarship to a school of their choice.

Dwight Garrett was born and raised in Kingsville, where he graduated from Henrietta M. King High School in 1971. After serving two years in the US Army Band (his primary instrument being the oboe), he was accepted to the Julliard School of Music, where he completed the required course of study towards a graduate degree in 1977. Upon graduation, he remained in New York, supporting himself with a series of engagements with various classical orchestras and ensembles, and teaching music at several private schools in Manhattan. In 1995, he married Gwen Carter Dixon, who worked for the investment banking firm of Cantor-Fitzgerald. A divorcee with two sons who were by then well-established in their own careers, the Garretts lived in an uptown condo a short distance from Mrs. Garrett's workplace in the World Trade Center complex. Upon her retirement from Cantor-Fitzgerald, the happy couple planned to tour the world, attending major music events such as Bayreuth and Glyndebourne Festivals. Alas, this was not to be; Gwen Garrett was one of the casualties of the terrorist attack on the World Trade Center, September 11, 2001. Unable to bear remaining in New York any longer, with smoke still rising from the ruins of the Towers, Dwight Garrett rented a car, packed it with a few belongings, sublet the condo and drove cross-country, intending to return to Kingsville. However, he was diverted onto side roads by a major traffic accident on IH 37 between San Antonio and Corpus Christi. Becoming hopelessly lost among a tangle of secondary roads east of Campbellton, he stopped for gas and directions at the Tip-Top Ice House, Gas, and Grocery, where he struck up a conversation with Coach Oatman. Coach Oatman mentioned that a dire need existed for a high school band music director. Being quite a forceful personality in his own right, Coach Oatman insisted straightway that Dwight Garrett come with him to the Luna City ISD offices and speak to School Superintendent Geraldo Gonzales regarding the opening. Upon seeing his qualifications, "Jerry" Gonzales tendered an offer of employment on the spot, and by the time the day was out, Dwight Garrett was settled into temporary quarters at the Cattleman Hotel. Before another two weeks had passed, he was filling Coach Oatman's role as well – and has continued to do so ever since.

A Quiet Family Dinner

Richard bicycled over to the Walcott's mansion the next day, after the Saturday morning breakfast and brunch crowd was done, noting with some mild resentment that Romeo's pick-up truck was gone from the Age of Aquarius – otherwise he would have bummed a ride, for the Walcott manse was a sprawling, architecturally jarring mansion, commanding the entire top of a hill a little way out of town. It was a long and exhausting haul on the mountain bike, but he arrived at it, feeling a little exhilarated, for he had made it all the way up the long, curving drive to the top of the hill only slightly breathless.

On the whole, he thought that he should go around to the front door and announce himself. Going to the back door and letting himself in – as he, Berto, and Araceli had done before on the occasion of the glorious beef Wellington catered dinner – might prove perilous, given local devotion to the principle of a home being a castle, and likely defended by anything short of heavy artillery. Given Clovis Walcott's devotion to the

Karnes Company Rangers reenactor group, Richard would not have been surprised if he <u>did</u> have an artillery piece of the old-fashioned 19th century solid-shot variety.

He rang the bell, heard it clanging within the depths of the house, like something in the bowls of Westminster, and presently the door was opened by the Walcott's youngest son. He was a lad of about fourteen, too young to be in the survival class, but Richard recollected him right away, from the beef Wellington event, although he couldn't for the life of him remember his name. The boy looked like a handsome juvenile edition of Clovis Walcott, but with dark hair and sloe-black eyes which had an epicanthic fold to them.

"Hullo – I'm Chef Astor-Hall. Your father has asked me to do a Sunday dinner for you. I'm sorry, I cannot for the life of me recall your name."

"Robbie," the boy replied. "Yeah, Dad called from Hong Kong to tell us you'd want to come over and check out the groceries. Mom's at the Players rehearsal," Robbie stood back from the door and allowed Richard to step into the terrazzo-tiled entryway, which went up two stories to a domed ceiling. Their footsteps echoed, and the solid thud when Robbie closed the door sounded like a castle drawbridge thudding into place. "She told me to let you in and help you to what you needed. So … the older kids were talking about your cooking class at the school. That's freaking awesome, Mr. Hall. I can't wait until I can take the life-skills class next year."

"I think you would find it a worthwhile experience." Richard said, momentarily baffled by the echoing and unpeopled spaces of the Walcott mansion. After the tidy, miniscule Airstream, this would be like living in an aircraft hangar, or in Paddington Station.

"Kitchen's through here," Robbie said, and Richard followed him, feeling considerable gratitude. "So what are you gonna fix for us, Mr. Hall?"

"Depends on what I find here," Richard answered, as they stepped into the huge, lavishly-equipped kitchen; all granite countertops and stainless steel-finished appliances in the latest fashion. "Your father said it was a special supper for your sister, so maybe you can give me an idea – what are her favorite foods? What does she like best to eat for dessert?"

"I dunno," Robbie shrugged. "Right now, she's not eating food at all ... but normally, she likes ice cream. *Tres Leches* flavor. And strawberries. When Bee and her friends go out for burgers after a game, she always has a grilled chicken sandwich – not a burger."

"Well, that's a start," Richard's mind was already moving to the contents of the vast refrigerator; the largest size available for home, rather than commercial applications, although it would not have surprised him in the least if Clovis' Little Bride had wanted one. The refrigerator beckoned to him. "Robbie, can you take notes? Here's my note-pad and a pencil. I was already considering chicken, for an entrée. *Coq au vin*, perhaps. I know that your father keeps an excellent cellar ... a good French Burgundy, or even a decent Pinot Noir ... of course, I could change it up and make it with Riesling, and the flavor would be somewhat less intense. Let's see ... excellent!"

"Mom an' Conchita went to the Costco in Karnesville yesterday, and loaded up," Robbie explained, as Richard pulled out a double-pack of fresh organic chicken, swathed in vacuum-sealed plastic.

"Excellent," Richard barely heard, so deep was he in consideration. "You know – the classic *coq au vin* demands rooster, but I don't suppose the Grants would permit me to sacrifice one of theirs, and that version demands a good long braising in a slow oven to taste like anything but chicken-flavored rubber bands. Ah ..." He slid open the vast vegetable bin. "Crimini mushrooms ... definitely the *coq au vin*, for the main dish. Everything necessary is here and for steamed buttered baby potatoes with parsley. Alas strawberries are out of season. It is always best to cook what is in season, at the peak of flavor and fresh from the source. Remember that, when you take my survival cooking session, Robbie. And herbs – I have a small selection growing out in back of the Café. I'll bring a selection of what is required tomorrow. Now about dessert. *Tres leches* … oh, yes, three milks." Richard shuddered. "Condensed milk; a disgusting concept, but acceptable in dire emergencies, I suppose. Personally, I'd rather drink good coffee black … But your mother purchased cream. Excellent – for coffee, I'd guess. Only barbarians drink coffee with that disgusting manufactured flavored chalk. Ah-ha! I have it! A simple *panna cotta*, with … let's see, what fruit did your mother buy that is in season … interesting; persimmons…"

"*Halmoni* – Grandmother likes them," Robbie explained, as Richard examined a bag of rich orange persimmons and pursed his lips.

"Not certain they would meld well. Ah-ha! Blackberries! Perfect! Fresh blackberries with a ginger-infused blackberry syrup over individual panna cotta servings. Before I leave, I would like to begin marinating the chicken pieces in … oh, what the hell – Burgundy. You can never go wrong in sticking with a classic, Robbie. Is your father's wine cellar available to me? Should he keep it locked, I suppose I could make do with that half-bottle …"

"It's not locked," Robbie looked at him in mild astonishment. "Why would you lock anything in Luna City."

"Well," Again, Richard was slightly boggled. "A house full of teenagers, a wine cellar full of whatever… doesn't your father ever worry about you and your sister … er – helping yourselves?"

"Why?" In his turn, Robbie was likewise boggled. "We've always had wine with supper, if we wanted it. Dad says – nothing is so tempting as that which is forbidden."

"I'm sorry that I assumed otherwise," Richard said, "Common sense these days has the charm of rarity. Lead me on and let me show you how to properly cut up a chicken…"

He coasted down the hill, with a sense of a good job, well-begun. With Robbie's help, he had ransacked the various cupboards, the pantry, the standing freezer and found all that was needful; every ingredient save the fresh herbs, which he would bring on the morrow. The cut-up chicken pieces were marinating overnight in a plastic zip-lock bag, saturated in a bottle of moderately good Burgundy. He had whipped together the simple and basic vanilla-infused *panna cotta* and constructed the flavorful essence of ginger and blackberries which would bathe fresh blackberries and the subtle, creamy mounds of *panna cotta* for the dessert. Oh, that the Café might one day have command of the high-end basic ingredients available in the Walcott kitchen and pantry! That would set Karnes County ablaze as a gourmet destination! Nothing but the best would do for the prosperous magnate-owner of the Walcott manse. Proof was stocked in serried rows on the shelves, in the wine cellar, and in neatly-labeled, vacuum-sealed packages in the deep-freeze.

He arrived mid-Sunday afternoon to start the chicken – browning the lardoons, the whole small onions, the quartered mushrooms, all his attention given to that absorbing task. A small pot of broth made from the less-succulent and bonier pieces of the dismembered chickens simmered away on the back of the stove.

"It's the natural gelatin in the broth that makes the final dish so succulent," he said aloud, to no one in particular. "It's a challenge to make it, in a country where the poultry is not sold feet-on…"

"You can get them in some of the ethnic groceries in San Antonio," observed a new voice. Richard was startled out of all countenance to find himself with company in the kitchen; a slightly plumpish young man, with the same dark hair and eyes as Belle and Robbie. "If you want, I'll buy a couple of pounds for you, next time I come home for the weekend. You're Rich from the Café. Robbie said you'd be fixing dinner for us tonight – he was impressed."

"And rightfully so," Richard wiped his hands on a clean towel. "I thought I had met everyone in Luna City by now."

"I'm just finishing up my last year at UT for a degree in nursing," the young man explained. "Heavy schedule – Jeremy Walcott. Everyone calls me Jerry."

"Pleased, I'm sure." Richard gave a quick stir to the mushroom quarters, now giving up their moisture and slowly turning a delicate brown. "Your brother was helping me yesterday with preparations for this. He insisted that he'd like to be a chef, too, someday."

Jerry chuckled in amusement. "Robbie would say that. He's interested in anything and everything. Soaks up information like a sponge. Today he'll want to be an astronaut, and tomorrow a long-distance truck driver, and the day after that, a rock star neurosurgeon."

Richard reflected that Jerry Walcott was abnormally even-tempered for a Walcott offspring. He had all of Clovis's quiet, solid self-assurance; nothing of Sook's hotly imperious temper.

Now Jerry asked, "So what are we having tonight, Rich?"

"Chicken cooked in red wine, for the main course. Your father told me that this dinner is to celebrate your sister's college prospects, and Robbie says that she is fond of chicken as ..." Richard gave a small, involuntary shudder, "a fast-food option, in preference to all others."

"That sounds fantastic," Jerry nodded, in approval. "And it already smells wonderful. That should tempt Bee into taking a bite, if nothing else will. Dad has fantastic ideas, sometimes."

"She won't be able to resist," Richard stated, all easy assurance. "I don't think anyone has ever come away from a meal of mine without being completely satisfied. Oh, there was the Duchess of Cambridge that one time, but she was newly pregnant and unable to keep down a single morsel..."

"*Hyperemesis gravidarum*," Jerry nodded, with grave sympathy. "It sure does do a number on some ladies. But this is different; Bee is on a hunger strike and Dad is hoping to persuade her out of it … with your food."

"What?!" Richard exclaimed, utterly horrified at being maneuvered into playing a part in some horrible family psychodrama. No, he didn't need this. He didn't need drama; his previous life had offered a surfeit of the same – tantrums, screaming, heavy objects thrown with force, showers of tears. He had been the initiator of some elements, the cause or object of others.

"I don't think Dad wanted to burden you with family baseball," Jerry allowed sympathetically. "See – it's not your job. It's his, or mine. But Mom went all overboard about Bee wanting to be a musician. Not," Jerry imitated his mother, or perhaps some stock Oriental character from a movie made a generation ago, "Honorable profession for finest-kind numbah-one family!" He resumed his normal soft-spoken voice and continued. "Mom has – well, ambitions for us all. She wants us to have the best, be the best, work hard for the best. She really trained us very well," Jerry added, acknowledging with a touch of pride, and Richard nodded in grudging comprehension. Yes; he could so totally understand that relentless urge to perfection. Jerry continued, "So, playing the horn was totes fine with Mom. First trumpet in marching band; A-OK and checks a box on the old college applications. Even performing with *Los Maldonados* – a bit down-market, but Mom and Dad approve of us having some kind of grubby summer job. That's how Dad says that you learn to appreciate some nice, high-paying white-collar occupation. Do it for a living for the rest of your life? Oh, hell no. Mom went absolutely bananas and took away Bee's trumpet. She forbade her to perform with *Los Maldonados* any more and even read the riot act to Coach Garrett, demanding that Bee is suspended from band. Not even rehearsal … and so Bee went on a hunger strike. Not that I can blame her," Jerry added, with a fleeting smile. "Mom is an irresistible force and she remembers growing up very poor and proud in Korea. Not even *Halmoni* – Granny –

can stand against Mom when she has the bit in her teeth. But Bee said that she wouldn't eat a single bite until she has her trumpet back and permission to play in band and with *Los Maldonados*. She's held out since Tuesday."

"A battle of wills, between stubborn women," Rich nodded. "Your mother has met her match, I suspect. I did not volunteer to be the focus-point of these issues. I was paid."

"Yeah," Jerry replied. "So Dad called and invited me home for the weekend to partake of a special meal. Then he laid it on me about Bee and Mom. Me, I'd rather be doing the art walk in Southtown with my friends. But family. You do what you can do."

"Thanks for putting me in the picture," Richard said, moving the sautéed mushroom quarters to a waiting warmed bowl. The marinated chicken sections were awaiting their final apotheosis; bathed in herb-scented Burgundy, nestled into the high-end Creuset covered casserole with their attendant vegetables. Jerry looked relieved, at this indication of comprehension.

"Thanks, Rich. I thought it would be best. You got a family back in England and I was pretty certain you'd understand."

"They're now living in the south of France, but yes, I do understand," Richard said, although he didn't, really. If he recalled correctly, his parents had merely sighed and written out a substantial check when he broke it to them that he wanted to study haute cuisine in Paris. "I hope it all works out, this plot of your fathers'," he added. "By the way, where is this special dinner to be served? Not in the formal dining room, I take it? I have everything timed for the meal to begin on the dot of 6 PM, not a minute before or after."

The formal dining room in Chez Walcott was a huge, cavernous place, capable of seating seventy guests.

"Hell no," Jerry grinned. "In the breakfast nook, through there. A modest little place, only seats twelve at a time. When it's just family, we keep things informal."

Richard had no idea if Jerry was being humorous or not; sometimes it was hard to tell with Americans. The breakfast nook was a pleasant small dining room off the kitchen, papered in a cheerful wallpaper print. A picture window looked out into the landscaped grounds of Castle Walcott, which in this direction featured Clovis' beautifully manicured putting green. According to local legend, Clovis had now and again beaned a marauding coyote with a well-aimed golf ball. A heavy old-fashioned dresser held a range of china plates, in colors that matched the wallpaper. Richard wondered vaguely if the paper had been custom-ordered to match the china, or the china custom-painted to match the wallpaper. The one jarring note in the room was the presence of a flat-screen television, with a DVR player and a whole stereo set, revealed behind the open doors of a painted corner cupboard.

He worked away in that state of work-bliss that he had come to associate with successful cooking events – a process in which he became so deeply engaged in his work and the pursuit of culinary perfection that time passed unobserved, and came up for air and conscious observation of his immediate surroundings when young Robbie appeared at his elbow, saying, with openhearted appreciation – which Richard felt was gratifying to an incredible degree,

"Hey, Chef, that smells amazing! Are we gonna eat soon?"

From across the room, Sook Walcott chided her son in Korean. She sounded as ferocious was her customary manner, but it didn't seem to have too much of an effect on her youngest son. Richard blinked and aroused himself from the delicate task of whipping in a judicious quantity of butter into that sauce formed from the natural reduction of wine and juices from the cooked chicken and vegetables. Clovis stood in the doorway between the kitchen and the breakfast nook, looking to Richard's distracted gaze as if he were torn between appetite and uncertainty.

"Five minutes, I would say." Richard answered, "But I do have the salad course ready, if you are hungry enough."

"Oh, yes!" Robbie said, and his parents echoed agreement, just as the older lady – Min Kim appeared in the kitchen with Belle, who to Richard's eye looked pale and wan. His heart sank a little. Belle's lips were set in a stubborn line. But Jerry had his arm around his sisters' slender shoulders; that was reassuring. Also reassuring was Jerry offering to bring in the plates of salad when everyone was seated; a small, still pool of considerate reliability in a jagged landscape of passionate and unconstrained temperament. Richard turned back to the last-minute preparation; a final sprinkle of minced parsley over the *coq au vin*, a spritz of melted butter over the boiled potatoes … his concentration was fatally broken by an ominous sound; a chair falling, the crash of a single glass against a hard tile floor, a startled exclamation in Korean, and Jerry's urgent voice, calling his sister's name. Richard, whose finely-tune sense of disaster already had all his senses pinging alarm like the submarine dive alert signal in an old war movie, slapped a cover on the casserole of *coq au vin*, and was across the room in a flash, meeting Robbie in the doorway.

"Belle's fainted!" he exclaimed; in the tableau beyond, Belle lay on the floor by the set table, Clovis and Jerry kneeling by her on either side. Min Kim struggled to rise from her own chair, and that was Sook, snapping impatiently in Korean with a glass of ice water in her hand.

"That won't help, Mom," Jerry was saying, supernaturally calm. "She'll come around in a minute … <u>if</u> she has only fainted."

"Hadn't you better call an ambulance?" Richard gibbered, unsettled by the portents of looming disaster. *No – not a good thing, having a diner laid out cold in the floor, even before having taken a single bite of a supper made especially in her honor.*

"I think we should," Jerry agreed. "She's not coming around ... and I do not like her color, at all."

"No – she only stubborn disobedient girl!" Sook went magically from calm into unappeasable fury in the space of an instant. "I tell her – no crummy musician, no crummy band! No starving in gutter for my daughter – no!"

Richard winced; Sook in a full tantrum outraged every shred of that British dignity, stiff upper lip, and *savior faire* encouraged in him since distant childhood, although doubtless a lot of her fury could be attributed to very real maternal panic. Clovis held his daughter's limp hand and begged her to wake up, and at that instant the doorbell chimed ... no, it gonged like a quarter-scale bells of Big Ben sounding the hour.

"Robbie, answer the door," Jerry directed him. "And bring down a couple of blankets from upstairs. Richard's right; we better call an ambulance. I don't like how her pulse rate is all over the place."

Robbie scampered off, being young enough to be excited by all the drama. Richard, regarding the potential wreckage of another promising dining event, could only be depressed. He took out the cellphone that he had barely used since Jess had presented it to him and dialed the emergency number for the Luna City Volunteer Fire Department.

"They're on their way, now," he reported, a minute later, after a terse conversation with a remarkably disinterested-sounding dispatcher. "They'll come around to the back. They know the layout of your place."

"Good," Jerry was still the calmest among them. "Dad, you could try raising up her feet – yeah, that's it. Prop them on that cushion. Mom – stop that carrying on, you're just gonna make Bee feel worse ..." To no avail; Sook, having collapsed onto the nearest chair, was sobbing nosily with her head in her hands.

"It's Coach Garrett," Robbie appeared in the hallway door, panting as if he had run upstairs and down again. "He says that he has something to show you, Dad."

"I'll get with him tomorrow," Clovis ran a distracted hand through his hair. "I'm sure that it can wait…"

"He says it's about Belle," Robbie said. With a thin edge of irritation showing, like steel under the velvet of good manners, Clovis replied. "Tell him to wait … my study is fine…"

"But …" Robbie started, as Coach Garrett appeared in the door as well. "I told him that Belle…"

"My God, Walcott!" Coach Garrett, for nearly the first time in Richard's acquaintance with the man, looked angry. Richard wondered if anyone would even notice if he went and poured himself a very large wine-glass – the size of a brandy snifter would do the trick – of the Burgundy intended to accompany the *coq au vin*. Only the prospect of going down the Walcott's steep and winding drive in a reality-altered condition on a bicycle kept him from doing exactly that. Although when Sook began to scream incoherently at Coach Garrett, he did reconsider.

Fortunately, the shriek of a siren approaching – faint at first, and then wavering in intensity as it circled around the hill provided a distraction, as did Belle opening her eyes and surveying the circle of faces looking down at her.

"What happened?" she whispered, in a voice as thin as tissue-paper.

"You fainted, Bee," Jerry replied, taking one of the blankets from his brother.

Belle – like her mother – began to cry. "I feel sick, Jere-Bear. And cold … is something bad the matter with me?"

"Well, you haven't eaten anything in five days," Jerry competently spread out the blanket over his sister. "Look, the ambulance is here. They're gonna take you to the hospital, but I'll be there. Don't worry – they're going to take good care of you. And I'll be there to make sure of that, 'kay?"

"Don't leave me, Jere-Bear!"

"I won't," Jerry promised. Richard had to hand it to him; he had that soothing and authoritative medical-expert-to-patient voice and manner down pat. "I'll follow the ambulance, all the way. You know that I will, Bee. My promise."

Meanwhile, in the doorway, Clovis was exchanging terse remarks with Coach Garrett. Richard couldn't hear what was being said. It was left to him to answer a knock and a shout at the back door. To his profound relief, Chris Mayall, authoritative in the garb of the LCVFD emergency tech, was first through the door, his heavy bag of medical gear slung over his shoulder, followed by the youngest Jaimie Gonzalez, still in a trainee status and jockeying one of those wheeled ambulance litters across the doorstep.

"Hi Rich," Chris said, without any preamble. "Through there? Thanks. OK, Jaimie, take your lead from me, and just do what I say. Hold the questions until we're back in the bus."

The litter rattled through the kitchen like an alien invader; Richard mourned inwardly for his *coq au vin* supper so carefully planned for the whole Walcott family and consoled himself with the thought that it could be put away and warmed up readily enough. It might even be more flavorful. Still, he could not give up hope entirely; he set the casserole in an oven set on low and lurked just outside the breakfast nook

It appeared that in the space of a few moments, Jerry completely filled Chris in as to what had been going on and Chris had consulted by cellphone with a doctor at the Med Center in Karnesville. Obviously, the command had been passed; Belle was installed on the litter, swathed in blankets, her face covered by a clear plastic oxygen mask. She made such a narrow mound under the heaped blankets, it looked as if there was no one on the litter at all, as Jaimie Gonzalez trundled it briskly through the kitchen.

"She'll have to be supervised very carefully, if she's gone that long without eating," Chris said, very quietly. "People have been known to collapse from the shock of suddenly eating again. We'd better take Miz Walcott, too. She'll soon have herself in a state, for certain."

"Right," Jerry agreed. In the corner by the window that looked out into the eastern aspect of the Walcott's grounds, Clovis and Coach Garrett were still disputing but at least they were doing so fairly quietly. Not so Sook Walcott, alternating between bouts of uncontrolled weeping and what sounded like ferocious verbal combat in Korean with Min Kim.

Nope, Richard concluded – this supper was now a historical event in both senses of the word. He resigned himself to the thought of ignominiously bicycling home to the Airstream and fixing himself a solitary meal. Although if Romeo was still around and not off playing grab-arse with Susannah the bunny-boiler, he could talk him into going over to Pryor's Meats and BBQ; that is, if they had anything left on the shank-end of a Sunday.

Now, Jerry took a set of keys from his pocket, and gently broke into the conversation between Clovis and Coach Garret.

"Dad," he ventured; a quiet voice, itself velvet over adamantine determination. "I'm gonna follow the ambulance in my car. I promised Bee I'd be with her. Chris says Mom had better go with Bee, but I think you better stay here and have supper like you planned; you still are jet-lagged as all get out, and we don't need you crashing in flames as well. Richard did a good job with prepping all this. I know it didn't turn out the way you planned, but Robbie and *Halmoni* need to eat, and so do you – and you have stuff to talk over with Coach. I have my cellphone; I'll call you as soon as we have everything sorted."

"I guess that would be best, Jere-Bear," Clovis answered, with an expression that hinted pretty broadly at being torn between family obligations, concern for his daughter, and his own physical exhaustion.

"I'll call as soon as I know what's up with Bee," Jerry nodded, grave and responsible, before flashing a quick smile at Richard. "Hey, don't let Dad and Robbie eat all the chicken. I want some for me, too." He nodded to Coach Garrett, added to Robbie, "Don't worry, little Bro – Jere-Bear is on the case and here to save the day."

It had the sound of a fond family joke, and with that, Jerry was out the back door, as the ambulance pulled away. The sounds of the ambulance engine and whatever Jerry drove diminished. Clovis sighed.

"Richard – you've done a damned nice supper tonight; you want to sit down and help us eat it? You too, Coach."

"I'll be happy to provide any assistance whatever," Richard replied, honestly grateful for the invitation, for he was hungry, and the supper was all but completed. At any rate, Robbie would be a totally satisfied client tonight, although as far as Richard recalled, hungry fourteen-year-old boys would cheerfully eat almost anything that didn't vigorously fight back.

Coach Garrett nodded, also agreeing. "Thanks, Clovis – but first, I'd like for you to listen to this," he said. "You need to accept just what an amazing talent your daughter has. She could be the next Alison Balsom." Without waiting for permission, he slipped the DVD into the player, worked some magic with the buttons on it *(audio-video technology had long been a mystery to Richard, who had believed for a decade that if he wasn't interested in it, why should he have to learn it?)* Titles flashed up on the flat-screen; a name – Isabelle M. Walcott, the date *(from the previous week)* and the name of a composer and musical selection, superimposed on a background which looked like sloppy folds of pink silk. It reminded Richard of the titles to some American TV comedy from so far back in time that it showed in black and white.

And there was Belle, confident and smiling on screen, with her trumpet in hand; not a shred of nerves, standing in front of a plain pale background, against which her dark hair, silver-button-trimmed short jacket and red silk sash stood out vividly – but not as vividly as the notes from her chosen instrument; if silver had a sound, that was it. Pure, clear, flashing as a waterfall over some tall mountain cliff … there was the first selection, the second, the third and the final … and Belle smiled into the camera. Richard was certain he had never seen the girl look so … alive. And then the screen faded to black, and Coach Garrett pressed the buttons that ejected the DVD.

Richard, who had meant to go and see to the last elements of supper, was the first to speak. "I can't think when I have heard anything so splendid. And I get free tickets – or I did get free tickets to the Proms, every year."

"She's good, then," Robbie enthused. "She's really, really good … I liked that part when she …"

"Stow it in your barracks-bag, Pip-squeak," Clovis said, with a fondness in his voice which took away any sting in the words. "Your sister is an artist. Don't start giving her a swelled head about it all."

Min Kim did nothing more than enthusiastically clap her old hands together, beaming rapturous approval, while Coach Garrett returned the DVD to its' case.

"Clovis – your daughter has a rare gift." Coach Garrett said, at last. "And she needs her music like ordinary people need oxygen. And food. Ordinarily, I wouldn't approve of teenagers manipulating their parents by pulling this kind of dangerous stunt like a hunger strike, but this case is as exceptional as your daughter. Don't take her music away from her; I beg you and Sook from the bottom of my heart."

"After this evening? I wouldn't dream of it," Clovis confessed. "Although … My Little Bride will be … well, perhaps she'll get over it once we point out to her the cachet that accrues to the mother of a world-class performing artist and she has time to think about it."

"She'll start making plans," Richard advised, only partly in jest, "Serious plans. The benefits of being an international celebrity are incalculable. So are the temptations – a watchful and guiding presence over the course of that career will be of inestimable value. I am certain that Mrs. Walcott will soon see the light."

"Wow," commented Robbie, in awe. "I don't understand what you just said, Mr. Hall, but it sounded serious. For real; Bee would be famous?"

"No guarantee of that," Coach Garrett admitted, in a judicious tone of voice. "But she would have a career in any one of a dozen top-flight orchestras, or as a studio musician and graduation from Julliard would make it a more certain possibility."

Clovis grunted, as if he had just felt something in his shoulder or shin twinge. "Then I had best start limbering up my check-writing hand. I don't suppose that tuition for a music school in New York is any less than a trade school in Texas? Didn't think so," He added, as Coach Garrett shook his head. "But if this is what Bee wants with her whole heart then she will have it, and I will so see to making My Little Bride see reason. That is, if Jere-Bear hasn't gotten her to see it already."

"He's a good boy, Jerry is," Coach Garrett acknowledged.

Richard added, "Bit of a Nancy, though. Surprised he didn't get bullied awfully at school," and was surprised and discomfited when Coach Garrett shook his head.

"No, he wasn't one of my band kids, but Jerry was never bullied. Likely he was the one making certain that other kids weren't bullied. He's strong, that way."

"It's why his nick is 'Jere-Bear'," Clovis added. "Because of that popular toy, you know – from a couple of years ago? The Care Bears. Jerry was always ... well, he was always looking out for people. He's ... he's a good person, a solid, trustworthy, honest person. So, he didn't exactly cover himself with glory with his career choice, and yeah, My Little Bride has certainly bent my ear over that, for the last three years, but Jerry – he's my son ... our son. It's his life to live. Now, I'll fall over fainting myself, if I don't have supper. I'm that hungry. Chef, you want to do the honors?"

"Of course," Richard answered.

Later that evening, as Richard pedaled down the hill from the Walcotts, with his bicycle headlamp casting a wobbly pale circle of light on the asphalted road ahead of him, he thought about the evening just past; about Jerry, quietly going his own way, Belle confident and joyful in her music, and Robbie who didn't know what he wanted yet of life. But Clovis and Sook would see that their offspring had something good in life, even if they couldn't quite agree on what that good might be, how to go about getting it, or even approving of those choices.

Struck by a sudden impulse, Richard turned his handlebars towards the grassy verge of the road where there stood several ancient oak trees, and some long-ago road authority had dictated there be established a pair of concrete picnic tables and benches in the shade underneath. He leaned the mountain bike against the nearest table, and sat down, taking out his cellphone.

Dialing a 1 and a country code, another long series of numbers, waiting while the distant telephone in another country rang, rang again.

"Hullo ... Mum? Is it that early? 3:45 – in the morning. No, nothing wrong, Mum – I'm fine. In the pink, as a matter of fact. I just ... I just wanted to call. I wanted to call and let you know that I was ... thinking about you. Thinking that I ought to say again how very grateful I am to you both."

Let No True Hearts Playbill

THE LUNA CITY PLAYERS PROUDLY PRESENT

LET NO TRUE HEARTS ADMIT IMPEDIMENT

AN ORIGINAL FARCE

OCTOBER 29, 2016
5:00

AT THE PAVILION – TOWN SQUARE
LUNA CITY, TEXAS

A Benefit Performance to Aid in Rebuilding the Parish Hall of Saint Margaret and Saint Anthony Catholic Church

FOR MORE INFORMATION, CONTACT: PATRICIA PRYOR AT PPRYOR@GMAIL.COM

9-11+15

"I know that it's been fifteen years as of last Sunday," Coach Garrett mused thoughtfully, hardly taking note of the beer in front of him. "But sometimes it's as clear to me as if it was yesterday."

It was a perfect, autumn afternoon – a Friday afternoon in mid-September, just beginning to turn cool. The VFW had visitors' night on Fridays, and now Richard sat outside with Joe Vaughn and Coach Garrett, at the splintery picnic table under the massive sycamore tree that shaded the back of the VFW.

"You were there in New York, weren't you, Coach?" Joe drank deep from his own beer. "You saw the Towers go down, up close and personal. Man … it was bad enough watching on TV in real time."

"Another life," Dwight Garrett shrugged, but something in the look of that otherwise undistinguished, middle-aged countenance warned Richard to embrace tact and circumspection in his further comment.

"It was a splendid day for me," Richard ventured, reminiscent for the world of just a little ago, but gone as distant now as the Austro-Hungarian empire. "I know ... the irony of it all. An evening in Paris – it was mid-evening. I had just won my first cooking contest and signed with a talent agency. Some of my old Charterhouse pals and I popped over to Paris to celebrate my excellent prospects. We were drinking in a bar in the Rue d Belleville, and wondering why they had a telly on, and tuned to some high-rise disaster movie. It didn't seem all that big a thing, not at first. The penny didn't drop until we saw the headlines in the newspapers the next day. In my defense, we were all enormously pissed that evening."

"I'll bet your hangover was epic," Joe said, not without sympathy. "I was at Fort Lewis. First assignment to the Second Battalion ... just driving into work, when it came over the radio. Airplane crashed into the World Trade Center tower. Swear to god, everyone thought it must be one of those little private airplanes, ya know, like a Piper Cub or something. The top sergeant said, 'Oh, man, they must have gotten hella lost!' And then someone turned on the breakroom TV, and there was this big ol' gash in the side of the tower and the smoke just pouring out... Top said he remembered hearing about a WWII bomber hitting the Empire State Building, but that was in a fog. Two big honking silver buildings – we just couldn't understand at first how it could happen by accident."

"It was such a beautiful morning," Dwight Garrett nodded. "Cool, crisp ... not a cloud in the sky. I had played a concert at the Alice Tully the night before, so I slept in. Gwen ... my wife didn't wake me up when she left for work. She left a note for me ... that we should meet for supper at Morton's on Washington Street, just around the corner, when she was done with work that evening."

"Didn't know you were a married man, Coach," Joe said, and Dwight Garrett sighed.

"Oh, yes – I left it late, sorry to say. Gwen and I were married for six years and three months. A dedicated career woman, and a divorcee with two sons she raised herself. We met at one of those musical soirees associated with a Mozart festival. Gwen was in finance. Did you ever notice that maths and music are deeply intertwined in some people? Anyway, we had a nice little condo in Tribeca, a stone-throw from where she worked."

"And?" Richard prodded. He had visited New York often enough during the high-flying years of his career as a globe-trotting celebrity chef and had only the vaguest notion of where Tribeca might me. It was not his favorite city on the American continent; that would be Vancouver, or perhaps Miami. New York was too crowded, too vertical for his taste.

"She worked at Cantor-Fitzgerald, in the North Tower," Dwight Garrett replied in perfectly level, dispassionate tones. Joe drew in his breath sharply, but said nothing, and Coach Garrett continued. "Even asleep, I heard the sirens – but so ordinary a sound in the city, I just went back to sleep. Until Gwen's son Jeff called from White Plains. 'Where's Mom?' he said, 'Did she go into work, today? Turn on the TV; there's a plane that hit the building she works in, all the top floors are on fire, and she's not answering her cellphone.' I told him to calm down. I'd walk over to the WTC and find her, make sure she was safe, and that everything would be all right ..." He took a long draw of his own beer, calm and meditative, as if he were telling a story of another persons' experience.

"The sidewalks along Vesey Street were full of people looking up towards the towers – both of them just gushing smoke. Like water coming out of a fire hydrant. I started walking as fast as I could. I could see nothing moving on the street, but fire engines, lined up as far as I could see, once I got close. I kept trying to call Gwen. I thought sure that they would let me through the barricades once I explained. The South Tower fell before I got to the end of the block. It was ... like a tidal wave of black smoke, dust, soot. A policeman yelled at us to run like hell. A bunch of us on the sidewalk ran into the nearest place – a coffee shop on Vesey, to escape it." Coach Garrett shook his head, slowly. "Outside that window it turned as black as you could imagine. And the lights went out. You couldn't see your hand in front of your face for about five, ten minutes. That policeman was in there, too. He had a flashlight, but it didn't help. When we came out everything was grey, covered with thick grey dust. We were all covered in it, too. Needless to say, they wouldn't let me come anywhere near the North Tower. There were too many people. And I think they were already afraid that the North Tower was going to fall as well."

"Did you find your wife?" Richard ventured. Coach Garrett shook his head.

"No. Not that day, or afterward. Nothing left – everything and most everyone on the floors just above the impact site were essentially vaporized. I accepted right away that she was gone forever, nothing to be done. No good going to the morgue or hanging around as they excavated the pile afterwards. It was almost as if our marriage had been a wonderful, fleeting dream, and she had never been … except for the boys, of course. And her clothes and things in the condo. It was just so … curious, how it happened out of the clear blue in the blink of an eye, on so ordinary day."

"Sorry, man," Joe said, after a long moment. "I never knew about your wife, and all of that. That why you left New York and came home to Texas?"

Coach Garrett nodded. "I couldn't stay. Not without Gwen. The pile of rubble burned for months. The whole place smelled of smoke and death. I packed a suitcase and took the express to White Plains a few days later. I signed the condo over to Jeff and his brother, rented a car and drove back to Texas. I meant to go back to Kingsville … but heard about a job teaching music here. It seemed like a good way to start fresh."

"You do what you gotta do," Joe agreed. "Another, Coach? My treat."

"Sure thing, Joe," the older man finished off his beer and looked into the distance; the blue, blue sky and the leaf canopy of the sycamores just beginning to turn gold and brown. "There's one thing I do regret about Gwen. I wish that I hadn't slept in – that I had fixed her breakfast, kissed her, said that I hoped she would have a good day, and that I loved her. I never for a single moment thought that she would suddenly just not be there. Love shouldn't end that way, on the flip of a coin."

"Nope," Joe agreed, and to Richard, it looked as if Joe had suddenly made up his mind about something. "You want another, Rich?"

"Only if you're buying." Richard replied.

"Cheap limey bastard," Joe grumbled.

The Luna City Players & And the Koenig Opera House

The Luna City Players are one of, if not the longest-established community theatrical groups in Karnes County, having roots in a small group of amateur performers known as "The Lunatics" who were famed for performing as a minstrel group in and around the local area in the late 1880s. The Lunatics also acted in farces and bawdy comedies, but around the turn of the last century turned to a more formal organization and more elevated materiel. In some years, they were able to mount three or four separate productions, with performances weekly, of classic and popular plays. With the popularity of motion pictures throughout the years since the 1920s, there was not so much demand for locally-sourced entertainments, yet the Luna City Players continued, with traditional theatrical presentations, and with short original presentations, tableaux, and skits to mark celebrations such as Founders' Day, the 4th of July and at Christmas. In the last half-dozen years, under the direction of Patricia

Wyler Pryor, the Players have begun performing original material by a selection of local South Texas writers and playwrights.

The Players performance space and rehearsal facility is the historic Koenig Opera House on Town Square – an intimate 200-capacity hall, which once was Luna City's movie theater, and remains the newest of the structures lining Town Square, dating as it does from 1922. Once merely a wide alley-way between the Cattleman Hotel and O'Byrne's Fine Haberdashery (now housing the Saints Margaret and Anthony Parish Thrift Shop) leading to a livery stable behind the Cattleman, the Opera House filled in that long, narrow space, adorning the façade on Town Square with colorful glazed tiles and a fabulously ornate marquee. The Koenig still hosts movie showings on a regular basis, showing mainly classic old black and white silent pictures, with live organ accompaniment. *(Consult the Chamber of Commerce website for a current schedule.)*

Those Wedding Bell Blues

"You should come to rehearsal on Friday," Araceli said as she and Richard wrapped up the Friday lunch hour at the Café. "It's a full dress rehearsal, everyone trying out their costumes – and Kate is going to take pictures of all the wedding party and the more important guests for the *Karnesville Weekly Beacon* Talk of the Town blog."

"I do not want my noble phiz on public media," Richard could barely keep himself from snarling. "I came here to get away from all that! How can you even think of – blowing my cover – as they say on those ghastly American cop shows?"

"Chef, I don't think that Kate wants your noble phiz – whatever that is – your ass, your face or anything else of yours on the internet," Araceli scowled. "Patricia wants the consult, after the dress rehearsal and the photography session for the final menu for the wedding buffet."

"Oh – that was all?" Richard drew up a long sigh from the depths of his being. After the near-disaster *coq au vin* dinner and the trauma of being door-stopped by Gunnison Penn and his friends, his nerves were understandably somewhat frayed.

"You have made up the buffet menu options for three to four hundred?" Araceli looked at him with severity.

Richard made a point of sighing heavily. "Araceli, my darling, of course I have – and ordered the basic foodstuffs. I have suggestions for upgrades to the dishes, additional elegant touches, and designs for a wedding cake, in keeping with the theme of the wedding. These final touches depend on Mrs. Pryor's approval … and of course, her budget."

"We're rehearsing the staged elements after Kate does the pictures, so I know that Patricia will be free during the picture taking. Say, four PM tomorrow at the school gym – it's the only place big enough with a video teleconferencing set up," Araceli added.

Richard was diverted. "Why a video teleconference?"

"Because Berto's friend Marigold – she's playing the bride? Her school in California is wrapping up their term. She won't be here in Luna City until the final run-through, so we've been doing her scenes that way. She's a fantastically good actress," Araceli giggled. "Don't tell a soul, but she's going incognito, too."

"I have no idea what you mean by that, and even less interest," Richard retorted. He had set aside his proposals for the theatrical presentation fund-raising dinner in the flurry over the smaller dinner; sufficient to the day were the menus thereof was his motto. No; time to reassemble those notes.

"So, what were you thinking of, besides the wedding cake?" Araceli asked. She was deftly slicing delicatessen meats and cheeses for tomorrow's sandwich luncheons, wrapping each sheaf of thin slices in waxed paper, and inserting them into a zip-locked storage bag, each neatly labeled as to contents.

"Definitely roast beef – carved on the spot," Richard replied. "Andy Pryor has that aspect all taken care of. He's donating the beef itself and providing it cooked, too, which is one less element for us to worry about.

He says his oldest boy can dress up in a white apron and toque and carve to order … so that's one less…"

"The Pryors do know how to serve up good beef. Good anything," Araceli nodded. "What else?"

"I'm torn between herbed roasted fingerling potatoes." Richard mused. "But with the costs involved in procuring fingerling potatoes in quantity it might be better to go with whole baked russets."

"There is the problem of wrapping every one of them in tinfoil," Araceli pointed out. "Although the committee of parish ladies has volunteered to help prep, so there is that. Go for simple mashed potatoes. It's what people expect, and we can make potato chowder for the luncheon daily special with any mashed potatoes left over."

"Salads; a choice of fruit, or green, with the expected toppings and several different dressings … all made in-house, of course," Richard said, with a reminiscent shudder. "None of those readymade bottled abominations."

"Some vegetarian and pasta options," Araceli nodded. "You know, there are people in Luna City who don't really care for beef."

"They don't?" Richard was appalled. "Heretics. I suppose I should consider some kind of herbed chicken as well. And there will be an *hors d oeuvres* table, of course. Little slices of bread, with crackers, and appropriate dips and toppings. Pickled Italian *giardiniera* vegetables, fruit and cheeses …there will be a particular dent put in my own stocks of Café-made *giardiniera*, but it can't be helped."

"It sounds as if you have it all in hand, Chef."

"Of course, I have," Richard returned, with serene confidence. "The venue will be in a pavilion in Town Square, just as it was for the *quinceanera* for those cousins of yours. We prepare and cook here, then just run the dishes and trays across to the serving line. Speaking of which; are we going to be civilized and serve on china plates and with real utensils?"

"Yes," Araceli nodded. "Saint Margaret and Anthony has been doing the spaghetti and meatball feed since time and memory began. They have service for at least 400 and the parish ladies have also promised to bus and wash up afterwards."

"Excellent," Richard said, much pleased. "The fewer services to be paid for, the greater the profits at the end of the game. You Yanks are marvelous for volunteering, you know. Part of your happy, inconsequent charm."

"Well, the parish hall won't rebuild itself," Araceli replied, tartly.

The next afternoon, Patrick obligingly drove Araceli and Richard to the school gym, after lifting Richard's bicycle into the back of the pick-up truck. This was the first time that Richard had anything to do with the Luna City Players, aside from being aware of the organization's existence. To judge by the familiar cars parked outside the Hernando Gonzales Memorial Gym, including Chris' little red coupe, Romeo Gonzales' familiar pick-up (*but not the black velvet Mercedes with the pink custom-leather interior, to his vast yet unspoken relief*) and the Walcott's enormous black SUV, a fair number of his Luna City acquaintances harbored theatrical leanings.

Richard could only suppose that his habit of retiring early so as to get up early had left him hitherto unexposed to this aspect of social life in Luna City. His disinclination to attend church services of whatever denomination, or to dress up in 19th century period garb likely cut him off from other aspects of small-town social life as well, although he recollected fondly how his mother had been such an active part of the Bickley Gilbert & Sullivan performing company, as she had a very pleasing contralto singing voice, and played Little Buttercup to perfection, the year that the company did *HMS Pinafore*. (*Richard himself, at the age of twelve, had a non-singing part as a very young sailor.*) But never mind; the Café and to a certain degree, the Age of Aquarius, and guest nights at the VFW encompassed his limited social life, and about as much of it as he could handle in good spirits.

The inside of the gym presented an interesting spectacle; the polished wood floor covered with canvas, the basketball hoops swung back and out of the way. One section of bleachers was run forward, the rest all neatly collapsed and flush against the walls. Most of the action seemed to be taking place at the end where there was a very large television set on a rolling stand, paired with a small video camera mounted next to it. A little beyond the television set, someone had set up a frame with a white drape hanging over it, and a couple of portable production light-stands with umbrella attachments on the business end. Miss Kate Heisel was in business, her camera also mounted on a tripod while a series of costumed cast members danced sequentially across the horizon before her lens, metaphorically speaking.

"Let me go and change, sweetie," Araceli tapped Kate on the shoulder and Richard had wondered why she was carrying a generously large gym bag. That mystery was resolved, when Araceli reappeared from the direction of the girls' changing room with her hair pulled into a modest chignon, makeup refreshed or freshly applied, and clad in a modest floor-length evening gown of a pale lavender color.

"What?" she said, upon noting Richard's expression. "I'm supposed to be the matron of honor and yes, Patricia recycled Maribel's dress from Beatriz' court. We gotta budget, you know. And," Richard would have said that Araceli was preening, "Two kids and I can still fit into a size-nothing dress."

"You look lovely," Richard said, "I wouldn't have recognized you as the same woman who was tearing stripes off my backside this morning for forgetting to put away the greens delivery from the Age."

"Late-season," Araceli snapped. "The last of their crop, and you let them sit on the back dock until they got all wilty from the sun beating down … honestly, Chef, if there's a man in this world who needs a keeper more than you, I hope that I never meet him. I couldn't stand the … Oh, hello, Sook, Clovis … all ready to break a tiny leg?"

Rich goggled and immediately attempted to hide the goggle. Sook was turned out in a flamboyant brocade gown – one of those ethnic Oriental numbers which he associated more with Philippines, or perhaps Vietnam – but with a lavish sable fur coat over it, and a delicate jeweled tiara in her dark hair. The coat looked real to his well-schooled eye, and the tiara very likely also real. Clovis Walcott hung watchfully at her elbow, his eyes masked in very dark sunglasses. Clovis wore an ostentatiously plain black suit, a small radio-communicator in the front coat pocket with a curly-whirly cord going up to an ear-piece and a carefully blank yet menacing expression.

"What is this passion that you have for dressing up?" Richard demanded, and to his frustrated and also strained amusement, the two of them took on their parts, or what Richard presumed would be their parts.

"Search him!" Sook demanded, in her familiar steam-whistle shriek, and then she confounded Richard with a broad burlesque wink. "He is threat to me!"

"If you don't mind, sir," Clovis advised in a confidential murmur. "Lift your arms, please." Richard obeyed, and Clovis swiftly patted down his sides and around his waistband. "All clear, Madame Chang-mai."

"Then you may kiss my hand," Sook extended her gloved right hand with a particularly operatic gesture. Richard thought he ought to play along, and bent respectfully over it, hoping to avoid an impact divot in his forehead from the doorknob-sized emerald cocktail ring on her middle finger. Sook favored him with a particularly wintery smile and a regal nod. The pair of them sauntered away, with Clovis lurking watchfully at her elbow; a lady of the undisputed blood royal, Oriental division with her ever-lurking, watchful bodyguard.

"They are having way too much fun with this," Richard murmured to himself, although it soon became obvious that all the members of the Luna

City Players were also having way too much fun, improvising their roles on the fly. Roman Gonzales the building contractor was snappily arrayed in a *Godfather*-style pinstriped suit with vulgarly wide lapels, a gardenia boutonniere, and two-toned wing-tip shoes with excessively pointed toes.

"Get you a good price on a truckload of hooch," he offered, also in the same confidential murmur. "Special price for my good friends, Ricardo. No? Can't say I approve of my nephew getting' hitched wid 'dis Kitty frail. I offered him … a lotta moolah to call it off. Offered her a lotta moolah to leave town wit-out any forwarding address." Roman shook his head sadly. "Kids today … tink dey know it all. You're a pal o' his, Ricardo. I can make it worth your while, you talk him out of it." Roman winked so broadly that Richard could almost hear his eyelid clunk and rubbed thumb and forefinger together.

"Er … thank you for your considerate offer," Richard answered, helplessly feeling himself being sucked into the madness. "I'm really here to talk to Mrs. Pryor regarding the menu…"

"I knew that," Roman allowed in his normal voice. "But hey, we gotta practice on <u>someone</u>, ya know? Come show time we'll be staging a hundred, two hundred little improvised dramas, never mind our scripted scenes, just so the guests can really feel part of the event. Hey, Romeo looks really good, doesn't he?"

"He certainly looks the part of an escaped criminal," Richard agreed; for Romeo was just now taking his turn in front of Kate Heisel's camera and holding up a small menu-board before him, of the kind normally provided for the obligatory mugshot when booking a criminal into jail. Romeo himself, slightly stubble-grown and wearing jeans and a white singlet, exuded the raw sexual glamor which had provided the basis for his nickname since he was in his early teens, according to Araceli.

Roman chuckled. "That's the suspense element for the presentation, you know. The groom may or may not arrive in time for the nuptials, though escaping from the Karnes County pokey. Ah, well; make the buffet spread as fine as for Beatriz and Blanca's *quince* and you'll have the Café on the culinary map of South Texas!"

"I'll endeavor not to disappoint," Richard assured him and made a game escape to have a real-life non-improvised discussion with Patricia Wyler regarding the buffet menu. "I know that you are terribly busy," he said – for she was; watching an exchange between Araceli, standing in front of the teleconferencing camera and TV screen, and a dark-haired young woman on the screen. The young woman looked vaguely familiar to Richard, who thought that he might know her from somewhere – although not as a former girlfriend or date; she was just too young for that.

(The prospect being charged for statutory rape afforded no thrills for him at all. He had a lively and well-founded distrust of very young-appearing women, ever since Pip Noel-Barrett had set him up with a date who ... well, if it hadn't been for a timely and discrete warning from a particularly sharp-eyed and worldly doorman at the Dorchester, Richard would have been up on charges as a pedophile at worst and for blackmail at best.)

The young woman and Araceli were conducting a scripted, yet enthusiastically-high-decibel spat.

"Not terribly," and Patricia Pryor turned that meltingly warm smile of hers upon him. Richard was reminded yet again of how much Patricia resembled the late Princess Diana; blond, serene, attractive, awesomely charismatic. Like Princess Diana, Patricia Pryor had the ineffable facility for making anyone who held her attention for even the briefest period of time believe wholly that he or she was the most fascinating person in the world to her. "Everyone is doing their bits, as they ought. My job is just to make it so, make it easy for them to do their jobs for this production. Give them just a hint of direction, to keep them going in a somewhat straight line. And we just got the word that Paw-Paw will match the sum of final profits for the presentation! Isn't that amazing? He's such a grouchy old bear when it comes to money! You have the proposed menus

… oh, excellent, you have made a copy for me! I know that Andy and the boys will manage the roast beef but give me a chance to review what you have worked out. Shall I come to the Café after the lunch rush on Monday, and we can sort the final details? I know that whatever you have proposed will be fantastic …" and Patricia's smile was most especially dazzling. "I'll have a good idea of attendance by then, of course. And I will leave the exact details of the cake to you. I know that you will do us proud; I trust you without reservation."

Richard knew at that moment why just about every male in town over the age of fourteen or so chastely worshipped Patricia Pryor; the uncrowned and crownless queen of Luna City.

Sook Walcott didn't have the ghost of a chance.

Invitation

Mr. And Mrs. Roland Dale-Barton
request the honor of your presence
at the marriage of their daughter
Katherine (Kitty)

to

Mr. Juan Belmondo

son of

Mr. and Mrs. Frederick Belmondo

Saturday, the twenty-ninth of October

two thousand sixteen

at five o'clock

At the Pavilion on Town Square

Luna City, Texas

(admit 1)

Celia Hayes & Jeanne Hayden

The Evening Program

Let No True Hearts Admit Impediment
An Original Farce
Presented by the Luna City Players
To Benefit the Parish Church of Sts Margaret & Anthony Building Fund
Town Square, Luna City - 5 PM
Cast

Family of the Bride & Friends	Family of the Groom & Friends
"Kitty" Dale Barton (Bride) . . . . Marigold Yasbeck	Juan Belmondo (Groom) . . . . Roman Gonzales
Jessie Dale Barton (MotB) . . . . Johanna Gonzales	Fred Belmondo (FotG) . . . . Anthony Gonzales
Roland Dale Barton (FotB) . . . . .Orlando Biggs	Juanita Belmondo (MotG) . . . . Marina Brodie
Matron of Honor . . . . Araceli Gonzalez Gonzales	Mikey "The Goth" Belmondo . . . . .Anson Pryor
First Bridesmaid . . . . Jessica Abernathy	Julio "Da Boss" Belmondo . . . . Roman Gonzales, Sr.
Second Bridesmaid . . . . .Linda Brodie	Best Man . . . . Sylvester Gonzalez
Third Bridesmaid . . . . .Caroline Brodie-Mills	First Groomsman . . . . Alberto Gonzales
Madame Chaing-Mai . . . . .Isabelle "Sook"Walcott	Second Groomsman . . . . Bob Huntingdon
Her Bodyguard . . . . Clovis Walcott	Third Groomsman . . . . Donovan Guthrie
Off-Key Wedding Singer . . . . Benjamin Cordova	Soviet Spy . . . . Bill Weitzman
Wedding Planner . . . . Patricia Pryor	Bitsy Bitterman (former girlfriend) . . . . . Marisol Gonzalez
Lost Tourist #1 . . . . .Georg Stein	Parole Officer .Dwight D. Garrett
Lost Tourist #2 . . . . .Annise Stein	Justice of the Peace . . . . .Hiram Abernathy
Forgetful Waiter . . . . Mark Stapleton	Arresting Officer . . . . Joseph P. Vaughn

Buffet catered by Luna Café & Coffee
Wedding Cake Design – Richard Astor-Hall
Serving Staff from the Parish of Sts Margaret and Anthony
Bartenders – Christopher Mayall and Hector Gonzales

495

The Best-Laid Plans

"We're sold out," Araceli reported, on Monday morning. "Just a week and a half to go and we're sold out entirely. That has never happened before, in the whole history of the Luna City Players. Patricia says they've already sold tickets to people coming from as far away as Waco and Houston. I suppose that we might squeeze in another thirty place settings, even more if we set up outside ... but it's going to be touch and go in the pavilion if it looks like rain."

"Do you have any notion of what brought all that on?" Richard paused, in the middle of dropping doughnut rounds into a vat of simmering fat.

(Mondays' breakfast specialty was in-house made-fresh doughnuts. Tuesdays was fresh butter croissants; Wednesdays – assorted muffins, Thursdays – crumpets dripping with melted butter and jam; Fridays – scones, and Saturdays was fresh, hot-from-the-oven Danish pastries.)

"I can't be entirely certain, but Kate put up the first pictures of the wedding party on Saturday morning," Araceli replied. "And she says that the picture of Romeo got such a response that it practically crashed the *Beacon's* server. Since then it has gone viral. Kate says that you would simply not believe some of the email queries they have gotten."

"Any publicity is good publicity," Richard hooked out several nicely-browned doughnuts and set them to drain and cool. "That's what Morty always said, but I believe that was mostly to cheer me up after another public relations flop. As long as your Luna City Players give the punters their money's worth, it's all to the good."

"You stayed and watched the whole rehearsal," Araceli brought over a shaker of confectioner's sugar and began baptizing the fresh doughnuts. "What did you think?"

"It's hard to judge, when it's a sequence of disjointed scenes," Richard mused, judiciously, "But I must admit that Romeo's entrance was definitely a show-stopper. But having Joe drag him in under restraints and in his capacity as a police officer ... isn't that abuse of authority, or something? How did Mrs. Pryor talk him into that?"

"She probably just asked him nicely," Araceli grinned. "Joe has a soft spot for Patricia. They were a pair in high school, 'til she went away to college and he joined the Army."

"Ah – explains a lot," Richard lowered another few doughnuts into the deep-fryer. "But I have to say that Joe really appeared to be enjoying that bit, all too much. Now, Mrs. Pryor is coming after the lunch rush today to review the final plans for the buffet and cake. I have several designs to show her. It is always best, you know, to give the client a choice between several differing options. I have prepared sketches for a severely traditional all-white tiered cake, for one with sprays of colored flowers ... and finally – I had a stroke of genius, after watching the rehearsals; one with comic figures in marzipan representing the various characters, and the groom himself in an orange jumpsuit with 'property of Karnes County Correctional Facility' on the back."

Araceli snickered. "That last one would be a riot and I would choose it but I think Patricia will favor something more traditional. She wants it all to look as much like a real wedding as possible. And Americans usually aren't all that enthralled with marzipan, anyway."

"Genius is never appreciated," Richard sighed. "Well, as long as none of Miss Heisel's publicity pictures feature me ... I prefer to do my work behind the scenes, as you very well know."

"Always, Chef!" Araceli returned smartly.

Araceli was right; Patricia chose the cake option with the colored flowers, although she did cheerfully agree that the same shade of orange that featured in correctional facility jumpsuits could figure highly in the design. She thumbed through her overflowing three-ring binder, bulging with lists, lay-outs, spread-sheets and designs, cheerily approved practically everything else that Richard had suggested, smiled brilliantly on them both and departed from the Café as if she couldn't bear to tear herself away, but simply had to.

Richard plunged himself into the all-absorbing task of preparation, and from that point on, took very little interest in anything else which didn't have to do with the all-important preparation. A vast white pavilion appeared in Town Square; string after string of lights, an acre of tables and a veritable sea of folding chairs. Everyone else was doing their part for the performance of *Let No True Hearts Admit Impediment*. This he was vaguely interested in and relieved to observe. Twenty volunteer ladies of Saints Margaret and Anthony Parish Church appeared on one afternoon to assemble ingredients under the direction of Araceli and Abuelita. They descended, chattered like a flock of grackles while they made swift and businesslike work of peeling, chopping, prepping, slicing and departed – also like a flock of grackles, leaving behind them not a Jackson-Pollocked stretch of pavement, but a walk-in refrigerator stuffed full of covered bowls, tubs and trays of ingredients, all ready for the final push on Saturday. They had even painstakingly labeled every single container with the contents, quantity in pounds and ounces, and date.

So Richard escaped being aware of just how far and wide publicity for *Let No True Hearts* had spread, world-wide on the internet, most especially that entrancing and appealing image of Romeo.

The Mug-shot the Rocked the World

From the Karnesville Weekly Beacon – October 10, 2016
By Katherine Heisel – Staff Writer

This website was responsible for launching a world-wide internet meme this last weekend, in posting a picture of Roman Victoriano "Romeo" Gonzales, age 39, and a native of Luna City. Mr. Gonzales was in costume and character as part of the cast of the Luna City Players' special production of *Let No True Hearts Admit Impediment,* which will be presented on the 29th of this month on Luna City's historic Town Square, a performance to benefit the rebuilding of the Parish Hall of St. Margaret and St. Anthony Catholic Church. *(see additional story on page 2 of our print edition.)*

Mr. Gonzales, a 1994 graduate of Luna City High School, where he was a member of the varsity Mighty Fighting Moths football team, plays the part of an escaped prisoner whose participation in his own wedding is a matter of considerable concern and suspense to his fiancée and family. His photograph and those of other cast members playing significant parts in the play were posted on this website Saturday morning, following the first dress rehearsal – but the picture of a soulful Mr. Gonzales had gone viral by evening, temporarily crashing the *Beacon's* server over Sunday. But by that time, his picture had been shared, and re-shared extensively on social media among smitten fans, and attracted admiring comments in fifteen different languages across four continents, of which only the mildest which can be repeated on a family-oriented website, such as, *"Oh, I could just drown in those beautiful blue eyes and swoon in his arms forever,"* and, *"If he were a flavor of liqueur, he would be cream-honey-Drambuie ... and I would have him ... on ice, every night and twice on Sundays."*

Reportedly, the demand for tickets for *Let No Hearts* skyrocketed over the weekend, as did overwhelming interest in Mr. Gonzales' personal life, although the overwhelming proportion of those women sharing and commenting sincerely believed that he is a convict in the custody of the Karnesville Correctional Facility. He is actually a long-time oilfield worker and skilled mechanic, completely law-abiding and currently employed as a driver and mechanic for Gonzales Auto Body and Maintenance. He is unmarried, which briefly lent hope to his many admirers – but in a confidential interview with this reporter, insisted that he is currently in a serious relationship.

In the interests of journalistic integrity, this writer has known him all her life, as he is a second cousin once-removed on her mother's side.

Showtime

Richard found it eminently satisfactory to look out from the front door to the Café and to see Town Square dressed for the event. How efficiently Patricia and her allies had planned this! There was even a parking-lot set up for the out-of-town guests, in an empty field by the Tip-Top Gas & Grocery, with the 12-passenger electric cart from the Wyler Ranch running guests between the venue and the parking-lot. The day itself couldn't have been better; one of those unspeakably lovely and temperate October days in South Texas, just cool enough to be comfortable, with tufts of pale cloud sailing in a brilliant blue sky. It would not have surprised Richard in the least to learn that Patricia Pryor had rung up God's private number and requested a beautiful day from Him as a special favor.

And of course – it was too good; there had to be just that one little blight, the fly in the Chardonnay, the un-resolvable kink in the lifeline … the absolute turd in the punchbowl.

Araceli, having worked into late afternoon in the Café kitchen with the final preparations, went to change out of her work togs and into her maid of honor dress in the quaintly old-fashioned ladies' room in the back of the Café. For some reason obscure to Richard, the ladies' room at the Café was a lavish one, wood-paneled, equipped with a well-lit mirror over a small dressing table and a fainting couch with slightly faded rose brocade upholstery.

"I'm just going across to check in with Patricia," she called from the door. Richard nodded, barely having heard. Show time – and time to start sending the trays of *hors de oeuvres* across to the buffet, set up all the way along the back of the pavilion. His wait-team were in readiness; Beatriz and Blanca, a handful of the parish ladies, all done up in the maid costumes that the inexhaustible Patricia Gonzales and her magical sewing machine had done up for previous events. Guests were already arriving, milling in the square, after showing their tickets *(disguised as wedding invitations)* at the barrier. He could look across and see Benny Cordova and Chris already opening wine bottles at the station designated to serve as the bar. Yes; all was in order. And since it was a buffet, to be supplied by relay from the Café over the course of the evening, the heaving lifting was already done. All he had to do was keep his eye on the clock and direct traffic.

That happy contemplation was shattered – well, not precisely shattered, merely rocked by the first crack of doom – when Araceli dashed back across the street, with Patricia in her wake. Patricia in her non-speaking role was cast as the professional Wedding Organizer, in a businesslike navy-blue skirt suit and sensible low heels, bearing with her the overflowing three-ring binder.

"Chef," Araceli panted. "Have you seen Romeo today? He was supposed to be here for curtain-call ten minutes ago, but no one can find him."

"Romeo?" Richard blinked at them, abruptly pulled from his zone of focus. "Not since … last night, I think. But his truck was still there at the Aquarius this morning when I left for the Café. He must be around. Where else could he be?"

"He didn't come to the final curtain-call meeting," Patricia tapped an impatient pencil on a page with a checklist upon it, and a dangerously threatening expression on her otherwise agreeable countenance. Richard sensed an increasing gathering of thunderstorms. And also detected a resemblance to her autocratic grandfather, Doc Wyler, which he had never noted until this very moment.

"I don't know," Richard protested. "I didn't know there was a rota to watch him! It's not like he is <u>my</u> cousin. Call Jesus at the garage; that's who he is supposed to work for, isn't it! And Sefton, at the Aquarius. He has a cellphone; he can tell you if Romeo's truck is still there. He doesn't go anywhere without he is driving that truck…"

"True," Araceli agreed. "But it's not like Romeo to leave people depending on him in the lurch. That just isn't him. He's always been reliable …"

"Not always," Patricia said, as she took out her cellphone. "He had a tendency to be distracted. Usually by his sexual conquest of the moment, or a promise thereof." She went to a number on her call list, and with an expression of adamantine concentration, waited it to dial and go through. "Curious," she remarked, after some moments. "It goes to voicemail. I asked that he call back – but if he doesn't in the next ten minutes…"

Richard was already dialing the number of Sefton's cellphone, while Araceli retrieved hers from her purse behind the Café cash-stand.

"I'm calling Uncle Jesus at the garage," she hissed, and Patricia nodded. "He might have tried to leave a message last night but there have been so many messages, my mailbox filled up entirely, overnight…" Richard lost the rest of it, as Sefton had just picked up.

"'Lo, Ricardo," he drawled. From the sounds in the background, he was out in the goat meadow. "Yeah, Romeo's truck is still here. He left it here this morning. He and Miz Wyatt went someplace in her Mercedes. She seemed in an awful hurry for some reason …"

"Did he say where they were going?"

"Nah," Sefton replied. "No idea, but he had a suitcase with him."

"Oh, Jesus!" Richard's blood ran cold, regardless of the scowl that Araceli sent in his direction for taking the Lord's name in vail.

Sefton continued, unruffled. "He gave me a note for Miz Pryor, though. but he didn't say it was urgent."

"What did you do with the note," Richard took a deep breath, then another, thanking his lucky stars that he was not standing next to Sefton and fighting back the strong urge to throttle the man.

"I left it with young Anson first thing. I saw him when I went past your place, with a load of eggs for the Café. Didn't he pass it on?"

"I guess not," Richard replied. Anson was the oldest of Patricia and Andy's sons, a strapping fourteen-year-old most often seen in the company of Robbie Walcott. "Thanks, Sefton. We'll track it down."

The two women were already looking at him, with matching expressions of dawning horror.

Araceli spoke first. "Uncle Jesus says that Roman asked for a couple days off to take care of business. Uncle Jesus told him to take the whole week – since he's been working day in and day out since he got here. Uncle Jesus figured that if he could say that Romeo was away for a week then maybe the garage wouldn't be getting so many calls for him, because of that picture of him – the one that went internet-viral…"

"And Romeo left with a suitcase this morning," Richard said. He thought he ought to get the worst out first. "With Susannah Wyatt. He left a note for you with Sefton, who says he passed it on to your son – Anson, is it? The tall boy. Didn't he pass it on?"

"It is a well-known fact," said Patricia evenly although she sounded as if she were clenching her jaw. "That your average teenaged boy has the attention-span of a fruit-fly. And that is being uncomplimentary to fruit-flies. I think that I shall go and speak to Anson. Don't worry; he is much too large for me to turn him over my knee and spank, especially in public."

Before she could leave the Café, her own cellphone rang. Richard and Araceli listened, breathless with hope.

A hope soon dashed, as Patricia's conversation with Romeo continued. "Romeo – thank God! No, I never got your message … no … What?! You're at Stinson, waiting on … your chartered jet? To New York!!! Are you out of …? How can we possibly arrange for a stand-in at the very last minute – yes, I KNOW you only have five minutes at center-stage and half a dozen lines!" Patricia sounded then as if she were in a titanic struggle to maintain an air of calm composure and control over events spiraling catastrophically out of control. "Romeo; listen to me. The curtain goes up here in five minutes. Two hours is a … yes, I know. A cover shoot for an international national men's magazine… yes, that's very nice. And … a live interview on *Good Morning, America* – even better. But how could you do this to the Players, when we are all counting on you?" Patricia very carefully damped down the disappointed fury that Richard knew absolutely had to be building. "Yes, I do understand; it's an incredible opportunity for you. And that opportunity would not have come your way without the Players … but yes, I <u>do</u> understand. Don't concern yourself with the production, Romeo. Of course, we shall cope. We all wish you the best in New York, and for your career in modeling. Yes, thank you. I have to hang up now, Romeo. I have a production to see to. Goodbye."

The tone of Patricia's voice in those last moments was so cold, Richard reflected – that one could have poured it into a bowl with cream, eggs, milk and vanilla extract and churned a very flavorful ice cream in the space of five minutes. He was profoundly grateful that such cold fury was not directed at him.

And then, he realized that both women were looking at him.

Oh, shit.

The Handsome Convict

(From the internet site – The Frisky – Posted November 3, 2016 at 4:45:00 EDT)

Oh, girls – stand down, and hand out the Kleenex. The handsome convict, whose ostensible mug-shot went viral last weekend, and darned near broke the internet is not a convict, and alas – not available. The picture of him which went viral was of Roman Gonzales, aged 39, an oilfield worker *(not much longer!)* from Texas, who *(sob!)* is in a committed relationship with Susannah Wyatt, the high-powered Venue Properties International marketing manager. The devastatingly handsome Roman – who goes by the appropriate nick of "Romeo" was participating in a local little-theater presentation in the dinky Texas burg of Luna City … swear on a stack of copies of autographed copies of *50 Shades of Grey* that I am not making that up. It's somewhere in the Panhandle country, I believe, but that's neither here nor there. The local newspaper put pictures of the various cast members in character on their webpage, and the rest is internet history.

The picture of "Romeo" Gonzales went so far, so fast … and with such devastating effect on the hearts of women across the world that within days, he was offered a contract as a male model for a major NY-based agency – and then for a cover on the classy men's magazine, GQ! Romeo and Susannah appeared on Monday's *Good Morning, America*, to talk about his blinding-rapid ascent into the public eye, their unlikely meeting and subsequent romance, and their plans for the future. Susannah intends to take a hiatus from her career with VPI and devote her attention to promoting Romeo's modeling career ….

Curtain Call

"No," Richard shook his head. "No, no, a thousand times no. I can't. I won't. You can't possibly think that I …"

"You have to," Araceli replied, with iron resolve. Patricia was no less determined, but more tactful, more … warmly persuasive.

"It's only five minutes, and half a dozen lines, Richard. I know that you're a pro entertainer and that you aren't a stranger to a large audience."

"No," Richard insisted, but under Patricia's persuasive wiles, he could feel his own resolve crumbling, crumbling, crumbling like the sugar crust on crème brûlée under the heat of a kitchen propane torch. "I simply can't … I came here to be a private man, my own person, a free man in Paris…"

"We're not in Paris, Chef," Araceli was momentarily befuddled.

"Give me three good reasons why I should do this!" Richard made a last-ditch and forlorn effort. "Why me, and not another of your Players?"

"All right, then," Patricia drew in a deep breath. "Because all the Players are already in costume, in character and out there, circulating. The guests have seen them, every single one. You're the only non-Player to have sat through the final rehearsal. And you are close enough to Romeo's age and general appearance to pass in his part; just for the entrance and the wedding itself."

"I don't look anything at all like him!" Richard protested.

Patricia looked at him with clinical detachment. "I can do splendid things with stage makeup," she said, with heart-chilling confidence and Araceli pleaded, "Say you will, Chef – for Luna City. You owe us ... just this one thing. Make an appearance, say the lines, then Joe will take you off-stage again, and it will all be done."

"I'll do it, damn you all!" Richard capitulated, inwardly condemning himself for being a soft-hearted fool. "But only for the five minutes! And I can't be recognized as the Bad Boy Chef. I've spent the last year and a half putting that absolute tosser behind me. I can't be dragged in again!"

"Wonderful, Richard!" Patricia favored him with one of those dazzling, heart-melting smiles, as pure relief flooded over Araceli's. "You have my word on it. Just a brief turn on the stage, and then ... safely backstage in the Café. Thank you, Richard. I thank you, the Players thank you, all of Luna City thanks you." She enfolded him in a sweet, perfume-scented embrace; *Diorissimo* – he was willing to swear to that and then immediately turned to business. "It will all be marvelous!" She consulted her cellphone for the time. "In ninety minutes, I will come to the Café with your costume and do your makeup and then Joe will come and bring you over in handcuffs. You don't have a problem with that? Oh, good; some of our Players do have a partiality regarding restraints but it's none of my business and I don't judge them."

With another smile, she and Araceli were gone, leaving him in the Café kitchen, a quivering, apprehensive knot of jittery nerves. The parish ladies came and went with their trays, keeping the table of *hors de oeuvres* well and bountifully supplied. It all seemed to be going well. At least, the food part of the show was going well. Curiosity led him to venture across the street and into the leafy green shades of Town Square; lively with balloons and crepe streamers, with happy people dressed in their very best.

To his relief no one spared him a second glance, anonymous in chef's white and a toque; just part of the furniture. The bar seemed to be doing a very good business; Chris spared him a conspirational grin, as he set up tray, after tray of wine-glasses. The only people who spoke to him was Martin Abernathy, nursing a small glass of white wine and standing next to Sylvester Gonzales, Luna City's resident computer expert and on-line gamer extraordinaire.

"Looks like it's going well," Martin nodded. It looked as if he didn't know that Romeo had pulled a runner. Richard thought he had best hold his tongue and not sow panic and demoralization among the troops. "This is quite a turnout, for a small-town event, you know. Hope you and your staff keep the food coming, Richard."

"I don't anticipate any problems," Richard lied through his teeth.

"Behold the power of the fully-functioning internet," replied Sylvester, a dapper vision of high retro-nerd fashion in his customary Buddy Holly thick-framed glasses and a vintage white gabardine sport-coat adorned with a pink carnation boutonniere. "Once that picture of Romeo went viral; I would have never thought something could go so viral, so fast. Uncle Roman might be able to get the new parish hall up by Easter – in time for the spaghetti and meatball supper, anyway."

At that moment, a dark-haired young woman in a long white dress flounced past them; yes, the girl playing the bride. It annoyed Richard that he still couldn't place why she looked so very familiar. In front of a half-circle of interested guests, the girl and an older woman in a matronly dark-blue lace dress with an orchid and babys' breath corsage the size of a small hanging basket pinned to her shoulder exchanged brisk remarks, which Richard couldn't hear very well over the murmuring of the crowd exclaiming that she was Kitty the Bride and that must be her mother.

"I keep thinking that I know that young woman from somewhere," he confessed to Martin and Sylvester. "Who is she?"

"A girl from college that Berto has a crush on," Sylvester replied, and something in his expression made Richard wonder if Sylvester was being entirely truthful. Well it wouldn't have been the first time that Sylvester had been less than candid. How Sylvester, Chris and Clovis Walcott had conspired to sink the summer's movie shoot and to keep Richard from knowing about it until the whole project came crashing down in the cross-dressing charge of the Karnes County Rangers was a memory still raw. "And it seems to be reciprocated. Her name is Marigold Yasbeck and Abuelita approves of her, even if she is an Anglo from California. Lucky for Berto, he is one of her favorite grandsons."

Granny Adeliza Gonzales, the supreme authority in the whole interlinked Gonzales/Gonzalez clan of Luna City. Young and old, male and female alike; when she commanded them to jump, the only possible response was a respectful request for clarification on the required altitude. Richard had a soft spot for Abuelita Adeliza, not least because she was his biggest local fan; her intervention on his behalf ensured and continued to ensure the comfort and livability of the old Airstream trailer, parked out at the Age of Aquarius Campground and Goat Farm.

"I have to say," Richard cleared his throat. "That really, everyone involved in this production is just fabulously well-turned out. On-point, as it were. Except for the Steins: I presume they are being ghastly simulacrums of tourists? Yes, I thought so. Socks and sandals with loud shirts, guidebooks, and many cameras are kind of a give-away. Otherwise, guests to our Majesty, Queen Elizabeth's honors garden party couldn't be any better arrayed. I suppose that Patricia Pryor saw to the costuming of the cast... but as for everyone else... Kudos, and all."

"Yeah," Martin Abernathy grinned and jerked his chin in the direction of Sylvester's vintage sartorial splendor. "Everyone loves a splendid occasion, and a chance to dress up a little. But no one under the age of seventy or so will get <u>his</u> reference, unless they're Marty Robbins fans. Ah, well. Looks like they're bringing out the main courses."

"Then I had better get back to my kitchen," Richard allowed, with a nod. Yes; the buffet table was ready for service; all the side dishes, neatly set out with the little chafing dish burners underneath, proctored by the relays of parish ladies, and by young Anson Pryor, deftly slicing off collops of beef. He ducked around the side of the pavilion and collided full-on with Kitty the Bride, Berto's student friend from California.

"Oh!" she exclaimed, startled and taken back, displaying a slight squint which suggested she was accustomed to wearing glasses. In that moment, a sudden burst of insight rang like a gong in his skull, temporarily driving the horrid prospect of being the prize exhibit in this farce, dragged in by Joe Vaughn and wearing convict orange.

"You!" he exclaimed. "I know you! We did a show together for … hang it, I can't remember! But we taped it at Disneyworld! You're Amy Butler!"

"Shush!" She hissed. He was aware that certain of the nearby guests had their attentions fixed upon them with the liveliest interest, certain that this was yet another extemporaneous scene and edging closer so as to catch every single word. "Don't blow my cover! I promised I'd do this under my own name as a favor for some nice people! And I know you, too! Rich Hall, the Bad Boy Chef!"

"Don't blow mine and we're even!" Richard begged in a whisper, to be rewarded by a dazzling smile and a brief peck on the cheek.

"That's a go, Rich!" she promised and dashed away, accompanied by puzzled commentary from the handful of guests sufficiently close enough to hear and observe.

"Do you suppose she is going to elope with the caterer?" was one of the loudest speculations ventured as Richard hurried back across to the Café. More than ever, his kitchen was a refuge from the madness.

He took good care to stay there, while the parish ladies came and went, cheerful and chirping together like birds, now and again acknowledging his presence and thanking him for his assistance. Almost against his will, he found himself liking the parish ladies; they didn't take any guff from anyone, not even himself. The youngest of the lot were about half-again his age and the oldest over twice that, but they knew what they were doing when it came to serving a multitude with metaphorical loaves and fishes, and of course, they were accustomed to work together. For restaurant amateurs, he was quite pleased with their work. Now he knew from whence Beatriz and Blanca had got their food-service work ethic.

He was quite resigned to his fate, when Joe Vaughn appeared from the back-dock area, casually spinning a set of handcuffs around a finger and Patricia Pryor came in from the front of the house, a largish case in her hand and a purposeful expression on her perfect countenance.

"Most everyone is finished with supper, Richard, and it was absolutely fantastic! Oh, hi, Joe; ready to roll on this? Romeo has run off to be a male model in New York, and Richard has agreed to be his stand-in. Good. Now sit down, Richard; this won't take a moment."

With the air of the condemned facing the block on Tower Green and a large masked bloke with a really sharp ax at the ready, Richard submitted to being sat in a straight chair under the brightest lights in the Café, which turned out to be in the Ladies' Toilet. He considered that he bore this humiliation with fortitude and grace, as Patricia swabbed his face with sponges, cotton-balls, and little brushes. At the end, she handed him an orange cloth pull-over shirt; yes, the one with Karnes County Correctional Facility stenciled in black across the back, and Joe lurked meaningfully at his elbow.

He definitely had no way to get out of this, now.

"Now, put this on – carefully, so you don't smudge ..." but just at that moment, a breathless parish lady pushed open the door, and gasped, "He's here! Romeo's here!"

Richard sagged in relief, for following her through the door was Romeo himself, in the flesh, also out of breath and the very picture of apologetic regret. "Hey, Patricia, I'm not too late, am I? I hated like hell to let you all down, but Sue kept saying how important it was to get to New York, once I had signed a contract and you know how it is with me."

Led around by your — Richard ventured silently to himself and Patricia astounded him by saying as much out loud and in pretty much the same words.

A crestfallen Romeo shrugged, and allowed that yes, that was pretty much his downfall, while Joe grinned. "Got it in one, Pat, but Miz Alice sure would have washed out your mouth with soap."

"But I made it in time, didn't I, Patricia? I came back and that counts for something, doesn't it?"

"I suppose it does," Patricia sighed. "I'd let Richard go ahead and stand-in, but I twisted his arm something awful and at least a third of the women out there bought tickets because they wanted to see you!"

"Great!" Romeo beamed from ear-to-ear, and deftly snagged the orange shirt to pull over his head. He struck a heroic pose, exclaimed, "Show time!" and then, "Owww!" when Joe snapped the handcuff on his wrist. "That hurt, Joe! What was that for?"

"Suck it up, cupcake," Joe replied. "For putting Pat and Ricardo to an evening of hell. Ready for your entrance? Jesus, you must have broken every speed limit there is, just to make it in time..."

"Sue hired a helicopter," Richard heard Romeo explain, as the door swung closed behind the pair of them.

In the mirror, Patricia herself looked almost limp with relief. Richard ventured, "So ... I guess I am relieved of duty, then?"

"You are, indeed! I can speak for the Players when I tell you how grateful we are that you agreed to step in. I know you didn't really want to, but ..."

"Not much choice." Honesty compelled Richard to agree. "You're a brick, Patricia. I can't promise that I would have saved the day, but it would have been disastrous, otherwise."

Faintly, from across the square came a roar of acclaim and applause, and Patricia gasped, "I must fly, but thank you again, Richard. I'll leave you some cold cream for clean up with."

And she was gone, leaving Richard to contemplate a half-full jar of cold cream, a box of tissues and his own countenance in the mirror.

"Not bad," he allowed to his reflection. "I might just have been able to do it ... assuming that everyone concerned had a sudden attack of near-sightedness. Ah, well – I've always believed I did my best work behind the scenes anyway."

New Love, Old Love

Under the starlit evening, a slight breeze stirred the tree branches, casting swaying shadows and blobs of light on the dancers below. The big event was done, the wedding performed, to a chorus of coos and happy sighs, the towering cake expertly carved and served to the multitude – and the groom, in his orange shirt removed from the scene by Joe Vaughn. Now it was time for dancing and unscripted celebration. Hardly anyone noted the departure of a single private helicopter, which rose from the empty goat-pasture by the Age of Aquarius and jetted away northwards at speed.

"I wonder how much it cost to rent a helicopter for that little jaunt," Joe Vaughn mused, to Jess Abernathy, as they slow-danced to the music of *Los Maldonados*. Jess answered, "I guess Romeo thought it was worth it and he could afford it. Or she could; good Lord, what an odd couple. Who would have thought it" An oilfield roughneck and a C-level executive for an international resort property company? But if they can make it work …"

"The odds are usually pretty even," Joe pulled Jess even closer to him, and Jess leaned her head on his shoulder. "Even for young love …" he nodded towards where Berto and Marigold – Amy – were dancing blissfully in each other's arms.

"They look so cute together," Jess sighed. "She's such a nice kid, too. Total pro – but still a nice kid. When Patricia asked her, she didn't even guess that she was – is – Amy Butler. Berto just said that he had a student friend who had done a lot of acting. She said she would do it for us because she had such a good time in Luna City shooting that movie over the summer."

"I do believe that she was the only one of the movie people who had a nice time," Joe agreed. Jess could feel, rather than hear the rumble of his laughter. She snuggled against him, again thinking how … safe she always felt, with Joe. Then, now and forever. Even when he was the star senior quarterback, and she was a gawky freshman at Luna City High, Jess saw him as one of the good ones; a nice-mannered, courteous, and reliable guy. She caught a glimpse of Berto and Amy; the latter luminescent in the white bridal gown, although she had sensibly ditched the veil and tiara once that the performance was over, before they were lost in the crowd of other dancers.

"They look good together, though," Jess ventured. "Yeah, but young love. Good luck with that."

"There's something to be said for old love," Joe protested. "You know, I've been thinking. Anything could happen, at any moment, to either one of us. I've come to a decision that you and I ought to get married for real, Babe."

"We ought to, yes," Jess answered, because every doubt and hesitation on her part had vanished like winter frost touched by sunlight with those words. Everything was clear and obvious. Of course, she and

Joe should get married, formally. They had been informally married in every other respect for years, they all but lived together. "But no fussing, Joe. We should just run away and get it done quietly. Privately. Then tell my folks and your parents and Uncle Harry in Alaska. I can't imagine putting up with all the fuss like what we were making fun of today. We have two households of stuff. It's not like we need wedding presents!"

"Fine by me," Joe agreed. They danced a few more measures in blissful agreement. "I do have a ring, though. Had it for years – my grandmother's. Thought I might keep it handy against a future need. I almost gave it to Patricia once, but we had already broken up, and she married Andy by the time I got to where I could support a family."

"You scoundrel," Jess teased. "You've been holding out on me all these years with a second-hand ring!"

"Nope. Cross my heart and hope to spit in your mess-kit ... sorry, Floyd."

"You love those old comedy records of your Grandpops', don't you?" Jess giggled. In Joe's house, inherited from his grandparents, the pride of place in the living room was held by the vintage stereo system and a collection of disks in worn covers, also inherited from Joe's grandparents.

"Funny stuff, Babe; out in the 'Stan, I used to do the old Hudson and Landry routines by memory to get the guys to laugh and they never failed. OK; when do we do the deed?"

Jess thought for a moment, utterly content. Now that the deed was agreed upon, only the place and date remained to be decided. After all the simulated drama of an elaborate wedding/drama presentation, the prospect of her own wedding was a relatively simple proposition. "I think maybe next month. Go to a JP, and then up to the Hill Country, stay in Fredericksburg at a nice B&B ... we can visit all the museums and wineries. Or maybe to the coast. Padre Island, Aransas Pass, even Galveston. Galveston for Christmas, maybe. North, or south. What's your preference, Joe?"

"North," Joe replied. "The coast can be dismal in winter. We'll slip away for a long weekend. Hey, Babe, where do we live afterwards, then? Your place or mine?"

"Yours' is bigger," Jess considered the practicalities. Even if her place was newer by thirty years and she was fond of it as her childhood home, it was also smaller; a plain post-war bungalow of no particular architectural merit or attraction. In contrast, Joe's grandparents' house was an utterly charming, classical Craftsman-era cottage, and had the additional merit of being renovated most recently. She sighed, deeply happy and deeply content. "A proper corral for my Sweet-Pea out in back, though. Non-negotiable demand. I couldn't possibly board Sweet-Pea somewhere where I didn't see her every day ..."

"Ah. Babe, you were seriously considering the Dallas job offer. Did you turn it down because of me, or Sweet-Pea?"

"Oh, Joe..." Now that she recollected what she had turned away from, Jess felt like bursting into tears. "No, I turned it down because of everyone. You. Pops, Gram and Grumpy. Sweet-Pea. Doc Wye. I thought it all over one night and I realized that I just couldn't. I couldn't go and live anyplace else and not be happy. I had to come back, just as you did. You went away to the Army, had all the adventure you could stand and came back to Luna City."

"So I did, Babe," Joe answered, his voice thoughtful, grave. "Bones and blood; this place is in them. Draws us all back, eventually."

"How did you know about the Dallas offer?" Jess was a little bit miffed. *Really, even if Joe was a cop, did he have to know everything?*

Joe chuckled again. "Look, darlin' – I wasn't hired on account of my staggering good looks. The Dallas headhunter called on the house's old land-line, about a month ago. When you were in the middle of that movie job. I think you had it listed with them as an alternate number. So, I answered, Poor young HR weenie; she blurted everything to me; wanted your final decision on behalf of some higher-up. I played the dummy; I think they eventually called your cellphone."

"But you didn't say anything to me about it? Didn't you wonder, just a little?" Jess demanded, with a touch of indignation.

"I figured you'd tell me when you made your decision," Joe replied, unruffled. "The fact that you didn't say anything at all, or even talk it over with me? I guessed that you had already decided not to accept the job."

"I see," Jess leaned against his shoulder, slightly ashamed of herself for not having confided in him. "I didn't want you to worry, you know? Have that on your mind, be distracted while trying to keep law and order. Police work and all that."

"Babe, Uncle Harry could handle police work in Luna City on normal days and still have time for a good afternoon nap," Joe said. "And he's eighty-nine. Gotham City, this ain't."

"I suppose," Jess giggled, inexpressibly comforted by Joe's level-headed solidity, by the feel of his arms around her. "Still; it's going to be a pain, moving. I am not looking forward to that."

"Do it in increments," Joe suggested, punctuated by a brief kiss. "Every single time you come over to my house – our house – bring something. Just pick up something of yours at random, every time. OK, so we might have to get a third party to help with the big furniture … but bring something over, each and every time. No pain, no strain – moving in installments."

"Sounds like a plan," Jess agreed, utterly content.

Yes, there was no place she would rather be – than in Luna City.

A New Direction for Mills Farm?

Katherine Heisel, Staff Writer – Karnesville Weekly Beacon

There have been rumblings of discontent within Venue Properties, International over management of their signature Texas property, Mills Farm. The source of this unhappiness comes from the highest corporate levels, according to a number insiders familiar with the company's operations. Senior-level managers and shareholders have been critical of VPI's abortive attempt to broaden the appeal of their resort destinations by investing in movie and television productions, notably this summer's movie fiasco, M.A. Lydecker's production of *The Road to San Jacinto*. There is also an increasing degree of unhappiness over Mills Farm's strong identification with Old Charley Mills, as the public face of Mills Farm. Presented as a benign, welcoming host of VPI's multi-million-dollar resort and event venue venture, the real-life Charley Mills was a bigamist, drunkard and malignant scofflaw – and it has long been suggested that he was also a member of several late 19th century outlaw gangs. Serious researchers and treasure-hunters alike have insisted for decades that Charles Everett Mills concealed a fortune in gold somewhere about the Mills property. VPI executives have gone on the record repeatedly, downplaying the existence of such a hoard as mere fantasy but chance discovery of a pair of 1892 $20 "Gold Eagle" coins *(worth over $30,000 in mint condition)* earlier this year gave credence to the treasure-hunters.

Such a close association with a man notorious for a dissolute and criminal lifestyle, argue a strong minority within VPI's senior directors and shareholders, is damaging to the public image of Mills Farm. With the recent departure of Director of Marketing Susannah Wyatt, the matter of a rebranding of Mills Farm has taken on a new urgency. Ms Wyatt was the chief proponent of the strategy of 'branding' each location by associating it with a particular character, to serve as the 'face' – a strategy which in the main proved to be enormously successful, especially in ad campaigns. Her place on the managing board, and as Director of Marketing has been taken by Lucien Dubois, the first manager of VPI's flagship property, Chateau Venasque, in France's region of Provence, and most recently the manager of their Castle Mountain resort at Banff National Park, Alberta, Canada.

Insiders at VPI are also exploring various means of increasing appeal to a larger market sector, especially at VPI's various American properties. One suggestion under consideration for the Mills Farm location is to expand the already extensive attractions by incorporating a water park, in the style of the Texas-based Schlitterbahn chain of water-themed resorts. This would be a marked change for VPI, which heretofore has been relentlessly upmarket in its clientele.

Autumn Lights and Winter Ghosts

Richard pedaled home in the quiet autumn twilight upon closing up the Café kitchen after the Luna City Players presentation, although there were still a handful of revelers dancing under the lights shining in their spangled strings from the oaks around the bandstand. The parish ladies had long finished packing up the plates and glassware that belonged to the church and taken them away. He was exhausted yet elated. Araceli and Patrick had offered him a ride, but after the days' alarms and excursions, he preferred to wend a solitary way through the darkened streets of Luna City, and out onto the indifferently paved back road that rambled past a scattering of houses and double-wide trailers, and eventually plunged headlong between a series of pastures and hayfields. There was a bare silver thread of a new moon, sailing in the dark sky, and his feeble bicycle headlamp illuminated a little of the road ahead of him, just enough to avoid the worst of the ruts and potholes. Now and again a set of bright eyes – some nocturnal and adventurous animal which may have been a racoon, an opossum, or a domestic cat gleamed at him from the undergrowth – then blinked and scuttled away almost soundlessly, about their own business.

Tomorrow would be Halloween; a corruption of All Hallow's Eve, and then the Day of the Dead. Richard secretly thought that the ornamented candy skulls and the elegant Catrina figures were strangely reassuring. In the medieval world, reminders of mortality were everywhere; this local custom put a macabrely cheerful aspect on the presence of death. This night marked the divide between summer and fall, this night when the length of day and night were equally balanced. Judy Grant referred reverently to it as Samhain, and assured Richard that this was the time when ghosts were most prone to walk. He supposed that they did, even if Judy persisted in saying it as 'Sam-main' instead of the correct 'Sow-in.'

Judy Grant had, as Richard had discovered quite early in his residence in the Age of Aquarius Campground and Goat Farm, embraced with great enthusiasm every New Age belief, practice and enthusiasm; not to exclude a form of Wicca, spiritualism, Native American sweat-lodges, auras, 'sex-magick', the use of Tarot cards and divination by any methods save utilizing the entrails of sacrificed animals. Although he had been living in Luna City for a year and a half, he no idea what, if anything, the Grants did in regular observance of Samhain, having made it a practice to retire early so as to be fighting-fit for an early morning at the Café. Likely it would be pretty spectacular, although not up there with the enormous bonfire and the sky-clad antics of the old Communards which marked the summer solstice. October, even in Texas, was apt to be too chilly after sundown for such activities, even by true believers.

There was little sound on this night but the faint whirring of his bicycle wheels on the road, the crunch as they went over a bit of grit. At a far distance, there was the brief blare of a car horn; someone on Route 123, and the faint. nearly imperceptible drift of music, music from a radio, or perhaps a television on in a house close to the road. Sounds carried far on a still evening like this. A ragged serpentine veil of mist rose from the river, tangled like old rags or drifts of seaweed in the thickets of brush that marked the banks. A small goat baa-ed sleepily in the Grants' pasture as Richard came up to the even more rutted turn-off that led to the pasture. Almost home ... such as it was. Damn, he was fond of the little Airstream, his personal patch of paradise; the trailer, the Gonzales-built patio before it, his view of the goat-pasture and river-bank beyond. It was trig, stripped-down, comfortable and just large enough for a single person with simple tastes.

At that very moment, he was arrested by a most unearthly sight; a dozen silent orbs of yellow light, at some distance across the field. Round, glowing, rising gradually, floating in complete silence. A slight breeze seemed to be pushing them towards the west in a loose and shifting formation. Richard watched, disbelieving; no, he was not hallucinating, nor was he drunk. He had only drunk a couple of glasses of wine from the bar in the pavilion after he had finished overseeing the last dispersal of cake to the waiting, hungry thong. The mysterious globes bobbed and vanished, lost beyond the line of trees along the river-bank. Richard shook his head, as if to clear the cobwebs away; now he wasn't certain if he had seen the floating lights, or merely imagined them.

Still, to be safe, he dismounted from the bicycle and set out on foot, rather than take a change on the uneven track. Before he had gone very much farther, a sound caught his attention; the sound of a horse neighing, and the soft and regular hoof-beats on ground softened by the rain which had fallen earlier in the week. No, there were several horses or something – several very large, very dark somethings – moving swiftly in the thickets on the far side of the goat-pasture and the meandering river, stirring the branches wildly with the fury of their passage. But there was nothing to be seen, but the branches moving, and the thunder of horses running and with a crawling feeling at the back of his neck, Richard remembered stories in his childhood, of Gran telling him about the Wild Hunt, of Old

Crockern riding furiously across the moors, following his baying hounds. He also recalled Judy Grant's tales of the Agua Dulce riders; ghostly men on ghostly horses, riding at speed along the river-bank.

This was altogether too creepy, especially on a night where the moon was a single silvery thread. Richard was not a superstitious man, but at that moment he wished devoutly to be inside sturdy walls or at least the Airstream's aluminum walls, bathed in the warm daylight glow of electrical lights. He walked faster, wheeling the bicycle past Romeo's abandoned Fifth-wheel trailer and a scattering of other caravans and tents – none of which showed any evidence of life within – lamenting that there was no congenial company to share his own trailer with, even if for just a short time. Disconcerting, as until that moment, Richard was not certain he really wanted to share it with another member of his species, long-term. It had never worked out before, he admitted to himself; experience being that dear school that fools would learn in no other. Of late, he had come to the despairing conclusion that yes, he <u>was</u> one of those fools.

He wondered briefly what Romeo would do with that battered and travel-worn Fifth-wheel. From what had transpired today, it appeared that the adoration-object of three continents would never have need of it again; *New address Easy Street, please forward all mail, and the staff will get to it, eventually.* But at the end of the day, Romeo was a Gonzales. Doubtless, someone in the extended clan would see to taking care of the trailer. Perhaps it would be parked in back of Gonzales & Sons Repair and Auto-body.

Now that he was on the Grant's rambling and extensive property, he could see lights again – golden light, flickering and flaring. These were not floating in the air, but torches, carried by ordinary humans; a reassuring sight, after the floating lights and the sounds made by invisible horses in the night.

Well, if Judy and Sefton and their friends of the old Commune could be said to be ordinary; a thing which Richard doubted with every fiber of his super-rational soul. The torches were being held aloft by a dozen men and women clad in long white robes, led by Judy, with her long hair unbound and streaming about her face and shoulders; a procession of Druidic figures, all along the boundaries of that three acres of rock-ribbed slope encompassed in the gentle bend of the river – the goat pastures, the campground, the wooded hillock crowned by a grove of trees, the yurt and the numerous outbuildings, huts and small enclosures that housed the Grant's hens, goats and gardens. Disconcerted and astonished by the spectacle – and also a little awed, since the otherwise cynical and down-to-earth Sefton Grant had been somehow convinced to participate in this mummery, Richard leaned against his bicycle and waited for them to pass by; amused, horrified and comforted in about equal measure.

As exasperating as the Grants could be with their outlandish eccentricities, especially Judy, they were also confoundingly decent and hard-working folk, held in respect and affection by their neighbors in Luna City. This continued to baffle Richard, even as he was grateful for their continuing hospitality. Now, as the procession passed within an arm's length *(the older and stouter of them puffing slightly with exertion)* Judy beamed at him with cheerful good-will.

"Richard, how went your event? Wonderfully, I hope! You know that a good application of the magick resolves almost everything..."

"It went very well, Mrs. Grant. There was not a place at a table unfilled, and Romeo made a truly spectacular entrance just in the very nick of time ... and may I ask just what you are doing?" Richard could not keep his curiosity in bounds for a moment longer.

"We're walking the boundaries with the torches," Judy replied, in complete earnest. "To set the wards and banish the bad spirits, you know – for Samhain. It's the end of summer, the autumnal equinox, and of the spirits of the dead visiting the living. Did you see our fire lanterns, by the way? Such a charming custom, and Seftie worked out such a clever way to treat the candle-wick so that they will stop burning at a certain altitude … we had such a set-too last year with the Fire Department…"

"Ah," Richard, his puzzlement regarding the strange drifting lights resolved, still wondered about the horses. "It may have worked, very well. I thought I heard the Wild Hunt riding along the river-bank – you know; the haunts on horseback, chasing after whatever it is that they chase after."

"Old Roman Gonzales' herd." Behind his wife, Sefton Grant chuckled; he seriously resembled JRR Tolkien's wizard Gandalf, in a long belted robe, what with his grizzled Willie Nelson beard and long hair. "I'll bet you that is what you heard just now. He brings them to a winter pasture, just across the river from us. Bet that young black stud-stallion of his has busted out of the barn and gone for a run."

"Seftie, sweetie, it could still be the Agua Dulce riders," Judy insisted, confidentially. "They've been seen; seen many times at this time of year. I've seen them myself … oh, very often. They're an omen!"

"Of old Roman having a busted barn door, usually," Sefton winked very broadly at Richard, who thought it might be time to be tactful.

"After you have walked the boundaries with torches, what do you do then?"

"Oh, we have a splendid feast," Judy assured him. "A harvest pumpkin stuffed with wild rice, spinach, beans and corn. Then, afterwards," she sighed, like a small child in happy anticipation of Christmas morning. "We work the magick. You are welcome to join us, of course."

"I regret that I will have to pass on the hospitality," Richard replied with a stab at his customary suavity. "I have already eaten … and it has been a very long day for me. I doubt that I could work … er-magick with any energy tonight."

"Of course," Judy appeared mildly disappointed. "We understand. Have a good night, Richard. Sleep well, in the assurance that there will be no otherworldly disturbances of the bounds tonight. Of course," she added, as she and the others gathered their robes and hefted their spluttering torches, "We must do this again tomorrow evening, and the night after, in order for the warding to have a lasting effect. You are welcome to join us, of course."

"I will consult my social calendar," Richard said and made his escape, although he did note Sefton's brief grin.

It was not wholly an untruth. Richard had eaten well, at mid-evening, dining on the perfectly-seasoned roast beef, carved expertly by Anson Pryor, along with the chattering company of parish ladies. As for the magick-working; that was a practice and topic best left unexplored, considering Judy Grant's thoroughly horrible cooking abilities with vegan cuisine and the inedible results. Sefton regularly slipped away to indulge himself in Karnesville with fast-food hamburgers, for which duplicity no sane person could blame him in the least. But Sefton had remained faithfully married to Judy for more than forty years, so likely her magick skills in that direction were much, much more finely developed.

Apropos of nothing at all, he did wonder when he met with Jess Abernathy for their regular mid-week morning planning meeting, why on earth there was a tall floor lamp with a stained-glass shade in the passenger seat of her car – the end of it sticking out of the passenger-side window, clearly visible as they sat at the *stammtisch*, with a clear view of Town Square outside. A sturdy crew from a San Antonio party rental company were making swift work of taking down the magnificent pavilion from the wedding event.

"Just shifting things between households," she said, with a slight evasive air. "Now, do you have the figures on last nights' buffet event?"

"Not until I get the final tally from the winery," Richard replied. "That's the only large supplier still owing an invoice. When we added fifty more places, I had to go back and plead on my knees for another ten cases of their finest red. I consider that it was worth it, though."

"I have to agree with you," Jess made a neat stack of the assembled receipts. "So far, it looks as if the presentation cleared over $10,000, after everything is paid for and most of our supporters also supported in kind, not to mention donors who bought items on the wedding registry. Doc Wyler promised to match total contributions with one of his own, and Roman Gonzales says that he will do the rehab at cost, plus two percent, as he does have a family to support."

"What's the bottom line, then?" Richard asked, and Jess tucked the stack into a folder, which tidily vanished into her purse-briefcase.

"Between the fund-raising, donations, insurance, support from the diocese and all," she replied. "It's a go for a new parish hall. We may be able to eat lavish helpings of Anna-Marie's signature *polpette* at the spaghetti and meatball feed in the spring in a new and entirely mold-and-asbestos-free parish hall."

"Anna-Marie?" Richard asked, still slightly boggled at how this small town in an out-of-the-way corner of an out-of-the-way American state still managed to be so bloody cosmopolitan.

"Anna-Marie Gonzalez," Jess replied. "She's Italian; a war bride, actually. Hector Gonzalez met her ... I don't know; sometime during the Italian campaign in WWII. He tells some amusing stories about it at the V after a couple of beers about how they first met. Something to do with laundry, German hand-grenades, and stomping grapes. She arrived in Luna City about 1946, with one suitcase and a bulging file full of traditional Italian family recipes. Eighty-something and she still oversees the spaghetti-feed, and God help you if the pasta is not precisely al-dente when it is taken off the stove and served up."

"A lady with exacting standards," Richard commented, strangely moved by this. "I should meet her ..."

"You have," Jess retorted, with what Richard thought was perfectly savage sarcasm. "She was one of the parish volunteers working in your kitchen last night."

"All right, then," Richard replied, after a swift reconnoiter of his memories of that spectacular evening. Yes, a rather elderly, diminutive and authoritative lady did feature in them. And yes, the whole-parish-ladies-in-the-kitchen had worked out rather well. Now he realized full-well how this miracle had been achieved, although he ought to have noticed that her accented English was not quite the same accent as that of the other old-age-pensioner volunteers. "I owe her … some generous service or gift. I know her by appearance very well now, so don't embarrass me by introducing us…"

"Good," Jess said, snapping the latches on her bag, and regarding Richard with something like what he thought should be an air of fondness. "And did you watch the news last night?"

"Better things to do," Richard scorned watching TV news, as it often seemed to dwell excessively on the freakish. "Like sleeping or reading Larousse. Why?"

"It seems that someone driving between Beeville and San Antonio on last Saturday evening filmed some mysterious lights in the sky, hovering over Route 123. They floated silently over the road, then rose in the sky and seemed to vanish. The guy that filmed it insists they must be UFOs. They had him on KSAT-12 last night and Pops started getting calls from media folks within fifteen minutes. This morning, Joe and Pops's work email in-boxes were just jammed with messages from people wanting to know about the lights…"

"Those lights? I …" Richard stopped short. "They were nothing but fire lanterns. The Grants and their friends launched them; part of their seasonal ritual."

"Did they? Good Lord almighty," Jess sighed. "I might have known … thank God it rained all last week. The trouble is, the true believers will never credit that those lights were something as simple as all that. They have UFOs on the brain, so expect additional customers until the fuss over the news story dies down."

"I can just tell anyone that asks that they were cross my heart fire lanterns," Richard suggested, and Jess sighed again. "You can try, but likely they will think you are just part of the government's cover-up of alien visitors. At least you sell them coffee and pastries while you try and reason with fanatics, so it won't be for nothing."

"Oh joy, oh rapture unforeseen ..." Richard warbled. Jess groaned. "Do not lay Gilbert and Sullivan on me, Rich. It's too early in the day for operetta."

"I protest, Miss Abernathy! It's never too early for *HMS Pinafore*. Now, we have treasure-hunters, UFO-investigators and who is next? Ghost-hunters, I expect. Judy Grant was talking about the Agua Dulce ghost riders, as well. The more the merrier, I say."

"Bite your tongue, Richard. We had enough silly season this year with those movie people over the summer."

Jess gathered up her coat – for the day was chilly, and left the Café, the bell over the door chiming softly in her departure.

Outside in the street, Richard noted a panel van with a serious-appearing satellite dish mounted on the roof and the banner of a San Antonio television station along the sides, as it circled tentatively around Town Square. Now it pulled into a vacant parking place by the larger van belonging to the rental company, and three people emerged.

Stone the crows, Richard thought; *And God save us all, the media has arrived.*

The Luna Lights?

By Katherine Heisel, Staff Writer, the Karnesville Weekly Beacon

UFO hunters and connoisseurs of the paranormal are agog this week nation-wide after learning of a possible Texas rival to the famed and mysterious Marfa Lights, after Ferguson Bittner, of San Antonio recorded a 2-minute long cellphone video of a dozen lights floating from east to west over Route 123, as he drove from Beeville last weekend. Mr. Bittner spotted the lights as he approached the bridge over the San Antonio River, and the turn-off for Luna City, close to the Tip-Top Icehouse, Gas and Grocery. There were several other witnesses to the lights – all travelers on Route 123 who have come forward, but only Mr. Bittner retained the presence of mind to pull onto the shoulder and begin recording. No local residents reported seeing the lights, which Mr. Bittner estimates were in sight for at least ten minutes. It was almost 11 PM and the Tip-Top had been closed for an hour. A small number of cars remained in the temporary parking-lot for the Luna City Players' presentation of Let No True Hearts earlier that evening, [see story p. 2 of the Metro section] but their owners had elected to remain overnight at the Cattleman Hotel when dancing to the music of *Los Maldonados* continued until well after midnight.

The lights appeared to float in a loose formation, and in utter silence, before hovering briefly above the road. They then appeared to gain altitude, before veering off to the southwest in the direction of Karnesville and vanishing from sight beyond the tree line. Mr. Bittner's brief video recording confirms the sighting, the relative number, size of the lights, and direction of movement, but the quality of the recording itself is too poor for a detailed analysis. Still, the sighting has caused great interest among UFO hunters – and many of the most dedicated are already heading to Karnes County to undertake their own investigations…

Road-Trip

"I have absolutely got to get away from the madness," Richard confessed morosely, to Araceli, Patrick and Chris, on a Sunday afternoon at the Gonzales' residence – which had become almost as comfortably familiar to him as the Age of Aquarius. "Even if just for a couple of days. It's becoming unbearable. That wretched Gunn person is glaring at me around every corner, as if it were all my fault."

"He must have heard that Collin Wyler is spending Christmas at the ranch this year," Araceli nodded in sage agreement. "Patricia says that's because he's between wives again. I suppose Gunnison Penn must think the hunt for the Mills Treasure is on in a big way."

"He was on *Coast to Coast* a couple nights ago," Patrick agreed. "And that's what he was all about … the treasure, and how the Wylers and VPI and whoever are all about deliberately sabotaging his search."

It was the second weekend after the Luna City Players' benefit performance, the second weekend after the sighting of what had become known across the pseudo-scientific tabloids as "The Mysterious Luna City

Lights." The Age of Aquarius – once a quiet, semi-deserted backwater save for a few days around the yearly solstices and equinoxes – was now a lively and exciting place, filled almost to overflowing with treasure-hunters, detectorists, and UFO hunters.

The Grants, of course, were mostly pleased. Even for what they charged for a day or a week, which was more of a token gesture for parking or camping there than a serious fee, their business accounts were profitably fattened to the point where Sefton was considering renovating the old conblock latrine and bathhouse, served by the hot spring which had given the impetus to the original owner of the property to think of setting up as a destination spa and resort. Sefton also grumbled about the constant racket upsetting the chickens and goats, but Judy was pleased beyond words, at having another outlet and audience for her Tarot cards, her organic simples and natterings about old-world "magick."

"I liked it out there because it was quiet," Richard continued, still simmering over how his own refuge had been sabotaged by the constant influx of strangers over the summer. "After days in the Café, and people coming and going, it's restful to go out ... well, it used to be restful to go out to the trailer and unwind. Watch the goats, listen to the chickens, the wind stirring the leaves. It was positively blissful. Now it's full of people, pottering around with their metal detectors, waving around their sensor wands and standing up in front of each other's video cameras as if they were on the B-Bloody-BC yammering on about their search for whatever. It doesn't even let up after dark, either; a good third of the wretches are hunting for ghosts, and they sit up in the bushes, whispering to each other. I swear, if anyone shows up looking for something like the Loch Ness monster living in the river, I'll give it up and sleep nights in the Café Ladies. And those bloody cameras give me the pip."

"That bad, uh?" Chris replied, with sympathy. "Look, if you really feel like that, you can crash at my place until it quiets down, some. All I hear is traffic on the road, and sometimes the crunch of someone hitting the bridge abutment … don't mind that at all, reminds me of home. I'm going up to Marble Falls for a marathon, the weekend after Thanksgiving – you'd have the place to yourself, then."

"I might have to take you up on it," Richard said, although he was not entirely in earnest – still, it was his chance to vent to a sympathetic audience. This was over a meal of hamburgers, skewers of barbequed chicken, fire-roasted whole ears of corn, and a number of hearty salads. Araceli and Patrick, with their circle of friends had long ago fallen into the habit of those Sunday afternoon cookouts. By degrees, Richard had fallen into the habit of joining them; on this particular Sunday, the other participants included Chris, Sylvester, Kate Heisel, Jess Abernathy and Joe Vaughn.

("Do you good to have a social life, Chef," Araceli had urged him some months ago, fixing him with that severely analytical eye. "You need to get out more – hang out with real people."

"Likely I do need to hang out with people," Richard replied in a waspish mood. "That is – with people who don't tell me I need to get out more and hang out with people."

"There, you see!" Araceli pronounced in triumph. "Exactly what I said. Come over on Sunday – steaks from Doc Wyler's cow, that we bought half of, this year. You'll be amazed at how good, grass-fed beef can taste.)

"You know," Patrick announced, with a broad grin. "I think it's time for a road trip. How about we all go to Marble Falls and cheer on Chris. I have that weekend off, you and 'Celi can close the Café. I mean, who's gonna be eating out over that weekend?"

"Where the hell is Marble Falls?" Richard demanded, and Patrick's grin widened even farther. "About two and a half hour's drive north. Heart of the Hill Country. It will be a blast. Let's do it, 'Celi – leave the kids with Abuelita, and have some fun! Like we used to do…"

"I'd be game," Joe set aside his beer, and exchanged a quick glance with Jess. "If we can stop over in San Antonio for an hour or so … Jess and me, we have an errand to do there. Y'all can show Ricardo the Alamo as long as he promises not to pee on it. We can meet up at Buc-ees in New Braunfels and convoy to Marble Falls together."

"Sounds like a plan," Patrick beamed. "Uncle Jesus says it's OK to borrow Romeo's Fifth-wheel and that thing sleeps six!" while Richard demanded, "What in hell is Buc-ees?"

"You have to pee to believe!" Patrick replied and laughed so hard that he choked on a mouthful of beer.

"Count me in," Sylvester said, and Kate chimed in agreement, adding, "I can do a quick report on it for *'Talk of the Town.'*"

"Look," Sylvester brought out his cellphone and worked some miracles of inquiry on it. "Got a nice RV park, near enough as to make no difference. Some rental cabins, too; are we game?"

"Call me a ten-point buck," Joe answered, with a distant look on his face. "Yeah, we'll be at Marble Falls to cheer for Squid Medic when he crosses the finish line but then Jess and I have some other plans, don't we, Babe?"

"We do," Jess replied, and Richard didn't even try to figure out what that was all about.

So that was how, ten days later, Richard tossed a small overnight bag with some toiletries and a change of clothes into the back of Chris' little red coupe. Chris didn't hit the gas until they were well out on the main road north, in deference to the tires and suspension system.

"Man!" he exclaimed, as they spurted a bit of gravel behind them, and the speedometer steadily climbed to a hair below the legal speed limit. "I wish Sefton could get one of the Gonzalezes to come over with a scraper and level that broke-ass driveway of his. I shit you not, Ricardo. I drove on better-graded roads in Iraq and that is saying something."

"No argument here," Richard agreed. "I just don't think the Grants really expected all the traffic this year. I know I didn't…" He was still simmering over the regularly-occurring medium-distance death-stare from Gunnison Penn, although they did their mutual best to avoid coming from within twenty feet of each other, under the terms of the legal injunction. Obviously, it still rankled with Penn.

"Well, never mind, Bro!" Chris seemed unusually lighthearted. "The open road calls! We meet up in New Braunfels at noon, hit Marble Falls by mid-afternoon, set up camp … and then then I gotta be ready at oh-dark thirty. I'm aiming to do the whole course in under four hours, based on my last half-marathon. Hey, you should join me sometime! You'd get a kick out of running and the exercise would do you a world of good."

"Riding my bike supplies that need, thank you," Richard answered. "Frankly, I couldn't see the appeal, even when I was at school. Run around and around the track, looking at the backsides of all the fellows ahead of you? Nothing more boring can be imagined, and since I'm not a poof, I didn't even get any jollies from the exercise."

"You could join a club or something," Chris shrugged, echoing Araceli's earlier words. "You need a social life, for sure. You could learn to drive, even. Widen your horizons beyond Luna City."

"I like my horizons just as they are," Richard argued. "I agreed to join you all on this little jaunt. Isn't that enough?"

"True, dat," Chris slanted a sideways look at him. "OK, so no more bugging you about getting out. Still, you ought to learn to drive, like a real American."

"I will take that advice into active consideration," Richard said, in such a flat monotone that Chris dropped the subject at last.

They zoomed northwards along Route 123, which angles north and west through the gently-rolling ranchland country, stretches of pastures and thickets of oak, cedar and hackberry trees, interspersed with small towns like Stockdale, Sutherland and La Vernia where it was necessary to slow down, and now and again obey the strictures imposed by a stop sign or a traffic signal light. Those towns all looked rather like Luna City absent the grandeur of Town Square, no matter if they went straight through the town center or around the outskirts; a row of businesses, a straggle of cottages and double-wide trailers, a sign boasting the prowess of the high school football team, and then out into the pastures and groves again, dotted with grazing cattle and the occasional small oil or natural gas well.

Until they came to San Antonio – which from the southern approach was not one of those sprawling cities, attended by a steadily denser concentration of suburbs, strip malls and industrial parks. It seemed to Richard as if Chris' coupe topped one last rise of the highway ribbon – and there was the city, a modest gathering of high-rise towers just ahead.

"I promised you a look at the Alamo," Chris grinned. "You can't say you've been to Texas without you see the Alamo..."

"I am breathless with anticipation," Richard commented with a complete lack of emotion. Half an hour later, after Chris had deposited the little coupe in a city parking garage, and they had walked down one street, turned an urban corner and sauntered down another, Richard brought much more feeling into it. "Stone the bloody crows – is that it? It's ... so small – it never looked like that in the movies!"

Chris was laughing in what Richard considered to be a completely heartless manner. "Ricardo, man; what you see before you <u>was</u> only the least part of a larger establishment – the post chapel of a frontier garrison, as it was. The original place? Well, the walls around it went all around the outside edge of this plaza; most of it mud-brick and a single room deep. The chapel and the long building next to it were made of stone. Prolly why they lasted so long. But come on – you gotta see the inside, and the list of names. There were some of you Brits fighting here at the last, you know. And a mad Scot who played the bagpipes, too."

Borne along on Chris' unaccountable enthusiasm, and interested in spite of himself, Richard submitted to being dragged along. It was barely mid-morning on a Friday; the pleasant and oddly-shaped plaza was not particularly crowded. The classically Victorian bandstand reminded him of the one in Luna City. At every few paces, Chris pointed out a significant place where something or other had occurred.

"You come here often?" Richard finally asked, as the heavy wooden door closed after them with an ecclesiastically serious thud.

"All the time, when I was at BAMC," Chris answered, in hushed and reverent tones. "Miz Alice and Miz Letty used to bring me, when I could get a day pass. There's a nice garden at the back. Miz Letty, she was doing some research at the Daughters of Texas library – that's around the other side. Miz Alice would get tired, and we would go sit in the garden, wait for Miz Letty to get done. And she would tell me stories about this place, about her family, and I'd talk about J.W., mebbe. And then we would walk around to this old-school deli place on Commerce and have Reuben sandwiches and real old-fashioned root-beer …"

"You sound as if you are fond of the place," Richard commented. "As well as being almost embarrassingly knowledgeable."

"I am," Chris laughed, sounding slightly uncomfortable. "Miz Alice made it sound … you know, real to me. And Miz Letty; she knew so much. Between the two of them, I could see it in my head, you know? They were just guys. Real guys. I'll bet they talked dirty, knew that likely they wouldn't ever see their families again, but that they trusted the ones to their right and left … and they had something to believe in, at the end. Did you ever see that Billy Bob Thornton move about the Alamo? I did. There was a bit in it that stuck with me; Colonel Travis saying that Texas was a second chance. That's just what Luna City was for me; a second chance. Bet it was for you, too. A second chance at getting something right in your life. Something meaningful to hold to and believe in, a chance for something real and good, for friends that believed in you …

well, anyway. This is the sacristy room – where the womenfolk holed up in at the last. And there's the list of the garrison. See any names you know?"

"Not a one," Richard replied. "Which was the crazy Scot with the bagpipes?"

The Road North

Richard did have to admit, even if only to himself, that he was impressed with Chris as a guide to a historical site like the Alamo – quite as much as he was with Chris's ability to zip the little red coupe through a number of very busy, vehicle-and-pedestrian-clogged city streets, around a few more corners and up a long, gentle ramp onto the expressway, a feat which Chris performed with the absent-minded expertise of a professional knife-thrower. Within a remarkably short time, the tall towers of downtown San Antonio were left behind them, although not the suburbs, apartment blocks, and industrial parks. Chris gestured towards a particularly and sprawling set of buildings, all enclosed behind a tall metal fence, saying, "BAMC – Brook Army Medical ... twelve years ago, I practically lived in that place. I still can't go past without feeling I ought to steer towards the gates and report in."

"It's a bloody big place," Richard said, awed. It was the most vertical military facility he had ever laid eyes on outside of a futuristic television adventure.

"Yep." Chris deftly swung into a center lane and around a huge pantechnicon van, which towered over the coupe like a motor-driven Goliath over a pint-sized David – then another, and another, all lumbering along, bumper to bumper. "Traffic's always like this along here, I'm afraid; this is the main north-south highway between the Mexican border and into Oklahoma, so ya see a lot of trucks."

"So how far is this place where we meet up with the others ... what did you call it? Bucky's?"

"About twenty minutes, now," Chris looked briefly sideways at Richard and grinned. "It's a travel plaza; a place to get gas, ice, and a sandwich or something."

"Like the Tip-Top?" Richard asked, and Chris chuckled.

"Yeah, like the Tip-Top. The Tip-Top on steroids and a city block long. Didn't you read the fine print, about everything being bigger in Texas?"

Richard was certain Chris was exaggerating; a conviction which held up only to the moment that Chris pulled off the highway. They continued on a surface street which paralleled the highway for a block or so, passing a self-storage place marooned between two empty green fields, and then Richard saw a small sign; the head of an anthropomorphized beaver with buck teeth and a red ball-cap perched jauntily and unrealistically on its cartoon head. Chris pulled into the turning lane; yes, the parking-lot would have taken up several city blocks and the structures in the center would have dwarfed the plaza in front of the Alamo. There was a warehouse-sized building set back from the roadway, a structure the size of the Costco in Karnesville – the largest building that Richard was familiar with since coming to Luna City. Set before it was a pair of long awnings raised on brick pillars covering the petrol pumps. Each awning stretched almost the length of the main building and sheltered twenty pairs of pumps. Richard started to count them, to be certain, and gave up before he reached halfway. Here again, the head of the red-capped beaver adorned the center of each awning.

"Buc-ees," Chris announced, somewhat unnecessarily. "There's Pat's truck, around the side. Looks like Joe and Jess beat us here."

There was Jess Abernathy's yellow Jeep Wrangler, parked next to Patrick's truck at the edge of the parking-lot in the shade of some spindly trees, with the Fifth-wheel hitched behind and taking up three parking places all by itself. Pat, and Araceli with Kate and Sylvester were there, talking to Jess and Joe.

Joe very deliberately made a show of studying his watch, as Chris drove up. "Now, I know y'all weren't speeding, Squid," he drawled. "You must have been giving Ricardo the whole tour, chapter, verse, appendix and notes. Did you give him the test, yet?"

"Naw, we were running late. Say, Joe, you are lookin' awful smug this glorious afternoon. Did you pass out lots of tickets before you got out of Karnes County this morning?"

"Not a single one," Joe replied, with a wholly uncharacteristic expression of satisfaction. "I had better things to do, Jess and me. We figured we'd give the speeders a freebie today."

Richard, looking from Jess to Joe, and back to Jess again, wondered why they were actually holding hands; they were two of the most reserved and undemonstrative Americans he knew. It had taken him weeks and some blunt statements to that effect from Araceli to make him see that yes, they were a couple and even longer before he credited such statements wholly.

"Joe and Jess got married!" Araceli exclaimed. "They sneaked away to City Hall in San Antonio and just did it! Didn't you notice the rings?"

"I can't say that I have, actually," Richard answered. Chris crowed as he punched Joe on the shoulder. "Go Army! Congratulations, Joe – Jess! Way to go, girl … but why did you keep it so secret?"

"Well, it was private," Jess admitted, blushing as pink as a primrose. "And honestly neither of us wanted some ghastly brouhaha like *Let No True Hearts*, in real life. Just the whole prospect of it; the white dress, wedding invitations, fighting over who would sit next to whom at the reception. The thought made my skin crawl."

"But your friends, your families," Kate said, her expression reproachful. "What about letting them celebrate with you? That's what weddings are for; the customary rituals… they shape our lives and all…"

"Y'all are our friends and we're telling you now." Joe said. "We'll telephone our folks tomorrow and tell them. But for now, let's go in and grab some lunch, and you know … I can't speak for y'all, but the latrines here are the best you'll ever see between here and Dallas-Fort Worth."

As one, the group walked across the parking-lot to the nearest appropriately massive entrance; glass double doors, and a soaring interior packed with everything possible for the discerning traveler, and everything on a sufficiently lavish scale as to render Richard temporarily speechless; the row of coffee and soft-drink dispensers which seemingly went on forever, even longer than the petrol pumps outside, the immaculate and spotless W.C.'s, the bakery counter, the deli counter, the offerings of free samples, and the stand in the middle of the place offering sliced BBQ brisket sandwiches, grilled sausage and other roast animal-protein delights. No, it was most decidedly not cordon-bleu, but the odors from the cookers and the meats being sliced were enticing … especially since Richard's breakfast had been eaten at least six hours before.

He did notice, that for some odd reason, Araceli and Kate were an unconscionably long time at the bakery counter. When they finally tore themselves all away from the counters and racks of Texas-themed snack foods, groceries and assorted souvenirs, Kate was carrying pasteboard pastry box and Patrick a large brown grocery bag.

"A treat for dessert tonight," Araceli would only say with an air of mystery.

To Richard's mild relief, they did not rejoin the highway after leaving Buc-ee's; they followed Jess's yellow Wrangler along a two-lane country road, one which led through a green and highland country much like that around Luna City – just rather greener and slightly hillier. Small towns slid by, beads on a macadamized thread; a traffic light, and a welcoming sign, the usual small businesses, and sometimes the tall billboards for one of the big chain stores. It was all strangely restful for Richard; not quite familiar as Bickley or London, or as absolutely alien as Dubai, or Singapore, or any of those places where the pursuit of fame had taken him.

"Almost there," Chris remarked; they were approaching the brow of a hill; coming over the top, Richard could see that beyond a traffic light the highway crossed a deep green river. The yellow Wrangler's turn signal was already blinking for a left-turn. "Now, the town is dead ahead. The marathon starts at the high school football stadium tomorrow morning."

"Is this where we're spending the night?" Richard asked. The place was quite plain, but still a much-better kept park than the Age of Aquarius, with paved lanes and parking areas, set in a scattered grove of oaks at the edge of a scenic and substantial river. In the passenger-side mirror he could see Patrick's truck with the Fifth-wheel trailing behind. Chris nodded.

"Hey, we'll have a fantastic view of the city, across the river from here," he said. "It'll be grand. Patrick's gonna snag one of the slots right by the water and there are two or three little cabins for rent. I think Jess and Joe are gonna stay there tonight. I really gotta thank you guys for coming along. It means a lot to me; this is a qualifier for the Boston Marathon and that's a biggie I wanna work towards."

"I can't speak for the others, but it's my pleasure," Richard answered, a little awkwardly. Consideration for others had never come naturally for him; he supposed it came from being an only child.

"Adopted sons of Luna gotta stick together," Chris said with a quick sideways grin. "You open your mouth, they take one look at me and everyone knows right away we're not from around here … but I hafta say, God bless 'em, it's never seemed to make any real difference."

They waited, while Patrick rolled his truck a little beyond the designated space, then deftly angled the Fifth-wheel into it. No doubt a simple travel trailer would be a piece of cake to a driver accustomed to maneuvering tanker trucks. As soon as Patrick had it in the right position, Sylvester, Kate and Araceli emerged from the pick-up. Chris parked the coupe as close as possible, saying, "I gotta be out first thing in the morning – y'all can take your time."

Richard had to admit it was a nice location. He only wished that the Age of Aquarius held pride of place on a similarly broad river, but still, that was home.

"I have never been able to figure out why traveling is so tiring," Araceli said. "You are sitting down all day! You need any help setting up, Pat?"

"I'm on it," Patrick replied, with his usual air of quiet competence. In the space of five minutes, long enough for Richard and Chris to walk down to the river-bank to stretch their legs and walk back, the Fifth-wheel bump-outs were extended and the awning opened. Araceli brought out folding chairs and loungers from the back of Patrick's pick-up.

Chris commented in admiration, "Slick, you guys, slick! This is the way to do a road trip."

"I always thought it wasn't a proper camp-out unless it was pissing down rain, you all were starving from not being able to cook over wet firewood, and the bugs were eating you alive," Richard ventured. It seemed a little unsporting, to have brought along caravan convenience, complete with heat and air conditioning, plumbing and a gas hob, along with comfortable beds.

"I don't play that game," Chris replied. "'Specially not after a couple deployments. Bring on the comfort, bring on the glam."

Richard did have to admit this road trip thing did have distinct advantages; in that the food was as good as it usually was at Patrick and Araceli's backyard barbeques, the lager was delightfully cold, and the view across the wide and lake-like river, with the lights of the city beyond, the highway bridge over it, and the stars twinkling faintly overhead – all good. There were swifts or possibly even bats flying overhead, their wings a dark flicker in the sky. This was a welcome respite from the various hunters of ghosts, treasure and UFOs, just as the autumn chill was a respite from the broiling summer heat of South Texas. At mid-evening, Araceli emerged from the camper with the mysterious cake box in her hands, followed by Kate, with two bottles of champagne and a stack of plastic wine-glasses.

"Dessert!" Araceli said. "It's special – they made it for you two at the bakery counter!"

"What did they make special?" Jess and Joe had managed to squeeze spoon-fashion into a single lounger, which sagged alarmingly under the double weight.

"Your wedding cake!" Araceli unveiled the confection in triumph; a small, two-tiered cake frosted in white, with some small pastel icing flowers on the top. "No, it's actually a dozen plain cupcakes. The girls stacked them together and frosted it as one cake. And champagne – Jess, you absolutely have to have some tradition … and you and Joe have to cut it together."

"I draw the line at smashing it into each other's face." Joe warned, as he and Jess disentangled themselves from each other and the lounge. He brought out the ka-bar knife from his ankle sheath, adding, "Will this suit?"

"Perfectly!" Araceli nodded. Joe and Jess, their hands together on the knife-hilt, gently drew the blade between two cupcakes, as Sylvester and Patrick made a contest of popping the champagne bottle corks, aiming the bottles riverwards. Richard thought he heard a gentle splash, but it may have been a lonely fish, down in the water.

"For your wedding album!" Kate's camera flash briefly lit up the night, and there was cake and champagne and merriment, under the twilight sky, under a waxing quarter-moon, sailing among the stars and the faint veil of the Milky Way. When Joe and Jess went towards their cabin, they went hand-in-hand, while Kate and Araceli, giggling, threw handfuls of rice after them.

Marathon Talk

Richard did not believe that he would sleep very well that night in the Fifth-wheel, shared as it was with five other people. A pair of narrow bunk beds folded down on either side of one end, separated from the main sitting room/kitchen where there was a pull-out hide-a-bed, and a generous double-bed in the bedroom area. The whole place wan only half-again the size of the Airstream – but it seemed that serious advances had been made in caravan technology in the five decades between the manufacture of the Airstream and the Fifth-wheel – it had about three times as much space on the inside, seemingly. He, Sylvester and Chris claimed the bunks, out of gentlemanly consideration for Kate, leaving her the privacy of the hide-a-bed.

"I'll have to roll out pretty damn early," Chris warned them all. "I'll try not to bother anyone when I do."

"Look, it will take more than that to wake me," Sylvester replied, stifling a yawn. "I brought ear-plugs."

Sylvester might have just as well not bothered. Richard was asleep as soon as he pulled the covers over himself – he woke for a moment or two, very early the next morning when Chris departed for the start of the run, but only until the sound of Chris' car diminished in the distance.

The tempting scent of coffee – strong and black, scrambled eggs, toast and sausage, the prospect of a breakfast eaten at leisure – eventually roused Richard from renewed slumber. He stumbled out of the bunk area to find Araceli and Kate already busy in the kitchenette. Kate, smiling, handed him a mug already filled with coffee. She handed him the cream jug with the other, and Richard exclaimed with a grateful flourish,

"My dearest Kate, Kate of Kate Hall, my super-dainty Kate! Hearing thy mildness praised in every town, I might be moved to woo thee for my wife."

"Not now," Kate retorted, "For as soon as the bathroom is free, I have to wash my hair."

"Temptress," Richard sighed, and Araceli laughed. "Lucky you, Katie; he's never that charming in the morning to me!" The door stood open to the outside; the windows likewise; the morning air was fresh and cool, the view of the city half veiled in a misty fog. Joe and Jess were already outside with Patrick, tucking into breakfast.

"We can take our time," Araceli reminded them. "If the runners began at seven on the dot, Chris won't be crossing the finish line until about eleven. We can cruise around downtown – "

"There's a brewery we can check out," Patrick called from outside; Joe and Sylvester voiced enthusiastic assent.

"Beer is proof enough that God loves us and wants us to be happy," Joe said, and Richard agreed; not that he had any better ideas for an interim recreation in a strange city, but the morning was already well-begun and breakfast continued on so leisurely a note that they never did get around to committing absolutely to the brewery tour.

"We have to cheer Navy Squid on," Joe finally drew a line under the discussion. "It's the whole reason for this road-trip. And who knows – he might have made better time than he thinks."

"Agreed," Kate patted her camera bag. They piled into Patrick's truck and Jess's Wrangler for a ramble through the city; twice the size of Luna City, and with a larger downtown core. The high school football stadium was twice the size of Moth Field and even more full of spectators, awaiting the arrival of the full-marathon runners.

"A place with a long sight line," Joe said, while Kate took out her all-purpose press badge and put it to good use whenever they came up to someone who looked as if they might be in charge. Eventually, they found a stretch of low chain-link fence, right next to the track; when the lead runners in the full marathon run appeared and dispersed, a fair amount of the spectator crowd dispersed likewise.

"Any minute now," Sylvester consulted his vintage wristwatch. "He's been keeping real close to his scheduled times, the last few runs."

A few more runners appeared in the final stretch, under the watchful eye of spectators and administrators of the run. Kate took out her most serious camera, the one with a telephoto lens nearly the length and circumference of a body-builder's forearm. She propped her elbows on the top of the fence to hold the monstrous thing steady and aimed it at the distant end of the stadium, where the runners came in from the long course. A scattering of them were to be seen, distinguished only by black and white numbers spread across their chests, almost at once Kate lowered her camera, saying,

"There he is!"

"Fantastic!" Sylvester exclaimed with an exuberant whoop. "He's made it a whole ten minutes ahead of what he aimed for!"

"That's our Squid!" Joe said, "Going for the silver, if not the gold!" he raised his voice to the authoritative parade-ground bellow and roared, "Pedal to the metal, Squid! Get your ass in gear!"

Now Richard could pick him out – the triumphant grin clear even at fifty yards, the blade-like prosthesis propelling him like a spring. He finished that last stretch in a dash, ramping up his pace from the steady, ground-covering lope that likely had seen him over the whole twenty-six-mile course, accompanied by the cheers and encouraging shouts from his friends and from those spectators still lingering at the track.

"Pretty darned good for a disabled guy," someone commented nearby. Joe rounded on the speaker at once.

"He ain't disabled, sport, he's just a damned determined runner!" Turning towards Chris, who was panting from exertion, Joe added, "Walk it off, Squid – don't stop, or you'll stiffen up."

"I know, I know!" Chris protested, but Araceli handed him a bottle of water, and Sylvester emptied another one over him, although his shorts and singlet were already sopping-wet with sweat in spite of the coolness of the day. Sylvester and Joe went around the barriers; with Chris between them, they walked on the track, the others trailing behind, exclaiming and congratulating him on his improved time, while Kate danced backwards ahead of them, snapping off picture on picture. All around them were other tired and triumphant runners, walking to cool down, and relieving the glory of having run a good race.

"You're gonna be a star!" she exclaimed. "Even more than Romeo! You'll have to beat off the lovelorn women with a stick!"

"Promises, promises!" Chris gasped, elated and exuberant. "Oh, damn, what a good run that was! I hit a good stride early on … and from there on – it was like I was floating on high! Oh, man, am I gonna sleep tonight and half of tomorrow…"

"Stay awake long enough for lunch," Joe advised. "'Cause we're gonna visit heaven this afternoon … a brewery!"

"No sh*t, Army? Life just doesn't get any better than this!"

No, it certainly doesn't, Richard agreed silently. He could not actually recall the last time he had experienced a day like this; the glory of a victory, even at second-hand, coupled with the pleasures of friendship, the openness of the sky above, the adventure of seeing something new. Perhaps when he was a schoolboy; the first day that he had captained the school sailboat at a race event. He thought about what Chris said, the day before, when they visited the Alamo – about second chances here, after having bungled life the first time out. Maybe there was something to it – and maybe not, but in the meantime, here was this one perfect day.

Sunday afternoon, as they prepared to return to Luna City, Chris complained of feeling, as he said it, 'totally wiped' – too tired to face the three-hour drive, and the weekend traffic on the highway.

"I'll drive!" Kate chirped. "You trust me with your little car, don't you? I'm a very good driver."

"She's never had an accident," Joe said, adding meaningfully. "Or a ticket. At least, not in Karnes County. Don't know about any in Crook – I mean, Cook County."

"None there, either," Kate replied, with a bright smile. "Although there was that parking ticket. But that wasn't my fault!"

"Sure, I trust you, Katie," Chris tossed her the keys. "Just look out for those eighteen-wheelers."

So, when they set off, waving goodbye to Jess and Joe who were going to continue their honeymoon in the Hill Country for another week, it was with Kate at the wheel of the little red coupe, and Chris sprawled out in the back seat. Well, sprawled out as far as it was humanly possible to sprawl in the narrow back seat. But Chris seemed able to manage and before they had gotten twenty minutes from Marble Falls, he was sound asleep. It was not an awkward silence between Kate and Richard, although he was reminded of the night that the two of them had spared the children's room. They had not been alone together since then; Richard couldn't think why, or entirely decide how he felt about Kate. She was nothing like any of his previous flings; a woman more unlike Sammi Colquhoun could hardly be found within the limits of possessing XX chromosomes.

Like the time before, Kate broke the silence.

"You ought to get out more. just like this, Rich. It would do you good to unwind, now and again."

"Well, it's kind of a challenge. I don't drive and I'm not certain I want to learn, at this stage of the game," Richard replied. "A couple of hundred miles on a bicycle in Texas is just not doable. Not in the summer, anyway."

"Araceli worries about you sometimes," Kate mused. It didn't sound particularly personal as her eyes were on the ribbon of country road unspooling ahead of them. "You work like a dog in the Café all day, and then you go off to that crappy little trailer and read your cooking encyclopedia. It's not healthy, she says. You don't have any social life at all."

"A gross overstatement," Richard answered. "And a calumny. For I do, as a matter of fact have a social life. I'm having one right now. And I taught a session at the high school, just last month. I even go to the VFW on visitor's night. I'm a regular social butterfly, I am, considering what running the Café demands of me."

"I suppose," Kate conceded reluctantly. She was silent for another few miles, as Chris snored in the back seat and the paving hummed under the wheels. "I've been thinking. I'd love to feature some of your stuff on *Talk of the Town* as a regular feature. You know, with special recipes, kitchen hints – showing people how you do stuff. It's not like you have trade secrets, and mystery ingredients … just plain good cooking with a French slant, something a little different from the usual Tex-Mex. People would like that as a regular feature."

"They have cooking shows all over television and the internet, doing exactly that," Richard answered. "It's hardly original."

"But it would be with a local twist," Kate argued. "And that would make all the difference. You could be a media star, again."

"But I don't want to be a media star," Richard protested. "I've been there once before; I don't want to go there again. It wasn't good for me, you know. I became the most unspeakable, insufferable twat. I couldn't stand myself anymore. I like cooking, my Kate of Kate Hall, and I like teaching people to appreciate fine cooking and good food ... but I simply cannot go out there again, be a perfect Guy of a performing monkey. It will drive me around the twist for certain."

"It wouldn't actually have to be you," Kate mused – no, once she had a project in mind, she pursued it relentlessly. "You could have ... a puppet or something as a surrogate. We ..."

"We," Richard cut in. "You keep using that strange word as if this is already something that I had agreed to do."

"You haven't," Kate agreed, amiably enough, although she sent a brief look sideways at him. "Not yet, anyway. But I think that you will."

"And how is that?" Richard demanded, quite irked. *Was he doomed to be manipulated shamelessly by every woman in Luna City – from Miss Letty, to Araceli, Patricia and now Kate ... his super-dainty Kate ... Oh, merciful Deity, belay that random thought!* It was simply not right that he could be so easily maneuvered by women that he had never slept with and had no earthly intention or chance in a blue moon of sleeping with.

"Because we are very alike," Kate had her eyes on the road again, confidant and serene. She signaled a lane-change, and the coupe surged ahead and past a laboring and battered pick-up truck hauling a livestock trailer with a pair of unhappy horses in it. The horses looked mournfully at the red coupe as it zipped past.

"How so?" Richard was doubly indignant at the very thought. Kate signaled a turn again, and deftly pulled into the lane ahead of the pick-up and horse-trailer, soon leaving truck and trailer a small and distant shape in the rear-view mirror.

"And different, of course," Kate continued, icy and analytical as a surgeon, as if the pause in conversation had never happened. "We're alike in that we are both driven to excellence. Even perfection. You in cooking; me in the provision of information of interest to a heretofore unenlightened public. But the difference is that I like people straight off the bat and you don't, much."

"I do like people!" Richard protested, in wrath and indignation.

Kate shook her head. "No, I don't think so, not really. Oh, you like some people well enough, once you have made an effort. I'd venture that you have friends and very dear ones. Everyone but total antisocial misanthropes do have pals, but you seem to me to be one of those who appreciates humanity in the general sense but is shit-scared of individuals. OK, so I am not licensed to practice psychology; that's Dads' Cousin Lester, the one with a comet-trail of academic credentials after his name – but I do have enough ground-level experience. Cousin Lester is totes OK, by the way. If you ever want to get your personal demons sorted out by a licensed professional, I'll give a recommend, and he'd offer you the friends and family rate. My own reading would be that you're basically a potentially nice person with a total dick outer shell. I'm not being paid to cure that ... just consider that an email from reality, 'kay?" And then she took the sting out of the words by looking sideways at him. "I kind of like you, Rich; you quoted Shakespeare to me in a personal way. *Taming of the Shrew*, if I remember OK. Which is nice, and sort of totally gallant. Charming, even. I'm a sucker for the classics. But ..." and she shot him a severe sideways look, as she prepared to overtake another slow-moving pick-up and trailer combination in that smooth indicator-acceleration-quick look out the rear-view mirrors – a talent that he didn't think that he could ever master. (*Must be one of those genetic things, bred into the bones and genes of Americans.*) "Don't think that such a fondness will get you anywhere, for now. You are an interesting person, Rich ... but nothing that I'd be interested in committing to, seriously at this point."

She added with another of those sideways looks – a warmer one, even slightly flirtatious, if he were any judge at all. "But I could change my mind about that, any time."

The Luna City Volunteer Fire Department

The Luna City Volunteer Fire Department is Luna City's oldest and most venerable civic establishment, established in 1878, beating out the Masonic Lodge by a matter of eight months, and the Catholic parish of Saints Margaret and Anthony by a full year. Arthur Wells McAllister designed a building intended to serve as a fire house at the south-east corner of Town Square. The building, now a retail space for several antique and crafters, was the firehouse for thirty years. The distinctive twin double-door entrances meant to facilitate a pair of horse-drawn hose and pumper wagons are still evident in the façade.

Arthur Wells McAllister, being a forward-thinking city planner, naturally made accommodation for every civic service and improvement required by the last quarter of the 19th century. In the days when cooking, heating, and lighting a home depended on wood or coal fires, oil lamps or candles, domestic fires were an all-too-frequent occurrence, and an organized firefighting company of some kind was a civic necessity secondary only to a law-enforcement function. A busy man himself, Arthur Wells McAllister presented the task of organizing a fire company to another founding member of Luna City, Madison R. Bodie. Bodie, who had originally been a ranch foreman at Captain Herbert Kling Wyler's Lazy W, had saved his wages and investment share into a business providing patent cattle feed, grain and hay to his former employer and other local ranchers. A native of San Antonio, Madison Bodie had been an active member of Milam Steam Fire Company #1, and thus had the ideal experience to take on organizing a new civic volunteer firefighting company.

Madison Bodie soon had recruited thirty fit and enthusiastic male volunteers and attracted the generous support of town merchants. A pair of horse-drawn steam-powered pumps was purchased from the Waterous Engine Works Company, of St. Paul, Minnesota. For many years, community celebrations featured a race between Engine #1 and Engine #2 around the perimeter of Town Square. The two engines faced their first serious firefighting challenge in extinguishing a fire at the mansion of Morgan Sheffield – like Arthur McAllister and Madison Bodie, a man who had expected more of Luna City's prospects than were eventually delivered. Morgan Sheffield, who settled on a small tract of land along the river, slightly to the south of Luna City, had found a natural sulphur hot spring in the course of building his home. He had entertained hopes of a hotel and curative spa on the site. Work had just barely begun on a bathhouse and hotel, when a lightning strike on the roof of his house during a summer thunderstorm set fire to the roof.

The volunteers, alerted by one of the workmen, raced to the scene, and were successful in extinguishing the fire. In gratitude and as a token of his esteem, Morgan Sheffield had a silver speaking trumpet engraved with the date, the emblem of the company, and presented to Fire Company Chief Bodie. The silver engraved speaking trumpet was a prized symbol of authority, and after it ceased to be a practical tool for directing firefighters, it was displayed in a special glass case in the firehouse.

Eventually, the original firehouse building proved too small and ill-placed to accommodate Luna City's first fully-motorized ladder and pumper fire trucks, which were purchased in 1920 and 1922. The fire department moved to its present location on West Elm Street, although the present-day fire house is the third building on that site. The first building on the site had to be extensively expanded with the acquisition of larger vehicles in subsequent decades. Embarrassingly, the second firehouse burned to the ground on the 4th of July, 1939, while all vehicles and volunteers were attending to a massive fire in a hay-barn on the Wyler Ranch. Many relics dating from the early years of the LCVFD were lost in that fire, including the silver speaking trumpet, and other artifacts and memorabilia.

The present Luna City VFD building accommodates a multi-purpose fire engine, a tender and a ladder truck, a brush truck for fighting grass and brushfires, a command truck and the ambulance, living quarters for full-time fire fighters, medics. and volunteers on regular shift, a classroom, storage area and wash-rack. There are six full-time paid professional firefighters; the remainder of the eighty-strong force are volunteers; either reserve, in training status or junior members. Junior members must be of high school age and participate in regular training sessions. They assist with fund-raising and educational outreach to the local community and are considered full-fledged members of the LCVFD after their 18th birthday. Training sessions are held weekly; Wednesday evenings from 6-9 PM.

The Dragon Who Guards the Hoard

"Richard, we need a forth for a round of golf tomorrow afternoon on the Mills Farm course," said Doc Wyler, on the Thursday morning, just three days out from Christmas. "You interested?" He posed it as a mild question, but as Doc Wyler was the wealthiest man in Luna City, the owner of the second most profitable (in the aggregate) local businesses after Mills Farm, and one of Richard's employers to boot – it sounded to Richard as more of a politely-phrased demand.

"I'm not all that certain I'm good enough a player," Richard demurred. "And I don't have a set of clubs." He left unspoken his private opinion that golf was a game invented by bored and drunken Scotsmen, and that the phrase, "Hold my whiskey, laddie, and watch this!" had been involved

"Nonsense," snorted the old veterinarian. "You're likely better than I am. I'll lend you Miz Alice's old set of clubs. You'll be fine." He looked Richard clinically up and down, adding, "Boy, you're looking right pasty-faced. You need to get out in the fresh air; it'll do you a world of good. You and I will be just along to keep Clovis and Collin company, anyway. They're the serious golfing fanatics. You met my son, Collin?" He jerked his chin at the man who sat across from him at the regulars' table, which Georg Stein jovially termed the *'stammtisch'*. "Collie, this is Richard, who runs the Café. Damn fine cook and a good sport. You have a lot in common."

"Pleased, I'm sure," Richard briefly shook hands, and wondered if Collin Wyler knew precisely how much they had in common, in both of them being ex-significant-others with Sammi Colquhoun, the one-time Page 3 girl turned reality-show star and ubiquitous media personality.

"Love to have you join us," Collin replied. He was in his late middle age – likely older, if he was the father of Patricia Pryor – but careful tailoring and an expensive fitness regimen knocked off at least a decade and a half. He was, in fact, a younger and less lined version of his father, and less abrupt-spoken. "Pop told me you are English, used to run a fancy place in London. We might have friends in common."

"We might," Richard allowed. "In London and here in Luna City, but your father got an injunction filed against him, so we haven't had a heart-to-heart chat lately."

Collin raised a single eyebrow and chuckled. "Gunnison Penn, that old fraud! Is he still around?"

"In the very flesh," Richard sighed. "And his RV is still parked at the Age with a mob of his treasure-hunting pals. To tell the truth, I'll consider myself fortunate in spending a morning on the links with you and Colonel Walcott. It's altogether too crowded these days, what with the regular old Communards come for the solstice, Penn and his pals, the ghost-hunting fraternity, and to top it off, just yesterday, a couple of berks who call themselves UFOlogists drove in!"

"Ufologists?" Doc Wyler snorted in derision. "What the hell is a that?"

"UFO-chasers, Pop," Collin exchanged a wry and sympathetic glance with Richard. "Sounds like a barrel of laughs, out at the old park ... when I was a young tadpole, it was that deserted place by the river where we used to go drink and smoke and scare each other with ghost stories."

"I tell you, I'll be glad for a stroll around the links," Richard confessed. "Just for the peace and quiet. Still, I've always thought Churchill had the right of it: an afternoon of trying to put a small round ball, into an even smaller hole, with instruments entirely unsuited for the purpose. But anything to get away from the mob."

"Splendid, splendid," Collin beamed hearty pleasure on them all. "We'll pick you up here – say, half-last one?"

"On the dot," Richard replied, with a distinct lack of enthusiasm, which fortunately neither Collin or Doc appeared to notice.

On the whole, the afternoon did not – once Richard had properly embarked on it in the proper seasonal spirit – turn out to be as dire an experience as he had feared initially. The day was one of those mild winter days. A refreshing breeze stirred the leaves of the live-oak, cypress and poplar trees that starred the gentle, rolling slopes of Mills Farm. More trees fringed the bend of the river which lovingly embraced the low heights, all immaculately landscaped and planted, lovingly maintained by a company of groundskeepers and gardeners. They were early for their tee-time, so Collin treated them all to a late sandwich lunch on the terrace of the Mills Farm Country Restaurant, which offered a sweeping view of the golf course and the countryside beyond. Richard, because of his devotion to the Café and the hours of daylight that he spent there, had never set foot in the restaurant. This place was in a more spectacular situation than the Café; entered through a soaring foyer *(repurposed from an old gin mill building, painstakingly relocated from a decayed small town north of San Antonio)* which also served as entryway to the Mills Farm Country General Store.

"Good Lord, what is that – remains of the local lake monster?" Richard squinted up at a framed display over the glass double doors to the Genera Store; a carefully articulated skeleton of a gargantuan lizard-something.

Doc Wyler chuckled. "No, son; that's the skeleton of one of Old Charley's pet alligators. He kept a half-dozen of the beasts in a pond, downhill-a-ways. Used to, I could point out the exact place, but they did so much terracing and reshaping, I'm damned if I could tell you where."

"Near where the eleventh hole sand bunker is," Collin said. "They found that skeleton when they were digging out the fairway and kept it as a curiosity."

"In particularly gruesome taste, that is," Richard said.

Doc Wyler chuckled again. "That was Old Charley. Any taste he had was all in his mouth, but my father always said he made damn-good bourbon."

"It was really his last wife who had the reputation for it," Collin grinned, and his father growled,

"Christ, Collie, don't you get started on Old Charley again. I've had enough of that old bastard's damned treasure."

"Maybe," Richard agreed, "But I wouldn't mind knowing where it is, just so that Gunnison Penn and his friends would leave us all alone about it. I was there when young Matty found one of the coins in the henhouse enclosure at the farm. Miss Letty told us once that her brother the historian thought that the gold was hidden for a time in the old farm pit-latrine."

"I'd heard something along those lines through the gossip grapevine," Clovis Walcott ventured, "Didn't the Mills Farm people excavate that pit? They found another gold eagle and a lot of old bottles, or at least that is what the local rumor mill said."

Doc Wyler snorted, in disparagement, as the hostess led them to a table and distributed menus among them. It was quite plain that three of the foursome were still interested in the Mills Farm treasure-hoard, in spite of Doc's expressed scorn for the subject.

"They did, indeed," Collin assured them with authority. In spite of himself, and despite Doc Wyler's disapproval, both he and Clovis were interested. Collin was the expert on Old Charley and his treasure, after all. "I bought one of Old Charley's gold eagles thirty years ago when I made my first million, and the letter that gave it provenance. Cost me a pretty penny, too, but I didn't grudge."

"How did the letter offer a provenance?" Clovis asked. "Whose letter was it? I'd always heard that the old stoat was next to illiterate."

"He could read and write," Collin replied. "He just didn't care to. The letter was between two of his sisters, concerning one of Old Charlie's by-blows who had the good sense to run away at the age of fourteen or so and turn up at Elizabeth Johnson's house in San Antonio in 1915. They were relations of ours, weren't they, Pop? Mama was an Everett, you know. The letter was to her sister Mary in Houston. Old Charley was in the habit of dumping his offspring on his sisters."

"The family black sheep, as it were." Clovis closed his menu and said over his shoulder to the hovering waitress. "Iced tea, unsweet, and a club sandwich."

"BLT for me," Collin said. "Ice water, with lemon, thanks. Why do you Brits never put ice in the water, Richard? Is it some kind of religious proscription?"

"Egg salad, and a Coke," Doc Wyler said.

His son remarked, "Pop, shouldn't you be keeping an eye on your cholesterol levels?"

"Screw it, Collie. I'm ninety-six and it hasn't killed me yet."

"I have no idea," Richard replied, with a despairing glance at the menu. "Why do you Yanks insist on pouring perfectly good tea over ice? I'll have the chicken salad. And lemon squash. Oh – OK, Sprite. Thanks again, love."

"So, how did the letter tie into Old Charley's hiding place?" Clovis Walcott persisted.

Collin explained, diving with relish into one of his favorite topics for the benefit of a fresh new audience, "The kid found Old Charley's stash in the latrine-pit, lifted a couple of coins, and used them to facilitate traveling to San Antonio. Elizabeth Johnson couldn't get a square answer out of the kid as to how much he swiped, only that it was in the latrine-pit and that single twenty-dollar piece was the last of what he took. Prolly spent the rest of it on movie tickets, ice cream, candy, and other unwholesome amusements, if I know fourteen-year-olds. He did tell her that there were several bags, all full to overflowing with gold. That's where the legend about the Mills Treasure started. People will talk."

"Interesting," Clovis planted his elbows on the table. "Of course, the reshaping of the original site would have obliterated practically everything from that time. That was an excellent job, by the way – speaking as a professional. You would have sworn, looking at the finished project, that this was all the result of natural forces. Did anyone ever interview the young man, later on? Try and find out from him where Old Charley would have moved the stash?"

"Never had the chance," Collin replied, an expression of mild regret on his face. "He enlisted in the Army early in 1918 and died in the flu epidemic later that year. No; likely Old Charley figured out that his sprout had raided the treasure and shifted it someplace else. Ah, well; it has kept treasure-hunters like Gunn busy for decades."

The waitress emerged with their sandwiches just at that point – the restaurant being practically empty. The conversation turned general, and episodic, mostly to do with personal plans for the Christmas weekend. Richard was mildly elated to take to the course with the other three, for it was a very pleasant day, and a very pleasant place. The afternoon turned so warm, they could take off sweaters, windbreakers and jackets, and play in shirt-sleeves – so not like the dear Home Counties! The greens were as smooth as velvet, the sand-traps miracles of pure white sand, the roughs also as carefully groomed, and the artfully-deployed water-traps equally as miraculous. Over their heads, the sky was that pure, cerulean blue, dotted with a flock of white clouds moving in it as peacefully as grazing sheep. They did the course old-style, walking and carrying their bags, although in deference to age, Doc Wyler pulled his on a little wheeled trolley. They proceeded in a leisurely fashion, having a party ahead of them on the links by several holes, a quartet far-distant and almost out of sight. Richard and Doc Wyler whanged their various small white balls into all kinds of incongruous places, while Clovis Walcott and Collin Wyler observed with indulgent patience.

Close to the eleventh hole, they came upon another party. From a distance, they had assumed they were another foursome, but upon coming closer, Richard groaned, "Here, too, oh Lord?"

"You know them?" Doc Wyler finished his swing, and squinted after the while dot, skipping and bouncing over the green-velvet sward in a completely random and unexpected direction.

"They're staying at the campground – a bunch of treasure-hunting detectorists. That's not a set of clubs they're lugging around, but a metal detector. Looking for the Mills Treasure is an absolute mania with these people."

"It is," Collin agreed, with an indulgent air. "But as manias go, relatively harmless."

"They'd better not be caught digging up the greens," Clovis Walcott scowled, thunderously. "VPI will have them flogged and then simmered lightly in oil. My Little Bride got pretty tired of hearing her pal Susannah complain about how they were always sneaking onto the property. She had this rant about damn dirty naked hippies tearing up her golf course."

Richard lingered behind the other three, as their foursome approached the industrious treasure-hunters. Mercifully, none of them was Gunnison Penn. They were a quartet of amiable young men who looked more like earnest graduate students, save for wearing tee-shirts with lamentable slogans printed on them; one of them announced *I Hate Pull Tabs* and another said, *I'd Rather Be Dirt-Fishing*. Doc was lining up his shot, with a great deal of bad-tempered comment. Collin Wyler strolled over to where the four young treasure-hunters were methodically going over a gentle slope below a sand-trap set at the top of the ridge like a dish full of diamond-white sand. The one detectorist with a narrow shovel hurriedly replaced a divot of turf into the hole they had obviously been inspecting.

"Any luck today, fellows?" Collin asked, all genial and non-confrontational curiosity. "I'm guessing you're looking for the Mills Treasure. Been looking for that myself, for years; it's a legend around these parts, you know."

"Not so far, sir," the tallest of the detectorists replied; a bean-pole of a boy with a straggling hipster goatee who must have been well-brought-up, since he spoke so respectfully to an older stranger.

"The trouble is," Collin nodded, in complete sympathy. "The usual run of machines can't really detect a significant small target if it's buried deeper than a foot or so. They did a lot of shifting of soil around here, thirty, forty years ago, to make this place."

"Did they?" The youngest of the detectorists appeared slightly crestfallen, and Collin nodded. *Really*, thought Richard, *he was very good with the young, almost fatherly and head-masterish*. It didn't mesh well with Collin Wyler's public image as a Master of the Financial Universe and bon-vivant, cohabitating his way through the alphabet of the nubile and not-quite-so-nubile female of the species.

"Show me what you have found so far, then. I used to do a fair bit of this myself, when I was your age." Now, Collin really did sound fatherly. At a nod from the boy with the goatee, one of the other detectorists presented a small plastic bucket containing their pathetic takings from the site.

"We pinged on some disturbed earth at the edge of the tall grass," the detectorist with the bucket. "An animal burrow, I guess."

Richard looked over the collection, as Collin took up each one; a couple of pointed animal teeth, a bent and corroded shotgun shell, a very old silver dime, some soft-drink or beer-bottle caps, also much corroded, and a single small brass buckle, with a short length of narrow and age-blackened strip of something that might once have been leather threaded through it. The buckle was a sturdy, solid thing. Collin looked it over with interest.

"Not a belt-buckle," he commented. "Unless it were a woman's belt. I have a shooting bag with a buckled strap that looks very like this. I suppose it could have come off a satchel. The dime's a 19th century one, though. You said you found it all by the edge of rough and the eleventh hole?"

"Right over there," the goateed detectorist nodded in pleased agreement.

"Interesting," Collin's face was a study, although in what, Richard had no idea. He looked as if he had been struck with a new notion. At last, Collin thanked the detectorists for sharing their paltry results of the day with him, adding, "Look, fellows, you know this is private property, so don't be too surprised if security eventually notices your presence …"

"Oh, we have permission from Mr. Cordova," the leader of the quartet assured him, all wide-eyed youth. "I guess no one before us had ever thought to, you know, <u>ask</u> if it was OK. He was very pleasant, especially when we said we would dig very carefully and replace the turf when we were done. The management of this place is practically fascist about having the turf damaged."

"Well, that's all right then. Just be careful about smoothing it all in again… and happy hunting!"

Richard and Collin rejoined Doc and Clovis Walcott. Doc did look sharply at Collin's thoughtful expression, as the latter was seeming to take a deep interest in the landscape and not in the direction of the twelfth hole.

"What's your major malfunction, Collie?" the old veterinarian asked. Collin shrugged, replying, "Later, Pops." It was Richard's turn to tee off, and it was such a mild and lovely day that he soon put the exchange out of his mind entirely.

***

As the sun slid down the western horizon later that day, illuminating the distant rooftops, church steeples, the water tower, and the notable façade of Abernathy Hardware, and the Cattleman Hotel *(the two tallest buildings in Luna City)* two men sat on the second-floor verandah of the Wyler home place, watching the sunset. This particular part of the verandah had long been the place that Doc Wyler favored as a vantage point to survey all that of which he was master, accompanied by the tall mint julep which had been his favored evening drink for almost eight decades. Now he regarded his son with an acuity which neither time nor the half-consumed mint julep had impaired.

"Collie, I b'lieve you figured out something about where the Mills Treasure is hidden, when you talked to those young fellers at the golf course today."

"I have, indeed, Pops." Collin Wyler took a deep swallow of his own julep and set the glass down on the table-top with a small, definite clink. "I'm about ninety-nine point nine per cent certain-sure of where Old Charley hid his gold stash after moving it from the latrine, way back in 1915, and where it has been ever since."

"Are you indeed?" his parent replied and there was a considering silence. "What are you going to do about it?"

"Nothing," Collin replied. "Nothing at all."

"Any reason?"

"A few," the younger man looked out on the gentle pastures, dotted with stands and thickets of oak, and hackberry. "First; it's on VPI property. I could make an offer to purchase the place, but why bother? I don't need actually need to dig up a small fortune in gold coins, or to go through the expense and hassle, since I am damn certain it's buried pretty deep, after all the earth-sculpting they did in the 1970s. VPI? The Mills Treasure is just a drop in the bucket to them, though I guess they'd get some good publicity from it, should they manage to figure it out. I'm doubting they ever will or want to. I'm not in the business of doing my rivals any particular favors, either. But that's not the principal reason."

"Ah, so now we get down to brass tacks," Doc Wyler sank another long draught of his julep. "What would that reason be, Collie?"

"The mystique of the Mills Treasure," Collin replied, his countenance alight with a passion most often reserved for his financial or sexual coup of the moment. "See, Pop; it's not the finding that matters to fellows like those we talked to, poking around the eleventh hole with their metal detector. The lure of the Mills Treasure gives form and shape, purpose to their lives. Just thinking that it may be out there, somewhere, still. It's the great golden whale of their imagining."

"Collie, son – you ain't had one or more of these before coming to sit out here? You are sounding right lyrical and that just ain't in your character."

"No, Pop, I'm serious as a judge, though maybe not quite as sober as the defendant appearing before him. I know or at least, I am mortal certain in my own mind of where Old Charley put his gold and I'm contented with that. I don't need to prove it to myself or anyone else by going to the trouble of digging it up, not when doing that would spoil everyone elses' fun. Leave it lie where it is, to the last turn of this old world."

"You might just have a point there, son." Doc Wyler looked out, seeing the bright sun, as golden as any of the 20$ eagles in Old Charley's hoard, slanting down into the horizon, attended by a few solicitous purple clouds, clouds trimmed with a line of brilliant silver around their edges. "You could relieve my own curiosity, though. I will swear to never reveal to anyone but my Heavenly Maker; just where did Old Charley put the gold, all these years ago?"

"Ah, that." Collin sank the last swallow of his julep and regarded his father over the empty glass. "Isn't a dragon the customary guardian for a hoard of gold? Yes, I thought so. Well, if you don't have a pet dragon or two … wouldn't you make do with what you have on hand?"

"Yes, indeedy, son," Doc Wyler answered, after a moment, comprehension dawning on his own face, breaking out into a wide smile – in contrast to the fading sunset. "Yes, I do believe that I would. To you, then, and the fabulous Mills Treasure. May it ever be long-searched for and never found, guarded by Old Charley's pet dragons."

The Hunters and the Hunted

If Richard had thought or even hoped that matters at the Age of Aquarius might have calmed down at least several degrees by the time of his return from the road trip north, he was doomed to be disappointed. For it was now the time of the winter solstice and all the old Communards gathered for their customary celebrations, only to find the campground's best places already taken by the ghost-hunters, the UFOlogists, the treasure-hunters and the obviously sensation-seeking. There was barely sufficient room for all, even after Sefton moved the goats from one of their accustomed pastures close in to the grove of trees which sheltered the yurt. He had one of Roman Gonzalez's cousins come in with a small tractor/bulldozer, scrape it level, and spread out a truckload of decomposed granite to provide a safe footing for tires. The cousin also gouged out the drive leading into the campground, filling in the deep-grooved ruts with the earth scraped from the ridges, and rolling the tractor over and over again, until it was all quite beautifully level.

"Yeah, but it won't last past the next heavy rain," the Gonzales cousin replied, with a doleful look, when Richard had remarked on the improved appearance of the long driveway and its' navigability on his bicycle. "Enjoy it while ya got it, Ricardo."

"I shall endeavor to my utmost abilities," Richard replied, wheeling the bike around the idling tractor. The excursion to Marble Falls had proved a brief respite. On the bright side, the Café was gratifyingly full of a morning. This very day, he had been buttonholed by a young Italian detectorist, who had insisted that his great-grandfather had once owned a hotel in Luna City.

"Do you know of the Gran' Palazzo Vittorio?" The man waved a very ancient, sepia-tinted postcard under Richard's nose. Richard had looked at it very briefly. The structure pictured on it very much resembled the Cattleman Hotel, cat-cornered across Town Square from the Café. "Cannot say truthfully that I have, old sport. Honestly, this really isn't the place for a Grand Palazzo Anything. I suppose you could try in Houston... they're said to have a taste for that kind of thing there."

"My grandfather was a prisoner in the POW camp at Hereford, in the second war," the young man insisted. "He told me when I was a child that he came back and visited in Luna City to see the property that his father and his father owned, but that was all so long ago..."

"Can't help you, old chap," Richard said, but he did note vaguely, before he returned to his kitchen to oversee providing of breakfast to the great rush of clients, that Miss Letty had overheard, and was rising with a struggle from her regular seat at the *'stammtisch'*. Ah, good – Miss Letty, the oldest person in Luna City and her encyclopedic memory of local places, items and persons; she would have this in hand. Richard counted this as a lucky escape.

He had good reason to rethink that situation when he bicycled back to the Age of Aquarius late that afternoon; Wednesday before Christmas, the night of the solstice, a half-moon looming like a half of a great golden Cheddar cheese over the trees and know, without a doubt, to the core of his soul that this night would be a night for the records. The records of the local asylum for the terminally bewildered at worst – at best the records of the *Karnesville Weekly Beacon*. The old Communards had gathered for their solstice rituals … the fire in Sefton's traditional Indian sweat-bath had been leaking smoke for days, up through the mud-plastered brush that made the circular wikiup on the far side of the yurt. What it was like inside, packed full of naked sweat-leaking septuagenarians recalling their glory days of protest in the streets, illicit herbal substances and wild sexual orgies, he refused to contemplate. These people were nearly the age of his Gran, a salty-tempered retired cotton mill-worker and once Land Girl. That most of them, he was given to understand, were otherwise respectably middle class and conventional with it only added to the considerable horror.

And then there were all the others, digging here and there, setting up motion-sensors hither and yon, with quite astounding carelessness. Only the other night, one of the poor tent-camping detectorists came stumbling in after a night of barhopping in Karnesville, with as strong need to use facility in the middle of the night. As he was a well-brought-up young man, he went stumbling to the bathhouse and tripped one of the motion-sensors set up by the ghost-hunting fraternity. The blare of the alarm, and the sudden blinding flash of lights had woken up half the campground and rendered the young detectorists' midnight excursion redundant, as he had promptly lost control of his bladder. Bladder only, fortunately.

Everyone's nerves were scraped raw. Richard knew as clearly as if it were neatly printed across the pages of *Larousse Gastronomique* that matters were absolutely going to come to a head and very soon. He just hoped that he could stay out of the way when it did.

But such hopes were fated not to be fulfilled; likely there was some kind of cosmic fitness in that it was the very day of the winter solstice. He came up the newly-smoothed drive, and passed Azúcar, the Grant's pet snow-white llama, moodily cropping fresh green grass from where it had begun sprouting up between the dried blades of last year's dried hay.

Azúcar raised his head and looked scornfully at Richard, while making a brief kind of gargling sound in his throat.

"Know the feeling, chummy," Richard commented. No, Azúcar was being made uneasy, too. Azúcar followed Richard, still making that grumbling sound, deep in his throat. Richard stepped up his pace; Azúcar in a bad mood still made him nervous, although Judy insisted that their pet was extremely gentle and so totally harmless.

The grove with the Grant's yurt, and the campground, once so quietly pastoral, now looked like Hyde Park Corner on a day when all the fanatics came out, closely followed by several sets of video documentarians. But no soap-box podiums; these were new age. Xavier Gunnison Penn even had a white-board on a stand, with a long pointer in his hand, outlining a map for the benefit of his friend with the camera. Beyond him, a pair of ghost-hunters – the ones who had sensored the bathhouse the previous week – were setting up more sensors along the line of brush which delineated the edge of the campground, also for the benefit of another with a fairly serious tripod-mounted camera. Their project also seemed to involve many coils of electrical extension cord, snaking hither and yon.

The UFOlogists were at it, also. Richard couldn't make out why they had to have a small gas-powered generator as well as a camera crew taping their activities, under the glare of a number of parasol-shaded lights on tall tripods, but at that very moment, they fired up the generator. The racket was horrific, ear-splitting. Immediately, Gunnison Penn tore the little microphone off his collar, screaming and waving his pointer.

"Do you mind!"

"Hey, Pops, take it easy!" shouted back the senior-ranking UFOlogist, which did not mollify the furious treasure hunter in the least, especially not when he tripped over a stray cord, which pulled over the ghost hunter's lights with a crash and a pop of an exploding bulb.

"Dammit! Do you have any idea of how much those things cost!" the anguished ghost hunter cried. "You owe us for that!"

"Balderdash!" Gunnison Penn roared, and swung with his heavy wooden pointer, which flew out of his hand and hit the second UFOlogist a glancing blow across the top of his head. In his clumsy attempts to rise, he pulled over a second light standard, which fell on his own film crew. It did not break the bulb but was hot enough to burn; Penn's cameraman howled in pain. The UFOlogist struck by Penn's wooden pointer was already bleeding copiously, a wave of scarlet streaking his face and saturating his shirt-front with gore. In an instant, the whole place was in an uproar, as more hunters, UFOlogists and Communards came running from everywhere. It was, thought, Richard, rather like a traffic accident; one frozen moment of silence, the silence of a dam about to break – the next moment, pandemonium.

"What was that for, you bastard!" Gunnison Penn yelled. Before Richard's horrified eyes, the dam burst. The brawl was on; in the rush, Penn retrieved his pointer as a weapon. In aiming a wallop at one of his combatants with it, he struck Azúcar across the neck in his back-swing. The effect was electric; Azúcar's ears went back, and if Richard thought that the llama made a grumbling noise before, this was more like the growl of an attacking lion. Azúcar bared his teeth and sank them into Gunnison Penn's backside.

Penn screamed. So did Judy. "He hit Azúcar, Seftie! Get him!"

At Richard's side, one of the naked Communards – obviously fresh from the sweat-lodge regarded the scene with appreciative interest, and asked, "Is this a private fight, or can anyone join in?"

"Be my guest," Richard said, taking out his cellphone with trembling hands. The brawl was now universal and indiscriminate. Even Sefton was getting tore in, stringy and tough old bastard that he was. The whole scene reminded Richard of one of those Breughel paintings, with strange figures in small skirmishes everywhere, a thread of smoke twining picturesquely through the trees shading the yurt as a surreal backdrop.

Richard thumbed through the contact numbers, preprogrammed on his phone. "Joe... Chief Vaughn. You better get out here to the Aquarius and bring as much back-up as you can muster. It's a battle zone out here."

In the end, Joe *(muttering many arcane military curses under his breath)* had to call for back-up from Karnesville, and make use of zip-tie handcuffs, as there were so many to be transported to the Luna City PD facility, sporting black eyes, bruises and abraded knuckles. Richard, his duty having been done, retreated to the shelter of his own tiny domicile. He watched the brawl and the efficient charge of the Luna City PD into the fray from the window over the dinette area with the detached attention of someone watching a reality television show in which he had little interest.

It appeared at once that many of those old Communards, hunters of ghosts, treasure and UFOs who had not been actively involved in the brawl objected strenuously to the arrest of their comrades. From across the Age of Aquarius Richard could sense Joe's exasperation, like the little wavy lines over a cartoon skunk indicating a palpable stink. They did, in fact, object so strenuously that Joe's men and the county sheriff's contingent wound up arresting another twenty or so as well. Richard poured himself a glass of Sefton's exquisite white mustang grape elixir, upon noting that the campground was deserted of all but a handful when the last LCPD SUV departed in a cloud of dust, followed by the county convict-transport bus – the one with bars over all the passenger windows.

He took his wine-glass out to the little terrace, and sat, relishing the peace and quiet for the first time in months. No boom-boxes blaring incomprehensible popular music. No roar of portable generators, or Gunnison Penn nattering endlessly on about the malign intent of those preventing him from finding the Mills Treasure, or the ghost-hunters declaiming their narration in stentorian tones for the benefit of the video feature being produced. All was peace and quiet. Even the wretched peafowl kept his screaming at a distance, as it had ever since Richard had borrowed a Super-Soaker water gun from Araceli's son Matty and drenched the wretched beast with a gallon of water.

He sat, relishing the renewed quiet for the better part of an hour. The mist was already rising from the river, twining through the trees like coils of smoke … was that smoke? It did smell rather like a wood fire. Must be the sweat-lodge. Just at the moment that he drained the last of the mustang grape wine, he saw Jess Abernathy's yellow Wrangler coming up the driveway and there was Judy coming out from the decrepit little trailer that housed her soap-making and herbal remedy brewing enterprise. Judy, most unusually for her, was dressed, and with one of those coarsely-woven bags of ethnic design over her shoulder. She had a cellphone in her hand. With her free hand, she waved and beckoned urgently to Richard. Jess beckoned also, and Richard sighed. No rest for the righteous. No one could ever say he had not been gallant when it came to the ladies. Well, actually they could, and cite a whole stack of tabloid front pages as evidence, but he had never failed in courtesy to women that he liked. And dammit, he liked Jess and Judy, exasperating as the latter could be.

"Come with us, Richard," Jess said. "Moral support – we're going to bail out Sefton."

"It was so unfair!" Judy exclaimed, pink with indignation. "It was because of that awful Gunnison creep! He hit poor Azúcar, can you imagine! That warmongering capitalist a-hole, hitting a poor innocent animal! And when Seftie tried to protect Azúcar – can you imagine? Gunnison hit him! And then the county sheriff arrested Seftie! We have to get my darling Seftie-baby out of jail! You can speak for him, Richard! You saw the whole thing."

"Madame," Richard sighed heavily, "As much as I dislike Mr. Gunnison Penn and his pals and as much as I would like to see him languishing in durance vile for the maximum that the law would allow, I cannot really swear truthfully before a magistrate that I saw him strike Mr. Grant and Mr. Grant responding in pure self-defense. Or llama-defense."

"Then fib a little," Judy said, gazing at Richard trustfully. "He hit Azúcar – and that is just not right. And I need to have my Seftie at home where he belongs ... my rock, my anchor, my love ..." Tears spilled over her eyelids, making tracks down her cheeks.

Richard succumbed. "All right, I'll come with you, just to get Sefton out of jail, but I absolutely refuse to tell a lie to do it."

"Shouldn't be necessary," Jess replied, patting her own voluminous handbag/briefcase. "I have his bail money right here. In cash; I had to go to the bank in Karnesville to get it. But if you come along and swear to Sefton's upright character, and that his wife desperately requires his presence ..."

"Oh, yes," Judy affirmed, starry-eyed. "Tonight it is the Alban-tide celebration, the time of the winter solstice and working the sex-magick is absolutely essential to our celebration of it."

"Excellent," Jess put in. "Making note of the religious aspect ... freedom of religion and all that. Let's get going. It will be dark soon, and you want Sefton back in time to perform the celebrations."

Richard groaned slightly, but only to himself, and only as he scrambled into the back seat of Jess's bare-bones Jeep. There was a sagging cardboard box in the back seat; a box full of books. He wondered briefly at that. But the sooner this errand was done, the sooner he could return, relishing the peace and quiet. And the discomfiture of Penn, the obnoxious treasure hunter; a fine reward for this errand of mercy.

Jess drove up to the very front of the Luna City PD building – a rather more utilitarian structure a block away from the scenic historical splendors of Town Square. There were a number of official vehicles parked in front. Oddly enough, the Luna City VFD ambulance was one of them, and parked just before the front door. Jess claimed the last empty parking slot, and he and Judy followed Jess.

"I'm here to get my baby Sefton out of jail," Judy announced, with maximum drama as soon as they came in the door. The front office was relatively un-chaotic, although from behind a heavy closed door at the back, the sound of acapella singing resounded faintly, as well as an occasional shout of protest.

"I have the bail money for Sefton Grant," Jess explained, in slightly less dramatic a fashion. "Of the Age of Aquarius Campground and Goat Farm, Luna City. If you will be so good as to produce him, Tina, we'll be out of your hair."

The duty sergeant, who also doubled as dispatcher *(her nametag read "Gonzalez")* was seated behind a counter that ran halfway through the room, also shielded from the top by a pane of plexiglass. She looked up at them in wary courtesy, instantly replaced by relief combined with amused resignation.

"Oh, hi, Jess," she replied. "Isn't this the limit? Yeah, sure – you can have him. One less to put up with."

"Is he all right?" Judy clasped her hands together, the very picture of a silent movie heroine registering anxiety. "He wasn't brutalized by the forces of capitalist aggression …"

"Nope," Tina Gonzalez grinned. "He and his buddies are having the time of their lives. Can't you hear them back there?"

At that moment, the door at the back of the room opened, to admit a very harassed Joe Vaughn, and Chris Mayall, maneuvering the LCVFD ambulance litter through the door and around the corner. The litter bore upon it – prone and complaining vociferously at every jostle and bump – Xavier Gunnison Penn, with his trousers lowered and a substantial wad of dressings and bandage crowning the pale and freckled eminence of his equally substantial buttocks.

Now Richard could hear the singing more clearly; an acapella male choir in full-throated chorus. "*I fought the law and the law won.*"

"Very nice," Jess remarked in approval. "Are they taking requests?"

"Don't encourage them," Joe replied, scowling dangerously, while Gunnison Pen yelped,

"I was savagely attacked by that brute of a beast – that wild animal! The creature is a deadly menace! I insist on charges being brought!"

"You'll insist on nothing," Jess replied, while Judy cried,

"You hit him, you … you blood-thirsty fascist! I saw you do it!"

Jess meanwhile had whipped out her cellphone and snapped off a series of pictures of Penn and his llama-savaged buttock.

"OK, then," she said, calmly. "Do you have any preferences as to which website these pictures should be posted to? Oooh, I can email the whole set to Collin Wyler; he would love an early Christmas present! And Kate – for *Talk of the Town*! Wouldn't you love this picture to go viral! Think of the publicity for your treasure hunt!"

"You …" Gunnison Penn turned beet-red.

Joe, whose scowl darkened, deliberately jostled his end of the ambulance litter. "Keep a civil tongue in your head, Mr. Penn, there's ladies present."

Outside, the LCVFD's alert klaxon sounded three times. Richard had already learned that was an alert for all volunteers within hearing. Something was on fire, somewhere in the limits covered by the volunteer fire department. Jess's cellphone peeped at almost the same moment. Tina Gonzalez' small switchboard suddenly came alive with lights, as Chris' teenage ambulance trainee, Jaimie Gonzalez came bombing through the outside door.

"Chris, man!" he shouted, in high excitement. "About three people from the campground just called! The Grant place is on fire and going up like a bonfire!"

To be continued … of course.

Celia Hayes & Jeanne Hayden

www.ingramcontent.com/pod-product-compliance
Lightning Source LLC
Chambersburg PA
CBHW032252020726
47495CB00001B/77